BATTLE FOR EKLATROS

REBALANCING THE COSMOS
BOOK 1

ALEX GALASSI

GALACTIC TREEHOUSE LLC

Battle for Eklatros

Published by Galactic Treehouse LLC

Aurora, CO 80015

Copyright ©2022 by Alex Galassi. All rights reserved.

Map by BMR Williams.

Cover by Derek Van Skyock.

This book is a work of fiction. Names, characters, places, business establishments, and incidents are the product of the author's imagination and are used fictitiously. Any resemblance to actual events; locales; or persons, living or dead; is coincidental.

No part of this book may be reproduced, distributed, or transmitted in any printed or electronic form or by any means, including information storage and retrieval systems without permission in writing from the publisher/author. Please do not participate in or encourage piracy of copyrighted materials in violation of the author's rights.

All images, logos, quotes, and trademarks included in this book are subject to use according to trademark and copyright laws of the United States of America.

No AI tools were used in the process of writing or editing this novel. Additionally, no AI tools were used in the creation of the cover art.

No AI training: Without in any way limiting the author's exclusive rights under copyright, any use of this publication to "train" generative artificial intelligence (AI) technologies to generate text is expressly prohibited. The author reserves all rights to license uses of this work for generative AI training and development of machine learning language models.

ISBN 979-8-9864178-0-6

BISAC: Fiction / Science Fiction / Action & Adventure

If you purchased this book without a cover, you should be aware that this book is stolen property. It was reported as "unsold and destroyed" to the publisher, and neither the author nor the publisher has received any payment for this "stripped book."

All rights reserved by Alex Galassi and Galactic Treehouse LLC.

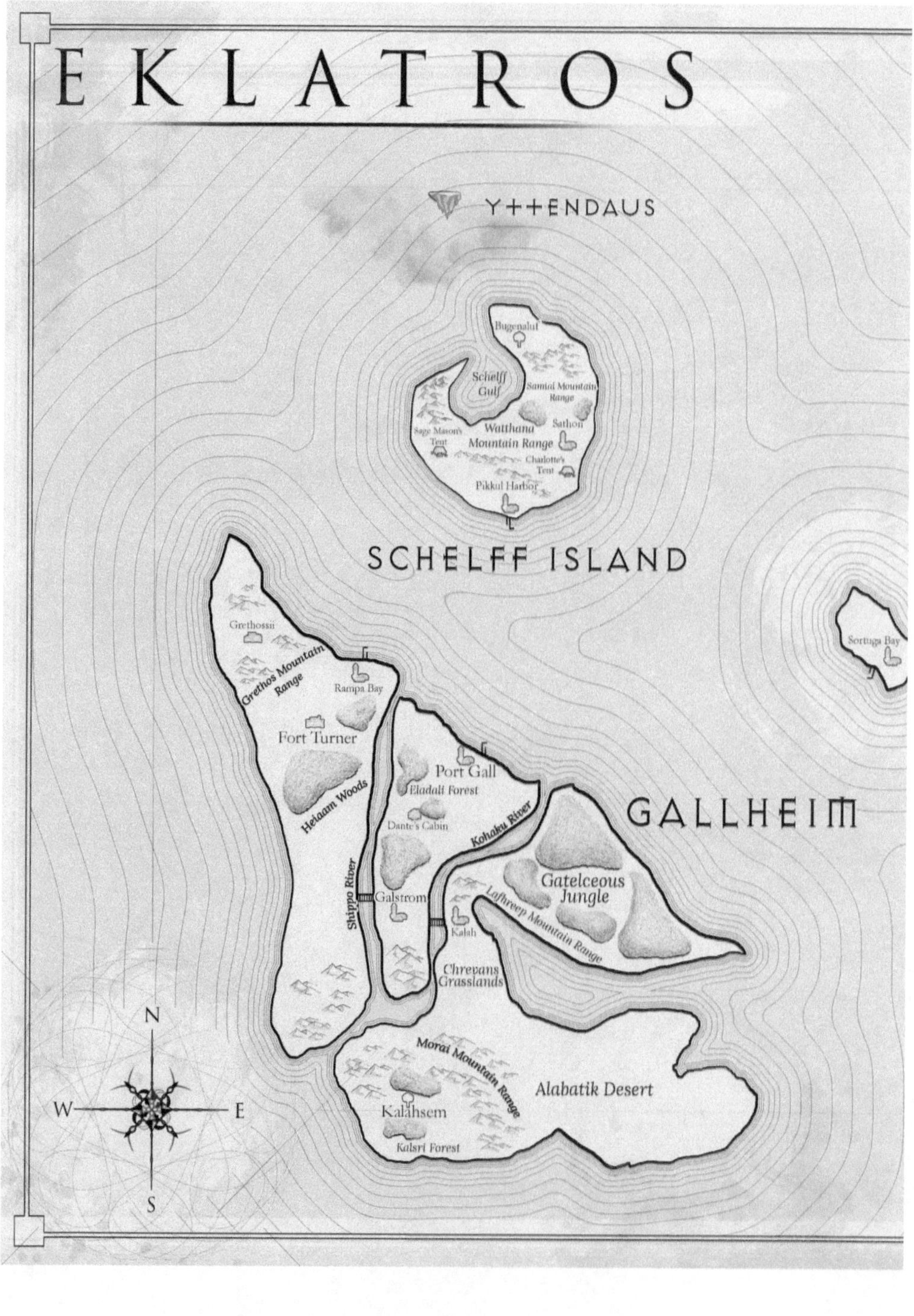

EKLATROS
YTTENDAUS
Bugenalut
Schelff Gulf
Samial Mountain Range
Sathon
Sage Mason's Tent
Watthana Mountain Range
Charlotte's Tent
Pikkul Harbor
SCHELFF ISLAND
Sortuga Bay
Grethossii
Grethos Mountain Range
Rampa Bay
Fort Turner
Port Gall
Eladali Forest
Helaam Woods
Dante's Cabin
GALLHEIM
Kohaku River
Gatelceous Jungle
Shippo River
Galstrom
Lafhreep Mountain Range
Kalah
Chrevans Grasslands
N
Morai Mountain Range
Alabatik Desert
W
E
Kalahsem
Kalsri Forest
S

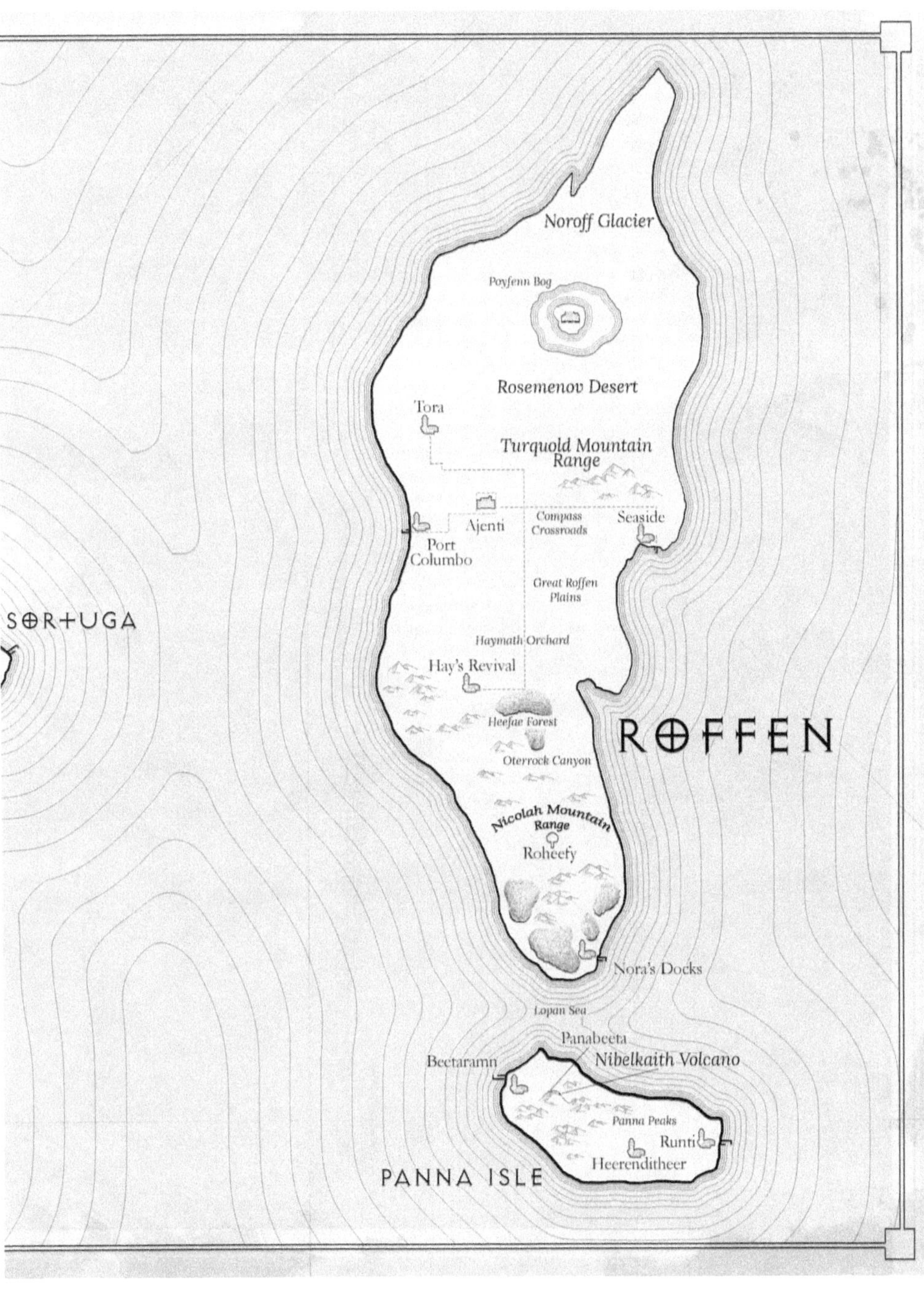

Noroff Glacier
Poyfenn Bog
Rosemenov Desert
Tora
Turquold Mountain Range
Ajenti
Compass Crossroads
Seaside
Port Columbo
Great Roffen Plains
Haymath Orchard
Hay's Revival
Heefae Forest
ROFFEN
Oterrock Canyon
Nicolah Mountain Range
Roheefy
Nora's Docks
Lopan Sea
SORTUGA
Panabeeta
Beetaramn
Nibelkaith Volcano
Panna Peaks
Runti
Heerenditheer
PANNA ISLE

CONTENTS

PROLOGUE
A BLINDING LIGHT

Her silent footsteps flutter down the hall. She's frightened—she hasn't been this scared in her entire life. It's as if darkness itself is trying to swallow her whole and consume her entire soul.

She loses her footing, slips, and falls.

A quiet whisper.

A small splash.

A blinding light.

She's surrounded by whiteness, and the stark contrast from the darkness momentarily blinds her. Her mind is hazy, as if she's floating in water, wading through the waves to reach the ocean that contains her thoughts—her memories.

Through the slushy mist, a voice calls out to her. At first, it's a faint call, but it quickly grows to fill her ears.

"*Ànifa...*" Her mind is swimming with the voice. It's flowing into every hidden crevasse. "*Can you hear me, Ànifa? Ànifa... Ànifa.*"

The voice repeats her name for what seems like an eternity. After many eons, Ànifa finds the strength to reply.

"*I'm... I'm here... I'm Ànifa.*"

As soon as she utters her name, the voice—its dark presence—

focuses with fierce intensity upon her. Darkness consumes the light around her as it creeps in from the edges of her mind.

"*Ànifa... give in to the flow, Ànifa... give into the flow and drown. Let the water cleanse your soul... let it cleanse your mind. The darkness welcomes you.*"

What's this about drowning? Suddenly, her body tenses, then flails, and she discovers that she's floating, pushing through a heavy substance—water.

"*Ànifa... you can't escape me... you can't escape my domain.*"

"*Yes... I... can! That's why I'm... that's why—*"

"*Ha ha ha ha ha... you can feel it, can't you? Give in to the water, Ànifa. Sleep now.*"

"*... I can...*"

"*Ànifa...*"

"*... I...*"

"*Ànifa...*"

"*... can... hold...*"

"*Ànifa!*"

"*... I can hold on!*"

"Ànifa!" A soft, caring voice breaks through the ominous haze. "Wake up, please wake up!"

1

BATTLE FOR MEMORY

Her eyes bolted open.

She panted heavily and was exhausted, as if she'd been swimming for a long time. It took a few seconds for her to calm down.

"Ànifa! You're finally awake!"

Ànifa sat up and looked around. She found herself in a strange bed, in a strange room. "Where am I? And who are you?" she croaked in reply.

"My name is Charlotte, and you are resting in my tent."

Ànifa studied the woman in front of her. Charlotte was sitting near the bed on a pink-cushioned stool. She looked to be in her mid-thirties. She had soft turquoise eyes with a small pair of silver-rimmed spectacles hanging off the end of her pointed nose. Her long, straight hair, covered partially by a purple bandanna, was a genuine silver. Ànifa noted that Charlotte was also wearing a purple dress with a long brown cape.

"Charlotte," she said slowly. Some seconds later, she asked, "Do I know you?"

"No, we've never met before, although I feel like I already know you well," Charlotte said, then paused for a moment before continuing in a softer voice. "I found you alone, a few days ago."

A few days? Had she been out there, swimming in the water, for a few days? She looked around the room frantically when Charlotte placed a warm hand on her shoulder.

"Ànifa, let's not worry about all that. You don't need to worry about anything. Now, do you need anything? Are you hungry or thirsty?"

Without warning, Ànifa's fatigue fully hit her and she laid her head on the pillow.

"I'm... I'm thirsty," she whispered.

"I'll get you some water straight away."

As Charlotte moved to get up, Ànifa slid her eyes closed.

That's right, she thought. *Someone was speaking to me before I woke up. Someone... else.*

———

A little while later, Ànifa was sitting at Charlotte's table, her belly full of soup, sandwiches, and tea. Charlotte sat across from her, watching her with a warm smile. "Now that we've gotten your needs taken care of, feel free to ask me any questions you want. Although, I don't know how helpful I can be."

Ànifa almost laughed. "But you've already helped me so much! And besides, any information would be greatly appreciated at this point. Please, tell me how you found me."

Charlotte smiled and brushed a tress of silver hair out of her eyes. "Well, as I somewhat said earlier, I found you a few days ago. You had washed up on the shore near my tent. At first, I thought... I thought that..."

Tent? Ànifa looked around and saw that she was indeed in a tent. A vast, well-furnished tent at that. It was all one large room. The table where she sat with Charlotte was adjacent to the bed she had been resting in. On the wall to her right, there was a set of wooden shelves stocked full of cans, jars, bottles, and other foodstuffs, while plates, cups, mugs, and utensils rested on the set of wooden shelves to her left. There was also a small desk with some potted plants and bowls on it, and a large bookshelf that was about to overflow. On the nightstand next to the bed was a large brown and green book titled *A Collective History: The Magical World of Eklatros.*

A small, oval mirror hung above the nightstand, and she took a moment to study herself in it. Her hair perfectly matched the color of the sky, creating a pleasant contrast to her lavender eyes. Her ears grew out and up by several centimeters and came to a point.

As she looked around the room, Charlotte remained quiet.

"What is it?" Ànifa asked, turning to face Charlotte. "You don't need to be afraid to tell me anything. I mean, you saved my life. I'm here now, and that's all thanks to you."

"Yes, well, it's traditional in this area to build a pyre for the deceased, so that's what I did. I gathered some wood and began building a fire. Soon, the fire grew and the surrounding area grew warmer. You were near the flame, and when I went to pick you up, you were shivering. I pulled you in closer and you huddled against me, your pale skin already regaining its color. I still don't know how, but you were still alive. I rushed you into my tent and have been taking care of you ever since. That was three days ago."

Ànifa closed her eyes and took a deep breath, feeling the air flow in, then out of her lungs. She was truly alive.

"Thank you for telling me all that," she said, opening her eyes once again. "It's... it's quite a lot to take in, but I'm glad I know now."

"Yes. That's why I wanted you to rest and recover before I told you. I didn't think you could handle that right away."

She thought back to when she first woke up, and of the other voice. It had called out her name, but Charlotte had also called her by name. *Could it be?*

She laughed softly. "No, I don't think I could have. But you truly have my deepest gratitude. Charlotte... I really don't remember much about anything right now. Not even who I am. But when I woke up, you called me by name. How do you know my name?"

"Yes, it's still strange to me as well," Charlotte replied. "The day after I rescued you, I returned from my errands to find a letter and a package by my tent. Here, let me get those for you."

Charlotte pushed herself to her feet and walked to a small desk. She picked up a long, skinny brown box and a pale green envelope and carried them over to where Ànifa sat.

"Here you go," Charlotte said as she handed them to her.

As she took both items, a wave of emotions surged through Ànifa. She was overcome with joy, then sadness, then puzzlement, then frustration, and then, as soon as it started, it stopped. Charlotte, softly plopping onto her small pink stool, brought her back to reality.

Ànifa pushed her dirty dishes away from her and then placed the package on the table. The envelope was made from a large dried leaf. Written on the back of it, in perfect script, was a single word: Ànifa.

"Ànifa—the name on the envelope."

"Exactly. I still don't know where the message came from. I even went back into town and asked about it. They all thought I was crazy —a strange message showing up outside my tent right after I find you on the shore. Nothing unusual ever really happens here. Anyway, go on. Open it."

Ànifa's fingers hadn't left it yet; she was still softly caressing the dried leaf. She turned it over, lifted the top flap, and pulled out a tiny piece of parchment. A warm and familiar scent washed over her. It smelled of trees and salty air. She closed her eyes, then opened them again and started reading out loud.

"'My dearest Ànifa, please accept your bow and quiver. May they be of use to you. Stay safe.' And it's signed JL. Do you know anyone that goes by JL?"

Charlotte twisted her silver hair through her fingers. "JL? I don't think I even know anyone with those initials."

"Hmm... A bow. I wonder what that could mean."

Ànifa examined the long, skinny box. Only a bit of string held the box together. She pulled at the longest end of the knot and it came undone with ease. She removed the lid and peered inside. A small gasp escaped her lips as she gazed upon the hickory bow, intricately carved with two trees, both twisting and turning around the other one all up and down the shaft. Next to the bow was a quiver of arrows —sixty in all. Ànifa picked up the bow to examine it even closer.

Charlotte leaned forward with wide eyes. "That's beautiful. What exquisite craftsmanship."

As Ànifa held it, her fingers slid into tiny grooves and locked in place. She smiled. This was her bow, and she knew this beautiful weapon well. She reached into the box and pulled out the quiver of arrows, then slung it over her shoulder.

"This... this is my bow." Ànifa examined it for a few more seconds, then turned to Charlotte. Charlotte leaned back on her stool, surprised by the intensity in Ànifa's eyes.

"Charlotte, is there a place I can go to train?"

"Are you sure you're feeling up to it?" Charlotte asked with hesitancy in her soft voice.

"Yes, I'm sure. Thank you so much for all of your help, and for telling me all that you know. But now I feel as if I must remember how to use this bow."

"I understand," Charlotte said with a nod. "If that's the case, I suggest heading into the Watthana Mountain Range. Monsters have been seen in the mountains recently and have caused all sorts of trouble for the locals. Judging by the intricacy of your bow, you must be a skilled archer. If it's not too much trouble, would you mind taking down a few of them?"

"I'll see what I can do," she replied with a nod. She felt a powerful urge to be outside, to be out in nature once again.

"That would be wonderful. And since you'll be in the area, would you mind doing me a small favor?"

"Of course. You've helped me so much, I'm only happy to help in return."

"Thank you. As you can see, I've recently run out of some special herbs," Charlotte said, pointing to a set of small empty glass jars that sat on the shelf to her right. "A man on the other side of the mountain sells them, and I haven't been over there since the monsters appeared."

"Are the monsters dangerous?" she asked in afterthought.

"To me, yes. Strange, nasty little things they are. But you seem like you can handle yourself. Now, when you exit my tent, travel west. Once you reach the foothills, there is a well-traveled path you can use. After passing through the mountains, go north. That's where you'll find Sage Mason. He lives in a tent much like mine. And please be careful."

"I will be. I think I'm pretty strong."

"Are you remembering?"

"Not really. No memories have returned, only feelings."

Charlotte smiled. "Well, it's a start. You may have woken up just a few hours ago, but you're recovering quickly. You are quite amazing. Although, I probably shouldn't be surprised."

"Why do you say that?" Ànifa asked.

Charlotte seemed a bit caught off guard by the question, but covered it quickly. "When I found you, you should've been dead. Your body must heal and recover quickly if you can survive such conditions."

"Fair point," Ànifa said as she stood up. "Charlotte, I don't know how to thank you. You—"

"Ah, don't dwell on it. The best gift you could give me, you already gave me. You're alive and well, and I couldn't ask for anything else."

Charlotte stood up and stretched. She reached into her pocket and walked over to Ànifa.

"Here, take this as well," Charlotte said as she took one of Ànifa's hands in her own. "It's not much. I think it comes out to be 187 koda. The herbs should only be about twenty. Keep the rest for yourself; you may need it. And please be careful. Don't even try coming back here tonight. The path to Sage Mason's truly isn't that long, but you can't go there and back in a single day."

"I'll keep that in mind," Ànifa replied. She took the bag of coins from Charlotte, reached into a small pocket of her trenchdress and placed the coins inside. She walked toward the opening in the tent, then looked back at Charlotte.

"Thank you. I'll return shortly."

Ànifa stepped out of the tent and took a few steps forward. She stopped, then looked behind her, back at Charlotte's tent. It was a pale orange color, as if it was made from the skin of a single large animal.

Everything around her was covered in a soft layer of snow. There was a small grove of pine trees to her left, and a substantial pile of firewood behind Charlotte's tent. There were no other tents or structures nearby, only Charlotte's tent.

She really did mean to burn my body, Ànifa thought. *I suppose that would be fine if I were dead.*

A snowflake drifted past her nose, interrupting her thoughts, and she watched as it fell onto her warm brown boot and melted.

Ànifa was wearing a long, light-brown jacket that hung to her knees. The bottom of her jacket flared out, almost like a dress, and was buttoned up in the front. Around her waist was a dark-brown leather belt. The inside of her trenchdress was lined with a soft white fur that puffed out at the collar and cuffs. Scattered along the inside were various pockets, all of them empty, except for two—the pocket with the bag of coins and the pocket that held the card from the mysterious JL.

These must be Charlotte's clothes. I'll have to return them to her once I get some of my own.

She took in her surroundings one last time, then headed down the path that lay in front of her.

About thirty minutes later, the path that she was on split into three. In front of the intersection, there was an old, worn-down signpost that held four planks of wood, each pointing toward a different path. One sign indicated that the path directly in front of her led to the Watthana Mountain Range, while the path to her right led to the nearby town of Sathon. The plank pointing to the path she had come from was labeled Charlotte Tuesti, and the plank pointing to the path to her left was nearly illegible aside from the word Harbor. Not only that, but the path itself was in rough shape, as if no one had traveled it for years. She turned toward the path straight in front of her and headed into the mountains.

She meandered down the path alone. There were only a few trees here and there, the soft call of distant birds, and the wind as it blew through her long blue hair. Above her was the cloudless blue sky, illuminated by the soft yellow sun.

I... I truly know nothing of myself, she thought. *I don't know what I'm doing, or why I'm here, but I can't deny that this area is beautiful.*

2

BATTLE FOR SAFETY

Theodore was alone in the snow and the cold. His traveling companion had abandoned him during the trek into the mountains. He didn't know how long Cecil had been gone before he realized. It could have only been a few minutes or an hour. All he knew was he had to return to the base of the mountains as fast as he could. Storm clouds threateningly loomed above him.

Not that I'm familiar with the storms in this area, he thought. *Either way, I'll freeze to death in the open. Maybe Cecil was the smart one for once. Wait, what am I thinking? Cecil is never smart. Ever.*

The wind howled past him, and he wrapped his long navy-blue cloak around himself.

Dagnabbit! Where in this frozen land are you, Cecil? Theodore trudged along the path, his boots filled with snow. He looked around and recognized a small group of trees. He was going in circles. Following his footsteps was only leading him astray.

Panic crept in, but Theodore pushed it away. *Now is not the time to panic. I must focus if I am to survive the night. If it's not the storm that does me in, the monsters will surely find me.*

The old wizard took a deep breath and closed his eyes. He held his scarlet staff out in front of him and felt the energies swirl around him. Water was not his specialty. Not only was it the most difficult element to control, but each of its forms required different magics. Yet, he could not give up simply because it was difficult.

Rather than focusing solely on water, Theodore used the surrounding wind to help him read the messages hidden in the icy crystals that fluttered all around him.

The wind howled, pushing him forward. *Yes, that's right! The slot canyon is this way!*

Theodore smiled and made his way toward the canyon. It didn't take long for him to reach the other side; he was finally out of the mountains. He used his staff to draw a circle in the surrounding snow, taking a moment to revel in the magnificent sight of the catalyst.

The outer layer of his staff was made of exceptionally durable glass. The glass was blown from the sands of the Rosemenov Desert, right at the boundary of the Noroff Glacier, and the unique sand in the region gave the glass its bright scarlet color. The core of his staff was made of fossilized wood harvested from beneath Ajenti University. There was so much magical energy in the fossilized wood that using the staff without the glass layer would cause certain death. At the top of his staff was a glass orb.

Once he was satisfied with the circle he had drawn, he aligned himself in the center and muttered an incantation. The wind picked up around him, blowing in a circle around the path he made in the snow. Soon a wall of snow surrounded him, quickly spinning clockwise. When the wind reached its climax, Theodore muttered a single syllable—Kwall—causing the surrounding air to freeze in place. Silence and darkness fell upon him simultaneously. He had created a small space for himself in the snow, but there was still one last step. He spoke the last incantation and the air around his small shelter shimmered, causing his shelter to disappear from plain sight. The only visible part of him was his long pointed blue hat, sticking out of the snow like a flag gloriously waving in the frozen mountain wind.

This'll have to do for now. I hope someone finds me soon.

He was physically and mentally exhausted. The magic he had just performed depleted his remaining energy.

Theodore closed his eyes, succumbing to sleep as the storm raged around him.

Ànifa turned a corner and found herself in front of the entrance to a narrow slot canyon. Standing akimbo, she looked at the top of the canyon and estimated the walls to be about ten meters tall. The road, which had been about a meter wide the entire way here, was narrowing to a small, single-use path. Steep cliffs rose high into the blue sky on either side of the canyon.

Snow covered the ground all around the area outside the path. The few scattered pine trees were small and shrunken, as if they had been there for hundreds or even thousands of years. They radiated with life—each tree brimming with small birds and squirrels, each minding their own business and chattering away at each other.

As Ànifa took in the scene before her, she caught something odd from the corner of her eye. She turned her full attention to it and was surprised to see a large, tattered blue sorcerer's hat lying in the snow. It looked as if someone had only recently placed it there.

Ànifa took a few steps toward it while absentmindedly muttering to herself.

"Hmm... what's this?" she asked herself.

Suddenly, the hat floated off the ground and spun around wildly, creating a miniature whirlwind. Ànifa screamed and hid her face behind her arms. Then, as suddenly as it had started, it stopped, and the husky voice of an elderly man called out to her.

"Hullo there!"

Ànifa was too stunned to move. She kept her face hidden, but after a few seconds, she felt foolish. She turned in the direction of the voice and saw a wizard dressed in fine blue clothing standing before her. He had a long white beard that trailed to his chest. His beard and hat covered his face, with only his small button nose and cerulean eyes showing. He wore a blue button-up shirt under his long navy-blue cloak with brown trousers held up by a large golden belt buckle. He was wearing the blue sorcerer's hat that she had seen resting on the ground mere moments ago and was holding a large scarlet glass staff. He was shorter than her by a head, but his sorcerer's hat made up for the loss.

"I apologize for the theatrics, miss, but I'm a lost traveler. I was sheltering myself from the storm that came through here last night, and also from the monsters, as I'm not much of a fighter." He lifted his scarlet staff in the air and gave her a deep nod. "I am Theodore Henry Caldwell, and it's nice to make your acquaintance. What's your name?"

Ànifa took a few seconds to compose herself and used this time to study the man in front of her. Although Theodore's actions and words made it seem like he was perfectly at ease, he eyed her curiously, keeping his staff raised as if readying for an attack. She realized how tense she was and smiled, feeling a bit ridiculous. She let out a sigh of relief and felt back at ease.

"I'm Ànifa. It's nice to meet you too," she said with a quick wave. "I haven't seen a single other person since I started on this path. So, you're lost then?"

"Yes, indeed," Theodore said while relaxing his stance. "I was with someone—a knight by the name of Sir Cecil Kloud. We were separated, and after wandering around in circles for a bit, I hid myself here. You said that you have seen no one else but me, but what about footprints? Any signs that there was someone else on this path recently?"

"I'm sorry. I haven't seen anything and I know nothing about this area. I'm on my way across the mountains to purchase special herbs for a friend. Would you like to join me?"

Theodore stood there for a moment, quickly and quietly analyzing her. After a few seconds, he nodded. "So, we are like twin wands, then. I'd love to join you, Ànifa, and I'm truly glad to have met you. But after we find these herbs, can you help me look for Cecil?"

"Of course!" Ànifa replied with a smile. "I couldn't accept your help without helping you in return."

"You are too kind."

"I'm just doing what I can. Shall we go?" she asked.

The wizard looked around, checking to make sure he wasn't forgetting anything.

"Yes, let us depart," Theodore replied after he seemed satisfied. "Now that the storm has passed, I don't want to wait around here any longer."

"Was it bad?"

"It was bad for me. I am not used to the cold or the snow."

"Neither am I. Let's hurry on," Ànifa urged.

Ànifa led the way into the slot canyon. The walls of the canyon were hauntingly beautiful—smooth from centuries of water erosion and composed of dark granite mixed with swirls of pink and white quartz. She suspected the canyon was carved by thousands of years' worth of melting and freezing water.

After only a few meters, they found a large tree trunk blocking their way. It was odd, since there were no trees in the slot canyon. It seemed as if it had been deliberately placed there.

"Is this from the storm you were talking about?" Ànifa asked.

"That would make the most sense. Still, it's strange that it wound up here. But, alas, it is in our way. Now, please stand back while I clear our path."

Ànifa nodded and took a few small steps backward.

Theodore stepped forward and centered himself in front of the fallen tree. He raised his glass staff into the air and cried, "Be gone, obstacle! *Firearaja!*" A burst of flames shot out from this staff, setting the log ablaze. After a few moments, Theodore put out the flames with a concentrated gust of wind so powerful it blew the flash-charred log out of the way.

"Whoa!" Ànifa exclaimed with wide eyes. "Very impressive. How did you do that? I didn't know humans could use magic."

"First of all, a sorcerer does not reveal his secrets. And that is what I am—not just a human, but a sorcerer! I am a B-Class Sorcerer from

Ajenti University. Yes... you have a true Ajentian wizard at your service."

Ànifa gave him a blank look. "I have no idea what that means."

She could see Theodore tense for a moment, then relax. "Not a problem. Just know that I am ready to assist you in the face of danger."

"I thought you told me that you weren't a fighter."

"Correct. I'm not a fighter. I'm an academic, which is even more frightening!"

Ànifa rolled her eyes. "Can you please drop the excessive showmanship?"

Theodore frowned. "Ah, yes, my apologies. Truth be told, I am exaggerating. I have had no one to talk to since Cecil ran off."

"Right, your friend. Did he really abandon you?"

"I don't know if I'd call him a friend. I think the correct term would be obligatory companion. But yes. One minute, he was there, following behind me. The next, he was gone. I don't know where he went off to."

"Well, maybe we'll find some clues."

"It's certainly possible."

Ànifa led the way further into the slot canyon. After a few hundred meters, she heard the call of a great raptor and glanced at the sky.

"Ah—it's a great white falcon! What a treat to see one," Theodore said, his cerulean eyes shimmering in delight.

As they continued, the slot canyon opened and they began climbing the mountain using a set of switchbacks. The terrain was rough at first, but the slope soon tapered out to an easy grade.

Wildlife was abundant. Not long after they left the slot canyon, they watched a large white bear and her two cubs peacefully strolling through the brush a few dozen meters away. They also came upon the tracks of a mighty beast, which Theodore enthusiastically identified as a woolly rhinoceros. At one point, Ànifa thought she saw one hiding deep in the shadows of the nearby forest. They also saw a few different groupings of unideer, each of their singular horns unique and beautiful. There was even a point when a winged ram glided above them. Theodore had explained to her then that the rams couldn't actually use their wings to fly. Instead, they used them to glide from one cliff to another.

Throughout all this, Ànifa was growing more and more calm and familiar with her surroundings. She was delighted by the wildlife—all of it new and wonderful to her.

"This has been a truly magnificent experience. To think, the woman who sent me on this journey, Charlotte, warned me of monsters. All we have seen are peaceful animals." Ànifa said with a contented smile.

"I don't know if I'd call a Schelff bear peaceful when they're chasing you. Or a woolly rhinoceros, for that matter," Theodore replied with a grim smile. "However, we have seen many animals out and about today. A rare treat indeed—most of the animals we've seen are typically timid and skittish."

"They haven't seemed skittish to me," Ànifa said. "That one unideer almost touched me."

"Yes, that was quite extraordinary. And your friend, Charlotte, is correct—there are monsters in these mountains. Cecil and I ran into some right before the storm hit. They were some truly ugly and terrifying creatures—nothing like I have ever seen before in my life. Nor did they resemble anything that any bestiary has ever mentioned before. I have absolutely no idea where they came from. I can only hope that our luck will continue and that we do not cross paths with any of those foul creatures today."

"I... I think you may have spoken too soon," Ànifa said as three large, bluish, bulbous creatures dropped onto the path in front of them. The stench was so rotten that she could hardly keep from retching. The foul odor was of decaying corpses and decomposing food waste.

The creatures were truly grotesque. They were large, gelatinous creatures with no discernible body shape. Their pale, nearly transparent bodies were a light shade of blue. They were small, about the height of a typical cockatrice, yet looked much more dangerous than the short, squat birds Ànifa used to hunt. The memory of her hunting sessions came and went in a flash—barely long enough for her to hold onto.

"Egads! Where did these foul beasts come from?"

"I don't know, but I'm not going to ask!" Ànifa said as she unslung her bow from her left shoulder, snapping herself out of a momentary daze.

As she held her bow in her hands, poised and ready to fire, she stopped for a moment, taking in the bow's beauty. In an instant, her hands had found their grooves—grooves that she had held many times before. The bow was as familiar to her as her own two hands.

As she stood there, the three monsters approached them. Ànifa fired. The arrow sang a swift song as it soared through the air. She hit the monster on the right side of what she could only call its face. Then, to her horror, the viscous monster absorbed the arrow.

"It looks as if your arrows are ineffective. Now, stand back, Ànifa! I can handle this!" Theodore cried as he stepped out in front of her.

Theodore shouted a phrase that she didn't quite hear and then drove his scarlet staff into the snow in front of him. A small burst of fire shot out of the staff, followed by two other fireballs, each one aiming toward a different gelatin monster. Upon impact, the monsters howled in rage and propelled themselves forward.

"It looks like we've aggravated them!" Ànifa yelled as she readied another arrow. As she drew her bow, she whispered under her breath, "Tekkhas Harmonias," and let the arrow fly. This time, upon impact, the lead monster stopped in its path.

Theodore took advantage of the moment and shot a stream of frozen air and snow toward the gelatin monster, freezing it.

"Ànifa, shoot the one on the left!"

"On it!" Ànifa said as she took aim and fired.

Theodore aimed and shot a ball of fire toward the arrow, encasing it in fire. The fire arrow punctured right through the monster, causing its form to break up and splash into the ground like a water bubble.

"Watch out!" Theodore cried moments before the third monster rammed into Ànifa. She fell flat on the ground, knocking the air out of her. Then, the monster was on top of her, smothering her.

The last thing she saw before she passed out was Theodore's scarlet staff bursting into flames.

"Ànifa..."

"Wh—who are you?"

"I am that which will destroy all life as you know it."

"What do you want with me?"

"I wish to eliminate you—to rid the universe of your pitiful existence."

"Why me?"

"You are the only thing in my way, the only thing keeping me from destroying this planet, the only thing keeping me from awakening my true power."

"So, why me?"

"You know why, Ànifa..."

"Ànifa!"

"Ànifa!" Theodore exclaimed; his eyes lit up in delight.

She sat up, coughed, then puked up water. "Ugh, nasty!"

"Are you alright?"

"Yeah, I guess so, besides this horrid taste in my mouth. What were those things?"

"Your guess would be as good as mine at this point. One thing is certain, though. We must not linger here."

"I agree." Ànifa nodded. "I don't want to deal with another one of those things."

Theodore helped Ànifa up and they continued down the path. Ànifa looked around for other jelly monsters, and since there were none in sight, she took a moment to study her surroundings. The path they were on was leading them through jagged peaks. Pine trees surrounded them, though the trees were spread too far apart for this area to be a true forest. From the path, Ànifa had a magnificent view of the peaks that surrounded them. And, off in the distance, if she squinted, she could see where the mountains met the shoreline. Ever since Ànifa and Theodore had run into the monsters, they hadn't seen any more animals. Even the songbirds had quieted.

Soon the path veered to the left, and all Ànifa could see was the land in front of her. As she trudged forward, she suddenly recalled what had been said to her when she was unconscious. This was now the second time that someone had spoken to her inside her head. And they had said something about this planet.

She turned toward Theodore to speak and caught a glimmer of movement in the corner of her eye. A moment later, the small black bat was on her, scratching at her face.

"Ah! Get it off!"

"Where did that come from?" Theodore cried as he swung his staff, smacking the bat in mid-air. It fell to the ground, letting out an ear-numbing screech.

Ànifa fell to her knees, clutching her ears. As the bat hit the ground, Theodore thrust the butt of his staff down, smacking it in the head. She didn't realize she had been screaming until the screeching stopped.

"Thank you, Theodore," Ànifa said, standing up as she combed her blue hair through her fingers, getting some knots out.

"Don't thank me yet. We've gotten ourselves into a situation."

"What—?" Ànifa turned around. The word caught in her throat as she saw the six massive jelly monsters looming behind her.

"Did you not smell them? These smell even worse than the ones from before." Theodore's face scrunched up as he gagged on the surrounding air.

"I haven't been able to smell much of anything since I passed out," she replied.

The six jelly monsters rushed toward them.

"We've got to move. Now!" Theodore commanded.

Theodore grabbed Ànifa by the arm and began dragging her until she caught her footing. They ran as fast as they could, Ànifa soon outpacing the elderly wizard. She glanced behind her and saw the jelly monsters following close behind.

"Ànifa, watch out!" Theodore cried, his face full of exhaustion and fear.

As she turned, all she saw in front of her was open air. She flung herself toward the ground, sliding to a stop right before the ledge of a steep cliff. Peering down, she estimated it would be a twenty-meter fall to the rocks below.

"What now?" Ànifa exclaimed as she stood, then noticed that the wizard next to her was frozen in stupefied fear. "Theodore, snap out of it!"

Theodore turned to her, wide-eyed, and looked back at the oncoming foe and gaped even wider. Ànifa followed his gaze and couldn't help but let her jaw drop.

Behind the six large jelly monsters, a massive dire sloth had appeared. It stood nearly six or seven times taller than her. A soft, snowy mist spun around it as it raised an arm thicker than a tree trunk and swiped at the six unsuspecting monsters with its three horrendously long, sharp claws. In a single swipe, the dire sloth tore the jelly monsters to puddles of gelatinous liquid.

Their way out was still blocked. The dire sloth stared at Ànifa. Ànifa met its gaze and smiled. The dire sloth stared back, its face still and unmoving. After a few seconds, the dire sloth turned and started clamoring down the path before it veered off into the scattered trees.

Ànifa and Theodore waited wordlessly for a few moments before they took a step forward. Then, still silent, the two companions swiftly continued their way down the mountain.

They continued in silence for about an hour. Their silence was eventually broken as a lamb-sized jackhorn crossed the snow-laden path in front of them. It looked similar to a rabbit, with pure white fur, but it sported two large antlers that looked like tree branches. If it wasn't for the patches of dark-brown dirt that stained the snow and marked the path, it would have been nearly camouflaged.

"Hold on, Ànifa. It's a jackhorn," Theodore whispered, pure excitement dripping from his voice. "I never imagined I'd be lucky enough to see one."

As Ànifa stared at the jackhorn, it stopped in its tracks and looked directly into her shimmering lavender eyes. She suddenly felt awash in purifying light. It was as if her soul itself was being cleansed, wiping clean her invisible scars. By the time she composed herself, the jackhorn was gone.

"That was beautiful... wondrously beautiful," was all Ànifa could say, her body still tingling with warmth.

"I can't help but wonder if all of these animal sightings could have something to do with you." Theodore stood there, his right hand stroking his long white beard as he leaned upon his glass staff. His wide-brimmed, dark-blue sorcerer's hat was slightly askew, making him look comical. "Yes—that would make sense now, wouldn't it?" he said, his cerulean eyes losing their focus.

"What makes sense? What do you mean?" Ànifa asked, snapping out of her daze.

"Well, I didn't want to be too forward before, but you are an elf, are you not?"

"An elf?" her right hand automatically rose to feel the pointed tips of her ears.

"Yes. The shape of your ears, your hair the color of the sky, and even your dark-brown skin differs from that of us humans. All are unique and only found in myths and legends. So, I can only presume you to be an elf, although elves haven't been seen in thousands of years." Theodore stood and looked in the direction where the jackhorn had gone.

Ànifa looked at her hands, studying her dark skin. Compared to the pale, white skin of the old wizard, hers was darker, more like umber. As she was comparing her skin tone to Theodore's, he caught her eye. Her expression must have startled him, as he almost choked on his words. "That's not to say that you aren't beautiful, of course."

She laughed. "Thanks. I... I don't remember too much about myself. But I believe you may be correct, Theodore, because I am certainly not like you."

"Well, few are. We wizards are a rare breed and becoming rarer and rarer nowadays. That makes us a rare pair indeed!" Theodore's eyes suddenly turned downcast. "Young folk are either disinterested in the old ways or too impatient to learn. The great university of Ajenti is now just a shell of what it was only twenty years ago. Yet I've gotten off-topic, and I would like to circle back to my original inquiry.

"I believe that your presence brought about these animal sightings. This is another sign that you are an elf. In the stories, elves are close to nature and can communicate with all animals—of Eklatros, of sea, and of sky—and can command them in both beautiful and malevolent ways. It is a magic that no human has ever learned, and one that is both revered and feared at the same time. For anyone that can speak to an animal can control nature itself."

"I don't think I know how to talk to animals, though. And what about the bat that attacked me? That animal wasn't behaving like the others."

"Yes, it's true the bat attack was erratic, and particularly peculiar, since bats are nocturnal. However, that dire sloth back there... it killed those six jelly monsters as if by your command. I know you may not know how, and you may not have even done it consciously, but I believe something inside of you called that dire sloth, and that is why it saved our lives."

"I... I do not know. But you may be right. All I know is that—well, after it happened, we looked into each other's eyes, and I learned her name—Maqinjinarii. I gave her my thanks, but I received nothing back from her before she left. And yet, moments ago with the jackhorn, our eyes met as well, and in that moment, I was filled with an intense, purifying feeling. I still feel warm from the sensation."

"See what I mean? Ànifa, you may not have your memories, but it's possible that the animals could help you in your quest to reclaim them."

"You may be right again. You sure seem to be a helpful companion."

"Not as helpful as yourself, Ànifa," Theodore said, his smile reaching his eyes.

She smiled back. "Well, we should continue on. I don't believe we are far from our destination."

"That's good. It's going to get dark soon, and I don't want to spend another night out in the wilderness," Theodore replied.

"I'm sure we won't have to. Let's go."

As they turned to continue along the path, a sunbeam cut its way through the mountains and reflected a myriad of colors on the surface of the shimmering sea.

I still may not know who I am, but I am obtaining answers. I'm safe, and I have met a helpful companion, she thought. *I believe I am exactly where I need to be. The reason I'm here should soon present itself. For now, though, I just want to enjoy the view. This may be the most beautiful place I've ever seen.*

3

BATTLE FOR ANSWERS

Ànifa and her new companion, Theodore, walked along a wide path. To their right were the mountains they had recently crossed, and to their left lay a scattering of pine trees and a quiet stream. Ànifa closed her eyes for a moment, taking in the tranquil melody of the serene landscape she found herself in.

They soon approached a set of stone stairs carved out of a small cliff. They climbed the stairs and approached a large, pale orange tent. To the left of the tent sat a large clay pot.

"This place looks nearly identical to Charlotte's tent. We must be in the right place."

"That's great," Theodore exclaimed. "Is there a way to knock?"

"Hmm..." Ànifa scanned the mouth of the tent and spotted a thick green rope. She gave it a tug and a bell chimed inside.

"Just a minute," a rough, shaky voice called out.

As she stood outside the tent, Ànifa took a moment to look around. To her left, she saw a bunch of logs and gnarled tree stumps she hadn't noticed earlier. It looked almost as if a colossal beast had torn the trees to shreds.

Before she could think any more on the matter, a small elderly man popped out of the tent flaps. The man was wearing a loose-fitting tan cloak with a white piece of string tied around the middle. He was bald but had a finely trimmed goatee and thick, bushy gray eyebrows that nearly covered his milky blue eyes. He was hunched down, with a hand tending to his back as if he was in pain.

"Yes—?" the man asked quizzically once he got a good look at them. "What do an Ajentian wizard and an elf want with me?"

"I... so you know what I am?" Ànifa asked.

"I know what you are, but I don't know why you'd be here. Though I can only guess..."

Although it had sounded like the old man was going to say more, he suddenly got silent, as if he was silencing himself.

"Well, I'm here on behalf of a recent acquaintance, Charlotte. She... well, she helped me out a great deal, and I'm running an errand for her."

"Ah, well, any friend of Charlotte's is a friend of mine. And who might you two be exactly?"

"I'm Ànifa."

"I am the B-Class Sorcerer Theodore Henry Caldwell of Ajenti."

"Ànifa. Theodore. It is a pleasure to meet you both. Now, let's get you out of the cold."

Ànifa followed the man inside, with Theodore following close behind her. It was much warmer inside, and she rubbed her hands together to warm them up.

"Excuse me," Theodore asked as he stepped inside, "but I don't believe you've introduced yourself yet."

The old man stopped in his tracks and turned around.

"By golly you're right! Where are my manners?" The old man cleared his throat and stood up straight. Ànifa was surprised to find him much taller than he had originally seemed.

"I am Christian Barthandaedlus Mason, Duke of Schelff Island, protector of the Dragolum Shrine, and purveyor of the best herbal remedies found this far north."

Theodore audibly gasped. "Duke of Schelff? Protector of the Dragolum Shrine? You are the great Sage Mason!"

"Yes, many know me by the name Sage Mason."

"But… Duke of Schelff Island. What an honor," Theodore said with a small bow.

"Please, it's a title I do not want. And besides, I have never needed to act as a Duke. It's nearly meaningless."

"Forgive me for saying so, but I fear that may not be the case for much longer," Theodore said.

As Theodore and Sage Mason continued talking, Ànifa looked around the tent. There was a large wooden table to her left, covered in dirty plates and beer bottles. The smaller wooden table to her right held about a dozen large glass jars, each filled with green herbs. Some were greener than others, while some had white, orange, or purple accents. Behind the table sat a small bed with brown sheets. A bookshelf, nearly overflowing with massive volumes, sat near the bed. And on the small nightstand directly next to the bed lay the same book that she had seen in Charlotte's tent, *A Collective History: The Magical World of Eklatros.*

Sage Mason grunted, and Ànifa snapped back into the conversation.

"I do not look forward to a meeting with those dimwits," Sage Mason growled. Directing his attention back to Ànifa, he feigned a smile and said, "Now, I believe you said you were here on behalf of our silver-haired friend, correct?"

"Yes. Charlotte said you had some special herbs for her."

"Indeed, I do," Sage Mason said, now with a genuine smile. Ànifa noticed he was missing a few back teeth. "I got them right over there for ya. Hold on for a quick second."

Sage Mason walked over to the table with the large jars. He opened a drawer and pulled out a small glass container. He then stared at the large jars filled with herbs for a few long seconds before he opened one of the jars, and then quickly put the lid back on.

"Sorry, not that one. That was some Forest Diesel," Sage Mason said. He then opened the jar next to the Forest Diesel.

"Yes, this is right. Blue Dream," he said as he filled the smaller jar with the green, pungent herb.

"My, what a strong fragrance," Theodore said, leaning in closer.

"Yes, this one is quite strong. It helps with joint pain," Sage Mason replied as he finished and handed over the jar. "Here you go, Ànifa."

"Tha—Thank..."

She couldn't breathe. It felt as if hands were gripping her throat, suffocating her. In a panic, she clawed at her throat as she fell to her knees. She tried to cough, but her throat was cemented shut. She closed her eyes and passed out.

"Ànifa... I knew you would fall into my grasp..."

She rolled her eyes. *"Really? You again? Can't you just leave me alone?"*

"You know I cannot do that. You are important to me, Ànifa."

"Look, I'm not afraid of you."

"You should be afraid... you should be, Ànifa."

Air quickly flowed back into her lungs and she coughed. All the while, she felt two pairs of hands on her back, rubbing and patting her. Before she could do anything, her eyes closed with sudden drowsiness. When she finally got a hold of herself, she found herself lying in a large brown bed.

Oh Eklatros, not this again.

"Ànifa!" Excited voices came from either side of her.

"I can't believe that—" before she could continue, she lapsed into another round of coughing.

"It's best if you don't talk, Ànifa. You've been through a lot," Sage Mason said.

Ànifa gave a weak nod in reply as she held back the urge to cough. Theodore handed her a glass of water and she gladly took it.

"From what Theodore told me, the two of you have been through a lot. I'm surprised you're both still alive," Sage Mason said. He paused for a few seconds and looked at the ceiling. "From what I can surmise, it happened when the gelatinous monster smothered you. A piece of it lodged itself into your lungs. You passed out because the piece inside you suddenly swelled up and blocked your throat. You're lucky you were here when it happened. If you had been out in the woods, it would have killed you within minutes. I am honestly astounded that it didn't happen earlier."

"Right. Well—" Ànifa said, then stopped when she caught the look in Sage Mason's eye. She nodded, then looked at Theodore. She then put her fingers to her head to mimic bunny ears.

"Yes, that's right. That must be it!" Theodore exclaimed, pounding his hand into his fist.

"What is it?" Sage Mason asked, with a note of impatience in his voice.

"Before we left the mountains, a large, pure-white jackhorn crossed our path, and it locked eyes with Ànifa. They stared at each other for a few seconds."

Ànifa nodded. A sharp whistling noise cut through the air.

"Ah, just a moment. The tea is ready," Sage Mason said as he stood from the stool he had been sitting on.

Ànifa looked at Theodore. She stared deep into his eyes.

"*Do you trust him?*" Ànifa thought.

Theodore softly nodded, his eyes wide in surprise.

"*Good, me too. I just wanted to make sure. Everyone here has been so nice to me.*"

"That's because we all care about you," Theodore whispered.

"Eh, what's that?" Sage Mason called as he approached, holding a mug filled to the brim with a dark steaming liquid.

"I was just telling her she's in good care here," Theodore said.

"Indeed, she is. Now, drink this."

Sage Mason handed her the mug. She took a sniff and smiled to herself.

I don't remember the names of these aromas, but they smell like home, she thought to herself.

"Now, it's quite bitter, and the liquid is pretty thick. It'll be—" Sage Mason began, but was cut short as Ànifa waved him off.

She brought the mug to her lips and took a small sip of the delicious nectar, followed by a large gulp, and then another, until the mug was empty.

As she handed the mug back to Sage Mason, his face wore an expression of shock and surprise.

"Most people throw up at least half of that stuff. It's wretched! How did you down that so quickly?" Sage Mason asked.

"Did you forget that I'm an elf?" she said, speaking for the first time since she'd passed out. "To me, that was the most delicious drink in the whole world. I think I used to drink a similar concoction quite regularly."

"Ah, is your memory coming back?" Theodore asked.

"I'd say it's more of a feeling than a memory. The taste was so familiar, but I don't remember actually drinking it."

"How did you end up here, if you don't mind me asking so bluntly?" Sage Mason asked, his eyes narrowing to a squint as he studied her.

"It's not a problem, although it may take a little while."

"I suggest we move to the table, then," Theodore said.

"Agreed. Let me clean up first, then we can start the story," Sage Mason replied.

"... and that's when we came across the jackhorn. When we looked into each other's eyes, I felt rejuvenated, down to my very core," Ànifa said, pushing away her empty plate. Sage Mason had served them a simple dinner—a fresh garden salad with pine nuts and a large grilled vegetable he had called a zuccuash.

"Jackhorns are sacred animals and are rarely seen. They do not come across the paths of humans by chance. Although you are not a human," Sage Mason said as he leaned back in his chair. "I think the jackhorn sensed you were under attack by that monster, and it temporarily healed you."

"It truly was a magnificent moment. I have witnessed nothing quite like it," Theodore said.

Sage Mason hummed to himself. "Few have. Now, Ànifa, I want to ask about the dire sloth you mentioned. As you said, her name is Maqinjinarii. She is the queen of the Watthana Mountains. Technically, all of Schelff Island is under her domain."

"Oh? Have you seen her?" Ànifa asked.

"Yes, a few times. The first time was many, many years ago; and on that day, I gained a new friend. She only comes around during times of significant change."

"Was she here recently? I noticed all of the fallen trees outside your tent," Ànifa asked.

"Yes, that was from Maqinjinarii. She was here, about three or four days ago. She was distressed—as if in anguish. At first, all she did was stare at me, the rage steaming off of her, and then she started ripping the trees into shreds. She came close to tearing my tent apart, but she suddenly stopped as quickly as she began," Sage Mason said.

"These tents... are they made from those dire sloths?" Theodore asked.

"You are quite perceptive. Yes, the hides we use are from the dire sloths." Sage Mason said.

Maqinjinarii was here three to four days ago, which was around the same time that Charlotte found Ànifa. She suspected her near-death experience caused Maqinjinarii's rage. If that was the case, then Maqinjinarii may have stopped when Ànifa awoke. She didn't understand the connection, or why Maqinjinarii took out her rage here. She thought back to the moment she and the dire sloth shared. Was there a hidden meaning to it all?

"Is Maqinjinarii a god?" Ànifa asked suddenly, interrupting Theodore and Sage Mason's discussion about the tent. She had no idea what prompted the question. She tried to focus on the fleeting memory, but it was already gone.

Sage Mason hesitated before he answered. "In a sense, yes, she is the god of all dire sloths. She is old—hundreds of years old—and there is still much life left in her. Maqinjinarii is highly intelligent, and does not help just anyone. You called her, Ànifa. Somehow you called her to help you."

"I... I don't know how. I was frightened of those jelly monsters... more frightened than I have ever been, as far as I can remember. I didn't want another one to attack me," Ànifa said, fear creeping into her voice. "And that strange bat, it attacked me too!"

"What bat?" Sage Mason asked, raising a bushy eyebrow in curiosity.

"Oh, it was only a bat. Though it may have been rabid," Theodore replied.

"Bats don't venture out in the daytime, even if they have rabies," Sage Mason said. He suddenly snapped his fingers, the sharp sound reverberating through the tent. "That's it! That's why they attacked you, Ànifa. Those jelly monsters—think about it. Their bodies must not be able to last long in the elements. I believe they seek out host bodies, plant themselves in the host, kill the host, and then possess the deceased body and use it to its own will."

Throughout Sage Mason's explanation, Ànifa sunk lower and lower into her chair.

"Ugh, to think that thing was inside me." An icy shiver ran down her spine at the mere thought of it.

"But even after it had infested Ànifa, I still had to kill it," Theodore explained. "That must mean the large jelly monsters must be able to infest many different hosts before depleting, right? It would probably take a far smaller amount to infest a small animal like a common cave bat than a fully grown elven woman."

"Very fair point indeed, Sorcerer Caldwell," Sage Mason replied. "But where did these monsters come from? Why are they here? What's their purpose, their goal? None of this makes any sense."

"No, none of this makes any sense at all," Ànifa said, rising out of her chair. "From what I can tell, *I'm* not supposed to even be here."

"You're not," Theodore replied. "Elves haven't been seen in thousands of years. You're more myth than history. There are many among my colleagues who adamantly believe the elves in all the old stories are just wizards and sorcerers. All poppycock to me. I believe elves are real; I always have, although I never thought I'd actually see one. And yet, now I have had the honor to become acquainted with one."

"Same here. Even I, protector of the Dragolum Shrine, never thought I'd ever see an elf, either. However, part of my responsibilities—the tasks handed down to me through the millennia—is to provide guidance and hospitality to any elf in need. And now I have done both. Life can be a funny thing," Sage Mason chuckled.

"So, why am I here, then? Why now? And these jelly monsters... why are they here?"

"Those are not questions so easily answered, especially right now. You'll need to figure them out on your own," Sage Mason replied.

"Yes—I suppose you're right." Ànifa sat back down in her chair and then looked at Theodore. "You know, I don't know if I ever even asked you why you were wandering around in the mountains, Theodore."

"Yes, I agree. I am quite curious as to why an Ajentian wizard of your caliber is here," Sage Mason turned his attention to the wizard.

"My lost companion, Sir Cecil Kloud, and I are on a mission. We are studying the Great Barriers and were in this area seeking information, which must be from you, Sage Mason."

"Indeed, and you found me," Sage Mason said.

"Is there anything you can tell us?" Theodore prompted.

"Very well," Sage Mason said with a sigh. "I will tell you what I know about the Great Barriers. Just keep in mind that this knowledge is kept secret for an important reason. Not even I know everything. However, my colleague Dante is the world-renowned expert on the Great Barriers. He lives just outside of Galstrom."

"Seriously? Galstrom? I was just there."

"Hohoo, I'm sure you were. Now, do you want to hear what I have to say or not?"

"Very much so, yes," Theodore replied, his eyes twinkling like a child's.

"Ànifa, do you know about the Great Barriers?" Sage Mason suddenly asked.

"I... I don't know," she stammered. The question caught her off guard.

"Well, maybe you know them by another name, and maybe you can't remember right now because of your memory loss. Their name has been nearly lost to history, but there are few that remember: Ekataramn.

"All Great Barriers draw their power from the original, the mighty Yttendaus," Sage Mason continued. "Some say the tree is so awesome in its power that it levitates the rock it sits on, creating the floating island. The barrier around Yttendaus is so powerful nothing can pierce it, not even wind or light. They say that Yttendaus has its own light source and even its own weather system, although no one can actually confirm this. What's more, the floating island lies just north of Schelff. It's not a secret by any means, although no one can truly observe it. I believe that may be where you came from, Ànifa. If you say Charlotte found you on the shore near her tent, it's possible you fell into the ocean from atop Yttendaus and the currents brought you to shore.

"But I digress. Now, for the rest of the Great Barriers. First, there is Kalahsem that lies in the southern portion of the continent of Gallheim. Next, there is Roheefy on the continent of Roffen, and Panabeeta on Panna Isle. Finally, there is Bugenaluf here on Schelff Island."

"I knew it! I knew that there was a Great Barrier here," Theodore exclaimed. "If only that dumbass knight, Cecil, didn't wander off on his own—"

"Slow down, Theodore," Sage Mason said, holding out a palm. "I am the guardian of the Dragolum Shrine. Did you not hear me? The tunnel below the shrine is the only way to reach Bugenaluf. And there is absolutely no way I am letting you go near the shrine. Not now, not anytime soon. Neither of you two are ready."

"But—" Theodore started, but a sharp look from Sage Mason shut him up.

"This is not a negotiation. It is I, and only I alone, that protects Bugenaluf. And it is said that once the chosen one is ready, the path will open. But now is not the time, although I am starting to believe you are the chosen one, Ànifa."

"Me? The chosen one?" Ànifa said, mostly to herself.

"Indeed. So even if you think you are ready, Theodore, she is not, and thus the path is not yet open."

Theodore crossed his arms and sighed. "That's disappointing. Yet, I understand. These are places that should be protected, and from what I remember, they are also extremely dangerous places."

"They're not only dangerous for those who venture near them— they are volatile and would cause widespread damage of apocalyptic proportions if they were to be set off."

"Ah—that I did not know. Good to know. By the way, I never even knew that the Great Barriers had names," Theodore said.

"Those names were not of the Great Barriers, but of the entities that dwell within—they are the reasons for the Great Barriers to be there in the first place. They are ancient names—the Ekataramn, the original Gods," Sage Mason said.

"Ah, sure. Those are not the names that the stories give them."

"No, the names are not for just anyone to know. They are powerful names, and must not be abused."

"Yes, of course. Also, I thought that there were seven Ekataramn, from what the legends say. You only named four," Theodore prompted.

"He named five. You're forgetting about Yttendaus, my home," Ànifa said.

"Ah, are you remembering?" Theodore asked.

"No, not really. But a floating island..." Ànifa trailed off, lost in thought, before she continued. "And from what Sage Mason said, even the name—Yttendaus—it gives me the feeling of home. I can't explain it."

"The elves must reside on Yttendaus," Sage Mason muttered quietly to himself. "No wonder we haven't seen them in thousands of years."

"But that's still only five, Sage Mason. What about the other two?" Theodore asked again.

"What?" Sage Mason said, snapping out of a daze. "Oh yes, the two other Ekataramn. I don't know anything about them. If you need to know more, you can talk to Dante. As I said before, he is the world-renowned expert on the Great Barriers and lives just outside Galstrom."

"I will keep him in mind. But you have been a great help too, great Sage. Being here was a revelation of sorts," Theodore replied.

"Of that I am sure," Sage Mason said. "Now, it is getting late, and I am old. I believe the time for slumber is upon us. Wait right here, I'll fetch you my spare bedrolls."

As Sage Mason stood up, his bones cracked in a steady succession, and he let out a satisfied sigh. He shuffled over to a small cabinet near his bed.

"Thank you, Ànifa, for helping me find this place," Theodore said to her when they were alone.

"No, it is you who brought me here."

"I can't explain it but... meeting you, and now us being here together..." he trailed off.

"Yeah, it feels right. Like all of this is supposed to be happening."

"Exactly," Theodore said, just as Sage Mason was returning.

"So, one of these is in far better condition than the other—" Sage Mason said, as he presented the two bedrolls.

It was true. One bedroll looked brand new, as if it had only been used a couple of times, while the other was visibly worn, as if it was decades old.

"I'll take the dilapidated one," Ànifa said.

"Are you sure?" Theodore asked. "I don't mind—"

"Nonsense. You are my elder."

"Ah, well, thank you. I appreciate it," Theodore said as he took the nicer bedroll from Sage Mason.

"And here's yours, Ànifa," Sage Mason said. "It's been through a lot. That's the same one I used throughout the vast majority of my traveling years."

"Yes, I can smell many of the places it's been, even if I've never been to those places myself," Ànifa said as she hugged the bedroll. She breathed in the aromas of past travels.

"I'm sure you'll have pleasant dreams on it," Sage Mason said.

Ànifa averted her gaze and looked at her feet.

Sage Mason hummed in concern. "Have you not been having pleasant dreams of late?"

"No, not really. It's always the same, but not the same." Ànifa shook her head and then looked up. Her eyes met his and she continued. "It's the same voice talking to me. I can never remember what it says when I wake up, aside from it repeating my name over and over again. I hear it constantly, even now. It started as a dull murmur shortly after I left Charlotte's home, and I have been able to ignore it for the most part. But—"

"But something like that does not just go away. It only gets worse as it gets stronger," Theodore finished for her.

"Indeed. This is not good, Ànifa. I wish you would have told me sooner. It'll take around twenty minutes, but I can whip you up a drink that will give you a dreamless night. It works for us humans, at least," Sage Mason said.

"Well, if it's not a bother," Ànifa said.

"No, no bother at all. It will only work for tonight, and this is not a remedy you can carry around with you. It's a special concoction that requires it to be brewed in an extremely specific way."

"You're not talking about tarnight, are you?" Theodore asked. "That stuff is poisonous!"

"Indeed it is, but only if one overdoses, or if they use it consistently. In small, controlled doses, it can give a great night's sleep. I thought you were an Ajentian wizard. Do they not teach this?"

"I uh, well, I've never taken a class on medicinal herbs and salves. So I never knew the specifics of it," Theodore said.

Sage Mason replied with a noncommittal grunt. "Well, the tarnight won't make itself. Give me about twenty minutes and it will be ready."

That night, Ànifa slumbered dreamlessly. When she awoke, the voice seeped back into the crevasses of her mind.

"*What do you want with me?*" Ànifa thought.

"*Ha ha ha... I thought you didn't want to talk to me. Isn't that why you took the tarnight?*" the voice replied.

"*Yeah, well, I want nothing to do with you. Leave me alone,*" she replied.

And with that, Ànifa turned her attention to Sage Mason, who was busy in the kitchen preparing pancakes, eggs, and a fresh local fruit called raspsteen.

After breakfast, Ànifa and Theodore prepared to head back over the mountains and into the town of Sathon. When she was almost ready, Sage Mason pulled Ànifa aside while Theodore was outside relieving himself.

"Ànifa. I wanted to tell you to be careful out there in the open world. Humans are not kind, and some are more evil than even the most rabid of beasts. They can be the real monsters. If anyone finds out that you are an elf... I can't imagine what a corrupted soul might do for a few koda. Please be careful out there."

"Thank you, Sage Mason, for your concern. I'll keep this in mind."

"Indeed. Here, take this." Sage Mason handed her a navy-blue bonnet. It was a similar color to her hair. "Use this to cover your ears. And I would suggest that you tie your hair back as well. Hide as much of it as you can. Your hair gives you away just as easily as your ears will, to the trained eye at least."

"My hair? What's so special about my—" Ànifa said, but as she ran her hair through her hands, she thought she saw it change shades, from a dark, navy-blue, to a bright sky blue. "How have I not yet noticed this?"

"Your hair doesn't change color all the time. I only noticed it this morning, for as you slept, it was the most brilliant shade of blue I have ever seen. And when you awoke, it suddenly got much darker."

Ànifa sighed. "That must have been because of the voice. I slept a dreamless sleep like you promised, but once I awoke, the voice seeped back into my mind. I couldn't control it."

"I feared that was the case. That's why I've also prepared these," Sage Mason said as he handed her a small jar filled to the brim with a brown-colored fungus.

"These are shuyukuii mushrooms. While not nearly as potent as tarnight, they produce a similar, albeit weaker, effect. Only a small bite of one should do. There is enough in there to last you quite a while if you ration it."

"Thank you. Truly," Ànifa said as she took the jar from him. "I will treat this with great care."

"And remember as well, just because you won't be dreaming doesn't mean that voice still won't be ever-present. And it will grow stronger every day. There may even be a possibility that those mushrooms will increase the speed at which it will gain strength. That is something I have never tested."

"Thanks for the warning. I appreciate it," Ànifa said just as Theodore entered the tent. She quickly slipped the jar into a large pocket in her trenchdress and then turned to Sage Mason. "How much do I owe you for all of this? I don't believe I ever paid for Charlotte's herbs yet either."

"Ah, right. Charlotte's herbs will be twenty koda. And the mushrooms are on me. I hope they help you."

"Thank you. I really appreciate it," Ànifa said as she reached into her trenchdress and pulled out twenty koda. She handed the coins to Sage Mason, who took them with a smile.

"Are you finally ready?" Ànifa asked, turning to look at Theodore. She placed her hands on her hips and gave him an impatient smirk.

"Yes, I believe I am."

"Then let's be on our way," she commanded.

Sage Mason held out an arm to stop her. "Please wait a moment. There is still one last thing I wish to speak to you about."

"What is it?"

"Your ability to speak with animals. On your way back across the mountains, I want you to test out your power. See if you can communicate with the wildlife around you. Start out with small, simple asks, and see where that takes you."

"I agree with Sage Mason," Theodore chimed in. "And don't forget to practice your archery also. Isn't that the reason you wanted to leave Charlotte's in the first place?"

"Yes, I had nearly forgotten. I will work on both of these things," Ànifa said, and with a slight bow, she thanked them both. "Sage Mason, is there any way I can repay you?"

"Being graced by your presence is payment enough... and, of course, the koda you gave me," Sage Mason said with a wink before getting serious again. "I never thought I would meet an elf. In a way, they were a forgotten truth. Until now, at least. It truly is a pleasure to have met you."

"Likewise. And I'm sure our paths will cross again," Ànifa said.

"That I do not doubt," Sage Mason replied. "And with you, Theodore, this will not be our last meeting either. I have much to discuss with you."

"And I with you. But we must be on our way. I must find Cecil," Theodore said.

"I understand. Until next time, then," Sage Mason said.

Ànifa nodded, took one last look around the tent, and then walked outside. She did not wait for Theodore. She marched forward, toward the new day, toward Sathon, and toward a new future.

I now know I'm here for a reason, and I was given many answers today, she thought. *But many more questions have arisen. I can only continue on this journey that I have been thrust into. And I don't think I would have it any other way.*

4

BATTLE FOR PRACTICE

Ànifa hurried down the wide path that led into the Watthana Mountain Range.

"Wait... wait I say!" Theodore gasped as he tried to catch up to her. "I can't keep up with this pace."

She stopped and looked at him. He stood a few dozen meters away, bent over with his hands on his knees, breathing deeply.

"Sorry. It's just that I finally feel like I'm where I'm supposed to be, even though I don't know where I really am. Does that make any sense? I don't think I'm making any sense."

Theodore stood and wiped his mouth with his large, dark-blue sleeve. "No, that makes sense. I feel similarly. I had already been on my quest, but now it's coming to fruition."

"Well, let's continue on, then," Ànifa said as she began walking forward again. "It's such a beautiful morning."

Theodore sighed. "Let's go at a slower pace, shall we?"

Ànifa nodded, then let the wizard lead the way. As the two companions headed into the mountains, the forest hummed with life. The songbirds were singing loudly as the squirrels, rabbits, and chipmunks chattered away happily. Even the trees seemed to purr as the wind rustled through them. "The forest feels exceptionally alive today."

"I think it's because of you. They could be playing off of your mood," Theodore replied.

"You think so? Shall I test my power?" Ànifa stopped and turned toward a large tree that held a variety of different birds. Ànifa stared at the tree for a few seconds, then cocked her head to the left and whistled softly. The chickadees immediately flew toward her. She held out her arms, and they happily landed on them and began singing.

"Quite impressive," Theodore said with wide eyes. He leaned on his staff and stroked his beard. "You truly have a gift."

"Yeah, but I feel like I'm just scratching at the surface. I feel like I can do so much more," Ànifa said. She dropped her arms, and the chickadees flew away, chirping wildly.

"It's just... I can't remember anything, Theodore. The only things I know are the things I've learned since I've awoken here. I can't remember anything. Not the names of the herbs that I recognized at Sage Mason's house. Not the names of the trees, or the names of the clouds. I can't even remember my full name, nor my parents... I don't even know if I had a family, or if I was alone. I remember nothing!" Ànifa's words were thick and wavering as she softly wept into her hands. "And yet, there's one thing I do know, and it's why I feel so happy, even through my pain and distress. I know I am on the right path." Ànifa took a deep breath, calming her emotions. "Now, come, Theodore. We're not going to get very far very fast by talking to songbirds."

"What did you have in mind, then?" Theodore asked.

"Keep up with me," she said, more sternly than she had meant to. "I don't think they'll venture this far out of the mountains. We'll have to go closer."

Ànifa dashed forward as Theodore sighed audibly. A moment later, she heard his weak footsteps behind her and hurried on. She didn't want him to see her tears.

She finally stopped at the point where they had run across the jackhorn. While she waited for Theodore to catch up, she held out her arms and closed her eyes. She breathed in deep, listening to the surrounding forest. The forest itself was breathing, and soon her breathing fell in step with the deep, long breaths of the forest. She remained in that state for a few minutes, her mind completely blank as she became one with the forest.

"Oh my nature!" Theodore exclaimed, breaking her out of her trance.

Ànifa took a deep breath and then opened her eyes. When she looked around, she saw that her outstretched arms were filled with songbirds and squirrels. She even saw a family of unideer scamper back into the forest.

"What on Eklatros were you doing?" Theodore asked.

Ànifa shrugged, scaring off the birds and rodents. "Waiting for you. I just closed my eyes and started breathing with the forest."

"It looks to me as if you were doing more than just breathing with the forest. You were joining into its collective consciousness."

"That would make sense," she said slowly. "I can't explain it, but the feeling that it invoked..." she trailed off in thought.

Theodore shook his head. "That's not something I can even fathom. What you did is taboo in Ajenti. No one is supposed to perform that ritual."

"Ritual? I was only *breathing*," Ànifa said.

"Right, but as an elf, I'm sure you have innate powers that human beings can never obtain, no matter how long we study. If you spent a few days at Ajenti, I'm sure you would learn more than even the headmaster knows."

Ànifa laughed. "I don't know about that, but I appreciate the sentiment. And now that you're here, I can call upon our mounts."

"Mounts?"

Ànifa closed her eyes once again and envisioned the woolly rhinoceros she saw yesterday. She held the image in her mind, and after a few moments, she heard the forest thunder around her.

"Uh, Ànifa? What's going on?" She barely even registered Theodore's uneasy tone beside her.

The thundering grew louder until it suddenly stopped. Ànifa opened her eyes, and before her stood two large woolly rhinoceroses. Up close, they were even more majestic than she could have imagined.

The pair she had summoned were mates—the bigger one was the female, and the smaller one was the male. In comparison, the male had a much longer horn. Its woolly coat was a wonderous mixture of green and brown hues, giving it the perfect camouflage in the forest. The female's horn was smaller and wider. Her coat was much darker —almost black—even though it was still a mixture of brown and green hues.

"That worked out well," Ànifa said with one hand on her hip.

"Are you out of your mind? We can't ride woolly rhino."

"Why not? Who is going to stop me?" Ànifa asked, laughing.

"That's not what I meant," Theodore sighed in defeat.

Ànifa ignored him and grabbed a hold of the female's wool. She hoisted herself effortlessly onto its back.

"See? That wasn't so hard," Ànifa said.

Theodore stood in place and gaped at her as she sat atop the giant beast.

"Quick, Theodore. Get on your rhino before we leave you behind," Ànifa taunted.

"You wouldn't dare. Even after all we've been through?"

Ànifa shrugged.

Theodore rolled his eyes in disbelief and cautiously approached the male rhino. "First Cecil, now Ànifa."

"That's it," Ànifa reassured him.

Theodore looked at the rhino in front of him, took a deep breath, and grabbed a hold of its coat, much like Ànifa had done. He then attempted the same move she had, only to land on his rump.

Ànifa burst out laughing and clutched her chest. The rhino beneath her snorted along in amusement.

"Oh, would you please stop laughing at me?" Theodore said, his brow furrowed in agitation.

Ànifa wiped her eyes. "I'm sorry, I really am. I'll be quiet if it helps you concentrate."

"Thanks," Theodore replied sharply and returned his attention to the matter at hand.

Theodore tried and failed again. After a few minutes of struggling, he finally made it atop the woolly rhino.

"Holy Eklatros. I'm riding a woolly rhino! How did he even let me climb onto him?"

"I'll be honest. He did not enjoy it. He wanted to run away a few times, but I was able to hold him back."

"Really, Ànifa, you truly amaze me. You only learned of this ability yesterday and you can already tame a wild rhinoceros. Your powers are awe-inspiring."

"Thanks, but you really don't need to compliment me so much. I still don't know what I'm doing."

"Which makes it all the more amazing."

"Shall we go?" Ànifa gave the woolly rhino a small tap on its left flank and it lumbered forward. The male followed slowly behind.

Ànifa sat atop the rhino, taking in the sights around her. The shimmering sun as it shone through the clouds. The creaking of the trees as they swayed in the wind. The thundering of the massive animal beneath her. The fluttering and chirping of birds. The chattering of squirrels. The rustling of the wind through her shimmering blue hair. She took a deep breath and smiled.

"You know, there's something I've been meaning to ask you," Theodore asked.

"What is it?" Ànifa asked.

"Last night, when Sage Mason was getting your tea… you spoke to me, but you didn't use any words. How did you do it?"

Ànifa gave a slight shrug. "I guess I somehow knew you could hear me. And you did."

"Can you communicate like that with anyone else?"

"I'm not sure. I think you could hear me because of your connection with the flow of energy."

"Hmm, that could be the case," Theodore said. "It was astounding nonetheless. Did I look shocked?"

"No, you looked like yourself."

"That's good. I went along with it, but I didn't really know what was going on," Theodore finished with a chuckle.

"Hey, can I ask you something?"

"Of course," Theodore replied.

"Last night you were talking with Sage Mason about the Great Barriers. What exactly are those?"

"Well, as the sage was explaining, each one coordinates with one of the ancient beings called the Ekataramn. It is said that one of the Ekataramn lies at the center of the Great Barriers. Sage Mason also went over that, which I had a strong suspicion was the case. But truth be told, we don't know all that much about the Great Barriers."

"Why are they called the Great Barriers?"

"Because they truly are the *Great* Barriers," Theodore said, waving his arms for emphasis. "Nothing can get past them. Not wind, not rain, and certainly not humans or animals.

"When I was much younger, I saw one. I didn't go near it, but being there, in front of that towering whirlwind, sparked my interested in them. I read a lot about them after that. And almost everyone that has ever approached a Great Barrier said it felt like the wind was going to rip them apart. Essentially, it's an impenetrable wall of wind, lightning, fire. It's pure maelstrom."

"Oh, that sounds scary."

"Indeed; they are quite terrifying."

Soon they came upon a small stream. Ànifa hopped off of her woolly rhinoceros and prompted Theodore to do the same, which he did much less gracefully. Ànifa guided the rhinoceroses to the stream, where they each drank.

Ànifa unhitched her bow, strung it, and walked back to Theodore.

"Can you watch the mounts? Make sure they don't drink too much."

"How much is too much for a woolly rhinoceros?" Theodore asked.

Ànifa gave him another shrug.

Theodore sighed. "Should have known," he said as he sauntered toward the rhinos.

Ànifa took out an arrow, aimed it at a tree, and loosed the arrow. It flew straight and true, sticking into the tree with a satisfying *thrum*.

I shot three arrows yesterday against the jelly monsters, she thought. *I never picked them back up. That means that I should have fifty-seven left.*

Notch. Draw. *Thrum.* Her arrow landed directly next to her previous arrow.

These arrows are much nicer than the ones I could make. Of course, I don't even remember how to make them.

She heard a rustling in the bushes in front of her and readied her bow. She loosed her arrow and heard a small squeal as she hit true. Moments later, Theodore stumbled out of the forest behind her.

"Hey, do you find it odd that we haven't seen any of those jelly monsters yet today?" Theodore asked.

Ànifa ignored the question. "Where are the rhinos?"

"They're coming," Theodore said as they rumbled out of the forest behind him. "What do you think about the jelly monsters, though?"

"I think that our new friends are keeping them at bay," Ànifa nodded her head toward the rhinos.

She scanned the bushes and spotted her kill—a large, plump rabbit. She smiled to herself as she picked it up by its hind legs.

Theodore whistled. "Good shot."

"Thank you. Now, can you make a fire? Let's have some lunch," Ànifa said as she pulled out the arrow and cleaned it against a large leaf. She retrieved the other arrows she'd used and followed Theodore back toward the path.

The rabbit crackled as it sat over the fire. While it cooked, Ànifa asked Theodore about his magic. Without getting into too much detail, Theodore explained he was an elemental wizard—a wizard capable of harnessing and using nature's elements, such as the fire spell he had produced to light the campfire. Along with his elemental spells, he could also produce energy barriers for protection. Ànifa asked if his energy barriers were similar to the Great Barriers, to which he laughed and told her it was impossible for any individual sorcerer to produce a spell of that caliber.

A strong sense of knowing suddenly washed over her. The Great Barriers were exactly what she was looking for. They held the answer on how to return to the floating island she had fallen from.

The rabbit was finally ready, and Ànifa portioned it. She handed the larger half to Theodore and then dug into her portion. The juices splashed onto her face as she tore off another piece of meat.

"I wasn't sure if you ate meat or not," Theodore said through a mouthful.

Ànifa finished chewing a large bite before she replied. "Of course I eat meat. I wouldn't be as strong as I am by eating leaves, nuts, and berries. Besides, I ate those eggs this morning." Holding Theodore's gaze, Ànifa took another large bite.

"Yes, but eggs are not meat like this rabbit here," Theodore said.

"Fair point," Ànifa replied.

They finished the rest of their meal together in silence. Ànifa walked to the grassy area where the rhinos were grazing and tied her hair back. "It's time to finish crossing these mountains. I'm afraid we may have lingered too long."

She noticed Theodore eying her movements curiously.

"Sage Mason suggested it," she said as she donned the bonnet.

"That's good, very smart of him," Theodore replied. "I was going to suggest the same thing once we got closer to town."

"Thanks. I wouldn't have thought of it otherwise. How do I look?" she asked, turning to Theodore.

Theodore's eyes widened as he nodded in approval. "Yes, well done. Now you look like a proper Pannian tourist."

"As long as I can blend in, I'm happy," Ànifa said.

"Well, I don't think that people from Panna Isle really blend into Sathon. But they do get some tourists every now and again from what I hear, so you won't be out of place, so to speak."

"Good. Now, let's hurry on. We should get through these

mountains as soon as we can," Ànifa said with a hint of urgency. "I feel a storm coming in."

"Yes, I feel it too."

The icy wind howled as they set off. Ànifa pulled her collar close and snuggled into it while pulling her bonnet down to cover her face. Within a few minutes, they were engulfed in a white-out blizzard. Luckily, their woolly rhinoceros mounts were accustomed to these conditions, so they could trudge forward while keeping a good pace. The wind was so loud, though, that any attempt at conversation was useless.

After about ten minutes, the storm blew out as quickly as it had come. But they weren't out of danger yet.

They were back in the slot canyon—the same one they had passed through to enter the Watthana Mountains. The canyon was just wide enough to allow the woolly rhinoceros to pass through single file. The walls of the canyon were smooth—far too smooth to climb—and were sparsely occupied with ledges too high for either of them to reach. Peering from those ledges were dozens of jelly monsters, each one glaring at them with intensity.

"I don't like this," Ànifa said under her breath.

"Neither do I. Why do they not attack?" Theodore whispered. "They could smother us in this narrow canyon. We'd be dead within minutes."

"I can sense that they want to attack. It feels like something is holding them back. It's taking everything in their power to do so."

"But why? And who could command them so?"

"Only a being far superior than both of us combined. Let's just thank the stars that they are allowing us through safely."

"Thank you, Holy Mother Eklatros," Theodore muttered.

Soon, the canyon widened, and the woolly rhinoceroses continued on with haste. They wanted to be out of this cave as badly as their riders did. The rhinos eventually came to a stop at the spot where she and Theodore had first met. Although it had only been a short time, it already felt like she had known the old wizard for years. And for all she knew, in a way, maybe they had.

"Ah, back to safety," Theodore said with a satisfied sigh as he finished dismounting.

Ànifa dismounted from her own rhino, then held out a handful of nuts and berries that she had gathered earlier. "Here, for your troubles."

The woolly rhinoceros each ate out of her hand and she laughed while their warm snouts brushed against her palms. She gave each of them a good pat on the head and stroked their sides. They turned and lumbered slowly back into the slot canyon.

"I hope they'll be fine against that army of jelly monsters we just passed through," Theodore said.

"They will be. I know it," Ànifa said, looking back in their direction. She smiled and turned toward Theodore. "Now, before we go to Sathon, I want to give Charlotte the herbs I got for her. I think it's closer from here to her place anyway. Plus, I'm not sure how long we'll be in town."

"Good point. Let's go do that really quick. Then we must find Cecil."

Ànifa tightened the strings on her bonnet and continued on. Within no time, they found themselves in front of Charlotte's tent.

"I'll wait back here," Theodore said, stepping off to the side. "I'll let you two chat."

"Thanks, Theodore. I won't be long," Ànifa replied with a smile.

Ànifa approached Charlotte's tent and took in a deep breath. Even though she didn't know this place well, it smelled like home to her.

"Charlotte?" Ànifa called out when she had reached the tent flaps. "It's Ànifa. I've returned from Sage Mason's."

"Oh, wonderful! I'll be there in a minute!" Charlotte called from within.

A few moments later, Charlotte stepped out of the tent, drying her hands with a small pink hand towel.

"It's so great to see you again," Charlotte said.

"Agreed," Ànifa replied as she leaned in for a hug. Charlotte wrapped her arms around Ànifa, and they held each other for a few seconds before letting go.

"It looks like you're ready to go into town, I see," Charlotte said, looking at Ànifa's blue bonnet.

"Ah yes, well, Sage Mason suggested it."

"That was smart of him," Charlotte said.

"I have those herbs you asked for. I believe that Sage Mason called it Blue Dream."

"Yes, very good," Charlotte said, taking the jar from Ànifa. "Thanks!"

"Charlotte, about this jacket—"

"Oh, don't even worry about it," Charlotte said, cutting her off. "It's much too big for me, anyway. And those boots are an old pair. You can keep all the clothes you're wearing—that's why I gave them to you."

"Thank you. I really mean it. I've met a few amazing people since I left here. One of them is waiting for me down the road. We're looking for a companion of his."

"Well, I hope you find him," Charlotte said. "Did you see the monsters I told you about?"

"Yes, we ran into quite a few. But we got lucky. And I'm sure Cecil did, too."

"I hope so," Charlotte replied.

"Yes, but I wouldn't have been able to meet all these people if not for you. I wouldn't be here if not for you. I—" Ànifa cut herself off this time, choking back her words.

"Didn't we just go over this yesterday? I told you, I didn't do it for your thanks. I did it because it was the right thing to do. And I'd do it again, a hundred times over."

"Thank you, Charlotte," Ànifa said, wiping her eyes.

"Don't mention it. Now, didn't you say that you had someone waiting for you?"

"I do. There's just so much I want to talk to you about now that I'm here," Ànifa said.

"And I would like to hear all about it. Come back here once you find who you're looking for and we can have a proper chat."

"Yes, I'll do just that." Ànifa gave Charlotte a quick hug.

"Well, I better be off, then."

"See you soon," Charlotte said, waving her hand that held the jar of herbs. "And thank you for this! You were a great help."

"Anytime," Ànifa replied. She took a few steps and saw the tent flaps waving when she looked back. Charlotte had gone inside.

This place truly feels like home to me, she thought. *I can't explain it. But I know I'll be back. Today has been a fantastic day so far. Now it's time to visit Sathon and see what a true human town is like. I'm nervous, of course, but I have Theodore with me. With him, I'll be fine, even if people look at me strangely. Cecil should be easy to find. Of that, at the very least, I'm sure of.*

5

BATTLE FOR SOBRIETY

Not long after they left Charlotte's tent, the two companions passed into the city of Sathon.

Theodore had explained to Ànifa on their short walk how Sathon was a small, simple town. And although it was the largest town on Schelff Island, it was nothing compared to Ajenti.

For Ànifa, it was one of the most amazing sights she'd ever seen. The first thing that caught her eye was the largest building in Sathon, the Sathon Inn and Pub. The ground floor was split in half—the left side was designated as the inn, and the right side was a pub. It looked as if the structure may have begun as two separate buildings. The pub was constructed from stone, while the inn, and the entire second floor, was built with wood.

To her right was a scattering of small residential homes. Each house looked nearly identical, with a dark-brown wood exterior and gray shingles. Each were two stories with a staircase on the outside of the building that led to the second floor. Ànifa presumed that each story contained a family, allowing two families to live in each house.

On the right side of the inn was a large red wooden building surrounded by cattle. These were woolly cows and bulls, and each one looked to be warm and content standing in the snow. Tending to the cattle were young men and women, each one hurrying about purposefully.

To the left of the inn stood a building made from stone—the only other building in Sathon built with stone. The sign on the building indicated it was the general store.

While Ànifa was looking around Sathon, she felt many eyes watching her. They weren't hostile or even curious gazes. Instead, she felt a warmth in them, as if they were pleased to see her. She now wished that she had asked Theodore more about what people from Panna Isle were like so she could better play the role of one.

"It seems like there are not a lot of places that he could be," Ànifa said, looking around.

"Let's start with the most obvious. We'll go to the pub first," Theodore said.

"Lead the way."

Cecil had lost track of nearly everything. Theodore had abandoned him. He had no idea how long he had been in the pub and he had lost track of how many beers he'd had.

At least I still have... wait, hang on, he thought. He peered into the stein in front of him and saw it was nearly empty. *Damn, I thought it was full a moment ago.*

He lifted the stein to his mouth, emptied it, and sighed contently. He was about to order another when a hand slapped his back, causing his armor to reverberate.

"Cecil, where in Eklatros have you been?"

He turned around and saw a long white beard.

"Oh, hey! It's my friend, Theo the Sorcerer," he slurred. Movement caught his eye, and he swiveled on his barstool to face the most beautiful woman he had ever seen. "My fair lady, I am Sir Cecil Kloud of the Guild of Exemplary Knights. May I have the honor of knowing your name?" he said through hiccups. He tried to take her hand, but she pulled away.

"Yeah, I'm Ànifa."

"Ànifa is it? Well, I must say that—"

"Cecil! Dagnabbit, listen to me, you drunken fool. How you ever got to be a knight I'll never know. Now, do you even know what you did? You left me back there!" Theodore exclaimed, his face red with anger.

Cecil spun to face Theodore and stared at him blankly for a few long seconds. "What are you talking about? You abandoned me," he said slowly, trying to not slur his words.

"What? Why would I ever leave behind my ever so trusty knight, assigned to me against my will, yet sworn to protect me?"

"And how do you think I feel? I never asked to be paired with an old hack like you."

Theodore took a deep breath and let it out slowly. "Cecil, you're drunk."

"Hey, you got one thing right, at least." he said, picking up his mug and waving it around. "Barkeep, another!"

"Cancel that order, ma'am. My friend here has had enough," Theodore said.

"Not a problem," the barkeeper replied. She looked to be about fifty, her hair a mix of gray and brunette. "That will be forty-five koda, please."

Theodore rolled his eyes. "How have you already had nine beers?"

"Oh, you know. I've been here since..." Cecil looked around and continued, "... yesterday. I think. You got me covered though, right, ol' pal? Theo, my good buddy?"

Theodore sighed. "Fine. But you're not off the hook for this."

"Whatever you say," he said with a large smile.

"Now, what do you mean by I left you?" Theodore asked.

"That you left me! It was only moments after the storm blew in. I was following close behind you, but I tripped on a rock. I fell and sunk into the deep snow, and it took me a few minutes to get out. I thought I would freeze there, and I didn't see you anywhere. I even called out to you for a while. But I knew I couldn't stay there, so I hurried back into Sathon."

"Well, I don't remember you falling. I remember you being behind me one minute, then you were gone the next."

"That's because I fell and you left me behind," Cecil said in exasperation.

"Ah well, I suppose I must apologize for my rude actions," Theodore said with a slight bow.

He let out a merry laugh. "It's fine, really. I've been happily entertained since I've gotten here."

"I'm sure you have been," Theodore said with a heavy sigh.

"But, really, Theo? I trip and fall, and then here you show up with this beautiful woman? I think you owe me a story."

"Yes, we do," Ànifa agreed.

"So, what happened then? How did you meet?" Cecil said, putting his elbows on the table, hands under his chin, and a big grin on his face.

"Stop that, you big imbecile," Theodore said.

"Why do you always have to be so mean, Theo?" Cecil asked.

"I thought I told you, don't call me Theo. It's Theodore."

"Lighten up a little, bud."

"I'm not your buddy!"

"Whoa, and didn't you just apologize?" Cecil jested.

"I apologize for leaving you. But I don't apologize for calling you an idiot since you very much are one. Why else would they have assigned you to protect me?"

"Hey now," he frowned and crossed his arms. "That's not very nice."

"No, it really isn't. But whoever called the Ajentian elite nice?" Theodore replied.

"Fair point," he nodded.

They fell silent for a few moments before Ànifa cut in. "Are you two done bickering?"

"We... yes," Cecil replied, dipping his head down.

"Good. Now, this is also an inn, right? Do you have a room, Cecil?" she asked.

"Nope."

"I shouldn't be surprised after all this," Ànifa said under her breath.

"What do you mean, 'after all this?'" Cecil asked.

"You know exactly what she means, fool," Theodore interrupted.

"Really, Theodore, can you stop?" Ànifa commanded, a bit more harshly than she meant to.

"Ah, yes. Sorry, Ànifa."

"It's not me you should apologize to, but that's beside the point. I'll go get us a room. It'll be better if we have somewhere quiet to talk alone. Besides, it's going to be dark soon. So just wait here, alright?"

"Sure, thing," Cecil said. He sat straight up and gave her a salute.

Ànifa gave him an awkward smile, then walked toward the door that led to the inn.

"So, are you going to tell me about this new lady?" He gasped for effect. "What would Tyrona think?"

Theodore slammed a fist on the bar. A slight giggle escaped his lips, and Theodore glared at him. "I already told you, it's not like that with Ànifa."

"Then please elaborate," he asked.

Ànifa stepped back into the dark pub. She had to wait a moment for her eyes to adjust to the darkness. It had been brightly lit in the inn's lobby. As her eyes adjusted, she took a moment to study her new companion. The armor Cecil was wearing was old, chipped, dented, and filthy. The armor was patchwork—the breastplate didn't match the bracers, and the bracers didn't match the greaves. Cecil had long, straight, dark red hair. Currently, his bangs were covering his right eye as he spoke with Theodore. She walked silently toward them and stopped a few paces away.

"No, that doesn't sound right at all," Theodore said impatiently.

"Theo, listen to me. It's true. She was totally into you," Cecil slurred.

"It just... it doesn't—"

"Doesn't my ass! It's like... I mean, it's like you're perfect for each other."

"I don't know if I'd go *that* far," Theodore muttered. "Besides, you've never met her."

Ànifa cleared her throat, causing the two men to jump.

"Ànifa!" Theodore exclaimed. "How long have you been standing there?"

"Only a few seconds, but long enough to know that breaking up that conversation is a good thing. Now, who's hungry?"

"Me!" Cecil exclaimed, bouncing on his stool.

"I am also quite famished," Theodore said. "That small rabbit we shared earlier wasn't nearly enough."

"Look over this menu. I'll get the barkeeper," Ànifa said, handing the menu over to Theodore. She looked and saw that the barkeeper was on the other side of the bar, chatting with someone.

Ànifa walked over to the barkeeper, leaving Cecil and Theodore to look over the menu.

As she approached the bar, she noticed that the mysterious woman at the bar had dark skin, almost like hers, but different. While Ànifa's was more of an umber hue, this woman's skin tone was much more of a vibrant golden brown. She wore a simple purple blouse with a plain white skirt and a pink bow adorned her long black hair.

"Excuse me," Ànifa said, breaking up a sudden bout of laugher between the two. "I'm sorry to interrupt—"

"Oh, no problem, my dearie," the barkeeper smiled. "I got lost in conversation with my new friend. What can I do you for?"

"I was hoping to order some food for me and my companions." Ànifa pointed to where Theodore and Cecil were sitting. "The wizard and the knight."

"Ah yes, of course. I'll be over to take your order right away."

"If you don't mind me asking," the mysterious woman at the bar interjected, "what are you doing with such company? It's not often you see one of us traveling with others not from Panna. My name is Afyna, by the way," she said, holding out her hand.

Ànifa smiled. She took her hand in her own. "Afyna, it's nice to meet you. My name is Ànifa."

"Ha, Afyna and Ànifa. It's like the old children's story," Afyna smiled.

"Oh—yeah! That's a strange coincidence, isn't it?"

"It's funny, I think," Afyna said before bursting out laughing. "But you haven't answered my question yet. I don't mean to pry. I'm just curious."

"No, it's fine. We actually met recently. It's been a crazy couple of days, but now we are going to be traveling together, for at least a little while I think."

"Oh, where are you going?"

"Galstrom, I think."

"Galstrom? Interesting choice. I don't think I've been there before."

"I don't know much about it, but there's something important we have to do there. I'm sorry, I can't get into too many details."

"No problem. And I don't mean to keep you, either. It looks like they're waiting for you," Afyna said, nodding toward Ànifa's companions.

Ànifa followed her gaze and noticed their impatient expressions.

"They must be sick of each other already," Ànifa said with a sigh, then looked back at Afyna. "It was a pleasure to meet you, Afyna."

"And it was a pleasure to meet you as well! If you ever find yourself in Beetaramn, look me up!"

"I'll be sure to do that," Ànifa said with a wave, and hurried back to her companions.

Well, that worked out well! It was nice to have a conversation with someone from Panna. This world of Eklatros truly seems like a wonderful one.

"Sorry to keep you waiting," Ànifa said.

"What were you doing over there? Telling her your deepest, darkest secrets?" Cecil asked.

"We were just talking. She's from Panna, and I'm pretending to be from Panna, so it was nice."

"Wait, what? Pretending?" Cecil asked.

"Let's get you upstairs. What room is it?" Theodore asked.

"Room 212," Ànifa said, then turned to the barkeeper. "I'm terribly sorry. Now you had to wait for me."

"It's not a problem. Now, what were you going to order?"

Ànifa picked up the menu and looked it over. Beside her, Cecil stood up, stretched, and headed to a seat near the wall. He picked up his battle-axe and put on his helmet. It partially covered his face, with his long red hair nearly finishing the job. Sprouting from the top of his helmet was a light green plume that looked to be made from dyed horsehair.

Ànifa turned to the barkeeper and ordered her dinner—an arugula salad with grilled sea bass.

It's been an interesting day so far, she thought. *Cecil seems like a peculiar character, but I think we'll get along well, despite his bickering with Theodore. It sounds like they have some things to work out. I wonder why they said that they were 'assigned' to each other, and what that all means. But I'm sure, with all the other answers I seek, that I'll find out one way or another. Life is funny that way.*

6

BATTLE FOR STORIES

Their room at the Sathon Inn felt like pure luxury to Ànifa. As requested, their room had three full-sized beds. At first glance, Ànifa had noticed that one bed was spaced slightly further apart from the other two beds and she immediately claimed it as her own while Cecil and Theodore picked from the other two.

After settling into the room, the three of them gathered at the small wooden table that occupied the center of the room. The only other furniture was an extensive wardrobe, a dresser, and a small, empty bookshelf.

Their food was delivered faster than expected and was followed by a wordless meal. Ànifa and Theodore had both been hungry from their day of traveling, while Cecil acted as if he hadn't eaten a solid meal since he'd arrived in Sathon. And, of course, along with his meal—a full rotisserie chicken and two baked potatoes—he got a large tankard of ale.

When they finished eating, Ànifa placed the dirty dishes outside their room, and when she stepped back inside, she locked the door behind her, leaned against the door, and took a deep breath.

I don't think I'll ever get any better at telling this story, she thought. *But Cecil deserves to know everything that's happened so far.*

When she was ready, she opened her eyes and returned to the small table.

"Okay, I'm ready, Sir Cecil," Ànifa said.

"Alright! I've been dying to know who you are. And please, call me Cecil," Cecil replied.

"I suppose I can take this off now," she said as she starting untying her bonnet. She slid it off her head and released her hair from its restraints, letting it fall straight. She softly shook her head to help straighten out her hair.

She looked at Cecil, and he began gaping at her while attempting to speak.

"Yes, I suppose I felt similarly, though I could control my words much better," Theodore said.

"But... wait? Really? How? You're an elf?" Cecil sputtered.

"Yes, I am. I washed up on the shore near Charlotte's tent a few days ago. After waking up, I remembered nothing—nothing at all. And to this moment, I still don't remember anything from my past. All I know now is what I've been learning," she began.

Ànifa told Cecil of the events that led up to their meeting. When she finished, Cecil simply stared at them in amazement.

"Cecil, did you come across any rabid animals?" Theodore asked.

Cecil snapped out of his stupor, then hummed to himself. "Yeah, I guess I saw something odd, but I didn't think anything of it until now. I saw a black squirrel that looked like there was something not right with it, and it was chasing some other squirrels."

"That could have been one of them," Ànifa said.

"One of what?" Cecil asked.

"As Sage Mason explained it to me, the jelly monsters infest a living host by implanting part of itself into its host," explained Theodore. "It then quickly matures inside the host, kills it, and then reanimates the host and takes full control of its body."

"That, and we discovered the smaller the animal, the less amount of... stuff the jelly monsters need to implant inside it. So, I think I probably got a good-sized dose. I'm so thankful to have it out of me now," she said.

"Right, that sounds like it was a horrible experience," Cecil said, "but can anyone tell me where these jelly monsters even came from and what they are?"

"Well, I've been thinking about that, and it has reminded me of a story. It's an ancient myth, and I saw the book in Sage Mason's tent."

"Are you talking about *A Collective History: The Magical World of Eklatros*, Theodore?" Ànifa asked.

"Yes, I am. That is a book read by nearly every citizen of this planet. For many people, it's scripture."

"Yeah, it's holy, written by the Lady Eklatrossii herself," Cecil said mockingly. "Now, what's the story, old man?"

"Right. Well, it's a common tale. It's the story of Kieth Angelcross."

"Really? Kieth Angelcross?" Cecil's eyes went wide, and Ànifa's head darted between the two in anticipation of the story.

"Exactly. Or do you not get it?" Theodore asked.

"No, not really."

Theodore sighed. "Well, said plainly, the tale of Kieth Angelcross is a simple one. The story takes place thousands of years ago in the ancient, forgotten age where human and elf lived side by side, and every citizen could wield their own form of magical abilities. During this age, the elves were in charge while the humans worked the lower-class jobs. Humans were servants, housekeepers, janitors, maids, and so forth. So, a group of humans grew tired of this imbalance of power and revolted. This kick-started a war that lasted for three years. Out of this war, a hero emerged. Fighting for equality, a human named Kieth Angelcross was the first to begin peace talks with the elves. Yet... something strange happened that altered the course of the entire war—the course of our entire history.

"It happened just when things were settling down. A treaty was being drawn up between the human and elf leaders that would ensure equality for all. A treaty that would change everything.

"Then, out of nowhere, came the race called the dark elves. They were not easily killed, and they controlled armies of hideous monsters. The dark elves were truly evil, and they all turned against humans. They not only began slaughtering them in droves, but they also somehow began removing the innate ability that humans had for magic. They did not hold back against regular elves either, and essentially extinguished them all together.

"This was a new war called The Dark War, as it was truly the darkest of times. It was only due to the prowess and might of Kieth Angelcross and his army that the dark elves could be beaten. Yet the world had already been ravaged. Humans had, for the most part, lost the ability to use magic. Only a select few remained. Their descendants would become the founders of the Ajenti University.

"As for the elves, it was presumed that they had gone extinct. But your presence here disproves that. And while I believe some of the story to be fiction, the monsters the dark elves controlled could have been these jelly monsters."

"I'm glad you told us that story, Theodore. It really puts things into perspective for me," Ànifa said.

"Not a problem." Theodore looked at her intently. "I have had something else on my mind recently, Ànifa."

"Yes?" She cocked her head a little to the left.

"Well, you certainly are here, there's no denying that. But how? How did you even get here? Remember the Great Barriers that I was telling you about earlier today? It is said that nothing can pass through those from either direction. So how did you fall from the most powerful Great Barrier of them all?"

"Wait. You came from the floating island?" Cecil asked.

"Yes, I did. I don't..."

Ànifa closed her eyes and passed out.

***

She was being chased down a dark hallway. She ran, blind to where she was going. All she knew was that behind her was that *voice*, the one that kept haunting her.

"Ànifa, why so gloomy?"

"You know why, you monster! Get out of my head!"

"Ah, but if you were to only give in... give in to the deep."

She ran faster, then tripped and fell.

She awoke with a start, startling Cecil and Theodore, who had been standing over her with concerned expressions. She had been passed out face down on the table. Upon waking, she sat straight up.

"That was it!" she exclaimed.

"What?" Theodore asked, backing away from her.

"Are you okay?" Cecil asked.

"Yeah, yeah, I'm fine," she said, waving him off. "I just remembered something—something from before." She stood and paced around the room.

"What did you remember?" Theodore asked.

"Before I fell, I was running. I was in a long hallway. It was pitch black and I could hardly see a thing. But I was running from something—an evil presence. It felt like the voice that I keep hearing when I dream. But as I was running away from it, I tripped and fell. That's all I remember, but that must have been when I fell from Yttendaus."

"That still doesn't explain how, though, but it's a great start. Now that you have remembered something, I'm sure more details will come back soon," Theodore reassured her as he returned to his seat.

Cecil plopped into a chair. "Yeah, that's good and all, but why did you pass out?"

"I'm not sure. I did take some tarnight last night—"

"Really? Tarnight would explain it then. It looks like it's finally fully wearing off," Cecil said. "I would know because... well, I've taken some before myself."

"Yes, you have tried all the drugs and libations, haven't you?" Theodore scolded.

"Well, a true knight needs to know what to look for when rooting up the rabble from the slums," Cecil replied matter-of-factly.

"Keep telling yourself that," Theodore replied, rolling his eyes.

"Yeah, I do hope that doesn't happen again though," Ànifa said. "I want nothing to do with that voice."

"What do you think it is?" Theodore asked.

"I really don't know. I just know that it's pure evil, and that it must be infesting Yttendaus as we speak. We must return as soon as possible."

"And just how do you propose to do that?" Cecil asked.

"She's going to help us in our search for the Great Barriers, I believe," Theodore said.

"Yes. I am," she stopped pacing. "I believe the Great Barriers contain many of the answers I'm looking for. I believe that, somehow, we can get back to Yttendaus through them."

"Well, it's definitely something more to go off than 'they just interest me.' That's all I've been hearing for weeks," Cecil complained.

"Hey, I knew they were important. And now we know that they actually are. Not only that, but our quest just became much more serious now that an elf is among our ranks," Theodore replied.

"Yes, it's surely going to be an interesting journey," Ànifa said, sitting back down at the table. "It already has been. That reminds me. That woman at the bar I met, she was from Panna. When I told her my name, she told me hers was Afyna, and then she said, 'like the story Afyna and Ànifa.' What did she mean by that? Does anyone know that story?"

"I've heard the story," Cecil said. "I can recite it to you."

"Thank you, that would be great," Ànifa said. "Knowing more about this world could help me fit in better."

"Alright, here it goes," Cecil said, clearing his throat. He took a final swig of his beer, set down the tankard, and belched loudly. Theodore looked at Cecil in disgust as he waved a hand in front of his face while Ànifa watched Cecil intently.

"So. This is a story of twin sisters, Ànifa and Afyna. These sisters were inseparable. They did everything together, but they never did the same thing together. They did not want to copy each other, so they would do the opposite of what the other did. For example, if

Ànifa ordered tea, then Afyna would order coffee. Then, the next time they went out, Ànifa would get coffee and Afyna would get tea. Yet many of these minor differences were not so simple as ordering drinks.

"When the sisters turned seventeen, everything changed. They met their mates. It happened on their walk home from school one day. They came across a pair of brothers, also twins. Their cart lay broken in the middle of the road and the sisters decided to help. Afyna ended up helping one of the brothers, Alberto, with fixing the cart itself, while Ànifa helped the other brother, Augusto, tend to the horses. After they mended the cart, the brothers offered to take the women home. Ànifa sat in the front of the cart with Augusto while Afyna sat in the back of the cart with Alberto.

"The next day, the sisters found the brothers waiting for them outside their cottage. Now, traditionally, this is the point where the sisters would swap and try the opposite of what they had done before. This time, they broke that streak, and in the end, broke the string of good luck the sisters had shared. Ànifa always rode with Augusto, while Afyna always rode with Alberto. The months went by, and spring turned into late summer. When autumn approached, the brothers announced they were going to part ways from each other, and wished for their new lovers to join them. Augusto was going east, into the high plains, while Alberto was going north, to the ancient city of Grethossii. The sisters were apprehensive about leaving each other, since they had never spent a day apart in their lives, but love blinded them, so they parted ways while promising to stay in touch.

"Now, this is the part of the story where things start going downhill... for Afyna, at least. Ànifa ends up living a happy life. She and Augusto live on a farm together, where Augusto tends to the crops while Ànifa raises the livestock. They have many children together, and they also regularly write letters to their siblings in Grethossii.

"As for Afyna, hers is a much darker tale. Once she and her lover reach Grethossii, Alberto goes psycho on her. He purchases a small house and chains her up in the cellar. He then... well, he then visits her down there, quite regularly and against her will. And it's not just him, but many of the men in town. Afyna ended up bearing many children to many different men during her imprisonment."

Tears welled in Ànifa's eyes and she averted her gaze by staring at the table.

"Twenty-five years go by, and the two sisters have fallen out of touch. Ànifa and Augusto decide their children are old enough to look after the farm on their own, so they set off to Grethossii to visit their siblings. When they arrive, they discover Alberto had died a few weeks earlier in a jail cell. Ànifa ends up tracking down Afyna but barely recognizes her sister.

"Afyna had spent twenty-five years in that cellar. She was weak and ashen. Her teeth had rotted away and her hair had fallen out. She was a shell of what she once was. Ànifa and her husband end up taking Afyna home with them, and Afyna lives on their farm for exactly one year before she dies peacefully in her sleep.

"And that about sums up the tale of Afyna and Ànifa."

Ànifa wept softly. "Wow, what a story. And this is a children's tale?"

"Yeah, mostly. Although the woman who told it to me likely exaggerated some parts to make it not-so-child friendly," Cecil replied.

"So, why would anyone want to be named Afyna then? She has such a tragic story," she asked, drying her eyes.

"It's a sad story, yes, but think about it," Theodore said. "Although Afyna ended up getting into a terrible situation, she survived. While most people would have given in to death, she clung onto life. She persevered, and the children she bore did wonderful things for this planet. Or so they say, at least. This story is many hundreds of years old, and while many believe it to be true, some find it to be pure fiction."

"Well, whether or not it is true, I suppose it was an uplifting story at the end, because it proves that even those who live in agony for most of their lives can still pass away peacefully," Ànifa said.

"Exactly," Theodore replied.

"Yeah, it's certainly a strange story, though," Cecil said.

"Yes, it is. But now I know why the woman at the bar had been so excited about it. It was as if she was meeting her sister, although we'd never met. Before we parted, she even told me to look her up if I was ever in a town called Beetaramn."

"Beetaramn is the largest city on Panna Isle, so if we journey there, we'll stay in that city without a doubt," Theodore said.

"Ah, good. We only spoke briefly, but she was a kind person."

"Most people from Panna Isle are kind and generous," Cecil said.

Theodore's loud yawn nearly interrupted Cecil. "Oh my, I'm sorry. But I have grown weary."

"It's no problem. It has gotten late," Ànifa said. "Plus, we have a busy day ahead of us tomorrow."

"What's the plan?" Cecil asked. "After talking about all this, I'm getting quite excited."

"Well, I want to stop by Charlotte's tent. There's much I want to talk to her about. Also, now that I have started remembering who I am, though just only a little, I want to go back and speak with Sage Mason some more."

"And then what?" Cecil asked.

"We search for the Great Barriers. We need to find Sage Mason's friend, Dante, who lives around Galstrom. Are you in?" Ànifa asked.

"Do you even need to ask?" Cecil replied. "Sure, I started on this journey reluctantly. I never wanted to leave Ajenti. But this old man pulled me away, and we started traveling together. It's been nearly two months now, and even up 'til this morning, I've been thinking about going back to Ajenti—if they'd even take me back—leaving this wizard behind on his own. In fact, if you hadn't shown up when you did, Theodore, I was going to take the next ride into Pikkul Harbor and charter a ferry back to Port Columbo. I know it would have been risky, but as you know, that's where my sister and her husband live. I'm sure they would take me in."

"Well, I guess I don't blame you. Even if we found Sage Mason together, he would have only sent us back to Galstrom anyway, and we were just there. We'd have been going in circles," Theodore agreed.

"Yeah, precisely. But now... now I'm sitting across from an elf. Now, our journey has purpose. And you know what? Those shitheads in the Guild of Exemplary Knights back in Ajenti can go kiss their own shiny metal butts."

"Here, here! I never liked those knights anyway," Theodore scowled.

"Does anyone? They're a bunch of assholes! I can't believe I worked so hard to get into that guild," Cecil said to Theodore. He turned his attention back to Ànifa. "So, even though we've only just met, I would follow you anywhere, my elvish princess!" He bowed, partly mocking the gesture.

"Well, thank you, but I don't think I'm royalty," Ànifa said.

"How do you know that?" Cecil asked.

"I'm not sure, but I feel like I'm not."

"I think you are, and that you haven't remembered it yet. For one, I've been watching your hair change colors all night. It's magnificent. But also, I mean, come on, all the beautiful heroines in all the myths and tales turn out to be princesses, don't they? Well, save for the story I told you about your namesake, and I suppose some other ones, too... but for the most part, the strong female character in those stories ends up being some kind of royalty or woman of high status," Cecil said, clasping his hands together with excitement.

"I do agree it is a common element in stories," Theodore said while stroking his beard.

"Well, just because it happens in stories doesn't mean it's true for me. But I suppose I can keep an open mind."

"Just what a princess would say," Cecil exclaimed.

"How do you know what a princess would say? You've never met one," Theodore said.

"Neither have you."

"I've met Headmaster Giovanna Kalherd Glauss Barrow of Ajenti University," Theodore snapped back.

"Using all her names, really? Also, I don't think she's true royalty."

"Maybe not, but she's one of the most powerful people on Eklatros."

"Yeah, but that still doesn't make her a princess," Cecil said.

"I know you two enjoy your bickering," Ànifa said, interrupting the two, "but I believe we were about to prepare for bed."

A few minutes later, all three of them were in their respective beds. Ànifa took a bite from a shuyukuii mushroom. Sage Mason had promised her that these mushrooms would give her dreamless sleep, and she hoped he was right.

The mushroom had a bitter, dirt-like flavor, but she didn't mind. She chewed the tough fungi thoroughly before swallowing and took a sip of water.

A couple of hours later, she woke with a start. She didn't know what prompted her to wake, but she was having a dreamless sleep. She smiled and closed her eyes again.

***

The first thing she noticed was the intense heat, followed closely by the bright light. It was blinding, and everything was so hot. She opened her eyes and peeked out.

She was standing amidst a burning structure. The flames licked at everything around her—a small pink bed, an overfilled bookcase, a nice wooden table.

This is Charlotte's tent, she thought with a sudden wave of fear.

She scanned the burning wreckage and saw Charlotte lying on the floor. She was in a corner about a meter away from the bulk of the flames. Ànifa ran over to her and tried to shake her, only to have her hands pass right through Charlotte's body.

Horrendous laughter seeped in among the shadows, searing her more intensely than the flames.

"You can't move her. You are not really here."

"But this is really happening, isn't it?"

"Yes. You are seeing the moments unfold in real time."

"*You bastard! What did you do?*" Ànifa stood and screamed into the flames.

"*I did nothing myself, however, it was my desire, and all my desires are carried out by my minions. You have met several of them yourself.*"

"*Those disgusting jelly monsters? You're the one behind them?*"

"*In a sense, yes. Yet their presence here was foretold eons ago. We are simply fulfilling our destiny.*"

"*To the void with destiny! I'll kill you!*"

"*Ha ha ha! You are one among few who can, but, in the end, it will not be you who will fell me. I will not be brought down by any living soul.*"

"*I'll just have to prove you wrong. Now, I don't want to talk to you anymore. Get me out of this dream.*"

"*I cannot wake you. Only you have the power.*"

"*Fine. I'll do it myself.*"

Ànifa looked at the surrounding flames, then at Charlotte's unconscious body.

I'll be back for you, Charlotte. I'm coming.

She closed her eyes and felt the heat slip away.

Her eyes bolted open. She lay in bed for a moment, panting heavily.

That was real, she thought. *I have never had a dream like that before. I was actually there... or at least, my soul was there. And that evil voice... it said the jelly monsters were its minions. And Charlotte is in danger. I need to wake up Theodore and Cecil, now!*

7

BATTLE FOR DESPAIR

She jumped out of bed and hurried to the other side of the room where Theodore and Cecil were sleeping. Both were snoring heavily. If this were any other situation, Ànifa would let them sleep. They looked like they could use a few more hours. But right now, all she could think about was Charlotte and the vivid dream she had just had.

She shook Cecil and yelled, "Get up! Wake up now, both of you! Charlotte is in danger!"

Theodore gasped audibly and sat up straight in bed, while Cecil simply just cracked his eyes open and glared at her.

"What time is it?" Cecil croaked.

"It doesn't matter. We need to go, *now.*"

"What's the rush?" Theodore asked with a yawn. He got up and peeked out the window. "Dawn is breaking. It'll still be a little while until the sun rises."

"What else can you see from that window?" Ànifa asked worriedly.

"I see... it's faint, but I can see a large plume of smoke coming from the south."

"That must be Charlotte's tent. We must hurry, please!" she begged them.

Theodore looked out the window for another second and jumped into action.

"Right, you heard her. Up! Out of bed, Cecil. Get your armor on posthaste. We have an emergency here."

Theodore rushed around the room. He threw off his nightclothes and put on the clothes he had worn the previous few days—brown trousers, a blue button-up shirt, navy-blue cloak, and wizard's hat.

At this point, Cecil was also out of bed, groggily stepping into his armor where it still lay in a scattered mess on the floor.

Ànifa prepared her bow, stringing it tightly. She checked a few of her arrows for good measure while she tried to patiently wait for the men to get ready. Then, as almost an afterthought, she tied her hair back and threw on her bonnet. Even though it was still early, there was a chance that they would run into a few people out in town.

About ten painstaking minutes later, Ànifa, Theodore, and Cecil left Sathon. Once they exited the town proper, Ànifa broke into a dead sprint. She heard Theodore and Cecil hurry after her. Her fear was dulling her senses and blinding her to reason.

Please let us not be too late... please let us not be too late.

When she reached the southeast end of the shore, Charlotte's tent came into view. Most of the flames had subsided, although it still emitted a mass of black smoke.

Ànifa frantically looked behind her for Theodore and Cecil and realized that she must have left them behind. She already knew that she could run faster than Theodore, but she supposed she must be faster than all humans, as a knight should have been able to keep up with her.

It was no matter. She was here, and she was going to help Charlotte. She hurried into the burning wreckage with little thought to her own safety or well-being.

It took a few frightening seconds for her to orient herself within the tent. Nearly everything was scorched, but there were still a few places that had been spared from the fingers of the flames. She took a moment to look around. The tent was beyond saving. The walls were a burning mass of flames while the ceiling looked like it could collapse any second.

Ànifa saw Charlotte lying in the middle of the floor, mostly unscathed. She quickly scooped her up and heard something fall to the floor. Without thinking, she picked up the object and ran out of the tent.

The moment the crisp morning air touched her face, she heard a loud crash, and a powerful force knocked her and Charlotte to the ground.

She yelped in pain and turned her head in time to see the tent collapse. She had gotten there just in time. Ànifa turned her attention to Charlotte, who was lying on her back next to her. She smiled and closed her eyes for a moment. She wished she could rest. All around her, soft snow floated to the ground, mixed with harsh off-white ashes. It was hauntingly beautiful.

A moment later, she heard the clamor of Cecil's full suit of armor. A small voice in the back of her head told her the noise should concern her, but at the moment, she had no worries. Charlotte was safe and alive. Ànifa listened to her soft, rhythmic breathing.

She stood and waved Cecil and Theodore toward her.

"She's only unconscious. From what I can tell, she's barely even hurt," Ànifa said.

Theodore tended to the woman and grunted to himself in approval. "Yes, she looks to be in good condition. You were very fortunate, Ànifa. Another second and you would have been crushed by the tent."

"I know. The force of it collapsing pushed me to the ground."

"What's that you got there?" Cecil asked curiously.

For the first time, Ànifa noticed what it was she was clutching onto—a book—*A Collective History: The Magical World of Eklatros.*

"Why did you save the book?" Cecil asked.

"I didn't even realize I was holding it until now. It must have been from when I carried Charlotte out of the tent. When I picked her up, I heard something fall to the ground, and I grabbed the item without a second thought," she said, turning the large green and brown book over in her hands.

"Very curious," Theodore said as he stroked his long beard. "As I was saying last night, that book is a critical part of our culture and history. Eklatros must want you to read it."

"Yes—" Before Ànifa could say another word, she felt a chill run down her spine. "Something is coming," she whispered before tossing the book aside.

The ground shook beneath their feet, much like when the dire sloth god Maqinjinarii had approached them. Ànifa feared the worst.

Out of the corner of her eye, she saw Cecil brush his red hair out of his eyes and lock into a battle stance, poised and ready.

"Get ready, everyone," Cecil commanded.

Three monsters rushed out of the foliage from behind Charlotte's tent, accompanied by a burst of deep, grotesque laughter. It differed from the voice that haunted her, but it was similar.

"Ha ha ha... you three little sprites are in for it now."

The voice had emerged out of the smallest and most hideous of the monsters. This was a monster she had never seen before. It was short and bulbous with a similar appearance to the jelly monsters, but this monster had dark green scales and a pair of hands equipped with long, sharp claws. It walked on three short, stubby feet. Accompanying this new fiend was a winged ram and a dire sloth, both possessed and reanimated. The dire sloth was much smaller than Maqinjinarii, but was still a massive threat to them.

Cecil stood his ground. "Go back from whence you came, foul beasts. How dare you poison our ears with your evil words."

The monster laughed mockingly. "Puny little man."

"You dare talk down to me. You're tiny, you puny little demon!" Cecil spat on the ground near his feet.

Ànifa could almost see the monster narrow its eyes as it glared at Cecil.

"That's it. I was ordered to hold back against you three, but how can I when this is going to be so much fun? Gnurargurts, attack!"

The winged ram and dire sloth rushed forward with impossible speed. Ànifa fired off an arrow; the dire sloth swatted it away with ease. Behind her, Theodore was shooting fireballs from his staff. Cecil yelled and charged, his battle-axe gleaming, illuminated by Theodore's fireballs.

The winged ram lowered its head and charged straight toward Cecil, baring its long, sharp horns. Cecil parried and slashed into the side of the winged ram. It doubled back and charged again, catching Cecil off guard as it rammed into his left side. Cecil crumpled to the ground.

Ànifa had no time to react, as the dire sloth was now upon her. It had its massive right arm raised, ready to swipe at her. Ànifa rolled away just in time. She heard Theodore shout before he shot a stream of fire at the large arm. The dire sloth screeched and reared back. Ànifa was on her feet with an arrow notched in her bow. She whispered, "Tekkhas Harmonias," and fired with precision. The arrow stuck into the dire sloth's back, but that didn't slow it down.

Beside her, Cecil staggered to his knees.

"There's no time to be weary," Ànifa said, quickly helped him to his feet.

"I'll sleep when I'm dead," Cecil replied.

"We're in deep trouble," Theodore said as he approached. "I don't know what to do. None of my elemental attacks are working."

"My arrows are having no effect as well," she said, slinging her bow on her back. She had to think of a new strategy.

"Hey guys, let's chat later," Cecil said as the winged ram fell upon them. Cecil blocked its winged attack with his battle-axe.

The dire sloth wasn't far behind. Ànifa looked at the scaly monster as it watched the fight and grinned. Ànifa glared at it for a second, then closed her eyes and clenched her fists at her sides. She silently whispered to herself in a language she didn't recognize.

She slowly opened her eyes and looked at her fists. They were ablaze in blue flames, but she felt no pain or heat. The dire sloth was nearly upon her. She skipped forward, held out an arm, and pushed the dire sloth to the ground with much more force than she had meant to.

She quickly unslung her bow from her back and notched an arrow. She waited until the dire sloth pushed itself upright, then aimed at its head and fired. The arrow burned brightly with a cerulean flame as it streaked through the air. It hit the dire sloth in the face, boring a hole through its left eye. The giant carcass fell to the ground.

Ànifa looked at the scaly monster. It returned her gaze, its face awash in fear and surprise. It released an earsplitting noise and dashed away. Ànifa fell to her knees, her flaming hands clutching her ears. She peeked out with one eye and saw the grotesque figure sitting upon the winged ram. The ram leaped into the sky and flew away. Streams of lightning and fire followed the fleeing foes. Ànifa stood up, readied her bow, and fired. Her arrow, tipped in cerulean flames, flew high and fast. For a moment she thought she had them, but at the last possible second the winged ram dodged her attack.

She stared into the sky after them, her ears still ringing from the scaly monster's debilitating screech. Through the ringing, she heard Cecil shouting. She turned to focus on what he was saying. With all of her attention focused on him, the blue flames on her hands extinguished, but she didn't notice.

"... just took her! That bastard! What would it need with Charlotte?"

Ànifa looked around in panic. Charlotte was gone. Only splotches of dark blood remained—and the Eklatros history book.

"What happened? Did you see what happened, Cecil?" Ànifa grabbed the knight by his gorget. She subconsciously noted that her hands were no longer on fire.

"I did," Cecil said, looking into her eyes. "It happened right after that *thing* made that horrendous noise!" His eyes motioned toward her hands, which still clasped his armor. Ànifa released him and stepped back. "After it screeched, it grabbed Charlotte and jumped onto the back of the winged ram. I thought those things weren't supposed to be able to fly."

"Maybe it can fly now that it's dead. The dead do not need to obey the same rules as the living," Ànifa said quietly. "I can't believe it took her."

"Neither can I," Cecil replied.

"What would it want with her? Why would it even take her? Why not just kill her? And what was that—a new type of monster? None of this is making any sense," Theodore said wearily. "Also, Ànifa, what did you just do? Your hands were on fire."

She examined her hands curiously, then stumbled forward. An intense wave of exhaustion overcame her senses and she crumpled to her knees. Before her eyes slid closed, she thought she saw a large white figure approaching from the west, but she was too exhausted to be concerned.

Right, I need to sleep now, she thought. *I don't know what I just did. My hands burned with blue flames and it made me more powerful... if only for a moment. And it felt good... really good.*

8

INTERLUDE: SVETLANA SLESARENKO

Declassification Disclaimer: the following document has been declassified for this usage only and has been sanitized. It has been translated accordingly for your understanding. To access the complete records, please contact Councilmember Ducutyk. His contact information can be found at the end of this document. Sanitized copy approved for release 82017/13/34.

From the desk of Professor Navacus Clums. Ramnkiln, Julinar 8, 82002 06:21:05:19.

Today is finally the day. In only two short hours, I'll begin working on my very first project with Foxaire Biotech Industries. I am exhilarated and nervous. It's been six months since they hired me alongside my best friend, Fumalli Qymberkon, and we'll finally be working closely together again. I am the project manager, with

Fumalli working directly under me, and we have six other well-trained assistants to help as well. I have a really great team accompanying me today.

First and foremost, the aforementioned Professor Fumalli Qymberkon. He's the best there is when it comes to micro-circuits and nanotech, while my expertise is in the overall planning and execution of the designs. He is a Nioavelli, and did most of his studying on his home world of Clendenic, at Kelhorr University, until he transferred to Nalpetalis University here on Melridion. For the official record, I will now describe Professor Qymberkon's physical appearance.

Fumalli Qymberkon, like most Nioavelli, has dark-blue skin with a large, egg-shaped head, two long, skinny arms, and three stocky legs. He has a long face with two big turquoise eyes and a wide mouth that is usually smiling. Overall, Professor Qymberkon is a jovial person and is just as excited and nervous about this project as I am.

Then, there are my assistants. Through their performance in the past three months, I have ranked them and will present them in order. Keep in mind that even the person in the last spot is extremely adept at their work, and this system of judgment is not perfect by any means.

The top spot goes to Sylcertiverner, the Kolythoanthaean from the planet Mishunaed. He goes by Syl and is the tallest among us at 200 centimeters. He has light gray skin, much lighter than most Kolythoanthaean. He is also very skinny, and his six-digit hands make him adept at soldering and placing micro-electronics onto micro-motherboards. Without a doubt, he is, by far, the best hands-on person among the assistants.

Then there is Poi, the first of three Harmertians. She is the twin sister of the next in line, Mac. She is the best when it comes to design. Her digital blueprints are nearly flawless, and she has a true knack for spatial construction. As with most Harmertians, she is tiny with gray skin and measures in at 58 centimeters. She typically stands on the tables when she has to work on hardware, but most of the time she's comfortable working at her computer. During this project, she will be the one overseeing the execution of the prototypes to ensure they are flawless. In a sense, Poi has the most important job, as we will rely on her to tell us how our executions of the designs are going, from a structural standpoint.

Working right alongside Poi is her brother, Mac. He will keep a close eye on the subject's vitals. If anything changes with her pulse or breathing, he'll be the one to let us know. He excels at implementing bio-hardware onto living subjects. It's almost as if these twins were made for this line of work.

For the sake of the recording, let it be known that what we are about to perform is barely legal. Any mistake and we could be in serious trouble.

Now, next in line is Grasberg. Like Professor Qymberkon, he is Nioavellian. His skin tone is much more of a dark purple than it is a dark blue. It's quite a wonderful color. Grasberg will help Syl, and together they will lay the foundations for the prototypes.

Then, there is the third and final Harmertian, Lyd. Lyd will monitor the build from up close. He'll be the one guiding Syl and Grasberg on where to place the right parts.

Let it be clear that not one of us has ever done anything like this on an intelligent subject. Many of us have worked on animals, but never with one of our own. We are breaking new ground and cannot be too careful. We must ensure the subject's survival by all means necessary. While she is currently stable and has been for four days, she could very easily have another seizure. Her body is at its limit.

Though, I digress. I will discuss the details of our project soon enough, for I will not leave out the last of the assistants here. And that would be Kurjon, a Kolythoanthaean. Unlike Syl, she has very dark gray skin, much like the color of the rocks that surround the compound. Her job in all of this will be to assist either me or Professor Qymberkon, whoever will take the lead at that point in time. I shall detail the build plan at the end of this recording.

Finally, I am Professor Navacus Clums, a Yggdrazim. Like most Yggdrazim, I grew up in Yolavien, the largest city in the Yggdrazim territory on the planet Strutheine, the sixth planet from the suns in the Vortex Solar System. While it is commonly believed that Strutheine is a cold planet, it is actually quite nice there. The suns' rays reflect off of Dunartera, the gas giant, and back to Strutheine, providing our planet with an adequate amount of warmth and sunshine.

My species, the Yggdrazim, is one of four that did not originate in the Vortex Solar System, yet has a large population in the system. The other three are the Harmertians, the Eridavlos, and the Ancilsan. Collectively, we are known as the refugee species. I'll now try my best to describe myself in as unbiased a manner as possible. I have the typical white-feather coat of the Yggdrazim. I am 142 centimeters tall and my light orange beak is long and flat. I also have black webbed feet and annoyingly short arms, but I've learned to make up for this unfortunate feature of my species. Of course, I'm typically wearing my white lab coat and white slacks, as it is the standard uniform for professors.

I had always known that I was far more intelligent than the schools on Strutheine offered, so I traveled off-world for my higher education. I went to the greatest university in the solar system, Nalpetalis University on Melridion. As I mentioned, it was there that I met Fumalli Qymberkon. We became friends quickly after meeting. At times, it felt like he was my other, better, half as we worked our way through school. After we graduated, we both enrolled in the same graduate program, where we would work closely with bioelectronics.

We were about a year and a half into our program when we were approached by Head Professor Yilvin, a lanky Kolythoanthaean. He was recruiting for a new branch of Foxaire Biotech Industries. After a surprisingly short interview process, we were hired together, as Yilvin liked that we worked well together. He said it would make our training go faster, and he was absolutely right. It was a brutal training, and I don't think I would have gotten through it without Fumalli by my side.

As I mentioned, I am thrilled to have his help today, along with our six assistants. We've already been working fairly well with them, but today is the day we have all been working toward.

And our beautiful, amazing subject that we will operate on is a Human woman by the name of Svetlana Slesarenko. Before her accident, she was a young professional accountant for a large law firm. From her file, it looked as if she was going places, but things didn't quite go her way.

Approximately two weeks ago, she was involved in a terrible accident on her home world of Carange. While she was waiting for the light-rail on her way home from work, there was a commotion behind her, and she got knocked onto the tracks right as the train was approaching.

Initially, the train tore off her right arm at the shoulder, exposing her ribcage. The initial impact also scraped off the top of her scalp, exposing her brain. Additional injuries included a crushed left leg, a fractured pelvic bone, numerous broken ribs, and a plethora of other minor fractures to various bones throughout her body. The emergency medical team and the surgeons and doctors on Carange did all they could to stabilize her. Now, it is up to us to save her life. If we do not succeed today, she will soon succumb to her injuries. It really is quite amazing that she continues to cling to life. That's why I believe she will pull through. And, if she survives, she will have the honor of being the very first true cyborg in the Vortex Solar System.

I still cannot believe that I will be the one performing this operation—the one leading the entire operation. If any one thing goes wrong, it could lead to a complete failure.

So, to start, Lyd, Syl, and Grasberg will lay the foundations. We are completely rebuilding her right arm and shoulder, right eye and ear, and lower left leg and foot. We will also reinforce her entire skeletal system, including major modifications to her ribcage, spine, and pelvis. At the same time, we'll add the wiring to her brain to prepare for her new ear and eye, and for the connections to her nervous system.

After we have laid the foundations, Professor Qymberkon will take the lead, and we will work on each appendage at a time, starting with her left leg and foot. Once the main exoskeleton has been built, we will move on to her right arm and shoulder, then her right eye, ear, and scalp. Once the exoskeleton is completed, we will take a short six-hour break. After our rest period, we will hopefully come back refreshed to finish every component. I will take lead again after the break. Speaking plainly, the parts I am most worried about are her eye and hand. Both are exceptionally complex.

I'll go into more detail in the post-procedure recording. At that point, I'll be able to more clearly state in technical terms what we did at every step. Not to mention, Mac will record the entire process, so I'll be able to review the tapes and graphs from his monitors.

After all of that, I will need to report back to Professor Dea. He is Head Professor Yilvin's assistant and the one in charge of my department. In other words, he's my direct superior. Professor Dea is an Eridavlos, one of few that left their home city of Ligthuria. Like all the refugee species, the Eridavlos reside on Strutheine. And like all Eridavlos, Professor Dea has no limbs. He is simply a torso with a head, both of which are frighteningly Human-like. He moves around using a unique organ that allows him to float up to a full meter above the ground. They really are quite an amazing species. And Professor Dea is a brilliant person. I feel like I have a lot to learn from him.

However, I believe that is about all the time I can spend on this initial recording. I now need to prepare for the operation. It should take about three days in all. It'll be a long three days, though it really is such a short time for something so groundbreaking. I'm about to change the course of the entire Vortex Solar System.

So, with peace, and love, and faith, I am Professor Navacus Clums, signing off.

From the desk of Professor Navacus Clums.
Eklakiln, Julinar 9, 82002 13:46:33:42.

The exoskeleton is now complete, and we are beginning our six-hour break. The foundations have all been laid, and Svetlana remains stable. There were no mistakes—everything went smoothly. This team really works well together. The only issue is that we are quite behind schedule, but that is no problem. We figured we should take the extra time to ensure the foundations have been properly laid.

I need to catch some sleep, though. I need to recharge. None of us have had any rest since we began, aside from quick ten-minute breaks here and there. We are exhausted.

Peace, love, and faith.

From the desk of Professor Navacus Clums.
Pjorkiln, Julinar 13, 82002 07:07:27:17.

I only have a few minutes until I need to meet with all three department heads. That means Head Professor Yilvin, Professor Dea, and Professor Bodeelch will all be there, even though Professor Bodeelch typically only oversees Professor Peal. Professor Peal's team is the only other department in the compound—aside from the department heads, as I believe they are working on their own projects.

This meeting today is a big deal. While we finished Svetlana a full day behind schedule, she was a remarkable success. She has yet to wake up, as she is still heavily sedated, but all brain functions are normal, even with the new wiring. Her eye and ear are even recording data even though she's still asleep. This is all so fascinating.

I can only imagine the meeting will go well. I just wanted to pop in here and say that we are finished. We have created the very first cyborg today. Svetlana Slesarenko is truly a pioneer. And I suppose my entire team is as well. Pioneering into a new era.

With peace, and love, and faith, this is Professor Navacus Clums, signing off.

```
From the desk of Professor Navacus Clums.
Pjorkiln, Julinar 13, 82002 09:43:09:52.
```

As expected, the meeting went well. It was brief, and not at all what I had been expecting.

To start, I was rewarded for my efforts with a nice monetary bonus, as well as bonuses for the entire team.

Head Professor Yilvin then went onto say that due to the astounding success of Svetlana, he is ready to move forward with the next subject. I almost interjected since we are only just beginning the post-procedure for Svetlana. However, I am not about to turn down another great opportunity. I got little information about this new subject, only that he is a Eusphyrchiian male that has blunt trauma to his chest. His natural auto-healing ability isn't working, so he's struggling. It sounds like another interesting case.

Now, I need to go help Professor Qymberkon and the rest with the post-proc.

Peace, love, faith.

```
From the desk of Professor Navacus Clums.
Ramnkiln, Julinar 24, 82002 19:25:24:41.
```

The post-procedure for Svetlana Slesarenko is now officially completed. Overall, she is performing well above expectations. She is talking with ease and responding well to her new eye and ear. We had to make some minor tweaks to each, but after those adjustments, she says that her senses are working better than ever. After we tested her hearing and vision, we tested the strength of her new arm. She literally crushed the empty aluminum can we had her hold on the first try. We then made some minor adjustments to her strength levels, as the arm was far overpowered. However, that has now been better calibrated to where she had been before her accident.

Finally, we got her on her feet. She struggled to stand at first but was soon walking around the examination room on her own with ease.

Mentally speaking, she is exuberant. She is still in pain, but also still on many painkillers. It will be about half a year until her pain completely goes away. She did not seem fazed by this information, but we'll see what she says after she's done taking these heavy doses.

We will keep her here, in the compound, for the foreseeable future. The Lakinceitian security guards—Bsarg and Nijork— already set up a room for her adjacent to Head Professor Yilvin's office. It seems as if she fully understands the situation, but I can already see that she is not happy with it. She desires to return to her old life. We explained to her it will not be easy, and it may take some time to be fully reaccepted into her community. While she seemed a bit saddened by this realization, she faced it the same as she has faced everything else—with a stern acceptance.

So, although Svetlana is complete, the work is not over. We will be preparing for the next project, West Kilinder, the Eusphyrchiian. It took two weeks to design Svetlana's attachments, but this time around, Head Professor Yilvin is demanding a week and a half. I hope we won't be rushed, but I understand Head Professor Yilvin's excitement, and we might as well keep going. I feel like we are in a pretty good groove right now.

But first, before all that, it's time to have a little celebration with the team. We all deserve it.

So, with peace, and love, and faith, I am Professor Navacus Clums, signing off.

For all inquiries, please use the contact information below:
Ducutyk@icos.gov
FBI@icos.gov
Please keep your messages under 500 characters. Attachments not allowed.

9

BATTLE FOR HOPE

Theodore couldn't believe it. Of all his experiences throughout the past few days, this was the most inconceivable.

Theodore held Ànifa's body close to him. She was surprisingly light, making it easy for him to hold on to the elvish woman while keeping a firm grip on the massive winged ram that was flying them over the mountains.

Everything had happened rather quickly. Within seconds of Ànifa passing out, a massive winged ram had landed nearby. This wasn't just any winged ram. It was three times larger than normal winged rams. This was the god Aerigasus. With little introduction, Aerigasus had knelt, allowing them to climb onto her back. Cecil had been hesitant at first, which was understandable. This had been Cecil's first experience seeing Ànifa's power with animals. However, Theodore knew in his bones that they should not linger by the smoldering tent. They had to flee as fast as they could, and Aerigasus was literally a godsend.

He had carefully scooped up Ànifa and hurried onto the god's massive back. Once Cecil had seen him do this, he followed quickly, cursing and muttering under his breath as he held the Eklatros history book under one arm. It didn't take long before Aerigasus was in the air.

Theodore had studied Aerigasus and the other animal gods when he was a student at Ajenti University. There were many of them scattered all over the world. And now he had met two in three days and was literally riding on the back of one. Theodore shook his head in disbelief. He was still processing everything, but it was hard to keep focus while Cecil whooped and hollered loudly next to him in a mixture of excitement, joy, and fear.

"Will you please quiet down? There could still be foes about. We don't want to attract any more attention than we already have."

"How can you not be loving this? It's like riding a horse, but like a thousand times better in every way! Look at how high up—"

Theodore interrupted Cecil with a loud shush.

"Did you really just shush me?"

"As I said, we must keep quiet," Theodore said as quietly as he could over the roar of the wind. "I understand that this is a once-in-a-lifetime experience, but I am not fond of the height. Please calm yourself until we get to wherever we're going."

"Hey!" Cecil called out. Theodore glared at him, so he continued in a quieter tone. "It looks like we're approaching a large tent," he said, pointing at the ground. Theodore glanced downward nervously and saw that they were approaching Sage Mason's tent.

"Of course. We must see Sage Mason immediately. Thank you so much, Aerigasus," Theodore said, using her name. He didn't remember many of the gods' names, but for some reason, the winged ram god's name had always stuck with him. Aerigasus bleated in response and descended.

Her thoughts were hazy as she lay in a soft bed, half awake. She could hear the muted tones of an intense conversation, but she didn't have the energy to focus. Instead, she needed to focus her unclear thoughts on the dream she'd just had.

It had all been so strange and alien, unlike anything she could even imagine. The evil voice hadn't been present, at least not that she'd been able to sense. This dream had been like listening to an old message with the visuals flickering in and out. Most of the time, everything was out of focus. Every now and again, though, she had clearly seen two strange blue alien humanoids, two tall gray humanoids, and three smaller gray humanoids. The old message had been recorded by a large, talking white bird. She knew somehow that the feathered being was in charge, leading the others, and they were doing something quite odd and grotesque to a wounded human woman. There were no other humans in the room, only the eight strange beings.

A loud clamor broke her concentration, and she lost her train of thought. She silently cursed to herself, but knew that it was probably for the best.

If I could hold on to that dream for as long as I just did, she thought, *then I'm sure I'll be able to recall it again later. I hope so, at least.*

Ànifa sat up and stretched, letting out a loud yawn. She felt her back pop as she reached her arms above her head.

"Ànifa!" By now, she knew the warm, familiar voice of the elderly wizard. He was right by her side. "How are you feeling?"

"I feel... fuzzy," she responded, letting her arms fall to her sides.

"It's no wonder. You used up a lot of your energy back there. In all honesty, we didn't think you'd be awake for at least another day," Theodore said.

"But this is convenient," an unfamiliar voice said.

Ànifa gasped audibly as the mysterious man stepped out of the shadows. Physically, he looked to be a haggard middle-aged man. While his skin was extremely pale, almost as white as daisies, it wasn't frail. He was, however, utterly filthy and smelled quite horrible, though she could tell that someone had tried to cover his odor with a bunch of different herbs. He was hairless—he didn't even have eyebrows and through his frayed hood she could tell he was bald. The man was wearing old, tattered clothes. In truth, they were much closer to rags than clothes. They were black and encrusted with dirt.

There was much more to this mysterious man than what could be seen on the outside. Ànifa sensed this was an ancient man. It wasn't just his soul, which was from antiquity, but the man—his body—was ancient. She also sensed something dark and resilient. It was a familiar presence, but one she couldn't fully identify.

"Who are you?" she asked the man directly.

The man stared at her blankly.

"Ànifa," Sage Mason said, nearing her bedside. It was at that moment Ànifa fully realized exactly where she was—back in Sage Mason's tent. More specifically, she was back in Sage Mason's bed. Theodore, the mysterious man, and Sage Mason stood over her. Cecil was sitting backward in his chair at the table, watching them.

"Ànifa, this is Dasch," Sage Mason said, motioning toward the mysterious stranger. "We have much to talk to you about. But you need not get up. Please, stay in bed."

Cecil stood from his chair, his armor clanking. He picked up his chair and set it next to Ànifa's bedside.

Sage Mason nodded in approval. "Yes, let's all sit around the bed." He picked up his chair and moved around to the other side of the bed. Theodore followed suit, while the mysterious man continued to stand there, still as stone, staring at Ànifa.

Once everyone was settled, Ànifa cleared her throat and said, "So, what's been going on? How long was I asleep for this time? I really wish this would stop happening."

"You were asleep for about three hours," Sage Mason replied. "It really is quite incredible, Ànifa. From what Theodore and Cecil have been telling me, you manifested fire out of thin air. You performed an ancient spell, one that requires years of study and practice to master."

"Yeah, well, I honestly have no idea how I did that. I don't think I could do it again if I tried."

"That may be the case," Dasch, the mysterious man, replied. "I suspect your power, for the time being, is not one that comes by your own will, but subconsciously, through your thoughts and emotions."

"That would make sense," Theodore added. "Otherwise, why would Aerigasus, the winged ram god, have appeared right when she did?"

"What?" Ànifa said in surprise. "What happened?"

"Right after you fainted," Cecil replied, "the winged ram god landed in the middle of the road. Of course, as a knight, I kept my cool."

"No, you clearly hesitated," Theodore snapped at him.

"Let's not get into the minutiae of who may or may not have hesitated. Point is, the winged ram god let us ride on its back as it flew over the mountains," Cecil said.

"I held onto you the entire time," Theodore said, looking right at Ànifa. "And her name is Aerigasus. You might as well use it while talking about her, Cecil."

"Ah, yes, Aerigasus. To be honest, I had forgotten its name," Cecil said coolly.

"*Her* name," Theodore snapped. "Please be respectful when talking about gods."

"Right, fine."

"Can we move on to something more relevant?" Sage Mason asked.

"Yes, please. You two can bicker later," Ànifa said. She sat up in the bed and looked at Dasch. "I want to know who this man is."

The man known as Sir Dasch Valentine had been alone for thousands of years, and he now found himself surrounded by people. He was nervous and tried his best not to let it show. A good soldier never shows weakness.

He nodded at Sage Mason, giving him permission to introduce him.

"This is Dasch. He arrived this morning. He came from the Dragolum Shrine itself, from deep inside. Apparently, he had been living down there, alone in the dark, for years."

"Yes. How long I was in there, I cannot say," Dasch added.

"How did you stay alive down there?" Sir Kloud asked.

"I do not require food to survive."

"What are you?" Ànifa asked.

Dasch eyed the woman curiously. Sage Mason had informed him she was an elf, and yet her aura was much stronger than the elven king of his day. "I am Dasch, a man from the past—a man that has been granted the cruel gift of immortality. Now that you are awake, I can tell my tale in earnest."

Dasch shifted his weight to his other foot and continued. "It is a tale you may have heard before, but never from a first-hand account. For I was one of Kieth Mason's most trusted advisers."

"Wait a minute. I need to cut you off right there. Did you just say Kieth Mason?" Sage Mason interjected.

From the moment Dasch met Sage Mason, he had sensed a connection between the sage and Kieth, yet the sage seemed completely unaware.

"Yes, that was his name. Kieth Mason, the Angel Crosser. They called him that because his mission was truly a holy one, and no one could cross him. At least, until the very end."

"The Angel Crosser. I see. We call him Kieth Angelcross," Sage Mason said.

"Kieth Angelcross. An even loftier name for a common man. But even the best of us have our faults, and Kieth's fault was one that changed the course of the entire planet."

Dasch paused for a moment and relaxed his stance. Telling his story was calming his nerves. It was refreshing to tell it out loud to an audience, rather than repeatedly churning it over in his head. He took a deep breath and continued.

"As I have said, I was close with Kieth. He was my truest and closest friend. We fought alongside one another through many battles. Yet the arrival of the Gnusar was something no one expected.

"I am not sure what you know them to be called, but I know them as Gnusar. They come in a variety of forms; the most common form is that of a gelatinous mass. Others are covered in scales, while some have wings. Each has its own name, but they are all Gnusar, and they are all controlled by an omnipotent entity called Gnusaramnii. I know not where this entity originated from, nor how ancient it is, but I suspect it is as old as the universe itself. It feeds by invading and taking over species and their planets.

"It was all we could do to vanquish them the first time around. Elves and humans, who only months prior were at each other's throats, were fighting and dying side by side. It was even worse when they started raising our dead—bringing them back to kill us. I had to strike down the reanimated corpses of many friends and allies." He bowed his head in a moment of remembrance.

"However, this story is not the story of the Gnusar or the war, but of Kieth and his greatest mistake. You see, Kieth was the best of us all —the best of the humans and the elves. His magical abilities were unmatched, as was his skill fighting with sword and shield. It was he, and he alone, that Gnusaramnii feared the most.

"Kieth had a chance to kill Gnusaramnii and end it all. He stood up to the most hideous creature I have ever seen. It is not a being I can describe with words. Its physical form would chill you to the bone. It can even control brain waves and thus control the consciousness and actions of those around it. We were all there— Kieth's Golden Army. We had it surrounded, but not a single one of us could move. We were all frozen in place—all but Kieth. He walked right up to it. And as he prepared to strike, he did something odd. He just stood there. It was almost as if he had come under its spell, but that wasn't the case. He was still moving—shifting from foot to foot as he was thinking—communicating with the monster.

"Kieth stood there in complete silence for about five minutes. Then, out of nowhere, Gnusaramnii lashed out at me and me alone. It killed me on the spot and then it brought me back to life. But I was no longer among the living. I was—I am something else now. For when Gnusaramnii revived me, it returned my memories and made me stronger than ever before.

"So I struck back. I buried my sword deep into the beast. And then it did something strange and completely unexpected. Instead of ripping me to shreds, Gnusaramnii left. It was as if it tore open a portal through time and space itself and walked through it, taking all of the smaller monsters with it. It was only after they were all gone that the other soldiers could move again.

"While we were overjoyed that the war was finally over, I was troubled, and so were a few others in our inner circle. There were three of us in total. Me, Sir Lindserick the Lancer, and the Elf King Waesjeon. We all approached our friend and ally. We asked Kieth why he didn't attack the foul monstrosity when he had the chance.

"And his response? That is something I will never forget. He spoke these words with a calm, straight face. Yet in his eyes, I saw something I had never seen before—madness. During his silent exchange with Gnusaramnii, he became tainted. This is what he told me that day." Dasch cleared his throat and spoke in his best Kieth impression. "'I made with them a most glorious deal of the highest caliber. They are going to leave Eklatros and they will let us all live happy lives, and our children will live happy lives, and their children, and their children, and so forth for dozens of generations. But one day, they will return to finish what they started.'

"'As for you,' Kieth had continued, speaking directly to me, 'I gave you the greatest gift of all. Gnusaramnii wanted a servant to stay here, and I told it to choose you. You, Dasch, who is the best amongst my army. Be pleased, my good friend, for you now have eternal life.'

"In response, I told him, 'I did not ask for this gift. And I fear for the time when they return.'

"Kieth laughed in my face and said, 'Why fear what you are now a part of? That was why Gnusaramnii gave you this gift, so it could have someone here for its return.'

"I pleaded with him, trying to get him to remember why we were fighting in the first place. 'Our mission was always to protect the Ekataramn,' I said. 'They were already damaged during our war for equality, and it will take a long time for them to recover. Perhaps these aliens plan to come back when they recover in order to draw more power and strength from them.'"

Dasch fell silent for a few moments. No one spoke, letting the silence hang around them, until he continued. "Kieth would not listen to reason, so I turned and left without another word. Those were the last words we ever shared. I never saw him again.

"And so, I watched from afar while all those I knew grew old and died around me. After I received word that Kieth had died, something changed inside of me, and I felt myself losing control. There was something living inside of me. It was keeping me alive, but it also wanted to kill me. The conflicting urges were driving me insane.

"So, I fought back the only way I could. I traveled north, to Schelff Island. I found an underground passage built by the elves and I shut myself off from the rest of the world. And in that darkness, alone, I waged the most intense battle of my life—a battle I just recently won. When I came to, the way out of the cavern was sealed by roots and rocks. So, I waited patiently until I either withered away to nothing or the path opened. The path opened this morning, possibly in response to the attack on Charlotte. I ventured outside, only to discover I am now in the age in which the Gnusar have returned. But do not fear. I am fully in control of myself. Gnusaramnii may have given me everlasting life, but I am not its minion."

"Gnusaramnii—" Ànifa didn't like the feel of the name in her mouth. It felt vile. "And Gnusar—are those the jelly monsters?"

"They are similar, yes. They are the most numerous of the Gnusar —it's the ones with the green scales that you should be worried about," Dasch replied.

"A green scaly monster? W-we were just fighting one this morning," Ànifa said, her voice shaking.

"Indeed. It is truly a grave matter. We were discussing it before you awoke," Sage Mason said.

"Until Cecil knocked his helmet off the table," Theodore added.

"Oh, so that's what the loud noise was," Ànifa replied, side-eying Sir Kloud.

"Yeah... sorry about that."

"You need not apologize, Sir Kloud," Dasch replied. "We required her input on the matter. We had been discussing the scaled monster, otherwise known as the Gnusar—the true Gnusar. While I may use the term Gnusar as a blanket term, the gelatinous monsters are called the Gnuelry. And when a Gnuelry infests and revives a host, that foul creature is called a Gnurargurt. Finally, there are the Gnureavers. These are also made by Gnuelry. On rare occasions, the Gnuelry finds its host does not need to be killed—it is already compatible in its current state. This creates a truly terrifying monster. Its strength and power are unmatched.

"While it is true that Gnureavers are rare, I feel as if this planet is ripe with those that are highly susceptible to becoming Gnureavers. And those are the gods. You have already met two, but there are many, many more. At any given time, there are always exactly one hundred eight of them, each a shimmering point in the fabric of our sacred planet.

"However, I have veered off topic. Now, Ànifa. To the heart of the matter. Your friend Charlotte. She was taken, and I have a theory as to why."

"What? Really? What could that demon want with her?" Ànifa asked, sitting up taller in the bed.

"Well, the aforementioned Gnureavers. In my previous life, many humans were turned into Gnureavers. If that Gnusar felt like Charlotte could become one, then it's possible that's why they took her," Dasch replied.

"If that's the case..." Ànifa looked at the bed for a moment before looking into his eyes. "If that's the case, then she's already lost. We saw close to fifty of those Gnuelry in the mountains the other day, Theodore and I. She must already be infested," Ànifa replied. He turned away as her eyes filled with tears.

"While that may be the case, a Gnureaver takes longer to brew, so to speak, than a Gnurargurt," Dasch looked back at Ànifa, then continued. "Unfortunately, Ànifa, from what it sounds like, you were going to turn into a Gnurargurt. Well, I suppose both are quite unfortunate, so there really is no better option. As for Gnureavers, they can take weeks or even months to turn. Of course, I also saw cases where Gnureavers were made within hours, so it can vary."

"Hmm, does that mean the dark elves in our stories were these... New Weavers things?" asked Theodore.

"It's *Gnureavers*. I am not familiar with the term dark elves, yet it is an apt description for when an elf becomes a Gnureaver," he replied.

"But what do we do about Charlotte?" Sir Kloud demanded as he stood from his chair. Everyone looked at him. "You know me, Theodore, I really am a horrible knight. I drink too much. I sleep too much. I eat too much. But I never stopped practicing my skills with the battle-axe. And I never stopped sharpening my thoughts. I've been learning while we've been traveling together these past few months. And what I've been learning is that our planet needs help. Eklatros needs help from people like us.

"If not us, then who's going to stand up for it? We all—all five of us in this tent—we know many truths that no other living soul knows. And this is not information that can be freely shared. So, it must be us. We must be the ones to stand against these demons— these Gnusar. We must find Charlotte and do everything we can to save her. But we must also continue our quest to uncover the truth behind the Great Barriers. That mission is becoming more important than ever before. It must be us."

The room fell silent again. It wasn't long before Theodore broke the silence with a loud snort. "Where did all of this bravado come from, *Sir Kloud*?"

"I know. I'm not the leader here. Ànifa is. But—someone needed to say it. We all need to be serious right now."

"But you're the one—" Theodore began before Ànifa cut him off.

"Not now, Theodore. Cecil is right," Ànifa said.

"I appreciate your support," Sir Kloud said, sitting back down.

"Indeed. The knight is correct," Sage Mason said thoughtfully. "And, luckily, you can achieve both of your goals in the same place."

"What do you mean?" Theodore asked. "Sure, that was inspiring, but what can we realistically do about Charlotte? We don't even know where she was taken."

Sage Mason looked at him, prompting him to speak. He cleared his throat. "As far as I know, a Gnureaver can only manifest in the presence of an Ekataramn. I believe the Ekataramn infuses the chrysalises with extra knowledge, allowing them to be fiercely intelligent. They are truly formidable opponents."

"So the Gnusar is taking Charlotte to one of the Great Barriers, then? Which one?" Sir Kloud asked.

"I believe they are going to the one on the southern tip of Gallheim—Kalahsem. That is why you must speak with my colleague, Dante. As I mentioned last time, he lives near Galstrom, and he is truly the most knowledgeable person on Eklatros when it comes to the Ekataramn," Sage Mason said.

"Why that one? Why wouldn't she be taken to the Ekataramn here on Schelff Island?" Ànifa asked.

"Dante told me many years ago that each Ekataramn has its own unique ability. I cannot recall the specifics, except for this: Kalahsem is the spirit of Eklatros herself."

Dasch grunted in approval. "I also believe that your friend is being taken to Kalahsem."

"Alright, it's settled then. How do we get to Galstrom, exactly?" Ànifa asked. "Is it far?"

"It will take us more than a few days, that's for sure," Theodore replied.

"Indeed, it will take some time. But the first leg will be quick. Pikkul Harbor is only about an hour's walk from here. And there are about three hours left of sunlight. That should hopefully give you all enough time to get there and find travel and lodging arrangements," Sage Mason said.

"What will you do?" Ànifa asked.

Sage Mason hummed in thought. "Well, before you all arrived, Dasch was advising me to flee into the underground space within the shrine, where he had slumbered for so long. And that is what I am going to do. I'll grab all the provisions I can carry there in my wheelbarrow. From what Dasch says, there is a clean well to drink from, so I just need food and my herbs. I'll be fine," Sage Mason said.

Dasch grunted. "From what I am told, elves have not been seen on Eklatros since my time, and yet here you are. It's possible the Gnusar are seeking those you come into close contact with."

"I hadn't considered that," Ànifa said, a hint of sadness in her voice. "If that is the case, then you must stay hidden and safe, Sage Mason."

"I'm already a hermit. I'm just trading my tent for a cave. I'll be fine."

"How are you feeling?" Theodore asked Ànifa in concern. "Are you able to travel?"

"Yes. I feel that I have regained much of the strength I lost before. I may not be at full capacity, but I'll be able to manage until tonight," she replied.

"Good. We must be on our way," Dasch said.

"You're coming with us, then?" Ànifa asked, looking him in the eyes.

"Yes, I must. You will require my aid."

"Right, I'm sure we will. Can you just wash off really quickly?" Ànifa asked.

"There is no time," he replied hastily.

"Well, there should be time," Sir Kloud responded. "I fear the attention we'll attract in town if we are traveling with one as foul-smelling as yourself. And you need new clothes, too, if you can spare any, Sage."

"Yes, of course, that won't be a problem," Sage Mason nodded.

"I suppose I do reek of the dead. It is not a pleasant odor to carry with you. I can spare a few minutes to wash in the river. Where is your clothing?"

"Right over here, in those drawers," Sage Mason said, leading the way. He pulled out a pair of tan trousers and a pale tunic, along with an old, dark green cloak. "Will these clothes suit you?"

"They will be fine. I'll be back soon," Dasch said as he hurried from the tent.

Once outside, he stopped for a moment and looked back at the tent.

After centuries underground, I find myself thrust back into the same war, he thought. *Kieth, why did you not slay the monstrosity when you had the chance?*

Ànifa, when the moment comes, will you be able to succeed where he and I failed?

Ànifa finally got out of bed and stretched in earnest.

"Ah, that feels good," she said. She spotted *A Collective History: The Magical World of Eklatros* lying face-down on a nearby table.

"Is that the book I retrieved from Charlotte's tent?" She asked, walking to the table.

"Indeed, the very same," Sage Mason replied. "Take it, it's yours now."

She opened the book and thumbed through its pages for the first time. Each section began with a full-page illustration, followed by a descriptive paragraph in a larger font size before it launched into a story. In all, she counted forty-two chapters. She wished she had the time now to read each one.

Dasch's entrance interrupted her thoughts. The quick wash had served him well. His pale skin was even paler without all the dirt, and the dark green cloak suited him well. Dasch had the hood up, fully hiding his baldness. To complete the outfit, Sage Mason lent him an old pair of brown high-top boots.

"I'm ready. Now let us depart," Dasch beckoned.

"Right, are we all ready?" Ànifa asked, closing the book. "Where's my bow and quiver?"

"Ah yes, right over here," Sage Mason said as he retrieved them from the foot of the bed. He also picked up a small, overly stuffed brown backpack.

"Here, I packed this while you were resting. It contains some food, a waterskin, and survival gear—everything you might need on your journey. I suggest you put the book in there, too."

"Thank you so much. This is so much more than I could have hoped for," she said as she took them from him. She slung her bow and quiver over her back, set the backpack by her feet, and took Sage Mason's hands in her own. "Thank you," Ànifa said again, looking into the old man's milky blue eyes. "I mean it. You've helped us all once again. I only wish there was something I could do to repay you."

"Not this again," Sage Mason replied, taking his hands from hers and waving one as if to dismiss the thought. "Didn't I tell you last time? As long as you and your companions survive, hope will survive. Hope lives within each of you. Hope lives within Dasch, for he awakened from his long slumber and is here now to assist us in this fight. Hope lives within the wizard, Theodore Henry Caldwell, for it is his guidance and knowledge that will lead your quest forward. Hope lives within Sir Cecil Kloud, for his faith has been restored, and he has found what it means to be a knight once again. Finally, hope resides within Ànifa," he said, taking both her hands again, "for she is the one who will save us all from our future of torment and destruction." He broke away from Ànifa and continued, holding an arm out for emphasis, "As long as each of you carries your hopes, you will inspire others around you to become hopeful once more. And hope is a powerful thing. Hope can mean the difference between suffering and salvation."

"Hope, is it?" Theodore said thoughtfully. "Yes, hope is what we all need right now. Thank you, Sage Mason."

Sage Mason nodded. "Now, you really must be off. I wish we could talk more, but you must be on your way to Pikkul Harbor before it gets dark."

Dasch, carrying the backpack, led them down a small staircase and onto the path toward Pikkul Harbor.

Ànifa looked at the position of the sun and determined that they had just under two and a half hours of sunlight left. They would have time to make it there, but she worried that they might have a hard time finding lodging.

This is the first time I've felt this worried in a while, she thought. *I think I may just be nervous, though. We'll be leaving Schelff Island tomorrow if everything goes well. I've known nothing else but this place since I awoke in Charlotte's tent. It may have only been three days, yet this place already feels like home. I'm glad somewhere feels like home on this planet.*

It's just... everything is still quite unfamiliar. And then there is Dasch. He's like me, in a way. An immortal being thrust through time into a strange and unfamiliar place. What he spoke of is true... I can fully sense the piece of Gnusaramnii that lives inside of him. I can't say why, but I fully trust he has control over it.

These foes we face truly terrify me. But as long as I can trust in my comrades, we'll be fine.

10

BATTLE FOR PASSAGE

Ànifa walked down the path toward Pikkul Harbor. Dasch and Cecil led the way, while Theodore trailed behind her. It was late in the day, and the setting sun cast long shadows. Ànifa watched Dasch and Cecil's long, distorted shadows as Cecil attempted to get to know Dasch. Without looking back, Ànifa sent a silent message to Theodore.

"What do you think of Dasch?"

After a few seconds, Theodore's voice whispered in her mind, *"I am unsure. I sense that what he told us is true, but I don't know if I can trust him."*

"I think I can trust him, but it never hurts to be careful. Can you keep an eye on him?" Ànifa asked.

"Yes, I can do that. Do you truly believe he should be with us?"

"Yes, I do. I don't know why, but I trust him. I feel he is similar to me. You gave me a chance, and I think we should give him a chance as well. But we must not let our guard down around him. It looks as if Cecil already has."

"Don't underestimate him. He may appear relaxed, but see how he holds his weapon? He's on edge, just like us," Theodore thought back to her.

Ànifa glanced at Cecil and saw that it was true. While he was laughing jovially along with the story he was telling, he clutched his battle-axe tightly.

"That one continues to surprise me," Ànifa said to Theodore.

"I feel the same. He may annoy the crap out of me, but I would not have made it this far if not for him. He is a noble companion when you need him to be."

Ànifa nearly giggled out loud but caught herself. A moment later, though, she caught a whiff of something truly foul and stopped in her tracks. Theodore nearly crashed into her. She saw Dasch had done the same and had forced Cecil to a stop.

"Egads!" Theodore exclaimed, "What's the big—"

"Quiet, Theodore," Ànifa whispered. "Something is coming."

Ànifa motioned toward Theodore, and they silently approached Dasch and Cecil.

"What is it?" Dasch asked without looking away.

Ànifa focused her eyes and examined the path they were on. After a moment, she spotted them—three snow foxes. They were small and hunched low to the ground, but they were moving fast. She could immediately tell they were not normal snow foxes, but had been reanimated by the Gnuelry.

"Three snow foxes, moving fast," Ànifa whispered to her comrades. "Wait, they've stopped."

"I see them too now," Dasch whispered as he unslung the backpack and threw it into the grass.

"Yeah, it's hard to focus on them, but I saw the movement stop," Cecil whispered as he brushed his burgundy hair out of his eyes.

"Why did they stop?" Theodore inquired.

"It looks almost like they are waiting for something. Keep an eye out, everyone," Ànifa urged.

She held her focus on the foxes while the others scanned the area. After a moment, she heard Theodore gasp in shock. The three snow foxes bounded swiftly toward them.

"The foxes are coming. Quickly!" Ànifa yelled.

"The reinforcements come from above! By the gods, Ànifa, look up!" Theodore exclaimed, his voice seeped in terror.

Ànifa tore her eyes from the three foxes and realized they had only been a distraction from the real threat. A massive cloud of crows approached from the north. The murder looked to be nearly five-hundred strong.

"I will handle the foxes. Everyone else, please keep us from being torn to shreds," Dasch commanded as he unsheathed his sword.

"Theodore, help me out here!" Ànifa cried as she unslung her bow and quickly drew and notched an arrow.

"With pleasure!" Theodore sprang into action.

Ànifa shot her arrow the next moment. At the same time, Theodore shot a stream of fire into the arrowhead, infusing it with an explosive punch.

The arrow flew true and hit a crow in its small reanimated body. Upon impact, the crow exploded and took nearly four others down with it.

"We need something stronger than that. They're nearly upon us!" Cecil exclaimed while waving his battle-axe in the air wildly. "Theodore, do that thing you did on Sortuga when you were hammered on that barley wine!"

"I told you never to speak of that," Theodore said with a twinkle in his eye.

Suddenly, one of the foxes was on top of Dasch. Ànifa saw him fall to the ground, but a moment later he had wrestled himself out from under the snow fox and sliced its belly open from its tail to its throat.

Ànifa watched all this unfold out of the corner of her eye as she was focusing on quickly shooting individual crows. It was inefficient, and she was running through arrows fast, but it was all she could do. She didn't dare try to do what she did at Charlotte's. She couldn't allow her energy to be drained again. Instead, she had to keep her cool and finish this with the help from her new friends. But the murder of crows was nearly upon them.

The deep snarl of a snow fox interrupted her thoughts. Dasch cried out in pain and crumpled to the ground as both snow foxes leaped onto him. The moment he went down, an electromagnetic pulse shot out of Theodore's staff and into the air above them. The burst of electricity went off like a bomb, felling dozens of crows, but there were still hundreds left.

Cecil let out a battle cry and rushed toward Dasch. A snarling snow fox turned in his direction and bounded toward him. Cecil lunged forward and swung his battle-axe, catching the fox on the side of its head. Cecil slammed the fox to the ground with a loud crunch, lifted his battle-axe and buried it into its exposed stomach. Blood sprayed onto his armor as he glanced toward Dasch. The man from the past was flat on his back, holding back the final snarling fox with his sword clenched in the beast's mouth. Before Cecil could react, Dasch tore the sword out of the fox's mouth and stabbed it in the eye with a dagger. Dasch grunted as the fox collapsed on him.

"Help me up," Dasch asked as black blood poured onto his face.

Cecil rushed over and shoved the fox off of Dasch, then held out a hand to help him onto his feet.

"Everyone! I think we need to run for it!" Ànifa cried.

While Dasch and Cecil had been focused on the final snow fox, Ànifa and Theodore had been throwing everything they could at the oncoming murder of death. She was down to her last twelve arrows and knew she had to make every one count.

By Ànifa's quick estimate, there were still nearly three hundred crows left. A few of the crows separated from the flock and hurled toward them at a truly impossible speed. Ànifa turned and ran, dodging the first of the deathly spearing crows. Its beak stuck straight into the ground and its body burst on impact, spraying the ground with chunks of blood, bone, and feathers.

"Wait!" Theodore called out with commanding power. Ànifa stopped in her tracks. "It's death if we run. Quick! Everyone huddle around me!"

Cecil and Dasch were the closest and quickly closed in on Theodore. Theodore had his head bowed and his eyes closed, and was quickly muttering a spell. A moment later, Ànifa was by his side.

She watched in awe as a purple tinted energy barrier enclosed around them. A second later, the first of the crows smashed into the barrier, spraying a cloud of blood and feathers. Theodore cried out in pain.

"Theodore! There's too many of them!" Cecil shouted to make his voice heard over the commotion of dive-bombing crows.

"I... I can... I can hold on!" Theodore managed to say through gritted teeth. This moment reminded Ànifa of a similar struggle, one she had recently. Her thoughts were unexpectedly flooded with water, and she was once again in the dark, murky sea where she had nearly drowned. Her keen eyes had found the moonlight, and she'd rushed toward the surface and swam ashore, where she had immediately passed out from exhaustion.

She remembered something else she had forgotten. Her memories were coming back.

Out of the corner of her eye, she saw Cecil move toward Theodore.

"Stop! Please, let him do this!" Ànifa pleaded. "Have faith in him." She glanced to Theodore. "I know you can do this, Theodore!"

Beside her, Dasch grunted softly. She barely heard him above the thundering noise as hundreds of murderous crows bore down upon them. At this point, she could see nothing beyond the energy barrier but a layer of blood, bone, feathers, and viscera. They were being buried under a mound of dead crows.

After nearly a full minute, the inundation of crows suddenly stopped. Ànifa looked toward Theodore and saw that he was barely holding on.

"Quick, everyone, prepare to be buried!" Ànifa rushed to Theodore's side and knelt, blanketing him with her body.

Cecil and Dasch threw their arms in the air to cover their heads. A second later, Theodore's energy barrier disappeared, causing the mounds of bone, flesh, and feathers to rain down upon them.

Ànifa wasted no time as she crawled out of the grotesque pile, pulling Theodore along with her. It took nearly all she had to not retch. The stench was horrible. Once she was out of the mound, she cradled the old wizard as gently as she could as she rushed away from the pile. When she was about ten meters away, she stopped and looked back. Dasch was helping Cecil out of the pile while Cecil shouted obscenities. Dasch talked with him to keep calm.

Ànifa gently laid Theodore on the ground and turned her head toward the sky. She glimpsed movement and noticed that some crows had escaped.

They must have remained airborne so they could report back to whatever sent them, she thought.

Ànifa turned her attention back to Theodore and crouched over him. She put her head to his chest and realized he wasn't breathing. Sitting up straight, she instinctively placed both hands over his chest and closed her eyes. A small blue light emerged from her hands for a moment before it descended into Theodore's chest. She had transferred a small amount of her life energy into the wizard. His upper body radiated for a moment, and then it heaved as Theodore took in a large breath. He began coughing, and Ànifa sighed with relief.

Cecil ran up to them. "How is he?"

"He's fine, for now. He's still out, though," Ànifa said.

When Dasch caught up to them, Ànifa quickly explained what she'd seen. They all agreed they needed to reach Pikkul Harbor as swiftly as they could. They had much ground to cover still and now had to deal with carrying Theodore. Dasch was the strongest, so he hoisted Theodore onto his back. Ànifa suddenly remembered the backpack and looked around for it in a panic. She spotted it lying in the grass, mostly untouched—it only had a few blood splotches on it. Cecil took the pack from her and they set off at a brisk jog.

It wasn't long before things got strange. It felt as if the sun was setting faster than it should. The elongating shadows grew sinister as a strange haze set in around them.

"Something... strange is... afoot here," Cecil was panting with nearly every word. "This is... not natural."

"No, it is not. There are ancient magics present," Dasch replied, breathing normally, even though he was carrying Theodore. "I have not felt anything like this since…"

"How much further until Pikkul Harbor, Cecil?" Ànifa asked after Dasch had trailed off into silence. Cecil's burgundy hair was sticking to his beet-red face.

"Like… maybe… um… twenty minutes?"

"Are you okay?" Dasch asked.

"Yeah… golden."

"Good. We need to pick up our pace," Ànifa instructed and began running. Cecil and Dasch followed her lead.

"Are you sure you're okay?" Dasch looked at Cecil again.

"Yes… don't… talk to me," Cecil managed as he panted heavily.

As Ànifa ran, she felt as if they were all being watched. She looked around but couldn't see anything, and suddenly she was falling.

The wind tore through her long blue hair, and her nightgown billowed around her legs as she plunged toward Eklatros. She saw a shimmer and then closed her eyes as she punched through the dense, invisible energy barrier. A split second later, she was engulfed within a massive cloud. Thunder struck close by, and her hair stood on end, doused with static electricity. She opened her eyes and saw the ocean's surface swiftly approaching. Maneuvering her body midair into a dive, she plunged into the deep.

She hit the ground face first. The impact knocked the wind out of her.

"Ànifa, are you okay?" Cecil asked, rushing to her side.

She rolled onto her back and sucked in a hard breath.

"I can't see a thing." She blinked multiple times in a row, trying to regain her focus. "My natural dark vision isn't working."

"That's because this darkness is unnatural," Dasch said. "Sir Kloud, help me set the wizard down for a moment."

Cecil was bent down beside Ànifa on his hands on his knees, gasping for breath.

"In... in a moment," Cecil said as he stood. He staggered toward Dasch and helped him hoist Theodore off his back. Dasch reached into his cloak and pulled out a torch and a flint.

"Where do you keep all that stuff?" Cecil asked.

"I have my ways," Dasch replied with a smirk as the torch crackled to life. "Besides, this is my only torch." The fire lit the surrounding area. Ànifa saw the path in front of them was littered with small rocks.

"That's helpful, thanks," Ànifa said as she stood and brushed herself off.

"I should have done it earlier," Dasch replied. "We must continue with haste."

"Agreed. Do you want me to carry Theodore?" Ànifa asked.

"No."

Ànifa shrugged, then helped Theodore onto Dasch's back.

"It shouldn't be too much longer now," she whispered to him. Theodore coughed, but his eyes remained shut. "We need to give him proper attention and fast."

"Then let's mosey!" Cecil declared.

The sun dipped below the horizon as they came across a small stream. They were all still covered in blood, feathers, and guts. Dasch set Theodore on the ground and stood watch, taking the torch from Ànifa, while they took turns to quickly wash off. Ànifa went first, followed by Cecil. Then Ànifa and Cecil worked together to help rinse off Theodore. After a quick rinse, Ànifa put her right ear to his chest. She heard his heartbeat and his soft, deep breathing.

"How is he?" Cecil asked.

"He's fine. We need to keep moving, though," Ànifa replied. "Dasch, rinse off really quick."

"I don't need—" Dasch began before Ànifa cut him off.

"No, you need to wash off. We can't go into town reeking of blood and death."

"As you wish," Dasch replied. He began to remove his cloak in front of her. Ànifa turned around quickly and said, "I'll just stand watch. Cecil, watch Theodore."

They made it to Pikkul Harbor without any other problems, aided by Dasch's torch. By the time they reached the city limits, night had fully set in. The unnatural darkness had dissipated, allowing the moonlight to shine brightly. Ànifa suspected the unnatural darkness had been caused by Gnusaramnii. She felt its power slowly growing stronger.

As they reached the outer fence of Pikkul Harbor, they came across many people. Some were lying on makeshift cots, trying to sleep. Others were begging for money, holding out bowls and cups in attempts to collect a little koda. There were elderly couples, young mothers with dirty children, and what seemed to be a group of orphans among the many others that made up the dense throng of bodies.

"What's going on?" Ànifa whispered to Cecil.

"Not sure. It wasn't like this when Theo and I came through here. That was about a week ago now," Cecil whispered back.

"What could have changed in such a short amount of time?"

"They could have been wrought with a similar experience as us," Dasch grumbled.

"I suppose that could be true. But they look different from the people of Sathon," Ànifa whispered.

"These people are not from Schelff Island," Cecil replied. "That much I can tell."

She felt a little uncomfortable with all the people around. Some even yelled at them, but a hard glare from Dasch, still carrying an unconscious Theodore, shut them up quickly. Yet nothing could have prepared Ànifa for what came next.

Once inside the city, it was utter chaos. People were everywhere. To her right, there was a small two-story stone building where a half dozen people were fighting outside. Some people cheered them on while others cried for them to stop.

Somewhere, Ànifa heard a baby cry, then another, and suddenly she heard children everywhere, crying out for their parents.

A woman wearing dirty rags with twigs and leaves in her matted hair approached them carrying a limp baby. She walked right up to Ànifa and held her baby out so she could get a better look. The child was filthy, and its breathing was raspy.

"Please help us. Please," she begged.

Cecil stepped in front of Ànifa and held out his arm. "Please miss, we are in a sorry state ourselves. We are not fit to help anyone but our own. I'm sorry. I truly wish we could do more."

"Oh, you're a knight!" the woman cried out, noting his armor and green plume. She held her baby out to Cecil. "Please, Sir Knight, take my baby boy. Raise him to be a strong man like you!"

Cecil crossed his arms. "Ma'am, I cannot take your child."

"But he'll starve!" the woman screamed. She tore a fistful of hair from her head while yelling in apparent agony and despair.

Dasch intervened. He grabbed Ànifa's arm and dragged her away.

"Sir Kloud, come. We must find the inn and pray there is space."

With Theodore still slumped over his shoulder and Ànifa's arm clutched tightly, Dasch pushed and shoved his way through the throng of people, using his elbows like lances while Cecil followed close behind. They headed toward the largest building in town—the inn. Once they neared the door, the mob of people that surrounded it suddenly parted to let them pass.

"What's going on?" Ànifa raised an eyebrow in confusion. She shook free of Dasch's grasp.

"Oh miss, we simply don't have the funds. Please, go on ahead. I hear there is still room," an elderly woman said to her in a warm and soothing voice.

Dasch hesitantly continued forward. Ànifa knew they were all a little uneasy. The crowd of people simply watched them as they made their way to the large set of double doors.

Cecil stepped in front of them and pushed the doors open. The air in the lobby was warm and heavy and stank of people. Dasch approached the middle-aged bald man behind the desk.

"Please, good sir, we need a room for four. One of us is gravely injured, as you can see," Dasch said, motioning toward Theodore, whose head was draped over his left shoulder. Theodore's large blue-tipped sorcerer's hat smacked Dasch's face and he batted it away.

"Ah yes. As you noticed, there are many people that need boarding, and other injured as well. However, I do have a room open that fits your description. It will be 750 koda for the night, per person."

"But that's three thousand koda! For one night?" Cecil roared.

The bald man shrugged. "If you can't pay, please leave. I can't have you blocking the way for any paying customers."

"Now, listen here," Dasch shouted, releasing out a torrent of curses.

Ànifa felt a tap on her shoulder. She looked to find a young teenage boy standing behind her. His dark gray clothing was dirty and ragged.

"Um, excuse me? Miss?"

"Yes?" Ànifa asked. "What is it?"

"I couldn't help overhearing. My pa told me he has room at our house. You can stay with my family tonight."

"Where is your father now?" Cecil asked, turning his attention to the boy.

"At home, helping my ma cook supper."

"And why would he send you out alone on a night like this?" Cecil continued his line of questioning.

"To find those in need. To help others," the boy said, standing up straight and placing a fist over his heart.

"I'm sure there are others more in need you can help," Ànifa said.

"I've already been asking around. No one seems to trust me," he said meekly. "And besides, you folk look like you could use some help. It looks as if you were in a war or something."

"Why should we trust you?" Dasch asked. Ànifa was so engrossed in her conversation that she didn't even realize Dasch had given up on getting the room. The bald man at the counter glared at them intensely, but said nothing.

"Well, why would I lie to people like you? It looks like any of you could easily overpower me."

"He has a good point. Dasch, let's go with him," Ànifa said.

"No," Dasch said fiercely.

"But why not? He seems—"

"Can't you sense it, Ànifa? Or has the crowd of people diluted your senses?" Dasch asked. "This boy is not to be trusted. We must get out of this place."

"Agreed," Cecil said. "I don't like the energy of this place."

"See? Even the knight can sense it," Dasch chided.

"Alright, I'll trust your judgment," Ànifa resigned. "My senses are quite overwhelmed."

"Let's get out of here, then," Cecil said.

"No!" the boy shouted. They all turned to look at him. "You're going to come with me!"

As the boy finished his sentence, six muscular men stood from a round table nearby.

"Time to go, now!" Dasch commanded.

"Right, let's do it," Ànifa replied as she hurried toward the door.

Dasch threw open the double doors and ran outside, followed closely by Ànifa and Cecil. As soon as they exited the inn, they were bombarded by the crowd of people that had just let them through. Many were shouting at them, claiming that they too had room and board. Others fully dropped the pretense and simply shouted that they would kill them if they didn't hand over whatever koda they had.

"We could really use the wizard right now," Dasch grumbled through gritted teeth as he fought his way through the crowd.

"Hang on to him tightly!" Cecil cried.

"I won't let anyone take him," Dasch replied.

"I can do it," Ànifa whispered.

"What was that?" Cecil asked as he punched a man in the face.

"I can do it!"

"No," Dasch commanded, turning around to look at her full in the face, intentionally tripping someone when he turned. "We're almost through."

"No, you're not," said a large, muscular man with short red hair and a bushy mustache. He was one of the six from the inn.

The man swung his arm, intending to punch Dasch, but Dasch swiftly drew his dagger and deftly sliced his hand off in a single fluid motion. The man howled in pain, clutching his bloody stump as blood sprayed out between his fingers. Suddenly, the man was mobbed by the angry crowd, engulfed in a torrent of hands, fists, and feet.

"Let's move!" Dasch commanded.

Using the injured man as a distraction, the three able-bodied companions tore through the crowd. Even after they got through the mob, they continued running toward the docks. While the docks were nearly empty of people, it was chaos in its own way.

The docks were absolutely crowded with ships of all shapes and sizes, from small dinghies to large trade vessels. It was so densely crowded that ships were literally on top of one another.

"This is chaos," Ànifa whispered. Her heart suddenly went out to all the people in the mob. She may not care for them, but it still hurt knowing they were all in distress.

"Where did all of these ships come from?" Cecil asked.

"Does it matter? Right now there seems to be a bigger problem. It's so crowded that some of these ships may never be able to leave the dock," Dasch said.

The full moon glowed in the cloudless sky. Vesten lurked in the shadows cast by the hodgepodge of ships that crammed onto the pier. He leaned against the hull of a large ship with his arms crossed, watching a group of strangers make their way through the crowded docks. Although it seemed as if they didn't know where they were going, they moved with purpose, unlike the other refugees that swarmed Pikkul Harbor.

They need help, he thought. *But don't we all.*

He shrugged and began to turn away when the dark-skinned woman caught his eye.

"Oh, there's someone. Maybe he can help us." The woman spoke in hushed tones, but the wind carried her voice over to him.

"I wouldn't fuckin' count on it, miss," he replied.

"Are you going to try and rob us, then?" the woman asked, fire burning in her soft lavender eyes.

"Nope. Guess again," he replied, then sighed. He stepped out of the shadows and walked toward the strange group. He stopped a few meters away and gave them a wave. "I'm Vesten."

Vesten quickly scanned the people in front of him. The knight in dented armor was on guard, gripping his battle-axe tightly. The red hair that partially covered the knight's left eye was a few shades lighter than his own red hair. To the knight's left stood a very pale man with no eyebrows. He wore a dark cloak with the hood up and had one hand on the hilt of his sword. An unconscious old wizard in blue robes was draped across the pale man's hunched back. The woman he was speaking to wore a long trenchdress with a navy-blue bonnet covering her hair. She stepped out in front of her companions and held her palm out in greeting.

"My name is Ànifa. We've got an injured companion and nowhere to go."

"And where would you like to go?" Vesten asked.

"Gal—" Ànifa began.

"Gallheim. We're on our way to Port Gall," the knight interrupted.

"I see you folks are a bit on edge. I can assure you that I won't fuckin' harm you, or rob you. I ain't like that mob."

"But you don't want to help us," Ànifa stated. Her navy-blue bonnet fluttered in the wind.

"Aye, I didn't want to. And part of me fuckin' still doesn't want to.

But it just so happens I'm on my way to Port Gall myself. And besides, I can tell you need help. Your wizard friend needs a fuckin' proper bed to rest in."

"Wonderful," Ànifa said with a smile. "Thank you very much!"

Vesten blushed and looked away. "Shit, well, come on then. We ain't got all fuckin' night. My dinghy's just over here." Vesten pointed at the small space between two triple-masted ships.

"Don't tell me you've only got a dinghy," the knight complained. He shifted his weight, causing his armor to clink together.

"Oh, fuck no. My ship is anchored offshore. I can't be having anyone trying to steal my darlin' *West Wind*." Vesten turned and led the way.

"Halt right there," the pale, hairless man demanded, causing Vesten to stop in his tracks. "How do we know you won't slit our throats in our sleep?"

Vesten looked the pale man in the eye. "Because I ain't no fuckin' pirate."

They stared at each other for a few long seconds before Ànifa interjected.

"Dasch, I know I led us astray earlier, but I trust this man. Besides, what other choice do we have? You saw the mob tear into that poor man you dismembered. We can't go back there."

"No, we cannot. I trust Ànifa," the knight replied.

"Trust or no trust, we need to get a move on. The fuckin' mob is finding its way over to us," Vesten said as he watched dozens of silhouettes making their way down the ramp that led to the pier.

"Dasch, we have to go," the woman said to the pale man with desperation in her fair voice.

The pale man grumbled, then nodded. Vesten quickly led them to his dinghy and prepared to cast off.

The full moon radiated above them as Vesten paddled the dinghy across the sea. The lights from Pikkul Harbor behind them and the moon above them cascaded into hundreds of lights that danced along the waves.

Ànifa sat across from Vesten, which gave her a chance to study their new companion.

Vesten had bright green eyes that shimmered in the moonlight. Tied around his head was a black bandanna, causing his dirty-red hair to stand straight up. His short, scruffy beard was lighter in color than his hair, making it look as if his face was covered in tiny burning embers.

He was wearing a green vest with the face of a sea dragon on each side with a plain white t-shirt underneath and sun-bleached blue trousers. On his wrists he wore brown armbands.

I really do trust this man, she thought. *Although he is vulgar, he seems to have a good heart. I am unbelievably happy we found him when we did. I don't even want to imagine what would have happened to us if not for Vesten's help.*

Seriously though, what a day. Charlotte... oh, how I wish that we could have saved you from the monsters. Yet I cannot change what happened. Or what I did. Though what I regret most about today is what I did not do. I held myself back in the fight against the crows. And what came from it? Theodore nearly died protecting us.

Theodore... although we just met, I don't know what I would do if I lost you. And I feel the same way about Cecil and even Dasch. These people are important. I must protect them with my life. I will not hold myself back again. I must do what I can to protect those I love.

11

BATTLE FOR PROTECTION

Ànifa sat in front of a small table with a large plate of food in front of her. There were scrambled eggs with onions and peppers, bacon, fried potatoes, homemade waffles with maple syrup, and a glass of fresh-squeezed orange juice. The meal had been prepared by their host, Vesten, whom she now sat across from. He looked much different today. His scruffy beard was gone, revealing a smooth, handsome face. He had also ditched the black bandanna, leaving his dirty-red red hair to fall to his shoulders. As for his clothes, he still wore a plain white t-shirt underneath his green dragon vest and blue trousers.

Dasch sat to her right while Theodore and Cecil sat to her left. Everyone around her was eating, but Ànifa was too busy thinking about the previous night.

It had taken them nearly an hour to get from the docks to Vesten's small passenger boat, *West Wind*. By the time they made it, Theodore was pale and shaking, even after Ànifa had spent the entire trip watching over him and keeping him warm. He still hadn't woken up by that point.

It took nearly another hour for Ànifa to calm the fragile, unconscious wizard. After she had put Theodore to bed, she stumbled into her room, munched on a shuyukuii mushroom and fell into a dreamless sleep. Before she fell asleep, she remembered thinking how crazy it was that the night before she had woken up peacefully in the Sathon Inn. Her already unbalanced world had been turned upside-down in a single day.

She had woken up groggily, and it had taken several minutes for her to remember where she was. As soon as she remembered, she sprung out of bed and barged into Theodore's room, interrupting a conversation between Theodore and Cecil.

West Wind contained four small bedrooms, each one connected by a hallway. Ànifa had taken one room for herself, and Cecil stayed with Theodore, giving Dasch his own room. The last room was Vesten's personal cabin. At the end of the hallway was the kitchen, which also contained a small dining area. Off to the side of the kitchen was a small lavatory.

"Er, miss, is there something wrong with your food? It's getting cold," Vesten said, breaking her out of her thoughts.

"No, it looks wonderful, really. I'm sorry, I was just thinking."

"Well, eat and think then, we're all fuckin' doing it," Vesten said as he shoved a forkful of waffle into his mouth.

After breakfast, the five of them sat around the table in silence. Ànifa broke the peace.

"Thank you so much for the meal, Vesten. It really was delicious."

"No problem! I got really good at cooking after my crew all up and fuckin' left me."

"Oh, I'm sorry to hear about that," Ànifa replied.

"Shit, it ain't really nothing now. That was many years ago now."

"Well, it's still a shame," Ànifa replied. "Vesten, why was Pikkul Harbor so overcrowded? Where did all of those people come from?"

"I'm not really sure myself. I've heard a lot of different things. Some said they were from Kalah, and that it had been burnt to the ground. Yet some claimed that was a fuckin' lie and Fort Turner had been pillaged, which, as you know, is over a hundred kilometers away. Some were even saying that the island of Sortuga had been destroyed. There are simply too many stories out there to know for fuckin' sure. But I'm sure there's some truth mixed in with all the bullshit."

"I wish I had been conscious to see it," Theodore said mournfully.

"No, you don't," Cecil said. "It was a living nightmare."

"Although we could've used your assistance," Dasch grumbled.

"Yes, well, I truly thank you for helping me, Dasch," Theodore said, holding out his hand. "Cecil told me everything. How you carried me the entire way here. I can't thank you enough."

Dasch crossed his arms and looked away, grumbling. After a moment, he lashed out a hand and slapped Theodore's outstretched hand.

"It was nothing, really," Dasch muttered. "Besides, I was rusty. I didn't fight as well as I should have against those foxes. I never should have let them get on top of me. The old me could have handled them."

"It's okay Dasch. It really is. None of us are truly prepared to handle our new foes," Ànifa replied. "Plus, in the end, we were saved." She turned to Vesten. "And I still don't know how to properly thank you."

Vesten smiled. "You know, it's been a long time since anyone besides my sorry ass has been on this ship. Just having some company is all I need."

"So, you're definitely not trying to murder and rob us?" Cecil asked, focusing intensely on Vesten.

"Didn't I tell you last night that I ain't no fucking pirate? At least, not anymore. Now I'm a privateer. I'm employed by a small outfit that operates out of Sortuga. Yet, truth be told, it's been weeks since I've gotten any commissions."

"And why are you helping us, exactly?" Theodore asked. "I thank you as well, but—"

"I get it," Vesten said with a wave of dismissal. "You don't fully fuckin' trust me. Well, that's just fine, because I don't fully trust you lot either. But I have my reasons for helping you all, aside from us heading in the same direction."

"And what is your business on Gallheim?" Ànifa asked.

Vesten squinted his eyes, then sighed and shrugged. "Trust has to work both ways, right? Well, to tell you the truth, I'm looking for someone—my cousin. We were separated a long time ago. But I know I'll find her someday. And I don't fuckin' know why, but... I think that you folk will help me find her. I know it don't make any sense."

"No, I think it does," Ànifa replied. "We're all together for a reason. I need to show you something."

"Are you sure that's wise?" Theodore asked, placing a hand on her shoulder.

"He's welcomed us into his home. It would be discourteous to continue the facade."

She turned away from him in her chair and untied the knots on her bonnet. After she removed it, she took the pins out of her hair and let her blue locks naturally fall. This morning her hair was a deep shade of blue that she figured must have something to do with her being on the ocean. She looked back at Vesten and saw him gaping at her.

"What the fuck is going on?" Vesten managed to say.

"I am an elf, Vesten. I fell from Yttendaus, the floating island, almost a week ago now. My companions have been helping me regain my memories, and we've realized that our paths are aligned. I believe you are meant to help us, Vesten. Otherwise, why would you have helped us in the first place?"

Dasch grunted noncommittally. Theodore stroked his beard while Cecil closely watched Vesten.

"I understand if you don't trust us, but I want to trust you," Ànifa continued. "For I dare not show my true self to just anyone, don't you understand? You saw the mob last night—how they jumped on that poor man after Dasch injured him. What would a crowd like that do to an elf? I didn't fully realize it, but humans terrify me. But I must trust my companions, and so I must trust you.

"Please, Vesten. Please grant us safe passage across the seas to our destination," Ànifa pleaded. She put her hands together and held them in front of her face as she bowed to him.

Vesten chuckled nervously, then scratched his shoulder blade.

"Hey now, I already agreed to take you to Port Gall. Don't get all fuckin' mushy on me now."

Ànifa unclasped her hands and giggled. "Thank you for believing in us, for believing in me."

"Don't fret about it. This here may not look like much, but *West Wind* can move pretty fuckin' hastily when she wants to. You're in good hands."

"How long will it take us to get to Port Gall?" Dasch asked.

"No more than seven hours," Vesten replied. "We can get there right before sundown if we leave soon."

"Then let's leave," Dasch replied impatiently. "We're achieving nothing by sitting on our hands here."

Vesten laughed heartily. "You make a damn good point! Let's get a move on! Give me ten minutes and we'll be sailin'."

Ànifa stood on the deck next to Theodore and watched as Dasch and Cecil raised the anchor. Vesten stood on the captain's deck, shouting orders at them.

"Good! Stop there. Now, let's fuckin' fly!"

The hull creaked beneath them as they moved slowly, but they soon picked up speed as the wind puffed out the sails. There was only one mast on the ship, and it sported two full sails, giving the small ship extra speed.

Vesten let out a loud, hearty laugh. "We're in luck! The wind is on our side. If it keeps up like this, we'll get to Port Gall ahead of schedule!"

Ànifa watched as Pikkul Harbor grew smaller in the distance. From this vantage point, the small port town looked almost peaceful. Suddenly, a thought struck her.

"Hey, Dasch. You're from the past, right? Like, from thousands of years ago?"

"Yes," Dasch replied. "What of it?"

"You don't really seem surprised by anything. Did you have ships like this in the past?"

Dasch nodded slowly. "Yes, we had all sorts of ships. Kieth's warship was far nicer than this ship is."

"Hey, don't talk down to *West Wind* while riding on her!" Vesten chided from behind his captain's wheel.

"Sorry," Ànifa called to Vesten. He flashed her a thumbs-up along with a grin.

"So, really though? Nothing has changed in over a thousand years?"

"No, not really. I'm honestly surprised by this. It seems as if innovation petered off when magic was drained from the lands."

"Hmm, that is a little odd," Theodore said. "You would think that even without magic, a civilization could advance on its own."

"If I'm to guess, it seems as if something has been restricting its evolution," Dasch said thoughtfully.

"What's all this now?" Cecil inquired as he approached them. He had been standing off on his own, watching the ship create its wake as the waves slapped against the hull. "Talking about how we humans are a bunch of dumbasses?"

"More or less," Ànifa said with a smirk.

"What do you know about this, Theodore? You studied at Ajenti. Did you learn anything about this?" Cecil asked.

Theodore thought for a second as he stroked his long white beard. "Nothing that I can recall. Nothing of importance."

"Hey, Cecil, would you come up here for a minute?" Vesten called from the captain's deck.

"Sure, I'll be right there." Cecil climbed the short flight of steps to the quarterdeck.

"What's going on?" Ànifa asked, looking at Vesten and Cecil.

"I don't know, but it seems like there may be a problem," Theodore said.

"Why am I not surprised?" Ànifa redirected her attention to Theodore. "How are you feeling today?"

"A bit queasy, but fine. I just need to focus on containing my seasickness."

"Ànifa!" Cecil called. "We need your eyes."

She nodded, then quickly made her way to the quarterdeck.

"What's going on?" Ànifa asked.

"We've only just left Pikkul Harbor, but it looks as if we're being followed," Cecil said.

"Fuckin' shit," Vesten muttered beside her. "Ànifa, look to where I'm pointing. Can you see them?" Vesten asked, pointing behind them.

Ànifa saw it immediately. There was ship pursuing them. It was smaller than *West Wind*, and it was quickly picking up speed.

Ànifa nodded, then replied, "I see them. They'll catch up to us within the hour."

"Damn. How many are there?" Vesten asked.

"Let me see..." Ànifa trailed off as she squinted.

The figures were small, but she could easily make them out. At the head of the ship was a stout middle-aged man with short black hair. Standing behind him were five tall, muscular men—the same men that had accosted them the previous night at the inn. *If they're on the ship, then I wonder...* she thought as she scanned the faces. Then, she saw him, the teenage boy from last night. Today, however, he was fully decked out in pirate garb.

"I see seven right now, but there could be more."

"Fuck! Why are they following us?" Vesten exclaimed.

"I recognize six people from last night. A teenage boy and five men."

"The ones from the inn?" Cecil asked.

"The very same ones," Ànifa replied.

"They must be really mad," Cecil replied. "Dasch killed one of them."

"Yes, it looks like they're out for revenge," Ànifa replied. "Dasch! Theodore! Prepare for battle."

"Battle? At sea?" Theodore was aghast.

"You're a wizard. What does it matter, on land or at sea?" Dasch asked him. "I'm the one at a disadvantage. I use a sword."

"I don't enjoy traveling by ship. I've been holding back my seasickness with magic," Theodore said.

"Then stop the spell. We are going to need your skills," Dasch replied.

The ship caught up to them much faster than Ànifa had anticipated.

"They're nearly upon us," Theodore cried out. He was perched over the ledge, coughing deeply. "Vesten, what are we to do?"

"You're the experienced fighters, aren't ya?" Vesten shot back from his post at the helm of the ship. "I haven't dealt with fuckin' pirates since I had a crew. Back then, I had people I could fuckin' throw at the enemy, but now it's just us."

"Theodore, focus! You can do this!" Cecil called, brushing his burgundy hair out of his eyes. He was standing next to Dasch and Theodore with his battle-axe drawn. His helmet's light green plume waved in the breeze.

"Yes, you can do it, Theodore!" Ànifa called from the captain's deck, lending her support.

"I... I can do this? I can do this!" Theodore exclaimed proudly, placing his hands on his hips. "For am I not Sorcerer Caldwell, B-Class Sorcerer of Ajenti?"

"Yes, that's it. Now, fire at them! Shoot a big ol' fireball!" Cecil commanded.

"Yes, sir!" Theodore replied. He absentmindedly pushed the tip of his large blue sorcerer's hat out of his face and readied his scarlet staff.

"I call upon the fire, deep within Eklatros. May I borrow her power!" Theodore cried.

The tip of his staff blazed a bright vermilion, then flared out with intensity into a circular formation. Theodore took control of the ball of fire by molding it with his hands and then sent it flying toward the pursuing ship. He hit the hull dead on, but before the ship could catch fire, it was immediately dowsed with buckets of water.

A loud laugh rang out from the ship behind them, and the voice said, "Are you really so naïve to think that we wouldn't be prepared for a fire attack from your feeble old wizard? Men, retaliate!" The short black-haired man was the one giving out the orders. On his command, half a dozen loud shots rang out from the enemy ship, and large metal crossbow bolts whooshed through the air toward *West Wind*.

"Yikes! I should've known they'd have some firepower," Cecil cried as he took cover behind the short bulkhead.

"If it's a bolt fight they want, it's a fucking bolt fight they'll get! Come at us, you fucking bastards!" Vesten's laughter bordered on hysteria. He pulled the wooden plate off of the captain's wheel, revealing a crossbow. The crossbow was chained to the wheel, but had enough slack for him to aim it in any direction.

"For fuckin' emergencies!" Vesten said, fire burning in his eyes. He strode to the port side of his ship while firing back rapidly, the crossbow automatically reloading from a small magazine. It didn't take long before they were fully engaged in battle.

Ànifa had taken cover behind a tall barrel and sat with her knees up and arms around her legs. She rested her head on her knees.

Think! What can I do to help? Ànifa thought. *I don't have enough arrows left for this fight! I wasted too many on those crows.*

"Is that all you got?" Vesten laughed as he continued to fire at the enemy.

I must do something! she thought.

She placed her hands on the deck, and then she felt it. A small pulse wave rose from the depths of the sea. It was so subtle that she wouldn't have noticed it if she hadn't known what to look for.

"Everyone, hold on to something! Now!" Ànifa instructed.

"Oh, mother Eklatros, what could it be now?" Theodore took hold of a rope that was firmly fastened to the deck and wound it around his wrist the best he could before leaning over the edge of the ship and vomiting.

"What? What's going on?" Vesten asked.

"You better do as the lady says," Cecil replied. "There's going to be a large animal arriving soon."

"A large animal? Wait, you don't mean—?"

The ship lurched sideways as an enormous shadow appeared beneath them. The firefight came to an abrupt halt on both sides.

"Oh, mother of all fuck. It cannot be..." Vesten said, his voice shaking and trailing off as the color drained from his face. He shoved the crossbow back into place and quickly grabbed a hold of the wheel once more.

A large wine-colored tentacle rose out of the sea, straight into the air.

"Take cover!" came a frightened call from the other ship. The tentacle fell swiftly and smashed into the enemy vessel. It exploded under the pressure, sending out a shockwave of splinters and bones in every direction. The bloody spray just missed *West Wind*. The tentacle sunk back into the sea, and the shadow disappeared as swiftly as it had emerged.

"One strike. That's all it took," Cecil said, completely in shock.

"Holy shit, I've never seen anything like that before. Do you think anyone survived?" Vesten asked, eyes wide. He still had a firm, white-knuckled grip on the helm.

"I wouldn't count on it," Ànifa replied with unshed tears filling her eyes. She burst into tears. "There was n-no other way, right?" she asked between sobs.

"No. They would have done much fuckin' worse to us. A quick death is a true mercy at sea," Vesten reassured her.

"I've never killed anyone," Ànifa said, calming a bit. "I know that I'm not Krakuluthosii, but I felt that tentacle fall as if it was my own limb. This was different from Maqinjinarii—I think because I was killing people, not monsters."

"Krakuluthosii—the God of the Sea. How can you fuckin' command it like that?" Vesten mouth hung open in fascination.

"I honestly do not know," Ànifa replied, while Theodore retched off the side of the ship. She glanced at him and wiped her tears with the back of her sleeve.

"We better be on our way again, captain," Dasch said sternly.

A startled Vesten looked at him and said, "Ah yes. Give me a moment to collect myself and I can get back to my post. And someone get the wizard some fuckin' water to drink before he dehydrates himself."

They approached land as the sun was setting. The orange sun and nearly cloudless sky made the ocean perfectly reflect the sunset, as if there were two suns, each one rushing to greet each other.

It seems as if we can't catch a break, she thought. *It has been one battle after the other. If I had known it was going to be this intense—*

No, I should have known from the beginning. That voice that haunted me—that still haunts me—it is powerful. And it's always there, at the edge of my consciousness, lurking in the shadows of my thoughts. Always there, but never present. Not since I started taking the shuyukuii mushrooms. I'm happy that they have been helping. But it's only been a few days and I can already sense a tolerance building.

But that's beside the point. I really shouldn't worry so much. Not now, at least. It's too beautiful right now. She gazed at the horizon. *And we're nearing land. We're another step closer in our journey.*

I only wish that I hadn't needed to kill all those people. But at the same time, I know I may need to kill more. She sighed, averting her eyes from the miraculous sight before her. *Humans, even those not possessed by any monsters or demons, can still be evil in their own right. I mustn't forget that. I mustn't forget Pikkul Harbor, nor our battle at sea. This has been a truly intense couple of days. I can only pray that we can get some respite soon.*

If only everything could be as peaceful as this sunset... as this moment.

12

BATTLE FOR DIRECTIONS

The wreckage of *The Sundering* bobbed up and down with the waves. Most of the ship had sunk into the deep, leaving behind corpses and sundries. Also among the flotsam were the two sole survivors, each holding onto the same piece of driftwood as they floated with the bones of the broken ship.

"What in the living fuck just happened?" the man with short black hair exclaimed as he tried to get a better grip on the driftwood.

"It was the great beast of the deep. The fabled God of the Sea," replied the man with a short blond beard. His red bandanna covered his dirty blond hair.

"Well, shit. Does that kind of thing happen often?"

"No. We must've really angered the gods."

"Look, I'm sorry, but I honestly don't remember who you are."

"I'm Bartholomew. Bart for short."

"Well, Bart, I'm Danai. And it seems as if I'm stranded with a lunatic of a pirate."

"I may be a pirate, but unlike you, I have love and respect for these seas."

"I thought you were all about killing and pillaging. That's why I hired you dirty lot to begin with. And now we're the only ones left," Danai said with a sigh.

"A lot of my friends died today, along with the local kid," Bart said, a hint of sadness in his voice.

Danai snorted. "They knew the risks."

"They did. But that doesn't give you the right to belittle their deaths," Bart replied curtly. He absentmindedly adjusted his bandanna with his free hand. "Why are we even out here to begin with? You never told us. Those who passed don't even know why they died."

"Right. I was going to tell you after we captured them. A few days ago, I ran into a silver-haired wench. She claimed she rescued a woman with blue hair from drowning or some shit and kept going on about a mysterious package. I decided to take matters into my own hands and track her down. As soon as I saw her, I immediately recognized her as an elf and knew that if I could capture her and sell her off in the underground auctions, I could make a fortune. So I hired you lot to help."

"An elf? Are you sure?" Bart asked.

"Fuck yeah, I'm sure! I saw her ears, and I saw her blue hair change colors right before my eyes. I'm telling you, she's an elf. And she's going to make me mighty wealthy."

"You are probably one of the worst people I've ever met. And I'm a *pirate*."

"So why don't you talk all piratey?" Danai asked.

"We don't all fall into that silly stereotype," Bart snapped back.

"Well, what do you suppose we do now?" Danai asked.

"Nothing we can do. Luckily, we weren't too far from the shore. Someone should come across us, eventually."

"They better come soon, then. I'm not going to be fuckin' fish food."

"That is not up to you," Bart said.

"Shut the fuck up."

There wasn't much else to talk about after that. All they could do was wait.

As *West Wind* sailed closer to Port Gall, Ànifa could tell that something wasn't quite right.

"Hang on everyone," Ànifa said as she stood on the quarterdeck next to Vesten, who was manning the helm. Theodore, Dasch, and Cecil stood on the main deck below, each trying to check out what was going on for themselves.

"What do you see?" Vesten asked her.

"There's smoke coming from the center of town. And it looks as if the docks are even more crowded than they were at Pikkul Harbor."

"Ah, I should've fuckin' seen this coming," Vesten said with a snarl. "Well, at least we aren't out of options. I'll take us to an old smuggler's cave I used to use back in my pirating days. It's not too far from here." Vesten spun the wheel to the starboard side.

"How out of the way is it?" Theodore asked from below.

"It's about an hour away from Port Gall. Now, the road to get there—"

"We're not going to Port Gall," Ànifa said, "We're on our way to visit a man named Dante that lives outside of Galstrom."

"Ah, I see. To Dante's it is, then. And thanks for finally trusting me," Vesten said with a grin.

"Weren't you headed to Port Gall, though?" she asked.

"It's no problem. As I mentioned, I'm fuckin' looking for my cousin, so that was my next destination in my search. Yet, that can wait. I'd rather not deal with those fuckin' crowds right now anyway."

"Do you think anyone can see us?" Dasch asked.

"It's possible, but there's little we can fuckin' do about it now," Vesten replied. "But this smugglers' cave was rarely used. It's possible no one uses it anymore."

"Let's hope that's the case," Ànifa whispered.

It was dusk by the time they approached the shore. Beside the shoreline, Ànifa could make out a small sea cave.

"This is the place. We made it here in fuckin' really good time too. The wind was on our side again," Vesten said.

"It doesn't look as if anyone else is here, from what I can tell right now at least," Ànifa said.

"That's good," Vesten said. "I don't want to deal with any more fuckin' pirates today."

"Agreed. At least that battle went quickly," Theodore said, looking at them from the bottom of the steps.

"All thanks to our elvish princess!" Cecil chimed in, shooting Ànifa a grateful look.

She rolled her eyes, but there was sadness in her voice when she said, "Yes, but I still regret killing all those people."

"They would have done much worse," Vesten replied.

"So you've said. But it doesn't really console me much."

"Shit, I understand. I've killed... fuckin' way too many people. I still see their faces at night. Honestly, I wasn't a good pirate."

"And I wasn't a good knight before I met Ànifa. Now, I want to be the best me I can be," Cecil said. "If you try, I'm sure you can be good at anything you want to be."

"If only that were true, good knight," Vesten replied, shaking his head softly.

They were nearing the mouth of the sea cave. As they got closer, Ànifa focused her eyes deep within the darkness of the cave. Just as she suspected, the small cave was empty.

"We're alone," Ànifa confirmed.

They dropped anchor and decided to spend the night on the ship. Ànifa ate a few shuyukuii mushrooms and fell right to sleep, exhausted from the day's events.

"Are you coming with us, Vesten?" Ànifa asked. She strapped her bow and quiver to the back of the backpack and hoisted it onto her back.

"Aye, I think I fuckin' will. She should be safe here," Vesten said, glancing over his shoulder at *West Wind*. He turned his attention back to the cave. "It looks as if this place hasn't been used in years."

"Good," she said with a nod. "I think we'll need you on this next leg of our journey."

"I don't know how I can help, but I'll do what I can. Are you sure you don't want any help carrying that fuckin' pack? It looks heavy as fuck."

"Oh, it's not that bad," Ànifa replied.

"Yes, but your weapons will be difficult to access if you need them," Cecil said. "I can carry your pack too."

"It's okay, really. I'm nearly out of arrows, and they've been doing little to help us, anyway. Besides, I want to see what I can do on my own accord."

"Fair enough," Theodore said. "Sounds like part of the training I had to go through in Ajenti. It takes much more effort to conduct magic without a catalyst, such as a staff or a wand. But it makes you a much better sorcerer."

"I'm sure it does," Ànifa said. "Now, are we ready to go?"

"Yes, of course," Theodore replied.

"Let's do this fuckin' thing!" Vesten exclaimed, a little too excitedly.

As they made their way out of the sea cave, Ànifa heard a soft rustling and squeaking above them. She looked and saw there were hundreds—if not thousands—of small bats above them.

"Ugh, bats," Vesten said with a shudder as he followed Ànifa's gaze.

"Not a fan of bats?" Ànifa asked.

"No, not at all. I'm going to hurry on ahead," Vesten said as he jogged toward the mouth of the cave.

She glanced at the bats and shrugged. None of these seemed to be corrupted by the Gnusar. There shouldn't be anything to worry about. Ànifa softly hummed to herself as she meandered out of the cave.

The morning sun nearly blinded her as she reached the mouth of the cave. It took a few seconds before she could open her eyes and look around. She stood in a small, grassy clearing lined by many different species of deciduous trees. She could hear the chattering of small woodland animals and the chirping of birds. Above her, the sky was a brilliant blue. Under her bonnet, Ànifa could sense her hair was changing to match the color of the sky.

"So, where do we go from here?" Theodore asked.

"Uh, well. Shit! There used to be a fuckin' path!" Vesten furrowed his brow as he scanned the ground.

"There's no path I can see," Cecil replied. "It's obviously been a long time since anyone's been here."

"Wait, hang on. I can faintly make out a path," Ànifa said, as she scanned the ground in front of her. "Here, follow me."

As soon as she began walking, she knew she had found what they were looking for. Even though it was completely overgrown, she could easily tell that all the growth in front of them was much newer than the rest of the foliage around them.

The others followed her in silence. As she made her way into the forest, the path became easier for her to see. She deftly wound them out of the forest and onto a road.

"Well done, Ànifa!" Theodore complimented her keen skills. "That was quite impressive indeed."

"I knew we could count on our fair princess!" Cecil exclaimed as he brushed his hair out of his eyes.

"Thanks, but I got some help from the animals."

"When?" Vesten asked curiously. "It didn't look like you were communicating with any animals."

"Oh, I wasn't speaking to them directly, but they were helping us along," Ànifa replied. "I know none of you can hear it, but each chirp from a bird holds a different meaning. I just listened to what they were saying."

"Ah, right. Well, fuckin' A. We're here." Vesten replied.

"Now, which way, sailor?" Dasch asked coldly.

"Shitfuck. I'm not really sure."

"It's this way," Ànifa said. "Right? We need to head toward Port Gall, right? Or away from it?"

"Oh, we need to go away from Port Gall. Galstrom is inland," Vesten replied.

"But is this even the right road to get to Galstrom?" Cecil asked.

"I really don't fuckin' know, man. I rarely come this way anymore," Vesten said.

"Look, it's okay, everyone," Ànifa said in a calming tone. "If we need to head away from Port Gall, then let's go this way," Ànifa said, motioning in the other direction. "I'm sure we'll find our way there, eventually."

"We'll find our way somewhere, that's for sure," Theodore replied.

They headed down the road away from Port Gall, Ànifa's senses leading the way. After a few hundred meters, their surroundings grew eerily quiet. Ànifa slowed her pace and the men behind her began looking around nervously.

"What is it?" Theodore whispered.

"What the fuck is going on?" Vesten whispered.

Ànifa shushed them and whispered back, "We're approaching something—some kind of Gnuelry."

"Are those the jelly monsters?" Cecil asked. "All those terms confuse me."

"Yeah, the jelly monsters," Ànifa replied in a hushed voice.

"Um, what?" Vesten asked quietly, his voice shaking.

"It's okay." She shushed them again and continued. "I can see them. It's two little ones. They look different, though. These are yellow; the other ones were blue."

"How do we know it's not a trap?" Cecil asked.

"We don't," she whispered.

"If it's just two of them, I can handle it. I think I know how to properly neutralize them in one shot now," Theodore whispered.

"Alright, go ahead, then."

Ànifa stepped back to let Theodore creep slowly in front of her. He peered along the path and caught sight of the two jelly monsters. "Okay, here we go," Theodore whispered.

Raising his scarlet glass staff high in the air, Theodore closed his eyes and muttered a quiet incantation. Upon finishing, he thrust his staff into the ground. A shockwave rumbled toward each of the two small jelly monsters loitering on the path. The two shockwaves struck at nearly the same time, causing an explosion of fire and dirt. The jelly monsters melted into a puddle within the crumbled terrain.

Theodore turned around and grinned at them. "Nothing to it," he boasted.

"That was a neat trick, wizard," Dasch said with a nod.

"Yeah, that was fuckin' awesome!" Vesten exclaimed. "I've never seen anything like that before."

"Theodore!" Ànifa cried. "It's not over yet!"

The Gnuelry that Theodore had attacked were merging into one large jelly monster. As the two puddles came together, it roared at them, spraying flecks of yellow ooze from its gelatinous mouth. Mounds of dirt and rocks were being picked up and melded into the gelatinous mass as it continued to grow.

"I take back what I said," Dasch grumbled.

"Shit! What now?" Vesten cried.

"Now it's my turn," Dasch said as he stepped forward. In one swift movement, he pushed his cloak back and unsheathed his sword. Cecil also stepped forward as he gripped his battle-axe firmly with both hands. "I'll be your support," the knight said, making eye contact with Dasch.

"Just don't get in my way." Dasch looked away and lunged forward. He raised his sword and cut a gorge into the gelatinous monster. The cut healed within seconds. Dasch cursed under his breath and jumped back a few times. He stood next to Cecil once again, and the massive Gnuelry was now lumbering toward them.

"It's as I thought. I'll need to use something more effective. Sir Kloud, keep it occupied," Dasch requested as he stepped back and knelt down.

"I'll do what I can," Cecil replied as he ran forward a few steps.

Ànifa stepped next to Dasch, bow in hand. She aimed at the Gnuelry's head, whispered "Tekkhas Harmonias," and fired. As expected, the spell was ineffective.

"I'll help keep it distracted," she said over her shoulder, "but I don't have many arrows left."

When Dasch didn't reply, she turned around and saw that he had his head bowed and his eyes closed; his arms were held out in front of him gripping his sword with both hands. Ànifa looked back at the massive yellow gelatinous creature. Cecil was fully engaged, slashing and defending himself with his battle-axe. The Gnuelry roared, becoming even more aggressive. She fired another arrow and notched another. Ten arrows left. She had to make each one count.

She was forced to use three more before Dasch was ready. Stealing a quick glance behind her, Ànifa saw his sword was now awash in golden flames. Dasch stood and muttered softly to himself as he stepped toward the massive Gnuelry. Cecil jumped back, avoiding a swipe from a long appendage that had grown from the monster. Dasch raised his golden flaming sword and sliced the appendage clean off. The limb burned away, creating a horrible stench as embers floated up into the air. The yellow monster roared again and reared back, but Dasch quickly brought his sword up and slashed across its midsection. It wailed as it burned away into a cloud of thick black smoke. Dasch covered his face with his cloak and hurried back to his companions. His sword's golden flames now extinguished, he sheathed his sword.

"Oh my nature, this smells awful!" Ànifa said as she pinched her nose shut with her fingers. It smelled like rotting eggs fermenting in woolly rhinoceros droppings. "Come on, let's get outta here!"

They ran ahead a few meters to fresher air. Vesten coughed and sputtered as he sucked in a breath he'd been holding.

"Shit, that was utterly fuckin' rancid."

"Keep it down," Cecil whispered. "You never know what could be listening from the forest."

"Oh, shit I'm sorry, that was just—"

Ànifa cut in. "I think he's right. Something could be coming."

The forest rustled around them on both sides of the road. The five companions froze where they stood, each ready to spring into action if necessary. Then, as suddenly as it started, the forest quieted. A few seconds later, a bird chirped, then another. The forest was full of life once again. Ànifa let out a heavy breath, one she hadn't realized she'd been holding.

"I think we'll be okay. Come on," Ànifa said quietly, waving everyone forward. "I think the smell will ward off other foes."

They continued along the path quickly and cautiously. About half an hour had passed when they were stopped in their tracks by the unexpected appearance of a unicorn standing in the middle of the road. Its silky coat was pure white, much like the jackhorn from the Watthana Mountains. Its horn was a perfect crystal cone, shimmering in a rainbow of colors.

No one said a word. Vesten and Cecil simply stood there, gaping open-mouthed in shock, while Theodore squinted his eyes and began combing his beard with his right hand. Dasch stood there frozen, his face firm like a mask of stone. Ànifa stepped softly forward. The unicorn turned toward her and whinnied.

The unicorn's dark black eyes stared straight into her own and then bounded away into the forest with a single leap. Curses spilled out of Vesten until a hard nudge from Cecil shut him up.

"What was that?" Theodore asked.

"Nothing good," Dasch muttered knowingly.

"It was a warning. She told me the lands were changing. The gods are beginning to willingly accept the Gnuelry—the jelly monsters. Some gods are even allowing themselves and their servants to be taken by them—to be turned into something even more fearsome.

"She warned of war. That soon, nature will be at war with itself. Come, we must get to Dante's as quickly as we can."

Ànifa ran down the path. They soon exited the forest and came upon a well-marked fork in the road and took the path toward Galstrom.

It soon became apparent that they were on the wrong path. After they had crossed a small wooden bridge, they spotted an enormous fortress in the distance. The fortress was surrounded by pine trees.

"We've been tricked," Cecil exclaimed, pointing toward the fortress.

"Yeah, some fucker switched the signs," Vesten seethed. "At this rate, we'll end up in fuckin' Fort Turner!"

"Well, we haven't gone too far. Let's just go back to the fork," Theodore suggested calmly.

The five of them turned around and headed back. As they neared the bridge, they could see it was now being blocked.

"We've definitely been tricked." Cecil shook his head in bewilderment.

Blocking the bridge was a massive brown dire wolf and two lesser black dire wolves. The larger dire wolf's eyes were bloodshot and it was foaming at the mouth. It stood nearly two meters tall, while the black dire wolfs were about a meter and a half tall. The black dire wolves' eyes were also red. They panted, revealing their long, sharp teeth.

"This must be what the unicorn warned me about," Ànifa said quietly. "This is Morokomii, the wolf god."

"It doesn't look friendly," Vesten whispered.

"No shit," Cecil whispered, turning to face Vesten.

Dasch stepped forward, his sword held out in front of him. "Give me the best you got, god," he taunted.

The two black dire wolves charged forward. Cecil stepped out to stand next to Dasch and crouched into his battle stance, gripping his battle-axe with a firm familiarity.

The two black dire wolves leaped into the air, each one targeting a different opponent. Dasch stepped forward and slashed across the wolf's exposed belly as he sidestepped away from the direction of the spray of entrails. Cecil let out a battle cry as he jumped into the air and swung his battle-axe, cleanly slicing off its head.

"Is that all you got?" Dasch yelled, mocking the angry wolf god.

Morokomii raised her font paws. The ground shook as she planted her feet back on the ground and belted out a deafening roar. Ànifa covered her large, highly receptive elven ears the best she could, but it was too much. She fell to her knees, clutching her head, screaming without fully realizing she was doing so.

She could vaguely sense her companions rallying behind her. It seemed they weren't affected the way she was. Without warning, her head dipped forward and she passed out.

A familiar maniacal laughter echoed in her thoughts.

"You should have known that you were no match. You are puny little things that cower before the might of Morokomii!"

"This god, Morokomii. You've twisted her mind. She wouldn't be behaving this way if not for you!"

"And how do you know, Ànifa? How do you know anything? You don't remember anything."

"I don't remember much about my past life, you're right. And I happen to think that it's largely your fault... Gnusaramnii."

"Ha ha ha... so, you know who I am. Good. That makes things easier."

"But does it? Look, I know you think you are a godlike creature. But come on, don't you realize that in the end, you'll be beaten?"

Gnusaramnii laughed. *"You know—"*

"No, I'm not finished, and I don't know how long we've got. Look, I'm really angry. I'm angry at you for causing all of this... for taking my memories. But mostly I'm infuriated that you would even think for one second you could march into my home and take what isn't yours!"

"But that's where you're wrong," Gnusaramnii replied. *"This planet is mine. It's more mine than yours. You'll understand one day."*

She awoke with a start, then cursed.

"Whoa, Ànifa! Since when do you curse?" Theodore asked.

"Since I've been around Vesten. But also, I had so much more that I wanted to say—"

"What? What do you mean?" Dasch asked.

"I... I've been talking to Gnusaramnii. That's who's been in my head ever since I woke up at Charlotte's. But I haven't heard its voice since I've been taking those mushrooms Sage Mason gave me to control my dreams. I haven't wanted to hear its voice, but now that I don't hear it, I have so much that I want to say." She looked around in confusion. "By the way, where are we? And what happened to Morokomii? And where is everyone else?"

For the first time, Ànifa realized that she'd been moved since she passed out. She was lying in the grass at the foot of a tree. Only Theodore and Dasch were with her. Vesten and Cecil were nowhere to be seen.

"Ah, well, pretty soon after you passed out, we were saved. Dante just... basically, he just showed up—" Theodore stammered.

"Holy Eklatros, I thought you were a more elegant speaker," Dasch cut in. "Right after you passed out, Morokomii began charging. Honestly, I thought we were all done for. Those black wolves were big, but nothing like Morokomii. Yet before she could reach us, a set of hooks plunged into her back. Suddenly, a man with black hair standing in a small boat appeared. He yanked on the chains and spewed out a string of ancient verses. It was the language of the Ekataramn, I believe. After that, the god wrestled free from the hooks and bounded away into the forest.

"The man introduced himself as Dante. Cecil and I picked you up and helped you onto his boat. We went down the river for a little while, then we docked and he led us to his cabin, which is just over there," Dasch said, pointing behind him.

Ànifa saw it for the first time. "Ah, I see."

"Yes. Dante said this tree has special healing powers, and it would be better for you out here," Theodore added.

"I do feel energized and refreshed, honestly," Ànifa said. She admired the canopy that stretched out above her. It was a wide-reaching weeping willow, its long tendrils dangling in front of her, swinging gently in the soft breeze. She whispered a silent thank you, and turned back to her friends. "How long was I out for this time?"

"A little less than an hour," Theodore replied. "You've only been under the tree for five minutes. We just got here."

"Yes, I thought you'd take much longer to awaken. But now that you are, I suggest we reconvene with the others inside."

"Yeah, let's do that. We have a lot to talk about," Ànifa said as she stood and stretched, raising her arms high above her head as she rocked back and forth on her toes. She picked up the backpack and hoisted it onto her back. "Let's head inside. Thanks for watching over me," she said with a smile.

"Of course. I really feel a kinship with you, Ànifa," Theodore said, his face growing slightly red.

"Aw, I really feel connected with you too, Theodore. But Dasch, I'm a little surprised you're out here with me."

"I needed a break from Vesten," Dasch said, his voice filled with exasperation.

Ànifa laughed. "I get it. He can be a bit much, but I like him."

I like everyone I'm traveling with, she thought. *I've really gotten lucky here. But, I'm a bit nervous now, honestly. I feel as if Dante has a lot of the answers I've been looking for. I hope he can help to unlock some more of my memories.*

13

BATTLE FOR KNOWLEDGE

Ànifa followed Dasch and Theodore inside Dante's cabin.

"Oh, um, watch your step, please," a voice grumbled from the darkness.

She looked inside and gasped. The cabin was in complete and utter disarray. There was almost no floor space to be had. Nearly every available space held something—a stack of papers, a barrel of assorted items, a pile of clothes, boxes of foodstuffs. In one corner was an immense pile of scrolls. The kitchen looked as if something had exploded—there were stains on the walls and all over the counters. The counters were stacked high with dirty plates, bowls, and cups. There was also a large bowl containing moldy fruit that appeared to have been sitting out for quite some time. Fruit flies buzzed all around the bowl.

Cecil, Vesten, and Dante looked quite awkward sitting together on the couch. There were two other chairs open.

"Please, take a seat. We have much to discuss," Dante said, his hand extended toward the chairs. His short, black hair was matted and dirty, matching his dirt-stained cheeks. Dark stubble covered his long face, perfectly accenting his narrow black eyes. He wore a dirty wool poncho with ratty wool pants. His unkempt appearance made

149

him look older than Ànifa suspected he was, which she guessed to be around forty.

Ànifa, Theodore, and Dasch gingerly made their way to the two chairs. Ànifa took one for herself. Dasch offered the last to Theodore, who examined the chair with a sour face before plopping down. Dasch stood behind them and crossed his arms.

"Right, so as you all know, I'm Dante Suebsanguan. I'll be brief with the introductions since we have little time to spare. I am a very busy man, you see. At least Cecil and Vesten have been filling me in so far."

Dante, who sat on the right end of the couch, turned in his seat to face Ànifa. "You must be the elf, Ànifa. It is truly a pleasure to meet you. I hear you have been having some frightening experiences with various monsters, beasts, and gods."

"Yes," Ànifa began. "So far, I've been in direct contact with four different gods."

Dante whistled. "Quite impressive. The average person will live their entire lives and never truly know that the gods are real. Of course, you are not human. Which ones have you had the pleasure of meeting?"

"Let's see..." Ànifa clasped her hands together in her lap as she looked at the ceiling. "First, there was Maqinjinarii, the dire sloth. Then, there was Aerigasus, the winged ram, although I was unconscious the entire time. After that, I called upon Krakuluthosii while we were sailing here—we were attacked by pirates. Then there was Morokomii, the wolf god. Unfortunately, she wasn't in control of herself."

"Indeed. It is quite unfortunate, but the gods have been turning. I'm glad I was in the vicinity and was able to help deal with Morokomii. It's good to hear that the other three you mentioned are still within the light, though."

"How many fuckin' gods are there?" Vesten asked.

"Exactly one hundred and eight. They are scattered all across this planet. Many live deep within the depths of the oceans, never seen by any land dweller."

Vesten let out a slow whistle. "Damn, that's a lot of gods. Why one hundred and eight?"

"I can't say the exact reason why, but that number represents unity in all existence," Dante replied.

"While that may be, I fear we will run into many more gods on our journey if what the unicorn said was right," Ànifa said softly.

Dante sputtered and coughed, then looked at her, wide-eyed. "What? You came across a unicorn?"

"Oh yeah, that was fuckin' neat," Vesten said.

Dante, who was sitting next to Vesten on the couch, glared at him and said, "No, lad. Unicorns are not neat, as you say. Seeing a unicorn is always a sign that something dreadful is coming. They are the harbingers of death, doom, and destruction. No one should ever wish to see a unicorn."

"Oh, that's not how they're made out to be in the stories," Vesten said with disappointment in his voice.

"Oh no, lad—nothing like the stories." Dante turned back to Ànifa. "What did it say to you?"

"She told me that the gods were turning against us. That they were siding with the jelly monsters—with Gnusaramnii."

Dante grunted and covered his mouth with his right hand. "Gnusaramnii... so it really is back."

"Yes," Dasch grumbled. "Gnusaramnii is back, and it is hungry. It's attempting to devour Eklatros itself."

"Indeed. I feared it was so, as I have seen these jelly monsters you speak of. Now, Ànifa."

"Um, yes?" Ànifa asked after a momentary pause.

"As an elf, you must already have the knowledge to defeat these enemies. But is there anything you can tell us about your past that could help us now? We are going to need all the help we can get, especially since you saw that unicorn."

"I... well, Cecil must not have told you this part, but I remember little about my time with the elves. All I remember is what has transpired since I woke up at Charlotte's. Additionally, I've remembered a few little things here and there, but not much."

"Have you remembered anything new?" Theodore asked.

"Yeah, actually. It's just been so chaotic I haven't gotten a chance to tell anyone yet. But it happened when we were fleeing from the crows. I tripped and fell, and I remembered that..." Ànifa struggled to recall her memories, her hands fidgeting in her lap. "So, the night I fell off Yttendaus, I was running away from something. I think I was terrified. And at that time, I also tripped and fell. That part is clear. As I fell, I punched through an energy barrier. It felt really strange. After that, I fell through a cloud, then I attempted to dive into the water, but I think I passed out from the impact. Before I could drown, I woke up and swam to the surface. I think I swam all the way to the shore before I passed out again.

"But that's all I remember. I still remember nothing about who I was, or about my family, or anything of the sort. I mean, I know I used archery, as I was given my bow and quiver of arrows from before. That weapon is really familiar to me."

"Hmm, there's quite a lot I want to talk about. However, I must ask this first. Who gave you your bow and quiver?" Dante asked.

"I don't know. The letter was wrapped in a large leaf and signed by someone named JL."

"Do you have the letter with you?" Dante asked.

"Yes, hold on," Ànifa said, reaching into her long trenchdress. She found the letter still safely stored in one of the inner pockets and handed it to Dante. His eyes widened as he held the leaf to his nose and inhaled.

"This is not from any tree I have ever encountered. This must be from Yttendaus. But this JL is a mystery. The name doesn't ring any bells?"

"No, it's still not familiar to me."

Dante placed his hand on his chin. "My guess is that this came from someone close to you, especially since they had access to your personal weapon."

"Yes, that is a fair point," Ànifa said.

"I also think she's royalty, but that's just my opinion," Cecil said.

"I could see it," Dante said. "Her hair is quite regal."

"I don't really know, but I just don't think I am," Ànifa said.

"You probably aren't," Theodore said.

"It would be really fuckin' cool if you were, though," Vesten said, grinning.

"Yes. Now, Ànifa. There's something else I wanted to ask. You said that you distinctly remember falling through an energy barrier?"

"Yeah, it felt really strange. It felt like… it was like my whole body was consumed in electricity, but it wasn't harming me. And the energy itself wasn't harsh, but gentle. It was strong, though. I could feel that. Like it had repelled many things throughout its existence."

"Indeed. Nothing is supposed to be able to cross through a Great Barrier. But you fell straight through the strongest one without so much as a scratch. That is impressive indeed. It's no wonder Sage Mason sent you on this quest. You really are the perfect ones for the job," Dante said.

"And what job is this, exactly?" Vesten asked. "I mean, I know what's going on, but… what's really fuckin' goin' on?"

"Right, well, I'm sure you may not even know this, Ànifa, but your arrival was foretold. It is a legend only known to a select few, for as you may know, knowledge in the wrong hands can be disastrous. Without getting into the details, the legend states that your true purpose is to awaken the Ekataramn. They have been dormant, lying asleep for thousands of years. The Great Barriers have been protecting them all this time, but now they must be awoken in order for Eklatros to survive. By awakening the Ekataramn, we can ensure that most of the gods will stay on the side of light and purity. It also may sway those who have turned from their true path to rediscover their way back into the light.

"However, do be warned. There will be gods that may be too far gone to save. If that happens, the best thing to do is to slay them as swiftly as you can before they cause any harm."

Ànifa had her right hand placed over her racing heart and her eyes closed. She tried to calm herself with deep breaths. After a few moments, she opened her eyes and looked into Dante's eyes.

"That's a lot to take in. Me, the savior of the Ekataramn? Maybe that's why my dreams have been..." she trailed off for a moment, then asked, "Is there an alternate way to save a god?"

"If the Ekataramn cannot help, then killing them is the only way. Once turned, there is no going back," Dante sternly replied.

"It really is a shame," Theodore said, shaking his head. "I have a question for you, Dante."

"What is it?"

"What do you know about the Great Barriers and the Ekataramn that lie within?"

Dante grunted. "I am the expert. Although, this will be the simplest explanation."

He stood and stomped through the mess on his floor, giving little care to what he was crunching underneath his dirty sandals. Dante walked over to the pile of scrolls and began looking through them, throwing the ones he didn't want over his shoulder, creating an even bigger mess of his already messy house.

Eventually, he found what he was looking for and returned to them. He handed the scroll to Ànifa, then returned to his spot on the couch. Before sitting down, he picked up the mysterious letter from Yttendaus and returned it to Ànifa.

She took the letter graciously and placed it in back in her trenchdress. Then she unrolled the scroll. It contained a map of Eklatros, but not just any ordinary map of the world. She laid the map on her lap. Theodore leaned over so he could look as well. She tilted it toward him so he could get a better look.

"What you got there is something special I've been working on. No one else has anything even nearly as complete as mine," Dante said, puffing out his chest a little. "As you can see, the map marks the precise location of every known Ekataramn. There's the closest one to here, Kalahsem. But don't get me wrong, it'll be a few days' journey from here to reach Kalahsem. I also have an explanation on how to get there, as there is no true path to get to any of these places. But I have left cairns and waystones along the way that I describe in the directions."

"This is exactly what I've been searching for this entire time,"

Theodore said with a large smile, his eyes wide with excitement. "The upper-class wizards always scoffed at me whenever I would bring it up. They would say, 'but there is no need for such a map, as there is no need to study them. We already know everything about them, and they are off limits,' and similar blather. I never liked any of them. Well, only one, but she's special."

"Oh? And who is this special woman?" Ànifa asked with a sly smile.

"It's not like that. And now is not the time for this," Theodore sputtered in exasperation.

"Agreed. Ànifa, do you have any questions about the map?" Dante asked.

"Yeah, I do. I've already skimmed through each set of directions, and it seems like it'll be fairly simple to follow them. What I am curious about is the large question mark in the center of the Rosemenov Desert."

"The Rosemenov Desert? What's there? I thought it was just a barren wasteland," Cecil said.

"Indeed," Dante replied. "That is what Ajenti wants you to believe. But don't believe what they say. There are strange, mysterious ruins lying at the center of the Rosemenov Desert. Haven't you ever wondered why the scorching desert turns into a freezing glacier, with only an absolute mess of a bog in between? Well, my theory is that the ruins are causing that strange weather shift to happen.

"Some believe there is a Great Barrier there, but my best guess is that there is not one. So, I do not believe that you need to worry about it. Besides, there was ever only supposed to be one Ekataramn per landmass. Of course, much has changed since the ancient times of Kieth Angelcross. For there used to be seven continents with seven Ekataramn. Of course, now there are five, one of which is on a floating landmass. Which leaves the four on each of the main landmasses.

"As I mentioned, Kalahsem is here, on Gallheim. Then, on the continent of Roffen, there is Roheefy. Panna Isle is home to

Panabeeta, and Schelff Island has Bugenaluf. Well, then there is Yttendaus, of course," Dante said. "Any other questions? Anyone?"

"I don't mean to pry, but it seems as if this map itself contains secrets that many at Ajenti are not aware of. Plus, looking around this room, I can assume that many more secrets lie in this filthy cabin," Theodore said, noting the immense pile of scrolls.

Dante shrugged. "You're not wrong. I see what you're getting at, and I feel as if you already know the answer."

"So, it's true... you are Dante—the Sorcerer Dante Suebsanguan. You were once almost headmaster of Ajenti," Theodore said, pointing right at Dante for a moment before quickly dropping his hand.

"Yes, in my past life. I was going to become the headmaster of Ajenti. Why do you think I left so suddenly?"

"It's said that you left for undisclosed reasons, and it is assumed those reasons were personal," Theodore replied.

"Yes, but what do *you* think, Sorcerer Caldwell?"

"I think you cracked. I think you didn't want the responsibility, but you felt inclined to take the position. In the end, you couldn't handle the pressure, so you left."

"Good guess. And it's mostly right too. But the real reason I left was because of the secret opposition. They knew that if I was going to get into power, I was going to reveal many secrets the Ajentian elite keep to themselves. This did not go over well with them and they threatened to kill me.

"I figured it was better if I didn't get brutally murdered by my peers, so I left one night without saying a word. Of course, I stole many scrolls when I left."

"So that was you, too? A couple of years ago, there was an extensive investigation into who stole nearly an entire shelf of the library archives."

"I knew it!" Dante laughed and slapped his knee. "I knew no one would go down there for a long time! The corner I stole from was in such a little hidden nook—but it was my hidden nook. It's where I stored the ones I was using for my research. So, I took as many scrolls as I could carry and hightailed it out of there."

Theodore chuckled heartily. "I know what you mean. There are too many hidden nooks in the library."

"Ah... but it is in those nooks that the best texts lie. Now, Theodore. What brings *you* out here? You, being an Ajentian sorcerer. Why are you venturing outside of Ajenti? I thought most sorcerers sat in their cold rooms practicing their dusty old spells over and over again."

"Yes, many of us tend to do that in our free time. It helps to keep the mind sharp. But as for me, I was sent on a special mission—"

"Oh, really, Theodore?" Cecil cut in. "How much longer are you going to keep up that lie?"

"It's better than the truth," Theodore spat. "How would you feel if you had the vast majority of your power stripped from you? Do you even know how it feels? Every day I wake up feeling naked. I am not my true self anymore, Cecil!"

Cecil looked at Theodore mournfully, then at his hands as rubbed them together.

"So, you're in exile then," Dante said.

"What? You're in exile? What does that mean?" Ànifa asked.

"It means..." Theodore sighed. "It means that I was exiled. Banned from Ajenti for life. And before I left, they stripped away the vast majority of my magical energy. Of course, they can't steal of all of my power, since it would kill me. Throughout our journey, I've been pushing myself, stretching myself to my limits. It's only a fraction of what I can do."

"Yeah, I mean, he *was* a B-Class Sorcerer, but from everything I know..." Cecil trailed off and then continued, looking at his friend. "Well Theo, you should have been at least an A-Class!"

"I know it. Oh, do I ever know it. But it's all thanks to deceitful Spell Master Prander! He has always had it out for me," Theodore grumbled.

"Why were you exiled, wizard?" Dasch asked.

"Ah, well, I was caught removing a book from the S-Class Library."

"An act that would get you whipped and banned from the library, for an S-Class or an A-Class Sorcerer," Dante added. "But for a B-Class, exile makes sense."

"Yes, and I am still happy about the fact I negotiated myself out of the whipping," Theodore said proudly.

"Well, you are an old man. I'm sure it would have killed you," Dante said matter-of-factly.

"You aren't so young yourself! You may still have your natural hair color, but that doesn't fool me. I know your lineage," Theodore shot back.

"Then you know why I'm helping you. I am the last of my line," Dante replied.

"No, not the last. Not anymore," Dasch said, looking deep into Dante's eyes knowingly.

"What? Who are you?" Dante asked.

Dasch lowered his hood for the first time since entering the cabin, fully revealing his face. Ànifa looked back and forth between the two, her mouth open in surprise. They looked as if they could be brothers, aside from Dasch's pointed ears.

"I may have lost all my hair, but mine was once as black as yours," Dasch said.

Dante's eyes went wide. "Dasch... you cannot be! Dasch Valentine, the warrior from *The Magical World of Eklatros*!"

Dasch grunted. "So I've heard."

"How do you still breathe, my kin?" Dante asked.

"I have a piece of Gnusaramnii tearing into my soul. Do not worry," Dasch said in response to Dante's gasp, "for I have learned to control it. I will never be rid of it, and I am sure that it will be what will kill me in the end."

Dante nodded. "I have heard the stories about the man that Gnusaramnii possessed for a short time. It makes sense that it would be you. You—Dasch Valentine—you are a true half-elf, are you not?"

Dasch nodded. "My mother was an elf."

Ànifa looked back at Dasch, who still had his hood lowered, and examined his ears. While his ears were small, like a human ear, they were tipped like an elf's.

"What?" Cecil threw out his hands, nearly slapping Vesten in the face. "That's crazy."

Vesten leaned away from Cecil and nodded in agreement. "Yeah, really fuckin' crazy."

"Why do you think it's so crazy?" Dasch asked them as he put his hood back up.

"It's just, first an elf, now a half-elf. A week ago, I wouldn't have believed any of this would ever happen to me," Cecil replied.

"What did you believe would happen to you then, knight? We may have just met, but I know your type. I know you would have drunk yourself to death," Dasch sneered.

"Hey, lay off of him," Theodore cut in.

"Why? You know that once a drunk, always a drunk. It doesn't matter how many years someone stays away from the drink. Eventually, the alcohol consumes them. I've seen it happen to better men than you," Dasch replied with a face of stone.

"Yes, it's no secret that I'm a drunk. But I haven't had a drink since Sathon. That was days ago, and I feel completely fine. No withdrawal or anything."

"How is that possible?" Theodore turned to his friend. "Sorry, it's like you said though, it's no secret what you are."

"Sage Mason gave me some medicine to help with the withdrawal, as well as his special herbs, which I've been sneaking here and there."

"Sage Mason has an herbal remedy for everything," Dante said with a grin.

"I should've known," Theodore replied, shaking his head at himself.

"But that doesn't change the fact that you are still a drunk," Dasch said.

"So what? I am who I am," Cecil replied.

"Shit, yeah you are!" Vesten said. "You be proud of who you are. I know I'm fuckin' proud of myself."

"No wonder you're so annoying," Dasch muttered under his breath.

"Yes, and it's a good thing if you really think about it," Theodore said. "When I was exiled, they ordered him to come with me. Essentially, they were exiling him with me."

"Yeah, screw them all. They just couldn't handle me," Cecil exclaimed with a smile as he brushed his hair out of his eyes.

"No, they couldn't handle how you handled your drink. You missed nearly every drill. You were barely holding onto your status as a knight. But that's exactly my point. If you hadn't been a lazy, good-for-nothing drunk, you wouldn't have been exiled with me, and we would have never ventured out on our journey together. We never would have met Ànifa, so none of this would ever have happened.

"So, in that sense, we are all exactly who we are meant to be," Theodore said.

"Well put, wizard," Dasch grumbled.

Ànifa only partly paid attention to the conversation as she continued to pore over the map. She focused on Kalahsem, the first of the Great Barriers that they would need to visit. After leaving Dante's cabin—marked with a small 'D' on the map—they would need to go straight past Galstrom, across a stone bridge, then pass through a small town called Kalah. After that, they would need to pass through the Chrevans Grasslands, then traverse across the Morai Mountain Range. Then they would reach the Kalsri Forest, where Kalahsem was located. Right now, they were in the Eladali Forest, which was north of Galstrom.

This map was truly helpful, probably the most helpful gift Ànifa had received on this quest—aside from her bow and quiver, of course.

"Hey, Dante, I have another question," Ànifa asked, interrupting Theodore, who had been arguing with Cecil about elegance. Dante turned to her and nodded. "Are the people nice in Kalah, and do they have a supply shop?"

Dante cast his eyes down. "Ah, well, about that..."

"Oh no," Ànifa immediately sensed what Dante was going to say next and placed a hand over her heart.

"That town is destroyed. It was only a few days ago. I saw the destruction myself. Otherwise, I wouldn't have believed it."

"What happened?" Ànifa asked, lacing her fingers together and placing her hands in her lap.

"The whole town... destroyed?" Theodore shook his head in disbelief.

"Oh shit," Vesten said softly. "So, it is true."

After a brief pause, Dante continued, "I used to frequently travel to Kalah. Even though Galstrom is a much larger city, and much closer, there are certain items you can only purchase from Kalah. The most noteworthy were the spools of fresh Lafhreep wool they sold, which is a truly amazing material. You see, being knowledgeable about this world does not earn me a living. So, to make koda, I would purchase lafhreep wool to make a wide assortment of useful items, such as socks, gloves, and blankets. I made the clothes I'm wearing now, but I digress."

Dante paused, giving Ànifa a chance to look around the room. Once she knew what she was looking for, it wasn't hard to find. The loom was already becoming buried by trash and dirty clothes, and she now suspected that there might be a sewing machine beneath the enormous pile of clothes next to the loom.

"As I made my way to Kalah a few days ago to stock up on wool, I saw a large plume of smoke. I hurried there as fast as I could, but it was too late. The town was burnt to the ground. In the center of the flames, I saw movement, so I quickly hid behind a boulder. These monsters were none like I had ever seen before."

"Let me guess," Ànifa cut in. "They were short, fat, and covered in scales, right?"

"Yes, exactly," Dante replied. "And it sounded like they were talking to each other. Not only that, but they seemed to be perfectly content within the flames."

"They must be immune to fire," Ànifa replied. "The one time we saw one, it was right after my friend Charlotte's tent burnt to the ground."

"Charlotte... do you mean Charlotte Tuesti?" Dante asked with sudden concern in his voice. "Is she okay?"

"We don't know. She was taken, and we're looking for her." Ànifa's tone was sullen.

"She was taken? Why?" Dante asked. "None of this makes any sense. An entire town, burned to the ground, leaving hundreds of people homeless. And now I learn monsters kidnapped my dear friend."

Theodore looked Dante in the eye. "If we find her, we'll let you know."

"I would appreciate that," Dante replied with a deep nod.

"Dante, what happened to the citizens of Kalah?" Ànifa asked.

"I'm sure they'll go anywhere they can. Port Gall, Galstrom, and Fort Turner would all make the most sense though."

"We ran into many refugees at Pikkul Harbor yesterday," Cecil added.

"Yeah, we even had to fuckin' avoid Port Gall. There were too many ships," Vesten said.

"Ships? That doesn't make much sense unless the monsters destroyed more than one town. Kalah was a farming town and was nowhere near the ocean. They are not seafaring folk," Dante said.

"Well, shit. See, when I was in Pikkul Harbor, I heard an assortment of different rumors. Along with Kalah, I heard that fuckin' Seaside was destroyed, as well as Rampa Bay and Heerenditheer," Vesten said.

"Hmm, I don't know about Seaside or Heerenditheer, but I'm sure that Rampa Bay is just a rumor. Fort Turner's standing army there is among the best I've ever seen, even better than Ajenti's soldiers," Dante replied.

"That doesn't much surprise me," Cecil said. "They may talk a big game in Ajenti, but honestly, they're all fakers and cheats. That's why I got so into the drink—because I couldn't stand my fellow knights. Each one was a massive asshole."

"Dante..." Ànifa began, then got quiet.

"What is it?" Dante asked.

"It's just that Sage Mason said you could help us find Charlotte, but from what you said, you don't know why she was taken."

Dante sighed. "I may not know *why* she was taken, but I suppose I could guess where they are taking her."

"Where? Sage Mason and Dasch both believe she was taken to Kalahsem." Ànifa said.

"Kalahsem would make sense," Dante said while rubbing the stubble on his chin. "Especially considering Kalahsem's powers."

"About those powers—" Theodore began.

"But why Charlotte?" Ànifa asked, cutting off the wizard and pounding her fist on the armrest of her chair.

"She's certainly a special woman. We met at Ajenti. Even though she was just a simple serving girl at my favorite pub, she was bright and special. She never studied at Ajenti, but she could have. Instead, she applied her knowledge and talents to other areas.

"We grew close, and in our time together, I told her much about my studies. It's possible the monsters want to exploit that knowledge."

"But what about you? Why did they not take you?" Ànifa asked.

"You may not have noticed, Ànifa, since you were unconscious earlier, but surrounding my cabin is an energy barrier. It is similar, in a sense, to the Great Barriers themselves, but much, much weaker. This energy barrier allows my cabin to stay hidden. However, I fear that even my energy barrier won't protect me from what is about to transpire," Dante said.

"Can I see your energy barrier?" Ànifa asked with a note of curiosity.

"Sure. We might as well prepare for the night, anyway. As you can tell, you can't sleep here. But there is a safe place nearby where you can set up camp."

Ànifa looked out the window and realized it had grown dark since they had started talking, and she was exhausted.

"Thank you, Dante, we appreciate it," Ànifa replied.

Dante stood up from the couch.

"Before we do that," Theodore interjected, "I would like to ask about the Ekataramn's powers. Sage Mason mentioned each one has its own special ability."

Dante sat back down and said, "I'm afraid I cannot divulge that information to you. That knowledge cannot find its way into the wrong hands."

"I can assure I won't share it with anyone," Theodore stressed.

"It's no matter. I have a responsibility to uphold," Dante said firmly.

As Theodore opened his mouth to speak, Dante waved him off and said, "I have one more thing to add before we end for the night. I'll be leaving here tomorrow morning before first light to travel to Fort Turner."

"That shouldn't be a problem. You've helped us out a lot today. Your information, and the map, have been invaluable," Ànifa said, placing her hands together and nodding deeply. "I have a quick request though," Ànifa added.

Dante sighed. "Sure, what is it?"

"You don't happen to have any arrows, do you? I'm running dangerously low."

"Ah, you're in luck. I also make arrows, but those I do not sell. I do most of my hunting and foraging on my own. The arrows I make are quite durable. How big is your quiver?"

"It can hold up to sixty arrows, and I only have seven left."

Dante raised his eyebrows and whistled. "A quiver that can hold sixty arrows? Now isn't that something. Yet I can't spare that many. Would thirty-five suffice?"

"Thirty-five is perfect," Ànifa replied. "How much do I owe you?"

"You don't owe me anything. Arrows are cheap and easy to make; it's not a problem," Dante said. He stood and trudged through the mess of his house. Ànifa dug into her trenchdress to look for the koda that Charlotte had given her. She found the small bag of coins and placed ten koda on the armrest of her chair.

The bright moon illuminated their path as Dante led them away from his cabin. He stopped in front of a set of trees.

"This is where my energy barrier ends. I feel a slight shock every time I go through, but that's only because I know what it feels like. Most others that pass through here don't feel a thing."

"Oh, shit? Let me be the one to test this," Vesten said, standing akimbo with a large grin on his face. Dante shrugged nonchalantly. Vesten walked forward, past the trees, and turned around.

"Yeah, I didn't feel a thing." He was disappointed.

"I told you. Most people feel nothing. Now, Ànifa, I'm curious if you'll notice anything," Dante said.

Ànifa nodded and walked past the trees. As she walked through the barrier, she felt a warm, tickling shock.

"Yes... that felt eerily similar to when I fell through the Great Barrier."

Dante smiled widely. "Ha! I knew it. It's basically the same principle as the Great Barriers, and it really wasn't that difficult to replicate. Now, the sheer amount of power and energy it would take to make a barrier akin to the Great Barriers... that's something altogether otherworldly. Now, let's continue on. The clearing isn't far."

Theodore and Cecil followed Dante with Dasch following behind them. As Dasch walked past the trees, Ànifa saw Dasch's eyebrow-less eyes widen slightly as he passed through the barrier.

They soon found themselves in a small clearing. The soft grass blew gently in the wind, and Ànifa thought she heard an owl hooting off in the distance.

As promised, Dante helped them set up camp. He had brought with him three canvas tents—two that slept two people and one single-person tent. After the tents were erected, Dante said his goodbyes and headed back toward his cabin.

Both Ànifa and Dasch declined to use the tents, so Theodore, Cecil, and Vesten each took a tent for themselves. Instead, Ànifa was perfectly happy to sleep in the grass, while Dasch didn't really sleep. Instead, he went into a meditative trance. Dasch took one end of the clearing, and Ànifa took the opposite.

She sat cross-legged, the large Eklatros Collective History book in her lap as she read. This was the first real chance she'd had to read it and was immediately engrossed in it.

She would have stayed up all night reading, but a visit from the owl god put her mind to rest. She closed the book, using a blade of grass to mark her page, and lay down. She took a deep breath and smiled. The clearing seemed to have its own protective barrier that blocked her negative thoughts. She would not need to take any shuyukuii mushrooms tonight.

It's been another long, eventful day, she thought. *Each day has had its own set of battles and adventures. And even though it's been frightening at times, it's been really fun.*

Although, I'm not sure if I deserve to feel happy right now. Charlotte is still out there. At least we now have a good idea where she may be. Charlotte, I will find you. You saved me, and I will save you. Please, please be at Kalahsem. There's been too much death and sadness lately. Having you back would be like a sunbeam finding its way through a rainstorm. And not just for me. Eklatros still needs you, Charlotte. I can feel it.

With the help of Dante's map, we should be able to reach Kalahsem in a few days. Please, hold on until then.

14

BATTLE FOR BALANCE

Ànifa awoke to the sounds of birds chirping close by. She opened her eyes and saw rows of songbirds lining the trees surrounding the clearing.

She smiled. She had been right—she had another dreamless night without the need for the shuyukuii mushrooms. And yet, even now in the morning peace, her mind swirled. The memories she had recovered recently were part of the reason, as were all the events that had transpired since Charlotte's abduction. There was also the matter of what she had learned last night by reading *A Collective History: The Magical World of Eklatros*. Finally, there was the presence of Gnusaramnii as it kept on chipping away at the corners of her mind. She needed more dreamless nights, but at the same time, she felt as if her dreams could be helpful. If not for Gnusaramnii, she would welcome her dreams.

All these thoughts battled for prominence in her mind, creating a furious haze. A loud snort beside her interrupted her thoughts. She turned to her side and watched as an elk with an impressive set of antlers ambled into the forest.

Ànifa stood and reached toward the sky, stretching out the minor aches she'd acquired from sleeping on the ground. *Today is going to be another long day. I can feel it,* she thought. *I'll let them sleep for just a few more minutes. I need some time to get my mind in order, anyway. Yet we shouldn't linger here much longer.*

The sun peeked out from above the trees as they made their way along the path. They passed Dante's cabin and followed the small trail that would take them to the main road.

As they walked briskly and quietly along the path, Ànifa took the time to reflect on what she had read last night.

The book began rather oddly, but not in a bad way. The first chapter was a peculiar poem that told how the Ekataramn—or the sentient trees, as the book had put it—were thought to be the first sentient beings on the planet. The second chapter was written as if it were a children's story, telling the tale of how the first elves established themselves in the forests. They had built wondrous structures, including giant staircases that wrapped around massive trees. Entire buildings and houses had been erected within the canopies of those ancient trees.

She had only made it part of the way through the third chapter before the owl god had lulled her to sleep. So far, the third chapter introduced the world of humans. Once again, it was written as a children's story, although much less detailed. It was easy enough to read, and the characters had been simple and two-dimensional, but there was much knowledge hidden between the words themselves. It was the message and the story that mattered. Now that she had begun the book, she was eager to finish it.

They exited the Eladali Forest and connected with the main road.

By this point, it was almost noon, and her companions were getting restless.

"Fuck, I'm hungry," Vesten moaned.

"Why didn't you eat more for breakfast, then?" Cecil asked.

"I'm not used to nuts and berries. I'm used to rich, full breakfasts. I'm talking about bacon, and eggs, and waffles. A nice glass of orange juice is really fuckin' nice every now and again too."

"Where do you get oranges from?" Theodore asked. "An orange sounds mighty tasty right now."

"I only ever get them when I'm at the Sortuga street markets, or if I ever wander down to Panna Isle where they grow them fresh. So not too fuckin' often. I served you some, remember?"

"I understand you two are hungry," Dasch grumbled, cutting Theodore off before he could reply, "but we really must keep our voices down."

"How about a rest, then?" Vesten inquired.

"No, we need to keep moving," Ànifa said curtly. Noticing her harsh tone, she turned around to face her comrades and continued in a softer tone. "I'm sorry. It's just that we are a long way away from Kalahsem, and I want to get there as quickly as possible, especially if Charlotte might be there." She spun back around and resumed her place at the head of the party.

"Yes, I agree. We must get there with haste," Theodore replied. "But a hungry body cannot move quickly."

"Fair point," Ànifa replied without looking back. "But I'm not stopping. If you want to stick with me, you better keep up."

Dasch snorted in laughter and picked up his pace. Cecil straightened his back, held his head high, and marched forward, looking like a true knight.

Theodore grumbled. Vesten sighed. Both continued forward, picking up the rear.

As they passed by the fork that branched off to Galstrom, they came across a caravan of wagons that was carrying a wide assortment of supplies to the city. The caravan had come from Port Gall. They received news that Port Gall was once again under control, thanks to Baron Von Skyock. He had brought the port city under control with hangings and decapitations. Apparently, the gallows had been running nonstop since the riots. The news didn't sit well with Ànifa.

While the caravan didn't stop, they had some runner boys that were selling some easy-to-get-to wares. Theodore, Vesten, and Cecil each bought a hearty snack, Dasch purchased a waterskin, and Ànifa got a small loaf of bread.

The snacks had given them enough energy to continue well into late afternoon. They eventually took a rest under a large willow tree that stood beside the path. They were only a few hundred meters from the wide stone bridge they had to cross to reach Kalah.

"Why are we stopping now? I can keep going," Vesten said.

"It's not that. My heart is racing," Ànifa said. She placed her right hand over her heart. "I need to still it before we go into Kalah. I may know what to expect, but I'm not ready for it."

"I understand," Theodore replied, placing a hand on Ànifa's shoulder for a moment. "Take all the time you need."

"How big was Kalah? Was it a large town?" Ànifa asked. She caught Vesten's eye and he looked away quickly.

"It's been fuckin' forever since I've been there," Vesten said as he examined the weeping willow's long tendrils.

"I would estimate that it was only about the size of Sathon," Theodore said.

"Oh, really?" Ànifa replied. "Sathon seemed like a pretty large city. So was Pikkul Harbor. I think it was smaller than Sathon, only much more crowded."

"Sathon is a good-sized city for Schelff Island, which has the lowest population of the five main landmasses," Cecil explained. "And your experience of Pikkul Harbor is not a good example. We passed over Port Gall so you never saw it, but Port Gall is bigger than both Sathon and Pikkul Harbor combined. And yet Port Gall is only about a third of the size of Galstrom."

Ànifa whistled. "That's a lot of people."

"That's nothing," Cecil continued. "Ajenti is about five times bigger than Galstrom. In total, I'd say there are nearly eight hundred thousand people in Ajenti. I've never been to Fort Turner, but I hear that it's a little more populated than Ajenti."

Ànifa didn't know what to say. The thought of so many people in one place boggled her mind.

"I knew humans had large settlements, but I didn't realize that they got that big. How do you know all this?" Ànifa asked.

"Being a knight is more than being skilled on the battlefield. It's also about knowing things. Knowing the populations of every city and town in the world is important because if a war broke out, any single knight could easily calculate the number of soldiers versus civilians an attacking city might have."

"That's a good point," Ànifa replied. "Are there a lot of wars?"

"Nope. There hasn't been a war in hundreds of years. But you never know. It could happen one day, especially in this climate," Cecil said.

"Do you think it was true what they said? About the public executions in Port Gall?"

"Sadly, I wouldn't doubt it. Baron Von Skyock is ruthless. They used to say that he'd do anything to keep Port Gall running smoothly, and apparently they were right."

Even though the subject was dark, talking with her friends eased her racing heart. Her mind was still in a haze, and she figured there was nothing she could do about it.

Ànifa took a shy step forward onto the stone bridge. It was firm beneath her, and it gave her the confidence to continue forward. She was a little nervous; the river they were crossing was raging below.

"You'll be fine," Cecil laughed. She must have looked stiffer than she thought. "Loosen up. This bridge may be old, but it's sturdy. Its age is how I know it's safe to cross."

"Agreed. This bridge may have even been built by elves," Dasch grumbled.

"Really?" Ànifa asked as she examined the stone bridge.

"It's certainly possible," Theodore replied. "No one truly knows the age of the two nameless bridges of Gallheim."

"Are they truly nameless?" Ànifa asked. Her heart began to beat wildly again, so she knew she had to keep talking. Focusing on the conversation was the best thing for her right now.

"No, not truly. I read somewhere they did have proper names once, but their names have been forgotten through time. Now they are just unofficially called the same as the river they bridge. So, they dubbed this the Kohaku Bridge, while the bridge west of us is dubbed the Shippo Bridge. But those aren't their real names," Theodore said.

"I'll try to remember that," Ànifa replied.

"Don't you already know all this, though?" Theodore asked. "From Dante's map, I mean."

"Yes, I saw what it said, but the map didn't explain it like you did," Ànifa replied.

The bridge was longer than she had expected—nearly three-quarters of a kilometer long. Even before they stepped off the stone bridge, they could smell ash in the air. Ànifa felt a strange sensation wash over her.

She looked in front of her and saw a firm, yellow jelly monster had jumped into their path. Without thinking, Ànifa swiped at the creature with her right hand, sending out a wave of destructive energy that tore right through the Gnuelry. It exploded into the air around the group. Theodore and Dasch were closest to Ànifa. Theodore shielded himself from most of the gelatinous splatter with his large blue cloak, while Dasch simply turned his back to it and let it spray him.

Ànifa hurried forward, her right hand still awash in blue flames from her attack. As she stepped through the ash, she looked at the footprints she was leaving behind, then stopped. She stood before the remnants of a building, its dilapidated heap still smoldering. She had known what to expect. But standing here, with the ash swirling in the surrounding air, she was hit with a wave of emotions as everything boiled up inside of her at once. Her missing memories. The ever-present existence of Gnusaramnii. Her anxiety about her dreams. The strange bird-like creature she had dreamt about. The loss of Charlotte. The mob in Pikkul Harbor. The news that some rich Baron was openly murdering people in the streets of Port Gall. The torrent of crows that had smothered them. The Gnusar monsters that were ravaging the world. The strange stillness of the destruction around her. The pirates and sailors that she had been forced to kill. The unicorn's grave message. The wolf god that had turned on them. The subtle cries of the world around her, from Eklatros herself as the infestation tore the harmonic balance of nature apart. And the knowledge that she was learning about this planet and how it had once been so much more.

Ànifa felt herself growing slightly warmer. She idly noticed that blue flames had consumed her entire body.

A blinding light overcame her senses.

"Ugh! So gross," Theodore exclaimed as the remains of the yellow Gnuelry splattered onto his outstretched cloak. "Ànifa, be careful of the spray."

"I don't think she can hear you," Cecil said softly beside him.

"What do you mean?" Theodore asked as he turned around. He was slightly annoyed that Cecil didn't have a speck of yellow jelly on him.

Then he saw her standing there, amidst the smoldering ruins awash in blue flames. The flames licked at every inch of her body as the tip flared out high above her head. "Dear Lady Eklatros, we've got to stop her!"

"Oh fuck, what's happening?" Vesten asked, his voice filled with shock and awe.

Dasch sprinted past Theodore as he stood there, gaping open-mouthed at what he was seeing. Ànifa was levitating off the ground. He shook his head and looked the others.

"Is there anything you can do, Theodore?" Cecil asked, his face full of fear.

Theodore tried reaching out to Ànifa through their mental link but couldn't reach her.

Ànifa stopped rising into the air. She hovered about four meters off the ground. She lowered her head and the surrounding air began spinning. The ash and dust around Ànifa rose into the air along with the charred wooden remains of buildings. She was creating a tornado.

"Holy Eklatros, she's going to fucking kill us!" Vesten cried. He turned and sprinted back to the bridge.

Theodore ignored the privateer. He looked at Dasch and saw he had his head bowed and his eyes closed. He held his sword in both hands with the blade pointed to the ground. He was softly muttering something, but it was impossible to hear over the rising wind.

"Theodore! We've got to get out here. We'll be ripped apart!" Cecil cried as he grabbed his friend's hand.

Theodore returned his grip and they turned and fled.

"Wait, what about Dasch?" Theodore asked. He tried to stop, but Cecil pulled him along, bringing him onto the bridge where Vesten was cowering on the ground, shaking in fear.

"I think he'll be able to handle this. We need to trust him," Cecil said. "I mean, freakin' *look* at him!"

"Hang on!" Theodore said. "I'll raise a barrier."

He thrust his scarlet staff into the cracks between the rocks of the stone bridge, muttered a familiar incantation, and erected an energy barrier to shield them from the debris.

Theodore turned to look at Dasch. He was now screaming into the air. His sword was fully aflame in golden fire, the tip of the golden flames towering high into the air, cutting through the tornado. The dust, ash, and debris that tore through the air seemed to miss him, choosing to swirl around him instead. Dasch's words somehow made it to Theodore through the torrent. It was nothing he could make out —it sounded like an ancient language. But Ànifa's whirlwind had begun to die down. It seemed as if whatever Dasch was doing was working.

"Theodore, are you sure this is okay?" Cecil asked, his brow furrowed in concern.

"It's fine. I can hold the barrier. Besides, it's dying down. Ànifa's regaining control of herself."

They stood within the shimmering barrier and watched everything unfold before them. Vesten had gotten off the ground and was huddling behind Cecil.

The whirlwind that had gathered around Ànifa had mostly

dissipated. Ash and debris floated to the ground in a cloud. Dasch remained firm where he stood, both hands gripping the hilt of his golden flaming sword as he held it into the air, still shouting the same incantation.

Ànifa descended, and the blue flames around her dissipated. She stirred up another little cloud of ash as she touched the ground. Her knees wobbled and she hunched forward. Dasch sheathed his sword and ran to her, catching her before she fell.

Theodore released the energy barrier and sprinted to Ànifa. Cecil followed behind, his armor clanking as he ran. Vesten followed meekly behind them.

———

The whiteness clouding her vision receded, and Ànifa found herself in Dasch's arms. He was looking at her with a mixture of surprise and fear on his face. Theodore, Cecil, and Vesten stood around them. She tried to move but found she was much too weak to even lift a finger.

"Wh-what happened?" Ànifa asked. She coughed and looked around, moving only her eyes. "Why is the air suddenly filled with ash?"

Dasch grunted. "Something stirred it all up."

"Ànifa, are you okay?" Theodore asked, his eyes filled with worry.

"Seriously, Ànifa, what was that just now?" Cecil asked as he pushed his burgundy hair out of his face.

"What do you mean? I—" she coughed hard, causing her chest to ache.

"It's nothing to fret about," Dasch said. "Now, we must continue. Let's get ourselves out of this dust cloud. Can you walk?"

"No, I can't move," Ànifa said. "But are you sure everything is fine?"

"Yes!" Theodore said with a reassuring smile. "Let's go. We were in a hurry, remember?"

"But wait—" Cecil began.

"Quiet!" Theodore cut him off. "Every time I feel like you've gotten some sense into you, you go and make a fool of yourself!"

"Hey, what's all this now?" Cecil was offended.

Ànifa smiled. She may not know what was going on, but the familiar bickering between old friends calmed her nerves.

Oddly, she wasn't afraid. Her friends' presence kept her fear at bay. Yet she had the feeling that something had transpired, and she'd been the cause. If she had hurt her friends without meaning to, she would never forgive herself.

But now was not the time to dwell on any of this. They had to keep moving. They had to reach Kalahsem as soon as possible. She suddenly felt a small tug at her heart and knew had it to be Kalahsem urging her forward.

You want us to come that badly, huh? Ànifa thought.

They continued silently through the wreckage of Kalah. Ànifa hid her head in Dasch's arms. She didn't want to see anything else. She couldn't let herself get emotional again. After a little while, Dasch stopped.

"Ànifa, you must see this." Ànifa felt Dasch's words as his chest vibrated.

"What is it?" Ànifa asked without looking.

"They're here for us, I think," Theodore replied.

"Yes, my elvish princess. You've called for our rides yet again," Cecil said, his voice filled with awe.

Ànifa lifted her head and peeked out. Five strange bird-like creatures stood before them. They each had four skinny reddish-orange chicken legs with long flat feet and sharp talons. Each creature stood roughly four meters tall and were covered in a fine layer of bluish-purple feathers. The feathers were so small and fine they almost seemed like hairs. They had long skinny necks with egg-shaped heads, dangerously sharp beaks, and two small beady black eyes. They were looking at the group expectantly.

"What are they?" Ànifa asked from Dasch's arms.

"They're called quetzalrong," Theodore replied. "They're

normally skittish around people and hide within the tall grasslands, or so they say. I've never actually seen them before."

"And they shall carry us across the long, wide, and terribly dense Chrevans Grasslands!" Cecil said with an arm stretched out toward the quetzalrong, his palm to the sky. "This is good luck, milady. These grasslands are notoriously dreadful to cross on foot. Some of the grass blades are so sharp they'll flay you to the bone."

"Why are you calling me milady?" Ànifa asked.

"Oh, you know, because I think you're a princess, and I won't stop thinking that until I have any formal proof to the contrary," Cecil replied. He turned his outstretched hand into an awkward bow.

"Well, that's fine, but please call me Ànifa," she said as she looked at Dasch. "You can set me down now, Dasch. I'm feeling much better now."

"No problem." Dasch set her on her feet.

They were out of the smoldering ruins of Kalah and were now standing in a wide-open field. The largest of the quetzalrong approached Ànifa and bowed before her. Ànifa gently grasped its lean neck and hoisted herself onto its back, one leg on either side of its neck. The quetzalrong squawked, sounding like a mixture between a songbird and a chicken, and shook its head back and forth.

"Let's go, everyone. As Cecil said, we'll use these glorious birds to help us cross the grasslands," Ànifa said.

After they each settled on their quetzalrong mounts, the group set off toward the grasslands proper. As they rode on, Ànifa began to truly appreciate their new animal friends. The grasses they were approaching were well over two meters tall. It would be nearly impossible to navigate through without them. She gave her mount a soft pat on its neck and urged it forward.

They tore through the grasslands at a comfortable pace. Soon, they faced the first of their obstacles—a giant green snake with a flat head sprung at Ànifa from the grass. She screamed, more surprised than scared. The quetzalrong she was riding stood on its back legs and slashed at the snake with its long, sharp talons, slicing the snake. The slithering reptile recoiled and retreated into the tall grass.

There were other snakes, and at one point, a large tortoise with sharp teeth and a rock-hard shell moved into their path and they had to skirt around it. They also crossed a small, deep stream one by one as the quetzalrong hopped across at a particular rocky point. And, as Cecil had said, they crossed through a patch of exceptionally sharp grass. The scaly legs of the quetzalrong were hard enough so they didn't get cut. She listened to the sharp blades of grass sing off the legs of their mounts as they tore through.

It took roughly three hours to cross the grasslands. Dusk was settling in by the time they made it to the foot of the Morai Mountain Range, so they made camp for the night.

While Cecil, Vesten, and Theodore helped to put together the campfire, Ànifa and Dasch scavenged for food. She was able to shoot four small rabbits. She had used one of Dante's new arrows for all four kills. His arrows were not as good as her previous ones, but were of high quality nonetheless.

Dasch had found some wild onions, peppers, mushrooms, and lettuce that they used to make a salad. Ànifa skewered and roasted the four small rabbits over the fire. It was a satisfying dinner and a good way to end the day.

Once everyone finished their meals, Ànifa broke the silence with a confession. "Look, everyone... there's something I need to tell you."

"What is it?" Theodore asked.

"Ever since I woke up in Charlotte's bed, I've been hearing a voice in my head, the voice of Gnusaramnii, as you called it, Dasch. I know you know about this, Theodore and Dasch, but I don't believe you two know," Ànifa said as she looked at Cecil and Vesten. "I've been taking some mushrooms Sage Mason gave me to help me sleep a dreamless sleep. If I don't, I hear its voice in my head. The mushrooms helped for a while. But I heard the voice again the other day when I passed out during the wolf god's attack. And ever since then, I've been feeling its presence more. It's always there, nipping at the fringes of my mind."

"Fuck. That's, well, that's fucked," Vesten said, shaking his head slowly.

"Ever so eloquent, are you?" Cecil said.

"Well, he's not wrong, Cecil," Ànifa replied. "It is messed up. Anyway, I just... especially after the events from today, I wanted you all to know. I don't want to lose my mind to it."

"I don't believe you will," Dasch said. "I've been fighting that demon off for centuries and I was never as strong as you."

"Thanks, that means a lot," Ànifa said with a nod.

A little while later, they each found a place on the ground to rest. Like the previous night, the moon was bright, which gave Ànifa enough light to read.

She finished the chapter she had started the previous night and read one more. The fourth chapter continued the story of the humans and how they eventually mingled with the elves, creating half-elves. It was a pleasant tale, enjoyably told, and was a good note to end her night on.

She laid in the soft grass and closed her eyes, deliberately deciding not to take any shuyukuii mushrooms. She immediately felt Gnusaramnii slip through the cracks.

I knew it, she thought with a smile. *If Dasch is right, I should be strong enough keep my mind straight. There's a lot I want to say to you, so have at me!*

15

BATTLE FOR PURPOSE

"*À*nifa..."

"*I'm here. I'm back, Gnusaramnii. And I'm back here willingly.*" She once again found herself in the familiar ethereal realm where she and Gnusaramnii conversed.

"*Ha ha ha ha... I can sense that. What changed?*"

"*I've been learning a lot—from my friends, from the gods, from the Eklatros history book.*"

"*You should not consider that book to be historical.*"

"*I don't. But you can still learn hidden truths through children's stories. And I think I'm starting to understand something.*"

"*Are you realizing how powerless you are before me? That you appear before a God more powerful than any of the puny gods you have met?*" Gnusaramnii's voice bore down upon her, but she stood her ground.

"*I believe you are more powerful than most. But I can't believe you are the greatest power there is in this universe. There is something stronger. There is someone besides me who is stronger. And you fear this other power. You fear it so much that you—*"

"*Silence! Do not dare lecture me about things you know nothing about. You presume too much. Did you ever stop to wonder why I have been speaking to you this way?*"

"I figured you wanted to stop me from dreaming. Because if I could dream without you butting in, I might actually reclaim more substantial memories."

"That has been a great beneficial side effect, but it is not the reason. I chose you, Ànifa, because you are powerful. You know this now, first-hand."

"But I don't remember—"

Suddenly, it all came flooding back. Her whole body had been ablaze with blue flames. She had levitated off the ground and caused a tornado. The whirlwind had been dreadful—full of ash, debris, and splinters of wood. Luckily, Dasch had stopped her before it had become too destructive. He had chanted a spell that brought her back to herself.

"That was me? That's monstrous!"

"And it was only the tip of your enormous well of power. If you learned how to harness that power and to truly wield it, you could far easily surpass me."

"Why are you telling me all this? And besides, I thought you wanted to kill me. Isn't that why you made me nearly drown in the first place?"

Gnusaramnii let out a stream of vile laughter. *"Are you still so blind to my intent? I shall not educate you on that. You will need to figure that one out yourself. But you are intelligent, Ànifa... use it!"*

She awoke with a start and smiled deeply.

I got it to reveal a lost memory to me. Even if it was recent, it was a start, she thought. *It may have its own intentions for me, but I can use Gnusaramnii to my benefit as well. I'll get it to reveal to me who I truly am.*

Plus, it didn't deny my hunch—there is something more powerful out there, and that is why it is here, drawing power from this planet, so it can fight that powerful entity.

For breakfast, Ànifa gathered some berries and seeds from around their campsite. She then mixed some oats with fresh water to make a sort of oatmeal. She had left her bonnet off today and allowed her long, flowing hair to wave with the wind. This morning, her hair color was a swirl of light blue hues mixed in with deep purple. She had idly thought about what that meant as she prepared their breakfast.

As Ànifa cooked the oatmeal, she and her companions sat in a circle around the fire. Theodore and Cecil bickered over whose quetzalrong had been the larger of the two. Then Vesten chimed in with his profanities. It was only then that things got serious.

"Vesten, why are you here? What is your purpose for coming with us?" Dasch asked him with intense seriousness.

"I... well, fuck. I mean, you know—"

"No, I don't. That's why I'm asking," Dasch grumbled. "We all have a reason for being here. What's yours?"

"I guess there ain't no fuckin' harm in telling you all," Vesten said with a deep sigh. "I've known you lot for less than a week and you already feel like family to me. But I suppose it's how it fuckin' goes with me. I'm hopeless..." Vesten trailed off as he stared into the fire. "My entire purpose in life, ever since I set out on my own, was to find someone—my cousin Patsy. I—I haven't fuckin' seen her in years. I'm worried about her, to be honest," Vesten said, choking on his words.

"Why are you worried about her?" Ànifa asked, still stirring the pot of oatmeal.

"You see, we were separated a long time ago. We grew up in a small town called Haymath, south of Ajenti."

"Oh yeah, I've heard of it," Cecil said sadly as he looked into the fire.

"Right, you've heard of it. But you probably ain't never been there since it don't fuckin' exist no more. And don't you dare try to argue with me that Hay's Revival is Haymath, because they are not the same fuckin' thing at all."

"Vesten, what happened?" Ànifa asked.

"Our town... it wasn't close to the shore, nor any other fuckin' towns. We thought we would never have any troubles. Yet one night... oh shit," Vesten said as he teared up.

"Don't worry, I can tell her. I am familiar with the story," Theodore said, placing a hand on Vesten's back.

Vesten simply nodded in agreement as he choked on a sob. "Fuck... I'm sorry."

"Don't be," Theodore said. "You see, while it's true that Eklatros is a peaceful planet most of the time, horrific tragedies do happen. I'd say it was about fifteen years ago now—"

"Thirteen," Vesten corrected through his sobs.

Theodore nodded. He removed his hand from Vesten's back and placed his hands in his lap. "Thirteen years ago, a large group of bandits tore through Haymath. They pillaged, defiled, and killed. Within a single night, nearly everyone was slaughtered."

"That's horrible," Ànifa said as tears welled in her eyes. "What happened to those responsible?"

"Many were caught and executed by various towns, most in Ajenti and Port Gall. But there are surely still some out there. That's beside the point, of course," Theodore said.

Vesten nodded and sat up straight. "Alright, I can continue. Sorry. Fuck. Now, as far as I know, there were only three survivors. Me, Patsy, and Patsy's older brother, August. August got us all the way to Pikkul Harbor. His plan was to take us to Sathon, but that never fuckin' happened. During the trip to Pikkul Harbor, August fell ill. We thought he'd recover once we hit land, but he didn't. He died a few hours after we got to the harbor. That left Patsy and me together. And we fuckin' stuck together, but only for four months. She... she was taken by some fuckin' black-market slavers. Fuck those vile people!" Vesten yelled, raising a shaking fist into the air.

Ànifa gasped, and a tear rolled down her cheek.

"I'm sorry... I didn't know," she said as she turned her attention to the steaming oatmeal, stirring it with a small wooden spoon.

"It's fine," Vesten said, choking back a final sob. "It's been fuckin' years. But I always return to Pikkul Harbor around the time she was taken. Which is around now. But then I met all of you. And I'm glad I met you."

"I'm glad we met too, Vesten," Ànifa said, placing her palms together. "We wouldn't have made it this far if not for you."

Vesten blushed and turned away, wiping the tears from his eyes.

"You still haven't properly answered my question," Dasch grumbled, catching Vesten off guard. "You told us you are looking for your cousin. That's fine, but why are you here, traveling with us? You've seen the foes we've faced, and I saw you cowering on that bridge yesterday. Why do you continue to travel with us? Why have you not fled back to the safety and comfort of your houseboat?"

Vesten looked at Dasch for a moment as he regained his composure. "Shit, you're right. I got caught up in the fuckin' story. But I am searching for her. I've been searching for years, and I still haven't found her. Don't ask me how I know this, but I know she is still alive. And I know she is well. But I just need to fuckin' see her again.

"And in order to do that, I need to be stronger. You're right—you are so fucking right, Dasch. I am weak and cowardly. But I dare say I am skillful with a blade. A dagger is best, but any knife will do. I was a pirate..." Vesten said proudly, then trailed off and slapped his thigh. "I did not enjoy my time as a pirate," Vesten said, nearly spitting out the word *pirate*. "I stole. I hurt people. I fucking killed people. I was a fucking horrible person to be around. I bullied my crew to the point where they abandoned my worthless ass. And they were right to do so. I may have been a fuckin' pirate... but even other pirates didn't want to be around me. How fucking sad is that?"

Vesten grew quiet and hung his head, weeping softly. "I'm fucking trash. I know it. So if you don't want me around, Dasch, I understand."

"I want you here," Dasch said, surprising everyone. "You have a role to play in all of this. I needed to make sure that you knew why you were here. Because if you didn't know your purpose, then you would drag us all down. But if your end goal is to become stronger, then you are right where you need to be."

"Shit," Vesten said, choking back a sob. "I've been a fuckin' wreck today. Tearing up all over the damn place. But thank you, Dasch. That means a lot."

Dasch grunted in reply. Ànifa beamed at him. Theodore gave him a deep nod. Cecil awkwardly threw him a thumbs-up and a wide toothy grin.

"Ah, thank you everyone," Vesten said, resigning himself to his emotions and letting his tears fall freely.

"That reminds me," Ànifa said, cutting into the lingering silence. She looked at Dasch. "I need to properly thank you for everything you did for me yesterday, Dasch."

"It was nothing," Dasch grumbled.

"Oh, it wasn't nothing," Ànifa replied with a sly smile. "Not only did you carry me through Kalah, but you are the one who calmed me down. You stopped me from accidentally killing all of you. I remembered everything last night, and I fear that if you hadn't stopped me when you did, it would have been impossible."

Dasch looked at the ground and sighed. "It was nearly too late. You almost slipped through my grasp."

"I did? That's… terrifying," she replied, rubbing her arms as she stared into the fire. "I'm terrified of myself. If I lost control of myself like that yesterday, then it could happen again. And maybe next time things won't go so well. I'm frightened of my powers… of what I can do. But you want to know the funny thing? I really want to master this power. I want to learn how to control it, so it doesn't control me."

Theodore gave her a big smile. "That, Ànifa, is what all students at Ajenti must come to understand before they are allowed to gain access to the more advanced classes and libraries. Power can be scary. And the fear of power is important. Without fear of power, a person can be consumed by it and do terrible things. It is your fear that will keep you balanced."

"Thank you. I really needed to hear that," Ànifa replied with her right hand over her heart.

"Fuckin' A," Vesten said as he stood. "Let's get stronger together!"

"Yes, let's!" she replied with a gleeful chuckle. Her hair turned navy blue in response.

"There's one more thing," Dasch grumbled. "If you truly mean to learn how to control your power, you mustn't do it yourself. One of us must be present."

Vesten looked around at the others and sat back down.

"Sure. I can agree wholeheartedly to that," Ànifa said. "If you hadn't been there for me yesterday, then everything would have been different. You're a hard man to get to know, Dasch. But under your quiet, rough exterior, you truly care for all of us, don't you?"

Dasch huffed, crossed his arms, and turned away from them. "Why should I care? What good did caring do for me before? I turned my back on my best friend. I don't deserve friends anymore."

"But you have them," Ànifa said. She didn't move from tending to her oatmeal, but she reached out to him with her heart.

Dasch turned back around and smiled. "Thank you, Ànifa. I think I might start caring again."

Ànifa returned his smile with an even bigger one, her hair color somehow becoming an even deeper navy blue. "It's why we're all here, to help each other."

"By the way, how did you do that, Dasch? How did you calm Ànifa?" Theodore asked. "That was a spell I am not familiar with."

"Nor should you be," Dasch said harshly. "My mother taught it to me. As I told you before, she was an elf. And she taught me a few of the spells she knew. Although, calling them spells doesn't give them credit. They are more like truths. Truths that you can speak aloud to make things happen. The one I used yesterday was one of those truths. I was essentially telling Ànifa she was in control of herself— she had power over her actions. A truth, spoken in such a way, can make anything be."

"But that—" Theodore began.

"Right. It can be easily abused. Which is why you'll not find such knowledge in any textbook, wizard."

"So, the thing you did with your sword the other day when you fought that jelly monster, was that also something your mom taught you?" Cecil asked.

"No, sir knight. That was simply something all the knights of Kieth's Golden Army knew. It's why we were called the Golden Army in the first place. It's not something that you can sustain for long, but it does greatly enhance your power."

"I would like to learn such a trick one day. Does it work with a battle-axe?" Cecil inquired.

"It works with any weapon. The power comes from within yourself. With focus and meditation, one can even call upon the flames while drawing their weapon. I plan on performing this meditation myself. It may be of use in the upcoming battles."

The oatmeal was ready, and the conversation trailed off to more mundane topics while everyone ate. When finished, they pored over the map one more time to acquaint themselves with where they were going.

They spotted the first of several cairns as they climbed the path that led to the highest peaks on Eklatros. According to Dante's map, the seven highest peaks were all grouped together, and they were called the Morai Murderers.

Essentially, the Morai Mountain Range made the Watthana Mountains back on Schelff Island look like mere foothills. The mountains were breathtaking. Ànifa hadn't even reached a point where she could see them in all their proper glory. She was looking forward to it. Mountains were a new wonder to her, and she reveled in their majesty. She was growing excited and optimistic. It looked as if the weather was perfect.

Dante's map warned to be mindful of the weather. These mountains supposedly had notoriously bad weather. At any point in time, it could rain, hail, snow, or even a mixture of all three. For now, it looked as if the weather would hold.

They didn't make it far before they faced their first set of foes. As they turned a bend, two large Gnuelry blocked the narrow path. There was no way to go around them. To their left was a steep cliff and to their right was an unscalable rock wall.

These Gnuelry were different once again. They were dark gray, much like the color of river stone. They were larger than the yellow or blue ones and much more viscous.

"These things again," Cecil moaned. "Why is it always the jelly monsters? And why do they keep changing?"

"I think they're adapting to their environment," Ànifa replied. "The yellow ones from the grassland and forests would blend in well with their surroundings, while these gray ones could appear as rocks if they wished to."

"That's a chilling thought," Theodore said. "At least these don't smell so bad."

"Fuck yeah, and they're not attacking us either," Vesten said.

"We cannot discount what Ànifa said," Dasch grumbled. "Other ones could be hiding among the rocks that line the path. The ones on the road may only be a distraction."

"Fuck!" Vesten cried. "Then what can we do?"

"There's nothing else we can do. We take the bait," Dasch said, unsheathing his sword. He held his sword out in front of him and closed his eyes. After a few moments, his sword burst into golden flames. Theodore's eyes went wide as he stroked his beard.

The two gray Gnuelry turned to face Dasch as he stared them down. "Sir Kloud. Ànifa. Vesten. Do you wish to share in my power?"

"Fuck yeah!" Vesten replied. He unsheathed two daggers and thrust them toward Dasch.

"Hold on," Dasch commanded. "Sir Kloud goes first, then Ànifa, and then you, Vesten. And come slowly."

"I'm at your command," Cecil declared. He brushed his hair out of his eyes, then held his battle-axe toward Dasch.

Dasch nodded and tipped his sword to the battle-axe. After a moment, Cecil's weapon burst into golden flames.

"Now, Ànifa, bring some arrows. I can light them for you. Quickly now, I can't hold the spell for long. Sir Kloud, engage as you will."

"Yes, sir!" Cecil said with a salute. He looked at his battle-axe in awe.

"Cecil, don't let your guard down!" Theodore shouted as he raised his staff into the air.

Ànifa turned her focus away from Dasch and saw the two gray jelly monsters steadily approaching.

"Leave it to me," Cecil said. He stepped up and swung his golden flaming battle-axe with both hands. He struck the bulbous mass and pierced its thick hide. Cecil belted out a battle cry and tore his weapon from the creature. He ducked, dodging the counterattack from its massive arm. Next to Cecil, the other Gnuelry was taking hits from Theodore's various elemental attacks.

"Dasch! Their skin!" Cecil cried without looking away from his enemy.

"It's just as I thought," Dasch replied. Ànifa held out seven arrows to Dasch's sword and each one erupted in golden flames. Vesten was right behind her and touched the tips of his two daggers to Dasch's sword.

"These are very tough for jelly monsters. Their hide is nearly as strong as scales," Theodore said through gritted teeth.

"Alright, then let's all move back for now," Dasch suggested. "Sir Kloud!"

"Sure thing—" Cecil began. A hard blow from the large monster sent him crumbling to the ground.

"Cecil!" Theodore yelled as he shot a lightning bolt at it.

"Theodore, hold your attacks! They don't look like they're working," Ànifa said as she approached him, her bow drawn and notched with one of the golden flaming arrows. "Aim for their weak points!"

She muttered "Tekkhas Harmonias" and fired the golden arrow. It flew toward the Gnuelry who was holding Cecil to the ground and sunk deep into its forehead. The Gnuelry seemed completely unharmed as it turned to them and roared.

"Ah, I get it!" Theodore said as he prepared for another attack. "Aim for the eyes!"

"We need to defeat these things before we can help Cecil," Ànifa cried as she readied another flaming arrow.

"Shit," Vesten said quietly. He was standing off to the side, looking back and forth between his flaming daggers and the battle.

Everything was happening so fast, but he had to do something. "I'll fuckin' do it!" He tossed each dagger into the air and caught them by their blade. He took a moment to be surprised that the golden flames weren't burning his fingers.

"Get off my fucking friend!" Vesten cried as he threw both daggers. One dagger missed while the other lodged deep into the monster's right eye. At the same moment, Ànifa's arrow struck its left eye.

The gray jelly monster howled in rage as it swung around wildly.

"Theodore! Cecil will be crushed," Ànifa yelled in terror.

Theodore lowered his head and held his scarlet staff in front of his face. He muttered a quick spell that created an energy barrier around Cecil. The blinded Gnuelry continued to thrash violently. It came into contact with the other jelly monster and pounded at it fiercely. Cecil, although protected by the energy barrier, was in danger of being crushed.

Ànifa turned to Dasch. "Can you do something?"

"The wizard is handling it just fine," Dasch replied without looking at her.

She glanced to Theodore. He had his head bowed and eyes closed as he muttered an incantation. Dasch tapped her shoulder and pointed at Cecil. Theodore was pulling the energy barrier that surrounded Cecil toward them.

They regrouped and stood off to the side and out of range of the berserk jelly monsters. The Gnuelry who had been attacked by the blinded one was fully retaliating. They were smashing and pounding into each other with a brutal strength Ànifa had never seen before.

Now that they had Cecil safely within their reach, Theodore dropped the energy barrier and crouched to tend to his friend. She knelt to help Theodore, but he waved her away. She crossed her arms and watched as the two jelly monsters slowly beat themselves to gravel. Out of the corner of her eye, she saw the golden flames extinguish from her arrows.

"So, they were mostly just fuckin' rocks?" Vesten asked.

"It seems that way," Dasch replied.

"Yeah, remember what happened when those two yellow ones merged in the forest, before Dante's?" Ànifa asked the group. "When they merged, they had integrated a lot of dirt and rocks from the path. It's possible that these two were comprised of several others, and when they merged, they incorporated rocks from these mountains."

Vesten raised his eyebrows and nodded. "Good point."

"How's Cecil?" Ànifa asked, turning her attention back to Theodore.

"He's fine. He was just knocked unconscious is all," Theodore replied. He was sitting cross-legged on the ground, cradling Cecil. Theodore had taken Cecil's helmet off, and Ànifa could see it was true—Cecil was barely bleeding.

"We'll have to carry him," Dasch said. "I say *we* since he is too heavy for me alone, especially with his armor."

"Why don't we just take him out of his armor?" Ànifa asked.

"But then who would fuckin' carry that?" Vesten asked.

"Not carry. Wear. And you, Vesten. You look like you're a similar height and age," Ànifa said as she looked him up and down.

"Whoa, I can't wear a knight's armor!" Vesten stepped back and waved his hands.

"Why not?" Theodore asked.

"It would be like sailing someone else's ship. It just doesn't fuckin' seem right," Vesten replied.

"Either way, we need to move," Ànifa said, looking at the sky. It had grown overcast and the dark clouds loomed above them menacingly. "The storm moved in quickly. We need to find shelter as soon as possible."

"Fuck it, I'll just help carry him then, Dasch!" Vesten said as he stepped forward.

"Alright," Dasch nodded. "You better keep up."

The sky cracked and thundered above them, followed by a deafening boom. The center of the storm was directly above them.

"We need to move out, now!" Ànifa commanded.

Vesten scrambled around while Dasch knelt and hoisted Cecil up. Vesten composed himself and wrapped his arm around Cecil's legs.

Ànifa set off, leading the way. She didn't look back. She moved as quickly as she could without leaving the others behind.

Hard rain pelted down on them. Ànifa stopped and looked behind her for the first time and saw Theodore was also helping Dasch and Vesten. The foursome moved together in an awkward scrambling fashion.

We can't keep this up for long. We need to find shelter. She scanned her surroundings and spied a small cave nearby. The rain had turned into peanut-sized hail. She dashed over to the others, took a hold of Cecil and led them into the small cave.

Once inside, they set Cecil on the damp ground and huddled together. They were all shivering. Theodore held out his staff and muttered an incantation. The glass orb on the end of his staff glowed brightly, sending out waves of warming energy.

The cave was just tall enough for them to stand upright. Theodore's hat fit snugly to the roof of the cave. They watched the hail as it grew into berry-sized chunks, then into walnut-sized chunks. The pounding of the hail accompanied by the booms of thunder directly above them made it nearly impossible for them to talk.

After a few minutes, Ànifa began to sense something moving behind them. She tapped Dasch's shoulder softly. He turned to her, and she pointed behind them and leaned into his ear to say, "I hear something behind us."

Dasch nodded with a serious look in his eyes and got Vesten's attention.

Ànifa walked past Theodore, who was still tending to Cecil, and went deeper into the cave. It was dark—much darker than it should have been. She stopped, aware that something was amiss.

Why can't I see anything? she thought. *I should be able to see in the dark. What's causing this haze?*

The unnatural darkness was similar to the time after the fight with the crows. As she tried to peer through the haze, Dasch appeared before her.

"Something's wrong. I think something is watching us," she said, just loud enough for him to hear her. Dasch grunted softly in return. He took her hand and led her back to the group.

"We aren't safe here," Dasch said.

"We aren't safe out there," Theodore said, pointing to the hail that was building up around the cave. He was still on the ground next to Cecil. "What do we do?"

"Believe me, we're safer out there," Ànifa said firmly. "There is something very wrong with this cave."

"Hey, do you fuckin' hear that?" Vesten asked.

"Hear what—" Ànifa began, but then she heard it. Seeping through the deafening roar of the storm was a deep, unfriendly growl. A slight breeze accompanied the growl.

"Oh my, what a stench," Theodore said, pinching his nose shut.

"It's the smell of death," Dasch said plainly.

A slight change in the air pressure told Ànifa that the attack was coming. She grabbed onto Vesten's and Dasch's shoulders, shoved them to the ground and then fell to her knees. A split second later, an immense paw sporting five sharp claws swept over their heads, right where they had been standing moments ago.

"Grab Cecil! We're getting out of here," she bellowed.

Dasch lunged forward and helped Theodore with Cecil. Ànifa clutched Vesten by the collar and tugged him to his feet. He was shaking with fear, but he seemed to be in control of himself. Ànifa nodded, grabbed the backpack, and quickly led them to the mouth of the cave. She looked back and saw Dasch and Theodore carrying Cecil. A flash of movement caught her eye.

"Watch out!" she yelled.

The impact took the wind out of her. Her head whipped back and the world spun. Through the haze, she noticed they had all been hit by the same attack. They were being pushed out of the cave by the beast's massive paw. The beast shoved hard, sending the five of them flying through the air. Rain and hail pelted them as they fell off the side of the cliff.

Stupid fool, she thought, criticizing herself. *When you ran into the cave, you noticed it was on the edge of a cliff. Now everything is over.*

She closed her eyes and embraced her fate. A moment later, she came into contact with something and felt herself rise into the air. She opened her eyes and found that she was lying on the back of the wyvern god.

You're Uswassisbaena, aren't you? she thought. *Thank you!*

She looked over and saw that Vesten and Theodore were with her. Beside them another wyvern had Dasch and Cecil clutched in its claws. Vesten was screaming obscenities, while Theodore had a look of pure bewilderment on his face as he looked at the sky above them. She followed his gaze and her jaw dropped. Above them flew dozens of wyverns, creating a barrier from the storm.

The wyvern god took them back to a large cave in the side of the mountain. The cave rose dozens of meters above them and housed nearly a hundred other wyverns. Some were flying in circles above them, and others slept on the ground.

Although the wyverns were friendly, they were still intimidating. Most were over three meters tall while sitting on their hind legs. At the ends of their long wings were their strong hands that sported deadly claws. Those that slept on the ground kept their claws outstretched, as if ready to strike.

The group found a quiet spot in the cave that was too small for any wyverns to get in, including the smaller hatchlings. They spoke little as they rested and waited for the storm to pass. Their backpack had gotten soaked from the storm, so they set everything out to dry. The Eklatros book was damp, but not ruined, as was most of their food—most of their vegetables were spoiled.

Once Cecil awoke, he thanked them for saving him, although he was disappointed that he'd missed the flight with the wyverns.

At this point, we've all saved each other, she thought. *What goes around comes around. We must continue to look out for each other or else we'll all fail.*

Everything happened so fast today, starting with the jelly monsters, then the storm and the cave... I think that was the wolverine god we intruded upon. And I don't think we've seen the last of it either.

16

INTERLUDE: WEST KILINDER

Declassification Disclaimer: the following document has been declassified for this usage only and has been sanitized. It has been translated accordingly for your understanding. To access the complete records, please contact Councilmember Ducutyk. His contact information can be found at the end of this document. Sanitized copy approved for release 82017/13/34.

From the desk of Professor Navacus Clums. Eklakiln, Caranar 9, 82002 04:64:72:14.

It's been three weeks since we completed Svetlana Slesarenko. During that time, we got half a week off for some rest. Without going into too much detail, the time off was quite relaxing and much needed. Fumalli and I could finally take an overnight trip into Nalpetalis. Of course, we still had to check in and do some tests on

Svetlana periodically during the break, but it was nothing like an average day of work.

Speaking of, our current subject's name is West Kilinder. He is a member of the Eusphyrchiian species, native to the planet Ijurvoll.

For the sake of thoroughness, I will briefly describe the Eusphyrchii, as their unique anatomy is quite important in regard to the overall designs. On average, Eusphyrchii are roughly 180 centimeters tall. This particular individual is above-average in height, standing in at 196 centimeters. Of course, this height includes his head, so he now would stand a few centimeters shorter. Hard exoskeleton covers their bodies. Its color is typically white; however, some range from light to dark gray. This individual's coloring is slightly off-white.

Typically, when a Eusphyrchiian loses a limb, they can regrow it back within a few months. From what I hear, the process is quite painful, but it is certainly much better than living without your arms or legs. Not only that, but if their exoskeleton is damaged or cracked, their bodies can heal themselves with little external aid. Overall, Eusphyrchii have quite an extraordinary ability to heal themselves.

However, the individual we are working with, West Kilinder, is unable to heal himself. He lost that ability when he lost his head. Normally, this type of injury would kill even a Eusphyrchiian. And yet, West still lives. It has been nearly two weeks now. No Eusphyrchii has ever lived so long without its head. This really is a fascinating and unique case.

Before his injuries, West Kilinder was a bounty hunter and an official member of the Intergalactic Bounty Hunter Association, or the IBHA. From the records I can access, he had a fairly impressive track record. However, his last hit went sour. From what I know, he was hiding on a rooftop with a sniper rifle. Right before he was about to pull the trigger on his target, he was attacked from behind by an unseen assailant. The attacker put up a real fight and nearly beat West to death with a metal pipe.

I shall now describe the extensive injuries West suffered. Blunt force trauma to the chest has caused a complete collapse of his right lung and a partially collapsed left lung. Roughly 65% of his internal ribcage is either broken or fractured. And as I previously mentioned, he is missing his head. And yet, the only personal item that was delivered with him was a large, white, wide-brimmed cowboy hat. I heard the bounty hunter that brought him told Professor Dea that it was his most treasured possession.

Currently, West is hooked up to a pacemaker to control his heartbeat, a ventilator to control his breathing, an electroencephalogram to monitor his brain activity, and an IV to help regulate his fluids. Essentially, he is a living vegetable devoid of consciousness and life. It is our task to give him his life back. I should mention here that Eusphyrchiian brains are located in their chest, next to their heart. Their head houses several important organs and glands, one of which controls their self-healing.

This time around, we are constructing only one major component, whereas Svetlana had several. We will start by reconstructing his inner ribcage by adding support and reinforcement throughout. We will also reinforce his spine and overall inner-body structure. As for his exoskeleton, we will mend it and strengthen it using protoplaster, an extremely durable and malleable substance.

Finally, we will graft an electronic chest-piece on his upper torso. There will be an on-board computer that will continuously monitor and, when necessary, regulate his heartbeat. It will also monitor his brain waves and overall health and wellness. It will also be able to record audio and video across the entire electromagnetic spectrum. We're not stopping there, as it will serve as a communication device, a calculator, or even a weapon if necessary. And, of course, since he lost his head, it will be his eyes, his ears, and his voice. I have dubbed his system simply the Life Support System, or LSS, but it truly will be much more than that.

We have almost finished all major developments on LSS, and have been running several tests nonstop for nearly four days. There are only a few minor tweaks left before it's ready to be grafted onto West.

This time around, Lyd and Sylcertiverner will lay the foundations, building the support and reinforcements in his inner ribcage. Mac and Professor Qymberkon will monitor his vitals throughout. While that is happening, Grasberg, Poi, and I will prepare LSS while Kurjon will prepare the solution to create the protoplaster.

Once Syl and Lyd are finished, Grasberg, Mac, Syl, and Kurjon will apply the protoplaster onto his exoskeleton. It will be applied heavily in the damaged spots and lightly in the areas with no damage. Since he can no longer regenerate his cells in the same way as before, we must ensure that his entire exoskeleton is protected.

Finally, we will graft LSS onto West. While this may sound simple, it will be the most complicated part of this process. We will need to connect it to his nervous system, circulatory system, respiratory system, and most of his major organs, the most difficult of which will be his brain. West will need complete control of LSS, so that means connecting to every single neuron.

I really am quite excited. The entire team is. We all feel great after our success with Svetlana.

I have been wanting to record an update on her status for days now, but it's been so busy I haven't gotten a chance.

Overall, Svetlana is doing very well, much better than our expectations. She has now fully adjusted to her new eye and she is getting stronger every day. She is also quite happy. She tells us quite frequently that she is the happiest she's been for a long time. She has been in contact with her family and friends but has encouraged them not to visit. Although I'm not sure if she is allowed to have visitors, she refused them without us needing to tell her so. I suspect she simply wants to grow accustomed to her new body before she is ready to show her family—whenever that will be, of course. That decision will be made by Head Professor Yilvin.

So, I am quite pleased with how Svetlana is doing. She's been a real joy to be around as well. I think she brightens all of our moods every time we see her.

Overall, Svetlana took two weeks and one day from start to finish, so from the day of the operation to the end of the post-procedure. That's seventeen days. LSS took about twenty twenty-hour days from inception to completion. Now Head Professor Yilvin is asking us to have LSS fully installed within two weeks. It's going to be another very intensive two weeks. At least we're being rushed for a good reason.

Currently, our security personnel on staff is at an all-time low. There are only four security guards, all Lakinceitian—Bsarg, Nijork, Sharg, and Jakog. Having an ex-bounty hunter on staff would be a great addition. I say ex-bounty hunter because it is in West's contract that after the procedure, he will stay at the compound for up to one year.

Our work will start in a few hours—at seven. I wasn't planning on getting here so early this morning, but I really couldn't sleep, so I'll spend the rest of this time preparing the operation room. I'll scrub everything down once again, to ensure full sanitation.

As for West Kilinder himself, he's being stored in a temperature-controlled room, which is adjacent to the operation room. I'm sure that if he was aware of what was going to happen to him, he would be as excited as we are. But we can only wait and see.

So, for now, with peace, and love, and faith, I am Professor Navacus Clums, signing off.

From the desk of Professor Navacus Clums.
Sarkiln, Caranar 10, 82002 10:13:11:19.

Just a quick update before a brief break. Lyd and Sylcertiverner have finished laying the foundations and support within West's inner ribcage. I jumped in to help after LSS was fully prepared. We also finished applying the protoplaster to his exoskeleton. We now must wait about two hours for the protoplaster to dry and harden.

Overall, West is doing spectacularly. His mental strength was always a strong point of his, as he is the only Eusphyrchii to have survived so long without a head. He was also able to survive and thrive in the IBHA for many years before his injuries. He is a strong individual, and his strength is apparent even now. We had initially predicted that laying the foundations in his inner ribcage would be quite stressful on his body, but his pulse remained consistent throughout the entire process. This tells us that even in an unconscious state, he can adjust his body's hormones in response to outside interference, something I thought would have been nearly impossible without his head. We had been fully prepared to administer multiple sedatives, but he only needed the initial one. It really is quite impressive.

Now, I believe most of the team is planning on getting a little sleep before the next round. I think I will do the same. We need to be fully refreshed and alert when installing LSS.

So, in the meantime, Professor Dea has offered to watch over West. He's on his way here now. I think he is coming from a meeting with Head Professor Yilvin and Professor Bodeelch.

And speak of the demons, Professor Dea is here now.

I'll be signing off then. With peace, and love, and faith, this is Professor Navacus Clums, signing off.

— You still use that phrase, huh? —

— It's habit. Thanks for coming. —

From the desk of Professor Navacus Clums. Dunakiln, Caranar 12, 82002 16:20:07:10.

Well, it's certainly been quite eventful since my last recording. I believe the last recording was right before Professor Dea began his watch over West. Well, once he arrived, Professor Dea did what only the Eridavlos can do and learned quite a lot about West. He discovered we had made some major errors in our calculations.

I believe I have previously mentioned in my recordings a little bit about the Eridavlos. And if I did, then I mentioned the unique organ they use for locomotion, since they do not have arms or legs. They simply float above the ground using the energy they produce. Additionally, they possess many more natural talents.

Aside from locomotion, Eridavlos can use their energy to gather knowledge from the environment around them. As Professor Dea explained it to me once, if an Eridavlos finds itself in a strange and unfamiliar land—even if every plant in the area is unknown to them—they can still find clues about where they are in the soil and the air around them. Or something like that, at least. I will admit I was slightly intoxicated when he was telling me all this, as it was at the grand opening party for the compound.

But I'm getting off-topic. Professor Dea discovered the supports and foundations we laid in his inner-ribcage were too weak. They would not fully support the weight of LSS for long.

Unfortunately, we were forced to forgo our break and clear away the protoplaster so we could add more support to his inner-body structure. Professor Dea was on hand the entire time, observing everything alongside Professor Qymberkon and Poi in the control room.

Suffice to say, after our second round of supports, we were quite behind schedule. But having Professor Dea, my direct superior, there with us helped to reassure Head Professor Yilvin that our delay was necessary.

However, because of the setback, it allowed for an opportunity to arrive. When it came time to graft LSS onto West, we had a full audience. Everyone was there watching—Head Professor Yilvin, Professor Bodeelch, and even Professor Peal and his assistants made it over. There was the Human, Surridge; the Nioavellian, Kalosse; the Eusphyrchiian, Kamarial; and the Kolythoanthaean brothers, Mahlvern and Walverm. I believe that is his entire team. There are six of them on his side, while there are eight of us on our side.

It was quite crowded in that small workroom. Luckily, the exciting part—grafting LSS onto West—was quick. Most everyone left soon after that. Only Professor Bodeelch remains.

Professor Qymberkon has taken lead on the slow process of

attaching LSS to West's nervous system and circulatory system. So, for now, I'm going to make my way back to the barracks to get some shut-eye. I've also sent Poi, Syl, and Kurjon back to rest. After they rest for a few hours, I instructed them to relieve Mac, Lyd, and Grasberg. We all need to keep up on our rest if we are to stay sharp and alert during the immediate post-procedure process.

So, with peace, love, and faith, this is Professor Navacus Clums, signing off.

From the desk of Professor Navacus Clums. Melrikiln, Caranar 19, 82002 16:41:03:08.

West Kilinder, the former agent of the Intergalactic Bounty Hunter Association and member of the Eusphyrchiian species, has now accomplished what no other has before. First, he conquered death by surviving his decapitation, then he stunned everyone when he continued to live. And now, West Kilinder is the second official cyborg in the Vortex Solar System.

Anyway. His Life Support System is fully installed to his nervous system, respiratory system, circulatory system, and major internal organs. It is fully a part of him now. We turned it on about an hour ago, and it's already exceeding our expectations. We have a full record of all his vitals and his blood pressure. Also, thanks to the second round of supports, LSS is putting a negligible amount of stress on his body. While I believe we caused a fair amount of stress to his body opening him up a second time, it was necessary. And, thanks to LSS' medicine, West is healing at a normal pace once again.

West is still unconscious. We plan on letting him sleep for another hour. We also want that time to gather more initial data through LSS.

We're going on a meal break now. Professor Qymberkon has

ordered everyone their own personal pies, so everyone got to choose their flavor. It will be a good meal.

With peace, and love, and faith, this is Professor Navacus Clums, signing off.

`From the desk of Professor Navacus Clums.`
`Pjorkiln, Caranar 29, 82002 21:04:19:44.`

I have not been able to make as many updates as I would have liked. We've been busy completing the post-procedure.

When we first woke up West, he was in quite a lot of pain and was extremely disoriented. He hadn't been fully conscious since his accident, and part of his mind still thought he was fighting his assailant. He nearly knocked Grasberg unconscious in his confusion. Once he realized where he was, he remained hostile and alert.

We had to call Professor Peal's assistant, Kamarial, to help calm him down. She was able to help to reassure him, Eusphyrchii to Eusphyrchii, that he was safe, and she also helped explain to him where he was and why he was here. Before she could learn too much information, I sent her away. I still haven't properly thanked her yet, but I will need to do so.

Once West calmed down and realized we were the ones who helped him, he became increasingly interested in LSS. During the initial chaos, West hadn't even realized that his head was missing. While things seemed off, he thought it was just from being disoriented.

Now, a little over a week later, West is using LSS as if it has always been a part of him. It's truly quite amazing. Not only that, but I even rigged a way for him to continue to wear his large white cowboy hat. Not only will it cover his neck wound and partially hide the fact he has no head, but it also gives him much more confidence.

Many times, West offered to pay us for LSS. We turned him down every time, as he unwittingly volunteered, so there is no way we could take his money. But a trade of services is a suitable compromise. Even if it wasn't written into his contract, I think West would want to stay. His last experience as an IBHA agent soured his experience with them. Plus, he admitted he was thinking about quitting before his incident. He felt like he was slowly becoming the outcast in his agency and suspects that his own partner sold him out and betrayed him.

Either way, I gotta say that the glamor aspect of the IBHA has faded for all of us since we have gotten to know West. It sounds like a horrible association to work for.

At this moment, West is beginning his initial training to become a security guard and to replace Sharg, who disappeared mysteriously about a week ago. He'll be training under Bsarg, who is now the head security agent, and alongside Svetlana. She has had little to do lately, and jumped at the opportunity to help out around the compound.

Head Professor Yilvin has been quite patient with us, though, despite how behind schedule we are. But, as always, the post-procedure is as important as the actual operation. The subject needs time to fully adjust—physically, mentally, and emotionally—to the enhancements. And while West quickly picked up the basics, it will take time for him to truly master his Life Support System. For now, though, he can easily switch between the different spectrums, so from visible to infrared to ultraviolet to x-ray. He can also fine-tune his hearing and focus on a single individual, which will come in handy when tracking down any future potential security breaches. Luckily, none have happened yet.

I mean, we are being sequestered out here in the Volgash Desert. And we are in a secret compound. If anyone were to break into this place, they would need to be exceedingly clever.

Sorry, I got sidetracked again. Aside from his vision and hearing, West is practicing using the energy weapon LSS can create. We've only tested it in small, weak bursts, but so far it looks like it can become a very dangerous weapon.

West will be a good security guard here, plus I look forward to seeing him and Svetlana more often.

Anyway. Now that West is complete, we will get our next assignment soon. We still haven't heard many details yet, but it sounds like something big is coming up next.

For now, at the very least, we get another well needed break.

With peace, and love, and faith, this Navacus Clums, signing off.

For all inquiries, please use the contact information below:
Ducutyk@icos.gov
FBI@icos.gov
Please keep your messages under 500 characters. Attachments not allowed.

17

BATTLE FOR SPIRIT

Ànifa stood before the Great Barrier of Gallheim. It was a massive, towering whirlwind; a tornado that had been spinning for hundreds of years. Streaks of lightning tore through the cyclone as it loomed in front of them, displaying its awesome power.

"So, this is a Great Barrier," Cecil said. His eyes widened as he pushed his burgundy hair out of his face. "This is quite the barrier."

"Yes, it looks much like the other one I've seen," Theodore replied. He was standing straight, his scarlet staff in hand, ready for anything.

"I guess this is what I should have been expecting. Even so, how are we supposed to pass through that?" Ànifa asked. "Also, how could Charlotte be inside of there?"

"It's possible that the scaly monsters have figured out how to pass through the Great Barrier," Theodore replied. "And if they can do it, we can too."

"Uh, what do you fuckin' mean by 'we'? I'm not going anywhere near there," Vesten said as he stepped back.

"Right, I don't think you should, either," Ànifa replied. "I think I may be the only one who can."

Dasch grunted. He had his arms crossed and hood up as he stood off to the side of the group. "Yes, I believe so."

"I... I suppose you're right," Theodore said as he leaned against his staff and stroked his beard. "At the very least, it's a pleasure seeing a Great Barrier again. It's been too long."

"You got my back, right?" Ànifa asked. She was not wearing her bonnet, and her hair color shifted from a light blue to a deep blue, displaying her uncertainty.

"Of course we do," Theodore said, placing a hand on her shoulder. "You should know that by now."

"I know. It's just—"

"It will not be easy," Dasch cut in. "But you can do it. Know that you can do it. Believe it, fully within yourself, and only then can you pass through the barrier."

It was mid-morning, and the sun was steadily rising above them into a clear blue sky. As she stood before the towering whirlwind, preparing herself for what was to come, she closed her eyes and reflected on her day.

She hadn't taken any of the shuyukuii mushrooms the night prior, and had expected to speak with Gnusaramnii. Instead, she had another dream about the strange white avian creature, Professor Navacus Clums. This time, Navacus and his strange alien team had been working on a creature she had never seen before. It had a hard white exterior, and it had been hooked up to many unknown machines.

It was a strange dream, but it had been *her* dream, without Gnusaramnii's influence. In fact, now that she was close to the Great Barrier, the presence of Gnusaramnii seemed much dimmer than usual.

After everyone had eaten a quick breakfast, the wyvern god, Uswassisbaena, had dropped the five of them off at the edge of the Kalsri Forest. Ànifa had thanked Uswassisbaena wholeheartedly, for without her help, they would still be making their slow way through the Morai Mountains.

The forest was dense, yet they had made it through fairly easily by utilizing Ànifa's dark vision. As she passed through the deciduous forest, Ànifa had the feeling that she had been there before, even though she knew it wasn't possible. The familiarity helped her navigate the group. She was even able to avoid several Gnurargurts; she had felt their presence before she saw them and was able to get everyone to hide before the possessed warthogs spotted them.

After that, they had made it to the Great Barrier with ease.

She took a deep breath, opened her eyes, and embraced her fear and excitement.

"Ànifa? It's okay, really, you can go on ahead. We'll be there if anything happens to you," Cecil said with a slight bow. "I mean, as you know, you are my elvish princess."

Ànifa smiled. "Thanks, Cecil. I think I'm ready now."

"*Keep an eye on everyone for me,*" Ànifa thought, directing her thoughts to Theodore.

"*I shall. Be safe, Ànifa,*" Theodore replied.

She took a step forward, then another. After half a dozen paces, the force of the surrounding wind picked up. After a few more paces, Ànifa felt the pressure drop significantly around her.

I can do this, she thought to herself. *I am the only one who can do this. Charlotte, do you hear me? If you're in there, I'm coming for you!*

Another two dozen paces and Ànifa crossed the threshold and passed into the wall of the Great Barrier.

It was an odd sensation. She felt as if a bubble had formed around her. The bubble was causing the wind and bolts of electricity to shoot around her without getting close. Although she was fully engulfed within the whirlwind, she was calm. She felt as if she was exactly where she was supposed to be.

The whirlwind was much quieter than she would have thought. There was hardly any noise, and it made her relax even more. She sighed in contentment, and as she looked directly in front of her, she could make out shapes through the windy haze. A silhouette grew bigger as she approached, and it also grew stranger. What she was approaching was obviously an immense tree, yet it there were parts of it that looked sentient.

She emerged from the Great Barrier and stood before the strangest being she had ever seen. She gasped, putting a hand in front of her mouth so she wouldn't offend the Ekataramn.

It stood nearly sixty meters tall, although most of the height was from the thick leafy green canopy—unnaturally rounded, as if it had been trimmed and shaped. Near the bottom were two large red fruits. They sat right above the lowest layer of the canopy, which was composed of a yellow and orange ring of leaves. With the two together—the two large red fruits and the yellow and orange leaves— it looked almost as if the canopy was smiling at her.

And that wasn't the only face she saw. On the trunk of the immense tree were two black unblinking eyes. The left eye was nearly five times smaller compared to the right eye, and both were staring right at her. She felt exposed as the tree's gaze pierced through her.

Below the two eyes was a chunk of bark that looked like a small hand. The bark covered a crack that looked like lips, as if the tree held a hand in front of its mouth.

Aside from the many branches supporting the canopy, there was only one other thick branch. This branch held a wide assortment of oddities. The largest of these was an enormous purple mushroom cap that had large yellow spots. Below the mushroom cap was the head of a strange lizard-like beast. It had scaly blue skin with a teal streak running from its chin to the back of its head. Bulging from the sides of the blue head were two large red eyes. The head was being supported by a group of supporting branches that came together to form a neck.

Below the blue lizard head was a large blue berry with a silver calyx. And finally, sprouting from the largest of the branches that held the canopy was a large red berry.

It was, without a doubt, not at all what she had been expecting to find. She had been standing in front of the tree for nearly a minute now, and the blue lizard head suddenly turned to face her. It opened its strange, toothy mouth and spoke to her. "Welcome, Ànifa. I am

Kalahsem, one of the Ekataramn. I apologize for not introducing myself earlier, but I didn't want to interrupt your thoughts."

Her hand fell away from her face, exposing her gaping mouth. The blue lizard head laughed softly, shaking up and down as it did so.

"I understand. I am quite the character, aren't I? But do not fear—I won't harm you. Although, that's not what you're worried about, is it?"

"N-no... that's not what I'm worried about. I was simply surprised to hear you speak. But you can do more than that, can't you? You can read my thoughts."

"Yes, I can read your thoughts, Ànifa, and only yours. I've been listening to you since you awoke on the shore near Charlotte's tent," said Kalahsem.

"Oh, Charlotte! Is she here?"

"In a sense," the blue head nodded. "She is not here physically, not yet at least. Instead, she is here spiritually, and I can assure you she is safe. I will explain more about this later. You have something else you want to ask me."

"Yes, I suppose I do," she said, placing a finger on her chin. "If you've been listening to my thoughts this whole time, then have you heard my conversations with Gnusaramnii?"

"No. Those interactions I have not been witness to. I will not allow that monster to know of my presence. However, when it is in the fringes of your mind, I can lie in those same fringes without it detecting my presence."

"Yeah, so all of this feels quite invasive," she said, rubbing her arms with her hands.

"Yes, it is quite invasive. Know that my intentions were never malicious. I simply wanted to guide you here. After your last experience with your powers, your mind was more attuned to my wavelength, which allowed you to feel my presence."

"Yes, I remember that. And you're right. You're not malicious, but..." she trailed off, staring at her feet.

"Indeed. Gnusaramnii wishes to claim you as its disciple. It wishes to corrupt you and turn you to its side," Kalahsem said.

She looked at the blue head and spoke firmly. "I would never let that happen."

"I know you would not, yet it won't ask you for permission. My presence has been helping keep it at bay while your mind is still weak."

"I suppose I should thank you, then," she said. She reached out and placed her right hand on the blue head in the space between its eyes. She closed her eyes, felt Kalahsem's presence within her mind, then took a few steps back. "You're so weak."

"In a sense, yes. I am vulnerable right now. All Ekataramn are. That is why we need your assistance, Ànifa. Only you can fully wake us. Your presence here is giving me strength. And there is more you can do."

"What is it?" she asked. "I'll do anything to help."

"I need you to answer three questions. Think through each before you answer in full, as truthfully as you can, at this moment," said Kalahsem. The blue lizard head bobbed up and down to emphasize its seriousness.

"Sure, I can do that."

"While the questions themselves may sound simple, each one uncovers a deeper truth. After you answer my questions, I shall grant you what you seek. Now, prepare yourself."

Ànifa smiled in excitement and fought the urge to ask about Charlotte again. She understood things were getting serious, and she had to remain calm. She closed her eyes and took a deep breath to steady her racing heart. Memories of the events leading to this moment swirled in her mind, from being saved by Charlotte and meeting Theodore and the others to the monsters she had fought. Everything she had been through had taught her much about herself.

She took another deep breath, then opened her eyes and nodded. "I'm ready."

The blue head lowered to her height, then said, "Who are you?"

Who am I? she thought. *That is quite the question.*

The blue head seemed to smile at her knowingly.

She pondered on the question for a few moments, and when satisfied, gave her answer.

"I am Ànifa, and I come from Yttendaus, from the last city of the elves. I may not remember much about who I was before, but now I am humbled. I woke up in this strange foreign land knowing nothing, only to learn that an elf like me has not been seen in thousands of years, and that there are vile people who would take advantage of me. And yet, the people I have come to know have all treated me with the utmost respect. They have been kind and understanding. All of my friends—Theodore, Cecil, Dasch, and Vesten—they have all supported me throughout our journey, just as I have supported them in turn. And although we all don't know each other well, a genuine bond has been formed. It is only because of that bond that I am who I am now. And who I am is an elvish woman who is humbled by her comrades and overjoyed at being in the presence of one as holy as yourself," she said, finishing with a slight curtsy.

The blue head simply stared at her. She couldn't pick up on any emotions on its stone-like face.

"Why are you here?"

Again, Ànifa took a few moments to ponder on the question.

"At first, I did not know my purpose, even after learning about the Great Barriers. I went along with Theodore because our paths aligned. Even after Vesten joined us, feeling similarly, I still did not understand. And Dante may have told me this, but I... I don't think I fully understood my true purpose until now—until this moment.

"I am here to awaken the Ekataramn, to revive our land, to give life back to Eklatros. In doing so, our planet will grow stronger and will be able to better defend itself against the invasion of Gnusaramnii and its monstrous minions. I am here so Eklatros does not fall into the hands of Gnusaramnii. And I am the only one who can do this... I am the only one who can save Eklatros. Well, me and my team, because I can't do it without them."

The blue head remained still.

"What do you seek?"

This time, Ànifa knew her answer, but still gave herself a moment to be sure before she blurted it out. She nodded to herself.

"There is a lot I am looking for—my lost memories, the next Great Barrier after I leave here—but most of all, right now, I want to find my friend Charlotte. She was taken and I don't really understand, but it sounds like she's here, so I want to see her."

The blue head stared at her for a long minute, then nodded deeply in approval.

"You are wise, Ànifa Tataluynnia Ekataramnii," Kalahsem said with a smile emerging on the blue lizard's face.

"Ànifa Tataluynnia Ekataramnii... that's me. That's my full name," she said as she studied her hands. Her hair was flashing quickly from a sky blue to a royal navy blue.

"Indeed. Princess Ànifa Tataluynnia Ekataramnii. Names are important. Keep it close. Do not share it, not even among your comrades, at least for the time being."

"But why not?" she asked, making a mental note that Kalahsem had just said 'princess'. So she *was* royalty.

"Names are important," Kalahsem reiterated. "And your ancient one holds a meaning. It's a truth that, if exposed, could be your downfall. Yet, it is important that you know your true name, which is why I have shared it with you. That, my dearest Ànifa, is my first gift to you.

"Now, heed my words, for I shall now share with you your three truths.

"You cannot do this alone. You need your teammates, just as they need you. They only make you stronger. I know you know this, but it is important to be reminded of this truth.

"You now know your true purpose, for you are the only one who can awaken us, Ànifa. Gnusaramnii is coming. It is not here, not yet, but it comes. You must prepare Eklatros for when that time arrives.

"Your last truth is twofold. Everyone you meet, you like. Even that dubious boy back in the Pikkul Pub. Which leads to the second part of this truth. You are too trusting. That trust may get you in trouble.

Yet trust in your friends, and trust their intuition. They will lead you along the right path.

"Now, there is one last thing I shall give you. Understand something before I do this, as this is my power; I can reach out with my soul and communicate with other souls. This is how I was able to reach you, and this is how I was able to reach Charlotte. I have her soul with me now, yet to retrieve her body, I will need your assistance," Kalahsem said.

She stomped a foot in the grass. "Yes, of course! I'll do anything that I can."

"Good. You are one of the few who can. Your soul is connected to hers, Ànifa. This happened when Charlotte saved your life, and it is how you were able to see she was in danger in your dream.

"Now, I will need you to approach me, Ànifa. Approach me and lay your hands on the top of my blue dinosaur head."

"Dinosaur?" Ànifa asked as she approached.

"Ah yes, it's possible you're not familiar with the term. Dinosaur is the name given to the majority of the animals that live in the Gatelceous Jungle. In fact, wyverns are technically dinosaurs, as they originated from the jungle. This particular dinosaur is a brontosaurus. Yet I digress."

Ànifa approached Kalahsem and stood before the large blue head.

"Now place your hands on the top of my head and focus on the energy within yourself."

"You want me to make my hands burn with blue flames?"

"Yes. I need your power to bring her body here."

"Where is it now?" Ànifa asked without moving.

"I do not know. Now, please, your hands."

Ànifa did as she was asked and placed her hands on top of the blue head. She closed her eyes, took a deep breath, and focused. Before she knew what was happening, she was engulfed in a sea of white.

When she came to, she was sitting under the cover of an aspen tree holding Charlotte. Charlotte was warm, yet frail and malnourished. She was unconscious, and her clothes were torn and dirty, but overall, she looked unharmed.

Ànifa sat there for a moment, holding Charlotte tight as she buried her face into Charlotte's silver hair. She wept softly, letting her tears flow down her cheeks. She was happy to have Charlotte back, and she couldn't even imagine what she had gone through.

After a few minutes, Ànifa realized she was alone with Charlotte. She thought it odd that she had only noticed this now. Still holding Charlotte, she got to her feet and walked forward. After a few steps, whatever haze she had been in vanished and she could suddenly hear the worried shouts and calls from her friends.

She called out to them and noticed how weak her voice sounded. She called out again, in case they hadn't heard her, but a moment later she saw them rushing toward her.

They were ecstatic to see her and completely dumbfounded that she had actually found Charlotte. Cecil even told her he didn't believe they would ever find her and expressed his regret that he hadn't fully believed in her. Theodore chimed in then, as did the others. She smiled, simply happy to be surrounded by her friends.

Dasch took out his waterskin and poured some on Charlotte's head. She was still unconscious, so she couldn't drink yet, but Dasch said the water should help her some. Ànifa handed Charlotte off to Dasch, and once her arms were free, Theodore prompted her to follow him.

According to Theodore, once Ànifa had entered the Great Barrier, things began changing. First, the whirlwind shone a deep blue. Cecil interjected, saying that he thought the color reflected her hair color at the time, and she nodded in agreement. Theodore, still leading the way, continued, explaining that there had been an extremely bright white light. After the light dissipated, the whirlwind was gone.

They reached the edge of a deep, dark maw that had appeared in the ground where the whirlwind had once been. At the center of the massive hole was a perfect circle of an island. Kalahsem sat proudly on the island, and it waved its blue dinosaur head at her when it saw them looking at it.

The circular island exposed Kalahsem's roots, and its roots were just as odd as its branches. Kalahsem had three main roots that branched out in three directions. One split off to become a large alligator head that eventually turned into more roots. The middle root became the head of a large elephant, again splitting out to create more roots. The last of the main three roots split off into multiple smaller alligator and elephant heads, each one creating more roots.

"Is that Kalahsem?" Theodore asked as he stroked his beard.

"Yes. It may look odd, but it's kind and understanding. We had a pretty amazing conversation," Ànifa said.

"It spoke to you?" Cecil asked with an incredulous look.

"Yes. It may look like a tree, but it is not a tree, nor a plant, nor is it truly an animal either. I think it represents all walks of life—the mushroom cap represents fungus and the various fruits represent the many colors of life. Then, of course, there is its dinosaur head as it called it—"

"It's kinda fuckin' creepy," Vesten said.

Ànifa giggled. "I can't deny that. But it's wonderful."

"You'll need to tell me what happened in there," Theodore said.

"I wish I could, but I was told to keep everything to myself for now. Knowledge in the wrong hands can be dangerous."

"I understand," Theodore said with disappointment in his voice. "If not now, then maybe another time."

A large cloud moved in front of the sun, blocking the sunlight from reaching them. Ànifa glanced at the sky and realized that it was nearing evening.

"How long was I in there?" she asked.

"A few hours. And it has been almost an hour since the whirlwind disappeared. We've been searching for you frantically all that time," Theodore said.

"Seriously? That's strange. For me it was only a few minutes."

"Time must have moved differently once you passed through the Great Barrier. I should have anticipated this," Dasch said.

"How? There's no way you could have known," Ànifa said. "Now, we should get moving again. Once we get closer to the mountains, I'll try summoning Uswassisbaena."

Ànifa stood there for another moment and gave a small nod to Kalahsem, then turned toward the Kalsri Forest. She looked at Charlotte, who was still unconscious in Dasch's arms, and smiled.

I've finally found you, Charlotte, she thought. You took care of me and now it's my turn to take care of you. And once you wake, maybe you can tell us what happened and where you were taken. Well, you may not know why, but your story will help to shed light on the situation nonetheless.

We need to take you somewhere to recover. But right now, we all must worry about getting back to safety. I fear this forest will turn treacherous once the sun sets. Hopefully, we can make it through with no trouble.

Meeting Kalahsem was a truly amazing experience, though. It gave me so much knowledge, and not only that, but now I think I'll be able to better decipher the shred of truths from the fabrications within the Eklatros collective history book. It may have gotten a little wrinkled from the rain, but the text was undamaged. Next chance I get, I want to really study that book. I think it may help us in the next leg of our journey. But now is not the time for reading. I must focus on the moment.

So let us go forth, my friends. Let us save this world together!

18

BATTLE FOR SPEED

Ànifa stepped into the Kalsri Forest, followed by her friends. She led the way, using her dark vision and expertise in forest terrain to guide them through. The forest was dense with flora with fauna. Each time they neared a big animal such as a warthog, a forest elephant, or a saber-toothed panther, she stopped the party so they wouldn't draw any unnecessary attention. Most of the time, she could ward the animals off by sending them subtle nudges, but some were overtaken by the Gnusar, and those they avoided the best they could.

They also came across many smaller animals, such as black flying squirrels, tiny forest frogs, lanky centipedes, magnificent spiders, colonies of worker ants, snails with wondrous spiral shells, and more. Birds flocked the skies, from small songbirds and woodpeckers to birds of prey. It felt as if the forest was alive—much more alive than usual. Kalahsem's awakening must have also awakened the forest.

Ànifa glanced back at Charlotte, who was still unconscious in Dasch's arms. Protecting her made them vulnerable. Ànifa picked up her pace, motioning for the others to do the same.

When they reached the edge of the forest, four snarling possessed warthogs blocked their path.

"Dasch, protect Charlotte," Ànifa commanded. "Cecil, stay close."

Cecil readied his battle-axe with a grin. "I'll protect you, Princess."

The lead Gnurargurt charged, and Cecil deflected the attack skillfully, sidestepping at the right moment. It continued charging straight toward Dasch, who leaped over the charging Gnurargurt with Charlotte still in his arms. He landed softly, picked up a large stone, and threw it with precision. The stone struck the side of the warthog's head and sent it reeling right into a tree, knocking it out cold.

This sent the remaining three warthogs into a frenzy as they charged forward.

"Hold on!" Theodore cried before Ànifa could react to the remaining warthogs. "I want to try something."

Theodore held his scarlet staff close to his body and muttered a spell, then thrust his staff out. A bright light shot out toward the warthogs, encasing them in a protective barrier. The three warthogs were trapped, unable to move the barrier from within.

"Ha! I thought that might be handy offensively," Theodore exclaimed with his chest puffed out.

"Great job, but we've got more incoming," Ànifa warned.

The attack had been a distraction. While they had been fighting, a ring of warthogs had silently surrounded them. "Well shit, what do we do now?" Vesten asked, gripping the straps of the backpack tightly.

The Gnurargurts were slowly approaching. Ànifa closed her eyes and reached out to the surrounding forest.

A deafening trumpeting sound cut through the tension. The warthogs froze for a second, then came at them from all directions. A moment later, eight forest elephants thundered out of the woods, trumpets blaring. Each elephant sported four massive tusks, each one as sharp as a spear. The elephants crashed into the warthogs, tossing them into the air.

"Now's our chance to run," Dasch yelled. "Lead the way, Ànifa!"

They charged through the violent fray, and within moments burst out of the forest. The Morai Mountains loomed menacingly before them. The sun was setting, elongating their shadows as they marched forward.

"*Uswassisbaena, please, if you can hear me, we need you. Heed my call!*" Ànifa projected.

"Hey, guys, we got more trouble a-brewing!" Cecil cried as he brushed his burgundy hair out of his eyes.

Ànifa broke her concentration with the wyvern god and looked around her. Once again, they were being approached on all sides, this time by a horde of porcupines. Their tongues lolled out of their mouths, grinning madly with dead eyes.

"We need to be careful! They can shoot their spikes!" Cecil continued.

"I called Uswassisbaena. Hopefully, she'll be here soon. In the meantime, Theodore, we need protection!"

"Right!" Theodore cried as he created another energy barrier, this time to surround and protect them all.

The porcupines fired off their spikes. A few rounds got through to them before Theodore's energy barrier was fully erected, striking Vesten in his left thigh. Vesten shot out a string of curses as he knelt to the ground. Ànifa rushed over to him and pulled out the needles.

"Careful!" Cecil warned once again. "They're serrated!"

"I've noticed," Ànifa said, cringing as the spike sliced open her thumb.

Dasch set Charlotte on the ground and began collecting rocks and stuffing them into his cloak.

A loud roar, echoed by dozens of others, pierced through the sky.

"Theodore! Put all that you have into the energy barrier, now!" Ànifa cried.

"Allow me to help," Dasch reached out and grabbed Theodore's staff with both hands. He cringed, then muttered an incarnation, sending waves of golden flames into the staff. The energy barrier shimmered in response.

Another loud roar, this time directly above them. The ground shook beneath their feet. A moment later, streams of fire engulfed them. The wyverns arrived, their flames scorching the porcupines where they stood.

When the torrent of fire ended, Theodore dropped the energy barrier and thanked Dasch.

"Come on, we need to move," Ànifa urged as Uswassisbaena crashed to the ground. "Dasch, grab Charlotte!"

The air reeked of burnt, rotted meat as they hurried to Uswassisbaena. Once all six of them were on her back, she took off. Most of the wyverns accompanying them followed, while smaller groups scouted ahead and above them.

The wind tore through Ànifa's sky-blue hair as they soared higher into the air. A gust of wind nearly threw her off, but Cecil caught her. A moment later, Theodore erected another energy barrier around them.

Ànifa breathed a sigh of relief. "I think we'll be safe for now." With the energy barrier around them, they could talk freely. "How long can you keep this up, Theodore?"

"Not long. Not if I want to keep up my strength for the next fight."

"Speaking of fights, here comes one now," Vesten said, pointing behind them.

The wyverns that were above them broke off and attacked their pursuers.

"Cecil, are those..." Theodore asked, unable to finish his thought.

"Yeah, buddy. We're in for a real fun time now," Cecil replied.

"What are they?" Ànifa asked.

"They're called dragolum. But they're more commonly known by their unofficial name—dragon drillers," Cecil said.

"Dragolum—like Sage Mason's shrine?" Ànifa asked.

"Exactly. On their own they're easily dealt with, but when they swarm together like this, they can be deadly. It won't be long until they catch up with us," Theodore said, gripping the brim of his hat.

"We're sitting ducks up here," Vesten whimpered as he gripped the hilt of his dagger tighter.

"I can handle this," Ànifa said as confidently as she could.

"I can use my spells, but I will need to drop the barrier first," Theodore replied.

Dasch grunted. "Then we'll wait until they are closer."

"Vesten, how many daggers do you have on you?" Cecil asked.

"Let's see…" Vesten patted himself down. "Six? No, eight. There are small ones in my boots, but those are meant for close combat."

"If any get too close, throw a dagger at it, if you can spare it. You're an excellent shot," Cecil commended.

"I have two daggers of my own. If needed, you can use those, too," Dasch replied.

"Alright, I'll see what I can do," Vesten said.

"Here they come!" Ànifa yelled.

All around them, the battle was raging. Wyverns were swooping upon on the significantly smaller dragolum, but the dragon drillers were faster. Most of them avoided getting crunched in the wyvern's claws or swiped by their strong tails.

Now that they were closer, Ànifa could better distinguish their features. They weren't dragons or birds, but small furry rodents with two tiny arms and one long tail that ended in a sharp arrowhead. Each one sported a large drill that was nearly two-thirds of its total body length and had four wings with full range of motion.

She watched in horror as a group of dragon drillers spun themselves in circles and sliced through the wyverns' scales. Moments later, half a dozen dragolum swooped down on their barrier and drilled into it, twirling their small furry bodies.

"Theodore, now!" Ànifa commanded, her bow aimed at the dragolum directly in front of her.

As Theodore dropped the barrier, three of the dragolum charged. Ànifa pierced one in the heart with an arrow, Vesten hit one in the neck with a dagger, and Dasch struck the last one with a rock.

Ànifa swiftly fired off arrows, keeping track of how many she used. She had thirty-two left and was running through them quickly, only hitting seventy percent of her shots. She had to be more efficient.

Beside her, Theodore was ferociously shooting bursts of lightning from his staff. Dasch continued to throw rocks, hitting his target every time. When any got too close, Vesten hurled a dagger at it. They were managing the swarm, but there were too many. Their ammunition would be depleted before they made it across the mountains. They had to do something drastic. Ànifa closed her eyes and called out to the wyverns flying around them.

After a moment, she turned to Cecil, who was the only one unable to attack.

"Cecil! Do you trust me?"

"What?"

"Do you trust me?"

"Yeah, why?"

"Sorry about this!" Ànifa said as she gave him a shove, pushing him off of Uswassisbaena.

Cecil cursed at her as he fell. Mid-curse, he was caught by a wyvern. She turned to the others, who were gaping at her.

"Take care of Charlotte!" she asked, then jumped off Uswassisbaena.

Ànifa closed her eyes and stretched her arms out wide, feeling the wyvern beneath her as it caught her. She opened her eyes, then commanded it to fly up so she could see the others. She flashed them a grin and flew off, heading straight toward a dragon driller. The wyvern screeched, then shot a blast of fire at the dragolum, scorching it in midair.

***

Theodore looked around him, utterly bewildered. He had never seen a wyvern before this journey, and now he was witnessing a truly unbelievable battle between wyvern and dragolum. And fighting in the midst of it all were Ànifa and Cecil, both riding on wyverns and commanding them as if they were experts. Well, Ànifa was at least. Cecil simply looked heroic as his wyvern thrashed around. Theodore looked behind him just in time to see Dasch jump off Uswassisbaena. Vesten carefully scooted closer to the wizard, his eyes wide with fear.

"You ain't gonna jump too, are ya?" Vesten asked.

"No, we need to protect Charlotte," Theodore replied.

"How? These fuckers are relentless!"

The wyvern Dasch rode on soared over their heads, unleashing a stream of fire into the frenzy of dragolum.

"Protect this god with everything you have," Theodore said through gritted teeth.

"Aye! I ain't never ridden on a wyvern, but it reminds me a fuck-ton like being on a ship during a raging storm." Vesten stood up, a dagger in each hand. "Here they come!"

Uswassisbaena set them down on the edge of the grasslands. A patch of dark clouds obscured the moon, making it hard to see. Before she returned to her roost, Ànifa had Uswassisbaena help them make three torches. They lit two of them and secured the third to the outside of the backpack.

The five companions headed toward the Chrevans Grasslands. Fireflies, moths, and mosquitoes swarmed around them, drawn to the torchlight. They reached the edge of the grasslands and stopped. The grass blades were razor sharp—they couldn't get through on their own.

"Maybe we can stop here for the night," Ànifa suggested. "Hopefully—"

Behind them, a low growl emanated from the darkness. Ànifa turned around and faced a large silhouette. They were cornered.

"It's the wolverine god from the other night. We disturbed its cave —" Ànifa began.

"—and now it wants to finish the job," Theodore finished for her. "At this rate, I fear we won't be able to rest until we make it back to the ship."

The ground shook beneath their feet.

"What's going on?" Cecil asked, tightly gripping his battle-axe.

"Help is on its way," Ànifa replied.

The wolverine god lunged forward and swiped at them, its massive claws glittering in the torchlight. Moments later, a towering quetzalrong thundered out of the grasslands and dove forward with its sharp beak. The wolverine god swatted the attack away, only to be raked by the quetzalrong god's long, deadly talons.

The wolverine god slunk back into the shadow of the mountains, clutching its wound.

Ànifa turned to face their savior and said, "You must be Quohuatzin." She bowed. "Thank you for coming."

"Yeah, that was great fuckin' timing!" Vesten replied.

In response, Quohuatzin squawked in a chipper tone.

"We should extinguish one torch before we head out," Ànifa said.

"I can put mine out," Vesten said.

"Sure, and then Cecil can continue to carry the other one," Ànifa said, volunteering for him.

Cecil nodded as Vesten shoved his torch flame first into the dirt.

A few minutes later, they each clutched a fistful of stiff feathers as the quetzalrong god carried them through the grasslands. Charlotte lay in a protective pocket between them while Ànifa and Dasch held onto her.

Quohuatzin moved much faster than the quetzalrong they had initially ridden, and they were higher off the ground, which gave them better protection against their many assailants.

Like the first time through, snakes attacked them, but this time the snakes attacked in twos and threes. The team worked together, coordinating their attacks. After the third snake attack, Ànifa instructed Cecil to put out the last torch.

Moments after the torch was extinguished, the moon emerged from under the cover of the clouds and shone brightly in the night sky. It was as if the universe itself was giving them the light they needed to see.

It took about two hours for Quohuatzin to carry them through the Chrevans Grasslands. Rather than stopping to let them off, the god took them straight through the ruins of Kalah and to the edge of the stone bridge.

They dismounted and thanked Quohuatzin for the assistance. Quohuatzin squawked and headed back to the grasslands.

"Let's hope there are no surprises on the bridge," Vesten said with a sigh.

"I'm not sensing anything," Ànifa said slowly as she concentrated on the bridge. "Quickly, we must cross."

The bright moon guided them across the stone bridge. Waiting for them on the other side were a group of four dire rabbits. Each one stood about a meter and a half above the ground. Towering above the dire rabbits at nearly three meters tall was their god, Nuralagusamii. As the group approached, the dire rabbits looked up at them with mouthfuls of grass.

Ànifa held out a hand, stopping her companions from reaching their weapons. "It's okay. They're here to help us, like the quetzalrong."

"Another beast we need to ride..." Dasch said, complaining slightly. "If only we could get something else to help carry Charlotte for us."

"I think I can arrange something," Ànifa said. She silently called out with her heart. A moment later, a loud screech rang out above them. A small wyvern descended and landed near the rabbits. The rabbits eyed the wyvern cautiously while they stood their ground. The wyvern was much smaller than others she had seen. She guessed he was still an adolescent.

"This little one has been following us since our battle with the dragolum. He should be able to carry Charlotte."

Although he was small for a wyvern, he stood about a head taller than Ànifa. She looked up into the wyvern's bright green and brown eyes. They shimmered in the moonlight, the radiance dancing in the dark-hued swirls. Ànifa looked at Charlotte, then back at the wyvern, and the wyvern nodded in response.

"Cecil, would you mind handing Charlotte over?"

"Sure. He's cute for a wyvern," Cecil said as he held out Charlotte. The wyvern launched into the air, then gently grasped Charlotte with both its claws and screeched happily.

"Alright, that's settled. Let's get moving," Ànifa said as she approached the dire rabbits.

They climbed onto Nuralagusamii's back. Two of the dire rabbits led the way, while the other two dire rabbits brought up the rear. Rather than hopping, the dire rabbits traveled by rolling head over heels. Nuralagusamii, with everyone on her back, had to slink along the ground. The wyvern carrying Charlotte flew above them, keeping watch for any assailants.

They followed to the road that led to Port Gall. This left them exposed, especially under the bright moonlight.

It wasn't long before a pack of five wolves, led by a large dire wolf, came at them from all sides. The dire wolf snarled and lunged at Nuralagusamii. One of the dire rabbits following behind them leapt into the air, striking the dire wolf. The wolves barked madly and rushed to tend to the wounded dire wolf where it lay in the grass.

"We must hurry!" Ànifa urged Nuralagusamii to pick up the pace. The two dire rabbits behind them pushed their god forward. As they hurried away from the wolves, the wyvern shot a stream of fire across the path, preventing the wolves from following them.

Ànifa whooped into the sky, thanking the wyvern.

"I wouldn't celebrate so soon if I were you," Theodore said, fear creeping into his voice.

Ànifa turned her attention back to the road and saw two more wolf packs blocking their way.

Before any of them could react—rabbit, wolf, human, or elf—a stampede of tusked beasts thundered across the path. Nuralagusamii stopped abruptly, nearly throwing them off her back.

They watched in amazement as the large herd flowed like a river in front of them. The wolves had fled, each pack going in a different direction.

"What are those things?" Vesten asked. "They look like rhinoceros, but they have different horns."

"They're called megacerops," Theodore explained as he stroked his beard. "They are rare to see and are typically independent animals. It's unusual to see them in such large numbers."

"It's Kalahsem. She's awoken this land—this entire continent. That's why everything has been so active tonight," Ànifa said with a smile.

"I figured that was the case," Theodore replied. Dasch grunted, agreeing with them.

"If it's been this active at night, I wonder what it'll be like during the day," Cecil asked.

"I'm not fuckin' waiting around to find out," Vesten replied.

They found their way back to the trail that led to *West Wind*, and then dismounted and thanked Nuralagusamii and her dire rabbits. The wyvern that had been carrying Charlotte landed on the path, allowing Dasch to take her once again. Once free of carrying Charlotte, Ànifa approached the wyvern and stroked his scaly snout. The wyvern screeched as it bobbed it's head up and down, then flew off toward the mountains.

They turned and headed into the Eladali Forest. The dense forest blocked out the moonlight, so Theodore helped Vesten relight his torch.

Dawn was breaking as they wound their way through the small, poorly marked path. The forest was alive around them. The birds were chirping and the owls were hooting. The squirrels were chattering and the cicadas were singing.

They made it to the cave without anything else attacking them and continued walking in silence, ready for anything. The light from the torch cast strange shadows throughout the cave, keeping them all on edge.

They reached a ledge where they could look upon *West Wind* and saw why it had been eerily silent.

Waiting for them on the rocky shore were three Gnusar, their small, port, scaly bodies glistening in the morning light that beamed into the mouth of the cave. Surrounding the Gnusar were sixteen small greenish-blue amphibians. They each had a spiked sailfin running down their backs, four long legs, and a fat spiked tail.

"Oh shit. Not these fuckers," Vesten exclaimed.

"What are they?" Ànifa asked.

"They are called brudobasu. They may be small, but they are deadly," Cecil replied. "My last experience with these things was not fun."

"You!" the deep, grainy voice called out from below. The Gnusar had noticed them. "Give us back that woman! We still need her."

"Never!" Ànifa called back. "She's under our protection now."

All three Gnusar croaked loudly, causing the brudobasu to leap into the air all at once. Their long legs propelled them high and far—they would easily reach them in a single bound.

"Incoming!" Cecil shouted as he prepared to defend himself. Dasch turned his back to the attack in order to better protect Charlotte.

Before the waves of brudobasu could overwhelm them, Theodore erected a barrier. The brudobasu, upon impacting the barrier, were shot back to the ground below.

After the last brudobasu was deflected, Theodore fell to the ground, panting heavily.

"I... I can't... keep this up."

"We're all exhausted, wizard," Dasch replied. "We can't falter now!"

"It's okay, Theodore," Ànifa replied as she watched the brudobasu preparing for another attack. "We got some help coming."

Behind the Gnusar, several large yellow, blue, and black spotted salamanders emerged from the waterline. They flicked out their long sticky tongues, catching the brudobasu and eating them.

In response, the brudobasu turned their attention to their natural predators and retaliated against the salamanders.

"Now's our chance." Ànifa waved them forward.

She led the party down the path. They reached the lower ground and had to make their way through the melee of brudobasu and salamanders.

"Watch out for the Gnusar!" Dasch cried as he drew his sword.

One Gnusar sneaked up on them and was rushing toward them with its long sharp claws.

Suddenly, a massive salamander burst out of the water—the

salamander god. She shot out her massive tongue, ensnaring the other two Gnusar and swallowed them whole. The Gnusar attacking them looked at the god in shock, allowing Cecil to rush upon it and bury his battle-axe in its back. The Gnusar squealed and cursed as Cecil tore his battle-axe out and buried it into the Gnusar's skull.

When they finally made it back onto *West Wind*, Theodore and Cecil went straight to their rooms and promptly fell asleep. Dasch carried Charlotte to Vesten's room and laid her down. Vesten was happy to give up his bed. He claimed he could sleep just as well on the deck of the ship as he could in his bed. Once they were all settled, Vesten expertly navigated them out of the cave and back into the open ocean.

Before she crawled into bed, Ànifa called upon the sea for protection. Answering her call was Krakuluthosii, the giant squid god who had helped them previously. Three other gods appeared as well —Mystiterachii, the blue whale god; Carchaselachii, the shark god; and Mochelioidae, the god of sea turtles. With all four gods protecting them, Ànifa felt safe enough to rest.

Whew! she thought. *That was intense. Gallheim is fully awake now. I wonder how the towns will fare with this awakening. I guess we didn't have time to visit any of the towns on Gallheim, huh? We never made it to Galstrom or Port Gall. Yet that's okay. I have a feeling I'll soon be around many, many people.*

We're now heading toward the continent of Roffen, specifically to Port Columbo. After that, I presume we'll go to Ajenti since it's close by, but we haven't gotten a chance to discuss that yet. We all need our rest. That was certainly an exhausting journey. We made it across nearly the entire continent of Gallheim in a single night, with lots of help, of course.

The unicorn was right. Its warning came true. Nature is at war with itself, and it may only get worse, the more Ekataramn we awaken.

But Charlotte is safe with us now... safe and secure. That Gnusar mentioned they wanted her back, and it was a Gnusar who took her in the first place. For all I know, that was the same one that took her. If Gnusaramnii still wants Charlotte, I doubt their pursual will cease anytime soon.

I think we can afford to take a rest. Having four gods as escorts is comforting. However, I don't feel the same amount of energy as I did on Gallheim. I think the awakening was limited to only Gallheim.

Well, I suppose I should turn off my brain now. Peace and love and faith.

19

BATTLE FOR IDENTITY

Ànifa stood on the deck of *West Wind* and gazed out at the shimmering ocean as they sailed toward Roffen. According to Dante's map, Roffen was the largest continent on Eklatros. While it could be argued that Gallheim was bigger, the prominent geologists claimed Gallheim wasn't a proper continent. Notes written in Dante's sloppy handwriting on the back of the map stated Gallheim was technically split into three separate landmasses. The Shippo River and Kohaku River cut Gallheim into three pieces—Khall, Heiaam, and Alabatik. That made Roffen the largest landmass. However, according to Dante's notes, about a third of Roffen was uninhabitable due to an expansive desert, a poisonous bog, and a large glacier.

"Oi, land ho! Won't be much longer now," Vesten called from the deck, breaking Ànifa's train of thought.

She smiled, then called out to their four godly escorts—Krakuluthosii, Mystiterachii, Carchaselachii, and Mochelioidae. She thanked them for being their sentinels throughout their lengthy journey. She knew they must be hungry as she watched them split off. Carchaselachii and Krakuluthosii, the shark and the squid gods, respectively, sped off quickly in different directions, while Mochelioidae, the sea turtle god, dived below them. The largest and slowest of the four, Mystiterachii, the blue whale god, seemed content to guzzle on krill a few hundred meters from their ship.

It was the morning of the fourth day out at sea. For Ànifa, it had been an enjoyable experience. Each day she spent a few hours meditating. By the end of the trip, she could send her consciousness down into the depths of the ocean and swim alongside the four gods. Dasch also spent his time meditating and training his mind so he could call upon his golden flames quicker. He tried teaching Cecil, but the knight was having a hard time grasping the concepts. As for Theodore, he spent nearly the entire trip fighting his seasickness. Vesten explained to them that he typically stops at the small island of Sortuga when he makes this trip, but they had to take care of Charlotte.

Charlotte was still unconscious; yet, the more time Ànifa spent with Charlotte, the more she felt sure she would wake up again. They decided to take her to the healers at Ajenti. Theodore told them the field of medical magic had been progressing steadily over the past few years, and many of those advancements weren't able to be performed anywhere else.

Ànifa was still bothered by the way the Gnusar had reacted to them a few days ago. Not only had they known where to wait for them, but they had been fully prepared to give their lives to recapture Charlotte. This made Ànifa want to awaken Charlotte even more. She wanted to know why her friend had been taken.

She hadn't spoken to Gnusaramnii since before Kalahsem. She knew its presence was still there, but it felt like it had taken a step back. She hadn't taken the shuyukuii mushrooms since then either. Initially, she had hoped she would regain more of her memories while she slept. Yet now, every time she went to sleep, she slept a completely dreamless sleep. The last dream she had was about Professor Navacus Clums and his odd alien helpers, and that had been nearly five nights ago. She suspected that, even though Gnusaramnii wasn't bothering her while she slept anymore, it was still stopping her from dreaming.

At the very least, Ànifa had read a considerable chunk of the

Eklatros history book on their journey. She learned much from the stories and myths. One chapter had even referenced Kalahsem and her large dinosaur head, although it was still fictionalized.

Her most important discovery was hidden underneath the facade of the stories. Sage Mason and Dante had both mentioned that each Ekataramn has their own power. As she found out firsthand, Kalahsem had the power to awaken and call upon souls. After studying the book closely, she discovered what each of the other Ekataramn's powers were. Roheefy had the power of rhythm, and Panabeeta had the power of the mind. Bugenaluf's was the power of reality, while Yttendaus, the largest and wisest of all the Ekataramn, contained the power of life itself.

While the book didn't mention the Ekataramn by name, she could understand which of the Ekataramn they were referring to, based on the geographical placement of them in the story when compared against Dante's map.

"Here they come! Remember what I told you, everyone," Cecil said, interrupting her thoughts.

Ànifa stared at the bow of the ship, watching as it cut through the waves. She snapped out of her trance and saw a small dinghy approaching. All four passengers were swiftly rowing toward them. Ànifa yelped, then ducked below the deck. She pulled her bonnet out of a pocket and put it on quickly, covering her hair as it changed shades.

Yesterday, while they had been eating lunch, Cecil informed them about the possibility of higher security at Port Columbo. It was a good assumption, judging from the state Pikkul Harbor and Port Gall had been in. He told them that even on an average day, Port Columbo was quite strict. Typically, there were guards at the docks that didn't let people into the town unless they provided them with either the proper identification or a large bribe. In other words, even before the streams of refugees, they didn't let just anyone into Port Columbo. Now, it seemed like they were speeding up the process by performing these inspections out at sea, a possibility Cecil had warned them about.

They had come up with a cover story and based it on an actual truth—they were going to visit Cecil's sister, Sarah. She lived in Port Columbo, close to the docks. For their cover story, after they met up with Sarah, they would travel to Ajenti together to get help from the wise healers. They would say they were looking for a cure for Cecil and Sarah's mother.

Cecil would tell them the truth, that he was visiting his sister. Vesten would get to tell the truth mostly—that he was simply the owner of the boat they had hired for the trip to Port Columbo. They had decided Theodore would play the part of Cecil's grandfather, while Dasch would be Cecil's estranged uncle. As for Ànifa, she would be the adopted sister from Panna Isle.

To help their roles, Theodore, Cecil, and Dasch had rummaged through Vesten's closet for temporary disguises. They wanted to seem wealthy but aloof, as many of the mega-rich on Eklatros were. Luckily, Vesten had stolen a lot of upper-class clothing and had held onto them, so it worked well for them. Ànifa was still unsure about the plan, but Theodore and Cecil were both quite confident about it. She was glad she didn't need to change clothes—her trenchdress would do well enough. Vesten was also going to continue wearing his normal clothes.

They had also decided that Theodore and Dasch should use different names. Theodore, since he had been exiled and technically wasn't even welcomed back in Port Columbo, would go by his middle name, Henry. As for Dasch, they decided his name was a little too unique, so they would call him Chris, after Sage Christian Mason. Ànifa could still use her name because of the story of Afyna and Ànifa.

It was now time to put their plan into action. She stood and watched the small dinghy as the four men rowed closer to them. Theodore approached her from behind, and when she turned to look at him, she couldn't help but laugh.

He had traded out his worn blue robes and floppy blue sorcerer's hat for a decoratively embroidered tunic with dark-brown slacks and brown shoes. The tunic was pale green and was embroidered with a swirly golden pattern. Rather than buttons, the tunic sported wooden toggles. He'd neatly combed his white hair back, which made him look regal.

"Do I look that ridiculous?" Theodore asked quietly.

"No, it looks quite good, actually. I'm simply not used to it," Ànifa replied.

"Neither am I. It's much too stiff for my liking," he said while tugging at his tunic. "At least we're sailing slowly. I don't think I'll get seasick today."

"Stop pulling at your clothes, they can see us," she said, eying the dinghy as it got closer.

Cecil and Dasch approached them. Dasch looked absurdly good in his neat black suit. To cover his elvish ears, he wore a black top hat. Ànifa wasn't used to him appearing as a gentleman. Cecil also looked like a gentleman, proudly wearing a light-blue vest with a white button-up shirt underneath. His trousers matched his blue vest.

"Ahoy!" a voice called out from the approaching dinghy.

"Ahoy!" Vesten called back from the captain's deck. "How be ye fine gentlemen?"

"Very well! Would you mind assisting us for a moment?"

"Sure, whatever you need."

"Just be ready to catch this rope," the man said as he held out a thick rope.

Each of the four men wore the same dark gray uniform with a circular badge on the right sleeve.

The man with the rope threw it, and once Cecil had the rope, he tied it to a metal brace.

"Very good! Now, prepare to be boarded."

Two of the men expertly climbed the rope while the other two remained in the dinghy. Once the two men were on board, they introduced themselves.

"Apologies for the intrusion. I'm Officer Berry and this is Officer Hood." Officer Berry had a neatly trimmed handlebar mustache and goatee, while Officer Hood was clean-shaven.

"It's a pleasure to meet you fine gentlemen," Cecil said, holding out his hand. "My name is Cecil. This is my grandfather, Henry, and my uncle, Chris. This is my adopted sister, Ànifa."

"Wonderful. Now, before we can tell you why we're here, we must first ask for your full cooperation," Officer Berry said.

"Absolutely," Henry—Theodore— replied.

"Wonderful. Now, what is your purpose for visiting Port Columbo today?" Officer Berry asked.

"We are on our way to visit my sister, Sarah. She lives in Port Columbo," Cecil replied. "Port Columbo is not our final destination. For you see, my mother is ill, and we are seeking help from the wise healers of Ajenti."

"And how have you come to know about these healers?" Officer Hood asked, speaking for the first time.

"Ah yes, well, you see, I used to study there... yet I did not..." Chris —Dasch—trailed off, his rough voice shaking and wavering.

"My Uncle Chris left Ajenti with a few screws loose. But while he was there, he was an apprentice to a healer," Cecil said.

"Where is your mother now?" Officer Berry asked, his face showing no emotion.

"In her bedroom. She's been unconscious for quite some time now," Cecil said, pointing to the steps that led belowdecks.

"What is she afflicted with?" Officer Berry asked.

"Sadly, we do not know. That is why we must seek help from the healers," Henry said.

Officer Hood hummed to himself and eyed them closely. "Where are you all from?"

"Rampa Bay," Cecil replied.

"Rampa Bay, very good. Now, the reason we have boarded your ship today is due to the recent flood of refugees. You wouldn't be harboring anyone else, besides the six of you?"

"No, sir," Cecil replied honestly.

"Hood, have a word with the captain. Cecil, would you be so kind as to take me to where your mother is?" Officer Berry asked.

"Certainly. Right this way, please," Cecil replied. "Grandpa, would you mind coming with us?"

"Of course, of course." Henry replied.

———

The inspection took about twenty minutes. Once they finished, the two officers instructed the group to follow them back to the docks so they could complete the necessary paperwork. Officer Hood stayed on *West Wind* while Officer Berry returned to the dinghy to reunite with the two other officers.

With Officer Hood standing on the deck with them, they weren't able to communicate freely, but Ànifa was able to silently chat with Theodore.

"How did it go below decks with Charlotte?" Ànifa asked him.

"It was fine. The officer could clearly see how ill Charlotte is. He did a few things to attempt to wake her—nothing that we hadn't tried before—so, of course, his methods didn't work. He seemed pretty satisfied, though," Theodore replied.

"So, is the process to get the paperwork done really just that? Cecil didn't mention this part at all," Ànifa replied.

"I have never heard of such a thing, either. We can only wait and see at this point. Even if they suspect we are lying, they don't have any proof yet. We mustn't give in to them," Theodore thought.

"Agreed," Ànifa said, then closed the link between them.

Once at the docks, Officer Berry and the two other officers from the dinghy secured *West Wind* to an open bay and led the party of five to a small office. Charlotte stayed on the ship. Officer Berry assured them he would take care of her paperwork, so there was no need to disturb her.

They followed Officer Hood into a small room. The walls were bare, and the only objects in the room were a table and four chairs. Ànifa, Theodore, and Dasch took three of the chairs, while Cecil and Dasch stood behind them. It soon became apparent that this was no innocent identity check. Officer Hood questioned them thoroughly about minor details. Why did they have a suit of armor in one of the rooms? Why did this look more like a houseboat than the typical charter ferries that people of their status typically rented out? For each question, they were able to provide a seemingly satisfying answer. Officer Hood peered at them through narrow eyes and was about to split them up so they could be interrogated one-on-one when a high-ranking official interrupted them.

As soon as the tall, skinny man popped into the room, Cecil's eyes went wide.

"Officer Hood, apologies for the interruption. Do you know where Captain Ledger is?"

"Rear Admiral Mont Simmons, sir! I last saw Captain Ledger in the mess hall, sir."

"Thank you," the Rear Admiral replied. Before he could leave, Cecil called out to him. "Hey, brother Briggs, it's been some time."

Rear Admiral Mont Simmons looked at them for the first time.

"Cecil, what are you doing here?" Rear Admiral Mont Simmons asked, his eyes wide.

"We're here to visit Sarah, actually. We were planning on having a surprise family reunion, but this officer has been interrogating us," Cecil said, tilting his head toward Officer Hood.

Rear Admiral Mont Simmons crossed his arms and glared at Officer Hood. "Is that so? What is the meaning of this?"

Officer Hood was caught off guard. "I, uh, they seemed mighty suspicious, sir. Even Officer Berry agreed."

"Well, you're not wrong. But I see little harm in a surprise family reunion. Please, release them into my custody."

"Yes sir, absolutely, sir. Please, go ahead, sir," Officer Hood nodded profusely.

"Well, come along then, everyone," Rear Admiral Mont Simmons said, opening the door wide for them. "Oh, and Officer Hood? Please find Captain Ledger and send him to my office."

Cecil nodded at the Rear Admiral and walked out of the room, prompting everyone to follow. Unlike most of the officers who wore simple gray uniforms, the Rear Admiral uniform was jet black and decorated with many badges and ribbons. He wore a peaked cap that sat neatly atop his well-cropped short blond hair and a pair of small black-rimmed spectacles balanced neatly on his small pointed nose. Overall, he looked like an important man.

The group silently followed the Rear Admiral across the docks. While the docks were mostly full of luxurious yachts, Ànifa spied ships similar to theirs as well. Rear Admiral Mont Simmons led them into a large building, down a hall, and into a large, extravagantly furnished and decorated office. He closed the door behind him, then turned to face them. Even though there were enough chairs for them all to take a seat, they chose to stand.

"Cecil, what is the meaning of this? Why are you back and why have you brought the exiled wizard with you?"

"Right. You see, we seek aid from Ajenti. We have a sick friend back on our ship that requires the master healers' attention."

Rear Admiral Mont Simmons sighed. "Cecil, you know the rules. By all rights, I should have all of you jailed and shackled for even being here. Simply speaking to you right now is an enormous risk for me. Luckily, Officers Hood and Berry are complete dimwits. Who are you all, by the way?" Rear Admiral Mont Simmons asked, directing his question to Vesten, Dasch, and Ànifa.

"I'm Vesten, captain of *West Wind*."

"My name is Dasch."

"And I'm Ànifa, and I suppose you could say that we're all together because of me."

"And who are you exactly, Ànifa?" the Rear Admiral asked.

"Just a simple traveler. Cecil and Theodore are a crucial part of our journey. We have had many encounters with a wide assortment of monsters, and we wouldn't have made it this far without their help."

Upon mentioning the monsters, the Rear Admiral's eyes widened, and he stroked his neatly trimmed beard.

"And you all still live? Just two days ago, some citizens of Port Columbo took it upon themselves to fight a large green jelly monster. Needless to say, none of them survived."

"She's a powerful fighter, Briggs. We all are. We've had many fights and we've defeated nearly all of our opponents," Cecil said.

"Is that so? Maybe I underestimated you, Cecil. Word is that even the Ajentian knights are having trouble with the monsters," the Rear Admiral said.

"Well, I have a really great team now," Cecil said, holding a hand out to Ànifa and the others.

"So it seems," Rear Admiral Mont Simmons said with another sigh. "Alright, since Cecil is family, I'll do what I can to help you out."

"Thank you very much, brother," Cecil said with a deep nod.

"Of course. Besides, if Sarah were to find out that we met like this without getting to see you, she'd force me to sleep on the couch for a year."

"I never understood how anyone could stand that woman," Cecil said, "but you know as well as I do, it's hard not to love her."

"That it is. Now, give me a few minutes and I'll get you all out of here. Did Officer Hood have you fill out any paperwork?"

"Paperwork? No. I thought that was a ploy to get us into that room," Ànifa replied.

"No, he's just a little prick. Let me get that for you so we can get out of here," the Rear Admiral said as he opened the door to his office. He stepped out and closed the door behind him.

"So, who the fuck is this guy exactly?" Vesten asked.

"My sister's husband, Brigsby Mont Simmons. I just call him Briggs, though, and I'm sure you can too. We've had our differences in the past, but after they married, we got pretty close. That was before I was exiled, of course."

"And he's a Rear Admiral? I knew he was important, but I never knew he was *that* important," Theodore said.

"Oh yeah. He's a bigwig for sure. But it's always been that way. He came from an affluent family, so he's always held a position of power in one way or another. I think that's part of the reason my sister married him—for his koda, I mean."

"Either way, he's been a great help. Why didn't you mention him earlier?" Ànifa asked.

Cecil shrugged. "I never know where he is. For weeks at a time, he can be off visiting other cities for political reasons. It's rare for him to actually be here, at Port Columbo," Cecil said as Briggs returned.

"Speaking of which, I'm heading over to Seaside tomorrow. Well, what's left of Seaside, that is. I'll be going to assess the damage and search for any survivors," Briggs said.

"So, it's true then. Seaside has also fallen," Theodore said as he stroked his beard.

"Yes. Sadly, the Guild of Seafaring Knights wasn't able to do anything about it. The attack came too swiftly. While I'm there, I'll be searching for clues to see if I can learn anything about our enemy," Briggs said.

"We passed through the ruins of Kalah a few days ago. It was burnt to the ground," Ànifa replied, doing her best to keep her emotions out of her voice.

"So I've heard. I've already dispatched a team to investigate. However, this is not the time for this discussion. Please fill out these forms and I'll take you back to my house."

———

About an hour later, Ànifa and the others sat comfortably in Briggs' house. His home was massive—the largest that Ànifa had ever seen. It was bigger than the Sathon Inn. There were rooms upon rooms upon rooms, and that was only the first floor. Overall, there appeared to be three or four floors. Charlotte was currently resting in a small bedroom near the large sitting room where they were all seated.

They had gone back to *West Wind* before going to Briggs' and Sarah's house. Four soldiers carrying a stretcher for Charlotte accompanied them. While at the ship, Theodore grabbed his robes and sorcerer's hat, Cecil donned his armor, and Dasch changed into his normal robes. Ànifa grabbed the backpack, and they all reclaimed their weapons.

As a bonus, Briggs had instructed Captain Ledger to put *West Wind* under his direct supervision. This meant Briggs could assign his own guards to their ship.

The sitting room they lounged in was luxurious. Elegant, soft white couches and chairs furnished the room. There was a large bookshelf lining one wall filled with volumes of military history and autobiographies. Scattered across the room were exquisite paintings of various styles and sizes. The painting in the center of the room was accompanied by a small plaque that indicated it was by an artist named Lyla Thein. When Cecil caught Ànifa studying it, he told her that this painting was one of his sister's most prized possessions. It was beautiful—the painting depicted a young family of four sitting beneath a tree having a picnic. The scene itself was simple, but captured the viewer's attention with its bright colors and evoked a feeling of home and family. It was a heartwarming painting and made Ànifa miss her own family, even though she still couldn't remember anything about them. Cecil told her that the family represented in the painting was very much like their own family— the older sister, the younger brother, and the happy parents. He seemed morose when he mentioned his parents, but she decided not to press the issue.

Briggs sat with them, lounging comfortably in an extravagant chair. He had sent one of the many servants to fetch Sarah for them. While they waited, two servants brought them platters filled with snacks and glasses of water. The servants wore simple white uniforms and were all young men.

"Where the fuck is my good-for-nothing brother?" a woman yelled from somewhere in the house. Ànifa could hear her stomping through the halls as she approached, muttering other curses along the way.

"Cecil!" Sarah shouted when she entered the room. "Why in holy Eklatros are you here? You're supposed to be in fucking exile. And for that matter, why is Theodore back here?"

"Honey, I told you—" Briggs began.

"Not. Now," Sarah cut him off, her gaze tearing into her husband.

Sarah was wearing a simple white summer dress patterned with daisies. At the moment, the dress seemed out of place on her as she spat at her brother, who sunk deeper into his chair. Sarah was sightly taller than Cecil and had wavy dark-brown hair that fell to her shoulders. She was wearing red lipstick and pink eyeshadow contrasted by black mascara and eyeliner that made her dark-blue eyes pop.

Sarah continued to cut into her brother, yelling insults at him, but Cecil seemed relatively unfazed by the torrent of curses. "You dirty little drunk, come over here and give me a fucking hug," Sarah said with a wide smile.

Cecil stood and wrapped his arms around her. "It's great to see you again, sis."

"You too, brother."

"Everyone, this is my sister, Sarah," Cecil said as he and sister released their embrace and turned to everyone in the room.

"It's a pleasure to meet you all," Sarah said with a small curtsy. It was as if she had become a completely different person, finally fitting snugly into her summer dress.

"It's great to meet you too," Ànifa said with a bow.

Sarah turned to her husband. "Sorry, Brigsby."

"You know you don't need to apologize," Briggs said as he munched on an hors d'oeuvre. "I understand how you get around your family."

Vesten, who was sitting next to Ànifa, leaned in to whisper, "Now that's my kind of woman."

Ànifa looked at Vesten and giggled while nodding in agreement.

According to Sarah, most newcomers typically spent a few days being interrogated by the dock's officers, so she told them they were lucky they ran into her husband. Briggs added that this was a new tactic. Because of the rise of monsters, they couldn't be too careful; though Briggs did not fully agree with the new methods.

Soon the conversation turned to their plans to enter Ajenti. Sarah and Briggs both stressed they couldn't just walk into the heavily guarded fortress with an exiled wizard and knight. Sarah suggested they stay the night. She explained that tomorrow morning would be the best time to slip in unnoticed, as it was the day the supplies were brought in from Port Columbo. Sarah had a friend, Alexia, who ran her own bakery. She might let them hide in her cart.

Sarah called in a servant and instructed him to send a message to Alexia while Briggs apologized and told them he must get back to work and prepare for his trip to Seaside.

After Briggs left, they talked a bit more about the state of the world. Sarah was well informed and could confirm that not only had Kalah and Seaside been utterly decimated, but also Runti, a small village on Panna Isle. That meant the Gnusar had already destroyed three towns.

Sarah told them how the Ajentian Knights were being deployed across Roffen. Each city and town would receive their own contingent of guards to protect them from the monsters. They were even in contact with Fort Turner to coordinate deployment to Schelff Island, Panna Isle, and Sortuga.

Besides the security measures, a world summit was being organized. This would be the first worldwide summit in over ten years. All the Dukes and city leaders were being summoned to Fort Turner to attend the summit. Briggs and many other high-ranking military personnel would be going and Sarah said she was considering going too.

After the conversation died down, Sarah stood and stretched.

"Is anyone hungry? I can get lunch started."

"Yes, that sounds lovely, thank you," Theodore replied.

"It's no problem," Sarah said in a sweet voice. "Wedge!"

A few moments later, a servant popped into the room. Ànifa recognized this servant to be the same one that had fetched Sarah for them earlier. He was short and chubby, with neatly cropped black hair.

"Yes, ma'am?"

"Please tell the chef to prepare lunch. I'm feeling a nice salad today, with some gazpacho. And tell her we have five guests as well."

"Certainly, ma'am. It'll be my pleasure," Wedge said as he bowed and took his leave.

"It shouldn't take long. Please, follow me into the dining room."

Lunch was delicious. The salad had been a pleasant mix of lettuce topped with nuts, a white crumbly cheese, berries, and a simple balsamic vinaigrette. The gazpacho that accompanied it had been made from a sweet summer squash.

After lunch, Sarah requested to speak to her brother alone. They had much to catch up on and many personal matters to discuss. Vesten had a few things he wanted to tend to on *West Wind*, and Dasch and Theodore also went off to do their own things. Ànifa didn't blame them—they had been together for days now. A break apart from each other would be nice.

She took a small bedroom for herself and read *A Collective History: The Magical World of Eklatros* and continued to learn about the past, although the chapters she was currently reading were silly stories that didn't tell her much about the planet itself. Though, she learned a lot about Kieth Angelcross. Many of the stories about him included a character named Dasch. He was portrayed to be the loyal best friend, though none of them truly captured his personality. She knew he was a different person back then, yet, even through the fictionalized account, something felt off to her.

Later that night, the group reconvened in the dining room. Each of them had returned to their original outfits, except for Cecil, who wore a simple green tunic and black trousers. Upon serving their dinner, Wedge informed them that Alexia agreed to take them to Ajenti. Briggs told them about the rest of his day while they ate. When he was finished, Vesten thanked Briggs for assigning top-notch guards to *West Wind*.

Yes, thank you, Briggs. You have been a great help, she thought. *I don't know what we would have done without you. Navigating this world seems extremely difficult. People really are unpredictable. However much I trust Sarah and Briggs, I still must not allow them to learn of my true nature. I just hope I wasn't too awkward when Sarah suggested I take off my bonnet.*

Anyway, tomorrow we'll travel to Ajenti, a place I have heard so much about. Though, truth be told, I'm really quite nervous. Today was fine— there really weren't too many people out in the streets. But I feel like it will be much different tomorrow. This is something I need to learn how to deal with. I need to do my best to blend in.

Most of all, I hope we can speak to a healer about Charlotte. Theodore seems confident they can help, but he is in exile. I'm worried about that as well, but he thinks it'll be fine. His plan is to search for his friend, Tyrona. He claims she'll be able to help us. I hope he's right... I hope everything works out for us tomorrow. I just want you to be okay, Charlotte. I want you to wake up... I want you to be your true self again.

20

BATTLE FOR ENTRY

Ànifa found herself scrunched into a small corner of the supply wagon they rode in. She held Charlotte in her aching arms, unable to move to redistribute the weight. Two white and brown spotted draft horses pulled the wagon, and the road was quite bumpy, making their ride that much more uncomfortable.

They had gotten up an hour before dawn, met Alexia in the arranged meeting place, and followed her to her small bakery. She had already begun packing the wagon full of assorted breads, pastries, cakes, muffins, bagels, and more. The cart smelled absolutely divine.

The five of them, plus Charlotte, had piled into the small wagon, trying to take up as little space as they could. Since six full-grown adults took quite a lot of space in her cart, Alexia and her wife Roxanne had to be creative packing the rest of their load.

They set off in time to join the caravan of other vendors as the morning commute began. A squadron of knights guarded the caravan, and Cecil pointed out that they were from the Guild of Chivalrous Knights. He could tell from the color of the plumes on their helmets. Cecil's guild, the Guild of Exemplary Knights, had light green plumes, while the Guild of Chivalrous Knights had dark red plumes.

Cecil explained that upon joining a guild, they only gave out the standard broadsword and helmet. The low-class knights had to provide their own armor. It was the helmets, and only the helmets, that distinguished a knight from one guild to another. In the higher ranks of the guilds, elaborate armor, capes, and robes with the guild's official color and seal on them were provided.

Having the knights along proved quite useful. Along the way, Ànifa heard three separate skirmishes. She couldn't see from her spot in the cart, but it sounded like they had fought some fairly large beasts.

It took about two hours for them to reach the walls of Ajenti, where they had to stop and wait in line for another half hour until they could make it through. For the most part, there were no inspections—it simply took a while for the carts to go through the gate one by one.

Once through the west gate, it took roughly another half hour until they reached Alexia's spot in the large weekly street market. Alexia and Roxanne had to unload most of their goods before they could exit the cart. Theodore was the first one out. His sigh of relief quickly became a fit of hacking.

"Holy Eklatros. Now I remember why I dislike this place," Theodore wheezed. "The air here is poison."

"Hush now. It'll be best if you stay quiet throughout the unloading process," Roxanne whispered.

Ànifa stayed with Charlotte in the cart until it was completely unloaded, at which point Dasch climbed back into the cart. He helped her gently hoist Charlotte onto his back. They thanked Alexia and Roxanne, then silently followed Cecil to a deserted alley where they could speak more freely.

"Welcome to Ajenti, milady," Cecil whispered.

"I thought it would be nicer," Ànifa said as she stretched—her body was still sore.

Red and white brick lined the walls of the alley. The few buildings she could see from the alley were made from the same red-white brick as the alley and had wooden roof shingles. The buildings were charming and unique. In stark contrast, the ground was strewn with litter and reeked of urine.

"There's really no pleasant part of the outer Ajentian slums. It always stinks," Theodore replied, his right hand covering his nose and mouth.

"Yeah, but it has its charms," Cecil said with a twinkle in his eye.

"What's the plan?" Dasch asked, steering them in the right direction.

"We need to get into that enormous castle, right?" Ànifa asked, pointing to the shadows that loomed above them.

"Yes, that's Ajenti University," Cecil added.

"Right, well, I don't think we should all go together. Some of us should stay behind."

"I'll stay behind," Cecil volunteered quickly. Theodore scoffed at him but said nothing.

"Fuck it, I'll stay behind also," Vesten said. "I wouldn't fit in, anyway."

"So then, Dasch, Theodore, and I will take Charlotte to the healers while the two of you wait out here. I'm not sure how long it will take though."

"It's no problem. There's a place nearby here that I used to go to quite often."

"No, Cecil, you can't go there," Theodore said with his hands on his hips. "That's the place that got you exiled in the first place!"

"But it's just so wholesome."

Theodore rolled his eyes. "Look, there are dozens of pubs in Ajenti. Can't you two wait at a different one?"

"So, you don't mind if we go to a pub?" Cecil asked as he rubbed his hands together.

"I can't think of a better place to lie low," Theodore replied. "Just try not to draw any attention to yourselves. And I think the best place for that is The Dark Horse."

"Ah, yes... that place. Yeah, let's go there, Vesten," Cecil said.

"Sounds good to me," Vesten said with a grin.

"We better do this, then. We'll meet up with you at The Dark Horse when we're finished," Ànifa said.

"Good luck, milady," Cecil said with a slight bow. "Take care of yourself. Same to you, Theo and Dasch."

Ànifa, Theodore, and Dasch, who was carrying Charlotte on his back, exited the alley onto a busy street. There were large carts pulled by horses, donkeys, and camels. Weaving around the carts were people on two-wheeled carts. Theodore sensed Ànifa's confusion and told her they were called bicycles. She watched as a bicycle spooked a horse, prompting the rider to throw out a slew of curses. As they made their way down the street, most of the people paid the three no mind. Yet the gazes she felt were not friendly.

"Are they going to the street market where we just were?" Ànifa asked.

"Oh no, this is simply the daily traffic," Theodore replied. "While this area is pretty poor, most everyone has a job to do. We just happen to be going through at one of the busiest times."

They continued along through the mass of people. Ànifa felt herself being pushed along by those behind her, eager to get wherever they were going.

"*How far away are we?*" Ànifa asked Theodore through their mental link.

"*Not very far. Once we turn down this next street, you'll see,*" Theodore replied.

The buildings that lined the street were all quite tall—each four to six stories. Many were built with brick, but some were stone, wood, and even mud and straw. It was a unique patchwork of styles, and when Ànifa looked closer, she could see why it was this way. From her deduction, the stone buildings were the oldest. For all she knew, they could be original structures from when Ajenti was first constructed. The brick seemed to be the next generation of structures, then it degraded from there, going next to wood, then mud and straw. Along with the stone buildings, the wooden ones were the only other structures built with columns, giving them a much more regal look than the others. On one particularly large building, every wooden column was intricately carved, each depicting a different scene from the founding of Ajenti.

Above the buildings were thick, dark tree limbs. She scanned all around for the source but couldn't spot any trees. Finding a tree in the dense city would have been quite surprising.

She felt right at home, even though it was her first time in Ajenti. Now she knew why Cecil had mentioned its charm. Although, he could have also been talking about being reunited with alcohol.

They soon turned right, heading deeper into the city, and then Ànifa saw it—the large black castle at the center of the fortress. As she stared at the large structure, she realized the branches she had seen earlier were coming from the castle.

She stopped in her tracks when she finally realized what it was, causing Theodore to bump into her and other people around her to curse about the sudden obstacle.

The castle in front of her was not actually a castle—it was a tree. A large stone tree. Its spires, towers, and battlements were its branches, while its main trunk was a gnarled hunk of stone. It was unbelievably massive. It had to be nearly fifty stories high and hundreds of meters wide at the peak of its canopy.

"It's truly impressive, isn't it?" Dasch said, surprising Ànifa and Theodore, who had stopped along with them.

"You've seen it before?" Theodore asked as a younger man brushed past him.

Dasch nodded. "I know this place well. It was ancient even in my time. Yet back then, it wasn't called Ajenti. It was Cascagrada—the Divine Tree. The stories say that it was an actual tree that turned to stone thousands of years ago."

"Cascagrada... that name has been popping up a lot in the book I've been reading," Ànifa said as she walked forward, prompting the others to continue.

"Yes, it was an important place during the war. Kieth and I spent a lot of time here with our forces, which is the reason this place is a fortress. Both elves and humans constructed these walls under

Kieth's command. It's impenetrable, even by the Gnusar. Just look around you. This city is alive. No one seems to care about anything that's been going on outside of Ajenti. Everyone seems very isolated here."

"Quite an astute observation, Dasch," Theodore replied. "Now, we're approaching the main entrance. Everyone, follow my lead. These guards look like rookies. Their guilds must really be stretched thin."

Theodore puffed out his chest and picked up his pace, walking with a sudden sense of purpose. Ànifa and Dasch followed suit. Ànifa noticed that these guards had light-blue plumes on their helmets.

When they were within earshot of the knights, Theodore called out to them.

"Hey! Hey, you there! Yeah, you!" Theodore yelled as the guards frantically looked back and forth at each other, each unsure of what to do. "Come here, you blathering idiots! We need your help!"

Theodore stepped aside, allowing Dasch through with Charlotte on his back.

"Oh my god!" one knight exclaimed. "Is she okay?"

"Not yet she isn't, you tin-headed dimwit! She needs to be brought to the infirmary straight away!"

"Not just anyone is allowed to—" the other knight began.

"Dagnabbit, do you know who I am?" Theodore bellowed while violently shaking his scarlet staff in front of them. "If you don't help us this instant, I'll tell your guildmaster about this!"

"Right, sir! Sorry, sir!" the knights exclaimed, snapping to attention. Theodore smirked, then furrowed his brow in frustration.

"Can one of you carry her?" Theodore asked.

"Our apologies, but we cannot leave our posts, not for any reason."

"Then let us through!" Theodore shouted.

"Yes, sir!" the two knights said in unison, then parted, letting them through. Theodore hurried through the large, intricately carved wooden double doors. Ànifa wished she could get a closer look at the doors, but they had a guise to maintain.

Once they were through, Ànifa found herself in a large atrium. The ceiling rose close to a hundred meters above them. It was supported by sets of large wooden columns, each one as intricately designed as the doors they just passed through. None of the columns rose all the way to the ceiling. Directly in front of them was a set of stairs, and they began climbing.

When they reached the middle of the staircase, Theodore slowed and said, "We need to be on edge now. There are many who will recognize me."

"Let us hope we can make it through unnoticed," Ànifa replied.

They made it to the top of the steps, then turned left and headed down a long hallway. The walls and floors were made of jet-black fossilized wood. If she didn't know any better, Ànifa would have assumed it was obsidian. The walls were bare besides the occasional torch or door. In all, it was darkly lit. She felt as if they were wandering through a cave.

"This place feels really strange," Ànifa whispered.

"That would be a combination of the various magics flowing through Ajenti, as well as her structure itself. This place is truly divine—that is not an overstatement. Our magics can blossom and grow in ways that they never could outside these walls," Theodore explained.

"So this place enhances magical energy?" Ànifa asked thoughtfully.

"Yes, and also no. Only those who can tune themselves to the frequency of Ajenti itself can truly master their own power. It's a feeling that is utterly indescribable, and the desire to maintain this feeling can be quite blinding to everything else around you. This is why most of us never leave once we are here. I've seen many of my peers lose themselves within these walls.

"And I know what you must think, but—"

"Halt!" a voice called out, stopping Theodore mid-sentence.

Theodore looked up and sighed. "Selma. Of course it's you."

"I should have known you'd be back," Selma spat. The woman that approached them wore light gray robes. Her blond hair was a matted mess and her wide blue eyes were wild. "You can't be here. Get out! I'll call upon Master Prander myself!"

"Please, Selma, you mustn't," Theodore begged.

"There's that whiny little Theodore that I know. And you even had the audacity to bring others with you. Be gone, all of you!"

Selma raised a small wooden wand. Theodore thrust out his staff in response.

"Please, Selma. We were friends once, remember?"

She spat at Theodore's feet. "Screw your friendship, Theodore. Who needs you?"

<hr>

Tyrona hurried down the hallway. Her intuition told her she was needed, and she never questioned her intuition. The urgency of this situation, while quite unusual, had a familiar tone to it.

Before long, she heard raised voices shouting at each other. She stopped mid-stride as the realization hit her.

Theodore! It's you, isn't it? she thought. *I knew you'd be back.*

Tyrona smiled warmly as she placed her left foot back on the ground. She closed her eyes and took a second to compose herself. She opened her eyes and brushed dust off her cloak, then took a few small steps forward, allowing her to identify the source of the second voice—Selma Wingert.

Of course, she thought. *The nosiest witch on all of Eklatros.*

"Selma!" she called out.

Selma turned to face her.

My word, you have let yourself go, she thought.

"You!" Selma shouted as she pointed a long, bony finger at her. "Why do you constantly defend this fool? Can't you see that he's—"

She watched as a small burst of electricity shot out of Theodore's staff and hit Selma in the back. Selma fell sprawling to the ground.

"Tyrona!" Theodore called out as he rushed toward her. Two people she didn't recognize followed him—a hairless man and a dark-skinned woman wearing a bonnet. The man was the palest person she had ever seen and was carrying a silver-haired woman on his back.

Tyrona was aghast. "Theodore, what did you do to Selma? You'll be..." She lost her train of thought as Theodore embraced her in a deep hug. "Oh Dorie, how I've missed you so!"

She hugged him back fiercely. Until this moment, she hadn't realized how much she had missed him. Theodore was the only friend she had.

Theodore ended their embrace. "I've missed you more than you know, Tyrona. But now is not the time for pleasantries. Your timing is impeccable, and we need your help. Our friend, Charlotte, is hurt." He pointed to the woman on the pale man's back.

Tyrona looked at the pale man and the dark-skinned woman and flashed them a smile and a quick wave.

"Thank you for helping to return Theodore in one piece," she said with a nod. "Now, what's happened to her?"

"She was taken by the Gnusar—the green scaly monsters. She's been unconscious ever since," the dark-skinned woman said.

"I understand. I'll take her to the healers right away," Tyrona said. "Dorie, I trust you remember the way back to my apartment. Wait for me there."

"I remember a few different ways," Theodore said with a smirk.

The pale man grunted. "We're in a hurry, right?"

"Yes, of course. Give her here," Tyrona said with her arms outstretched.

The pale man lowered Charlotte into her arms. Tyrona closed her eyes, feeling the woman's weight. She focused on that weight while moving an oval-shaped saucer of air held together by vibrational energy underneath her.

Tyrona opened her eyes and dropped her arms to her side. The woman floated in mid-air in the same spot she had been holding her moments ago.

"Before I go, I'll need her full name," she said.

"It's Charlotte Tuesti," the dark-skinned woman said. "And I'm Ànifa."

"Nice to meet you, Ànifa, but I'm afraid the introductions will need to wait. I'll be on my way now. See you soon."

"Wait, what will you tell the nurses?" Theodore asked.

"I'll think of something on the way. I mean, it's me," she said with a playful tone.

"And you're honestly the only other person in the world I can trust right now. So I know you can do it," Theodore replied.

"Thanks. Now, see ya later, Dorie!" she said, then turned away and hurried down the hallway. Charlotte's unconscious body floated behind her. She heard Theodore say something and, without hesitating, manipulated the vibrations around her to send a wave of undisturbed air in his direction, allowing her to eavesdrop on them. Ajenti's magics were so powerful, you could be four meters away from someone and you wouldn't be able to hear a single word they were saying.

"Now, follow me. There's a secret passage over here," Theodore said.

"Lead the way. That woman—I remember you and Cecil fighting in the Sathon Inn about her. From the way I heard—" Ànifa was cut short.

"Nothing has happened," Theodore said. "She's just like that."

"But, I mean, really? Dorie?" Ànifa asked.

"As I said, that's how she is. Now, come on," Theodore commanded.

A soft popping sound let her know she was out of range. Tyrona smiled to herself.

Oh Dorie, welcome back.

Cecil and Vesten sat across from each other at a small, round wooden table. The Dark Horse was dimly lit and sparsely occupied. They sat in a corner of the small wooden bar, apart from everyone else. On the walls were a strange assortment of items. Some made sense—a horseshoe, a whip, a pair of boots with spurs on them. Others were completely random—a toy raccoon, newspaper clippings, framed currency, and even a tattered cloak. The walls were nearly completely covered with an assortment of random objects.

He was on this fourth beer while Vesten was only on his second. The world was getting that familiar spin to it, and his head was aching in just the right way.

"Ah, this is the life," Cecil said.

"Aye. I spent many a day in dive bars similar to this one across the world. There's one particular spot in Sortuga that I have to go back to nearly every fuckin' time I visit," Vesten replied.

"Yeah? What place? You're not talking about The Broken Well, are you?"

"No, but I do enjoy that place. I'm talking about Gurdy's."

"I'm not sure if I've been there. I mean, I've only been to Sortuga twice."

"Yeah, I can't even say how many fuckin' times I've been there. Hundreds of times at this point, I'm sure," Vesten said as he finished his beer.

"For sure, for sure," Cecil said, nodding in agreement. "So, why don't you carry alcohol on your ship?"

"I dare not bring any alcohol onto *West Wind*. My mind must be sharp if I am to sail her properly. Care for another round?"

"Always," Cecil replied, lifting the mug to his mouth and finishing his beer. "Ah, nothing compares to a good Ajentian Pale Ale."

"Agreed. This next one's on me," Vesten said.

They stood and made their way to the bar when the door opened. Sunlight streamed into the dank pub, followed by stomping boots and clamoring armor. Cecil glanced up and noticed their light green plumes. His eyes widened, and he ducked behind the bar. The other patrons of the bar quickly paid their tabs and left.

"Don't look at me, Vesten. Just order the drinks."

Vesten nodded, looking forward.

"You should've seen that shithead! He just laid there, moaning, like 'oh, good knight, please don't take my goat, oh, not the goat.'" A burst of laughter rang out among the four knights.

"Ah, that was too funny. Some people, man," another knight chimed in.

The bartender ignored Vesten and approached the knights first.

"What'll it be today?"

"The usual! You should fucking know this by now, Ed!"

"Sorry sir, I'll fetch it right away."

The bartender got to work fixing the drinks. Cecil, still crouched behind the bar, glanced at Vesten and realized he was staring at the knights. He grabbed Vesten by the trousers, but it was too late.

"What? You see something funny?"

"Oh, no, sorry," Vesten said.

"Don't you mean 'sorry, *sir*'?" another knight asked.

"Ah yes, my apologies, *sir*."

"Hey! What's with that attitude?" one of the knights said. He stomped over to Vesten, then slammed his fist onto the bar.

"You better start showing us a little respect, pal."

Cecil cursed, then stood up straight. "Decker, can't you be a shithead somewhere else?"

"Where in the fuck did you pop out from? Boys! Look who's back!" Decker exclaimed.

"If it isn't that little drunk-ass shitbag Cecil Kloud!" Cecil glanced in the voice's direction and frowned.

"How ya doing, Ethan?"

"Oh, you know, swell, swell. Doing better now that I get to pound my fist into your fucking face. You're not supposed to be here, you know," Ethan said.

Cecil sighed. "Yeah, I know. But it couldn't be helped. And, you know, I was really trying to avoid you lot, but now that you're here... yeah, let's do this!"

"Whoa! Cecil, what?" Vesten exclaimed. "I would totally fuckin' fight alongside you. But I'm the only one here without armor."

"Yeah, stay out of the way, fire-hair, unless you want to fucking die," Decker said.

"Wait, please wait!" The bartender interrupted. "Not in my bar, please. Take it outside if you must."

"Well, you heard the man. Let's take this outside, bitch!" Ethan said as he pounded back his drink. The others did the same, then slammed their mugs on the bar.

"Keep our tab open, Ed. And don't you fucking say we ain't never done nothin' good for ya now, ya hear?" Decker said.

A knight with long black hair approached Cecil and started pushing him to the door.

"Come on, Reggy. I can walk," Cecil said as he took a step toward the door.

"Then fucking move!"

Cecil was being herded out the door by the four other knights. Before he left the bar, he attempted to turn around to face Vesten. "Vesten, don't forget the backpack!"

An hour later, Cecil lay aching inside a jail cell. From his assessment, he had three broken ribs, a black eye, and a bloody lip. They had pulled some of his hair from his head, leaving a crusty, bloody mess on his scalp.

At the time, he actually thought he was going to die. As much as he fought and struggled, Decker and the others were too ruthless. Any knight that soured the Guild of Exemplary Knight's status deserved to be put down. It was in their creed.

Seriously, screw them, he thought. *Screw all the guilds. They're all rotten to the core.*

Even the guild who had saved his ass was not without its own corruption. The Guild of Policing Knights, better known simply by the police, had intervened right before he was about to get his face stomped in. Now he was in debt to the police, which was not something anyone desired.

The situation he found himself in reminded him of the time before he was exiled, but this time he wasn't alone. Vesten was in this mess as well, even if he managed to come out of it in slightly better shape. He had only gotten a black eye and a broken nose because he had spent most of the skirmish cowering behind some barrels. Cecil understood—he knew he should have done the same. But he was a knight; he would not back down from a fight, even if he was sorely outnumbered.

And yet, the worse part about all of this wasn't his injuries. It had been his first day drinking in nearly a week. He had missed his poison and drank more than he should have. If he had been sober, he knew he would have fared better. Not only that, but he also would have defended Vesten. He had let his friend down today.

I must stop drinking. For good this time. I can't keep making stupid mistakes, he thought. *There are other lives at stake, lives I care about.*

Cecil's thoughts turned to Theodore, Ànifa, Dasch, and Charlotte. He hoped they were having better luck than he was.

Ànifa's thoughts wandered as they wound their way through the Ajentian maze.

This place is truly amazing, she thought. *I can feel the energy flowing through these walls. I'm amazed that Theodore knows how to navigate this place. Every staircase has looked the same, every hallway has been nearly identical. Every single door is unmarked. There must either be a very high learning curve, or there's another way to navigate this place that I'm not yet aware of. Maybe the magics of the structure itself can guide those who know how to listen.*

It's quite interesting. I wish I knew more about this place. If it hadn't been for Tyrona's help, we may have been thrown out altogether. And Charlotte wouldn't be getting the help she needs. I don't know what it was about Tyrona, but even if she wasn't Theodore's good friend... I have a feeling that I would trust her. I know I trust too easily, but she seems like a good person with a pure soul. If only there were more people like that in this world.

21

BATTLE FOR FRIENDSHIP

Ànifa followed Theodore through the winding maze of Ajenti. She cleared her mind and allowed herself to listen to the subtle messages that swirled around her. It was as if the walls themselves were pouring knowledge into her. She was seeing things she shouldn't know. For instance, the third time Theodore threw open a door that led to a staircase, Ànifa saw the broken first step and knew that a wizard named Quentin Holland had broken it three hundred sixty years ago when an ore manipulation spell he'd been casting had gone wrong. She had also seen a scratch on a spiral staircase that she knew had been put there by a witch named Yolanda Hillsborough after she had failed to kill a despised peer. She'd been caught and thrown into the dungeon, where she was ultimately forgotten about and died alone in the dark.

The stories kept coming to her, and she let them in, consuming all the knowledge she could.

This place is trying to tell me something through random stories, she thought. *But, the more I absorb, the more confused I get.*

She shrugged and followed Theodore to yet another door. Fully expecting another staircase to appear, Ànifa was surprised when a brightly lit and well-furnished room was revealed. It was a stark contrast to the dark hallways.

Theodore stepped into the room and ushered the others in. "Come on, quickly! We've got to get inside."

Ànifa followed him in, with Dasch bringing up the rear. The first thing that caught her eye was an oval vase decorated with scenes straight out of the Eklatros history book.

Dasch grunted audibly while taking in the room. "Interesting place."

"Yes, please be careful," Theodore said while shooing Ànifa away from the intricate porcelain vase. "Tyrona is quite particular about her living space. Everything needs to be tidy and stay in its rightful place. So, while I know she welcomes all of us in, please be sure not to disturb anything."

Ànifa took a proper look around and noticed that it was exceptionally clean, especially compared to some of the hallways they had ventured down. The white shelves, pink decorations, and purple couches beautifully contrasted the same jet-black stone as the rest of Ajenti. Everything was in an orderly fashion; from the way the trinkets were displayed on the shelves to the placement of the pictures on the walls. There was a small, immaculately spotless kitchen on the left and a hallway to the right with four closed doors.

"What will she do to us if we touch something?" Dasch asked with a devious look in his eyes.

"Oh, nothing at first. She'll simply tidy up silently while biding her time for the perfect moment for revenge. And believe me, she knows exactly when to strike," Theodore said, knocking his staff on the floor to emphasize his point.

Dasch grunted in approval.

"So, what's your deal with her?" Ànifa asked with a twinkle in her eyes.

"As I said earlier, we're just good friends, contrary to what Cecil may think. We've known each other for a long time now. We were in the same entry-level courses together, but we didn't talk much back then," Theodore said as he stared off at nothing and stroked his beard.

"Huh, she looks younger than you," Dasch said.

"Oh no, we're right around the same age. She likes to use her powers to make herself appear younger. A lot of the sorceresses do that. Just don't let her jovial nature fool you. She can be ruthless."

"Hey, Theodore," Ànifa asked. "I'm curious—is there a difference between a wizard and a sorcerer?"

"There used to be. But now they're essentially interchangeable terms. Sorcerer is just a more official term, while wizard is more casual."

A small noise at the door silenced the conversation. The door creaked open and Tyrona popped her head into the room before fully opening the door. She stood there with a sly smile on her face.

"I had a feeling I could catch you all off guard. And hey, nice! No one's touched anything," Tyrona said as she stepped into the room and closed the door behind her. She made a slight hand movement, magically binding the door closed.

"Yes, I told them not to," Theodore said.

"Thanks, Dorie!" Tyrona said as she made her way to the large purple couch. "Oh, and Selma is fine, by the way. I checked up on her on my way back here. She was livid, but I helped her calm down."

"Yeah, by altering her memories, I'm sure," Theodore said as he crossed his arms in disapproval.

"You know it!" Tyrona said gleefully, then patted the cushion next to her. "Now, get yer butt over here! It's been too long."

Theodore took a seat next to Tyrona, Ànifa sat on the couch across from them, and Dasch, of course, chose to stand. There was a small white table between the couches with pink and purple candles burning in the center of the table and some books resting neatly to their right. Somehow, even the candle wax seemed to melt in an orderly fashion.

"So, you know you owe me an explanation. Big time. Do you know how hard it is to convince that blubber-headed master healer about anything? She is strict, but she's helping your friend."

"Thank you, Tyrona," Ànifa said with a deep nod. "Thank you so much, I really appreciate everything you've done for us so far."

With Tyrona sitting across from her, Ànifa got a better look at her. Now, up close, she could see the telltale signs of her age, yet they were hidden well. Her youthful face had several faint lines few would notice. And while her hair was a shimmering black, her roots were gray. She really was stunning—her dark umber skin contrasted well with her long hair and deep jade eyes. She wore a small-brimmed violet witches' hat. It was smaller and more effeminate than Theodore's and perfectly matched her deep violet dress robes.

"It's no problem," Tyrona said, smiling. She tilted her head to her right and asked, "Now, if I may be so bold... who *are* you? There is something very different about you."

Before Ànifa could answer, Theodore laughed heartily, causing Tyrona to glare at him.

"My apologies," Theodore said with a grin. "It's just been a really crazy adventure since I left."

"So, tell me. What happened? Why are you back here, and who are these people you are with? Because this one is also very odd," she said, pointing her thumb at Dasch.

Dasch grunted ambiguously.

"Alright then, I'll start from the beginning."

Theodore dove in, starting from when he and Cecil departed from Port Columbo. First, they had gone to Sortuga, then caught a ride to Port Gall. They then traveled to Galstrom, where Theodore and Cecil searched for answers about the Great Barriers, but to no avail. It was there that he heard about a knowledgeable Sage that lived on Schelff Island. Shortly after that, they met Ànifa.

After Theodore told Tyrona of how he and Ànifa had met, he prompted her to remove her bonnet. It was the first time she had revealed her color-changing hair and pointed ears to anyone since Dante.

Tyrona gaped at her unabashedly. "It can't be!"

"And yet it is," Ànifa replied.

"I don't get it." Tyrona shook her head in disbelief. "How?"

Ànifa told her part of the story up until she met Theodore. She and Theodore continued together after that point, with the random grunt from Dasch.

When they finished telling her everything, Tyrona simply stared at both her and Dasch.

After a moment, Tyrona closed her eyes and shook her head, then opened her eyes and said, "Okay. So. There's a lot to process there. Especially with you, Dasch. I have a lot of questions for you." Tyrona turned to face Theodore. "But Theodore, I'm not sure if you realize what this means. For one, you were exiled. You were told to never come back here, not under any circumstances. They also told you to cease all outside learning. You were to go into hiding, much like Dante Suebsanguan, of which you all met. That's what exile means. But you went off and did the exact opposite. You continued looking for the Great Barriers... even though uncovering knowledge about them was the whole reason you got exiled in the first place.

"And it *worked*. You met Ànifa, and you met Dasch, and from what it sounds like, you are all on your way to changing this planet. And to do so, you will need your full powers."

"But it's like you said, Tyrona," Theodore said. "I'm in exile. I'm not supposed to be here."

"Yes, but I'm sure you know that there is a way to get your powers back. It's never been done before, but there is a way. And the way to do that is to go to the high council and tell them everything that you just told me."

"What? We can't do that!" Theodore exclaimed. "I can't be seen in front of Spell Master Prander, not to mention Speech Master Fritta! Do you know what they will do to me if they see me again?"

"But that's the thing, Theodore. Ànifa is an elf, but she's not an ordinary elf. You see, I've been researching the Great Barriers myself since you left. As soon as I could, I read the book that you tried to steal."

"Ah! And what did you learn?" Theodore asked with wide eyes.

"A lot—fantastical things that I thought to be just exaggeration.

But her *hair*, Dorie," Tyrona turned to face Ànifa. "Ànifa... your hair. Do you know what it means?"

"I'm afraid I still don't remember a lot from before I fell," Ànifa replied, her hair swirling between dark and light-blue hues.

Tyrona nodded. "Then let me explain. Every thousand years or so, there is an elf that wields more power than any single individual should be able to—elves, faeries, and angels included. And that elf's hair is the color of the sky, and it can change shades with her emotions. That elf is you, Ànifa. Your journey here on Eklatros has been foretold for centuries; yet, it is not common knowledge. It took many hours of studying ancient, brittle texts to learn this much."

"It is true. Do you know how long I searched for that book?" Theodore said, throwing his hands out for emphasis. "Sure, I had to hide from everyone that approached me, since I wasn't supposed to be in that library in the first place... but I searched those stacks for nearly a full day before I found that volume. And right after I found it someone spotted me from afar. I panicked and grabbed the book and ran. Looking back now, it was a really stupid thing to do."

"And yet, if you hadn't, you wouldn't have been exiled," Tyrona said, placing a hand on Theodore's knee. "Also, where are the knight and the privateer you mentioned?"

"They're down in the slums at The Dark Horse," Theodore replied.

"Really? That shithole? We need to find them. If I am to call a meeting of the high council, I want to make sure I know where everyone is who's involved."

"Wait, what?" Theodore stammered. "You're serious?"

"Of course I am! I don't care what you say, Dorie. You need your powers. I mean, those crows? And all those gods and monsters that you've been fighting? Dorie, you need to be who you are meant to be. And, of course, I'll be joining you all as well."

"What?" Theodore asked as he stood from the couch.

"Oh, do you not approve?" Tyrona asked with a sly smile.

"I-I wasn't expecting you would want to join us."

"After that story, who wouldn't want to join you? Besides, I've spent too many years cooped up in this room. I need to get back out into the world." Tyrona sat up straight, looking serious.

"I'll admit it is quite a liberating feeling," Theodore said, sitting back down on the couch.

"We'd be happy to have you, Tyrona," Ànifa said as she looked into her eyes.

"Thanks," Tyrona said.

"So, are we going to find Cecil and Vesten?" Ànifa asked shooting to her feet.

"Yeah, let's go," Tyrona said, standing up, "Well, not you, Dorie. You should stay here. Ànifa, Dasch, and I should go."

"I see how it is," Theodore replied, crossing his arms. "But I understand. I'll just wait here then."

"Great! If you touch anything, be sure to return it to its proper place," Tyrona instructed.

"Oh, I know, Tyrona."

"And I know you do, Dorie. But you know I gotta say it."

Tyrona pulled a short white wand out of a hidden pocket and waved it at the door, unsealing the magical binding.

Ànifa donned her bonnet once again as she and Dasch followed Tyrona out the door, opposite the way they had arrived.

"Oh, we came from the other way, I thought," Ànifa said as she followed.

"You can tell?" Tyrona said slyly, then continued, "I should have known Dorie would go that way. No wonder it seemed like you had just arrived."

"Yeah, we were wandering around this place for a while," Ànifa said.

"That way is the longest, but it also helps to ensure that you wouldn't be seen. The way we're going is the quickest if you're trying to go into town."

"Is it okay if we're seen?" Ànifa asked.

"Don't worry about it. I'm A-Class, on the cuff of being S-Class. Not that I really want that. S-Class is much too elitist for me. As long as you're with me, no one will ask questions, and if someone does, I'll just tell them off," Tyrona said as her long purple dress flared out behind her.

"This place really is big, isn't it?" Ànifa asked quietly.

"Yes, no one knows its true size," Tyrona replied. "As far as I know, there are places that have never been visited. There are doors that have never been opened. Of course, there are doors that have also been sealed shut, but that's different, even if no one knows what's behind most of those doors anymore.

"This place is absolutely amazing. I love it here. But I've been getting a feeling lately like it's time to leave." Tyrona paused, then continued in a softer tone. "I'll be honest with you two. I don't leave my room very often. Today, though, I felt a strange urge to go outside. Of course, I never made it out. I ran into you all instead. I know it may sound strange, but I feel like Ajenti itself told me to find you."

"I wouldn't doubt it," Dasch grunted.

"Have you been here before?" Tyrona asked.

"Many times," Dasch replied as he looked at the black ceiling. "This place gave me many answers, though it raised many more questions. Most of the time I spent here I was in the Golden Auditorium. I don't know if you've been there before, but it was very thought provoking."

"Oh, I wish I could have seen it," Tyrona said sadly. "It sounded wonderful. You see, soon after this place became a university, the Golden Auditorium was vandalized. A group of witches doused it with dark magic and it's been closed off ever since. That's one of the few stories that has stuck around. That place is simply legendary."

"It was quite spectacular," Dasch replied.

"This place *is* quite spectacular," Ànifa whispered to herself.

Cecil's lips were chapped and crusted with dried blood. He hadn't had a proper drink of water since before he had been thrown into the small jail cell. Vesten sat across from him in another cell, and the cell block was constantly guarded. Any talking resulted in a backhand across the cheek. Vesten had already gotten nearly four of them. He just didn't know when to stop cursing sometimes.

The clanking of keys on his cell door startled him into alertness.

"Welp, your time here is nearly up. It'll be the gallows for the two of ye," the deep-voiced knight said. He was from the Guild of Ajentian Knights. They dealt with all of Ajenti's major security issues. They really were in a tight spot.

"Hey..." Cecil croaked, then cleared his throat. "Don't I get a say in any of this?"

The knight laughed sharply. "And why would you?"

"Because I'm on a holy mission from Eklatros herself! And so is my friend in the cell across from m—" The guard opened the cell door and slapped him across the face. His previously split lip burst open, causing blood to pour down his chin.

"Shut it, or I'll end you right here. I swear to Eklatros. Then we'll see if you're on a holy mission or not, Kloud!" The guard laughed as he stepped back out into the hallway.

"Leave him... alone," Vesten croaked from the cell across from them.

"Oh, you want some now too?" the guard said, slamming Cecil's cell door shut. "Hey, Preston! Get over here and teach this fool a lesson."

When there was no response, the guard tapped his foot in frustration. "Preston! Come over here, now!"

"Hang on a second, boss," a distant voice called back.

"I'll be right back to beat your ass bloody." The guard stormed down the hall, his footsteps echoing and his armor clamoring.

"I wonder what the fuck that was all about," Vesten whispered.

"Hopefully something good for us," Cecil said. "Because if not, we're going to die soon. And there's very little we can do about it at this point."

A few minutes later, the guard who had hit him and another guard he assumed was Preston approached their cells.

"I guess it's your lucky fuckin' day. Who knows, maybe Lady Eklatros is looking out for you after all."

"Ah, I knew it," Cecil sighed. "She couldn't let us die." He was referring to Ànifa, of course, though the guard wasn't aware of it.

"Religious nut-job. Preston, get these two shitheads out of my sight."

The party stood together outside of the jailhouse. The sun was setting, casting long shadowy tendrils from Ajenti's branches across the city.

"I can't believe they arrested you!" Ànifa was shouting. "I thought you said you weren't really in exile."

"Yeah, I thought that was the case at first, but I guess not," Cecil said as he shrugged and strapped on his right shoulder plate. Upon his release, Cecil had received his suit of armor and his battle-axe. Vesten had also gotten all of his gear back, as well as the backpack and most of its contents. Only some of the food was missing, which they could easily replace.

"What I can't believe is that they were going to fuckin' kill me, just for being associated with him," Vesten said.

"This whole situation is quite messed up," Tyrona said. "We must all return to my room within Ajenti."

"I still can't believe you're here. I've heard a lot about you," Cecil said with a sly smile.

"I hope it was all good," Tyrona said, returning his sly smile with her own. "Now, come on, let's hurry back before it gets dark."

Tyrona led them back through the slums toward Ajenti University. The jailhouse was located in one of the most dangerous parts of town, especially at night, so they moved quickly. Once they made it inside, Tyrona efficiently led them back to her room without running into a soul. Ànifa didn't quite understand how, but she was already becoming familiar with the maze. Even though everything looked the same, she mentally cataloged every small variation they passed.

When they opened the door to Tyrona's room, they were

surprised to see Theodore sitting with two other people. They were teenagers—a boy and a girl. The girl had short blond hair that reached her shoulders. She had fair skin that was spotted with an assortment of light-brown freckles. The boy had short brown hair with a vaguely familiar face. They were sitting facing them, while Theodore sat on the couch that faced the opposite wall.

"Eric! Kelso! I wasn't expecting you today," Tyrona exclaimed as she closed the door behind her, binding it shut.

"Actually, we had a lesson planned, Sorceress Knorse," Kelso replied.

"Did we? Oh shoot, it's the seventeenth, isn't it?" Tyrona said, pounding a fist down in the air. "You're right. I got completely distracted. Well, I see you've already met Theodore."

"Yeah, they just barged in. It really surprised me," Theodore said, turning to look at Tyrona.

"They are the only two that know the way past my binding spell," Tyrona said.

"Oh no! Cecil, Vesten! What happened?" Theodore exclaimed once he noticed the bruises and cuts on their faces.

"Well, first, we got slightly drunk at a bar. Then we got the shit beat out of us. Then we got arrested and thrown in jail. And then we were almost hung in the gallows, but our highness Ànifa and our new friend, Tyrona, saved the day," Cecil said, ending in a slight bow.

Theodore stood and walked over to Cecil. "I'm sorry, my friend. I dragged you back here—"

"It's not your fault, Theo," Cecil said as he waved him off. "We're all on the same journey here."

"Fuckin' A!" Vesten chimed in.

Tyrona walked over to the couch where her two students sat.

"Eric, Kelso... I'm sorry to have forgotten about today. It's really unlike me. But as you can see, I've gotten caught up in something. And I'm actually glad that you're here since I do need your help."

"Sure. What do you need us to do?" Kelso asked.

"I need you to take a message to the masters. We need to call together a meeting of the High Council. Theodore must get his full powers back, and Cecil needs to be avenged for how he's been treated."

"Sure, we can do that," Eric said. "But, are you sure? If this backfires—"

"I know. I'll lose a lot of the respect that others have for me and I won't be able to become S-Class. Who gives a damn?" Tyrona shrugged. "I'd happily give that up for something that matters, which is exactly what I'm doing. I know I'm new to all of this, but this does matter. Now, everyone, bear with me while I write up the formal letter."

Tyrona went over to her clean white desk and picked up a piece of parchment and a quill. After a few minutes of writing, she presented the letter to everyone in the room. When she looked up, about to read from it, she noticed a few items around her apartment that had been displaced. She narrowed her eyes, sighed, then held the letter out in front of her and cleared her throat, then dropped her arms down.

"Before I start, I should probably tell you all what's about to happen, since I'm sure most of you aren't aware. What I did was write a letter that, when read out loud, will bind the eight of us together in this pact. After I read it, we all must sign our names to solidify the pact. The signatures will contain magical traces that the masters can use to determine the authenticity of what we are saying. Does everyone agree with these conditions?" Tyrona asked.

There was a murmur of agreement.

"Good. Oh, and one more thing. I needed to use everyone's full names in this letter. However, I don't know Ànifa's or Dasch's full names."

Dasch grunted. "Valentine. I'm Dasch Valentine."

"Oh, okay, let me make that quick amendment," Tyrona said as she stepped back to her desk.

"Oh well... I know my full name too," Ànifa said.

"You do? When did you remember?" Theodore turned to face her.

"Well, it wasn't that I remembered. Kalahsem told me my true name. Princess Ànifa Tataluynnia Ekataramnii."

Cecil burst into laughter, bending down to slap his knee. "I freakin' knew it!"

"Yeah, you were right, somehow," Ànifa shrugged as Cecil continued to laugh heartily.

Theodore glared at Cecil with his arms crossed. "Yes, you were right, but now is not the time to gloat about it."

"Uh, right, sorry Ànifa," Cecil stammered.

Ànifa shook her head. "No, it's okay."

"The amendments have been made," Tyrona said, walking back to the group once again. "My apologies. One of my innate powers is to discern who someone is upon first meeting them. It comes with my ability to manipulate thoughts and memories. For some reason I couldn't fully discern your names."

"It's okay, I mean, neither of us are human," Ànifa said.

"True," Tyrona said, raising her eyebrows and nodding her head. "I've never used my power on an elf before. I hadn't considered that. Well, here we go, then." Tyrona cleared her throat and held the letter with both hands.

To the High Council of Ajenti -

Heed my plea. It is I, the A-Class Sorceress Tyrona Claire Knorse, who writes to you this day of Ektember the seventeenth of the year eight thousand eight hundred eighty.

I have discovered information of the utmost importance. The exiled B-Class Sorcerer, Theodore Henry Caldwell; and the banished knight, Sir Cecil Johnathan Kloud of the Guild of Exemplary Knights, have returned to Ajenti. They are accompanied by a privateer named Vesten James Teixeira, a half-elf named Dasch Valentine, and a true elf—Princess Ànifa Tataluynnia Ekataramnii.

Also in witness to this testimony are my students, Eric Franklin Mason and Kelso Mackenzie Spinner.

What I write is the truth. The elves have returned at this dire time of need. Eklatros is suffering. Ànifa and her party are the only ones who can stop this suffering.

In order for them to complete their quest, I urge you to restore Sorcerer Theodore Henry Caldwell's full powers and reinstate Sir Cecil Johnathan Kloud into the Guild of Exemplary Knights. Their statuses must be restored for the sake of our planet.

Look inside yourselves and know this to be true.

Please, call together a meeting of the High Council and we will share our story with you.

Please heed my request. Our request is Eklatros' request.

Tyrona took a deep breath. "Now, we must all sign." She took the quill, dipped it in ink, and signed her name. She handed the quill to Ànifa. "You next. It'll carry more weight. Then Dasch, then Theodore, then Cecil, then Vesten, then Eric, and finally Kelso, in that order."

"Alright," Ànifa said, as she took the quill, signed her name, and handed it to Dasch.

After everyone signed, Ànifa glanced at it and noticed one of the names.

"Eric Mason? Are you related to Christian Mason?" Ànifa asked.

"Yes, he's my uncle," Eric said.

"Huh, that seems significant," Ànifa said.

"Indeed, it is," Tyrona said with a smile. "When you were talking about Sage Mason earlier, I knew then that it wasn't just chance that I was assigned Eric Mason as my pupil. As it is said, everything happens for a reason."

"Agreed," Ànifa replied.

Tyrona took the letter, placed it in an envelope, and sealed it with wax. She handed the letter to Eric, causing Ànifa to remember that she needed to send a message to Dante. She wrote a quick note, telling Dante they had found Charlotte and gotten her to safety. After that, Eric and Kelso headed out to deliver the messages.

At this point, it was nearly midnight. The day had gotten away from them.

Tyrona explained that they would get an answer sometime within the next few days, and then it might be a few days before they could actually meet with the council. In other words, they were going to be here for a little while, and she wanted to make sure they were all comfortable.

Tyrona led them down the hallway she had noticed earlier to four small spare bedrooms. Ànifa took the last bedroom, allowing her and Tyrona to have a word in private.

"So tell me, Tyrona. This place, Ajenti, how well do you understand it?" Ànifa asked as she sat on the bed. Tyrona sat next to her.

"That's a deep question from someone who just arrived here earlier today. In which case, I'll simply throw the question right back at you," Tyrona said.

"Well, when I was walking through the halls and stairwells, I was flooded with stories about this place, about its residents. At first, I thought it was all random... but I now understand what Ajenti was trying to tell me—that even though everything looks the same, nothing is the same. And it is those minor blemishes that can tell you where you are in this labyrinth."

"Impressive," Tyrona said with a nod. "It takes most of us years to figure that out. Of course, you're not a regular person, are you? I mean, you're not even a regular elf. So, I shouldn't be surprised.

"Now, to answer your question. I know a lot about this place, a lot about its history, and a lot about how its inherent magical energy works. But it's not anything I can explain to you now.

"However, your name. Beyond the fact that you are royalty, your name proves you are meant for more than a typical elf is capable of. Ekataramnii means you are a true child of this planet. According to the ancient records, the Ekataramnii were the names of the elvish dynasty back in Dasch's era. I saw it on his face when you said your name—he definitely recognized it, too," Tyrona explained.

"But what does it actually mean?" Ànifa asked. "I may know my name, but it sounds like you and Dasch know more about my family history than I do."

"Well, if they make you wait a while to see the High Council, you will have some time to read up on it. I have many books in my personal library that I can show you tomorrow. Now, go to bed, dearie. We'll talk then." Tyrona placed a hand on her knee for a moment, then stood and stretched.

"How do you think Charlotte is doing?" Ànifa asked.

"She's in good hands. I'm sure we'll hear about her condition at the meeting. We must be patient until then."

"I understand."

Ànifa nodded goodnight as Tyrona closed the door behind her. The small bedroom only had a bed, a dresser, and a desk with a chair. It was furnished similarly to Tyrona's apartment—black walls, white furniture, pink and purple embellishments.

This place... I still can't get over it, she thought. Its magical energy is so familiar, yet nothing like I've ever felt before. Kalahsem and even Yttendaus, from what I remember, felt similar to this, but just inherently different. This place feels older, and much more powerful. It's almost as if this place is the birthplace of the Ekataramn... and maybe even Eklatros herself.

And if what Tyrona says about my name is true, then I can only guess she must know more about me. I hope we can stay here for a few days so I can learn as much as I can. At the same time, we cannot linger here for long. We must keep moving. Knowledge is tempting, but we must not lose focus.

I'm glad Tyrona has joined us. We could use some help for what's to come; I can feel it. Plus, it'll be nice to have another woman around. Not that I've really minded being around everyone... they are loyal friends.

Now, I really must be going off to sleep. And let's see what happens. I mean, I think I'm done taking those mushrooms, anyway. Let's see if I can dream about anything related to this place. Ajenti, tell me more about you.

22

BATTLE FOR REDEMPTION

The next morning, Eric and Kelso returned with the reply. It turned out the High Council was extremely eager to meet with them. They scheduled the meeting for tomorrow afternoon. While that was excellent news, since they could get on their way again sooner, Ànifa was slightly disappointed. She knew it was selfish, but she hungered for knowledge.

Last night, she had dreamt for the first time since the night before Kalahsem. That had been nearly five days ago. And while the dream itself didn't tell her much, it was a dream, which felt like a huge win.

She didn't remember much, but she remembered being in a forest. She had been with other people, people that she was close to. It felt as if they were hunting together, fully trusting each other in their hunt. What she had been hunting, she didn't remember, but it was the feeling of security in that circle of people that she remembered the most.

It was the same feeling she had when she traveled with her companions now. Yet, it had felt as if the bond in her dream had been stronger, much more established.

After a quick breakfast with the others, Ànifa asked Tyrona to show her the books she had mentioned the night prior. There were quite a few, so she picked two of them that Tyrona highly recommend. She also found a book on the history of Ajenti and a book on the history of Roffen, and took all four books back to her room.

She read for the rest of the day, ignoring everything else. As Dasch had said, Ajenti was once called Cascagrada, although even that name wasn't original—its original name was currently lost to history, or so the book claimed. About three hundred years after the Great War, as this book called it, the structure was repurposed. Under the name Cascagrada, it had been a cathedral—the holiest place of worship on all of Eklatros. After the war, religion changed. People grew less interested in mass worship and started following more personal beliefs and rituals. Cascagrada fell to the wayside.

Before Ànifa could finish the passage, Theodore burst into the room and dragged her to dinner. As soon as she finished eating, she excused herself and returned to reading.

Cascagrada desperately needed a change. That was when a man named Mirke Ajenti converted the cathedral into a university for the magical arts and changed its name to Ajenti. For a time, the university flourished. And it had been a real university, full of professors, instructors, and students.

Ànifa had asked Tyrona about this later that night, and she told her Ajenti was deteriorating. Tyrona explained she and Theodore had been part of one of the last true classes. Shortly after they graduated, the admissions nearly stopped, forcing the university to change. And so, they decided that in order for people to continue to live in Ajenti, they had to have students when there were students to be had. Yet, even those rules had fallen to the wayside. Tyrona guessed that there were a little over four hundred people that called Ajenti their permanent home, but there were only approximately sixty students and most were in pairs, like her two students.

Ànifa asked if Theodore had had any students. Tyrona said he had a single student before he was exiled, and that student was now under the tutelage of Theodore's brother, Cedric. Ànifa hadn't known Theodore had a brother.

Before she could dwell on it for long, though, Tyrona added that she felt as if Ajenti was going to go through a major change again soon. The state of the world now indicated how poorly prepared they were. Three towns should not have lost so swiftly. Even the knights, of which there were thousands, were wholly unprepared. That was another reason Tyrona wanted to travel with them—she wanted to do all she could to help save not only Ajenti, but the planet as well.

After she talked with Tyrona, Ànifa returned to her room and read up on her family. She recognized some names from the Eklatros history book, yet the book she read expanded on them profoundly. While she knew she should only take the information with a grain of salt, it truly captivated her. She learned much about the Ekataramnii dynasty that night and discovered that good deeds accompanied bad ones. Some family members were pious individuals that wanted equality for everyone. Other family members wanted only to make the elf race stronger by enslaving humans.

Her family was ancient, as old as time itself. And the more she learned, the sadder she grew. When she finished the book, she closed it softly and shook her head. She had to remind herself that the book was authored by a human, and much could have been altered. If she was going to learn anything about her family, she wanted to do it the right way, not from an old history book.

"Welcome back, Ànifa."

"Gnusaramnii... you're the one that's back, not me. We are talking within my mind, right?"

"Indeed, we are. I see you have learned a lot since we last spoke like this. A lot about Eklatros and a lot about yourself."

"Yes, I have. Does that scare you? Is that why you're back now, to taunt me?"

"No, I wanted to remind you of something... something that used to be a core part of who you were."

"Yeah, and what is that? The knowledge of who I really am?"

"You never knew your true identity, and you still do not. No one can tell you that. You must find that out on your own. No, Ànifa, what I speak of now is your ability to discern fact from fiction. I see you struggling with that now... you want to believe some things that are false, and you scorn things that are true because you do not fully agree. Everything you read today has been important knowledge, yet you cannot decipher what it means."

"I really don't understand you, Gnusaramnii. First, you try to kill me. Now you are giving me advice? Helping me be who you want me to be? Nothing you do makes sense."

"My actions have always been necessary. This, too, is necessary."

"Whatever. I mean, I know you're probably right, but that's the thing. Why do you always have to be right? Why can't I simply think my own thoughts, without them being read by you, or whoever else might be in my head?"

"You wish for freedom, and that you cannot have. You will understand in time."

They spent the next day getting ready for the meeting with the High Council. Ànifa didn't have much of a chance to dwell upon her conversation with Gnusaramnii, but she didn't really want to. This meeting was important—right now, it was all that mattered. The hunger for knowledge she felt the day before was sufficiently satisfied.

Yesterday, when she had been reading, Theodore had slipped back to his old room to grab a change of clothes. He looked rather dashing in his clean navy-blue cloak. On the back of the cloak were symbols that represented the various elements. The hat he wore was slightly smaller than the previous one but was firmer and more pointed at the top. Overall, it was a similar look, but much cleaner. He had also grabbed fresh robes for Dasch that were similar in color to the robes Sage Mason had lent him—dark green. Small pockets lined the inside of the cloak, allowing Dasch to store even more hidden rocks and daggers.

Cecil and Vesten, both of whom were covered in bruises, decided to display their wounds proudly. Tyrona had offered to cast a quick spell to cover up their bruises, but they refused. They thought it might help their case if the high council could see what they had gone through. Instead, Cecil had spent the morning meticulously cleaning his armor, wiping away every spot of dirt and grime. This prompted Tyrona to wash all of their clothes, which made them look much more presentable.

They held their heads proudly as they made their way through the maze-like halls and stairways of Ajenti. It didn't take them long to reach a large set of double doors—the first set of doors Ànifa had seen like it in the entire place.

Ànifa placed a hand on the door, but Tyrona stopped her.

"We're a few minutes early. Besides, we have to wait for Eric and Kelso. They should be here anytime now," Tyrona said.

"Holy Eklatros, I'm nervous," Cecil said as he bounced from one foot to the other.

Theodore crossed his arms and nervously tapped his right foot. "I am as well. I don't want to get my hopes up, but the thought of getting my full powers back is exhilarating."

"You'll be fine," Tyrona said, gently placing a hand on his shoulder. "Besides, why else would they have fast-tracked the meeting like this? It's quite unheard of."

"I think it will go well also," Ànifa said. "Plus, I would really like to see you two reclaim what was taken."

"That's partly why I'm nervous," Cecil said. "I don't know if I'm ready to be back in with that guild."

"Well, maybe you can switch guilds then," Ànifa suggested.

"That's not how it works," Cecil said. "But I think I would if I could at this point."

Tyrona shrugged. "I'd say it's at least worth a shot if the opportunity arises. Go for it."

"Fuck yeah, man. I agree," Vesten said with a grin.

A moment later, Eric and Kelso joined them outside the council chamber.

"Alright, is everyone ready?" Tyrona asked. Without waiting for a response, she raised the large knocker on the right-hand door and knocked three times, then pushed open the set of double doors and strolled through.

Ànifa followed her in, with the others following behind. They entered a large room with gray stone floors—the first difference in architecture she had witnessed since wandering Ajenti's black halls. Surrounding the open area were dark-brown wood walls. Sitting in raised chairs above the walls were six people. They stared at the group as they entered.

The door slammed shut behind them and latched loudly. There was nowhere they could go—they were forced to stand in the middle of the open area and crane their necks up to see the masters.

Sitting in the center was an elderly woman, dressed regally in lush crimson robes. On her right were two men, one dressed in black robes, the other in blue robes. The man in the black robes was frail and had a long white beard, while the man in the blue robes was middle-aged and sported a wide black handlebar mustache. Sitting to the left of the regal woman were the remaining three masters, the closest of which wore orange robes. He had a scornful look plastered on his face. Next to him was a muscular man in brown robes with thick brown sideburns and a young woman with light auburn hair and a fair complexion who wore dark green robes.

"Welcome, Tyrona Claire Knorse, and thank you for your request. We have heeded it well," the woman wearing the crimson robes said in a loud, clear, and commanding voice. "Welcome, Princess Ànifa Tataluynnia Ekataramnii of the elves. Welcome, half-elf Dasch Valentine. Welcome, Theodore Henry Caldwell. Welcome, Cecil Johnathan Kloud. Welcome, Vesten James Teixeira. And finally, thank you, Eric Franklin Mason and Kelso Mackenzie Spinner, for bearing witness here today.

"Presiding over you today is I, Headmaster Giovanna Kalherd Glauss Barrow. To my right are Grand Master Kyle Chinn and

Speech Master Elbert Fritta. To my left are Spell Master Jamm Prander, Scout Master Murdock Everhart, and Medicine Master Kaila Gomez.

"The five-hundred-and-third meeting of the High Council shall now commence.

"Please, tell your tale, and tell it truly. We'll start in the order established in the letter. Each of you will say your piece. Tell us about the journey you have been on, and your role in it.

"Princess Ànifa, please begin."

Ànifa stepped forward and cleared her throat. She took off her bonnet, exposing her ears and hair, which was currently a light baby blue with dark navy swirls. Gasps filled the room, and she took a deep breath to calm her rising nerves.

She began her tale by explaining how Charlotte had saved her. With great detail, she told them of all her experiences until this point, including her strange dreams about Professor Navacus Clums. The only thing that she did not disclose was her connection to Gnusaramnii.

When she finished, Dasch stepped forward. He began with his relationship with Kieth Mason. He told them how he and his troops had hunkered down in the Golden Auditorium, and how after three nights of nonstop barrages, he led the counterattack and cut down the enemy as they took advantage of the blinding sun. From there, Dasch explained his disagreement with Kieth and how he lived in darkness for many lifetimes as he fought to control the parasite inside of him. Dasch continued from there, telling his side of the events.

Next, Theodore told his tale, starting from when he was exiled. He nearly stopped after he explained how he met Ànifa until a prompt from Headmaster Barrow made him continue. He then told the rest from his perspective.

After that, Cecil went, followed by Vesten.

Then, by request, Tyrona explained how she met them yesterday. She included what had happened to Selma, saying she agreed with Theodore that it was necessary.

Once they finished, the high council's chairs silently slid away into an unseen room.

No one spoke. The silence that hung over them was commanding them not to speak. Ànifa didn't know how long they waited—time itself seemed to be suspended.

When the masters finally reemerged, Grand Master Chinn, the frail, bearded man with black robes, spoke first.

"Theodore. You know full well why you were exiled. And part of being in exile is ceasing the search for knowledge. Your academic days were supposed to be over. And yet, you continued your search and have found yourself in the middle of a quest that you have no right to be a part of.

"Even after taking all that has been said into consideration, I cannot grant you your full powers. Nor can I grant the knight his guildship. My vote is nay."

Next, Spell Master Prander spoke. "Theodore, as you know, I was the one who cast you into exile. It was one of my books you stole—a book you did not have access to as a B-Class Sorcerer. Not only did you engage in theft, but also in trespassing.

"I heard your story, and I weighed it out. I cannot in good faith grant you your full powers. My vote is nay."

Speech Master Fritta spoke next. "Theodore, Cecil, Ànifa, Tyrona... everyone. I welcome you all to this hall in the most ancient and holy of places. I heed your words, and I heed them well.

"Theodore, I know that we have had our differences. And you know what rules you broke and why you received the punishment you did. And yet, I can only believe that was all part of the grand vision of Eklatros. Ànifa, you standing here right now is all the proof I need to know that what you speak of is the truth. There is a great evil descending upon us all, and I believe in you and in your comrades. I can only agree with Sorceress Tyrona.

"Theodore must have his full powers restored, and Cecil must reclaim his guildship. My vote is aye."

It was Scout Master Everhart's turn to speak. "As my title states, I am the Scout Master. It is my duty to keep the area around Ajenti safe from bandits and thieves. Lately, my duties have included monster tracking and slaying. I have lost many good scouts to these foul beasts.

"And yet here you all stand before us now. All of you, raw and untrained in your own ways, are stronger together than any force I could ever muster.

"There is only one obvious answer here. We must trust our lives, the fate of Eklatros herself, to you all.

"Besides, an elf leads you—a true elf. If I could, I would follow you on your journey, but my post is here, protecting Ajenti. My vote is aye."

The young woman in the green robes, Medicine Master Gomez, spoke. "I must begin by thanking you, Tyrona. If you did not get Charlotte to us when you did, we may not have been able to help her. She was very far gone, but we were just in time, even considering my initial opposition. Charlotte is recovering well. She still has not awoken, but this morning my assistants noticed her stirring in her sleep. This is a good sign. She is now struggling to wake, which means she is slowly regaining control of herself.

"Her case was much like yours, Dasch Valentine, although, I can only presume her dosage to be nearly tenfold. It is a pure miracle that she survived. My healers are doing everything they can to remove the monstrous entity that has taken root deep inside her.

"Ànifa, I cannot thank you enough, for I believe it was because of your presence, your soul itself, that she kept up her strength for so long. If you did not rescue Charlotte when you did—if you did not bring her to me when you did—she would be lost to us all.

"I tell you this now because I want everyone in this room to understand the gravity of the situation. These are dark times, the darkest since your era, Dasch, which is why I believe you were brought here to this time to aid us now in our fight.

"We need all the help we can get. I have mended many of Scout Master Everhart's scouts. Many of the survivors are crippled, both physically and mentally.

"We cannot handle these monsters alone. Your journey to awaken the Ekataramn is truly essential in our fight. I believe it in my soul that you are our saviors. If you cannot do this, no one can. Theodore Henry Caldwell and Cecil Johnathan Kloud must be redeemed. My vote is aye."

A few moments of silence hung in the air before Headmaster Barrow spoke. "Everyone, I cannot thank you enough for being here today. And your timing on this matter is perfect, for we are all—minus Master Everhart and Master Gomez—headed to the world summit in the next few days.

"The news you have delivered to us today is highly essential. What you are all doing is highly essential. I will relay the stories you told us today to the world summit. As Master Gomez said, these truly are dark times. Before I received Tyrona's letter, I did not have hope. Now my hope has been restored. I believe once again that Eklatros can make it through this. We can all make it through this.

"I only wish the circumstances of this meeting were different. It should be us coming to you for aid, not the other way around. I am truly humbled today by every one of you. I may be Headmaster of Ajenti, but I am in awe of what you have accomplished together.

"Theodore, I deeply apologize for what we have done to you. Your plea for your powers to be returned has been accepted.

"Please know that what is about to happen has never been attempted. Never before has an individual stripped of their power been given it back. And so, I cannot predict what will happen. It is possible that you will remain handicapped for the rest of your life. Or, it is possible that by returning these powers to you, you will become stronger.

"That said, I believe this is essential to our survival.

"After this meeting has ended, please go to your quarters and wait for our call. This is something you must do alone.

"As for you, Sir Kloud, granting your guildship back will be much simpler. I believe you were in the Guild of Exemplary Knights. Do you wish to remain in this Guild?"

Cecil cleared his throat before he spoke. "Um, no, Headmaster. I do not wish to be a part of that guild any longer."

"Then what guild do you wish to be a part of? I am sure Scout Master Everhart would gladly accept you into his guild, the Guild of Ajentian Knights."

"Actually, I had a bad run-in with them recently. They were the ones that nearly executed me a few days ago," Cecil replied.

"I feared that was the case," Scout Master Everhart said. "I will discover who did this to you and reprimand them accordingly."

"So, speak. What guild would you like to be a part of?" the headmaster prompted.

"I was actually thinking that I could start my own guild. As I was thinking about this, I realized that the reason I was a bad knight was that I didn't relate to any of the guilds. I wanted to be knight... but none felt right. I honestly only chose the Guild of Exemplary Knights because of their name."

"And what would be the name of your newly proposed guild, Sir Cecil Kloud?" Headmaster Barrow asked.

Cecil hummed to himself for a moment. "I was thinking that it could be the Guild for Eklatros. Not the Guild of Eklatros' Knights—simply the Guild for Eklatros. We would be the protectors of Eklatros herself. We would go where we are needed and fight the true, honest fight for the planet."

"I see. And what does this entail, the 'true, honest fight for the planet?'" Headmaster Barrow asked.

"We would do right by the planet. If there were no disputes to settle, we would help where we could. Perhaps a farmer in Sathon needs a hand tilling his fields. He could call upon us. Perhaps a miller needs a hand with her flour delivery. She could call upon us. No matter would be too small. No problem too big. We would help with everything that we could."

"What say you all?"

A chorus of voices spoke out at once. Unsurprisingly, everyone voted the same as they did previously.

"Granted. You are henceforth the guildmaster of the Guild for Eklatros. When you return from your journey, we will begin the enlisting process."

"Actually, may that start now? This is not something that should wait for me, as I may never return. If there needs to be a guildmaster in Ajenti, let Scout Master Everhart take the role. Of course, only if he wishes to take on another guild."

"I cannot accept," Scout Master Everhart said with a shake of his head. "No matter where you are, you are the guildmaster, Sir Cecil Kloud."

"Alright," Cecil nodded.

"I can assist you, though," Scout Master Everhart continued. "I shall speak with my guild members and see which ones would like to join your cause. I cannot say that the other guildmasters will do the same, though."

"That's fine. As long as word gets out, I'm sure there are those who will flock to it," Cecil said. "Thank you, Headmaster Barrow, and thank you, Scout Master Everhart, for granting me my requests today."

"It is our pleasure," the headmaster said. "After our meeting concludes, have Eric take you to the tailor and blacksmith. We'll get you a proper suit of armor."

"I want to join your guild," Medicine Master Gomez said suddenly.

Cecil laughed. "Of course! This guild is not meant only for knights. A guild needs more than knights. It needs academics and healers, sorcerers and farmers. It needs all types of people to truly be a representation of Eklatros."

"That is true. I shall allow this as well. It's time we finally got back to the original guilds' roots," Headmaster Barrow said. "Are there any other matters to discuss?"

"I have one more thing," Cecil said. "My brother-in-law, Rear Admiral Brigsby Mont Simmons, helped us get here. I would like to grant him and my sister membership into my new guild, and I would like them to know that the resources that my guild has are theirs to utilize as well. Oh, and Eric and Kelso should join too."

"Granted. We shall send word to your family. We will perform the ceremony to allow Eric, Kelso, Scout Master Everhart, and Medicine

Master Gomez into your guild after this, as well as your comrades, and anyone else here who wishes to join."

"I truly appreciate it," Cecil said with a bow.

"Is there anything else?" the headmaster asked again.

The silence that followed answered the question.

"Then it is settled. Theodore Henry Caldwell will reclaim his powers and will henceforth be promoted to S-Class. We will also promote Sorceress Tyrona Claire Knorse to S-Class. Guildmaster Cecil Johnathan Kloud will need to be given a seal, and then all those who will now join the Guild for Eklatros shall be officially admitted.

"I thank everyone for their presence here today. This meeting is now concluded. Now, those who will *not* join the Guild for Eklatros, please leave the room."

Spell Master Prander and Grand Master Chinn stood up and left the room. Before he left, Spell Master Prander shot Cecil a cold look.

"Now, everyone, please feel free to be less formal than before. Sir Kloud, can you describe your seal?" Headmaster Barrow asked.

Cecil looked up at the ceiling and rubbed his chin as he thought for a moment. "Well, if the Ajentian Knights are already using Ajenti as their image... Yttendaus. I want my seal to show the floating island of Yttendaus, for that is where Ànifa is from, and that is where our journey will lead us in the end."

"Then it shall be so," Headmaster Barrow said.

She took out a large stamp from within her red robes and held it in her hand. A bright light shone, transforming the stamp into the official seal for the Guild for Eklatros. She pulled out some paper and used magic to inscribe each sheet with the official messaging that would allow those present to join Cecil's new guild.

"Now please, each of you sign your copy," Headmaster Barrow said, using her magic to send everyone in the room a copy of the document and a quill readied with ink.

After everyone signed, the headmaster sent them all to Cecil, where he signed his name on the indicated line. Finally, Headmaster Barrow took the papers back and signed her name onto all of them.

She sent the documents back to Cecil, along with the newly created seal, and Cecil stamped them all.

On this day, the Guild for Eklatros was officially born.

Ànifa settled into Tyrona's comfy purple couch, with Vesten and Dasch sitting next to her. Tyrona and Kelso sat across from them. They chatted while they waited for the others to return. Eric had taken Cecil to the tailor, and they were going straight to the blacksmith once they finished. As for Theodore, it would take all night for his powers to be restored.

Even though Tyrona seemed at ease, laughing at something Vesten said, Ànifa could sense how tense she was. Ànifa was also nervous—she sent Theodore her loving thoughts. Somehow, she felt as if Ajenti would carry her feelings to him. Perhaps that's why Tyrona seemed so calm—maybe she could feel Theodore's presence through Ajenti as well.

When Cecil and Eric returned, Cecil showed off his brand-new armor. Since his previous armor hadn't been made to fit his frame, it had breaks between the sections that had left him exposed. This new armor covered him from head to toe. It shone brilliantly against the dark black walls, making him look regal. His new helmet even had a small catch to prevent his hair from falling into his eyes. Sprouting from the top was a rainbow-colored plume.

Cecil went on to explain that the forge his armor was made in still contains traces of ancient magic, which is how it was forged so quickly.

Along with his new armor, Ànifa congratulated Cecil on starting a brand-new guild. When she asked him how he had thought it up, he had said, "Truth be told, I have never been inside the Ajenti University before, but once I entered, I started realizing that everything I knew about Ajenti was just... wrong. My experience in jail and almost getting executed helped spur these thoughts, and I realized that the whole structure of the guild system is flawed. Why are guilds only for knights? Guilds should be for everyone. Everyone should have a way to feel empowered and to make real change, and to do that, there needs to be a support system in place. Thus, The Guild for Eklatros."

Now that they were all guild members, and founding guild members at that, they had access to reserves of supplies and caches of information that would have been inaccessible before. Plus, with Theodore and Tyrona now S-Class, they could go wherever they wanted inside of Ajenti. In order to display their rank, they were each given a silver necklace with the S-Class seal.

Tyrona displayed hers proudly. Even though she had said only a few days ago that she cared little about it, Ànifa could see the pure joy on her face.

Before bed, Ànifa lost herself in a simple book of fairy tales that she had taken from Tyrona's bookshelf. The stories were simple and fun, yet behind the brave knight and the damsel in distress were some ominous tones. She went to sleep conflicted, deciding to take a bite from the shuyukuii mushrooms to settle her thoughts.

Today was truly an amazing day, she thought. *So much good happened. Theodore is getting his powers back, and he is now an S-Class Sorcerer. Tyrona is also now S-Class, and Cecil created a brand-new guild. Our quest has been approved by the Ajentian masters, and they have shown us an amazing amount of generosity.*

And yet I wasn't able to tell my full story, as truthfully as I should have. I haven't even told Tyrona about Gnusaramnii yet.

Damn you, Gnusaramnii. I don't want you in my head any longer. Even throughout the meeting today, even throughout tonight's celebration, I felt you lingering in the corners of my mind.

I promise you, Gnusaramnii, Theodore will regain his powers. And with him, Tyrona, and everyone else, we will come for you, and we will defeat you once and for all.

23

BATTLE FOR REUNIONS

They were up early the next morning, eager to get on their way. Now that they had accomplished what they had to do in Ajenti, there was little keeping them there.

When Tyrona was about to send Eric to check on Theodore, they heard a knock at her door. Tyrona unsealed and opened the door to find an exuberant Theodore.

"Good day, my friends! How are all of you this fine morning? Splendid!" Theodore exclaimed, after seeing everyone smiling at him.

"Dorie!" Tyrona cried as she threw her arms around him. After a few seconds, she stepped back to get a better look at him. "You look well today yourself."

Cecil approached Theodore and placed a hand on his shoulder. "It's good to see you again, Theo."

"It's good to see you again as well. I see your new armor fits you nicely," Theodore said. In response, Cecil stood akimbo and looked at the ceiling, beaming.

"Thank you, everyone," Theodore continued. "I must say, I feel better than I have in a long time. Although, I suppose part of it could be the herbs Master Gomez gave me after the procedure."

"What happened? If you don't mind us asking, of course," Ànifa asked.

"Not at all. It was excruciatingly painful for a little while. During that time, I don't remember much. But that's pretty much irrelevant now," Theodore said as he waved a hand in dismissal. He walked into the center of the room and continued. "Essentially, they had me in a small room, strapped to a wooden table with a stone base. Surrounding the table was a moat of water. Torches lined the walls and there was a constant breeze. Finally, the room was surrounded by an electric barrier. See, I am an elemental wizard, which means I manipulate the elements. So, by having the stone, wood, wind, water, fire, and electricity in the room with me, I was in the presence of the major elements of this world.

"When they took my powers from me... well, suffice it to say, I was not able to reclaim those same powers. It's not like they kept them in a bottle. After they stripped me of my powers, they were gone, returned to the planet. So, to return my powers back into my body, I had to be inundated by the elements themselves, but not directly, for that would kill me. It was the essence of these elements—some could even say the soul of the elements themselves—that I needed to regain what I had lost.

"Once again, it's not the same power as before. It's still a bit confusing to me. I don't think that my innate abilities have been altered, but the source of what I draw from now is different from it was before. I think I'm stronger now than ever before. So, I want to test my powers, and in order to do that, we need to find some monsters to fight. Is everyone ready?"

"Yes, I believe we are," Ànifa nodded. "We just finished repacking the backpack, with some special help from Tyrona."

Tyrona smiled and laughed. "It really wasn't much. I simply made it more efficient and easier to carry."

"Oh, I see," Theodore nodded knowingly. "You used your magic to turn it into a magical pack that can carry a nearly unlimited number of items, didn't you?"

"You know it, Dorie," Tyrona said with a wink. "It's also essentially weightless, and it can shrink down really small."

"Yeah, it fits right into one of my pockets," Ànifa said as she patted her trenchdress, "which is good news, because now Vesten won't need to be the one to carry it anymore."

"Oh, I didn't really mind it, you know. But I don't mind not having to fuckin' carry it anymore either," Vesten said.

"Yeah, it'll be really nice this way. Before we leave, I want to make one stop," Ànifa said.

"What do you need?" Theodore asked.

"Arrows. I am nearly out, and Vesten and Dasch need to replenish the daggers they lost on our race across Gallheim. With our upgraded backpack, we can even carry extra ammunition."

"Ah, good point. I know of a good armory we can go to. Plus, now that we're S-Class, we may get an extra discount," Theodore said.

"That would be great," Cecil said. "The headmaster said that as a new guildmaster, I get access to the stocks as well, but it would depend on who's guarding the military stocks today."

"Follow me, then," Theodore said, waving them toward the door.

"Take care of yourselves," Tyrona said to Eric and Kelso. "Remember to lock this place up tight when you leave."

"Take care, Sorceress Knorse," Eric and Kelso replied.

As they left Tyrona's room, Ànifa took one last look around and smiled to herself. She had enjoyed her time in Ajenti. This place was special to her. She knew that if all went well, she would return here after everything was settled. There was much that she wanted to learn and experience here, but they had a mission to accomplish. She tapped Tyrona's shoulder, who was also taking a long last look at her apartment.

As they headed down the wide staircase that led out of the university, they ran into Cedric, Theodore's brother. Cedric was slightly taller than Theodore and was completely clean-shaven. He wore dark gray robes with a small black academic cap.

The two brothers said little to each other; they simply gave each other their warm regards. Theodore spoke to his previous student more than he did with his brother, but Ànifa could tell that Cedric didn't mind. It seemed as if the two brothers had an understanding between them that could only be shared between brothers.

Once they were outside Ajenti University and on the streets of the town, Theodore headed toward the armory he had mentioned.

Ànifa still wasn't quite used to the sheer number of people yet, but she felt surprisingly calm. The crowds were dense around the university but thinned out once they began winding through the streets and back alleys.

"We're getting close now," Theodore said as they turned a corner. Vesten, who had been walking in front of Ànifa, stopped suddenly, causing her to bump into him.

"Vesten, what's the hold up?" Ànifa asked, rubbing her nose.

"Holy fucking shit. I think that's her," Vesten said, staring at a woman wearing dirty clothes as she hurriedly made her way down the street they were about to turn off from.

"Who is it?" Ànifa asked.

"It's Patsy. It's fuckin' Patsy!" Vesten said as he chased after her.

"Hey, Vesten, wait!" Theodore called after him.

"Theodore, let's follow him. The armory can wait. Come on, everyone," Ànifa said, running after Vesten.

Ànifa caught up to Vesten when he caught up to his target. He slapped his hand on her right shoulder and crouched back in time to dodge a punch from the woman.

"Who the fuck do you—"

"Patsy!" Vesten broke out into laugher as he stood and faced her.

"Holy shit! Vesten!" Patsy was exuberant as she threw herself into his arms.

Ànifa smiled, and tears welled in her eyes. She couldn't believe Vesten had found his cousin. As she watched them, she looked Patsy over. She had long unkempt mahogany hair full of tangles and frizzles. She wore light-brown baggy pants with a light-gray shawl and a plain-white shirt underneath. Her ivory skin was covered in small red freckles that perfectly accented her beautiful green eyes.

When Patsy broke away from Vesten, her gaze met Ànifa's, then scanned the rest of them. Her face grew suddenly downcast.

"Oh... shit. Shit. Fucking shit. Shit," Patsy repeated.

"Stop saying shit, cousin. What is it?" Vesten asked.

"Are they with you?" Patsy asked.

"Aye," Vesten nodded. "You wouldn't believe—"

"Shut it. Come with me, now," Patsy commanded. "Hurry!"

"Um, shit, okay," Vesten replied. Patsy turned and began walking fast, going in the same direction she'd been headed before. Vesten glanced back at the group quickly, then followed her.

Ànifa shrugged. "Well, I guess this is happening."

They followed Patsy into an alley, then down a wooden staircase and through a basement door. A large, bronze-skinned, muscular man latched each of the door's seven padlocks.

"What is this place?" Vesten panted.

Patsy had brought them to a wide-open room. The floor was scattered with an assortment of couches and tables. The wood-paneled walls had missing slats, exposing the dirt underneath. Across from where she stood, there was a door guarded by a tone woman. Her brunette hair was tied in a bun, and she wore denim overalls with a green shirt underneath.

"Welcome, dear cousin, to my sanctuary," Patsy said.

"Don't you mean *our* sanctuary, boss? Why did you bring these people here? You told us this morning that we were to avoid them at all costs if we were to see them," the large man who had bolted the door shut said as he stomped over to them, his brow furrowed.

"Yes, Money, I did, but that was before I learned my bone-headed cousin was one of them."

"So, what in the actual fuck is going on?" Vesten asked. "I'm excited to see you again, Patsy, but I think we're all very fuckin' confused here."

"Right," Patsy nodded. "Word around the slums is that there is going to be a big fight. Some asshole named Danai has it out bad for a group of people perfectly matching your description. He's planning something big—he plans on crushing you guys."

"Danai? Who could that be?" Cecil asked.

"I think he's from the pirate ship I decimated," Ànifa said, her eyes downcast. "I killed many people that day. I suppose it only makes sense that one of the survivors is seeking revenge."

"Oh, those guys," Cecil said. "He's really tenacious for a pirate."

"You don't know pirates very fuckin' well, then," Vesten said. "Once a pirate has their eye on a prize, they don't know how to quit. In this case, the prize is us."

"You? A pirate? Eh, I guess I could see it, actually," Patsy said. "You still look weak to me, though. For a pirate."

"Fuck you," Vesten shot back with a smile. "I'm no pirate, not anymore."

"Well, I'm glad you ran into me, cousin," Patsy said, pulling Vesten in for another quick hug. "What I told my crew this morning was true at the time. But now it's personal. It sounds like Danai is putting together a huge gang. He's hitting all the underground hubs. Last we heard, he's got pirates, smugglers, bandits, gamblers, and even fuckin' slavers on his side. You all may look strong, but you'll need all the help you can get."

"And we'll gladly take it," Ànifa said. "Just... I don't want to kill anyone. I hope that won't be a problem."

"We don't want to kill anyone either," Patsy said. "That's not our way. In which case, I believe we're overdue for some introductions."

The tall dark-skinned muscular man guarding the door was named Trevonn, but most of the time, he was called Money. He had a thick black mustache with bushy eyebrows. He was wearing a green sleeveless shirt with black canvas pants.

The brown-haired woman guarding one of the only other doors in the room was Annalyse, Trevonn's wife. Patsy told them that before the monsters arrived, the two were rock climbers. They had summited many dangerous mountains in the nearby Turquold Mountain Range. Now they were two of the best monster slayers in Ajenti.

Patsy introduced the rest of her crew, who were sitting on a large couch together—Tushar, a short man with dark hazelnut skin, and was the lead strategist of the team; Anqi, a skinny woman with short black hair and a small round face; Martin, a large man with thinning blond hair, a round face, and a button nose; and Dale, a short woman with long blond hair. Patsy told them that Dale was her girlfriend of two years, and it had been the two of them who started this crew and they ran it together. Dale operated from behind the scenes and Patsy was the face of the operation.

"I'm sorry. This probably wasn't the reunion you were expecting, cousin," Patsy said.

Vesten laughed. "I never have any expectations with you."

"Smart man," Patsy replied with a grin.

"But... are you?" Theodore jabbed at Vesten.

Patsy laughed, then grinned at Vesten. "So, who's the tin-head?"

Vesten introduced all of them and told his cousin and her crew an abridged version of what led him and his friends to her. According to Vesten, they were seeking each of the Great Barriers to help stop the monsters, and that the two sorcerers were the key. Ànifa supported his cover story, for it would have been too much to fully explain everything to them, even though she felt guilty. Since Patsy was Vesten's cousin, she deserved to know the truth, but now was not the time to tell her.

Once the introductions were over, Dale brought out a large map of the area surrounding Ajenti and placed it on a nearly empty table. She used an assortment of empty bottles and mugs to keep it from rolling back up. Tushar placed figurines on the map to mark where Danai's gang was gathering. It was determined that the attack would take place in the middle of the Compass Crossroads.

Ànifa and her group would come from the western road, heading east. The Compass Crossroads split off in four ways—Ajenti was on the western road, Seaside was on the eastern road, Hay's Revival was on the southern road, and Tora was on the northern road.

Through Martin's and Anqi's underground connections, the two had gathered quite a bit of information. Anqi estimated there could be close to thirty-five or forty opponents. In response, Tushar suggested that if there were really that many foes, there may be people who do not wish to fight, so persuading them with some extra koda may be necessary.

"We won't need to use any koda," Tyrona cut in. "I possess the ability of suggestion, meaning I should be able to persuade a good number of them to leave. They won't realize their minds are being interfered with and will leave on their own accord."

"What a scary power," Patsy replied. "How does it work?"

"It's quite complicated. There are many layers to creating a powerful suggestion, but the core of it relies on slight memory alterations."

"That's even scarier," Tushar said with wide eyes.

"At least she's on our side," Dale said as she studied the map. "Now, we need to formulate a plan."

Everyone agreed they shouldn't simply charge into the crowd. Danai and his goons were expecting Ànifa's party to be there, but not Patsy's. That meant they had the advantage.

Luckily, the area surrounding the Compass Crossroads had a fair amount of cover in the form of large boulders. That allowed for Trevonn and Annalyse to scale the boulders—boulders that they had climbed dozens of times before. There was a small cave in the largest boulder that faced away from the road. Annalyse would lead the climb up and set the top rope, which would allow Trevonn, Patsy, Martin, and Anqi to climb up easily. It would be a tight fit, but they would have enough room to spend the night there.

The plan was for Ànifa and her party to approach the Crossroads, seemingly unaware of the situation. After being spotted, Tyrona would use her powers of persuasion to send off a majority of the opposition. Once Ànifa gave the signal, Patsy and her crew would barrage the remaining enemy with rocks, allowing for Ànifa's party to escape.

Dale and Tushar would stay behind. Neither of them were fighters, so they were to guard the hideout.

According to Martin's information, Danai's gang was already setting up camp in the crossroads. That meant Patsy and her crew had to leave soon to set their trap.

Vesten and Patsy said their goodbyes. They had only just reunited and were now about to be split up again. Though they knew they would see each other soon, there were no guarantees when it came to battle. Nobody wanted to kill anyone, yet Danai's gang most likely didn't feel that way. They all would do what they had to in order to make it out alive.

After Patsy and most of her crew left, everyone else had time to kill before the fight.

"There's no way I'm letting any of you go anywhere tonight," Dale said when Ànifa spoke of going out. "If any of Danai's posse sees you, the plan is shot."

"Yeah, but you see, we were on our way to the armory," Ànifa said. "A lot of us are low on supplies."

"What do you need?" Tushar asked. "We have quite the stockpile of goods in the room back here."

"You're lucky Annalyse isn't here to hear you say that," Dale said.

"Yeah, I know she'd whoop my ass. That's her responsibility, you see, but Patsy is going out of her way to help you folk, so I can't imagine why we can't help resupply what we can," Tushar said. "In the end, though, it's up to you, vice-boss."

"I think that if Patsy were here, she'd agree. I'll fetch what you need. Aside from Annalyse and Patsy, I am the only other person allowed in the storeroom. What do you all need?" Dale asked.

"Well, I'm really quite low on arrows. How many can you spare?" Ànifa asked.

"We have hundreds of arrows," Dale said with a wave of her hand. "How many do you need?"

Dale gave Ànifa eighty arrows, and Vesten and Dasch both got a few more daggers, while Cecil obtained six throwing hand-axes. They were also able to refill their two waterskins and restock on nuts and oats.

A short while later, Ànifa asked Theodore about the encounter with his brother earlier. She had thought it had been quite brief, with little regard for the other. When she said this, Theodore simply laughed and told her it was just how it was between them. Cedric was his younger brother, and they had never gotten along well. But over the years, they had learned to tolerate each other. Cedric was also an elemental wizard, but he specialized in the power of water. Theodore said that his powers suited his personality, as Cedric had always had a quiet determination.

After a simple dinner prepared by Dale and Tushar, Ànifa dove into the Eklatros history book. She finished Kieth Angelcross' story, as this book told it.

According to the book, Kieth felled a massive demon. And it was a demon of epic proportions—it had eight powerful arms, four massive wings, four sturdy legs, and dozens of heads. Some of the heads breathed fire, others breathed ice, while others breathed lightning. The rest of the heads spit poison and acid.

Somehow, Kieth slew the monster with little help from anyone else. Sure, the character known as Sir Valentine helped, while a platoon of humans and elves barraged it with arrows of every kind— poison-tipped, fire-tipped, arrows that exploded into sickled shards upon impact, and arrows made from pure stone. But, it was Kieth's sword, burning in pure golden fire, that did the most damage. Kieth hacked off limbs and heads and delivered the final blow by destroying the crystal that served as the beast's heart.

It was pure fiction, through and through, but Ànifa enjoyed the story for what it was. At the same time, she was saddened to know that this was being passed off as history. She knew that others who read this must know it to be an exaggeration, yet it still buried the true threat that was Gnusaramnii.

Of course, Ànifa didn't actually know what Gnusaramnii looked like, but she had a feeling that it probably looked similar to the Gnuelry and Gnusar that they had been fighting, and nothing like the monstrous beast that the book described.

She had seven chapters left when she closed the book for the night, and each chapter would tell the story of a different notable individual from Kieth's time. She saved these for another time.

Well, tomorrow we need to fight more people, she thought. *I don't understand these people. Why do they choose to fight us when there are actual monsters that need to be stopped?*

I am curious as to Danai's motivations. I know he's seeking revenge; that much is obvious. It's just... why would he gather a gang so large just to stop us? Even after talking about it with the others, it still doesn't really make sense.

But I guess it's how it is. I simply don't fully understand humans. I hope it goes well tomorrow—and quickly—so we can be on our way. We need to get the next Ekataramn awakened before any more towns are destroyed.

We must be swift now. The Gnusar are getting stronger and the Gnuelry are evolving. We must stop the invasion before it's too late.

24

INTERLUDE: NORMAN HARRISON

Declassification Disclaimer: the following document has been declassified for this usage only and has been sanitized. It has been translated accordingly for your understanding. To access the complete records, please contact Councilmember Ducutyk. His contact information can be found at the end of this document. Sanitized copy approved for release 82017/13/34.

From the desk of Professor Navacus Clums. Eklakiln, Ohocinar 1, 82002 06:26:42:07.

It's the first day of the month and the official start of our third major project, Norman Harrison. I have just about fifty more minutes until we begin.

Before I delve into our newest project, I want to record an update on West and Svetlana.

First, Svetlana. Last Dunakiln, a visitor from Foxaire Biotech Industries headquarters arrived. He's a Human named Carl Feng, and he is a personal assistant to Lord Foxaire himself. Typically, someone with such a high stature would prefer to be referred to by their title, but Carl simply goes by Carl.

Carl has been inspecting the entire compound. He spent about three days with Svetlana—talking to her, training her, testing her. Afterward, he told me he is quite impressed with the results. He also proposed a few upgrades, all of which have been fully approved by Svetlana herself. Some upgrades are fairly basic, such as improvements to her eye and arm. He also wants to install additional add-ons, such as extra limbs. Additionally, he wants us to build her a helmet that can provide additional sensory information to her brain and while increasing her eye's megapixels, zoom, and focus.

These upgrades are all across the board, so it will take us some time to plan them out. However, since they are just add-ons, we won't need to set up additional support for her spine and ribcage, even with the potential of additional limbs. Svetlana was our first, so I think that we may have been heavy-handed with the support system for her current bio-hardware. So, I believe that having additional limbs and add-ons shouldn't add any extra stress to her body. Although I should plan on looking at the supports, just to double-check. So, that will be our next project after Norman.

A few hours from now, Carl will begin inspecting West, so I also expect some changes for him soon.

Speaking of West, he is doing quite well. About a week after the post-proc, Head Professor Yilvin had West stationed at the front door as a security guard for the compound. It is a definite step down from the Intergalactic Bounty Hunter Association (IBHA), but I think he's enjoying it nonetheless.

Even though he's working, West is still in pain. He is still recovering and adjusting to LSS, so it will be some time until his pain is completely gone. In the simplest of terms, LSS serves as West's new head. It is his eyes, his ears, and his voice. The strangest part for West has been his voice. We did our very best to match the speech unit to his natural voice by using recordings that were lent to us by the IBHA. Even though it sounds good to us, for West, it's just simply not the same. There is a dummy AI embedded in his speech unit, so, in time, we hope it will learn the inflections and nuances of his speech pattern to sound more natural and organic.

Aside from his voice, West has also been experimenting with his upgraded vision. In a way, his vision is now very similar to Svetlana's, as both can see most of the electromagnetic spectrum. The only exceptions are within the radio waves, yet they can see some radio waves.

West's white cowboy hat has been a big part of his recovery. Since it was a part of his old life, he enjoys having something familiar around. It also grounds him in the reality of his new life without a head since the hat no longer rests on his head, but on a special mount we installed onto LSS specifically for the hat.

I have about fifteen more minutes before I need to prepare for Norman Harrison.

Carl Feng changed our initial plans for Norman when he arrived, which is why it has taken us a little longer to reach this point. First, I need to explain some things about Norman Harrison before I get too far into what we'll be doing.

Norman Harrison is a male Human from Carange. He is 172 centimeters tall and has pale skin with reddish-brown freckles. His hair is such a bright shade of red that it's nearly orange.

Rather than using skypods like we do on Melridion and most of the planets in the Vortex Solar System, most Humans on Carange still use vehicles that crawl along the ground with wheels. It's not practical, but, for some reason, many Humans prefer them to typical flying vehicles. Whatever the reason, they are simply much more dangerous. Vehicle collisions happen quite frequently on Carange and kill many Humans each year. It's really quite absurd to me. Anyway, Norman Harrison and his fiancée, Kate Thomas, were in a vehicle collision about a Carange-week ago, which equates to roughly four days here on Melridion. As a result of the collision,

Norman lost both of his legs. Kate, who had been driving, made it out relatively undamaged.

Kate arrived with him, which was unusual. I haven't seen much of her since the first day, but I heard from Professor Dea that they gave her a room in the barracks. Since the vast majority of what is in the compound is secret and confidential information, she can't be exploring unattended, and no one, including the security guards, has time to babysit her. I also hear she won't be staying long, and will return to Carange within the next few days. I overheard Carl saying that he'll arrange special travel arrangements for her. I'm sure Foxaire Biotech Industries can afford to give her a nice private shuttle for the three-day trip back to Carange.

Now, back to Norman. In our initial plans, the legs we designed for him were not detachable. Carl proposed the idea to make them detachable so we can construct different attachments that would allow him to adapt to different situations. This pushed our initial timeline back. For the past ten days, we have been working on the base component which we'll graft onto the bottom of Norman's torso. All the attachments, which we have yet to start building, will connect to the base.

So, rather than simply adhering to his biological form, having detachable parts will allow Norman to be much more versatile. Since our initial design was only his legs, we'll build them first. Additionally, Carl has proposed two additional attachments. One is a vehicular attachment with a set of buoyant treads, so he will be able to quickly traverse both land and water. The other attachment will allow Norman to float like an Eridavlos. This attachment will be the most challenging. I have to say, I rather like this plan. I just wish I had thought of it myself.

I need to prepare for today—we are grafting the base component onto the bottom of Norman's torso. Mac and Poi will be in charge of monitoring Norman's vitals. Our task is tricky, as we will be working close to his genitals, but the Harmertian twins will ensure we won't damage anything important.

Qymberkon will take lead on the graft, with Lyd, Grasberg, and Kurjon assisting. Syl and I will oversee the entire operation.

It should take about a day and a half to complete the graft. It's not just a simple graft onto his thigh stumps, as we will connect all his nerve endings to the bio-hardware as well. Theoretically, he'll be able to feel each of his attachments as if they were part of his body.

With peace, and love, and faith, this is Professor Navacus Clums, signing off.

From the desk of Professor Navacus Clums. Melrikiln, Ohocinar 3, 82002 00:23:49:21.

It's late, and we are all exhausted, but the graft was successful. Carl dropped by about an hour into the operation and stayed until the end, silently overseeing everything.

It was quite nerve-wracking to have my boss' boss' boss—or however it works—watching over my work, but I feel like it was good to have him there—it kept us focused.

Norman's graft was completed about an hour ago. Everyone else went off to bed, but Carl stayed back and talked with me about the upcoming attachments. He reiterated that he wants us to work on them next, before Svetlana's or West's upgrades.

He also mentioned one other curious thing—that he was interested in letting me in on a side project. He didn't say much more than that. It sounds to me as if they are quite impressed with my work. I'm extrapolating here, but I think they want me to design something for Lord Foxaire himself, which would be quite the honor.

Anyway, I'm very tired.

Peace, love, faith.

From the desk of Professor Navacus Clums.
Gnuakiln, Ohocinar 23, 82002 14:65:39:54.

We finished the first few rounds of tests on Norman with his new legs. Overall, everything is working well. He can even feel his legs, though he claims the sensation is different from before. He's walking fairly well with the guiding handholds, but he still cannot fully walk on his own.

Carl popped in for a few minutes during the testing process. Professor Dea and Professor Bodeelch stopped by briefly as well.

While he was here, Professor Bodeelch told Norman that they had sent Kate home during his procedure. This frustrated Norman; he wanted to see her before she left. In response, Professor Bodeelch assured him that Kate would call when she got back home to Carange.

I do hope she calls. Norman's mood has worsened. After Professor Qymberkon and the others finish with the adjustments, we'll be sedating Norman. His body needs rest after the stress it took today. At the very least, Norman did not need any skeletal strengthening, as all of his attachments are below the waist. Although, some of our tests are to ensure that this decision was correct. I'm mostly concerned with his spine. I think the real test will be with the other attachments. The good thing is that if we do need to strengthen Norman's spine, we can use non-invasive nanoparticles.

That's about it for now. I should get back to helping my team.

With peace, and love, and faith, this is Professor Navacus Clums, signing off.

From the desk of Professor Navacus Clums.
Pjorkiln, Ohocinar 29, 82002 20:59:43:71.

We have been hard at work designing and creating prototypes for the other two attachments. So far, the treads have proven to be the easiest, as we had all assumed. They are quite simple, really—treads with a small jet-propulsion system that works on land and on the surface of water. The propulsion system has been the trickiest aspect, but earlier today Sylcertiverner came up with the solution we needed. So, it's been Syl, Poi, Kurjon, and I that have been working on this attachment.

The hover unit is still a work in progress. That attachment is being led by Professor Qymberkon, with Grasberg, Lyd, and Mac assisting. They have been successful with their prototypes—getting a small sphere of metal to hover using a miniaturized version of the stabilizing gravity devices that are used on the vast majority of spacecrafts.

The hard part is the control. Specifically, what nerves do we need to connect to that will communicate properly to his brain to control his hovering? The other two attachments—the legs and the treads— are both familiar to Humans. Yet, no one has ever emulated an Eridavlos before. We are once again breaking new ground.

This morning, we ran a few more tests on Norman. He's continuing to adjust to his legs and finally has full control over his balance. Since then, Norman has been with Professor Dea, Professor Bodeelch, and Carl. They have been running their own tests, which is fine with us, as it gives us time to focus on the attachments.

I think it will be a few more days before we can finalize the treads. I still think it's too early to start swapping out attachments. I want to give Norman another week to adjust to his legs before we switch it up on him.

I couldn't be more relieved that Head Professor Yilvin relaxed our deadlines. I think that Carl's assessments of West and Svetlana made him realize that strict deadlines do not produce the best quality of work.

Now, it's time for me to head home. Tomorrow will be another big day.

With peace, and love, and faith, this is Professor Navacus Clums, signing off.

From the desk of Professor Navacus Clums. Eklakiln, Ohocinar 33, 82002 13:26:09:10.

We finally finished the vehicular attachment this morning. We'll be running field tests in about fifteen minutes, which I am very excited about.

I realized I haven't discussed how the attachments actually work. The base we grafted onto Norman is the only actual piece that is physically attached to him. When he doesn't have any attachments, he's just Norman. In other words, the base adds nothing to Norman.

When he has an attachment fastened to him, it securely hides the base. The attachments are adhered using a specialized set of mechanical screws. In addition, the base is electromagnetic, which helps to hold it together while the screw mechanism is in operation. After the screws are in place, there is a seal that has been built into the top of each of the attachments that cover and surround the base. We don't want the attachments to look like attachments.

It's a fairly simple yet strong mechanism. During each test of an attachment, we examine the attachment mechanism, and nothing slides or shifts around. Everything is solidly locked in. We can thank Professor Qymberkon for the ingenious concept and design.

Throughout the past week, Norman has grown stronger and more confident in using his robotic legs. He's walking on his own now, without any handholds or walking rods. He says it still doesn't quite feel the same, and I don't think it ever will.

As I mentioned, we are soon starting our first field test outside. So far, all the tests have been around my lab and the halls of the compound. Now, we'll be doing a field test in the open desert. First, we'll test his legs on the uneven surfaces. Then, by order of Carl and Head Professor Yilvin, we will swap out his legs for the vehicular attachment. We plan to only leave them on for fifteen minutes, as it will be a big and unnatural change from what he has been getting used to. Personally, I think it's still a bit too early for this, but I may be proven wrong.

Anyway, I plan on popping back in here after the field test for an update. I'll be back shortly.

Peace, love, faith.

From the desk of Professor Navacus Clums. Eklakiln, Ohocinar 33, 82002 16:54:72:40.

I meant to get to this earlier; we've been busy making adjustments to Norman's attachments. Overall, the field test went well. Norman was able to walk on the uneven surfaces of the desert with ease. It was his first time outdoors since he arrived at the compound, and he enjoyed the fresh air. Norman told us he was from a desert region on Carange, so the terrain was familiar. However, this thought process led him to think about Kate, who still hasn't contacted him. Norman has been holding up better than I thought he would. He was furious at first, but now I think he's accepted that she will call when she is able to.

Anyway, after we tested his legs outdoors, we swapped out his legs for the treads. As I had expected, he had a lot of trouble with them. We had to make some on-the-spot adjustments to the connections—all done remotely by Mac and Poi using their tablets. Once the adjustments were finished, Norman was able to successfully accelerate forward, though he was unable to move in a straight line. We only kept the treads on for twelve minutes, at which point he was completely exhausted. He's been resting in his private quarters ever since.

I think I might get some rest myself. We've been working on the hover attachment since we got back to the lab, but the heat really did a number on me. I, for one, am simply not used to this heat yet. Granted, I rarely go outside. The walk to the barracks is covered, so I'm never in direct sunlight. Having such thick plumage, I can't really be out in the desert heat for long. Luckily, we were only outside for about an hour, which is honestly all I could handle.

So that's what I'm going to go do—take a much-needed nap.

With peace and love and faith, this is Professor Navacus Clums, signing off.

From the desk of Professor Navacus Clums. Eklakiln, Ohocinar 33, 82002 17:12:07:55.

Well, I never made it to the barracks, but I will go after this. I just wanted to pop back in here for another quick update.

I ran into Carl on my way to the barracks. He was present at the field test today, and once again wanted to congratulate our team for all of our hard work. Carl asked to speak to me privately, so we returned to my office. He spoke more about the side project he had mentioned about four weeks ago now.

The thing is, it doesn't sound like a side project—it sounds like he is recruiting me for something major. He explained that if I were to accept, Professor Qymberkon would take over the bulk of my responsibilities, and Sylcertiverner would be promoted to Professor Qymberkon's current position. I wouldn't be completely leaving my team, but my role would be more of an overseer, a big picture managerial role rather than lead decision-maker. He gave me until Rikiln to think about this, and ordered me to keep it secret. I don't see any harm in speaking about this to my private datalogs. I don't think anyone will ever listen to these things, honestly, as everything we're doing here is highly classified.

I mean, on the surface, Foxaire Biotech Industries is the leading producer in nanoparticles, nanopharmaceuticals, and pretty much any other form of nanotechnology. That is how Lord Foxaire made his fortune, and it's when he began dubbing himself Lord Foxaire, which I hear is similar in pronunciation to his actual name.

Anyway, this whole compound is a secret. And now I'm being recruited for an even bigger secret. I am really curious, but I haven't decided what I will do yet. I mean, Carl left my office less than ten minutes ago. My biggest question is, where will this new project take place? There's not much room in the compound. Maybe there's another facility somewhere nearby?

Well, either way, I have a few days to mull it all over.

So, with peace, and love, and faith, this is Professor Navacus Clums, signing off for the night.

For all inquiries, please use the contact information below:
Ducutyk@icos.gov
FBI@icos.gov
Please keep your messages under 500 characters. Attachments not allowed.

25

BATTLE FOR POSSESSION

Ànifa woke with a start. For a moment, she couldn't recall where she was, but as she looked around, she remembered—she and the others were in Patsy's hideout, resting until they had to face Danai and his gang.

She lay on top of the unpadded sleeping bag that was flush against the hard stone floor and sighed, staring at the pockmarked ceiling.

She had another dream featuring Professor Navacus Clums. This had been the third of such dreams, and she already felt a kinship toward Navacus. He may be a completely different species, far away on a distant planet, but she knew he wasn't simply a manifestation in her dreams. He was real and he was important to her, although she couldn't say why. She suspected he had something to do with Gnusaramnii. Could it be that he was the only other being in the universe that could stop Gnusaramnii?

Whatever it was, she was scared for him. She had gotten a really bad feeling from the black-haired human, Carl Feng. She wished she could tell Navacus not to take the offer, although she knew it was more than futile. He would take the offer, and there was nothing she could do about it.

Ànifa stepped out of the way as Vesten ran past her. He almost lost his footing as he skidded over a piece of paper.

"Vesten, calm down!" Dale yelled as she rushed to catch up with him. "You'll destroy our hideout."

"Why didn't you wake me up?" Vesten moaned as he dashed around the room.

"It's not like we didn't try," Theodore said calmly as he dipped his spoon into his porridge.

Ànifa smiled and focused on her task—double-checking every arrow she had received last night for quality assurance. They had time to spare before they needed to leave. Tushar had agreed to help her, and she enjoyed the company.

They were all nervous, especially Dale. Tushar explained to Ànifa that Dale always worried about Patsy, but this time it felt different. Ànifa nodded in agreement. She knew too well how dangerous humans could be. Yet they had to trust in their plan, and trust that Patsy and the others wouldn't be caught.

Once Ànifa and the others were ready to leave, they thanked Dale and Tushar for their hospitality. Ànifa led her party out of Patsy's hideout and into a dark alley. It was early, and many of the streets were still dark as the Ajentian University loomed over them, shielding the group from the rising sun.

They had to act like they knew nothing of Danai's plot, so they didn't hide. Tyrona, Theodore, and Cecil joked amongst themselves, while Ànifa spoke to Vesten about Patsy. Dasch, in his typical style, walked alongside them quietly. As they headed toward the east gate, the morning light broke through Ajenti's canopy, casting a bright light upon them. As she chatted with Vesten, Ànifa could feel many eyes watching them. When she chanced a glace into the crowds, all she could see were townsfolk rushing about.

They made it through the east gate easily and exited Ajenti. Once they were out of earshot, Cecil leaned into the group and said, "Oh man, that was weird. Typically, there are always groups of people coming and going from the east gate at this time of day. Today, we're the only ones."

"Danai must really have it out for you all," Tyrona said. "He must have paid off the guards. I could feel them watching our every move."

"I still don't understand it," Ànifa replied as she adjusted her bonnet. "Why would Danai go to all this effort just for revenge?"

"Well, maybe you can ask him," Cecil said. "We're getting close now."

It wasn't long before they reached the Compass Crossroads. As expected, there was a large crowd standing in the center of the intersection. The ruffians were openly harassing a young family as they attempted to head back into Ajenti.

As predicted, well over fifty bandits, thugs, and pirates had gathered there. They certainly made for an intimidating presence. Ànifa glanced at the tall rock towers where Patsy and her team hid. The towers really were in the perfect position for an ambush. Ànifa squinted as a flash of light emerged from a dark shadow. It was a signal from Patsy, letting them know they were ready.

Ànifa and the others were still a short distance away, and none of the bandits had noticed them yet. They were focused on raiding a family of what little goods they had. A sharp noise cut through the air —one bandit had slapped the helpless woman. Ànifa clenched her fists and ran toward the gang.

"Hey! Leave them alone," Ànifa shouted, no longer caring about the plan. She heard the clanking of Cecil's armor and the footsteps of the others as they ran to catch up to her.

"Well, looky here boys!" A short, bald man with a large potbelly exclaimed. "Is this the one, Danai?"

The broad man with short black hair looked over and shot her a crooked grin. He was holding a woman by her neck as she screamed and struggled. Other bandits were holding down the four other members of the family—a man, his son, and his two daughters. "Yes. Finally."

"Whoooey! Issa two-fer-one day today!" exclaimed a bandit with a scar shaped like an *x* on his left cheek.

By this point, Ànifa's comrades had caught up to her. Cecil readied his battle-axe, and Tyrona and Theodore drew their catalysts. Dasch remained seemingly unguarded, though Ànifa suspected he was hiding his sword underneath his new dark green cloak. When Vesten caught up, he panted, then yelled at the bandits, "You heard the lady. Let them go!"

"And why would we ever do that?" the bald man said.

"Shut it, Beck. Can't you keep your big mouth closed? You're already on Danai's shit list," said a man with a short blond beard and a red bandanna tied around his head.

"But Bart, they're completely outmatched!"

"If you don't rest your fat tongue, Beck, I'll rip it out of your face," the man with short black hair said.

Ànifa squinted as she studied him, and she remembered seeing him before. "So, it really is you. I'm sorry, Danai. I never meant to kill anyone."

"Well, you did, bitch. And now we're going to repay the debt," Danai replied.

"Tyrona, can you use your special powers?" Ànifa whispered.

"The situation isn't ideal, but I'll do my best," Tyrona whispered back, a small fire burning in her jade eyes. She stepped forward and held out her intricately carved white wand, holding it with both hands. She closed her eyes, bowed her head, and began muttering incoherently.

"Oh looky, they're sending out the magic users!" Beck laughed.

Danai dropped the woman to the ground, then stomped over to Beck and grabbed him by the neck. He held the squirming man up in the air, then reached into his mouth and tore out Beck's tongue. Ànifa wanted to retch, but instead she turned away and motioned to the terrified family to come to her quickly.

"Please, leave this area as quickly as you can," Ànifa said as she whipped out her bow and notched an arrow.

"Thank you, we will never forget your kindness," the woman said as she and her family hurried toward Ajenti.

"Our playthings have gotten away," one bandit said protruding his lower lip in a mocking gesture.

"Tyrona, anytime now!" Ànifa whispered loudly.

"Don't interrupt her," Theodore said. "She needs to concentrate."

"Concentrate faster," Cecil muttered loudly under his breath.

Danai released his hold on the tongueless man, who landed on the ground with a thud. Beck screamed in agony, spewing foam and blood. Danai laughed, then kicked Beck in the stomach.

"Danai, stop it!" the man with the red bandanna shouted.

"Oh, don't you start with me too, Bart," Danai said. "You've been on my ass ever since *The Sundering,* I won't hesitate to stop you if you stand in my way!"

"Who said anything about standing? I'm leaving!" Bart fumed.

"Then you can expect a knife in your back!" Danai yelled back at him, pulling a knife out of his baggy gray pantaloons.

Ànifa released her arrow, striking the knife out of Danai's hand.

"Leave him be!" Ànifa commanded, then notched another arrow.

"Those of you who wish to leave, that time is now!" Tyrona cried as a bright light burst from her white wand. When the light abated, nearly a third of the bandits had dropped their weapons and were running north toward Tora. Among them were Bart and Beck.

"Fucking pussies!" Danai shouted as the remaining bandits yelled their own curses.

A rock hit a bandit in the face, then another rock made impact with another bandit. Moments later, rocks rained down upon them. Patsy and her team had made their move.

In response, Theodore, exercising his full powers, caused the ground below the bandits to quake and ripple. It was as if the rocks were falling into a pond, causing a cascade of waves. The bandits screamed obscenities as they were tossed into the air.

Tyrona walked gracefully to Ànifa, held out her wand, and told her to speak. Ànifa put away her bow, cleared her throat, then tore off her bonnet. Her deep-blue hair proudly waved in the wind. She spoke into the wand as it amplified her voice. "Do you see what happens when you anger Eklatros? Your interference has gone far enough. Leave this place and never again attempt to defy the will of our Holy Mother Eklatros!"

Ànifa motioned to Theodore, who ceased the quake, then waved a hand and returned the ground to exactly how it had been, leaving no trace. Patsy's torrent of rocks also abated.

The bandits lay on the ground in a daze. Tyrona shouted a spell—equalybrious malirarbium—causing a stream of sparks to shoot out of her white wand. The sparks shot toward each bandit, restoring their balance and equilibrium. The remaining bandits stood and ran toward the ruins of Seaside.

Only Danai remained. He stood akimbo, his neck thrown back as he laughed deeply. "I am not scared of your tricks! I know you do not want to kill me, but I want to kill you. Let's see whose will is stronger!" Danai drew a cutlass and charged.

"For Ànifa!" voices cried as Patsy, Trevonn, Annalyse, Martin, and Anqi descended the rock from a rope.

Danai continued his charge, uninterested in the increased resistance.

"Stop this instant!" Tyrona shouted as a blue light burst out of her wand. Danai froze in place, his left leg awkwardly dangling in the air mid-step.

"Why are you doing this?" Ànifa asked as she walked closer to him. "I never meant to hurt your friends. You were the ones chasing us, and Vesten claimed you were going to kill us."

"I was only going to kill your companions! I had other plans for you," Danai replied with maniacal laughter. "You were going to make me rich! So, I'm not angry at you for killing my *hired help*. I'm angry at you simply for what you are. Elves should be extinct! They serve no purpose in this world. All elves must be eradicated!"

Ànifa stopped in her tracks and stared at him.

"Uh, Ànifa, what are you doing?" Cecil asked.

Theodore placed a hand on Cecil's shoulder. "Let her focus."

Patsy and her crew approached Vesten, who was standing in the back of the group.

"Ànifa's an elf? What the fuck is going on?" Patsy asked.

"Be patient, Patsy," Vesten said. "She's up to something. You'll learn the truth soon enough."

Ànifa quieted her mind as her friends gathered around her. She needed all of them with her if this was going to work. As she stood before Danai, who was still frozen mid-step, she closed her eyes and let the wind blow through her baby blue hair. She listened to the distant calls of birds as they chirped and played about in the wind. She heard the leaves as they rustled across the dirt path. She felt the heartbeats of the ten souls that surrounded her, the souls of established and newfound friends.

Through her thoughts, she heard Danai as he continued to laugh uncontrollably. She focused on his voice, then opened her eyes, sending him a piercing look that cut to his bones. She saw him physically shiver as he remained motionless.

She allowed the warmth that burned in her soul to alight her body in blue flames. For the first time, she felt a genuine connection to the flames. She now knew the flames did not burn her since the flames *were* her. The blue flames were the manifestation of her life force, of her passion for Eklatros and the people she befriended, and of her desire to show this man that he was on the wrong path. And yet, the blue flame was not just hers. It was everyone's—everyone carried this flame within them.

She took a deep breath, then rose into the air and said, "Danai, don't you see? It is you who is on the wrong path. These ten that stand behind me, they know the truth. The truth of this planet, and the truth of what's to come. Please, let us show you this truth."

Danai broke free of the spell and collapsed to the ground. A moment later, he rose into the air as if he were being pulled by marionette strings, his arms outstretched awkwardly as he rose to his feet. His head lolled back and forth as he rose, his neck moving clumsily. His face had grown pale and was locked in a maniacal grin. When he returned to his feet, he hunched forward, then raised his head. Danai's mouth broke from his concrete grin and opened wide as he laughed.

"Ànifa!" The voice that emanated from Danai was not his own, but the deep, haunting tones of Gnusaramnii. "Ànifa, you're mine!"

Two daggers thrown in quick succession punched into Danai's chest. A moment later, a third buried deep into his skull. Danai crumpled to the ground.

"Patsy, what did you do?" Vesten said, aghast.

"What in the living fuck was that thing?" Patsy cried in horror, her left hand still gripping a dagger. "And why is Ànifa floating? And why is she on fire? What the fuck is going on?"

"Patsy!" Trevonn shouted. "Please, calm down. I'm sure there's a perfectly logical explanation for everything that just happened. At least, there better be."

Patsy heaved a heavy sigh, then broke out into tears. Ànifa descended from the air and focused back within herself, calming the flames.

"Patsy... everyone. I apologize for not telling you sooner. Yes, I am an elf. It's just... I must continue to hide my true identity," she said, her blue hair swirling between light- and dark-blue hues. "Only those I trust can know my secret, and I trust you all now, including Dale and Tushar. They don't know, but they deserve to."

"Know what?" Anqi asked. "I agree with Patsy. This has gotten really out of hand."

"I'm sorry you feel that way, Anqi, but I had good reason. I know that what I just did was not part of the plan. But at the moment, I felt it was the right thing to do."

"If you knew you could do that, then why the fuck did you ask for our help?" Patsy asked.

"We needed you all here. We had no idea what to expect with a gang that large. Luckily, Tyrona was able to get a lot of them to leave with her first mind trick. And then your combination attack, Theodore and Patsy, that was a true masterpiece."

"That really threw me off guard at first, honestly," Martin said as he scratched the back of his head. "But it worked, and no one got seriously injured. Well, aside from the black-haired creep."

"That is Danai—and yet not Danai," Ànifa said, glancing at the body. "He was possessed by the entity that has haunted me since I first awoke on Schelff Island, under Charlotte's care.

"You see, I am an elf. But I have almost no memory of who I was. The mission we are on now is to restore my memories while awakening the Ekataramn, the entities that dwell within the Great Barriers."

"So, you're an elf, and you're trying to save the planet," Patsy said, with one hand resting on the hilt of a dagger. "I get all that now, but I've never heard of an elf who could burn in blue flames and float in the air."

"Yes, I don't fully understand it myself. While I know my lineage may has something to do with it, it doesn't answer all my questions. That's part of my mission."

"Yeah, that was only the second fuckin' time she's done that. And the first time she did it, she was not in control of herself," Vesten said, his eyes wide as he shook his head.

"Last time, I was drawing the power from my soul, so that's why I lost control. This time, I used all of your passive energies to support me. That was the only way I could stay in control the entire time. So, I must thank you all."

"You can use my passive energy anytime, Princess," Cecil replied. The group burst out in laughter, erasing the tension.

As they said their goodbyes, Patsy handed Vesten her scimitar.

"Here, take this, cousin."

"I can't fuckin' take this. It's yours," Vesten said as he waved his hands and backed up a few steps.

"Take it. You're going to need it more than I will. Take good care of Skimither."

Vesten laughed at the name, then nodded and took it from Patsy. "Thank you. I will."

"Don't fuckin' laugh. She's a good sword."

"Don't worry about it. Skimither will be in good hands."

As Vesten embraced his cousin, Cecil approached and asked Patsy if she wanted to join his new guild. While she was intrigued, Patsy turned down the offer. Cecil then mentioned the world summit, and encouraged them to check it out if they had the chance.

The two parties split into three groups. Patsy, Trevonn, and Annalyse headed north toward Tora to pick up some supplies and to replenish what Ànifa and the others had taken. Martin and Anqi headed east toward Ajenti to regroup with Dale and Tushar. Ànifa and her comrades headed south toward Hay's Revival, which would take them to the road leading to Roheefy, the next of the Great Barriers they sought.

They left Danai's body where it lay. Ànifa, Cecil, and Dasch had all tried to approach it, but none of them could get close. Danai may have been dead, but a strong evil energy surrounded him. Theodore even tried to bury the body using his ground magic, but not even his power could break through the dark aura. They had to simply leave him. Ànifa wasn't happy about it, but she was happy that it was over and that Patsy and the others understood. She had known that it wouldn't be easy for any of them to hear the truth, but they seemed to take it well.

The sun was reaching its zenith as they headed south. A prompt from Cecil reminded her to don her bonnet once again. She closed her eyes, took a deep breath, and listened to the world around her as she walked, the sounds themselves showing her the path to take.

It's been quite the day already, she thought, then laughed quietly to herself. *That gang... I really thought that they would put up more of a fight. In the end, they were all cowards, which is not inherently a bad trait. I am glad that they realized the folly of their actions. And those who remained to hear my speech, they got to see me for who I truly am, but I'm not concerned. I doubt many people will believe their stories. Besides, Patsy, Anqi, and the others will spread their own stories. Then, like any big tale, other tangents and fictions will be born. This story will be good for the people of Ajenti. I hope it will restore their faith in Eklatros.*

And yet, I could not save Danai. Although, I don't believe he could ever have been saved. I never expected Gnusaramnii to show up. Honestly, I'm glad Patsy felled him when she did. The moment I heard his voice, I couldn't move. I was as frozen as Danai had been. And Patsy saved us all. Now I get to enjoy the rest of the day—or so I hope.

26

BATTLE FOR RESILIENCE

They continued along the path that led to Hay's Revival, a small farming town. They were still about a day and a half away from the town; they first had to cross the Great Roffen Plains.

Vesten told them stories of his childhood as they traveled. The town he and Patsy grew up in, Haymath, was destroyed when he was young. In the wake of that destruction, a new community sprung up and rebuilt what they could. This settlement became known as Hay's Revival, but, according to Vesten, it still wasn't anything like the place he grew up.

Vesten told them he had visited Hay's Revival during his search for Patsy and nothing had been the same. While some buildings had been rebuilt, most of the structures were brand new. The town was populated by people from the surrounding towns—Ajenti, Tora, Seaside, Port Columbo, and even Nora's Docks—and Vesten and Patsy were the only known living survivors.

"Vesten, please stop talking," Dasch growled.

"What? Oh shit, aye, sorry. I've been chattering away for a fuckin' while now," Vesten said.

"It's not that," Dasch said. "We are about to enter the Great Roffen Plains."

"Aye. I've passed through here many times before. If we stay on the road, we'll be fine," Vesten said. "Besides, three times a year, large caravans from Hay's Revival pass through here."

"Don't forget that the Guild of Ajentian Knights protect the caravans," Cecil added.

"Hmm... then maybe things have changed since my time," Dasch replied. "I remember the animals here being very territorial, especially the large diprotodon."

"Aye, those things are dangerous. But this is a well-traveled road. I'm sure we'll be fine," Vesten said.

"Maybe," Cecil said. "Some rookie knights would use this area as a training ground. It was rare, but some never returned. I never felt the need to prove my masculinity in this way though."

"Ànifa, what do you think?" Theodore asked as he stroked his beard.

"It's hard to tell," Ànifa replied as she scanned the surrounding area. "I sense the presence of many animals, but I don't see anything. It's strange."

"That's not strange for these grasslands," Dasch said. "We must be on guard."

"I agree with Dasch," Tyrona said. "I feel a sorrowful energy from this place... the animals are in turmoil."

"Can your powers extend to animals too?" Ànifa asked.

"Not really," Tyrona replied with a shake of her head. "I can sense them though, maybe like you can, but I don't know how to explain it."

"I can't explain it either," Ànifa replied.

Dasch shushed them. "I would suggest we continue on in silence."

Dasch scanned the area. Even during his time, the plains were notoriously treacherous. Diprotodon were exceptionally territorial and would blatantly attack anything that got too close. Luckily, he had experience fending off the large brown beasts.

As they marched on, Sir Kloud's armor clinked together with every step.

"Can you do anything about your armor?" Dasch asked, shooting the knight a dirty look.

"I'm stepping as carefully as I can. At least it's quieter than my previous armor."

Dasch sighed, then stopped in his tracks, causing Vesten to bump into him.

"Shit, hey man. What's the—" Vesten was silenced by a bellowing roar. Following the sound came a deep thundering; the ground shook beneath them.

"Everyone, prepare yourselves," Dasch instructed. "Aim for their large black noses, it's their weak spot."

Dasch focused his thoughts on his weapon, then drew his sword. It burned in pure golden flames.

"May the light guide my hand," he whispered to himself. It was a phrase he had uttered many times before battle.

Beside him, he watched as Ànifa's notched arrow burst into blue flames. He grinned—she was learning quickly. Behind him, Theodore began to set up a large barrier, while Tyrona chanted incoherently, holding her wand out in front of her. Sir Kloud readied his battle-axe, while Vesten drew two daggers and gripped them tightly.

"Everyone, this barrier is special. We can shoot out of it, but nothing can get in," Theodore explained.

"Great!" Ànifa replied.

Dasch turned his focus to the first of the large diprotodon that thundered toward them. Mucus spewed from its large nostrils, and its wide eyes were bloodshot. This was no normal diprotodon—this was a Gnurargurt.

A flaming blue arrow punched through Theodore's barrier and penetrated the beast's left cheek. The diprotodon continued its charge unfazed. Dasch took a deep breath and moved into a battle stance as two more arrows shot toward the raging beast.

The diprotodon slammed into the barrier, creating a sharp

ringing that pulsed through the dome of energy. The beast stumbled back onto its haunches. Dasch gritted his teeth and dashed out of the barrier, slicing deeply into the beast's exposed belly. The beast screeched in agony and fell onto its back. Golden flames continued to smolder on the wound, creating an acrid stench.

The thundering ground alerted Dasch that more were on the way. He glanced behind him and saw Tyrona had condensed the sound waves from the diprotodon's attack into a small, swiftly rotating sphere.

Three more diprotodon approached. Ànifa fired blue flaming arrows at each target, while Sir Kloud expertly threw a hatchet. It struck the nose of a diprotodon, but it continued its wild charge.

"Uh, I thought you said to aim for the snout," Sir Kloud said, his voice wavering in fear.

"These diprotodon have been corrupted by the Gnusar. Normal rules do not apply," Dasch replied.

"I got this one," Tyrona said confidently.

Dasch stepped to the side as Tyrona hurled the sphere of energy toward the charging beasts. She hit it square in the face, causing it to stumble forward and smash headfirst into the ground. Tyrona whooped excitedly.

"Stay focused, Ty."

"Sorry, Dorie."

Ànifa continued to quickly fire off arrows, though they were doing little damage. Two diprotodon slammed into the barrier simultaneously, causing it to shatter into dust.

Theodore wasted no time as he gathered the shards of the barrier and flung them at the diprotodon. Dasch nodded, then flung himself forward and stabbed his sword into the left eye of a diprotodon. Beside him, Sir Kloud cried out, "For Eklatros!" while Vesten chanted his own battle cry.

The diprotodon who had been hit by Tyrona's attack stood back up and bellowed. Dozens of diprotodon emerged from the grasslands.

"What do we do now?" Tyrona asked.

In response, a deafening roar cut through the air.

Dasch looked behind him and saw a massive saber-toothed lion charging toward them, accompanied by a pride of thirteen lionesses.

"It's Sparassotereon, the lion god!" Ànifa exclaimed. "Help is on the way. And I think she means for us to ride on her back."

"Our savior!" Vesten cried.

"What in the world?" Tyrona said in disbelief. "Does she mean that, Dorie?"

"I'm afraid so. I thought I told you how we had to ride Aerigasus and Nuralagusamii, along with wyverns and quetzalrong and many others," Theodore replied.

"Yeah, but—"

Dasch shoved Tyrona out of the way, shouting "Pay attention!" A moment later, he sidestepped a diprotodon and slashed across its left side. The diprotodon stumbled forward and crashed into the spot where Tyrona had stood only moments prior. A saber-toothed lioness leaped onto the beast's back and dug its fangs into the back of its neck.

"Come on! We've got to move. Now!" Ànifa yelled from Sparassotereon's back.

Even while kneeling, the lion god towered over Dasch. He grinned to himself as he hoisted himself onto her back, then turned to help the knight.

"Tyrona, watch out!" Theodore shouted.

Dasch glanced at the sorceress and watched in horror as a diprotodon smashed into Tyrona's chest. She flew into the air, but before she could hit the ground, Theodore sent a stream of air hurtling toward her. Tyrona's limp body rose into the air toward them. Dasch reached out and grabbed her.

Once Tyrona was safe, Theodore hopped into the air and sent a burst of wind from the bottom of his staff, propelling him onto the lion god's back.

"I'm... so sorry..." Tyrona said, cradled in Dasch's arms, then burst into a fit of coughing, spewing droplets of blood.

"Is she okay?" Theodore asked as he settled onto the lion's back, his concern clearly showing on his face.

"I think she has some cracked ribs," Dasch replied as he examined Tyrona. "We need to get out of here."

Sparassotereon ran along the path, flanked by her thirteen lionesses. The diprotodon followed behind them but soon vanished into the brush. Ànifa couldn't sense any other large animals approaching. They had a clear, open path, but they all remained on edge. Ànifa could feel they were being watched the entire time, and she knew Sparassotereon and her pride could sense it as well.

They were making good time now—Sparassotereon moved much faster than they could on their own. Ànifa guessed that if they continued at this pace, without running into any other fiends, they would reach Hay's Revival sometime during the night.

Three hours into their journey across the Great Roffen Plains, Ànifa spied the first animals since the diprotodon. They were small, carnivorous marsupials with dark-brown fur and gray stripes called thylacoleo. They followed the group from a safe distance until they abruptly stopped their chase.

Not long after the thylacoleo had bounded off, they saw some enormous animals with dense coats made up of spines and had long, beak-like snouts called dire echidna. Similar to the thylacoleo, the dire echidna tracked them for a short while until breaking off.

The sun began to set, casting long shadows across the plains. In the fading light, Ànifa spotted a large group of kangaroos with grayish-blue tinted fur. Unlike the thylacoleo and the dire echidna, the blue kangaroos were fast enough to keep up with Sparassotereon and her pride.

"Whoa, watch out!" Cecil cried. "There's a large one blocking our path—it must be their god!"

When Ànifa's mount, Sparassotereon, came to a stop a dozen meters away from the kangaroo god, she locked eyes with it and saw that the mob of kangaroos were corrupted with the dark purple hues of the Gnusar.

The ground shook as the diprotodon god joined the kangaroo god on the path. A moment later, Carnivexion, the thylacoleo god, joined them. The diprotodon god stood nearly four meters off the ground, dwarfing the two and a half meter tall thylacoleo god. What Ànifa had assumed was a large bush near the side of the road lumbered to its feet. The dire echidna god turned its thick coat of spines toward them.

The various gods—kangaroo, diprotodon, thylacoleo, and dire echidna—surrounded them from all sides, creating a wall of bodies that was impossible to pass through.

A nudge from Sparassotereon told her they needed to dismount. Ànifa jumped off and said, "Everyone, we need to hop off. I think she's trying to do something. Theodore, pass me Tyrona."

Throughout the day, Tyrona's condition had only worsened. She remained in a lucid state, dipping in and out of consciousness as she mumbled to herself.

Ànifa took Tyrona out of Theodore's arms and held her close. Theodore hopped off, landing next to Dasch and Cecil. Vesten was the last one off, and as soon as he dismounted, Sparassotereon roared, showing off her four massive canines. Her thirteen saber-toothed lionesses echoed her roar.

In response, the herd of animals bellowed back, deafening the field for nearly a full minute. Without Tyrona's abilities to control sound waves, they were forced to endure the cacophony.

Ànifa set Tyrona on the ground in front of her, then crouched into a ball and covered her ears the best she could. Dasch, Theodore, and Vesten knelt and covered their ears. Cecil wildly attempted to remove his helmet, but after a few moments he grew limp and slumped to the ground.

"Cecil!" Ànifa cried as she rushed to him. A moment later, Dasch joined her in examining the fallen knight. Theodore hurried to Tyrona's side, picked her up, and approached the others. Ànifa slid Cecil's helmet off and found that he was unconscious and bleeding from his ears and nose, and he had a large gash on his head.

"Vesten, get over here!" Theodore shouted, but it was no use. Vesten couldn't hear them through the noise and had his eyes glued shut.

"I'll get him," Dasch shouted. He grabbed Vesten by the arm and dragged him to the others.

All the while, the five animal species continued to roar, screech, and howl at each other. Without warning, the herd of various animals surrounding them lunged forward all at once. Chaos erupted. The saber-toothed lionesses tore at the throats and soft underbellies of their attackers, spraying blood wildly, intending to blind their foes.

"We need to get the fuck out of here!" Vesten shouted to the others, his face pale with fear.

"I'm working on it!" Theodore replied.

Theodore thrust his scarlet staff high in the air and began chanting. The wind picked up around them, encasing them within a small whirlwind that created a barrier around them. It was unlike any other Ànifa had seen Theodore create—visibly thick with a metallic sheen to it. Once the barrier was formed, the wind outside its confines began picking up speed.

Ànifa could barely see anymore, although she could notice that the whirlwind wasn't affecting any of the air outside of it. The whirlwind's energy was being directed inside the eye of the whirlwind, causing the barrier to lift into the air. The attacking animals seemed to have taken notice—a group of kangaroos and a dire echidna broke through the defenses of the lionesses and charged at the whirlwind. Upon impact, the whirlwind threw them backward with such a force that Ànifa could hear their bones shattering through the roar of the surrounding wind.

With intense concentration, Theodore directed the whirlwind and the energy barrier they were encased in to rise high into the air, then down the path.

The last glimpse Ànifa got of the ensuing battle were the four corrupted gods joining into the bloody fray. Ànifa prayed that Sparassotereon and her pride would survive.

They would have been killed without Theodore's quick thinking and ingenuity. His restored powers had saved their lives, yet it took a heavy toll. They made it about half a kilometer before Theodore lowered them. When they were close to the ground, the barrier and the whirlwind disappeared, causing the six of them to drop half a meter to the ground.

Theodore crumpled to the ground. Half of their team were down, leaving only Ànifa, Dasch, and Vesten.

"What do we do now?" Ànifa shook her head in despair as she checked on Theodore's condition. "How can we go on like this?"

"We must. We must go on Ànifa," Dasch replied as he bent down and picked up Cecil. "Otherwise, all of this was in vain." He slung the limp knight over his right shoulder with ease and grunted in approval. "Sir Kloud's new armor is much lighter than before. Ànifa, grab Tyrona. Vesten, you take Theodore. We must not linger here."

Ànifa nodded, wiped her tears, and picked up Tyrona, cradling her in her arms. Vesten grumbled a few curses, then picked up Theodore, cradling him as well.

The three of them set off down the road as the sun dipped below the horizon. The light was fading fast. They had to push on if they meant to survive the night.

"Ànifa, are there any other gods that can help us?" Dasch asked quietly.

"I've been trying, but I can't reach anything. I fear this land is nearly fully corrupted by the Gnusar," Ànifa replied.

"It was a fuckin' miracle that those saber-toothed lions were able to help us, though," Vesten said.

"Yes, but at what cost? I fear they won't make it out of that battle," Ànifa said.

"That may be, but Sparassotereon knew what she was doing," Dasch said gently. "She's a true martyr and savior."

"What will we do if we don't find anyone that can help us?" Ànifa asked.

"Then we won't survive the night," Dasch said. "We must find some aid and shelter soon."

They pressed on, albeit much slower than they would be able to if they didn't have to each carry a fellow team member. They reached a large, dark river as the last of the day's light faded into darkness. Clouds blocked the moon and the stars, making it an extremely dark night.

"Hold up here for a minute," Ànifa said to the others quietly. "I'm not seeing a bridge."

"There should be a wooden bridge... is it not there anymore?" Vesten asked. "I can't see a fuckin' thing right now."

"No, it looks like there was once a bridge here, though. I'm also sensing something... something is coming, and it's not a friendly presence."

"Fuckin' shit," Vesten cursed. "We're not going to make it, are we?"

"It's looking pretty grim," Dasch replied. "This one of the worst situations I have ever been in."

"I agree," Ànifa replied as she scanned the river in front of them for their new foes. Even with her dark vision, the river was like a black hole.

"If we die tonight, I'm fuckin' honored to have been able to fight alongside you all," Vesten said.

Ànifa turned to face her friends. "Same. I'm happy to have met you, Vesten and Dasch."

"Ànifa, look over there," Dasch whispered loudly, pointing to their right.

"I see it," Ànifa said, nodding. She set Tyrona down behind her and drew an arrow, then lit the tip of the arrow in blue flames.

Dasch set Cecil on the ground and drew his golden flaming sword. Vesten clung onto Theodore.

"I can't see shit. I don't think I can be much help," Vesten said as he shirked back in fear.

"It's okay. Protect the others," Ànifa said softly, then fired an arrow. It struck true, hitting the beast between the eyes. It fell into the wide river and didn't move again, but many more were approaching.

"It's a pack of bunyippo," Dasch grumbled.

"Fuck. That's literally the worst fucking thing that could attack us right now," Vesten exclaimed as Ànifa fired another arrow.

Ànifa notched her bow and quickly fired another arrow. "Dasch, there's one coming toward—"

"I see it!" Dasch said as he lunged forward and slashed the large hairless amphibian-like creature with his sword.

"Everyone, hold on!" Ànifa cried out as another presence approached them.

A massive duck-billed animal burst out of the river. Ornithor, the platypus god, screeched and prodded the attacking bunyippo with her wide beak. The bunyippo roared and descended upon Ornithor. Once the bunyippo entered the water, they thrashed about in confusion and screeched in pain. All the while, Ànifa continued to shoot arrows, each one tipped with blue flames. The platypus god bellowed as the remaining bunyippo retreated, rushing down the river away from them.

"What happened?" Vesten asked. "It sounds like something intense just fucking happened."

A moment later, dozens of platypuses burst from the river and tended to their god. Ornithor was undamaged and chattered at her paddle of platypuses.

"We were saved by Ornithor, the platypus god," Ànifa said. "I think the males were stinging the bunyippo underwater, which caused them to flee."

"Thank Eklatros! Thank the gods!" Vesten praised.

After tending to her paddle, Ornithor motioned for them to follow her.

Ànifa and the others huddled together in Ornithor's cave. The male platypuses lay in a circle around them, protecting them, while Ornithor slumbered deeply in the back of the cave.

Tyrona had awoken when they entered the cave and shivered

with pain. Ànifa gave her a few bites of her shuyukuii mushrooms, which put Tyrona to sleep quickly. Ànifa had used a lot of energy to keep her arrows constantly awash in blue flames, so she took a few bites as well.

Today was a true challenge, she thought. *Theodore, Tyrona, and Cecil all went down. And it's hard to tell who is worse off right now. Theodore pushed himself too hard, too fast, which quickly depleted all of his energy. Tyrona was hit hard by that diprotodon... hard enough to take her out for the rest of the day. As for Cecil... I fear his eardrums may have ruptured. I think that's why his ears were bleeding. And the gash on his head from when he collapsed only makes matters worse. And yet we all made it through, thanks to Dasch and Vesten.*

Oh, Vesten. You continue to apologize about not being strong enough. I hope I can someday convince you of the truth, that you are stronger than all of us in your own way. You have the strength of resilience to face the enemy head-on, even if you feel unmatched. Your strength today helped us all push forward.

But now... now I must rest. We all need our rest. We cannot do much in the state we are in now.

With peace, and love, and faith.

27

BATTLE FOR PRAYERS

Ànifa woke from a restful sleep, slightly sore from sleeping in an awkward position. She repositioned herself and listened to the snores and heavy breathing of her friends and their platypus protectors. She quietly stood and stretched, popping the kinks out of her joints.

"Good morning, Ànifa," a soft voice whispered.

"Oh, Tyrona. I didn't realize you were awake," Ànifa whispered as she knelt next to the woman. "How are you feeling today?"

"Much better. My chest is sore but I'll manage. Ànifa... I'm really sorry. I feel like an idiot, getting hit by that diprotodon. I shouldn't have hesitated."

"Tyrona, it's okay, really. That was the most challenging battle we've ever faced. It was a lot to handle on your first day with us. You're not at fault."

"But that's why I feel bad. I could have helped. I... because of me, Theodore pushed himself too hard, and I can see Cecil was also injured. I can't help but think that if I wasn't..." Tyrona trailed off.

"Tyrona... it's not your fault," Ànifa reiterated, placing her hand on Tyrona's shoulder. "No one can predict what will happen. Both

Theodore and Cecil fought bravely. In fact, if it wasn't for Theodore and his quick thinking, we'd all be dead. We owe him our lives."

"That's my Dorie, always looking out for everyone else, with no thought to his own safety," Tyrona chuckled.

Ànifa smiled and removed her hand from Tyrona's shoulder. "Yes, he's a really good man. I can see why you love him."

"What?" Tyrona feigned a look of surprise, then sighed. "Oh, I suppose I can't hide it from you. It's just—"

"It's just nothing. Tyrona, he loves you, too. He really missed you."

Tyrona shook her head. "Honestly, I didn't realize how strongly I felt about him until he left. Once I realized I felt helpless, and I knew he was vulnerable from losing his powers... well, that's all in the past now. Theodore's powers have been restored, and I'm here, with all of you now. I couldn't be happier."

"That's the spirit," Ànifa nodded. "We need you for what's about to come. I can feel it."

"Thank you. I—" Tyrona paused and held out her palm. "Ànifa, something's wrong with Cecil."

"What?" Ànifa said sharply and turned to the red-haired knight. Cecil was shivering and dripping with sweat. "Tyrona, rouse everyone quickly."

"What can we even fuckin' do?" Vesten asked after everyone was up. "I mean, fuck, what about the platypus? They have those stingers, right?"

Most of the smaller platypuses were cleaning and pruning themselves, while Ornithor continued to slumber peacefully.

"They're poisonous stingers," Theodore said dryly. Now that he was awake, Theodore was essentially back to his normal self.

"Shit. Well, what about their god?" Vesten asked.

"Only the males have stingers," Tyrona replied as she absentmindedly pressed out the wrinkles in her dress.

"Right, and all the gods are females," Ànifa added.

"Oh," Vesten sighed.

"Although, since she is a god…" Ànifa trailed off. She walked over to where Ornithor slumbered, rested a hand on her thick brown fur, and reached out with her mind.

Ornithor awoke and Ànifa hopped back quickly as the large platypus god rolled over and yawned. The smaller male platypuses swiftly dodged their god with familiar ease.

As Ornithor unfurled, Ànifa spied two large spurs on her hind legs.

"*Ornithor… can you hear me?*" she thought.

Ornithor turned to look at her and blinked expectantly.

"*Thank you very much for your assistance yesterday. You saved our lives.*"

Ornithor yipped and nodded.

"*I must ask you for another favor. Our friend is ill. We suspect his eardrums have ruptured and have possibly gotten infected. I don't know if your serum can help, but if you can, please, I beg of you, save Cecil.*"

Ornithor looked over at Cecil and whined. She looked around her den and spied the largest of the male platypuses and called him to her. They waddled to the knight. Ornithor turned around and exposed her spur located on the inside of her right ankle. She gently stung Cecil in his left arm and moved out of the way. A moment later, the male platypus stung Cecil in the same spot.

"Hey, watch it!" Vesten exclaimed.

Ànifa put a hand on his shoulder, calming him. "It's okay. It's possible that a mixture of both venoms can counteract the infection."

Theodore slowly nodded as he stroked his beard. "If he truly does have an infection, that makes sense."

"Of course it's an infection! His fuckin' eardrums ruptured," Vesten cried.

"Hey guys," Cecil croaked, "don't fight over me."

The mixture of both platypus venoms had worked quicker than expected. Cecil was already awake, and the color was quickly returning to his face.

They let Cecil rest for a little while longer. The infection may have been treated, but he was still in pain from his ruptured eardrums. He told them he couldn't hear well—it sounded like everything was really far away. He also had a headache and couldn't stand straight.

Ànifa and Tyrona helped steady Cecil as he forced himself to his feet while Theodore urged him not to push himself. Cecil argued back that he had to press on—it was his duty as a knight to see the quest all the way through.

When everyone was ready, they said their farewells to Ornithor and headed out of the platypus den. Dasch supported Cecil out of the cave, letting the knight lean on him while they made their way back to the southern path. Once they reached it, Ànifa pointed them in the right direction.

Cecil soon shrugged off Dasch and attempted to use his battle-axe for support, but he tripped over the blade a few paces in, forcing Dasch to help him once again. Cecil grumbled, but accepted his friend's help.

The morning sun cast a warm light on their surroundings, making the area feel safe and secure. It was as if the dangers and enemies they had faced the night before could never take place in this land, especially not on this peaceful morning.

It wasn't long before they exited the Great Roffen Plains and passed through the Haymath Orchard, which turned into the Heefae Forest, and beyond that lay the Nicolah Mountain Range.

As they passed farmlands, Vesten explained that the Haymath Orchard contained the most fertile farming land in all of Eklatros. After each harvest, large caravans of carts traveled to Seaside, Ajenti, and Tora to sell their wheat, corn, oats, and other crops to merchants. Those merchants distributed the crops all across Eklatros.

It took about an hour to reach the turnoff to Hay's Revival. The town was a little less than a kilometer away and they could see the smoke rising from the chimneys.

"Cecil, do you need to stop and rest here?" Theodore asked, placing a hand on his shoulder.

"No, I'm fine," Cecil said, brushing him off.

"Are you sure?" Ànifa asked. "We can find a doctor to take a look at your ears."

"No, it's fine, really," Cecil insisted.

"Why are you being such an idiot? Go get checked out," Tyrona urged. "In fact, I think you should stay here while we continue. We'll need to pass through here again on the way back, right?"

"That's a great idea." Theodore's eyes lit up. "We will need to return this way, so let's do that."

"No!" Cecil shouted, stunning them all. "Look, I really appreciate your concern, but I can't see a doctor, not now. I just... I need to do this. Please."

"But Cecil, you're not well!" Theodore cried. "Tyrona, can you—"

"No," Ànifa said sharply. "Theodore... everyone, let's please respect Cecil's wishes. Besides, I wouldn't be comfortable leaving him behind. We don't know what's about to happen, so if he wants to stay with us, I think we need to let him."

"Thank you, Ànifa," Cecil replied. "Look, Theo, I understand your concern. But I must continue on with everyone."

"Alright," Theodore conceded, throwing his hands into the air. "It's just—"

"I'll be fine, Theo," Cecil said softly. "I can hear pretty well now, and I feel like I am becoming more stable as I walk. So let's continue on."

"We don't have to go into town? Fuckin' A," Vesten added. "I really don't want to go anywhere near there."

"This road looks thin. We'll have to be on guard," Dasch said as he walked toward the southern road.

It was true—the main road turned right toward the town of Hay's Revival while the road that continued south turned into a simple hiking trail.

As they made their way along the trail, they heard the cries and howls of animals. These were not menacing cries, but cries of pain and suffering.

"Come on everyone, we need to see what's going on," Ànifa urged, leading them closer to the calls of distress.

As they turned a corner around a grouping of aspen trees, they saw a large group of animals clustered together in a small meadow.

Ànifa hesitated, then continued cautiously. These animals were related to the thylacoleo that had attacked them last night. Although Ànifa didn't see any thylacoleo, she could identify the species. The smallest of them were the tasmanileo, and they were huddling around their larger kin—the dasyuricines and thylacines.

"What's wrong with them?" Cecil asked.

"They're lost and aimless. It's like they have no longer have the will to live," Ànifa replied softly.

"Wasn't their god among that large fuckin' group that attacked us last night?" Vesten asked.

"Yes," Ànifa nodded. "Their god was there. Carnivexion."

"I remember that, too. That was one of the last things I remember from yesterday," Cecil said. "Did something happen to their god?"

"I fear that may be the case," Ànifa replied.

As they approached the large gathering of marsupial dogs, one member of each species approached them cautiously. They kept their heads low to the ground, looking at the group with mournful eyes. The tasmanileo was small for its kind and was trembling as it stood in front of them. The largest of them, the thylacine, had a fresh set of scars on its dark-haired cheek; they looked to have been caused by a saber-toothed lion. The dasyuricine had the same set of scars on its back and was limping as it approached them.

"What's going on?" Tyrona asked. "Are they communicating with you, Ànifa?"

"I think they want us to follow them. They want to show us something. Come on, everyone," Ànifa said as she urged them forward.

The three marsupial dogs turned around and walked slowly forward.

The path they were on grew thinner and the trees grew thicker around them, turning from aspens and other deciduous trees to pine trees. They were now entering the Heefae Forest. The trail sloped up as they climbed one of the foothills surrounding the Nicolah Mountains.

Their marsupial leaders stopped multiple times along the way and trembled in fear. The tasmanileo kept its tail between its legs as it trudged forward. Even though the marsupials were terrified, they were determined to lead them. Ànifa sensed that their entire species depended on these three individuals.

Soon the path became even thinner as they made their way through a dense section of pine trees. The needles poked at them as they pushed through.

"Ugh, I just got sap all over my gloves," Cecil said in disgust. By this point, Cecil was walking on his own with only a slight limp.

"Shit, be careful. These fuckin' trees can kill chipmunks and birds and shit if they get caught in the sap," Vesten said.

"Oh, well, that's just fantastic," Cecil exclaimed. He shook off his gloves and hung them on his belt.

"We're almost through," Ànifa said to her friends as they followed along single-file behind her.

Ànifa broke through the trees and found herself in a small clearing. They faced a large limestone rock wall, split down the middle by a narrow slot canyon. Trees lined the remainder of the clearing.

Ànifa stepped into the center of the small clearing, followed by Theodore, then Tyrona, Cecil, Vesten, and Dasch. Their three marsupial leaders stood in front of the entrance to the slot canyon and howled in pain. The tasmanileo slumped to the ground and wailed loudly, causing Cecil to stumble forward. Theodore caught him before he fell to the ground.

"Thanks, Theo. I'm sorry, it's just, why do they have to be so loud?"

Ànifa approached the thylacoleo and shushed them. "Please, we have an injured friend. I know you are in pain, but if you can, please keep it down."

The animals' howls turned into pitiful whimpers as they huddled together.

"That's the saddest thing I've ever seen," Tyrona said, her voice wavering. "Let's find the source of their sadness and kick its butt or whatever we have to do."

"Agreed. Luckily, this is the way to Roheefy," Ànifa replied.

"I do not think it is luck. I think something is drawing us here—into this canyon," Dasch said.

"You mean they're trying to box us in?" Cecil said. "Those are some intelligent monsters, then."

"We've heard the Gnusar speak, Cecil," Theodore said. "Who knows what they are capable of."

"Yeah, that's a good point," Cecil replied.

"We better be on guard," Ànifa said. "Is everyone ready? Cecil?"

"Yeah, I'm fine. Like I've been saying, don't worry about me," Cecil replied as he shrugged off Theodore.

"Okay then, let's go, everyone." Ànifa waved goodbye to their thylacoleo allies.

"*I wish you well,*" she projected to them.

The narrow slot canyon reminded her of the slot canyon she and Theodore passed through together in the Watthana Mountain Range. Back then, they had been riding woolly rhinoceros, at least on the way back from Sage Mason's. Everything had been so much simpler then.

The slot canyon they were entering differed vastly from the one they passed through in Sathon. This canyon was composed of dark gray limestone and snaked through the land as if they were following an ancient riverbed. The walls were rough and uneven, and Ànifa thought she spied small fossils of shellfish scattered about. She wanted to examine the fossils more closely, but now was not the time.

As they traversed the canyon, they followed a fresh trail of blood. The deeper into the canyon they got, the heavier the atmosphere grew. It felt as if they were walking straight into a nightmare.

They turned around a bend and the canyon opened into a small egg-shaped space. Standing at the opposite end of the canyon was a grotesque humanoid that looked vaguely similar to Danai. Surrounding him were two other similar creatures—Gnureavers.

While each Gnureaver was slightly different in appearance, they all had the same basic features. Their arms were nearly one and a half times as long as a typical human for their size, and each hand sported six curved claws. They waved their arms as if they had no bones, yet they stood slightly hunched over, their spines bending under their new monstrous forms. Four thin insectile legs supported their twisted bodies, each limb containing dozens of sharp thorns. Their skin had turned a sickly gray as if they were living cadavers, which they essentially were. Jutting out of their wide mouths were sharp fangs, and their eyes glowed bright red.

The Gnureaver, formerly known as Danai, was standing on top of the decapitated corpse of Carnivexion, the thylacoleo god. Now Ànifa knew why the tasmanileo and the other canine-like marsupials had seemed so lost and aimless. Their god, their leader, their source of love and protection was dead, murdered by the hideous Gnureavers.

The monstrous Danai held Carnivexion's head out in his right hand and the decapitated head of Sparassotereon in his left as he laughed maniacally.

"Welcome, my dear friends!" Danai's mouth moved, but it was Gnusaramnii's voice that emanated from the body.

"Gnusaramnii!" Ànifa shouted. "What have you done?"

"After this beast and the others failed to kill you all last night," the being once known as Danai said as he shook Carnivexion's head up and down, "I had this one bring the head of that lion bitch to me and then I took its life. It no longer served any purpose after it failed me."

"You murdering bastard!" Vesten shouted.

"Oh? And you haven't killed anyone? Now, isn't that hypocritical. You'll get what's coming to you. You will all get what's coming to you, for you have arrived at the place where you will die, only to be reborn as my minions!" The Gnureaver threw its head back and laughed.

"Gnusaramnii!" Ànifa shouted back. "I thought you told me a few nights ago that you didn't really want to kill me."

"And you believe everything I tell you? Well, I have never lied to you. I don't want to kill you, Ànifa, not yet. But I will if I must. And Dasch, why do you not join your brethren?"

"I am not your kin," Dasch growled angrily as he brandished his golden flaming sword. "Gnusaramnii may have made me who I am, but I am no slave to it!"

"Indeed," the Gnureaver said. "You can no longer be controlled; thus, you no longer serve any purpose. Die now."

A loud screech drowned out Dasch's reply. A fourth Gnureaver had jumped from the top of the canyon walls and fell to the ground. It landed behind them, its long insectile legs absorbed the hard impact. Towering above them, standing nearly three meters tall, it blocked their only means of escape.

"Fuck. We're in a tight spot," Vesten said.

"Yeah, a really tight spot," Cecil replied as he raised his battle-axe, wincing as he forced himself to his feet. He gripped the metal shaft tightly with his clammy hands.

"Be careful, everyone. We have little room to work with. We must be smart about this," Ànifa said as she readied her bow.

The deformed Danai broke out into another fit of maniacal laughter.

"Enough! I'll show you what I'm made of!" Dasch charged forward, blinded by his rage. Ànifa tried to grab his arm, but he shoved her away, knocking her back into Cecil.

"Yes. Come to me, my children," Gnusaramnii said, extending one of Danai's arms. Danai's hands now had long, sharp claws where his nails once were. "Come and meet your maker."

When Dasch reached Danai, he swung his golden flaming sword, intending to slice off one of his legs. Danai blocked the attack with his long claws and shoved him back.

The two Gnureavers surrounding Danai leaped into the air. One descended upon Dasch, while the other propelled itself toward Ànifa and the others. Theodore, with his staff raised in the air, shouted an incantation. But, before he could cast a spell, the Gnureaver bore down on top of him. Theodore hit the ground with a thud.

Ànifa hopped forward just in time, dodging the Gnureaver's aerial attack. She turned around and shot an arrow awash in blue flames at the attacking foe. The arrow struck its chest and buried in deep. The Gnureaver screeched and turned to face her.

Ànifa pulled another arrow from her quiver. Before she could notch it, Tyrona bumped into her, causing the arrow to fall to the ground.

"Sorry!" Tyrona cried as she raised her wand and attempted to cast a spell.

"We have no room!" Ànifa replied.

A moment later, a powerful gust of wind thrust the attacking Gnureaver into the air. Theodore stood and prepared to cast another spell.

"We need to trap them in a barrier. It's the only way!" Theodore panted. "Tyrona, give it all you got!"

Gnusaramnii's vile laughter echoed between the canyon walls. "Your efforts are futile."

The Gnureaver that blocked their retreat slashed at Vesten as he tried to defend himself with his scimitar. Vesten was pushed back into Cecil and they both crumpled to the ground.

Dasch continued to wildly attack Danai, but the monster effortlessly dodged each of his attacks. Dasch screamed, stepped off to the side, and slashed across Danai's stomach, finally landing a hit. It cried in pain, then lashed out, swinging its limp right limb wildly.

Dasch had no time to raise his sword to defend himself. The impact hit him square in the chest, sending him flying back into Tyrona and Theodore, once again interrupting their spellcasting.

Ànifa drew another arrow as she shouted at Dasch. Without warning, Vesten crashed into her as the rest of their team bowled over them.

Danai burst out into maniacal laughter once again. "Don't you see, Ànifa? You have had much time to grow, yet you are still weak! And your companions are weak! You cannot save this planet—no one can!"

"Shut the fuck up, you fuckin' bastard!" Vesten shouted as Cecil helped him to his feet.

"Finish this," Danai commanded his minions.

The Gnureavers pounced on them, knocking Ànifa into Cecil and Vesten as the group collapsed to the ground.

"You'll never defeat us," Ànifa said through gritted teeth. "We will defeat you."

"And yet it is you who have been defeated," Danai replied. "I will control this planet soon enough. Now that one of the Ekataramn is awake, the others will awaken soon enough. I don't need *you* to awaken them for me anymore."

"Is that what you truly believe?" Ànifa replied from the tangled mass she lay in. "We are connected, you and I, whether I like it or not, and I know a great deal about you now, Gnusaramnii. I know you are scared. I know you are only here, on this planet, because you are scared."

"Do you not sense my excitement? We are approaching the end of Eklatros. Can't you feel it? Now, my children, die!"

"No, wait!" Ànifa shouted.

All four Gnureavers stood over them and raked at them with their sharp claws.

So this is it then... she thought. *"If you can hear me, please save us."*

Come on, come on, come on, come on... hurry! Hurry, Joan! I've got to make it! For the Princess!

Joan de Ligtheramnii soared through the sky on outstretched wings toward the Oterrock Canyon. She held Ekatalal, the Divine Hammer of Justice in her right hand, and Halahkahna, the Divine Shield of Protection, in her left. She had never been away from Ànifa for this long before. They had always been together, and she was excited to see her again.

After Ànifa fell to the lands below, Joan had been ordered to stay back and observe from afar. While she served Ànifa, she could not disobey a direct order from King Vyereth and Queen Stella, the leaders of Yttendaus and rulers of Eklatros. They recognized Ànifa had to journey on her own, for they believed Yttendaus cast her out for a reason. Joan had fiercely argued that Ànifa needed her protection and convinced the royalty she could interfere only on one condition—when Ànifa and her companions were on death's doorstep.

That time had come. Joan flew as fast as she could, hoping that she wouldn't be too late.

Danai cackled heartily. The last thing she would hear would be Gnusaramnii's hideous laugh.

"Ha ha ha ha! Die now—"

"Not on my watch!" Joan cried as her hammer connected with Danai's skull. Danai's head exploded, shooting shards of brain matter and bone into the remaining Gnureavers. His limp, headless body slumped to the ground. Joan screamed in triumph, then soared to the nearest Gnureaver. It was over within seconds.

Ànifa looked at their gleaming, blood-stained savior. The angel was awash in white flames. She smiled as she stared into the eyes of her oldest friend. Joan smiled back at her. Ànifa closed her eyes and sighed in relief.

Welcome back, my good friend, Ànifa thought. *It's been too long.*

28

BATTLE FOR RHYTHM

Ànifa awoke, feeling refreshed and energetic. She hadn't felt this good for as long as she could remember. She lay under a tree in a peaceful forest. Birds were chirping above her as they quickly darted from branch to branch. She breathed in deep, smelling the crisp morning air.

She sat up and smiled at the angelic woman staring back at her. Joan wore a suit of intricately decorated armor. Upon looking at it, Ànifa knew it was made from the hard bark of Yttendaus itself. The armor was a combination of wood and steel that was finely interwoven together. The material was called Ytteniron and was exceptionally rare. It could only be created in the specialized forges of the angels. Joan's particular armor was a shimmering gold with black accents. Covering her legs was a skirt made from long brown strips of Ytteniron. It provided protection without causing any restraints in mobility.

Joan's long, curly blond hair fell gently down her back, nearly reaching the base of her expansive, white-feathered wings, which, even though they were folded neatly, rose a few centimeters above her head. The stark whiteness of her wings contrasted well with her delicate walnut skin. Joan's hazel eyes glowed warmly as she smiled.

"Joan, you came for us," Ànifa said, her voice heavy with emotion.

"Princess, I know your memories still allude you, but know I would never let anything ill fall upon you. It is my duty as your guardian to protect you."

"I may not remember much about our time together, but I do know that."

"Then that is what is most important," Joan said, placing a hand on Ànifa's shoulder. "I will help you with your memories in due time. For now, you must awaken Roheefy and restore rhythm to this land."

"We've finally made it thanks to you," Ànifa said, placing her hand on Joan's.

Joan smiled, then gave her a quick hug.

"I am so relieved that you are safe, Princess. You were close to dead when I found you. All of you were. I nearly depleted my magical reserves healing and restoring you all to full health. Your friend, Sir Cecil Kloud, barely made it."

"We are fortunate you arrived when you did. Thank you, Joan," Ànifa said, embracing her angel in another hug.

"I was only doing my duty."

"Joan," Ànifa said, pulling away from her. "Joan de Ligtheramnii. You're JL. The one who gave me my bow."

"Yes, Princess. I had to deliver it in secrecy. It was the only way your parents would allow it."

"Thank you. I don't know what I would have done without it."

"It was a necessity. Now, let's rouse the others. We have a big day ahead of us."

When everyone was awake, Joan and Ànifa explained what had happened and their relationship with each other. Some of the information was even new to Ànifa.

"As you may know, elves evolved from humans. In other words, all elves and their subsequent variations derived from humanity. Yttendaus is home to four variations of elves," Joan explained. "First and foremost, there are the elves—typical everyday elves. They are led by an ancient monarchy. Currently, Queen Stella Tshaila Ekataramnii, Ànifa's mother, holds the reigning title. Then, there are the faeries—elves who have, over time, evolved into winged creatures. Most faeries can change their body size as well—shrinking to the size of a hummingbird, or growing to be the size of an elf. Also, a faerie's wings are much more akin to the wings of butterflies than any other creature.

"Which leads me to the angels, the highest and most divine form of elf. An angel is a truly holy being, one touched and blessed by Eklatros herself. We cannot change sizes like the faeries, and our wings are akin to swan wings, as you can see. Angels have the innate ability to heal wounds and illnesses."

"Thank you, Joan," Tyrona said with a slight bow. "You truly are a godsend. We owe you our lives."

"You can repay me by finishing your quest. And I will be here right beside you," replied Joan.

"Thank you, Joan. Your help will be greatly appreciated. I don't believe you finished your story, though. You only told us of three elvish variations."

"I suppose you're right," Joan said. "I will explain this quickly, then we must be on our way.

"Now, keep in mind I do not enjoy talking about this. For it both saddens and angers me," Joan sighed, then continued. "The fourth variation of elf are the dark elves. These are the elves who choose to live in the dark underground, deep within the roots of Yttendaus. These elves have forsaken their birthright and cannot truly be called elves... nor have they fallen so far to devolve into humans. And neither are they akin to a half-breed," Joan glanced at Dasch. "Dark elves are strange, malevolent creatures that deal in the dark arts of death magic and necromancy, or so we have been led to believe. If I'm being honest, I haven't seen a dark elf in ages. No one has. But we all know they still exist. This is what angers me—not knowing the truth about them.

"Now, we must be on our way. We have an Ekataramn to awaken."

After a quick bite to eat, the seven companions followed the faint trail to the Great Barrier of Roffen. Joan led the way, her wings folded neatly on her back and her shield, Halahkahna, secured safely to her left arm. A strong, specialized magnet secured Ekatalal, her Divine Hammer, to her waist.

"I believe you all may know this, but each of the seven Ekataramn holds its own special power," Joan explained as they walked. "Only when all of the Ekataramn are working harmoniously together will Eklatros truly awaken, and it's indescribably beautiful. You have already awoken Kalahsem, whose power is that of the soul. Awakening Eklatros' soul first was the right decision. And now, you are approaching Roheefy, whose power is rhythm. In other words, Roheefy regulates the constant ebb and flow of all living things and their souls during life and after death. All life is subject to the rhythm of all other life around it and subsequently changes the world around it by simply existing.

"This ebb and flow has continued since Roheefy entered her dormant state, due to Roheefy's lingering consciousness. She continues to whisper, although only few can hear. If you hadn't been in such close proximity to Roheefy, it would have been much more difficult to find you. True, I can always sense Ànifa's feelings, but only in the moment. Roheefy is the one that tells us angels and elves about the inner workings of Eklatros.

"We must awaken Roheefy and give Eklatros her voice back. She needs to have a say in this world again, especially now that Gnusaramnii has corrupted dozens of different gods. I hope Roheefy will help restore balance to these gods so they can see the error of their ways."

"We were told that wouldn't be possible," Ànifa said.

"Anything is possible, Princess. The future is never set in stone."

The forest they passed through was not a natural forest, but a part of Roheefy. Roheefy was the largest of the Ekataramn, aside from Yttendaus. Its enormous canopy, which spread above them even though they were still not yet at the walls of the Great Barrier itself, had to be supported by various other flora, from tall trees to dangling vines that clung onto smaller shrubs and bushes. The animals that lived in the region enjoyed a peaceful life. Brightly colored peafowl crossed their path, blissfully ignoring the intrusion. There were also large serene tortoises nibbling on the undergrowth, tiny gray koalas that hung from vines, and tall brown giraffes that munched on leaves.

It didn't take them long to reach the Great Barrier. It was similar to the Great Barrier that had surrounded Kalahsem—a wall of wind, lighting, and fire. Jutting out of the Great Barrier were the thick branches of Roheefy as the canopy spread out above them. The branches were more like limbs of massive animals, as they were all covered in a thin layer of brown hair.

"It's been a very long time since I've been here," Theodore said solemnly as Tyrona leaned against him. "Visiting this place when I was young sparked my interest in the Great Barriers. And now I'm back. It's been quite the journey."

Ànifa looked at Theodore and smiled. "It really has been an amazing journey."

"Are you ready, Ànifa?" Joan asked.

Ànifa turned to Joan and nodded. "Yes. I am." She glanced back at her friends. "I'd say I'll see you all in a few minutes, but last time it was hours, so... I'll see you all when I see you."

"Yeah, see you soon," Cecil replied. "At least this forest seems safe. And we have an angel with us now."

"I'm going with Ànifa," Joan replied, surprising everyone.

"You are?" Ànifa asked. "I thought—"

Joan laughed softly. "Ànifa, you are special and unique in many ways. There are powers that are inherent to only you. But passing through the Great Barriers is not one of them. True, normal elves cannot do it, but elves like you and your family can, as well as all angels."

"If others can do it, why haven't they been awoken before?" Theodore asked. "Why let the Ekataramn go dormant in the first place?"

"It wasn't a decision made lightly," Joan replied. "And besides, by that point, humans had nearly forgotten of our existence, outside of the myths, of course. We couldn't appear without causing an uproar."

"So why me? Why now?" Ànifa asked.

"Eklatros chose you because, at this point, you are the only one who can wake them. Not even I can awaken them in your stead. You, and only you, can do this task."

"Fuckin' A," Vesten said, breaking the silence.

"That's our princess!" Cecil exclaimed.

"Thanks everyone," Ànifa replied, then she took a deep breath. "Let's do this, Joan."

"See you in a bit," Tyrona said with a wave, as she looped her arm through Theodore's.

Ànifa gave her a knowing smile and then turned to face the wall of chaos that spun silently in front of her.

"Let's do this," Ànifa repeated to herself, then took a step forward. She looked back and saw Joan following her. Theodore, Tyrona, Vesten, and Cecil were waving, and when she met Dasch's eyes, he nodded deeply. Joan stepped beside her and took her right hand.

"We go together, Princess."

Ànifa nodded, then turned and plunged into the maelstrom. Similar to before, when she stepped into the whirlwind, the wind rushed past her without touching her. The major difference about this whirlwind was the added bursts of charged electricity that soared through the whirlwind whenever two lightning bolts crashed into each other. Ànifa idly wondered how the entire whirlwind wasn't simply a wall of electricity.

She gripped Joan's hand tightly as they walked deeper into the malevolence.

Theodore lounged against a tall tree. Tyrona sat beside him with her hand resting on top of his. Dasch, Vesten, and Cecil were sitting in a circle together, a short distance away from them.

"You know Dorie, you certainly got caught up in something phenomenal."

Theodore chuckled. "Indeed, I have. It's what I've always wanted —to have a purpose, to do something for the good of the planet... to feel needed."

Tyrona caressed Theodore's hand with her thumb. "You were always needed. You've always had a place in this life."

"Well, it certainly didn't seem that way when I was exiled. And over such an idiotic mistake, too. I should have known better," Theodore said, placing his palm on his forehead.

"Don't be so hard on yourself, Dorie."

"I know Ty. It's just… that was the lowest I've ever been. The only way I could keep myself going was by throwing myself into my research."

"And I'm glad you did."

"Yes, but it's been very dangerous. We all almost died yesterday. I… I don't know what I would do if I lost you… if I lost anyone."

"Theodore," Tyrona said sharply, catching him off guard. She looked deep into his eyes. "I chose to accompany you. No one asked me to. And if I remember correctly, you didn't really protest."

"I was being selfish," Theodore said. "I simply wanted to spend more time with you. When you got hurt the other day, and I had to hold on to you while the saber-toothed lion god whisked us away—rest in peace, Sparassotereon—I don't think I've ever been so scared in my life."

Tyrona leaned in and kissed Theodore on his cheek.

"You're sweet," Tyrona said, then she sighed as she repositioned herself against the tree, snuggling closer to Theodore. "You know, after the events from yesterday… well, I've been thinking—"

"Hey," Cecil called as he stumbled over to them, followed by Vesten and Dasch.

Tyrona quickly distanced herself from Theodore.

Cecil looked at the sky and blushed. "Oh shit, I'm sorry to interrupt—"

"What is it, Cecil?" Tyrona said harshly.

"Yeah, so we've been talking."

"Obviously. About what?" Tyrona said, glaring at him.

"What do you all think about Joan?" Cecil asked.

"Oh," Tyrona said, her annoyance fading. "Well, she saved all of us, didn't she?"

"Yeah, she did. But where did she really come from?"

"Cecil, she told us she came from Yttendaus, that she's Ànifa's guardian angel," Theodore said.

"Yes, but why now? Why didn't she intervene when Charlotte was taken, or when those crows attacked us, or during our crazy race across Gallheim?" Cecil asked. "We've been in a lot of dangerous situations and, what, Joan was up there watching the whole time, doing nothing?"

"She did tell us it was only because of orders from the king and queen that she stayed behind," Dasch said.

"Right," Cecil said, "but as I said earlier, I don't know if I really buy that."

"Aye, me too," Vesten said. "Listen, I think that she's cool and all, but it seems too fuckin' convenient. That whole trap set by... whatever the fuck Danai turned into."

"You're suggesting that Joan set it up?" Theodore said.

"Fuck, why not? What do we really know about Joan?" Vesten said.

"You knew nothing about us, and you took us all in," Theodore said. "Why are you judging now?"

"Did anyone else see how easily she killed those monsters?" Cecil exclaimed. "She tore through them like a knife through butter."

Vesten nodded. "Aye, and that voice that Ànifa was familiar with—"

"Right, Gnusaramnii, the voice she hears sometimes," Theodore said.

"Yes, right," Cecil said. "There's that, too."

Tyrona sighed. "I don't know why you're all conspiring against an angel—Ànifa's *guardian angel*. I don't doubt her for a second."

"Perhaps it's not her we should be doubting," Dasch suggested. "I also believe in Joan. Angels were only a myth in my era, but I have found no reason to doubt her."

"Maybe you're right, Dasch. And yet this whole situation feels fishy," Cecil said. "Something is definitely going on here."

"I understand what you're saying," Theodore said. "It's been a lot to process. I'll keep my mind open, but I'm with Tyrona on this one, honestly." Theodore glanced to Tyrona, who shot him a quick smile.

"Right, that's all I'm saying," Cecil said. "Just keep an eye on her."

"Yes, we all should," Dasch grumbled. "Whether or not Joan set this up, I have a strange sense that there are strings being pulled by higher powers."

Ànifa and Joan emerged from the Great Barrier. They stood in front of a massive tree, if it could even be called a tree.

Its thick brown trunk was nearly fourteen meters across. Oddly, the trunk only had three branches, one of which turned into the head of a green dinosaur with a bone-like beak. The dinosaur cocked its head sideways and squawked like a crow. One of the other branches appeared to be Roheefy's nose, as underneath the trunk was a wide white grin with two large green ovals set above it. Growing from the end of the nose was a round, pale green bush.

Above Roheefy's eyes, there appeared to be a mossy green beast biting into the thick branch. Yellow teeth-like leaves jutted out from its mouth, grinning with macabre amusement. Branching out from the mossy beast were the dozens of smaller branches that supported the canopy.

The dinosaur head cackled as it bobbed up and down.

"Welcome, Princess Ànifa Tataluynnia Ekataramnii and Joan de Ligtheramnii. I have been expecting you," Roheefy said, her voice emanating out of the white grin that sat beneath the nose-like branch.

Upon hearing Roheefy's voice, Joan knelt and bowed her head low to the ground. Ànifa followed suit.

"We are humbled to be in your presence, divine one," Joan said, her head still bowed to the ground.

"I am humbled to be in yours. Now please rise, Joan and Ànifa, and place your hands on my iguanodon head."

Ànifa rose to her feet and looked at the 'face' of Roheefy. A moment later, the green dinosaur head with a bone-like beak approached. Ànifa placed her hand on its head, and motioned for Joan to do the same.

"Why are you humbled, if I may ask?" Ànifa asked.

"Ànifa, you are my dearest sister. Your coming has been foretold, and I have been waiting and observing. You have journeyed well to get here. Do not be dismayed by the deaths, both human and animal. Sparassotereon sacrificed herself and her pride for your safety. Do not mourn for her. Instead, celebrate her, for she died a truly heroic death.

"As for the humans you killed indirectly by Krakuluthosii, you should not feel sorry for them either," Roheefy continued. "They made their choice to fight against Eklatros the moment they sided with that vile man, Danai Simasathien."

"But I don't want anyone to die, whether they're good or bad," Ànifa said softly. "Everyone deserves a chance at life."

"My sweet sister, you are pure. You cannot see the evils that lie in the shadows, even when the greatest of these evils speaks to you subconsciously."

"Gnusaramnii. I know he's bad, I really do..." Ànifa said, trailing off.

"Sister, your intentions are good, yet there are some that are too far gone. If you cannot learn that, your journey will fail," Roheefy said.

"I will not let that happen," Joan cut in. "Not under my watch."

"That decision is not up to you, guardian. You cannot protect her from everything. Now, let us end this discussion. You sought me out for a reason, and that reason has been accomplished. The whirlwind will dissipate soon. Now, please be prepared."

The iguanodon head cackled loudly as it withdrew. A moment later, a wave of energy hit Ànifa square in the chest. She flew back hard, only to be caught by Joan. Joan used her wings to encase them both in a protective shield.

"This is the reason I'm here, your grace," Joan said to her. "Even you cannot survive the torrent of energy that's flooding from Roheefy."

"Thank you, Joan. Thank you for protecting me," Ànifa replied, huddled against Joan's chest.

"I do everything in my power to protect you, Princess."

"Please call me Ànifa."

"But you are a princess."

"I guess I am. I'm just not used to it."

"I understand, Princess."

The noise of the great roaring whirlwind grew so loud it drowned out all other sounds. Even through the feathery encasement of Joan's wings, Ànifa could feel the raw energy pulsing out of Roheefy. Centuries worth of vibrations were flowing out of the Ekataramn, let loose simply by Ànifa's presence. The roaring continued for what felt like hours, although it could've only been minutes.

"Ànifa. Joan. You may come out now," Roheefy said.

Joan cautiously unfurled her wings, releasing Ànifa. Ànifa blinked, allowing her eyes to adjust to the light. She looked around and saw that the whirlwind was gone. Where it had once stood was a deep trench. It was slowly being filled with water from an unseen spring. The trench was deep and wide—too deep to climb into and too wide to jump across, yet there was one spot in which a large root was exposed, creating a bridge across the newly created chasm.

"Thank you," Ànifa said as she turned toward Roheefy.

"Nay, thank *you*, sister. Now, I believe your friends are waiting for you."

Ànifa turned to Joan. Joan smiled at her, then screamed in agony and clutched her hands to her head and fell to her knees.

"Joan!" Ànifa cried, squatting next to her. "What's wrong?"

"Now that my rhythm has been restored, Joan is experiencing an overload of information from all across Eklatros," Roheefy said. "Don't worry, she'll recover shortly."

"Joan," Ànifa called softly as she rubbed Joan's back.

"Princess... don't... ugh! Don't worry... about me." Joan collapsed to the ground.

"Joan!"

A moment later, Joan opened her eyes and got to her feet.

"My deepest apologies, Princess. It was a lot to process, but now I know where we must go next. Come, Princess Ànifa. We must get to Panabeeta quickly."

"The sooner the better," Roheefy said. "Gnusaramnii is getting stronger by the hour and its hold on the gods is growing. There isn't much time."

"Can you do anything about the gods it corrupted?" Ànifa asked.

"I cannot help those that have fallen, but I can help to protect those that still stand true; however, my influence is limited. I can only do so much," Roheefy replied.

"Which is why we must go. Now," Joan commanded.

"Okay. Lead the way."

Goodbye Roheefy, Ànifa thought. *I know you can hear my thoughts... just like Kalahsem and Gnusaramnii.*

You called me sister, and I feel akin to you as well, although I cannot explain it. I believe we are connected, like everything on Eklatros is connected. And if everything on Eklatros is connected, then you are correct. We must awaken the next Ekataramn. We must fight back with everything we have.

29

BATTLE FOR FLIGHT

When Ànifa and Joan returned to the others, they found them sitting under a tree, deep in conversation.

"Everyone, we must be on our way," Ànifa said as they approached, finally letting go of Joan's hand.

"You're back already?" Tyrona exclaimed, looking at them in surprise.

"Yes. Vesten, stand up. We must be on our way," Joan commanded.

"What? Where are we going?" Vesten asked.

"Back to your ship. We're going to need it," Joan replied.

Vesten stood up, stretched, and produced a deep yawn. "Well, fuck, why don't we all just go together, then?"

"Oh, we're not walking. We're flying there," Joan said as everyone got to their feet.

"Oh shit. You mean..." Vesten said, trailing off.

"That's right. You're going for a ride. Do you have any goggles or protective eye-wear?" Joan asked.

"Uh... no?" Vesten replied, raising an eyebrow in confusion.

"Do we have anything in that magic backpack of ours?" Cecil asked Ànifa.

"I'm not sure. Let's check," she said as she reached into her trenchdress.

"Remember, you have to say the spell to enlarge it to its actual size, which is *projorviidae*," Tyrona said with a small wave of her finger, mimicking her wand.

"Right. *Projorviidae*," Ànifa said, causing the backpack to expand in her hand. She was momentarily surprised that even though it was back to its normal size, it still weighed next to nothing.

"Alright, let's see. What are we looking for?" Tyrona said. She reached into the backpack and pulled out two pairs of snow goggles. "Will these work?"

"Yes, that will do just fine," Joan said, taking one of them and handing it to Vesten.

"What the fuck is this for?" Vesten asked as he took the goggles.

"Do you want your eyes to dry up and fall out of their sockets?" Joan asked.

"Uh... fuck no."

"Then put those on."

Vesten stared at the goggles for a moment longer, then hastily slipped them over his head.

"Do you need the other pair?" Tyrona asked, holding the goggles out to Joan.

"No, just the one is fine. Thank you, Tyrona," Joan said. "Do you have any extra cloaks in there?"

"Sure I do," Tyrona said, reaching into the maw of the backpack and pulling out a long, deep purple cloak. Joan took it and secured it to her belt.

"Are you ready, Vesten?"

"Aye, I suppose so."

Joan wrapped her arms around Vesten, holding him tightly, then leaped into the air and took off with Vesten screaming curses.

"What was all that about?" Theodore asked as he watched them fly away.

"On our way back here, Joan and I devised a plan to get us to Panna Isle by tomorrow morning," Ànifa explained.

"How will that be possible?" Cecil asked.

"I don't fully understand it, but Joan will be able to make *West Wind* fly, and she needs Vesten to pilot it. We'll be meeting on a quiet beach near Nora's Docks."

"And how are we going to get to Nora's Docks?" Theodore asked. "It's at the southernmost tip of this continent. We're a long way from there, even if we didn't have to pass through a mountain range."

"We're catching a ride ourselves," Ànifa replied. "Tyrona, can you shrink the backpack again?"

"Sure, no problem."

"Thanks," Ànifa said as she took the miniaturized backpack from Tyrona.

Ànifa closed her eyes and took a deep breath. She called out to both Roheefy and Kalahsem. She was going to need all the help she could get. Ànifa had called upon gods before, but nothing like this. She was preparing to summon Hartipavoh, the peafowl god. The Eklatros history book also called her the Ruler of the Skies and even The Divine Rainbow in some passages.

"*Roheefy... Kalahsem... heed my call. I need your divine powers, my sisters,*" she thought. In response, she felt the two separate energies converge upon her. "*Hartipavoh, hear my plea. We need your assistance, for the sake of Eklatros!*"

A sharp peal rang through the air above them, and a moment later they were cast in shadow as Hartipavoh flew over them. She turned around and descended to the ground softly.

Hartipavoh was beautiful. Her feathers, unlike other peafowl, were truly the colors of the rainbow, displayed in an intricate mandala pattern. She proudly displayed her uniquely striped tail feathers as she held her head high. Her crest was purple with pinkish tips.

The others stood behind Ànifa in awe as she approached Hartipavoh and gently stroked her chest. Hartipavoh stood nearly three times her height and looked at her with her large black eyes.

"Alright everyone. It's time to fly."

Vesten was thankful for the goggles. Only now he wished he had an entire face shield.

The wind tore at him as they soared across Roffen. He thought he'd be used to the wind, being a sailor and all, but this wasn't even on the same level. It was an unrelenting torrent of wind unlike anything he had ever experienced. His jaw ached as he clenched it tightly to prevent his mouth and throat from getting ravaged.

Two painful hours later, they arrived outside Port Columbo. Joan landed in a small alcove on the beach to prevent anyone from spotting them.

"Now what? I don't think you can just walk into Port Columbo with those fuckin' wings."

"That's what I got the cloak for, dummy," Joan replied as she untied the cloak from her belt.

"Ah, right. Hey! Who the fuck you callin' dummy?" Vesten cried.

Joan draped the cloak over her wings. "Only a dummy would curse in the presence of an angel."

"Hey, I don't care about that shit. I talk how I talk. Of course, I don't curse quite as fuckin' much as I used to, I suppose."

"I wouldn't know," Joan said as she finished tying the cloak's sash and threw on the hood. She stood with her arms slightly outstretched and said, "How do I look?"

"I mean... a little hunchbacked, but good overall."

"As long as I don't look like an angel."

"Well, you are angelic, but I don't think anyone would guess you're a fuckin' angel."

"Thanks, dummy," Joan said with a grin. "Now, let's go."

"So, where's your ship exactly?" Joan asked as they walked toward Port Columbo.

"Should be at the dock where I left her, unless Briggs had her moved for some fuckin' reason," Vesten replied.

"Good. Let's be quick about this now. Ànifa and the others might already be at Nora's Docks by now."

"Nora's Docks?" Vesten asked, stopping in his tracks. "Just how the fuck are they gonna get there?"

Ànifa held on tightly as Hartipavoh flew through the Nicolah Mountain Range. Cecil, Theodore, Tyrona, and Dasch clutched on behind her. Hartipavoh was large, and her body was wide, allowing them to have room to themselves as they held fistfuls of her dense and durable plumage. Tyrona and Theodore rode beside each other, allowing them to talk between themselves.

Hartipavoh flew at a comfortable pace. They didn't have far to go, now that they had wings to take them there. If all worked out as planned, they would reach Nora's Docks just before Joan and Vesten returned with *West Wind*.

Ànifa gazed out at the land beneath them. From above, everything looked much smaller and more peaceful. From this vantage point, it was hard to see the corruption taking place below.

"It's certainly an amazing view, isn't it?" Dasch said. He had crawled along Hartipavoh's back to sit next to her.

"Yes, this planet is absolutely beautiful," she replied.

"There's something I wanted to talk to you about," Dasch said after a moment of silence.

"What is it?" Ànifa asked.

"Before, when you were gone, the others were expressing their doubts about Joan."

"Oh, like what?" Ànifa asked.

"They believe we were set up, and Danai had only drawn us into that slot canyon so Joan could come and save us."

"They believe that someone is behind all of this—someone besides Gnusaramnii?" Ànifa asked thoughtfully.

"Yes. And while some of the others have their doubts about Joan herself, they think—"

"They think it could be someone in my family," Ànifa said, jumping ahead to the most logical conclusion.

"Yes. Could it be possible?" Dasch asked.

"I don't remember anything about my family, Dasch. For some reason, the memories of my family still allude me after all this time. Even when Joan mentioned the names of my parents, there was nothing. No memories at all."

"Some could say that in itself is suspicious," Dasch said. "If someone is controlling everything, perhaps they are the ones blocking your memories."

"You're not wrong," Ànifa replied, then shook her head. "I don't know. All I know is that once I remembered who Joan was, I was immediately comforted. Joan has been by my side my entire life. I firmly believe that she would never do me any harm."

"Not knowingly," Dasch replied.

"Yes. Not knowingly. I suppose even angels could be manipulated. If I've learned anything from Gnusaramnii being in my head, it is that anyone can be manipulated."

***

Vesten led Joan through the crowded streets of Port Columbo. No one was paying them any attention as the throngs of people went busily about their day.

Joan followed silently, taking it all in. These were sights, sounds, and smells she had never experienced. All she had ever known was Yttendaus—there were no angels during the time of the Great War. Rather, angels were a byproduct of that war, evolving as a necessity to be a higher governance for all living things. She had been one of those eight angels. She didn't even know if any new angels would ever be created. They were meant to be forever pure with no means of reproduction.

For the most part, Joan paid little attention to humans, but Vesten was certainly a special man. He had remained pure-hearted even after his losses and regrets.

"Alright, we're almost there," Vesten called back to her as they stepped onto the docks.

They walked past the rows of ships, each one anchored in an orderly fashion, and headed to the end of the docks where *West Wind* was anchored. As she and Vesten neared the ship, they approached two guards.

"Halt!" the male guard called out. "Stop right there!"

Vesten and Joan stopped immediately.

"State your name and your purpose!" the female guard commanded.

"My name is Vesten Teixeira. I am the captain of this ship, *West Wind*. Rear Admiral Briggs put this ship under his authority as a favor for my friend, Sir Cecil Kloud."

"You must mean Rear Admiral Mont Simmons. He said there were five of you. Where are the others?" the male guard asked.

"We're meeting the others at Nora's Docks," Vesten replied. "It's a long way from here, as you know, so we must get on our way quickly."

"No one may step foot on that ship without Rear Admiral Mont Simmons' direct permission and the Rear Admiral is not here. He left Captain Ledger in charge. Officer Gillian, go find the captain."

"At once, Lieutenant Leonhart," Officer Gillian said with a salute.

"I apologize for the delay, but I'm sure you understand," Lieutenant Leonhart said as he adjusted his weight.

"It's fine, honestly. I'd rather have it this way than the fuckin' opposite. I'm glad she's getting taken care of real well."

"It has been an unusual assignment, looking after a civilian's ship in this way. You must be on an important mission."

"Yes, which is why we must be on our way," Joan said, speaking for the first time.

"I understand ma'am, but orders are orders."

It didn't take long for Officer Gillian to return with Captain Ledger in tow. He was a handsome man with blond hair that fell to his shoulders.

"Ah, you must be Vesten. And is this Ànifa with you?" Captain Ledger asked.

"No, this is Joan. Ànifa and the others are on their way to Nora's Docks." Vesten said.

Captain Ledger raised an eyebrow in surprise. "Nora's Docks, is it? You must be on your way, then."

"Thank you, Captain Ledger, I appreciate your help," Vesten said. "Where is the Rear Admiral, if I may ask?"

"Rear Admiral Mont Simmons has taken several others to Fort Turner for the world summit."

"I see. Thank you again," Vesten said. He motioned to Joan as he stepped onto the ramp that led to *West Wind*'s deck.

"Travel safe!" Captain Ledger replied with a wave.

Once they were on board, Vesten looked around, took a deep breath and smiled.

"Home sweet fuckin' home," Vesten said. "Now, what is it you have to do?"

"First, you must take us out to sea. I can't do anything here," Joan replied.

"Aye, let's get on with it, then. Help me raise the anchor, would ya?"

About fifteen minutes later, Vesten and Joan were sailing away from Port Columbo. Vesten steered *West Wind* south, toward Nora's Docks.

"So, you're going to make my girl fuckin' fly, is that right?" Vesten asked incredulously.

"Indeed I am," Joan said as she threw off Tyrona's spare cloak and secured it to her belt. "This ship has a lower level, right?"

"Aye, right this way," Vesten said, leading Joan down to the lower deck.

Joan stopped before the small broom closet that lay between two of the bedrooms. "This will do. All I need is a small space to focus my energy. Please stay below deck during the transformation," Joan said as she stepped into the closet and shut the door behind her.

Vesten looked around *West Wind* in bewilderment. "The fuck? What fucking transformation? Oh shit, what's going to happen to you, girl?"

Hartipavoh landed on a soft sandy beach about six kilometers west of Nora's Docks. Ànifa and the others dismounted and said their thanks. Hartipavoh gave them a friendly cry, then spread her wings and leaped into the air.

"What an absolutely majestic creature. Fare you well, Hartipavoh," Tyrona said as she gazed at the rainbow god.

"I gotta say—her feathers really match my plume," Cecil said proudly.

"You're right," Ànifa said as she examined Cecil's plume. "Who designed it anyway?"

"I believe it was a gift from Headmaster Barrow."

Before them stretched the Lopan Sea. The sun was high in the sky, making the shimmering sea a brilliant, vibrant blue. Ànifa idly noticed her hair change shades to match the color of the sea. She hadn't worn her bonnet since Joan's rescue, and it felt liberating to have her hair flow naturally about in the breeze once again.

"It's beautiful here," Ànifa said softly, breaking the silence.

"It really is amazing, isn't it?" Cecil said. "I've always wanted to come here. All I have ever heard about Nora's Docks and its surrounding area is that it's one of the most beautiful places on Eklatros."

"From this, I would agree. Let's see," she said as she pulled out Dante's map.

It had been about three and a half hours since they parted ways with Joan and Vesten. They probably had about thirty minutes or so until they would get here if Joan had been correct about the timing.

"So, we really aren't too far from Panna Isle from here," Ànifa said as she studied the map.

"Yeah, we're pretty close," Cecil replied, glancing at the map. "If Vesten and Joan arrive soon, we really might be able to get there by tomorrow morning."

"I'm looking forward to seeing a flying ship," Ànifa said.

"Me too. I really can't wrap my head around it yet, honestly." Cecil replied.

"Well, no one has ever flown before. Not really, at least, not in a ship," Theodore said. "It'll be a first for Eklatros."

"Yes, it will be," Tyrona echoed. "Would anyone mind if we take a little time to ourselves while we wait?"

"I was going to suggest the same thing, actually," Ànifa said. "I want to try and finish the Eklatros history book soon."

"Ah yes, you should," Tyrona replied. "What you learn may even come in handy."

"Yeah, it's certainly possible," Ànifa said. She took out the miniatured backpack from a pocket inside her trenchdress.

"Well, come on then, Dorie," Tyrona said, tugging at Theodore's sleeve playfully. "Let's go over there." She pointed down the beach to a rocky outcrop.

"Alright, I'll see you all later," Cecil said, giving Theodore and Tyrona a wave as they headed off. "Oh, and same to you, Dasch!"

Dasch turned toward them as he slipped away. "Yup. See you later," he grunted, then continued to go off on his own.

"Well, I suppose it's been a while since I've trained with my battle-axe. I think now is a good time to get back into it," Cecil said. "I also want to practice that golden flaming trick Dasch does. Hopefully, I'll get it one of these days."

"Yeah, hopefully. See you in a bit," Ànifa said, then returned Cecil's wave.

Ànifa stretched wide, holding her arms out above her, then bent down to touch her toes. She did a few other stretches and then said the spell to enlarge the backpack. She pulled out the book, *A Collective History: The Magical World of Eklatros*. It had been with her since Charlotte's, and now she was ready to finish it.

She opened the book to chapter thirty-five. This chapter was the first of seven chapters that followed a different historical figure from the Great War, and it introduced a woman named Eliziana Lockhart. She was born into a humble family of locksmiths and key makers. When the war began, Eliziana rose to be a leader in her community and rallied those around her to fight and defend their small settlement, Quail. In the end, Eliziana died during a particularly intense battle in a foreign land and was honored posthumously as Quail's one and only queen.

A half hour turned into an hour, then another passed, and still Joan and Vesten hadn't arrived yet. The sun dipped toward the horizon, causing the ocean to shimmer in the evening light.

Ànifa had only two chapters left. Aside from Eliziana, she had read about four other heroes who played a part in the larger victory that had been led by Kieth Angelcross. Like Eliziana's tale, the others had humble beginnings—a sheepherder, a seamstress, a cobbler, and a fisherman. Ànifa felt as if the stories told the message that anyone, anywhere, can be a hero and a leader. All it takes is a willingness to stand for what you believe in and fight to turn those beliefs into a reality. If everyone back then had submitted to the invasion, this planet would have fallen long ago. Yet Eliziana, Kieth, Dasch, and the other heroes of the past kept that from happening.

As Ànifa was mulling over these thoughts, Cecil's armor clanked as he sat next to her.

"Oh, Cecil!" Ànifa cried as she tensed in surprise. "I didn't hear you approach."

"Really? Even with all the clanking?"

"I must have been lost in my own world."

"I'm sorry for interrupting you, milady. I'm just worried about the others," Cecil said solemnly. "They should've been back by now."

"Yes, according to what Joan had estimated," Ànifa replied. "I'm not worried, though. She also said that she had never performed the magic she intended to use on *West Wind*. It could be she underestimated just how much it would take."

"Yeah, that's true. You know her pretty well, I suppose," Cecil said with a slight shrug.

"Yes, I suppose I do. It's a strange feeling, though."

"You never forget those closest to your soul, no matter what," Dasch said with a grunt as he strolled up behind them, startling both Ànifa and Cecil.

"Holy Eklatros," Cecil said, holding his right hand to his heart. "You appeared like a shadow."

"Perhaps I am a shadow," Dasch replied.

"Well, talk about an angel and you'll hear her wings. Here they come now," Ànifa said, pointing off into the distance as *West Wind* sailed toward them.

"Well, what do ya know. I'll go fetch Theodore and Tyrona," Cecil said.

"No, it's fine. I'm sure they have noticed by now too."

"Oh, right. Yeah, I guess I already did interrupt them earlier today. They deserve some time to themselves," Cecil said.

"Indeed. Have more tact," Dasch grumbled.

"Hey, what do you know of love?" Cecil shot back.

"What do you know?" Dasch replied, shutting Cecil up.

The sun finished setting as the party regrouped on the upper deck of *West Wind*. Joan had completely remodeled the sails and the mast so they could gyrate in any direction to catch the wind. The sails were now more rounded and aerodynamic. Even the body of the ship was more streamlined.

Vesten laughed as the others took in the newly remodeled ship. "Welcome to the new and improved *West Wind*! Joan did a fuckin' mighty fine job, wouldn't ya say?"

"I'm happy you approve of the changes," Joan replied. She looked tired as she slumped forward, her wings touching the ground for extra support.

"So, it works then?" Theodore asked. "This ship can now fly?"

"Fuck yes she can! It's magnificent! The most extraordinary experience of my life!"

"Yes, I just wish it hadn't taken so much out of me," Joan replied. "That's why we're late. I got the ship to fly, but the transformation took more energy than I had anticipated. I couldn't keep the ship in the air for long."

"That's not a problem," Ànifa replied. "You're here now, and that's all that matters. Besides, it's getting dark. We may as well rest here until morning."

"That would be most wonderful," Joan replied. "I should be back to full strength by then."

West Wind lay anchored off the southern tip of Roffen. Ànifa let Joan share her bed with her, as they had done before when Ànifa was younger.

Before she went to sleep, Ànifa finished the final two chapters of *A Collective History: The Magical World of Eklatros.*

At the end of the book, scribbled in what appeared to be a woman's handwriting, was a short note:

I had a strange dream after my last read-through. A woman, shining brightly and descending from the skies, came to visit me. It felt so real and so powerful.

— Charlotte Tuesti, Ciditember 14th, 8867

Ànifa knew it was the year 8880. It was clear Charlotte had foreseen Ànifa's coming.

Charlotte, I hope you are well, she thought. *I hope the medics at Ajenti have healed you by now. I'm sorry I'm not there with you, but know I care. And I know you care about me, too. If you had this dream, maybe you were waiting for me... maybe that's why you lived off on your own, in your tent. I wish I got to know you better before you were taken away. I hope I can see you again, after all of this.*

As for now, we must complete our mission. Panabeeta is next, on Panna Isle. And then, according to Joan, we need to return to Schelff Island. I hope we make it in time.

30

BATTLE FOR DESIRE

Joan was up about an hour before dawn. She wanted to get a head start on the day. Even though they only had about two hours of flight time ahead of them, she had a feeling it would be a long day.

Ànifa slumbered deeply as Joan quietly got out of bed. She could sense a darkness in Ànifa's dreams, so she let her hands hover a few centimeters over Ànifa's head and urged Ànifa's thoughts to calm so she could sleep peacefully for the rest of the morning. Joan watched Ànifa's body relax, then smiled to herself and quietly exited the room.

Joan closed the door softly behind her and quietly crept to what she now thought of as her navigation console, although it still served as Vesten's broom closet.

"You're up early, I see," Vesten said, standing in the doorway of his room, wearing nothing but his red polka-dotted briefs. He yawned as he stood there, scratching his unshaven face. His light red beard was starting to fill in, and it suited him well.

"Ah, Vesten. I'm sorry to have awoken you," Joan said, looking away quickly. Her eyes had lingered for too long on his figure, and her face was growing warm.

"You didn't, I was already awake. Plus, I can hear everything that

385

happens on this fuckin' ship. She is my baby girl, no matter what. She's new and improved now though," he added, raising his eyebrows.

Joan couldn't help but smile. "Your 'baby girl?' Is that right? I appreciate you letting me take control."

"Honestly though, under any other circumstances, I wouldn't have. No one steers or harms *West Wind* and gets away with it, or so I fuckin' thought. But you're different. You can be my co-pilot any day."

"I appreciate it. I really must be getting to it. We have a long day ahead of us, and I want to get moving."

"I'll let you get to it, then," Vesten said, then gave her a quick nod. "You don't need my permission; although, I suppose you already fuckin' knew that. I'll go raise the anchor now. Alone."

"Yes, thank you. That would be helpful. I'll talk to you soon, Vesten," Joan said as she stepped into the closet.

She had been caught off guard. She wasn't expecting to see anyone this morning, and certainly not a half-naked Vesten. She shook her head and took a deep breath to collect her thoughts. She had to focus. Yesterday she had been tired, and she hadn't focused well. She had nearly crashed *West Wind* into the ocean—it had taken everything in her power to settle *West Wind* down gently.

But that had been a test flight—the only test flight. Now it was time to make this ship fly.

Joan focused within herself and allowed her consciousness to expand. She wrapped it around *West Wind*—let it consume *West Wind*. Joan was becoming *West Wind*, in the ethereal sense.

Joan felt the ship as if it was her own body. She knew the placement of each nail and how every wooden plank fit together. She knew the cracks and where the pests gathered. She knew its secrets.

Joan opened her wings—the sails of the ship—and, in her mind's eye, watched as the ship lifted off the surface of the ocean. She let the wind flow underneath the ship and raise it into the upper jet streams. She had to get above the clouds to escape the worst of the weather, a feat she had yet to fully accomplish.

Joan knew in her soul she could do this. There was no question of failure.

***

As soon as Vesten finished raising the anchor, he felt the ship lurch underneath him as it rose into the air. An energy barrier appeared over the outer deck of the ship, which would allow Vesten to continue watching safely without fear of being blown overboard by the strong winds.

"You don't have any time to waste, do ya?" Vesten said out loud to Joan. Although she wasn't present, he sensed she could hear him. "This is a fuckin' beautiful sight, though."

Vesten watched—feeling like a kid again, full of innocent wonder and excitement—as his ship soared into the sky. His gaze followed the retreating shoreline as it faded into the distance.

Suddenly, they were immersed within a cloud, and Vesten watched in wonder as the puffs of condensed water vapor streamed past them. A moment later, they burst out from the cloud cover and settled down to sail effortlessly on the top of the cloud, as if it were the ocean itself.

"Fuckin' A. I knew you could do it, Joan. I know you were tired yesterday, but today, you did it. *West Wind* can fly as high as any bird, or angel for that matter," Vesten said out loud to himself. He jumped in surprise when a voice answered him.

"Yeah, this is absolutely incredible," Cecil said as he appeared next to him. Cecil was wearing his pale green underclothes.

"Fuckin' shit," Vesten said as he clutched his heart. "You scared me. I didn't realize anyone was up."

"How could I sleep? It was quite tumultuous. The movement woke me right up."

"Yeah, I'm sure she'll get better with that eventually. But where else can you get a view like this?"

The clouds continued to stream beneath them as they sailed

ahead. Behind them, the sun was rising, casting its initial morning rays ahead of them and lighting their way forward.

"Yeah. It's really amazing. You may want to put on some clothes soon, though, before anyone else gets up," Cecil said as he kept his gaze on the spectacular view.

Theodore lay back on the bed, sweating. He was old, and it showed. He huffed and wheezed, then coughed deeply and wheezed some more.

"Oh, I'm so incredibly sorry, Tyrona. Nothing ruins the mood more than an old man's hacking."

"Dorie, if I cared about any of that, I wouldn't be with you. I love you for you," Tyrona said as she snuggled close to him.

"And I... I love you too. I only wish that I had admitted it sooner," Theodore said quietly.

"It's okay. We have the rest of our lives to say it again and again."

"Yes, well, even so. It's not like we're getting any younger."

"Well, you definitely made me feel young again," Tyrona said as she kissed his bare chest.

"It feels like we're moving," Theodore said suddenly. "Are we moving?"

Tyrona laughed. "Of course we are. We've been flying for about an hour now. It woke me up, and then I got you up after that."

"Huh. Our activities must have masked the movement. It must be an amazing sight, though, flying above the clouds without having to hold on for your life. I've ridden many animals and gods now, from winged rams to wyverns to the peafowl god. All amazing experiences, but I wouldn't exactly call them enjoyable."

"Really? I rather liked our trip here on Hartipavoh. That was real flying."

"Yes, but it is too much work, holding on for dear life like that. But traveling through the air by ship? Now that is convenience."

"Yes, it's been quite convenient, for us especially."

"What do you mean?"

"We're the first people to make love above the clouds," Tyrona said, giggling.

"Well, I'll be," Theodore said, chuckling. He sighed, then wrapped his arm around Tyrona. She snuggled in closer.

"As much as I want to go out there, I don't want to ruin the moment," Tyrona said. "I'm thankful for this time with you."

"I'm glad to be with you, too."

They grew quiet as they silently enjoyed their time together.

"You know, after we both graduated, we didn't see each other as much," Tyrona said breaking the silence. "Yes, we kept up, and we would visit each other every month or so. But even when we were together back then, we weren't truly together. You were preoccupied with your research, and I was afraid—afraid of what you would think if I confessed to you how I felt.

"But now, everything has been working out. From the moment I saw you, with Ànifa and Dasch, I knew things were going to finally change. Of course, I never could have predicted any of this."

"None of us could," Theodore. "I mean, a flying ship—an airship? That's not something anyone could have predicted."

Tyrona sighed, then sat up, the sheet slipping off her, exposing her bare body. "We should get up, though. It's getting late. I'm sure the others are starting to plan for today."

"I suppose you're right," Theodore said without moving. "But I've already got a splendid view."

"Oh, Dorie... come on, let's get up. We can lie together again next time we fly. For the entire ride."

"Well, I'd say that's a pretty good deal." Theodore moved over to the edge of the bed, then swung his feet to the floor. "Airships," Theodore muttered to himself. "Who would have ever thought? At least I can't get seasick on an airship."

"Right, because then it would be called airsickness." Tyrona giggled.

"*Ànifa... Ànifa!*"

"*What is it, Gnusaramnii?*"

"*You did well, Ànifa. You faced your toughest foes yet, and you made it through.*"

"*Only because of Joan's help. And you know what? Some of my friends have their suspicions. They think you pulled the strings to make that all happen.*"

"*Of course I did! I'm the one who took over that stupid weasel of a man. I'm the one who led you to that particular slot canyon. There were other, safer, paths to take to reach Roheefy's forest, you know...*"

"*Maybe there were. But you're right. I couldn't stand by and let you get away with murdering two gods.*"

"*Do you really think of those beasts as gods? They are the pinnacle of their species, the alpha, and nothing more. They are no more godlike than your angel is angelic.*"

"*I won't let you trick me like that. I know them to be what they are. I know of their powers, even if you don't. And yet, you are continuing to take them over.*"

Gnusaramnii laughed. "*Why stop what is simply pure fun? Sure, I make my Gnuelry create Gnurargurts—I do that on all the worlds I've inhabited. But corrupt a god and you get an entire army along with it. That is one of their powers I do admit no other animal has.*"

"*You're a worthless piece of trash, you know that?*"

"*Never have you been more wrong. I am necessary, a constant that this universe could not go on without.*"

"*Holy Eklatros. You know what? If you're really that all-powerful, then get me out of this dream.*"

"*Ha ha ha ha... your angel is already in the process of pulling you out...*"

Ànifa awoke feeling refreshed, having been able to sleep peacefully after Joan's assistance.

She was in a conundrum. She didn't want to speak to

Gnusaramnii anymore, yet she was dangerously low on her shuyukuii mushroom supply. And on top of it all, she really wanted to dream and sleep without any worries. Joan may have helped her this morning, but she knew it wasn't a solution. She couldn't rely on her all the time. This was something she had to figure out on her own.

She shook her head and got out of bed. When she stepped out of her room, she felt the slight tremble of the ship as it soared through the air. Light emanated from a closed door—Joan was behind that door, making the ship fly.

Ànifa smiled and laid her hand on the door, then sent Joan some good thoughts. In response, she felt the ship slightly increase its speed.

Ànifa walked up the steps that led to the upper level and found the rest of the crew standing around on the deck.

"How did you sleep?" Dasch asked in his gruff voice. He was standing at the top of the stairs, his dark green cloak helping him blend into the shadows.

"Fine," Ànifa replied as she reached the top of the steps. "I see I'm the last one out here."

"It's no problem," Dasch said. "We all needed the rest. Tyrona and Theodore joined us not too long ago."

"Ah, I see. I'm happy for them."

"We all need a little more love in this world, especially in this state."

"Dasch, who are you to talk about love?"

"You're right, I'm not an expert by any means, and I don't like getting close to people."

"You are right, though," Ànifa replied. "I was only teasing you. Love is important."

"Love has connected us all so far," Dasch grumbled, "In one form or another, of course."

"I just hope our bond is strong enough to get us through. And we're going to need all of us to do it."

"Been reading up on our next destination, have you?"

"Just reading over Dante's scribbled notes," Ànifa replied. "He says there is no clear path and no way for him to build any cairns or mark any landmarks, due to lava flows and geysers. He also mentions there are a lot of other dangers on the volcano."

"I believe it. Our battles have only been getting tougher."

"Is there a plan of attack?"

"We were waiting for you. You are our leader, of course," Dasch said.

"Yeah, but you could always plan amongst yourselves."

"Yes, I know. Honestly, everyone's been preoccupied with the view. Go and fully check it out. It's quite magnificent."

"Alright. Well, we'll talk soon then," Ànifa said, as she stepped out onto the deck.

Cecil and Vesten were chatting while Theodore and Tyrona enjoyed the view off on their own. The only protection between them and the surrounding atmosphere was a thin, transparent energy field Joan had raised to protect them from the strong winds.

Ànifa looked over the edge, her long indigo hair falling down over her chest as she peered out. White clouds streamed below them. They were riding on the edge of a cloud. Below them lay the ocean, majestically shimmering in the morning light. Even though they were nearly half a kilometer in the air, Ànifa could make out the shapes of dolphins and whales as they leaped into the air.

Beside them, a flock of albatross flew in a V-shaped pattern while cawing at each other. Suddenly, the flock dived and plunged into the sea below. Ànifa's elvish eyes tracked the albatross to the surface of the ocean, where each one emerged victoriously, clutching large fish in their long beaks.

While Ànifa had flown before—a few times now—this was incomparable to her previous experiences. This was luxury flying— the travel of the future.

Without warning, *West Wind* lurched as they began their descent. Ànifa looked out into the distance and saw a landmass coming into view.

"We're there already?" Ànifa asked, turning to Cecil and Vesten.

"We've been flying for nearly two hours now," Cecil said, brushing his burgundy hair out of his eyes. He had set his helmet on the deck to better view the surrounding landscape.

"Yeah, now I gotta get back to my post. I'm sure Joan's been giving me commands," Vesten said.

Ànifa followed him to the upper deck. "Joan's able to talk to you?"

"In a way. She can project her voice out through the helm of the ship, so if she needs me to turn the rudder, I can do that. But the past half hour we've just been flying straight and true. The wind has been real fuckin' nice," Vesten replied as he took the wheel.

"Wow, that's pretty cool," Ànifa said with raised eyebrows. "Joan really is your co-pilot then."

"Ha yeah, 'cept lately it feels like I'm fuckin' co-pilot to her. But hey, Joan's the only other one I'd ever let steer *West Wind*," Vesten said. A moment later, Ànifa heard Joan's voice emanate from the helm.

"Vesten, hold the wheel steady while we descend."

"No problem!" Vesten replied, putting both hands on the wheel to secure it in place. "See what I fuckin' mean? She's the one giving me commands."

"That's cute. But, why her? You've only known Joan for a couple days. Why are you so willingly giving up control of your ship? Especially after your doubts about her yesterday."

"Yeah, sure, I fuckin' had my doubts. But then she flew me from Roheefy to Port Columbo. I was wrapped in her arms for quite a while. We didn't speak much, but in a way, we grew closer, more comfortable... shit, I don't really know."

Ànifa giggled. "You like her?"

"Fuck. I don't know. She's an angel. And she's beautiful, sure. But I'm just a lowly fuckin' sailor. I ain't no match for her."

Ànifa shrugged. "You don't really know that." She sighed. "I don't know, Vesten. I'm sure you'll find love somewhere."

"We'll fuckin' see," Vesten replied.

The clanking of Cecil heading up the short flight of stairs

interrupted them. Behind him followed Theodore, Tyrona, and Dasch.

"So, what's the plan?" Cecil asked as they approached.

"Right. Joan, can you hear us?" Ànifa asked.

"Aye aye, Princess!" Joan replied, her disembodied voice once again emanating from the helm. "Vesten, one turn to port."

"Aye, one turn to port," Vesten said as he spun the wheel one spoke. "Sorry, continue."

"No worries," Ànifa replied. "Now, what can anyone tell me about Beetaramn?"

Vesten sailed *West Wind* the rest of the way into Beetaramn's port. Approaching Beetaramn was much more relaxed compared to Port Columbo. There were no guards or sentries, no security officers to guide them to port. Instead, an old withered man with a long wispy beard wearing a dirty white t-shirt sat in a small dinghy and simply pointed toward the dock they should head to. Vesten sailed them in smoothly.

A short time later, they had *West Wind* fully docked and secured. They left their ship and headed out into the streets of Beetaramn.

According to Dante's map, they were looking for a small A-framed cottage on the edge of town. It was the home of Bishop Farag.

Ànifa knew Beetaramn was a large town, but having just come from Ajenti, it felt small. There was only one main road through town, which they took to find the cottage.

A mixture of shops and residential homes lined the main road. The structures were built with black bricks mixed with dark gray stones. After they passed a unique smithy, Ànifa realized the bricks were constructed from molten lava, cooled into shape by molds. The roofs of the buildings were made from dirt and straw.

"How are you feeling, Joan?" Ànifa asked as they walked.

"I admit, that trip took a lot out of me," Joan replied as she held her head high, "but not nearly as bad as the first time. I just need a little time to rest, and I should be fine."

"Don't push yourself now," Ànifa said sternly.

"I'll be fine, Princess."

As they traveled along the road, everyone they passed greeted them warmly. Ànifa spied people hiding in alleyways—they looked to be refugees from Runti. The crowds lessened once they reached the cottage. It was easy to spot—it was the only wooden building in town.

Ànifa knocked on the door of the small A-framed cottage. Hanging on the door was a wooden sign that read THE BISHOP'S.

She waited for an answer—none came.

"Maybe she's not home," Theodore suggested.

"Try knocking again, just to be fuckin' sure," Vesten said.

"I agree," Joan chimed in.

"Yeah, I'll try that first," Ànifa said.

She knocked again, harder this time. A moment later, a voice shouted back at them.

"Calm your britches! I'll be out shortly," the woman's voice shouted.

We're almost there. We've almost made it to Panabeeta, she thought. *It's been a long journey, but I'm glad we've acquired a faster way to travel. Our journey is important, and time is increasingly becoming a factor. Hopefully we'll make it to Panabeeta soon.*

31

BATTLE FOR COURAGE

The door opened, revealing a petite elderly woman with short, frizzled white hair. She wore large thick-framed spectacles and was dressed in the purple garb of a high-ranking clergy member—thick robes with long, wide sleeves and a small circular hat that sat at the top of her white hair. Panna Isle was known for its religious hierarchy. The sign on the door indicated that this woman was the Bishop of Beetaramn.

"Ah! A group of newcomers. Well, get inside, the lot of you! If you mean to talk, we do it inside," The Bishop said forcefully as she stepped out of the doorway.

Ànifa shrugged, then walked into the small cottage. A plethora of religious paraphernalia adorned the interior, whether it was tacked to the wall or on a shelf. As she was gazing around, Theodore quietly explained that these items were typical for a devotee of the Holy Church of Eklatros. Their symbol was a birch tree, and there were many images of birch trees around the Bishop's cottage. There were also images of Kieth Angelcross, and Ànifa even spied a small portrait of who she assumed was Eliziana Lockhart.

As soon as all seven of them were inside, The Bishop hastily closed the door.

"Now! Let's see the lot of you. Take off your disguises, those of you who have them."

Ànifa hesitated and looked over at Joan, who nodded and pulled off the purple cloak she was wearing. Ànifa removed her bonnet and untied her hair, letting it flow freely again.

"Ah, so the rumors have been true. You are indeed the chosen ones. What are your names?"

Ànifa introduced everyone, ending with herself.

"It's a pleasure to make your acquaintances. I am Tanaq Jayne Farag, commonly known as The Bishop around here," said The Bishop.

"You're the Tanaq!" Cecil exclaimed. "It's an honor to be in your presence, divine one!"

"Now, now, don't get all formal on me. We're in my home. I may be Tanaq, yet I was also once the Bishop of Beetaramn, which is why the name has stuck."

"It's a pleasure to meet you, Tanaq Farag," Ànifa said. "We are here to ask you a question."

"You seek Nibelkaith," The Bishop replied knowingly.

"Yes. Our end goal is the Great Barrier, and beyond that, Panabeeta."

"Ah, so it's true. You have been awakening Eklatros' children. Then yes, you must climb the volcano. And you all look strong enough. You will need to work together and help each other, of course."

"That's what we've been doing for a while now," Theodore said.

"Good, good. Before you set off, there are some things I must tell you all. Please, sit," The Bishop said.

A row of eight wooden chairs lined the wall to her left, so Ànifa took one and the others followed suit. There was one reclining chair in the room, and The Bishop took it for herself.

"Now, I like the mix of you all. Elf, half-elf, angel, sorcerers, a knight, a sailor... a unique and strong group. That's what I can sense. Yet, as strong as you all are, you must heed my warning, for if you do not know about these dangers, they may well be the end of you all."

The Bishop described the various creatures they needed to watch for, including nible fire ants, rock crabs, dire wolf spiders, dire scorpions, and dire armadillo. She also warned them to be wary of geysers and lava pits.

"Yeah, that all sounds fuckin' scary," Vesten said.

"It's not going to be a walk in the park, that's for sure," Tyrona replied.

"Indeed, it will not be," said The Bishop.

"Is there anything else we need to know?" Ànifa asked.

"The volcano is sacred. Yet, I know that with an elf and an angel in your group, you will treat it with the respect it requires."

"It requires respect?" Vesten asked.

"Most certainly. Many of those that have lost their lives on Nibelkaith have done so by their own design."

Ànifa nodded. "We will heed your words. Thank you for your help, and for giving us permission to climb Nibelkaith."

As they were preparing to leave, The Bishop prepared a waterskin for each of them, then an extra for the entire team.

"Use these as sparingly as you can," The Bishop said. "This is all I can offer you."

They said their thanks and goodbyes and left The Bishop's cottage, making their way to the trail that would take them to the Nibelkaith Volcano. From there, they would have to make their own way to the top. There were no roads once they reached the base of the volcano.

Ànifa and Joan traveled without their disguises, as there was no one on the volcano to see them. They talked freely amongst themselves to keep calm on their journey.

"It's amazing that the town was built so close to the volcano," Ànifa said as she noted the sheer amount of dried lava flows they passed.

"I'm sure they've seen their fair share of disasters," Theodore replied, "yet these people are resilient."

"Runti wasn't," Ànifa said looking down. "Everything has a breaking point."

"Runti isn't Beetaramn," Theodore replied. "I know that might not count for much, but living in the volcano's shadow has hardened these people in a way no outsider can really understand."

"Are you really so sure about this?" Cecil asked his friend.

"Tyrona can back me up on this. I once had a student from Beetaramn. He told us much about its culture and traditions. Well, as much as he could before he was expelled."

"Right, I remember that," Tyrona said.

"What did your student do?" Vesten asked.

"He almost killed another student," Theodore replied. "It's my fault, really. I should never have introduced him to that form of magic."

"You mean, the form of magic I've mastered?" Tyrona replied. "Messing with someone's mind takes finesse—finesse that Nitin didn't have."

"If you don't mind me asking, where is your family from, Tyrona?" Ànifa asked.

"My family comes from Heerenditheer. My mother moved to Ajenti when she was just a baby, when my grandmother was accepted into the University. I had always wanted to visit, but I've never made it there."

"I'm sure that once all is said and done, you'll get a chance to visit," Ànifa replied.

"I would love that."

The trail came to an abrupt stop. Beyond them lay a maze of sharp lava rocks and black dirt.

"This is the end of the line," Cecil said.

"Everyone, follow me," Ànifa said. "Dasch, you take the rear—if you see anything, give us a shout."

"A shout would be an unwise decision," Dasch grumbled. "If anyone approaches, I'll whistle, like this." Dasch whistled like a sparrow.

Ànifa eyes widened in surprise. "That certainly works. I didn't know you could whistle like that."

Dasch shrugged. "Let's move—we don't want to get caught out in the dark."

It was mid-morning and they had a long journey ahead of them. Their way forward grew rockier with each step. Ànifa led her party cautiously, making sure each rock she stepped on was stable before moving on. She also scanned the patches of ground for any sign of nible fire ants and rock crabs.

While Ànifa was scanning for all the known dangers, she nearly overlooked a fiend that they hadn't been warned about—a jet black Gnuelry. It was camouflaged nearly perfectly against the black lava rocks.

"Wait!" Ànifa cried out. "There's a jelly monster hiding among those rocks."

"A jelly monster? Haven't seen one of those in a while," Theodore said.

"Don't let your guard down—it sees us too," Ànifa said. "A battle is unavoidable."

"There shouldn't be too many of these things left," Dasch grumbled. "Let's make sure that we can stop this one."

"Agreed," Ànifa nodded. She unslung her bow and notched an arrow, then focused deep within herself, making the arrow burn in blue flames. A moment later, the jet black Gnuelry lunged at them. It was massive—the largest Gnuelry they'd seen yet.

"No Gnuelry can grow that large on its own. It must have merged with many others," Dasch explained as he drew his golden flaming sword. "Be careful everyone."

Ànifa whispered, "Tekkhas Harmonias," then fired her arrow, burying it into the jelly monster's thick body. The Gnuelry continued to charge forward, unfazed. It raised a large limb. The limb expanded swiftly as the Gnuelry propelled itself forward. Ànifa jumped off to the side, dodging the attack at the last moment.

Theodore held his scarlet staff in the air as he muttered a spell. He raised his arms, causing two large volcanic boulders to rise into the air. Theodore lowered his arms quickly, causing the boulders to fall and smash into the jelly monster. The boulders exploded, shooting shards of sharp rocks at them. Tyrona targeted each rock with an equalizing sound wave, causing them to drop to the ground in midair.

"Sorry! Thanks!" Theodore cried as he looked back at Tyrona.

"Anytime," Tyrona replied with a wink.

The Gnuelry exploded out from underneath the rock pile, shooting even more razor-sharp rock shards at them. Theodore quickly created an energy barrier. Some shards ricocheted off the barrier and shot back at the Gnuelry, who roared in response as it rose high in the air.

"Uh, it looks like you made it fuckin' stronger!" Vesten yelled.

Dasch rushed in, burying his golden flaming sword deep into the Gnuelry while Ànifa shot another flaming blue arrow.

Vesten cursed as he flung daggers at the enemy. Joan placed her hand on Vesten's shoulder, halting him from throwing another dagger.

"Don't waste any more daggers," she said. "Stand back everyone, let me handle this foul creature!"

Joan clutched Halahkahna, the Divine Shield of Protection, in her left hand and Ekatalal, the Divine Hammer of Justice, in her right. Joan jumped into the air, stretching out her wings.

The jet black Gnuelry was nearly a meter taller than them now and was producing multiple limbs while using the two it had already to swing at Dasch and Ànifa.

"Take cover!" Joan commanded as she brought Ekatalal down hard on the Gnuelry's head. The Gnuelry screeched, then shot a dozen vine-like limbs at Joan. As each limb attempted to grab her, Joan swung her shield and cut through the limbs.

Ànifa notched another arrow. She focused on the arrowhead and it burst into blue flames. She took a breath and fired, hitting the Gnuelry in its left eye. The jet-black creature roared and flailed its limbs wildly. Dasch expertly wove through the berserk black limbs, cutting each one off. Joan flew in and smashed into the Gnuelry with her hammer, knocking it to the ground.

"Theodore, Tyrona! Can you hold it down?" Joan asked.

"On it!" Tyrona replied. She raised her white wand and Theodore raised his scarlet staff.

The two sorcerers sent a combined attack at the Gnuelry as it struggled to get up—Tyrona shot a barrage of high frequency sound waves while Theodore created a powerful stream of wind that thrust into the monster.

Joan swooped in and threw Ekatalal with all her strength, hitting the Gnuelry hard in its chest. It burst into dozens of smaller Gnuelry that immediately attempted to flee.

"Don't let any escape!" Ànifa shouted as she shot at the ones closest to her.

Vesten belted out a battle cry, then charged at the small black Gnuelry with Skimither. Cecil, who had been standing guard in the back, keeping an eye out for any other fiends that could be attracted to the battle, jumped into the fray.

In the end, they may have let two or three slip through, but they destroyed the majority of the jelly monsters.

"That Gnuelry," Joan said. "It was looking for a god. That's why you haven't seen many Gnuelry lately—they've been merging together and taking over gods; it takes a lot of effort to possess a god and break its willpower."

"Does that mean there's a god nearby?" Tyrona asked, looking around.

"Possibly, but we must keep moving."

The heat of the sun was relentless. Cecil panted heavily within the confines of his armor, while Theodore trudged on slowly, drenched in sweat. Before long, they spied a rocky overhang—the first bit of shade they had come across. After searching the area for any dangers, Ànifa enlarged the backpack and passed around bags of oats and nuts to snack on while the others drank from their waterskins.

"We should have accounted for this heat," Theodore sighed.

"Can you create cloud cover for us?" Tyrona asked.

"Possibly. Don't know why I didn't think of that before," Theodore replied.

"The sun is draining," Dasch said. "It can steal your wits as easily as your strength."

"Indeed. Ànifa, you must be careful as well. I know we are more resilient to the temperature, but we can still get heatstroke," Joan said.

"I'll keep that in mind," Ànifa said. She unfastened the top few buttons of her trenchdress. "I've been fine, but a little relief from the heat wouldn't hurt."

Theodore took a swig from his waterskin, wiped his mouth, and said, "I'll try to whip up some clouds. Of course, making the clouds is the simple part. Having them follow us, while keeping them from evaporating from the heat, will be the tricky part."

"Uh, Ànifa," Cecil said warily. "I think I see one of those fire ants."

"Where?" Tyrona squealed as she jumped into the air.

"On that rock over there. That's one of them, right?" Cecil said, pointing at it.

"Hand me the snacks," Ànifa demanded. "We must leave now. Theodore, if you're going to make clouds, now is the time."

Theodore picked up his staff and stood. "Indeed. But first, a little gift for our ugly friend."

Theodore sent a stream of wind to the nible fire ant, knocking it off the rock. He thrust his staff into the air, holding it with both hands. "Cumulus Returtunous!"

Billowy clouds formed above them, swirling around in the air as they condensed together.

"Let's go," Ànifa said as she stuffed the shrunken backpack into her pocket.

Waves of fire ants swarmed the area. Ànifa and the others hastily jumped from rock to rock as they fled, doing their best to avoid stepping on any patch of ground for fear of any nible ants lurking in the shadows. Fire ants crawled from rock to rock in pursuit, but the group was faster. They lost the ants after a few minutes of scrambling.

Theodore's cloud coverage followed them as they moved along, keeping them protected from the harsh sun, although the cloud coverage obscured the true color of the rocks. As Ànifa hopped along, she nearly landed directly on the back of a large rock crab.

"Watch out! That's a crab!"

The crab didn't seem to notice them, so they quietly worked their way around a large boulder. When Ànifa rounded the boulder, she was nearly trampled by the rock crab god. The god was locked in a fierce battle with Chactochactas, the scorpion god. The gods attacked each other with pincers as large as boulders. It was a one-sided battle, but Chactochactas was putting up a fierce fight. It was surrounded in a ring of rock crabs, each one snapping at the scorpion god if it got too close. Ànifa wanted to help—she wished ever so badly that she could intervene.

"Ànifa, we must go," Joan whispered. Ànifa looked around and realized the others had passed her by and were currently hiding amongst the rocks. Only she and Joan remained standing in the open.

"Can't we do something?" Ànifa replied.

"That would be suicide, even for us. Now, we must take our leave," Joan said, tugging at Ànifa's sleeve.

Ànifa tore her gaze away from the battle and nodded. As they hurried to the others, three rock crabs turned to face them, wildly clacking their pincers together.

"We've got to get the fuck out of here!" Vesten shouted at them from behind a boulder.

"Go! We're right behind you!" Ànifa shouted back, then whispered "Sorry, Chactochactas."

They were able to easily outrun the rock crabs as they leaped from rock to rock. After a few minutes, Ànifa spied an exceptionally large boulder and climbed to the top.

"I think we're safe here for now," Dasch said. "How are you all faring?"

"I need a breather," Cecil wheezed.

"Damn," Vesten said. "I thought you were in shape."

"It's just... really hot. Even with Theodore's cloud cover, this armor is quite warm," Cecil replied.

"About that... I can't keep up the clouds for much longer," Theodore said. "It's been a bigger strain than I thought it would be."

"Don't worry about it," Ànifa said. "Save your strength. We may need it."

"Alright, I'll disperse the spell," Theodore said, relieved.

"Hey!" Cecil objected as the clouds quickly evaporated.

"Sorry, Cecil. It's simply too much for me right now," Theodore said. "I can't sustain it."

"It's fine," Cecil said with a wave of his hand. He drew out his waterskin and took a long drink.

"Does anyone know if we've made any actual progress?" Ànifa asked. "Everything looks the same."

"I-I think so?" Tyrona replied as she scanned their surroundings.

"Yes, we've been doing alright, Princess," Joan replied. "I can lead the way if you wish. I know where we need to go."

"Alright, lead the way, then," Ànifa said.

Joan flew ahead while keeping an eye on the others. Ànifa trailed closely behind her, followed by Vesten, Theodore, Tyrona, Cecil, and Dasch. Joan led them upward, to the mouth of the volcano. She made her own switchbacks, even though she was in the air, to ensure the way up wasn't too difficult for the others.

Flying gave Joan a few advantages, along with one major disadvantage. The major benefits were that Joan could better watch the landscape around them for any suspicious movements, and, of course, she could move much more quickly. The drawback was that she could be easily spotted. Joan's white wings and metal armor stood out like a sore thumb against the black lava rocks.

On several occasions, Joan almost got blasted by fiery steams as hidden geysers erupted beneath her. After the third such occurrence, Joan joined the others and leapt from rock to rock. It was hot, and without Theodore's cloud coverage, they were nearly baking.

The heat didn't affect Joan as much, though she knew the humans were taking a heavy toll. While she was tired—she still hadn't fully recovered from flying *West Wind* to Panna Isle—she didn't allow her fatigue to show. Joan was about to leap to another boulder when she heard the whistling of a sparrow behind her.

Joan looked back and noticed that Cecil and Vesten were nowhere to be seen. Dasch was standing high on a rock with a hand over his eyes as he whistled and scanned the area while Ànifa had stopped to help Theodore and Tyrona. Joan doubled back.

"What happened? Where's Vesten and the knight?" Joan asked.

"That's the problem. We don't know," Dasch grumbled.

"What?" Joan said in surprise. "I thought you were leading the rear, Dasch!"

"I was," Dasch replied. "They were there, then they weren't there."

"I'll go find them. They couldn't have gotten far," Joan said, leaping into the air.

Joan kept low to the ground, skimming above the rocks. She was trying not to worry. She knew they'd be alright; they had to be. Before she could start second-guessing herself, she spied a large boulder and swooped around it.

Cecil and Vesten were lounging in the shade, each one sipping the last drops out of their waterskins.

"Vesten! Cecil! Are you okay?" Joan asked upon approaching them. She remained hovering above the ground.

"Ah! Yes. If it isn't the beautiful angel faerie princess," Cecil said in a serious tone, then pointed to a small round white rock. "Good. We've been trying to break into this egg here. Do you know why it won't crack?"

"That's a rock," Joan replied. "Are you really okay? Take off your helmet, knight."

Joan landed on the rocks, then knelt to feel Vesten's forehead while Cecil clumsily took off his helmet.

"Vesten, you're burning up,"

"You're burning up! You're so fuckin' sexy, with your wings and fuckin' bunny ears..." Vesten slurred as he trailed off.

"We have to get you back to the others, now." Joan picked up Vesten and leaned him against the boulder.

"Hold on to me," she told Vesten, who grabbed her right wing.

"Ah, that's not what I meant. Just don't twist anything."

Joan picked up Cecil by his shoulders and leaned him onto the boulder as well.

"I can't carry both of you at the same time."

Joan took Vesten's hand off of her wing, leaped into the air, and saw the others had followed her, so she lowered herself back to the ground.

"You can actually sit again," Joan said.

"Ah, fudge-nuggets!" Cecil said, slumping.

"That sounds so good right now!" Vesten said, bursting into a fit of hysterical laughter.

"Ànifa!" Joan called as she turned the corner. "They have heatstroke."

"They need water and shade. I suppose we'll need to linger here for a little while," Ànifa said.

"I have little water left," Theodore said. "What about you, Ty?"

"I just finished it off," Tyrona replied.

"Mine is still pretty full, and we still have the extra," Ànifa said. "It's possible the one in the backpack might have some water too."

"I have extra as well," Dasch said. "I can share mine with anyone who needs it."

"I can help too," Joan said. "I haven't had that much either."

Joan handed her waterskin to Vesten, who began to chug it.

"Hey, not so fast," Joan said, tipping the skin away from his mouth. "You'll make yourself sick."

Ànifa brought hers to Cecil and helped him sip it.

"Something's coming," Dasch said as he perked up. "I can feel the vibrations. Whatever it is, it's big." He was the only one standing on the ground. The others were up on boulders.

A loud roar cut through the air. A moment later, a herd of corrupted dire armadillo came bounding over the horizon toward them.

"We must move!" Ànifa yelled.

"I'll take Vesten," Joan said. "Ànifa, can you help Cecil?"

"I'll assist also," Dasch said.

Joan grabbed Vesten in a bear hug, then leaped into the air. She looked back and saw that the herd was seven adults strong with four adolescents. Dire armadillo weren't naturally aggressive, but if caught with their young, they were fiercely protective.

"Let's go! This way!" Joan commanded.

She led the party as quickly as she could while keeping pace with the others. In the air, she could travel double the speed she could while walking on land, even while carrying Vesten, so she had to restrain herself. He wasn't much of a burden, though. She was getting used to holding him while she flew.

"Tyrona, can you distract them?" Ànifa asked.

"How?" Tyrona replied.

"You can manipulate sound, right? Can you create a loud noise near the herd?"

"Yes, not while I'm moving, though," Tyrona said. "Dorie, get ready!"

"Right, Ty!" Theodore said.

Joan stopped and looked behind her. Theodore stood a few meters away and was creating a focused energy barrier. Ànifa readied her bow, while Dasch let go of Cecil and unsheathed his golden flaming sword. Cecil looked around in confusion.

"What's happening?" Vesten asked, delirious in her arms.

"We're trying to escape a herd of dire armadillo."

"Oh shit," Vesten said. "I'm flying again, aren't I?"

"Yes. How are you feeling?" Joan asked.

"Better, especially now," Vesten replied.

"Good. Once we reach a safe spot, I can put you down."

"Yeah, no rush."

Tyrona had her ivory wand raised in the air. She faced away from the charging herd and muttered a spell. Seemingly out of nowhere, a loud screech emanated above them. A moment later, two large boulders crashed together as Theodore pushed them toward the herd.

The herd of dire armadillo turned and sprinted away.

"Great job, Tyrona!" Ànifa said.

"Thanks! I figured a combination would be best in this case," Tyrona said.

"That worked well. Now, we must continue on," Joan said.

"Thank you for leading the way, Joan," Ànifa replied.

"It's not a problem, Princess," Joan said.

They continued on. Cecil was able to walk on his own, but Joan continued to carry Vesten. With Vesten in her arms, Joan found that her mind had wandered to places it shouldn't be. Which was how she nearly led them right into a massive nible fire ant colony.

"Oh shit," Vesten said under his breath.

The mounds were nearly a meter high and were crawling with fire ants. Joan yelped in surprise, then turned around and motioned for the others to steer clear of the anthills.

"Joan!" Ànifa called out as she stopped in her tracks.

"My deepest apologies, Princess!" Joan called from above.

"We need to run for it," Cecil said, frozen with fear.

"It won't work, not this time," Ànifa said softly. "At least they haven't noticed us yet."

"No, they have, Princess," Joan said, then flew down close to the others. "Theodore, we need a barrier!"

Theodore nodded, then thrust out his scarlet glass staff and quickly raised a powerful barrier.

Joan set Vesten on his feet and turned to Ànifa. "Princess, only you can save us now."

"How can I help?" Ànifa asked.

"You must find us some aid. We won't last long here."

Almost as if on cue, eight fire ants leaped at the barrier. All were shot back violently and splattered against the rocks, but there were thousands of fire ants and only seven of them.

"We must find aid," Joan repeated.

"Alright, let's go," Ànifa replied.

She stepped forward into Joan's arms. A moment later, she was being lifted off the ground. They passed through Theodore's energy barrier and flew into the air.

"Where should I go?" Joan asked.

"Anywhere—choose a direction. I'm leaving the flying to you. I'll do everything I can to find some help," Ànifa replied.

Ànifa cleared her mind as Joan carried her across the rocky terrain. For a fleeting moment, she felt the scorpion god they had passed, Chactochactas, but the presence faded almost immediately.

I'm sorry, Chactochactas... you will be avenged, she thought.

"I'm not getting anything over here," Ànifa said.

"Alright," Joan said, turning.

"I'm still not... wait," Ànifa said softly. "Yes!" she pointed toward a steep cliff. "Over there, hurry!"

I hope we make it in time, she thought. *This volcano... it's nothing like I had expected, but we have been making progress. All of this hasn't been for nothing. We'll find help, and we'll return to everyone. Please, stay safe.*

32

INTERLUDE:
ACAMPACHETLIAN SPECIES

```
Declassification Disclaimer: the following
document has been declassified for this
usage only and has been sanitized. It has
been translated accordingly for your
understanding. To access the complete
records, please contact Councilmember
Ducutyk. His contact information can be
found at the end of this document. Sanitized
copy approved for release 82017/13/34.
```

```
From the desk of Professor Maximilianus
Peal. Sarkiln, Kampanar 2, 82002
08:00:38:72.
```

Ah, good morning Melridion. It's good to be back.

Apparently, this is a new thing that Head Professor Yilvin wants to start—these recordings, I mean. I'll just get into it then.

Last night, my team and I returned from Acampachetli. It was my third time there, but for most of my team, it was their first. It really is a wild planet—no intelligent species live there. It's simply a natural landscape, filled with natural horrors and dangers. It's beautiful, don't get me wrong, but just about everything there can kill you.

The purpose of our mission was to gather different species for experimentation. I'm excited to say that we got a really good haul, much better than I had expected, including a bonus that surprised all of us. It was quite the trip for the six of us.

My team is led by Kalosse and I. Kalosse a Nioavellian and studied right here at Nalpetalis University, class of 81998. He's my lead biologist—he knows everything there is to know about Acampachetli and its diverse ecosystems. Next is Elizabeth Surridge, the only other fellow Human here at the compound. She's both brilliant and beautiful. She studied at Delgrious University on our home planet of Carange. Surridge is my gifted botanist—she's the expert in rare and mysterious plants. Then, there is Kamarial, a Eusphyrchiian. She's our lead entomologist. Her primary focus of study is in arachnids, though, she is also well studied in many other species. Finally, there are Mahlvern and Walverm, the Kolythoanthaean brothers. Mahlvern is our topographer. Acampachetli is mostly uncharted, so he is working on creating more complete maps of the small planet. His knowledge and expertise, while it may not seem like it gels well with what we're doing here, will be essential to our overall success. Walverm is our anatomist—the one who will be leading the eventual dissections that come from our bountiful haul.

And finally, I am Professor Maximilianus Peal from Starofsky, Carange. It's a small, humble town that's known for its tobacco farms. Where I grew up, my parents owned a lot of land, which gave me the freedom to explore. I've been interested in nature since I was very young. After my father tragically died in a tractor accident, I began thinking about how we can use nature to help us directly, whether it's with venom, saliva, sap, or knowledge.

That is my ultimate goal—to gain knowledge from these animals and directly learn from nature. If we can speak to the animal, and it can speak back to us, imagine what we might learn. Now, how do we accomplish such a feat?

For a long time, this was a challenge I could not overcome. That was, until I read about an experimental serum created by two master chemists, Doctor Sareyse and Doctor Poulson. They passed away after they published the report, and their serum was lost to the universe. So, although the report itself doesn't explain how to make the serum they invented, I have learned enough to recreate it—for my own purposes, of course.

The serum Sareyse and Poulson created made any animal docile and able to understand the common tongue. In their report, they explained how they gave the serum to a school of fish and got them to write out words and create extremely intricate designs through simple verbal commands.

What I'm trying to accomplish is different, but their ideas and knowledge have been a real jumping-off point.

We finished making our own version of the serum three weeks ago, on Melrikiln, Teinianar nineteenth. And we have been eager to test it.

We will perform our first round of experiments on the Curik. They are a species of horned beetles and can grow up to nearly half a meter long. We were fortunate enough to capture a dozen of them. Walverm will dissect four of them, and the other eight will be injected with the serum.

We also have ten Phasmatodaedalus. They are odd stick bugs that, when fully mature, can grow as large as trees. These bugs do not stop growing, and the knowledge I wish to gain from them is how they are able to do so. Walverm will dissect three, and we will inject seven with our serum.

The last of the insects that we collected were dangerously poisonous spiders called Dark Therids. We have eight of them. All eight will be injected with the serum. These freaks were way too hard to catch. Plus, a single bite from a Dark Therid can kill even a fully grown Ancilsan. Just one small bite. Their venom is that strong. And it's not just their venom—they have an amazing ability to spin a wide variety of different silks with various strengths and properties. My hope is that we can make at least one of them speak to us.

We were able to capture three different species of animals as well. The first I will mention were the sixteen Zubba that we captured. These creatures are fascinating, albeit much less intelligent than the Zubula—a very similar species. Half of the Zubba we caught will be dissected. I hope to learn as much from the dissections as I can from speaking to one.

Zubba have the body of a bat, with its wings and ugly, furry little head and everything. That is fused onto the back of a large scorpion. The coloring on the scorpion and the bat were always different, and each half seems to have its own personality.

We observed the Zubula and Zubba for quite a while and witnessed them interacting with one another socially. It was the Zubula that were giving the Zubba commands. You see, with the Zubba, they only have the bat's head. Their scorpion part doesn't have a head. Yet the Zubula have both a bat head and a scorpion head, so they command the Zubba as if they were their slaves, or so it seemed. We were not fortunate enough to capture a Zubula—they were too clever. The Zubba were much dumber, which is how we managed to nab sixteen of them.

We also captured six Loxocemae. They are a unique species of snake, with blood-red scales and a dark-brown underbelly. Only one will be dissected by Walverm, and we will inject the remaining five with the serum. The Loxocemae are masters at strangling their prey by squeezing them. They first consume their victims' eyes, carefully gouging them out with their fangs, and then devouring their preys' bodies.

The last of the fauna we captured was a stunning dark violet Neutortous. This was our biggest prize and was most unexpected. While we were watching the Loxocemae, the Neutortous appeared, hunting the snakes. That gave us a unique opportunity to capture the Loxocemae's predator, which we did successfully, thanks to Walverm, Mahlvern, Kalosse, and myself, who all jumped on it. It was a dumb strategy, but it worked, which was all that mattered in the end.

The Neutortous are large, lizard like animals. This is the largest Neutortous I've ever seen, at 250 centimeters long and 50 centimeters wide. We will inject this one with the serum.

Last, we captured a unique surprise—a seemingly sentient ivy plant. Even Surridge wasn't able to identify this ivy. It moved on its own in a calculated manner. We had captured a large haul of Grumantrus, which are similar to praying mantises. Yet, due to this ivy's meddling, they all escaped, and we weren't able to capture another one. However, we did manage to capture the ivy. Even after Mahlvern cut it off from where it was latched, it continued to writhe, so we drugged it with the same tranquilizer we used on the Neutortous, and, surprisingly, it worked. We were able to bring it back to our ship and lock it away securely before it awoke again.

Today, Mahlvern will take the lead by creating a unique terrarium for each species we captured. We will recreate their natural habitat the best we can, so when we experiment on them, they are as comfortable as possible in this unnatural place.

From the desk of Professor Maximilianus
Peal. Pjorkiln, Kampanar 13, 82002
20:19:10:10.

It's been a busy few days, and we've been quite successful.

For the past three days, we've been dissecting the Phasmatodaedalus and have been learning a lot about their anatomy. We discovered the secret behind their never-ending growth—a special set of muscles and glands on either of its ends that secrete a growth hormone when it's asleep. This most likely means that a Phasmatodaedalus can only grow while it is resting or asleep. In turn, that means the biggest Phasmatodaedalus are the ones that get the most rest, and closest in proximity to their food and water sources.

Once again, the full results of our experiment can be found in the database.

Today, we tested the serum on the Phasmatodaedalus.

As with the Curik, we started high, with twenty milliliters. The first one died, so we lowered the second dosage to seventeen. The second subject died within a minute. We lowered the dosage to fifteen, and once again the subject died.

We lowered the dosage to seven milliliters for the fourth subject. This one survived and seemed to understand what we were saying, but it could not speak—it continued to make the same scratching noises. This subject still lives and has been dubbed Stick-Brain by Mahlvern.

For our fifth subject, we upped the dosage to ten milliliters and the stick bug began talking. Immediately after the injection, a series of curses flew from its mouth.

We have our first success, and I couldn't be more thrilled. I knew the serum would work. We have named our success Denoptace after the Lakinceitian word that roughly translates to first winner. This one I named.

However, our final two subjects, the sixth and seventh, both failed, even after we injected them with the same dosage of ten milliliters. Rather than speaking, they killed themselves, much like how one of our Curik subjects killed itself. These will be handed over to Walverm for dissection.

Although Denoptace survived and can speak and understand us, we still don't fully understand why this subject was successful and the others were not. We need to go back and review the recordings of the experiments to see what the conditions were for Denoptace, and what differed for the other two. The more we know, the more we can perfect our successes.

We are running low on serum, so I am planning on making another batch. Each batch takes about four days to make. I might tweak the formula a bit. There have been too many deaths by either poisoning or suicide, so I'm going to see what I can do to lower the rates of death.

That being said, we are not keeping Denoptace with Stick-Brain. We moved Stick-Brain into a new terrarium that Mahlvern specially constructed. Denoptace will reside alone in the main Phasmatodaedalus terrarium. We don't want our subjects mixing after the experiments—we don't know how Denoptace will handle seeing another of his kind.

Denoptace has been fairly rude and unpleasant since he has been able to speak, but it's not surprising. I hope he will be calmer tomorrow so we can start a meaningful conversation, or at least start the groundwork to get into meaningful conversations.

```
From the desk of Professor Maximilianus
Peal. Gnuakiln, Kampanar 15, 82002
09:22:03:64.
```

Denoptace has proven to be an interesting creature.

He continues to throw curses at us and has been altogether unhelpful, but, even so, we have learned several things from him.

First, and most importantly, was that we needed to adjust the new serum. I believe we had a slight imbalance of chemicals, which is what made many of our subjects commit suicide while others died immediately. It also explains Denoptace's rage. When compared to a regular Phasmatodaedalus, such as Stick-Brain, their demeanors are completely different. Stick bugs, especially Phasmatodaedalus, are typically quiet, docile creatures, but Denoptace acts like he's seconds away from murdering everyone in the room.

This, in turn, led us to discover just how much the serum can change the personality of the subject, as this was an unexpected result. And through the cursing and insults, we have learned a bit about the Phasmatodaedalus culture. Denoptace keeps on referring to his queen, which would be a unique feature for stick bugs. He has also referred to an unusual ceremony. While we don't have any details, both of these pieces of information lead us to believe that the

Phasmatodaedalus are social creatures. The extent of this social behavior is still unknown, but we are making progress.

These discoveries have slightly delayed the creation of the next batch of serum. Until then, we will continue to run tests on Denoptace, and the other two surviving test subjects—the Curik, Salty Susan, and the other Phasmatodaedalus, Stick-Brain.

From the desk of Professor Maximilianus
Peal. Ramnkiln, Kampanar 24, 82002
07:74:48:69.

Today we are starting to work with the Dark Therids, and we are changing our initial plan. Originally, we were not planning on dissecting any of the Dark Therids. However, we have since discovered that half of our subjects are males, and the other half are females. So, we will dissect one male and one female. Walverm is preparing for that now. Kamarial will assist, as she is our resident arachnid expert.

I will report in later about today's test results.

From the desk of Professor Maximilianus
Peal. Ramnkiln, Kampanar 24, 82002
19:56:39:77.

Today went interestingly.

First of all, the dissections went well. They gave us insight on how the Dark Therids can weave webs of many different strengths and properties. While normal spiders spin between four to seven different types of silky strands, Dark Therids average to about thirty. We discovered Dark Therids have four extra glands in which their silk is made from, and twelve different sets of spinnerets. This diversity is what allows the Dark Therids to spin such a sundry amount of silk strands.

Now, as for the serum injections—well, it's safe to say that the new version of the serum is quite different. Out of our six test subjects, four survived—three females and one male. The two other males, which were smaller to begin with, did not survive.

None of the four survivors can speak, but they are exhibiting interesting behavior. Two of the females attacked the surviving male, while the other female protected the male. We have since moved all four Dark Therids into their respective cells for the rest of the night.

Tomorrow, Walverm will dissect one of the two aggressive females to see if anything changed internally since introducing the serum. We have already set that one aside so she will not get a name. However, the other three have received names, thanks to Kamarial this time around. The male will be named Ados, and its female protector is Adok, named after the ancient lovers from Eusphyrchiian mythology. The aggressive female has been named Penny.

One thing about today is that we are no longer calling survivors from the serum failures. If a subject survives, whether or not it can speak, it is a success. Especially after observing the Curik, Salty Susan, and the other Phasmatodaedalus, Stick-Brain. A few days ago, we put them in a terrarium together. At first, they were both timid, but now it seems as if they are communicating with each other. Interspecies communication has never been observed before, so we are breaking new ground in areas that we never expected.

Next, we will move on to the Zubba. We will move from insects to animals—most of which are reptiles. We may decide to tweak the serum again. I am speaking with Professor Bodeelch about this tomorrow.

From the desk of Professor Maximilianus
Peal. Sarkiln, Kampanar 26, 82002
16:20:19:42.

Just wanted to make a quick update. First of all, the Dark Therid dissection yesterday proved quite insightful. After administering the serum to the Dark Therid, we observed many internal changes.

First and foremost—the female Dark Therid that Walverm and Kamarial dissected had eighteen silk-producing glands, up from the twelve before dissection. The Dark Therid also changed to have sixteen spinnerets, and there was evidence of more glands and spinnerets growing as well.

Not only did the Dark Therid change internally, but she grew in size—from weighing close to 90 grams to weighing 140 grams, a nearly 65% increase in weight, along with a 28% increase in size.

This made us take a closer look at our other survivors. First, the Curik has been evolving. Curik, like all beetles, have wings, yet typical Curik have evolved to be unable to fly. Yet Salty Susan has been recorded flying in its terrarium. Stick-Brain, the Phasmatodaedalus in the terrarium with it, has been growing exponentially. When we captured this particular Phasmatodaedalus, it was 18 centimeters long. In the thirteen days since we administered the serum, it has grown to be 42 centimeters long. Mahlvern is already working on a new terrarium to allow for this exponential growth.

In stark contrast, Denoptace hasn't grown a millimeter. He has also become much quieter and reserved. Kalosse and Surridge, of whom I have tasked with observing and monitoring our subjects, haven't been able to get him to talk for almost two full days now. Since he has exhibited nearly zero physical changes, it leads us to believe that his changes have all happened internally.

As for the three surviving Dark Therids, we need more time for observation. They are proving to be the most interesting of our subjects. Kamarial is monitoring them closely and has been providing me with periodic updates.

As for the serum, Professor Bodeelch approved the modifications we proposed. This new serum will be ready in about a week. Once the serum is ready, we will move on to the Zubba.

```
From the desk of Professor Maximilianus
Peal. Eklakiln, Kampanar 33, 82002
21:39:37:04.
```

It's been a busy and productive few days.

Starting on the thirty-first, Walverm began the Zubba dissections, with Kalosse assisting. I could not oversee the dissections this time around, due to unforeseen problems with our newest batch of serum. Yet Surridge, Kamarial, Mahlvern and I were able to address and solve most of the problems without much of a setback. The full details about what went wrong with the serum are in the database.

We dissected eight Zubba in all. I still need to fully review the data, but Walverm and Kalosse have already made some very important discoveries.

The most important of these discoveries, which I'll touch on briefly, is that the scorpion head of a Zubba is underdeveloped. We discovered eye sockets and partially-developed chelicerae. All of this is hiding underneath its scaly shell, but it proves my theory that we can make a Zubba use both heads like a Zubula. That will need to be an experiment for another time.

As for today, we injected the remaining eight Zubba with the newest version of the serum. Once again, full details are in the database, but I'll explain the results for this recording's sake.

Overall, we had five deaths. Two died immediately from the dosage, and the other three died over an hour later. All three that died in this way seemed perfectly fine—they showed zero signs of change. Walverm will perform dissections on the deceased tomorrow, but my theory is that the serum was affecting the subjects internally, and within their scorpion half, rather than within the bat half. As we have been discovering, we can use the same dosage on the same species and we will get two different results. Nothing seems consistent with the serum; although, we have not been using the same formula every time either. But our formula changes do not inherently change the serum—all we have been doing is adjusting it accordingly for the new species that we are experimenting on, making slight adjustments with the amino acids and hormones.

As for our three surviving Zubba, two seem relatively unchanged. Yet one of the Zubba has shown signs of comprehending our language. This Zubba has also attempted speech, although its thoughts only come out in broken words and syllables. It's possible that, in time, this Zubba will be able to communicate fully with us. We have named this Zubba Blood Bat, courtesy of Walverm. Blood Bat is named for its dark rusty-colored bat fur and its bright red scorpion.

We have not named the other two surviving Zubba yet, as I am not confident they will live through the night. If they do, they will receive proper names for easier classification.

From the desk of Professor Maximilianus
Peal. Melrikiln, Kampanar 40, 82002
20:03:64:12.

We are ramping up the pace of our experiments. Professor Bodeelch is eager for us to finish. He's visited us every day since the thirty-fifth.

Today we worked with the second to last species that we have in our captivity—the Loxocemae.

We dissected one and learned very little. This was not due to the dissection, but because Loxocemae have almost no discernible differences from other snakes. While most Acampachetlian species are unique, it appears as if the Loxocemae are generic snakes.

We tried a different approach in administering the serum. Rather than starting with a high dosage of the serum and moving down, we are tailoring each dosage to the specifics of the Loxocemae's measurements—their mass and dimensions.

Out of the five test subjects we had to work with, there was only one death this time, but only one was an overwhelming success— our first genuine success since Denoptace. In many ways, this Loxocemae was much more successful.

Her name is Sassafrass. We did not give her this name—she told us her name. She also told us she is female, which we already knew, but it was interesting that she mentioned it.

Sassafrass is highly responsive and has already provided us with an abundance of information. All of the conversations we've had thus far with Sassafrass can be found in the database. However, I would like to play a small clip for this recording:

PROFESSOR PEAL: *I HAVE A FEW MORE QUESTIONS FOR YOU AT THIS TIME, IF THAT IS OKAY WITH YOU.*

SASSAFRASS: *YES, PLEASE CONTINUE.*

PROFESSOR PEAL: *CAN YOU TELL ME ABOUT YOUR UPBRINGING?*

SASSAFRASS: *CERTAINLY. AS WITH MOST OF MY KIND, I HATCHED FROM AN EGG IN A COLONY OF ABOUT SIXTEEN. AS SOON AS WE ARE HATCHED, WE DO NOT REQUIRE ANY SUPERVISION. WE ARE FULLY CAPABLE OF RAISING OURSELVES.*

PROFESSOR PEAL: *SO, YOU DID NOT GET ANY AID FROM YOUR SIBLINGS?*

SASSAFRASS: *THIS CONCEPT OF SIBLINGS IS UNKNOWN TO ME. NO SIBLINGS, JUST COMPETITION—I DEVOURED THREE OF MY FELLOW HATCHLINGS. WE MUST CONSUME IMMEDIATELY AFTER HATCHING TO SURVIVE.*

PROFESSOR PEAL: *WHAT HAPPENS WHEN YOU COME INTO CONTACT WITH ANOTHER OF YOUR KIND?*

SASSAFRASS: *WE EITHER FIGHT OR RETREAT. WE DO NOT INTERACT WITH OTHERS.*

PROFESSOR PEAL: *SO, WHY ARE YOU SO WILLING TO COMMUNICATE WITH ME?*

SASSAFRASS: *YOU ARE NOT SNAKE.*

PROFESSOR PEAL: *IN THE TERRARIUM, YOU LIVED WITH FIVE OTHER LOXOCEMAE FOR NEARLY A FULL MONTH.*

I found this part of the conversation fascinating and insightful. That recording took place about an hour after administering the serum to Sassafrass. This is a good example of how when we get the serum right it can do exactly what we intended it to do.

As for the other surviving Loxocemae, none of the others are exhibiting any signs of speech or understanding our language. Each has been given a unique name, all of which can be found in the database.

Today's experiments taught us much about the serum itself. It's too bad we only have one more test subject to work on—the Neutortous. We are going to create a specialized formula for our Neutortous by integrating the new insights into the serum. We are going to attempt to make the serum focus its effects directly on the speech center of the Neutortous' brain and nothing else. We only have one test subject, so we must make it count.

From the desk of Professor Maximilianus
Peal. Dunakiln, Julinar 4, 82002
20:03:64:12.

Today did not go as expected. And yet, the Neutortous is, by and large, our greatest success. We are going to need to study her closely to see how this came to be.

I'll rewind a bit. The morning started out well. The serum finished during the night, and we were running our initial diagnostics on it when Head Professor Yilvin and Professor Bodeelch arrived. They came to observe today's experiment, but their presence ultimately changed the entire experiment.

First of all, the Neutortous is by far the largest subject we've ever worked with, with a mass of nearly 120 kilograms. It took a lot of sedatives to sedate her. After we sedated her, we strapped her to the operating table.

This is when the trouble began. When Professor Kalosse was carrying the syringe containing the serum to the operating table, the syringe slipped out of his hand and smashed onto the floor. We lost nearly all of our freshly made serum.

Upon this accident, Professor Bodeelch demanded that we continue if we had the means to do so. And we did.

While I would not have even considered doing this in any other situation, we ended up combining the little bits of serum that we had left over from all the previous batches, including the little bit we had left from today.

The combined mixture was roughly the same volume as our original dosage at 42 milliliters. The original volume was 45 milliliters, so we administered this serum to the test subject.

I will say this—the results were completely unexpected. Immediately after administering the serum, the Neutortous began thrashing around and broke out of our restraints—the same restraints that could hold her at her previous full strength. After breaking out of her restraints, the Neutortous calmed down and apologized. She told us her name was Newtus, and she thanked us for giving her the power of speech.

The serum, somehow, was successful. I need to determine how this happened. I wish we had a small sample of the concoction left.

Needless to say, Head Professor Yilvin and Professor Bodeelch were both extremely impressed. And, after settling Newtus into her terrarium, I let Head Professor Yilvin and Professor Bodeelch observe Denoptace, Blood Bat, and Sassafrass. Professor Bodeelch even spoke with Sassafrass for a few minutes. That recording is in the database.

Now that we are finished administering the serum to our test subjects, we will spend much more time with our successes.

For now, Professor Bodeelch has approved us to take some time off —which essentially just means reduced hours. We still need someone here on a 25-hour basis. This work will be divided between Kalosse, myself, and a rotation of the compound's four security guards. My shift begins in two days. Until then, I'll be enjoying a much-needed break.

For all inquiries, please use the contact information below:
Ducutyk@icos.gov
FBI@icos.gov
Please keep your messages under 500 characters. Attachments not allowed.

© Foxaire Biotech Industries. All Rights Reserved. Any unauthorized copying, alteration, distribution, transmission, performance, display or other use of this material is prohibited. Any unauthorized use of this material will result in a minimum 70,000 munit fine and 6-week incarceration period, followed by heavy surveillance.

33

BATTLE FOR CONSCIOUSNESS

The nible fire ants were relentless. Wave after wave, they pounced onto the energy barrier, spraying acid upon impact, only to be zapped and thrown back into the sharp volcanic rocks. Although each ant was tiny and dealt minor damage, in mass they were a genuine threat.

Tyrona looked over at the man she loved as he put everything he had into maintaining the magical barrier. A few minutes ago, Dasch had sent some of his energy into Theodore's staff, momentarily enhancing the barrier, but his assistance wasn't enough. The onslaught was too much.

"Hang in there, Dorie! You can handle this," Tyrona called to him.

"And, you know, what if he can't?" Vesten asked, causing Tyrona and Cecil to glare at him. "Look, it's a fair fuckin' question."

"It is indeed," Dasch said, nodding in agreement. "My aid did almost nothing, and we don't know how long Ànifa and Joan will take to return. My power is drained... I cannot even enhance your weapons with my golden flames if I wished to."

"I can raise another barrier," Tyrona replied. "Dorie, let me know when you can't hold it any longer, and I'll back you up."

"I... I can hold out for a bit longer..." Theodore replied through clenched teeth.

"Well, this is certainly going to give me fuckin' nightmares," Vesten said quietly as he watched the berserk ants assault the barrier.

"I absolutely agree," Cecil replied. "I've always hated bugs."

"Who doesn't?" Vesten replied.

"Insects have their place," Dasch said harshly. "Even these ants play a vital role in this ecosystem."

"Yeah, that doesn't fuckin' matter to me much right now," Vesten said. "I just don't want to fuckin' die by fire ants is all."

"I'd kill every last one of these shitheads if it was up to me," Cecil said.

Tyrona rolled her eyes. "Can you guys please stop yapping? We need to let him concentrate."

"Sorry, Theodore," Cecil said, looking downcast.

"Its... fine," Theodore panted.

"Don't speak, Dorie," Tyrona said, placing a hand on his back. "Just focus."

They fell silent. The only sounds now were the scuttling of the fire ants, the spitting of their venom, and the zaps as they dived into the barrier. Tyrona took out her wand and waited. She looked at it closely, spinning it around in her hand.

This wand had been her grandmother's and had been passed down to her. Her parents didn't study magic. Ever since she was young, her grandmother had fascinated her. Often, when it was only the two of them, her grandmother would do everything with magic— dust the house, stir the pots, wash the dishes, and so forth.

This wand was old. They didn't make wands like this anymore. Most wands were made of wood now. Hers was ivory, carved from the tusk of a felled woolly rhinoceros after a deadly mating battle with a larger male.

The pattern on it depicted that battle. Starting from the bottom, the rhinoceroses met, then charged, then fought, then died as the image spun toward the tip.

Her wand was also unique in another way; since most wands only ever have one owner, it was rare for one to work for two separate sorcerers, including family members, but this wand had always responded to her as if it had been made for her.

Theodore grunted and fell to one knee. "Ugh! Tyrona!"

"I got you!" she replied as she sprang into action and immediately raised a barrier. Whereas Theodore's had been made from mostly static electricity, hers was made from pure vibrational energy.

As soon as her barrier was raised, Theodore's barrier dissipated, and he fell to the ground.

"Theodore!" Cecil cried as he rushed over to his friend.

"How's he doing?" Tyrona asked as she braced herself from the onslaught of fire ants. Her barrier worked differently—rather than zapping a fire ant and throwing it back, this time the ants simply slid down the barrier upon impact. Furthermore, the ants' acid stuck to Tyrona's barrier, held in place by the same vibrations that formed the shield. Once adhered, the acid ate away at it.

"Oh, shit!" Vesten cried as he watched in horror. "The fuck do we do?"

"Calm yourself," Dasch said as he placed his hand on Vesten's shoulder. "We'll be okay."

"How the fuck do you know that?"

"Uh, guys... the barrier," Cecil said, his eyes wide with fear.

The ants were focusing their attacks on a singular spot in the barrier. They would be through within minutes.

"How the fuck are we going to be okay now?" Vesten cried.

"Because our saviors are coming," Dasch said.

Tyrona looked through her barrier and spotted Joan flying swiftly toward them.

As Joan descended, Tyrona made an opening in the barrier's ceiling, allowing Joan inside, then closed it immediately. In doing this, Tyrona restrengthened the entire barrier, buying them a little more time.

"Where's Ànifa?" Vesten asked.

"On her way," Joan replied. "Until then, I need everyone's strict attention. We will not have much time to pull this off. These fire ants are out for blood, literally. They have gone berserk and will not calm down until they kill something, no matter how many of them have to die first.

"Ànifa is coming with a pack of dire wolf spiders. As soon as the spiders have surrounded us, that's when you need to drop your barrier, Tyrona. Then everyone needs to get on a spider. They'll carry us out of here quickly and safely."

"Yeah... did you just say dire wolf *spider*?" Cecil asked.

"Will that be a problem?" Joan asked.

"I mean, fucking yeah! I don't want to ride a giant spider!" Vesten exclaimed.

"Too bad," Joan replied with a shrug. "They're our only option. Get ready, Tyrona."

"Ready when you are," she replied.

The dire wolf spiders had come into view. They attacked the nible fire ants as they fought their way through the berserk colony.

Ànifa's body ached as the giant wolf spider she rode on bounded across the rocky terrain. On several occasions, they had to leap over free-flowing lava rivers and hidden geysers.

During the rough ride, Ànifa caught mental visions of strange creatures—a blood-red snake; a frustrated stick-bug; a strange bat-scorpion creature; and a giant, deep purple lizard. Through her intuition, she knew the visions were originating from the same place as Navacus Clums, but she could not understand why she now saw a different professor. The constant shaking from her giant spider mount didn't help her concentration.

Ànifa rode the female pack leader. Although she was not a god, she was a strong, fierce leader. Her loyal cluster of seven smaller male spiders skittered after them. Joan had flown on ahead to prepare the others.

She raced onward as fast as she could, moving naturally with the spider beneath her as they flew across the volcanic landscape.

We must make it in time! she thought.

She saw the nible fire ants before she spied her friends.

"Disperse!" Ànifa shouted. In response, the spider beneath her—she had chosen to name her Chitter—relayed her command with a series of clicks and hisses.

The powerful male wolf spiders attacked the nible fire ants by shooting needle-like hairs from their legs. The hairs pierced the ants, killing them on impact. Many of the hairs skewered multiple fire ants, stacking them like a macabre kabob.

The ants retaliated against the spiders, causing the ants surrounding the barrier to disperse. The wolf spiders closed in and surrounded the barrier, Chitter among them. Even though Chitter wasn't able to shoot leg hairs like her male companions, Chitter could spit acid. Judging from the pools of melting fire ants, the poisonous acid was quite effective. The dire wolf spiders had the energy barrier completely surrounded.

"Now!" Ànifa cried. A moment later, the barrier fell.

Dasch was the first on the back of a dire wolf spider, followed immediately by Theodore and Tyrona. Cecil cursed, and then climbed onto the back of one of the male wolf spiders.

Vesten stood in place, frozen in fear. Next to him, Joan hovered in the air worriedly.

"Vesten!" Ànifa shouted as the fire ants descended on him.

"There's no time," Joan said as she picked up Vesten and carried him into the air.

"Let's move!" Ànifa shouted. Chitter and her pack skittered over the fire ants, stomping them with their sharp, hairy, hook-like feet. Ànifa looked back and saw her friends clinging onto their own spiders.

"Let's climb, Chitter. Take us to the top."

<hr>

They reached the top of the Nibelkaith Volcano by sunset. Even though it was quickly growing darker, enough light emanated from the mouth of the volcano for everyone to see. Their wolf spider mounts would take them all the way to the Great Barrier. By this point, even Joan and Vesten each rode on their own spider. It had taken Vesten some convincing to do so, but Joan needed her rest. Ànifa knew that it was quite taxing on Joan to fly with someone in her arms, even though she wouldn't openly admit it.

Ànifa led her friends as they traversed the wide mouth of the volcano. There was only one way to reach the center of the volcano, where the small floating island was located, and that was by a long, rickety rope bridge with wooden slats. Even though she could see it, they were still close to two kilometers away from the bridge.

They were making great time riding the spiders, nearly doubling their walking speed. Ànifa was coming to learn how each spider had its own unique personality. For instance, the spider Theodore rode on was treading carefully, ensuring its rider was safe the entire time. In comparison, Dasch's spider was completely unruly, and when Dasch tried to change spiders, it wouldn't let him. After that, the spider settled down a bit.

Vesten and Cecil were not enjoying the ride, but they admitted it was better than walking. On the way up the volcano, the group passed many more mounds of nible fire ant colonies. A smaller one they passed was being ravaged by a group of dire armadillo— gobbling any fire ant they could with their long sticky tongues.

As they approached the bridge, they saw it was guarded by a massive wolf spider—the spider god. It stared at them with its eight enormous eyes, but after a moment stepped out of the way to let them pass.

"She must be the guardian of this bridge," Ànifa said as she looked warily at the wide rickety bridge. "If such a strong creature is guarding the bridge, it must be safe, right?"

"I would hope so," Tyrona said. "If you want, I can test it."

"No, it's fine. I'll do it," Ànifa said. "Besides, I think Joan and I should be the only ones to go across. You should all wait back here."

"Yeah, that's not happening," Theodore said. "Did you forget that the whole reason this quest began was so I could investigate the Great Barriers? I'm seeing this one up close, too."

"And I'm going with him," Tyrona said.

"We'll be safer as a group," Dasch grumbled.

"Ah, alright then. Just be careful everyone. I'll check the bridge first."

Ànifa patted Chitter on her back, signaling for her to continue ahead. The rope bridge was wide enough for the large spider to fit with little room to spare. Chitter made it a short distance across the bridge. It felt steady beneath them. The bridge was quite long—Ànifa estimated it to be nearly a half kilometer.

"Yeah, it's safe," Ànifa said as she made Chitter stop, then looked back at her friends. "I think we can all go."

"Are you sure?" Cecil asked. "I don't want to plunge into the molten lava below."

"Well, if you're that concerned, the next person can follow me in five minutes. I should be across by then."

"I'll go with you, Princess," Joan said, dismounting her spider.

"No. I think we need to use these spiders," Ànifa replied. "Why else would their god be the one safeguarding this place?"

Joan settled back on her dire wolf spider. "Be careful, Princess."

"I will be," Ànifa replied. "See you on the other side."

Ànifa nudged Chitter forward. The rope bridge swayed beneath her. Chitter's hook-like feet latched onto the planks and absorbed some of the swaying.

This bridge would be a death trap without a wolf spider ally, she thought. *I hope everyone else makes it over safely.*

"Well, that was... certainly terrifying," Tyrona commented as her wolf spider stepped off the bridge. Theodore and Dasch were behind her.

"Yeah, I don't want to do that again," Cecil replied.

"We still need to make our return journey," Joan said.

"Ah, fuck," Vesten sighed. "I didn't even consider that."

"Now that nearly everyone is here, we should start examining the barrier," Joan said.

"Can we get off our spiders yet?" Vesten complained.

"Do you want to tumble into the lava?" Tyrona asked. "In case you haven't noticed, the ground is extremely slick."

Ànifa motioned to Joan as they made their way along the side of the narrow ledge. The Great Barrier encompassed the vast majority of the small floating island, leaving only a small sliver of open ground. Tyrona was right—there was no way any of them could stand on the island without slipping into the volcano. The spiders' specialized feet were hooking into the small cracks and grooves, allowing them to continue along smoothly.

"What's this?" Ànifa said softly. She had spied a peculiar oddity in the Great Barrier. Like all the other Great Barriers, this one was made of wind and electricity. Somehow, though, there was also a rock floating in mid-air amongst the torrent of wind.

"That is a magical defense system," Joan explained. "Anyone who steps into the barrier that should not will get smacked by one of these."

"How is it just floating there?" Ànifa asked.

"The same way this rock we are on is floating, and the same way that Yttendaus floats. You see, these rocks are not originally from Eklatros. These are meteorites that fell from space. From my understanding, they are slightly less dense than our atmosphere, so they float above the ground. Sometimes, when you get large meteorites together, they can create a floating island like this one."

"That's crazy. Rocks from outer space with paranormal properties are a bit out of my range of expertise," Ànifa joked.

"I think we can all agree with that," Joan chuckled.

"Oh hey, there you are," Tyrona said as she appeared from around the bend. "Dorie arrived, and Dasch is nearly across the bridge. What's the plan?"

"We're heading in," Ànifa said as she continued to gaze at the floating rock.

"Be careful," Tyrona said.

Ànifa turned to look at the beautiful, dark-skinned sorceress. Behind her, Theodore was coming into view.

"I will. Keep an eye on the others," Ànifa said.

Tyrona laughed. "I will. Can't leave the boys by themselves, can I?"

"Hey, I heard that," Theodore shouted.

Ànifa laughed then looked at Tyrona one last time before venturing forward. "I'll see you soon."

Ànifa turned to Joan, nodded, and then she and Joan plunged into the maelstrom. A clear pathway emerged free of wind, lightning, and debris.

"Well, this is certainly nice," Ànifa said softly to Joan as they continued forward.

The tree-like being that stood before them was unlike the other two Ekataramn Ànifa had encountered—Panabeeta did not have any branches, dinosaur heads, or other strange limbs. Panabeeta was simply a large, thick tree trunk, split near the top into two diamond-shaped holes. Two black spheres stared at them, each one floating in the center of the diamond-shaped holes. Above the eyes was a large, green tower of leafy canopy. At the top of the canopy was a strange bird-like creature. It seemed to be infused with Panabeeta. Ànifa saw the bird's large head move to get a better look at them.

"Welcome, Princess Ànifa Tataluynnia Ekataramnii. Welcome, Joan de Ligtheramnii. Please, dismount from your arachnids."

Ànifa and Joan dismounted. Their wolf spiders skittered away, retreating to the back of the enclosure.

"Greetings, noble one," Ànifa said as she gave Panabeeta a deep bow. Beside her, Joan gave her the angelic salute.

"We've been awaiting your arrival for quite some time," Panabeeta said.

"Pardon me, but what do you mean by 'we'?" Ànifa asked.

"Ah yes, of course you wouldn't know. I do not dwell here alone, fair Ànifa. Alakana rests here with me. She watches you from above, for she is attached to my canopy."

Ànifa glanced at the brown bird-like creature above them.

"How did Alakana come to be in this state?" Joan asked, aghast. "I knew there were some Ekataramn unaccounted for, but this is unexpected."

"Indeed. Alakana is here with me. If not, she would have perished long ago. She was gravely injured in the distant past, before this barrier existed, and even before this floating island."

"I see. I am thankful that you have cared for her," Ànifa said.

"Yes, for if not, Eklatros would be lost. Now, Ànifa, are you ready for what needs to be done?" Panabeeta asked.

"That's why we're here. To awaken the Ekataramn and protect Eklatros from Gnusaramnii," Ànifa replied.

"That is part of the reason, yes. Eklatros needs us. Now more than ever it is vital that we all return to our former glory."

"Yes, of course. What can we do to help?" Ànifa asked.

"We need you to activate your soul power, Ànifa. You as well, Joan. With both of you together, place your hands on my trunk. Listen closely, and listen well. This act will have grave consequences. There is a price that must be paid. This price is non-negotiable. It is the only way that Alakana can fully take flight, and for me to truly reawaken."

"I understand. What is the price?" Ànifa asked.

"A soul for a soul," Panabeeta replied. "Alakana cannot awaken without a sacrifice. Do know that what will be taken will be returned in time."

"May we have a moment?" Joan asked. She took Ànifa by the shoulder and led her away from the Ekataramn.

"What is it?"

Joan put a finger to her lips. "Keep your voice down, Princess. I have a bad feeling about this."

"What other option do we have? You said it yourself—we must complete our mission, and quickly."

"Yes, the quicker the better. Although I wasn't aware of this price."

"I wasn't either. It'll be okay, Joan. She said that what will be taken will be returned."

"A cryptic message that could mean many things. Yet, the choice is ultimately yours. I follow your lead, Princess."

Ànifa nodded. "We must complete our mission, no matter the cost."

"Yes, Princess. No matter the cost."

She broke away from Joan and approached Panabeeta. "I agree to your terms."

Ànifa closed her eyes, then focused within herself, feeling her flame of life burning within her. She called out to it, then opened her eyes. She was awash in blue flames from head to foot.

"You next, Joan," Ànifa commanded. "She needs both of us."

"Yes, of course. You have amazing control now, Princess. That was quite impressive."

"Thanks," Ànifa replied, then stepped closer to Panabeeta, approaching its thick trunk. What looked like wood from afar wasn't actually wood, but a thick animal hide, similar to elephant skin. Joan approached her, awash in a pure white flame.

"Together now," Panabeeta instructed.

A blinding light.

What happened? she thought. *Did it work? Everything is white... Joan? Joan, are you there? Is anyone there?*

Wait... Tyrona? What are you doing here?

34

BATTLE FOR LOSS

"You know, Dorie, this place really is quite spectacular," Tyrona said as she clung onto the back of the dire wolf spider.

Surrounding them were the Panna Peaks, their jagged summits poking out through dark gray clouds. These mountains were too warm to hold any snow, allowing them to clearly see their rugged features. Beyond the mountains lay the small settlement of Heerenditheer and the now destroyed town of Runti.

"You can find beauty in anything, can't you?" Theodore replied as he tried not to look down into the volcano.

"Think about it. Below us is a pool of molten rock, the same material that created the landmasses we live on. Eklatros' constant churning and gyrating is continuously reshaping and changing the landscapes. Take Panabeeta as an example. Those thousands of years ago, when Panabeeta was in its true state as a mighty Ekataramn, it was planted firmly in the ground. The continents have shifted and changed much since that time. Eklatros truly is alive, just as much as you or me."

"Eklatros must be alive, for it is only because of her that we can draw and use magic," Theodore replied. "We cannot even begin to comprehend the majesty that is Eklatros, and that's why we must protect her."

"No matter the cost," Tyrona said quietly.

Tyrona gazed out and took in the sights—the steep inner walls of the volcano and the lava bubbling below. The lava emanated a bright and clear light that allowed them to see unhindered in the dark of the night. The plumes of steam and smoke rose into the starry sky above them.

A strange tingling sensation washed over her. She looked down and gasped. Her entire body was emanating a bright white light.

"Dorie... what's happening?"

"Tyrona!"

Her lover's voice was distant, as if he was calling to her from the midst of a long Ajentian hallway. She had a vague feeling the others were approaching, yet all of her cares and worries seemed silly now. Why did she ever worry about anything? Everything was going to be okay now.

Ànifa stepped back from Panabeeta, still awash in blue flames. Beside her, Joan, awash in pure white flames, also stepped back from Panabeeta. Above them, a loud screech emanated into the starry night sky. She glanced at Panabeeta's canopy, where Alakana sat. The bird-like creature was moving—it opened its wings and screeched once more.

"How can Alakana fly?" Ànifa asked. Around her, the Great Barrier was dispersing into the air.

"We are not originally from this planet," Panabeeta replied. "We came here a long time ago, from a planet very far away. Back then, we were nothing more than humble spores. This planet was rich in the elements we needed to grow and thrive, and its residents were kind to us. Until the greed began."

"You're not from here? Are you from the same planet as Gnusaramnii?" Ànifa asked.

"No, that vile entity has a different origin. It matters not where we are from, not at this moment. Now is the time for you to return to your friends," Panabeeta said.

Alakana soared high into the sky, feeling alive once again. Fully refreshed and rejuvenated, Alakana flew through the clouds, heading northeast. The land she had once been rooted to was now submerged under hundreds of meters of water, but there was still one place she could go. It would be cold there, but she would manage. She had been through much worse than cold.

Alakana stretched her wings wide and screeched as she soared high into the air.

"Tyrona! Tyrona! Where are you?" Theodore shouted into the night sky. Tears welled in his eyes as a sharp pain gripped his heart.

Cecil, Dasch, and Vesten surrounded him. Part of him wished they would just leave him alone, but he needed them now more than ever. He grabbed hold of the spider he rode on.

The dire wolf spider that Tyrona had been riding on was spinning around in panic and confusion, scanning the molten lava below them.

"Are you sure she disappeared?" Cecil asked from the back of his wolf spider.

"I already explained what happened! Do you not believe me?" Theodore shouted unnecessarily, but he simply didn't care.

"I... well..." Cecil mumbled.

"I can confirm. Tyrona glowed brightly, then a moment later she was gone," Dasch said.

"But... how? What the fuck is going on here?" Vesten exclaimed.

"I can only presume that her disappearance has something to do with the Great Barrier dispersing," Dasch grumbled in reply.

"But how? We've seen other Great Barriers disperse. Why would this time be any different?" Theodore asked, his bloodshot eyes wildly scanning his friends.

"I'm sorry, Theodore... maybe Ànifa and Joan know what happened," Cecil suggested.

"If they do, they better have a good reason for taking her away from me." Theodore seethed in anger as tears streamed down his cheeks. He felt the pure rage cut through his sadness.

"I'm sure it wasn't their fuckin' fault," Vesten said. "They wouldn't willingly harm any of us."

"Maybe it was that damn angel!" Theodore shouted. "She must have something to do with this."

"Calm down, Theodore!" Dasch commanded, pointing a pale finger at his chest.

A small burst of magic washed over him, momentarily reducing his anger. Theodore looked at his hairless friend, too stunned to say anything.

"Now, listen closely," Dasch continued. "Whatever happened, there must be a good reason. Do not doubt our comrades. I can assure you neither one of them meant Tyrona any harm."

Theodore cleared his throat. "We'll see about that."

Ànifa and Joan rode back to the others, finding them easily without the impeding Great Barrier. Theodore approached them, breathing heavily as he wiped tears from his eyes.

"What did you do to Tyrona?" he shouted.

"Theodore, what happened?" Ànifa asked with a dreadful feeling in the pit of her stomach.

"You better damn well know what happened, or else—"

"Theodore!" Cecil shouted, using his knightly voice. "Calm down!"

"Why should I? Tyrona is gone!"

"What do you mean, Tyrona is gone?" Ànifa asked, although she knew it to be true.

"I saw it happen," Dasch said clearly. "I heard a shout, so I came immediately. I watched Tyrona burst into a bright light then disappear."

"Tyrona... so, that's what she meant," Ànifa said softly.

"You do know something, don't you!" Theodore shouted, urging his wolf spider forward. He stopped centimeters away from Ànifa and glared into her eyes.

"Theodore! If you do not calm yourself, then I will do it for you, and you won't like it!" Joan commanded, stretching her wings out wide for effect.

"*You!*" Theodore said harshly, turning to Joan. "I'll deal with you later, you—"

"Dimentryion Pantamine!" Joan exclaimed.

Theodore sat up straight, his arms pinned to his sides.

"Wha—hap—" Theodore attempted to say.

"You'll find yourself unable to move or speak for the next twenty minutes. I suggest you use this time to listen rather than rage."

Dasch looked back and forth between Theodore and Joan with an approving look.

Ànifa turned to Joan. "Will he be okay?"

"He'll be fine. Remember, I used to do this to your sisters occasionally."

"My sisters? That's a mean trick to play."

"Yes, it was quite cruel," Joan nodded. "Right now, though, this is just the thing Theodore needs."

"I understand. Theodore," Ànifa said, turning to face the old wizard. His eyes were sunken and brimming with tears. "I am so sorry that Tyrona is gone. But, please understand, there was no other way. And I didn't know what was going to happen. Panabeeta said a price must be paid... but she also said that what's taken will be returned in time. So, I don't believe she is dead. I believe we will see Tyrona again."

"But where did she go?" Cecil asked. "And how did she disappear?"

"Alakana. I'm sure it was Alakana. She has the power of space... she can physically transport people and objects to anywhere in the cosmos. And coupled with Panabeeta's power of mind and consciousness, she could be anywhere," Joan said.

"Alakana? The Ekataramn? It was here?" Dasch asked. "Is that what flew into the sky around the time Tyrona disappeared?"

"Yes. I'll explain on the way," Ànifa said. "We need to return to *West Wind*. We can't stay the night out here, it's too dangerous. Our dire wolf spiders will take us there much quicker than we can on our own, especially in the dark."

"Lead the way, Princess," Joan said.

Theodore's body ached as anguish poured from his heart. He remained frozen with his arms locked at his sides, while Ànifa led his spider across the rickety rope bridge. Dozens of unanswerable questions looped through his mind. Why Tyrona? Was she alive? If so, where did she go? He tried to shake his head to clear his mind but was still paralyzed, so he took a deep breath instead, then let it out slowly, releasing his anger in the process.

His hand twitched. The paralysis was wearing off.

"How are you feeling?" Joan asked as she approached with Tyrona's spider. Joan was the last of the group to cross the bridge.

"A bit sore," Theodore replied as he rubbed his arms, "but my mind is clearer now. I'm still confused, but I understand we shouldn't linger here either. I only wish that I could have traded places with her."

"We'll see her again, Theodore," Ànifa replied with certainty, then waved to the wolf spider god as they passed by Panabeeta's guardian.

"In truth, Panabeeta was vague," Joan replied as they continued down the volcano. "However, I also believe that we will see her again."

"I can handle vague better than nothing at all. I'll go with that. I… I apologize about before," Theodore said, placing his palms together.

"You have no reason to apologize," Ànifa replied. "You were scared and confused. I wasn't prepared for this to happen either."

"I'm glad you've returned to your senses. We're going to need them." Joan quickly turned her attention to the mountainside. "Ànifa."

"I see it," Ànifa replied.

"What is it?" Theodore asked as he scanned the dark landscape.

"A large, mangled scorpion," Dasch replied.

"To be precise, it looks like Chactochactas, the scorpion god," Ànifa replied. "I felt her die earlier, so this is no longer Chactochactas, but a Gnurargurt."

"We don't have time for this," Theodore said as he urged his dire wolf spider forward. "Where is this monstrosity?"

"Down there," Ànifa pointed. "Can you see that large boulder? It's hiding behind it."

"There's a large boulder? Perfect. Stand back, everyone. I need to release some stress."

"Are you sure that's wise?" Joan asked.

"Definitely not. I can't see a thing," Theodore replied. "But I don't much care right now."

"I can relate," Cecil replied. "If I could see, I'd help you."

"The way you all can help is to be quiet and stay still. I need to focus."

Theodore prompted his spider to kneel, then hopped off its back. He planted his feet firmly in the volcanic dirt and closed his eyes, taking in a deep breath. He used his magic to reach out through the ground and search for vibrations. After a few moments, he felt the corrupted scorpion god as it crept out from behind the boulder.

He smiled to himself, then raised his scarlet staff high into the air and silently muttered an incantation. He visualized his staff's fossilized wooden core in his mind, feeling its raw power. A moment later, thunder boomed above them as a bolt of lightning struck the scorpion in its abdomen. The creature wailed in pain as Theodore prepared for his next attack. He thrust his staff into the ground and sent a small shockwave through the dirt, striking the boulder. Through his connection with the ground, he felt the boulder crack near its apex. He quickly pulled his staff out of the dirt with both hands and pointed the glass orb at the boulder, sending a stream of air toward it. Chunks of boulder rained upon the scorpion god while Theodore readied his final attack. He held his staff out in front of him and spun it in a circular motion as he muttered to himself. The glass orb illuminated as a stream of fire shot toward the pinned Gnurargurt. The onslaught continued until only ash remained.

Ànifa closed her eyes and sent Chactochactas her thoughts.

Theodore wheezed as he hoisted himself back onto his spider's back. "That was fun."

"That was overkill," Joan said.

"But it felt great," Theodore replied.

"Oh, is it over?" Cecil said. "That was really loud."

"Really fuckin' loud!" Vesten echoed.

"Quiet, all of you!" Ànifa whispered harshly, cutting through the building tension. "We need to get moving, now. We'll have attracted a lot of attention to our position."

"How can we move if we can't fuckin' see?" Vesten asked.

"Trust your spiders. They will lead you. And besides, three of us can see, right? We'll each watch after one of you."

"I'll watch the knight," Dasch replied. "He may need a lot of supervision."

"Good call. I'll watch Theodore," Ànifa said.

"What, hey!" Cecil cried.

"Then I'll watch Vesten," Joan replied.

"This feels so unfair," Cecil mumbled.

"Shut it, knight," Dasch whispered. "We don't have any other options."

"That doesn't make me feel any better, but thanks anyway."

Ànifa led the group, keeping Theodore directly to her left. Cecil and Vesten followed, with Joan and Dasch taking the rear. Once they began their descent, the smoke obscured the stars. While there was no unnatural darkness, Ànifa still had trouble seeing. She worried about Dasch—she hoped his dark vision was more elvish than human.

Despite the circumstances, they made their way down Nibelkaith without any other confrontations. They had to skirt around a few potential adversaries, including slumbering dire armadillo and hidden snakes. The wolf spiders could sense everything before they got too close. A short distance into their journey, Theodore, Cecil, and Vesten nodded off to sleep. Joan ensured they wouldn't fall off their mounts by magically making each of them hold on tightly.

They made it back to Beetaramn before dawn. Ànifa dismounted from Chitter and shook Theodore awake.

"Alright, alright, I'm up, I'm up," Theodore said with a massive yawn.

"Let's go. We can sleep once we reach *West Wind*," Ànifa replied. "We all deserve it."

They said goodbye to their spiders. Ànifa thanked each of them individually—they had taken them much further than they had expected. The spiders were exhausted, but seemed happy. She smiled, then turned toward Beetaramn.

As they reached Beetaramn's outer gate, they saw The Bishop as she performed a series of stretches and exercises in her front yard.

"Ah, so you've all returned," The Bishop said as they approached. "I'm feeling mighty chipper this morning. Much more energetic than usual. I think I have you all to thank for that."

Ànifa approached The Bishop. "Yes, we've awakened Panabeeta... and Alakana. They were both up there, but it cost us dearly."

"Yes, I can see that. I'm terribly sorry for your loss," The Bishop said as she placed her palms together.

"Thank you," Theodore replied with a yawn. "Now, we must be on our way."

"Oh yes, of course. Though, I do have a bit of news for you all, if you care to listen."

"What news?" Ànifa asked.

"They held the world summit yesterday."

Cecil yawned. "Oh right, I remember Sarah was talking about that."

"Yes, it was the first world summit in many years," The Bishop said. "And I am sure you all were the main topic of conversation."

"Seriously?" Ànifa replied. "The masters at Ajenti were talking about the world summit also. Why were you not there?"

"My place is here," The Bishop said. "I sent an envoy in my place. A young woman by the name of Afyna."

"Afyna? I wonder if it's the same Afyna I met in Sathon," Ànifa mused.

"Indeed, she spoke highly of you."

"Well, I'm glad she's there representing you."

"Indeed," The Bishop nodded. "Now, return to your ship and rest. You all have had a long night."

***

As soon as they made it onto to *West Wind*, each of them marched straight to their rooms. Cecil offered to bunk with Theodore, but he said he needed to be alone, so Cecil shared a room with Dasch.

Theodore lay in his bed, alone, caressing Tyrona's side of the bed.

"You said that we would spend the entire next ride in bed together... we were supposed to be here, together, right now. But now you're gone. I... I can't handle it. I'm really not okay, not at all. But... I need to be. I need to be okay. For Ànifa, for Eklatros... and for you, Tyrona. I need to be strong, for you."

Theodore spoke to himself, barely listening to his own words. He ranted on for a while, then sobbed uncontrollably. He curled into a ball and cried himself to sleep.

***

"Joan, did I mess up today? Were you right to caution me, and was I wrong to have ignored your warning?" Ànifa asked once they were alone.

"No, Princess. Your call was the right one. I was wrong to have doubted Panabeeta."

"But Tyrona is gone, Joan. She's gone. Where did she go? How will we even see her again?"

"That I cannot answer, yet there is one being that would know. She is called Mau, and she resides on Yttendaus. We can ask her when we get there."

"Yttendaus… my home. But, it doesn't feel like my home anymore. *West Wind* feels like my home. My friends feel like home. Eklatros is my home."

"And Yttendaus is a part of Eklatros, just as this ship is. We are all part of Eklatros. I know you still have memories that allude you, so know that when we return, nothing will be the same. Eklatros is waking up. The Ekataramn are reclaiming their powers once again."

"And Gnusaramnii. We need the Ekataramn to fight against Gnusaramnii."

"In a way, yes. The Ekataramn will give power to Eklatros, which in turn will assist to repel Gnusaramnii and banish it from our planet for good."

"I hope so. I really do. Because after today… I just can't lose anyone else."

"I understand, Princess. You have a big heart. But try and sleep now, you need your rest," Joan said as the sun began to rise.

"So do you, if you plan on flying this thing," Ànifa replied.

"Yes, I need my rest as well. Have a good sleep, Ànifa."

"You too. Goodnight, Joan."

Goodnight, Tyrona, she thought. *I… I thought it was going to be me— that I would be the price. A price I would pay as many times over. I thought I was the key… but I should have known that my story would not end yet.*

Why you, Tyrona? Right when you and Theodore… and now I've taken that away from you, from both of you. I wish I was not the cause of such pain, but I am.

Theodore... if you grow to hate me, I will understand. I hate myself right now. I hate this laughter that's creeping into my mind... please, Gnusaramnii, not now... just this once, please listen to me.

35

BATTLE FOR ACCEPTANCE

"À*nifa...*"

"*Not now... please, not now...*"

"*Ha ha ha ha... it's seldom a good time for you...*"

"*Right, and now is just—*"

"*Now is the perfect time for us... the pain and despair you feel... use it, Ànifa.*"

"*Use it for what? I want to know the truth... why did Tyrona need to be taken?*"

"*Use your pain and search within yourself... you will find the answer you seek.*"

"*She's... she's paving the way forward?*"

"*Ha ha ha... see, that wasn't so hard... now you know the truth.*" Gnusaramnii burst into another fit of laughter as his presence waned.

"*Wait... Gnusaramnii, wait!*"

"*You can never get what you want, can you?*"

———

Ànifa stood on the quarterdeck of *West Wind* as it descended gently out of the wispy clouds. Joan was setting the ship down around twenty kilometers from Pikkul Harbor so they wouldn't draw any unnecessary attention.

Vesten, Cecil, and Dasch silently accompanied her on the deck. No one knew what to say or do about Tyrona. All they knew was that they had to continue. No matter the cost, right? Isn't that what she had said, before agreeing to Panabeeta's conditions?

She had to stick to her word. She would not let Tyrona's disappearance be in vain. It had to mean something, and there had to be a reason why it was Tyrona.

Theodore remained below decks with his door firmly shut. He needed time to process what had happened. They all needed time, really. But there was no more time to be had.

West Wind hit the surface of the ocean with a loud splash. The ship rocked jarringly, but quickly settled as Vesten retook control. He looked into the sky for a moment, near the spot they had descended from, then said, "We'll be there shortly. It looks like the wind is on our side."

"Good. Full speed ahead, then," Ànifa replied.

Ànifa walked down to the main deck to give Vesten some room. Cecil and Dasch accompanied her.

"You know... I gotta say, it feels weird to be returning to Schelff Island. It may be where I... where most of my memories begin, but we've been all around Eklatros now. In a way, it feels like I'm going home," Ànifa mused.

"I feel the same," Dasch replied. "I resided in that shrine for millennia. It's not my home, and yet it feels strange to be returning, as you said."

"I can't really say I feel the same way but it was where I met all of you, so it's a kind of homecoming for me as well," Cecil said.

Ànifa heard a noise behind her and turned around. Joan was coming up the stairs to the main deck. She looked tired, swaying slightly as she approached. They had flown for nearly ten hours, all of which Joan spent focused on keeping *West Wind* in the sky.

"How are all of you doing?" Joan asked, her voice a little hoarse.

"Fine, it looks like it'll be nice day," Cecil said.

The sun was just beginning to rise, illuminating *West Wind* in its morning light. Upon their return from the Nibelkaith Volcano, they had slept nearly the full day. Joan had woken around sunset to start their journey to reach Schelff Island. They had traveled all through the night, preparing for what was to come.

"Yeah, we're doing well. How about you? You look tired," Ànifa said.

"I am. But I'll be fine. We have a full day ahead of us. Are you ready, Ànifa?"

"I think so. We were talking about how strange it is to be returning to Schelff Island before you joined us."

"Not just Schelff, Ànifa, but Yttendaus. If all goes well, we'll be in Yttendaus by tonight."

"Oh, tonight, is it?" Ànifa said. "That's much sooner than I thought."

"Well, we have little time to spare," Joan replied.

"How are we going to get there?" Ànifa asked.

"First, we need to journey to Bugenaluf," Joan explained. "Once we are in close proximity, Bugenaluf will transport us to Yttendaus. In other words, Bugenaluf is Yttendaus' gatekeeper."

The remainder of the trip went by quickly. In no time, they were docking in Pikkul Harbor. Unlike the last time, Pikkul Harbor was calm and quiet. It looked as if order had been completely restored.

Ànifa remembered about her bonnet and pulled it from her pocket.

"You don't need that anymore," Joan said as she placed a hand on Ànifa's arm.

"Why not?" Ànifa asked.

"I have a feeling… I believe people are becoming aware of who we are. We don't need to hide anymore."

"Are you sure?" Ànifa asked.

"As sure as I can be. All I know is that I don't want to hide my wings anymore. It's too much of a hassle," Joan replied as she shook out her wings. "Besides, our journey is nearly complete. Let's revel in it."

"Yeah, alright, I can go along with that," Ànifa replied.

As they debarked from *West Wind*, Ànifa gazed back at the ship for a long moment before turning to the others. "We're heading to Sage Mason's, right?"

"Yes. We shouldn't dally. We must be on our way if everyone is ready," Joan replied.

"What's the rush? Honestly, though, I know we're saving Eklatros, but what's the real rush?" Theodore asked.

"Don't you want to avenge Tyrona?" Cecil asked.

"Yes, of course I do. I thought I could handle it, but it's just..." Theodore trailed off as he stared at his feet.

"I'm sorry about Tyrona. I really am. But the threat is real. Bugenaluf, our next destination, is undefended right now. We must reach it quickly," Joan said.

"Then let's go," Ànifa said, breaking away from the group. "Come on, Theodore. We need you. Think about it... if it had been the other way around, and you were gone, do you think Tyrona would give up?"

"No... no, you're right, Ànifa. Of course, you are right. I apologize," Theodore said with a deep nod.

"There's no need to apologize," she replied. "We all lost a friend. I know she meant more to you, but we're all dealing with this in our own way."

As they made their way through Pikkul Harbor, Ànifa spotted a few beggars here and there, but it looked as if the city was nearly empty. It was mid-morning. Pikkul Harbor should have been bustling with activity, but it was a ghost town.

"Where is everyone?" Ànifa asked.

"Hey, Ànifa. Perhaps I can answer your question," Dale said, surprising her as she emerged from behind a small cart with Tushar in tow.

"Dale! What are you doing here?" Ànifa asked the pretty blond woman. "Where's Patsy?"

"She and the others are in Sathon," Tushar said. "Ànifa, your hair, though... Patsy had told us but, it's quite spectacular in person."

"Oh, thanks," Ànifa said as she combed her hair with her fingers.

At the moment, her hair shone a deep royal blue. "Why aren't you with Patsy?"

"Do you not know?" Dale asked.

"Know what?"

"Sathon is under attack, and it's bad. It's real bad," Tushar said sadly.

"An attack?" Theodore cried. "In Sathon? What's going on?"

"Is Patsy okay?" Vesten asked.

"I'm sure she's fine. According to the locals, a large swarm of those jelly monsters descended upon them, accompanied by a cloud of crows, packs of snow foxes, and even some Schelff bears. It was all-out chaos," Dale replied.

"We must help!" Ànifa cried.

"Agreed. I'm ready to kick some ass," Cecil replied as he twirled his axe in his hands.

Joan placed a hand on her shoulder. "Ànifa, wait. We must not get distracted."

"But—Sathon! We must come to their aid," Ànifa refuted.

"Think about it. This sounds like a trap," Joan replied, crossing her arms.

"It is indeed a trap," Sage Mason said as he approached them, accompanied by Charlotte. "I see you've made more friends, Ànifa."

"Charlotte! Sage Mason! What are you both doing here?" Ànifa asked, then ran to embrace Charlotte. "I missed you."

"I missed you too. I'm glad to see you are well," Charlotte replied.

"Hey, that's my line!" Ànifa laughed.

Charlotte took her hands in her own and looked into her eyes. "Ànifa, I'm sorry... I am so, so sorry."

Sage Mason cleared his throat, bringing them both back to attention.

"We'll talk later," Ànifa whispered, confused by Charlotte's sincere apology.

"We just returned from the world summit, held in Fort Turner," Sage Mason said.

"You must have stayed for an extra day, then," Dale said. "We arrived yesterday, and have been waiting here until we hear from Patsy or Rear Admiral Mont Simmons."

"Speaking of Briggs, here he comes now," Cecil said.

"Hey everyone!" Rear Admiral Mont Simmons called as he jogged over to them. "You have great timing. I have news from Sathon."

"The fuck do you people keep popping out from?" Vesten muttered under his breath.

"How's it going over there, Briggs?" Cecil asked.

"Cecil, it's wonderful to see you again. Where is Tyrona, though? And... I'm sorry, is this an angel that's accompanying you?" Briggs asked in confusion.

"Right. Everyone, this is Joan. She's my guardian angel. Joan, this is... everyone," Ànifa said.

"It's a pleasure to meet you all," Joan said with a wave.

"Where is Tyrona?" Charlotte asked. "I was hoping to thank her. I mean to thank all of you, of course—"

"Charlotte," Ànifa said, embracing her in another quick hug. "It's really great to see you again. I'm thrilled you've recovered."

"It's all thanks to you all," Charlotte said.

"It's not a problem, really," Ànifa replied.

"And Tyrona?"

"She's... Tyrona is no longer with us," she explained.

"Oh, I'm sorry to hear that," Charlotte replied.

"I'm sorry, too," Dale said softly. "She was nice."

"This might complicate things," Briggs replied.

"How so?" Ànifa asked.

"You see, the world summit was mostly focused on your efforts to protect Eklatros, and Tyrona was a major part of that."

"What about Sathon?" Cecil prompted, noticing Theodore's increasingly downcast eyes.

"Ah yes, right. There's a lot going on right now, my apologies," Briggs said. "We have been victorious at Sathon. Everyone came together to fight off the attack. The guards I had deployed here were of great assistance. Most of the Ajentian guilds had a presence there as well. It got really hairy for a while, but there were a few locals who really shined. They were the true heroes of this fight. Without them, it would have been a much more difficult battle."

"I'm glad the battle was won," Ànifa said. "I'm sorry we weren't there to help."

"It's not a problem," Briggs replied. "The Sathon residents were surprisingly strong."

"It demonstrates the strength and resilience that all humans have," Sage Mason replied, looking right at Dasch.

"Yeah, humans are strong," Dasch replied. "They used to be stronger. From my observations, humans have grown weak."

"And yet it was the everyday locals that outshone Ajentian knights in Sathon," Briggs replied.

Dasch grunted. "We'll see if that strength persists when the real fight comes."

"Well, if the battle is over, then Tushar and I best be heading out. We're to regroup with Patsy," Dale said.

"Tell Patsy that I owe her a drink real fuckin' soon," Vesten said.

"Allow me to accompany you. There may be foes along the road," Briggs said.

"How did you get here so fast, Briggs?" Cecil asked. "Last time we were here, we had to pass through the Watthana Mountains to get to Sathon."

"Ah, well after Pikkul Harbor became flooded with refugees from Seaside and Runti, the governing bodies of Pikkul Harbor and Sathon met and finally decided to clear the rockslide and fix up the path that connects the two towns, allowing the refugees to travel to Sathon more easily," Briggs explained.

"Indeed, it will make everything easier now," Sage Mason said.

"Well, Dale, Tushar, Briggs. It was a pleasure seeing you all again. Please take care, and send Patsy our regards," Ànifa said.

Ànifa and her companions accompanied Sage Mason and Charlotte back to Sage Mason's tent. As they traveled, Charlotte and Sage

Mason told them more about the world summit. While there was a lengthy discussion on how to handle the refugee crisis that Fort Turner, Heerenditheer, Tora, and Nora's Docks were still experiencing, the majority of the summit focused on Ànifa and her efforts. Sage Mason explained that Sarah, Patsy, Charlotte, Cedric, and himself were all asked to speak on stage about each of them. Although the summit ended abruptly upon receiving the news of an attack on Sathon, the summit had essentially decided that all available resources would be given to Ànifa and her party when the time was needed. Even with the summit officially concluded, Sage Mason—Duke of Schelff Island—had to meet with the other Dukes about other, more mundane matters.

It was a lot to take in that the main topic at the world summit was about her and her friends. Ànifa was happy to know that she had a lot of support, although she had never asked for it. It meant those who supported her had hope. What Sage Mason had told them the last time they had seen him had come true. Because the people had hope, they were able to defend Sathon. For the first time, she finally realized the true power of hope. Only with hope could Eklatros truly be restored.

Aside from conversing about the world summit, Ànifa finally had time to chat with Charlotte. When Ànifa asked why she had apologized earlier, Charlotte explained to her how Patsy and the others had told her about the encounter with Danai. Charlotte couldn't help but feel as if that entire battle was her fault.

"If I had never spoken to that creep about you, that whole situation never would have happened," Charlotte said, wiping tears from her eyes.

Ànifa placed her arm around Charlotte as they walked slowly forward. "It's not your fault. He wasn't in the right state of mind. He was possessed by the Gnuelry."

"Yes, but he wouldn't have been following you if not for me," Charlotte replied. "I knew I shouldn't have trusted that man."

"Charlotte, it's okay, really. Now, if you don't mind me asking... do you have any idea why the Gnusar took you?"

Charlotte silently watched her feet as they continued along the path. For a moment, Ànifa thought she wasn't going to answer.

"They knew who I was. They knew everything about me, from my childhood... to my dreams. They knew I foresaw your arrival..." Charlotte said, trailing off into silence.

"Right, I read your note at the back of the history book."

Charlotte hummed. "They wanted to know if I had foreseen anything else... namely, Gnusaramnii's arrival. I remember little else... aside from the debilitating pain."

"I'm so sorry that—"

"Don't be," Charlotte said with a warm smile as she brushed a tress of silver hair out of her eyes. "I'm blessed—I saved our savior."

"How did they know who you were?" Ànifa asked.

"I'm not sure, but if they could somehow read my memories..."

"They could know everything about us," Dasch added.

"Indeed. Now, I don't mean to spoil your reunion, but we must not speak on this topic anymore. We don't know who or what may be listening," Sage Mason said.

It was snowing as they approached Sage Mason's tent. The snow drifted slowly from the dark sky, stilling the surrounding air.

As they entered the tent, a surprised Eric leaped from his chair, spilling potato soup on himself.

"Uncle Chris—everyone! You surprised me."

"We can see that," Sage Mason replied as he pointed to the stain on Eric's shirt.

"Oh, it's not a problem," Eric replied as he wiped himself with a napkin. "How was the summit?"

"I'll fill you in later. We have more important matters to tend to," Sage Mason replied.

"Okay. Hey, where's Sorceress Knorse?" Eric asked as he looked around the room.

"She's gone!" Theodore cried in anguish. "She's gone, and we are trying to find her! How many more people must we educate about this matter?"

"Whoa, sorry, Sorcerer Caldwell. I didn't know," Eric replied meekly.

"It's okay, Eric," Ànifa said, placing a hand on Theodore's back. "I'm sorry... but it is true. Tyrona is gone. And there might be a chance to find her."

"Yes, there is a chance," Joan replied.

"Good to hear," Sage Mason said as he puffed on a small wooden pipe. "Now, I'm sure everyone is eager to get to the matter at hand."

"I know I am. I don't want to stand around here talking all day," Theodore replied, looking in Eric's direction.

"Indeed," Sage Mason replied. "Now, last time you were here, I spoke to you about the Dragolum Shrine. Back then, you were not ready to enter. Now I believe you are ready. Tell me, which of the Ekataramn have you awakened?"

"Well, Kalahsem was our first, then Roheefy. We recently awakened Panabeeta, and Alakana as well. It turned out that Alakana and Panabeeta were residing together."

"Wonderful," Sage Mason nodded. "Then you truly are ready to enter the Shrine. Only those who are prepared, both physically and mentally, can enter the dark tunnels that lead to Bugenaluf."

"Very true, Sage. The dark is not for the weak of mind," Dasch replied.

"It's not only the dark. Each of you will be tested in your own way," Sage Mason said. "Only those who are deemed worthy can pass through the tunnels."

"So, will we all be okay, then?" Vesten asked. "What if one of us isn't deemed worthy?"

"I believe in all of you," Sage Mason replied. "You've all traveled together for some time now. You have developed a strong bond. There is strength in numbers. So, while each of you will go through your own set of trials, the presence of your comrades will aid you."

"Hmm, that will be an interesting test," Dasch replied.

"Right. I'm sure you will be fine, Dasch. You've been down there before—you lived down there," Vesten replied. "I'm fuckin' worried about myself. I don't know if I'll be worthy."

"You can't think like that," Joan replied. "Worthiness comprises all parts of the whole, and your mindset is part of that whole. You must believe in yourself. If you do not believe in yourself, then you will not make it through."

"What do you know about this, Joan?" Charlotte asked. "My apologies, I don't know a lot about your kind."

"No apologies are necessary, Charlotte," Joan replied. "It's a fair question. I know little about the Dragolum Shrine, but I have a good idea of how its magic will work. It sounds similar to certain sections of the Ytten Forest—the forest that surrounds Yttendaus itself."

"That's a possibility," Sage Mason replied. "I have only been down there twice myself, and I do not wish to go down there ever again. It is not a pleasant place."

"That it is not," Dasch replied.

"Do we have to pass through it?" Cecil asked.

"Indeed. It is the only way to make it to Bugenaluf alive. Of that, I am certain," Sage Mason replied. "The mountains that span north are much different than the small range that runs through the center of Schelff. They are jagged, ruthless peaks, towering over five kilometers high. They are not to be taken lightly."

"Sage, you mentioned we will go through a set of trials. What does this entail?" Ànifa asked.

"Once again, I cannot fully say. I only know that each of you will experience something different. Perhaps you'll need to face a fear, or be confronted with a painful memory. In either case, be prepared for some sort of hallucination."

"Great," Cecil replied. "I hope everyone has a strong mind."

"Yeah, fuckin' hope so," Vesten said warily.

"Vesten, be strong. I know you can do it," Joan replied. "We all know you can do it."

"Thank you, Joan," Vesten replied, looking into the angel's hazel eyes. "I'll do my best."

"That's the spirit," Charlotte replied. "I may not know you personally, but I believe in Ànifa, and so I believe in you as well."

"Thanks, everyone," Vesten said, his face turning red.

"So, what's the plan then, exactly?" Theodore asked. "When are we doing this?"

"If you can spare a few minutes, I would like to whip up some lunch for you. I'm sure you'll need the energy," Sage Mason said. "Eric, can you help me make some pad seewu?"

"Classic. I just ate, but that sounds really good," Eric replied.

As promised, lunch was quickly thrown together. It was one of the best meals Ànifa had in a long time. After they ate, they refilled their waterskins and said their goodbyes to Sage Mason and Charlotte. Ànifa didn't want to leave Charlotte again. She feared something might happen again, and she still had so much that she wanted to speak to her about. But she couldn't stop now, not when they were so close to their goal.

They left Sage Mason's tent and headed away from the main path, walking along a ledge with a frozen river below. Eric led the way. It was snowing lightly as they trudged through snow left from previous storms. The ledge quickly narrowed out, and they had to continue along single file until they reached a rope ladder. Eric went down the ladder first, then Ànifa, and the others followed.

At the bottom of the cliff, Ànifa stood on a small, enclosed riverbank. Upon closer inspection, only the top of the river was frozen—the water still flowed gently beneath the ice.

"Here, this way," Eric said, motioning toward a small cave. "If you enter that cave, you will reach the Shrine. I am not permitted to go any further, so I must leave you here."

"Alright," Ànifa replied. "Thanks for taking us here."

"It's part of my duties as the Shrine Protector's apprentice. I may live in Ajenti now, but I will need to return here after my studies are over to take my uncle's place."

"I see," Joan said warmly. "I wish you well, Eric Mason."

"Yes, good luck. You'll need it, I'm sure. Remember to keep up your defenses," Eric said. "And please, find Sorceress Knorse."

The cave was wide and shallow. At the back of the cave was a large doorway. On either side of it stood a small dragolum statue, complete with strange drill noses and pointed tails. The doorway was currently blocked by a large slab of rock.

"Is this where you came through, Dasch?" Cecil asked.

"Yes. When I exited the Shrine, I passed through this way. At that time, the way was open."

"We'll need to find a way through," Theodore replied. "I might have some ideas."

"Why is this place called the Dragolum Shrine, anyway? I thought that dragolum only live in Gallheim," Vesten asked.

"I've been wondering the same thing myself," Cecil echoed.

"Dragolum may only live there now, but back in my time, dragolum were common. They appeared across Eklatros and were highly revered and worshiped. This shrine is the same shrine I entered all those years ago, although the landscape surrounding the shrine has completely changed," Dasch replied.

"Yes. Dragolum are very special creatures. If properly trained, they can be great assets," Joan said.

"A trained dragolum? Now that sounds fuckin' scary," Vesten said as he scratched at his red beard.

"It's not unheard of," Cecil said. "There used to be a small underground ring of dragolum fights before it got shut down. The knights involved were exiled and stripped of their titles and honors."

"I remember hearing about that, too," Theodore said. "Now, are we going to enter the shrine or stand around talking about it? Like I said, I think I know of a way in."

"What do you have in mind, Theodore?" Ànifa asked.

"I was thinking I could use my magic—" Theodore began.

"No. No magic," Joan cut in. "This door will not respond to that."

"Then what can we do?" Cecil asked.

"I think... I think I know what to do," Ànifa said.

"After you then, Princess," Joan replied.

She nodded to her old friend and stepped up to the large stone slab blocking their way. She placed both of her hands on the stone slab and focused within herself to find her inner flame. In response, the slab lurched forward a few millimeters, then lowered into the floor. Once the way was clear, Ànifa stepped forward into the darkness.

This is the final stretch, she thought. *We've passed through forests and grasslands, sailed across oceans and climbed mountains and volcanoes. We've fought Gnusar and Gnuelry, and we've fought those they have corrupted—animals and their gods alike, even humans. This journey we've been on, everything we've been through, has been to put an end to the suffering. At first, I only knew that I wanted to find my way back home, and now I am returning home... returning home and finishing the mission I have been on. That we all have been on.*

Tyrona... this is for you. And Charlotte, I'm incredibly happy I got to see you again. Sage Mason and Eric... Dale, Tushar, Patsy, and Briggs... everyone that has helped us along the way, I thank you all. We couldn't have done this without all of you.

36

BATTLE FOR VISION

Ànifa led her party through the darkness and into the inner workings of the Dragolum Shrine. It was pitch black, and while Ànifa, Joan, and Dasch could see, the humans could not. Ànifa was about to enlarge the backpack to grab a torch when Joan stopped her.

"Not now. This is not a place for magics. We must continue in darkness, for now," Joan explained with her hand on Ànifa's arm.

"Fuck, really? This sucks," Vesten said.

"Do you have any torches hidden in your cloak, Dasch?" Cecil asked.

"No, not at the moment."

"It'll only be for a little while longer. We'll be your guides," Joan said.

As they made their way through the inky darkness, Ànifa and Joan regularly gave out verbal assistance when they came across an obstruction on the path. Dasch followed at the rear of the group to ensure that Theodore, Vesten, and Cecil made it along safely.

The walls of the hallway were lined with stone. In some areas, the stone wall was exquisitely constructed, complete with intricate designs. In other areas, it appeared to be hastily thrown together. Every now and then, a large root stuck out of the ceiling or the wall and they had to squeeze around it. Littered along the way were signs of Sage Mason's recent stay—an apple core, some breadcrumbs, a used tea bag.

"Fuck!" Vesten whispered loudly as he stubbed his toe against a rock. "It's too damn dark in here!"

"Yeah, can you do something about this, Theodore?" Cecil asked.

"Of course I can," Theodore whispered in reply, "but Joan told us we can't use magic, remember?"

"I think you'll be fine now," Joan said. "We should be past the magical checkpoints."

"Well, in that case..." Theodore stopped in his tracks and turned around.

Ànifa watched as Theodore, fumbling in the dark, raised his staff into the air and shouted, "Luminous Radius!"

Light pulsed out of his staff as it glowed a deep red. The light emanating from the staff was enough for the humans to see.

"That's better," Theodore said with a contented sigh.

"Fuck yeah," Vesten replied. "This is so much better."

"Agreed," Cecil chimed in. "Why couldn't we do this earlier?"

"This shrine is sacred," Joan explained. "Around its entrance and exits are strong magical barriers with periodic checkpoints along the way. Only those deemed worthy can enter this shrine, and so anyone who tries to force their way inside with magic or brute force will be met with a set of deadly traps."

"Ah yes, we definitely don't want to set any of those off," Cecil said.

"Let's hurry on," Ànifa prompted. "I don't want to linger down here."

"Yes. We mustn't loiter any longer than needed," Dasch replied. "This place... we are approaching where I resided. The sooner we get through here, the better."

"Oh yeah? Is there anything we need to know about this place?" Ànifa asked, hearing the tension in Dasch's voice.

"It's just affecting me more than I had anticipated."

After a few hundred meters, they reached a dilapidated wooden door. The iron castings holding it together were rusted from disuse and the door was nearly falling off its hinges.

"We are here," Dasch grumbled softly to himself.

She hesitated in front of the door for a moment. Dasch pushed past her and shoved the door open. It creaked and groaned loudly as it swung forward on its rusted hinges. She followed. They emerged into a wide-open circular room where there was a path split three ways.

"Which way do we go?" Ànifa asked.

"Forward," Dasch grumbled, pointing to the path that lay directly in front of them.

"Where do the other paths lead?" Theodore asked.

"To the left is the well of fresh water that sustained me during my stay. To the right is the room where I meditated."

"So, this is the place, huh?" Cecil asked as he wandered through the open room.

"Indeed. I do not relish being back here."

"Did you ever attempt to go down this path while you were down here?" Joan asked as they finished crossing the open circular room. They now passed into a narrow tunnel. This time, the walls were simply dirt.

"Many times. I wandered everywhere I could. Yet both paths—the one we just came through and the one we're going down—were always blocked by a dense system of thick roots.

"When I first left this place, the roots retracted, allowing me through. I believe the roots blocking this path should do the same for us this time."

"Let's hope so," Ànifa said. "It looks like we're approaching the roots now."

Ànifa turned around a bend in the tunnel and came face-to-face with a mass of tangled roots.

"I could never get past here," Dasch replied. "I don't believe anything has gone this way in long time."

"Strange, though, that Sage Mason never mentioned this, nor the large room we just passed through," Cecil said.

"I don't believe he ever made it this far. Remember, the dark plays tricks on people's minds. I believe we've only gotten this far unhindered because something wants us to pass through here," Ànifa said.

"What? What the fuck is doing this?" Vesten asked.

"The Ekataramn," Ànifa answered. "These roots must be Bugenaluf's."

"How? We're still kilometers away," Theodore asked.

"Remember, the Ekataramn are not typical trees... they really aren't trees at all," Joan replied. "They are unique."

"I was told that they don't even come from Eklatros," Ànifa replied.

"So they're aliens, then? Like the Gnusar?" Vesten asked.

"Yes, they are aliens and no, they are not like the Gnusar. Yet I believe they are connected somehow," Ànifa explained as she placed her hand on the blockade of roots. She whispered softly, inaudible to all but herself and the Ekataramn in front of her, "It is I, Ànifa Tataluynnia Ekataramnii. Please allow us to pass through safely."

In response, the roots slithered into the ceiling, floor, and walls. After a few moments, the way forward was clear.

"Just as I suspected," Dasch grumbled. "You are the only one who can clear the path."

"It seems to be the trend," Ànifa replied. "Now, stay close, everyone. Theodore, do not let your light go out. I have a feeling that once we move on, we'll be inundated by those hallucinations and visions Sage Mason mentioned."

"I can feel this as well," Joan replied. "Ànifa, please allow me to go first. I'll lead the way."

"Sure, but please be careful."

"Always. You be careful too, Princess."

Joan de Ligtheramnii stepped forward, leading the way. As soon as she began leading the group, a strange feeling washed over her. She wanted to look back, to make sure Ànifa and the others were following her, but she found she had no control over herself. She felt like a prisoner trapped inside her own body while observing her movements from afar.

"What is this?" Joan shouted into the void. "What's going on?"

"Ha ha ha ha ha…" The vile, gnarled laugh was like poison to her ears.

"Who are you? Show yourself!" Joan commanded.

A grotesque creature appeared in front of her. Its leathery skin, covered in boils and warts, was dark purplish-brown. Its body shape was that of a typical Gnusar, yet it was more akin to a slug. If this creature had feet, they were completely engulfed in its enormous bulk. Aside from its bulbous head, it sported two fat arms with small, skinny hands and long claws.

"It's you, isn't it?" Joan asked.

"Yes, my dear angel. It is I, Gnusaramnii, appearing before you now in this ethereal plane. You see me now in my original form, only because I allow you to see me for what I am."

"And why do you grant me such a privilege?"

"You are strong, Joan de Ligtheramnii, and yet, you are so very weak."

"Some say that one's weakness is actually their biggest strength."

"It is only the weak who say such things," Gnusaramnii snarled.

"Yeah, I'm sure everyone is weak in your eyes, isn't that right? Your power blinds you, Gnusaramnii."

"I am not the one who is blind."

Suddenly, images of Vesten filled her thoughts. She saw him stumbling through the dark, alone. She watched in horror as he tripped on a rock and fell to the ground, bashing his head open on a large boulder. Blood gushed from his open wound, and Joan watched his pulsing brain cease moving.

"Stop this at once!" Joan cried. "What you show me are lies. You seek to deceive me. I will not succumb to your hallucinations!"

"As I said, Joan, you are strong... you see through me."

"But right, I'm weak, aren't I? And what, you're going to convince me I'm weak because I care about others. Listen to me well, you vile, disgusting creature. Dependence on others is not a weakness, it is a strength. A strength that you will never understand."

Gnusaramnii laughed again. "Prove me wrong, then. Prove to me I am not the most powerful being in this universe."

"I will. You can count on it!"

Joan opened her eyes. She didn't even realize she had them closed. She stood alone in front of a stone door. The door was intricately carved, depicting a large tree. Surrounding the tree was an assortment of wildlife—birds, butterflies, dragolum, and wyverns flew in the sky, while unideer, rhinoceros, stegosaurus, and saber-toothed cats surrounded the tree on the ground. This door was ancient—as old as herself, if not older. A message in an ancient language was inscribed on the door—the language of the elves. It read: THROUGH ME THE WAY TO REALITY'S CLAIM. THROUGH ME THE WAY TO ETERNAL FLAME. YE WHO GATHER HERE, SEVEN MUST THERE BE FOR THE FATES TO DECREE.

She made it through. Now she must wait and pray that the others also make it through safely.

Vesten Teixeira was back in Haymath—back among the flames of his former hometown.

He stood in the center of town, taking in the destruction that raged around him. He had come here for a reason. He was looking for someone, and from the town center, it was easy to get anywhere.

That's right—he was trying to find his way home. Vesten oriented himself in front of the fountain centerpiece. The fountain had once been a glorious thing, depicting a great saber-toothed lioness. She sat on her haunches regally, looking in the direction of the sunrise. Home was to the left of the lion's gaze. Vesten headed in that direction, bowling through surges of flames. He wound his way to his home and saw the shadows of people standing among the smoldering ruins.

Vesten rushed forward, calling out to his parents. When he got closer, he grew more hopeful, seeing the silhouettes of both men and women. Vesten got even closer, only to realize that what he was seeing was wrong—it was totally and completely fucked.

He watched as three different men defiled his half-dead mother. He ran forward, ready to fight the larger men, only to realize that he wasn't an adult—he was a small child who was utterly powerless against these men. Vesten simply fell to the ground and wept.

He realized why he was back here now. It was so he could die with the rest of his family. That was it, wasn't it? He never deserved to live. He never deserved to survive when his loving parents did not.

Vesten remained on the ground and watched as the flames crept closer. He was ready—he was ready to die. He had been ready for his long sleep for some time now.

He heard his name being called. It was distant. He wasn't sure if he had actually heard someone call for him, or if he had imagined it.

Suddenly, a face flashed into his mind. Patsy! That's right, if he was back in Haymath, then Patsy must be here too!

Vesten rose to his feet and sped off back to the center of town, calling out for Patsy as he ran.

He neared the center of town and once again saw silhouettes of multiple people. Suddenly, another name came to his mind.

Ànifa!

Vesten ran forward, pushing through the smoke and flames.

There, in the center of town, with orange flames licking at the large fountain, he found his friends. They were all there—Ànifa, Joan, Theodore, Cecil, Dasch, and even Tyrona.

He felt a flash of guilt as remorse washed over him. Why had he been so ready to die just moments ago? It wasn't his time yet—there were people that depended on him. People who needed him.

Vesten opened his eyes and sighed with relief.

Theodore Henry Caldwell found himself back on the floating island that sat within the Nibelkaith Volcano. He was sitting on a dire wolf spider. For how hideous it was, it had been quite good to him and had become a welcome companion and ally.

He shook his head—this wasn't about the spider.

He looked around and his heart lurched. Tyrona! She was back and she was safe!

"Tyrona!" he cried. "You're okay! What happened to you?"

Tyrona looked at him, then closed her eyes and smiled. She opened her eyes and stared at him without saying a word.

"Tyrona? Is everything okay?" he asked.

Tyrona grimaced in pain, and a moment later, she popped out of existence.

Before he could shout a curse, Theodore found himself transported to another plane of existence.

He was floating. He felt no solid ground beneath him—he was in a void. Pure blackness surrounded him. Theodore spun in place, scanning the darkness. He gave a shout as he spied Tyrona. He tried to run to her, but the harder he tried, the further away she seemed to get. She soon became too small to see. Theodore sighed, then spun around.

Tyrona floated behind him. She was bound to a strange device. Each limb was fastened by a rope that was connected to a gear. The gears began to turn and stretched each limb to its breaking point while Tyrona writhed in agony. She was being torn apart.

"Stop it! Please stop this!" Theodore shouted. "This isn't real! This isn't what happened!"

The device continued to creak and groan, and Tyrona's left arm was torn from her body. A moment later, her right leg gave way.

Theodore clenched his eyes shut and calmed his breathing.

This wasn't real. Tyrona was gone, but she wasn't dead. She hadn't been tortured. She hadn't been killed or eaten by a beast. She was alive. He knew it—he felt her presence.

Theodore opened his eyes and saw his friends. They were all there, everyone was together again. Ànifa, Cecil, Dasch, Vesten, Joan, and Tyrona, who stood in the back, apart from the others. When she saw him look at her, she waved, and then turned away and walked into the blackness.

"Goodbye, Tyrona. Take care of yourself. If all goes well, I'll see you again soon."

Theodore looked back at his friends. They were smiling, urging him forward. Theodore smiled back and took a step.

His foot hit solid ground, creating an echo.

Sir Cecil Kloud lay on the ground. No, that wasn't right. He wasn't a knight yet. But soon Cecil would become a knight. All he had to do was put up with a few hazing rituals and he'd be in. It was like this with every guild. Yet the Guild of Exemplary Knights weren't calling themselves that to be boastful—they touted that they truly forged exemplary knights through their initiation course.

He had completed all but the final task. That was why he was on the ground. He had been ordered to do so while blindfolded and wait for a special surprise.

Judging from the previous tasks, he figured he'd have to face another ferocious animal, like a saber-toothed lion or a juvenile centrosaurus. He listened intently but heard nothing at all.

He felt a swift impact to his stomach and recoiled. A moment later, an impact struck his back. He cried out in pain.

A faceless man pulled his blindfold off and Cecil found he was surrounded. His feet and hands were bound in iron shackles while six knights stood in a circle around him and took turns kicking him.

"Get up!" they cried. "Stand up and defend yourself. This is your final test. If you can stand up and fight us off, you will become a member of our exemplary guild!"

This felt wrong. Wasn't he supposed to be wearing armor? And how could he get up and fight? His hands and feet were locked in chains. Cecil tried to cry out and found that he was gagged. A dirty rag had been stuffed into his mouth.

The assault was unrelenting.

Screw this! Why do I have to put up with this? This isn't exemplary at all. This is downright abhorrent! Why would I ever join this guild? I was alone back then, that may be true. But I'm not alone now!

Using all his might, Cecil spat out the gag. He screamed and broke his hands free of the shackles, then shattered the shackles that bound his feet.

Cecil rose to his feet and fought back—kicking, punching, and screaming. He would survive no matter what. He had a mission, a purpose, a destiny to fulfill. He would protect his princess at all costs.

He came to realize that there was no resistance and stopped fighting. He looked around and realized that he wasn't surrounded by his enemies at all. The six faceless figures that had surrounded him had become the six faces of his team—Ànifa, Theodore, Dasch, Vesten, Joan, and Tyrona. They smiled at him.

These are my friends... this is my family. These are the people that I would die to protect.

This is right. I am home.

Cecil breathed in deep, then coughed. The air was stale and dusty.

Dasch Valentine walked forward, into the open circular room he had just passed through. It was the same room where he had spent thousands of years, moving only from one wing to the other when he needed to drink, rest, or relieve himself. Although, near the end of it all, he had simply relieved himself wherever he was when the urge struck. His cleanliness didn't matter, only his sanity. But that was then and this was now.

Dasch knew he was experiencing a hallucination, but he was unsure if he was strong enough to break away from it. Already he felt it taking hold. He felt the darkness creeping in as the thing inside of him clenched at his chest.

For the first time in a long time, the remnant of Gnusaramnii inside of him stirred. He was unprepared, and the Gnusar began to spread.

Panic washed over him. He no longer knew what was real and what wasn't. For all he knew, he could actually be back in the circular room. It was possible that he never even left.

Yes, that's right. When did he leave? And how, exactly? There were no exits—he had checked and checked and checked again.

It all made sense now. It had all been a dream. A long, detailed dream at that, but just a dream. He was still locked in a fierce, never-ending struggle with the sliver of Gnusaramnii that dwelled within him.

But something was off. Things weren't as they seemed. Dasch realized he was holding a small, miniaturized backpack and wearing new clothing.

He hadn't been carrying the backpack. Why did he have it now?

Wait, what backpack? And why was it so small? It had to be a toy —a backpack made for a doll.

But the backpack was important. It meant something important.

Dasch looked up and found himself sitting in a grassy field. The sun was shining, warming his metal armor.

"...yes, that's right, Eliziana," a familiar voice was saying.

Dasch looked to his left and saw Kieth sitting next to him. His heart lurched seeing his old friend again.

He and Kieth were sitting in a circle with five others—Eliziana Lockhart, Sir Lindserick the Lancer, an elf by the name of Hedrou Silkweaver, and two squires.

"Any magic cast, even magics with long-lasting binding spells, disperse after the caster is dead. Meaning that, in order to get through the powerful barriers that oppose us, we need only kill the magic-user who cast that spell. That is much more easily said than done, since it can be assumed that the casters are hiding behind said barriers. Which thusly poses a problem..."

That's right. How had he forgotten? And why was it so important?

Still sitting in the circle, Dasch unclenched his right fist and found that he was holding the backpack once again.

He looked to his left and saw a warm face smiling at him.

Ànifa... that's right! Ànifa! And the others, everyone was here, even Tyrona.

He now realized the significance of the backpack.

Dasch moved to stand and was transported back to the long, dark underground hallway he had started off in.

Ànifa Tataluynnia Ekataramnii pushed through a heavy substance. The situation felt familiar. She was cold, and she was wet. She was underwater, swimming, fighting against the current as it strove to push her into the depths of the ocean. She would not die here. She could not drown now.

A voice washed over her, seeping into her pores.

"Ànifa... Ànifa..."

"Gnusaramnii... is it you? Or is this all just a hallucination?"

"Ha ha ha ha... both. Neither. Take your pick."

"That's entirely unhelpful," she said. "Yet I am speaking out loud when I'm supposed to be underwater, so this isn't real."

A moment later, Ànifa stood in the middle of a barren field. The field was scorched, dusted in a fine layer of ash, and pockmarked with large gouges and muddy pathways.

It looked as if there had been a battle, and then the bodies came into view. There were dozens of them—no, hundreds, possibly even thousands.

The corpses stretched forward, toward the horizon. Ànifa cried out in horror as she looked around, only to find that she was engulfed in a sea of death.

Among the dead were faceless men and women, even Gnusar, Gnureavers, and Gnurargurts. There were gods among them as well. She spotted Sparassotereon, the saber-toothed lioness, and even Uswassisbaena, the wyvern god.

"What are you trying to tell me?" Ànifa shouted into the still, cold air.

"Ha ha ha ha ha... don't you know, Ànifa? The bodies that surround you are deaths you caused. You killed all of these people and animals. Even my own minions, but not me. I still live. I survive when all else withers away."

"That's great and all, but that can't be true. I didn't cause all of this death. That was you, and you alone."

Gnusaramnii burst into another fit of laughter. "That's a lie and you know it."

"Yeah, 'ha ha' right back at you, you big laugh-factory! I'm so sick and tired of your endless laughing! What's so damn funny?"

"Look again, Ànifa... look again at those you have killed and then you'll see."

Ànifa rolled her eyes and looked down again. Suddenly, the faceless beings were no longer faceless. Instead, they were her friends, her allies.

Among the dead, she spotted Joan, Dasch, Theodore, Cecil, Vesten, and Tyrona. But that wasn't all. Charlotte and Sage Mason, Patsy and Dale, Sarah and Briggs—everyone she knew, everyone she'd befriended—dead.

She was about to shout at Gnusaramnii when another face caught her eye—her own.

Suddenly, all the faces became hers, and they all turned to look at her.

Gnusaramnii laughed insidiously.

"This doesn't make sense! None of this makes any sense. Joan! Theodore! Cecil! Where is everyone? Don't leave me!"

"Ànifa!"

She turned and saw Charlotte looking at her.

She was back in Charlotte's bed, just like when she first woke up.

"Charlotte? What's going on?"

"Hey, Ànifa! You're... wait, how do you know my name?" Charlotte asked, backing away from her.

"Charlotte? It's me, Ànifa! You know me, I saved you, after you were taken by the Gnusar!"

"I think you're confused. I saved your life," Charlotte said tenderly. "You awoke only seconds ago. You've been asleep for a few days now."

"What's going on? I've already woken up. None of this is real!" Ànifa cried, shutting her eyes.

When she opened them, she found herself hovering above the smoldering ruins of Kalah. She was engulfed in blue flames and she saw her friends below her as they shouted at her. They were afraid.

She was afraid. She had no idea what was happening. Why was she seeing these events all over again? Why could she not wake up and return to her friends?

"Ha ha ha... that's the joke. Don't you get it by now?"

"What? What's the damn joke?" Ànifa shouted.

"You haven't woken up yet. You still lay slumbering in that pink bed. What you know are all lies... fantasies dreamt by a broken mind —*your* broken mind, Ànifa... a mind that may never recover."

"Yes... I... can! I can recover! I can make it through this! I *will* make it through this!"

Ànifa opened her eyes and was standing in front of her friends. They smiled at her in the dark, dusty underground tunnel.

So I'm back... am I? she thought. *This isn't just another dream, another hallucination? No, of course this isn't. Tyrona is still gone. And we're on our way to Bugenaluf. It looks like we only need to make it through this last door... this final door.*

37

BATTLE FOR REALITY

Ànifa stood in the dark, dusty hallway and faced her friends. All six of them had made it through the trials. As she approached them, she noticed they were standing in front of a large door with ancient markings on it.

"Ànifa, you made it!" Joan exclaimed. "We were getting worried."

"Really? I went in after you, didn't I?" she asked.

"Yeah, you did," Theodore said. "We all remember you going in after Joan."

"Fuckin' yeah, and the weird thing is that I went second to last. It was Dasch that went last, but I went second to last, and I fuckin' ended up here before everyone else. Well, Joan was the first one here, but I was the second," Vesten rambled.

"That's really strange," Ànifa said. "We all made it through, though, and that's what counts. What's the situation with the door?"

"The inscription mentions that seven need to be present for the door to open," Joan explained. "I think we need to place our hands on the door, but there are only six of us."

"If only Tyrona was here," Theodore sighed.

"Do you still have the backpack, Ànifa?" Dasch asked.

"I should. Hang on, let me get it for you..." she trailed off as she delved into the inner pockets of her trenchdress. She found the backpack and held it out to Dasch.

"Here, did you need something out of it?"

"No. In my vision I remembered something Kieth had told me a long time ago," Dasch said. "He explained that any long-lasting spell, such as a binding spell or miniaturizing spell, would end upon the caster's death. This backpack is still miniaturized, and Tyrona was the one who cast the spell. This means she is still alive somewhere."

"Is that true?" Ànifa asked.

"For the most part, yes," Joan replied. "There are some exceptions, such as the Great Barriers. However, I believe what Dasch claims is true. If Tyrona was really gone, the backpack would be full size again."

"Plus, it would probably explode due to how many things we stuffed into there," Cecil added.

Theodore nodded as he stroked his beard. "That is not always true these days, as there have been cases of sorcerers dying with their magically bound lock-boxes still sealed."

"Did these sorcerers actually die? Or did they simply move on to a different plane of existence?" Dasch asked. "I've seen cases of that happening in the past."

"Whatever the case may be, this is a good indication Tyrona is alive. It's possible we can use her magical energy contained in the backpack to pass through the door. Good thinking, Dasch," Joan said.

"I agree. Let's try it," Ànifa said. "But first, I think Theodore needs to take the backpack. He has the strongest connection to Tyrona."

Dasch nodded and handed the backpack to Theodore. Upon taking it, Theodore studied the backpack, turning it over in his hands.

"Are you ready, Theodore?" Ànifa asked. He turned to her and nodded.

"I'm ready, too," Cecil replied.

"Aye, let's fucking do this," Vesten added.

"Alright. Everyone, place a hand on the door... now!" Ànifa said.

Theodore placed both hands on the door, holding the backpack with his right hand. As they touched the door, the lettering on the door glowed brightly. A moment later, the door slid into the ground, revealing the way out of the underground tunnel.

Theodore handed the backpack to Ànifa. "I felt her presence, if only for a moment."

"I did as well. She truly is still with us."

They wound their way out of the twisting tunnel and emerged into a wide-open area. Surrounding the exit was a fine layer of snow. Behind them loomed the large, twisted peaks of the Samial Mountain Range. A dense layer of dark clouds obscured the peaks. If they were on the other side of the Samial Mountains, then they must have traveled beneath the Schelff Gulf.

There was a single path leading away from the shrine, so they followed it. After a few minutes, Ànifa spotted a large, circular dirt groove cut into the ground. Past the dirt line, the ground was clear of snow. It looked as if it hadn't snowed on the grass for years.

"This is where the Great Barrier must have once stood," Ànifa pointed out. "We should approach Bugenaluf shortly."

"Ànifa, can you feel it?" Joan asked.

"Yes. Something isn't right. It feels as if Bugenaluf is frightened... I think it's in danger."

"We must proceed with caution," Joan replied. "With the Great Barrier gone, anything could be waiting for us."

"Why can't we see it now?" Vesten asked. "The others were pretty fuckin' big."

"They're all different and unique," Ànifa replied. "We don't know what to expect. Let's continue on, with caution."

Ànifa led the way. The ground soon sloped into a crater-like depression. As they descended, the twisted upper branches of Bugenaluf were revealed. The branches were completely barren— not even a single leaf hung from them.

"This is different," Ànifa said, remarking the terrain.

"Bugenaluf is special," Joan replied. "It's not like the other Ekataramn. It serves as the gateway between Eklatros and Yttendaus. That's why it's in this depression—for an extra layer of protection."

As they continued, they began to see the trunk. Bugenaluf was the most tree-like of all the Ekataramn Ànifa had come across. Its branches were arranged in a twisted mess. In a way, it reminded Ànifa of Ajenti University. Ajenti had been much bigger, though—Bugenaluf was quite small in comparison to the other Ekataramn. They approached the face of Bugenaluf. He had two small, dark-brown eyes. The only foliage on Bugenaluf was a dense, mossy beard.

A loud whistle cut through the air. Ànifa looked at Bugenaluf, but the voice came from behind them.

"Welly, welly, well. Looky here, boys!"

They spun around and spotted a green scaly Gnusar standing in the center of the path.

"You there!" Dasch cried out as he drew his sword. "You have made a critical mistake by showing yourself!"

"Do you think I'm alone, dummy?" the Gnusar replied. "There's a whole horde of us waiting for you!"

The ground rumbled as a distant thunder stampeded toward them.

"What is this?" Ànifa asked.

"This is your doom!" the Gnusar replied with a laugh. "There's no getting out this alive, not for any of you!"

Gnusar approached from all sides as they poured down the hillside surrounding Bugenaluf. Some were riding corrupted woolly rhinoceros or corrupted Schelff bears while others moved along the ground. There were other Gnurargurts as well, including snow foxes, unideer, winged rams, and dire sloths. Also among the horde were Gnureavers—humans who had been possessed while alive and turned into the Gnusar's unwilling army.

"The fuck did they come from?" Vesten exclaimed.

The Gnusar laughed again. "You have your tricks, and we have ours."

"Everyone... best of luck to you all," Ànifa managed. She didn't know what to say—the force was simply overwhelming.

"I'll protect us," Theodore said reflexively.

"Don't worry about a barrier," Joan commanded Theodore.

"There's too many. We need you at full strength. We need to focus on simply holding them off as long as we can."

"Sure, I suppose that's probably the better plan of attack here," Theodore replied warily.

"Do not hold back," Ànifa commanded. "Everyone, let's give it our all."

Theodore nodded, then turned his attention to the oncoming horde of enemies. They would be overrun within minutes. He held his scarlet staff high in the air, then slammed it into the ground. A shockwave emanated outward, and the ground rippled violently. Those caught in the tremors were thrown about and tossed high into the air. The ground erupted, violently spewing clods of dirt and rock into the air. From the skies, lightning bolts rained down, obliterating anything they touched.

The attack was heavily damaging, but the opposing numbers were too great.

"What about the Ekataramn?" Dasch asked as he brandished his golden flaming sword.

"Right. Leave that to me. I'll make sure they don't touch Bugenaluf," Ànifa replied. "Everyone, take care of yourselves."

She took a deep breath, closed her eyes and reached within herself. She found the flame and coaxed it out, allowing it to fully consume her.

When she opened her eyes, she was floating above the ground, fully awash in blue flames.

"Let's do this," she whispered to herself.

She had never flown before but quickly got the hang of it as she willed herself forward. Before she could protect Bugenaluf, she wanted to do one thing. She flew straight toward the Gnusar who had taunted them earlier. It tried to run from her, but she was faster. She smashed into it as hard as she could and watched its limp body crumble to the ground. She flew into the air again and headed toward Bugenaluf.

Dozens of Gnusar and Gnuelry were taking advantage of the situation, focusing their attacks on the Ekataramn.

Bugenaluf! she called out to the divine being. *I'll protect you!*

Joan had prepared herself for the upcoming battle by unholstering her hammer and shield. Ekatalal and Halahkahna, respectively, were her responsibility. These were among the most divine weapons upon Yttendaus, even all of Eklatros. Her hammer, Ekatalal, was forged in part by her. All eight angels created it when they were less than a century old, back when their power was still raw and untamed. Halahkahna, on the other hand, was even more ancient. Many among the angels believed it originated among the first elves to ever grace Eklatros. Normally, these weapons were meant for the leader of the angels, Juliana. Yet she was granted access to them when she first began protecting Ànifa.

Joan needed her weapons now more than ever. This was an army unlike anything she had ever faced. Beside her, Theodore slung his spells at the throng, causing massive damage with ground, lightning, fire, and wind spells. Dasch gripped his golden flaming sword with his eyes closed, meditating for the best outcome. Cecil had his battle-axe out and ready, while Vesten awkwardly held his scimitar, Skimither.

"Best of luck to you all," Joan said as she flew into the air. "May the grace of Eklatros be with you all."

"As onto you," Cecil replied as he twisted his battle-axe in his hands.

"Wait, Joan! What do I do?" Vesten cried. "I'm not cut out for this shit!"

"None of us are!" Cecil exclaimed. "The only way we can hope to survive is to rely on each other. We need you, Vesten."

"I'll do my best," Vesten replied.

"Listen well to Sir Cecil Kloud! We're a team, and as a team, we stand for Eklatros!" Joan cried.

"For Eklatros!" Cecil cried.

Joan gripped Ekatalal as she swung down on the skull of a dire sloth, then spun and raised her shield to protect herself from an attacking Gnureaver.

The battle had begun.

"Ànifa, you must forget about me; protect yourself," Bugenaluf said to her as she soared past the Ekataramn, mowing down enemies along the way.

"I can't leave you! Our entire mission has been to protect you. We can't abandon you!"

"And yet you must. Circumstances are less than ideal. You cannot win this battle. Their power is too great. Even as I speak to you, the gods of Schelff Island approach. They have all been turned—Maqinjinarii, Aerigasus, Kadopodzi, even Qirinocorn. They come here now with their followers."

As Bugenaluf spoke to her, Ànifa continued to soar through the air, using her blue flames to propel her forward. She punched through Gnusar and Gnurargurts alike as she spun around Bugenaluf's trunk.

"Ànifa, you and your friends must make it to me," Bugenaluf continued. *"Only by touching my trunk can I transport you to Yttendaus. Normally, I'd make you go through your own set of trials, but there is no time for that now."*

"No, this is trial enough," she replied. *"I'll see what I can do. What about you, though?"*

"I'll be fine. I have my own way of defending myself."

Sir Cecil Kloud fought with a mad, uncontained rage. He would not allow Eklatros to fall. He would not fail. He slashed with his battle-axe, chopping off the tail of a snow fox, and then turned his body and parried an attack from a charging woolly rhinoceros.

Beside him, Dasch fought bravely, spinning his golden flaming sword with frightening dexterity.

Cecil spared a quick glance to check on Vesten. He was doing better than expected. Vesten held his scimitar in his right hand and a dagger in his left. As he swung the scimitar, cutting the belly of a Gnusar, he stabbed the monster in the eye with a dagger.

The battle had only lasted a few minutes, and their chances for survival diminished by the second. Before the doubt could set in, Ànifa burst through the wall of foes and flew straight toward them.

"Everyone! We must move, now!" Ànifa commanded.

"Where?" Joan cried, blood dripping off of her hammer.

"To Bugenaluf! He'll get us out of here!" Ànifa replied.

"Right! Let's move!" Cecil cried. "All together now! Don't leave anyone behind!"

He rushed forward while deftly cutting through any foe that got in his way.

"Joan, with me!" Ànifa cried as she led the way, shoving enemies aside.

"I'm here!" Joan said. She had her shield raised as she tore through the horde.

"We must make it through. It's the only way," she said.

Ànifa looked behind her and saw Cecil with Vesten and Theodore following closely. Dasch led the rear, holding off any enemy that tried to attack them from behind.

"This is utterly fucking insane!" Vesten exclaimed.

"We're almost there. Hurry!" she cried, urging them on. "Bugenaluf! We're coming!"

"Be careful. The enemy is forming a defensive circle around me," Bugenaluf replied, his deep voice cutting through the deafening noise of the horde.

"I can't believe this is actually happening," she whispered to herself.

Ànifa cut through a jelly monster, then another, then shot a wave of blue flames at a trio of Gnusar. As she approached Bugenaluf, she saw the defensive circle was composed of three different layers.

The outer layer was a ring of different Gnurargurts—snow foxes, dire sloths, woolly rhinoceros, Schelff bears, and winged rams. The second ring was composed of all kinds of Gnuelry—blue ones, green ones, hardened gray ones, and acidic yellow ones. The final ring was made of only Gnureavers, each one grotesquely twisted in their own way.

Ànifa was far more afraid of the meaning behind the numbers than dying from the horde. If the enemy truly had this large an army, Eklatros was on its last legs. They really were running out of time. Soon, it wouldn't matter if they completed their mission or not. There would be nothing left to save.

"Ànifa, above you!" Joan cried.

She had been focusing on the first ring as she approached it. The murder of crows that descended upon them had caught her off guard.

"I've had enough of this! Let us pass!" Theodore screamed and unleashed an electrical pulse. The spherical shockwave emanated from his body and burst outward, paralyzing surrounding foes.

Theodore fell to his knees. "I—"

"I got you!" Joan said as she swooped down and picked him up.

"Let's move!" Ànifa shouted. They needed to take advantage of the situation.

She flew on ahead, straight toward Bugenaluf. The shockwave had incapacitated the first two defensive rings, but the third ring stood strong.

"Ànifa, with me!" Dasch said as he sprinted forward, holding his flaming sword close against him.

She lunged forward, side-by-side with the half-elf from the distant past. Dasch cried out in an ancient elvish language and shot a stream of golden flames out of his sword. Ànifa drew an arrow and held it out in front of her like a wand and unleashed her energy from it. Combined with Dasch's attack, they were able to quickly cut down the third ring.

"Very good," Bugenaluf said, urging them forward. "Feel the strength running through you. You've almost made it."

"They really can talk!" Theodore laughed in Joan's arms.

"Yes, they can," Joan replied.

They had made it—they had finally reached Bugenaluf's trunk.

"Now, all hands on me, and I'll transport you out of here," Bugenaluf prompted. "Ànifa, I need you to call upon the other Ekataramn."

Ànifa reached out with the tendrils of her mind.

"*Kalahsem, Roheefy, Panabeeta, Alakana... if you can hear me,*" she thought, "*we need you. Please lend us your divine powers.*"

Bugenaluf absorbed the energy from the six travelers, condensed it into an unstable orb, and released it. The energy burst forth out of his trunk, disintegrating the Gnusar and its minions.

Now go, my saviors, Bugenaluf thought.

38

BATTLE FOR FAMILY

Ànifa stood in the Grand Hall of Yttendaus, disoriented and confused. It took her a moment to remember how she had arrived. She looked around and found her friends standing around her. A heavy haze surrounded them, obscuring the surrounding area.

"What just happened?" Cecil asked, holding a hand to his head. He had taken off his helmet and was holding it under his left arm.

"We have been transported to Yttendaus. We stand in the Grand Hall—the throne room," Ànifa answered. She couldn't see it well through the haze, but she recognized the deep bronze marble floor they stood upon.

"That was an unusual experience," Theodore said, "but I feel good as new. I haven't felt this alive in years."

"Yttendaus has the power to restore your energy," a soft voice echoed around them.

"Who the fuck said that?" Vesten exclaimed.

"Be mindful of your words, *human*," the voice replied.

"That would be my mother. Please try to refrain from speaking in her presence," Ànifa said.

"I understand. As humans, we are outsiders here," Theodore said. "You, Joan, and Dasch—"

"Even I am an outsider," Dasch replied.

"At this point, we are all outsiders," Ànifa said to her friends.

The hall was bound with powerful magic, making it difficult for Ànifa to discern how far away she stood from the throne. Everything appeared distorted and out of focus. As she tried to make sense of their situation, her mother's face filled her vision.

"Mother, it's me. I'm back, and I've brought some friends. Will you please stop the spell? We're already quite disoriented, and your magic is only making it worse."

"For you, daughter, I will."

The haze dissipated, and the hall came into focus. Ànifa blinked and took a moment to reacquaint herself with the Grand Hall.

Large pink quartz support pillars towered above them, each one intricately carved with its own unique images. Some pillars told the story of past kings and queens, while others were decorated with carvings of ivy, flowers, and trees that supported a variety of animals.

The ceiling rose nearly fifty meters above them and was intricately painted. The fresco depicted the seven Ekataramn, each labeled by its divine symbol. The Ekataramn were arranged in a heptagram, and in the center of the seven-sided star was Eklatros herself.

Ànifa's mother, Queen Stella Tshaila Ekataramnii, sat on the high golden-plated throne. The throne to her left was empty. Standing around Queen Stella were six guards, three on either side of her. The elvish guards were dressed elegantly in shimmering green armor with dark-brown and yellow embellishments. Their helmets obscured their faces.

The Queen looked especially regal today. She wore an elegant dark-blue dress with a tight leather bodice. Her long golden hair was peppered with small, tight braids held together with light-blue bands. Atop her head was a silver-blue tiara that signified her status as queen. Her dark-brown skin shimmered and shone in the sunlight that fell upon her from the large glass windows above her throne.

Ànifa turned to Joan, only to find that she and the rest of her companions were still stuck in her mother's spell. She saw their mouths move, though they made no sound. Only Queen Stella could hear what transpired within the haze.

"Mother, what's going on?"

"Dearest daughter, whatever do you mean? I welcome you back home only to be questioned?"

"This... this is not the welcome I was expecting. Where is father? Where are my sisters? And where is Grungo?" Ànifa asked as memories came flooding back to her. Grungo was her mother's pet dragolum, and it had followed her everywhere she went.

"Ànifa, you have been gone for too long. Much has happened in your absence. Sadly, Grungo has returned to his ancestors. Your sisters are fine—they wait for you in the antechamber. As for King Vyereth... your father committed treason against the crown. He was tried and executed for his crimes."

"What? Father was always so kind spirited. He would never do any harm—"

"And yet he did. He disobeyed a fundamental law to our society. That is why we do not honor his tainted memory," Stella said. Normally, whenever a member of royalty passed on, the hall would be decorated with white roses. To Ànifa, the barren hall was an insult to her father's legacy.

"I don't believe you," Ànifa replied fiercely, her hair shifting from baby-blue hues to dark indigo. "Something is not right. Joan... I need to speak with Joan."

"I will release your friends from my spell shortly. In the meantime—"

"No, mother. Release my friends now. Joan told me you have been watching my journey. So you must know how important they are, not only to me, but to Eklatros."

Queen Stella grunted and waved a hand in dismissal. "Have it your way."

"What the fuck?" Vesten said loudly as the spell was lifted.

"I have warned you once, human. Do not curse in this sacred hall," Queen Stella commanded.

Vesten took in a breath of surprise. "My humblest apologies, Your Royal Highness."

"At least you have some semblance of respect," Queen Stella chided as she glared at Vesten.

Joan placed a hand on Vesten's shoulder. "I apologize for my companion, My Queen."

"Is that all you apologize for? You have much to atone for, Joan. You disobeyed a direct order."

"If I hadn't, Ànifa and her friends would have been killed," Joan said confidently. "Besides, I was told I could only interfere under such circumstances."

"That was King Vyereth's command, not mine," Queen Stella said coldly. "Now that my husband has passed, I rule Yttendaus alone. My word is absolute."

"Mother," Ànifa said softly with a slight bow. "We stand before you, humbled in your presence. What is your command?" She glanced at her friends, urging them to bow along with her. Joan met her glance and bowed to Queen Stella. The others followed suit a moment later.

Queen Stella nodded in approval. "As you all know, Bugenaluf transported you here. Rest assured that Bugenaluf is safe and sound. The foes you faced have been destroyed by the same burst of energy that brought you here. Your arrival confirms an ancient prophecy— that those from above and below will come together to stand and fight against Eklatros' demise. Seven companions were to come together to restore the seven Ekataramn to their full powers. However, one Ekataramn has been misplaced, and so one companion has been misplaced. You've already awoken five of the Ekataramn. Now you must awaken Yttendaus."

"Yes, Yttendaus is the final stage of our journey," Ànifa said. "We must awaken the divine one as soon as we can."

"Aren't we already on Yttendaus?" Vesten asked. Upon receiving a sharp glare from Queen Stella, he added, "My apologies, Your Highness."

"Indeed. You stand in the Grand Hall of Yttendaus," Queen Stella replied as she stared at Vesten. "The island we reside on may be called Yttendaus, but in order to awaken the Ekataramn, you must journey to its location. This is no different from the other Ekataramn you've awakened."

"Apologies, mother. This is a new experience for them," Ànifa said.

"Understand that I will not tolerate another outburst from the sailor, or any of these foul humans, for that matter. The disgusting half-elf included." Queen Stella looked Dasch up and down in disapproval. Dasch glared back at her, his face shadowed by his hood.

"You have my word," Joan replied.

"Why do you stand up for these humans, Joan? Well, I suppose it matters little. Once the journey is complete, you will return to your post. That is an order."

"Understood, Your Grace," Joan bowed.

"Take Druder with you. He will help to protect you from the dangers of the Ytten Forest."

Upon hearing his name, the guard standing directly to the queen's left stepped forward and took off his helmet.

Joan gasped. "A dark elf! Your Grace, what is the meaning of this?"

"For too long, our societies have lived separately. And yet, Yttendaus is one floating island. We should all be one people. Besides, we are on the cusp of our complete and total destruction. We must come together to fight this vile evil that avails us. The ruler of the dark elves and I convened yesterday. I provided her with six of my finest guards, and she provided me with six of her own. Druder here is the strongest among them."

He glared at them forebodingly. Druder's skin was jet black. His long, dark ears came to a sharp point, much more so than normal elf ears. His long, silver hair was a stark contrast to his dark complexion.

"Your Grace, but what of the prophecy you spoke of?" Joan asked. "Seven of us there were, and now six remain. If Druder were to join our ranks—"

"Druder will not be joining your... outfit," Queen Stella said, waving her hand in the air as she decided on the right words. "He'll simply be providing additional protection from the foes you may face. This is my command."

Queen Stella nodded at Druder, who stepped forward stiffly and joined the others. Joan stepped back a few steps as she stared at the newcomer out of the corner of her eye.

"Understood, mother," Ànifa said. "Is there anything else you require from us?"

"That will be all. Now, begone from my presence, humans. Ànifa, it was a pleasure. We must catch up once the battle has been won."

"Of course, mother. I look forward to it," Ànifa said with a bow. Her hair continued to swirl from one shade of blue to the next, displaying her uncertainty. "Come along, everyone."

Ànifa led her party out of the Grand Hall and into the antechamber, where her sisters squealed and threw their arms around her.

"Ànifa! We can't believe you've actually returned! Mother told us you were coming, but I didn't know it would be so soon!" Pearla rattled off.

"Pearla, calm down and let Ànifa breathe," Nayeli said with a wide grin, unable to mask her own excitement.

Ànifa laughed. Her loving sisters, Pearla and Nayeli, were nearly identical. Nayeli's face was narrower compared to Pearla's round face, and Nayeli's ears were slightly longer and rounder than Pearla's, but they had the same eyes, the same small nose, and the same wide, dimply smile. Both sisters wore their dark green hair in a large bun that sat at the back of their heads. This hairstyle designated them as royalty that wasn't directly next in line to the throne.

"Nayeli, Pearla... it's so wonderful to see you again," Ànifa said. She stepped aside and introduced her companions.

"It's nice to meet all of you," Nayeli said, her eyes lingering on Druder. "Now, if you all don't mind, we'd like to talk to our sister alone. Joan, can you take everyone to the atrium and wait for us there?"

"Of course, Princess," Joan replied.

Ànifa followed her sisters back to their private quarters. When they entered, Raveen, Nayeli's boyfriend, stood from the couch awkwardly.

"Oh, um, hi Ànifa," Raveen mumbled.

"Raveen! It's great to see you again!" Ànifa exclaimed and gave him a hug.

"Oh, it's... it's nice to see you again, too," Raveen said as he glanced at Nayeli with a confused expression before turning back to Ànifa.

"Could you give us a few minutes?" Nayeli asked.

"Sure thing, love," Raveen said as he hurried out the door, leaving the three sisters alone.

"Ànifa... what was that just now?" Pearla asked with a sly smile.

"What? I was just saying hi to Raveen," Ànifa replied.

"Ànifa... you don't like Raveen," Nayeli replied. "You've never approved of me dating him."

"Huh, really? From what I can remember—which is much more now that I've returned home—we got along fine."

"Pearla, raise a barrier," Nayeli instructed.

"Oh right, I nearly forgot." Pearla closed her eyes and furrowed her brow as she raised both hands into the air above her head, then made a circle with her arms as she slowly brought her arms down to her sides.

"Okay, we should be good now," Pearla said with a satisfied nod.

"Is this... is this a sound barrier that we used to make as children?" Ànifa asked as she gazed at the thin, opaque barrier.

"Yes. It would annoy the crap out of mom and dad," Pearla said with a slight grin. "This is the only way we can assure that no one is eavesdropping."

"Speaking of mother and father, what's wrong with mother? She didn't seem herself," Ànifa asked.

"She's been like that since your disappearance," Nayeli said. "At first, we thought it was because you were gone. As soon as Joan left to help you, Grungo mysteriously died. Then, the very next day, father was tried and found guilty of treason. He was executed immediately, in private. Ànifa, we never even got the chance to say goodbye."

"Oh, I'm so sorry," Ànifa said as she embraced her sisters in a hug.

"Not only that, but the official cause of his death is he succumbed to a mysterious illness. The truth is being covered up," Pearla said with a sigh. "What happened to you, though?"

"It's a long story, and we don't have a lot of time to spare," Ànifa replied. She then went on to tell an abridged version of her journey across Eklatros and how she and her party returned to Yttendaus.

"I know this is an odd question, but how sure are you that the memories you've regained are really your memories?" Nayeli asked.

"I... I guess I can't really be sure," Ànifa replied, "but you mentioned it was odd that I gave Raveen a hug."

"Not odd—extremely unexpected," Pearla replied.

"The day before you disappeared, you and Raveen got into a huge argument over something really stupid. I don't even remember what it was about," Nayeli said. "But you were both screaming at each other. Father had to send four guards to break up the fight."

"So, yes, me suddenly giving Raveen a hug would seem out of place, then," Ànifa said thoughtfully. "I suppose there were a few times my memories seemed a bit off. I had almost no memories of our parents before returning to Yttendaus, but I remembered the two of you. It didn't make sense to me why I could remember you and not them."

"I think something has gotten to mother," Nayeli replied. "She's always been the strongest magic user in our family. For all we know, she could influence your memories."

"How is that even possible?" Pearla asked.

"Believe me, Pearla, I've had many voices in my head. Between Gnusaramnii and Kalahsem and the other Ekataramn... even Theodore. The next step beyond that would be manipulation," Ànifa said with certainty.

"With all those voices inside your head, it made your mind malleable," Nayeli explained. "It could be how mother influences you so easily."

"Look, I don't deny that something is wrong with mother," Pearla said. "But how can we be so sure she's been in Ànifa's head, messing with her memories?"

"It's what makes the most sense to me," Nayeli replied, then sighed. "I don't want to believe it, though."

Joan and the others stood in a circle in the palace atrium. Lining the atrium were statues depicting former kings and queens, including King Waesjeon the Wise and Queen Beatrix the Brave. Joan sighed. She was happy to be back in a familiar setting, especially considering the peculiar interaction they had with Queen Stella, but Joan knew better than to speak of this now. Instead, she crossed her arms and glared at Druder. Druder stared back, expressionless.

"So, Druder. What's your story?"

Druder stared blankly at her for a few seconds before answering in a thick accent. "I am your Queen's new bodyguard. Hand-picked by my village elder, I am here to represent our Supreme Leader Eridame III. Even living among Yttendaus' roots, we feel Eklatros changing."

"You live in the root system?" Joan asked.

Druder nodded. "Yes."

"Then you are familiar with Yttendaus."

"Yes. Those of us that live underground learn much from Yttendaus. She shows us the way."

Joan narrowed her eyes. "I was taught that the dark elves only practice restricted spells, including spells that can cause instant death."

"All simply stories, to be sure," Druder replied. "On a similar note, we were taught that the elves who lived above ground had been misled and are no longer able to hear Yttendaus."

"That may be partially true," Joan replied with a sigh. "Many of the common elves cannot hear Yttendaus."

"So, I guess you're not all bad, then," Vesten said as he softly punched Druder's arm. Druder simply glared at Vesten, who shirked back and hid behind Dasch.

"Indeed. What we were taught may have been a lie. But that doesn't mean I can trust you just yet," Joan replied.

"I understand. Take your time," Druder replied.

The conversation devolved from there, and a few minutes later, Ànifa and her sisters entered the room.

"Alright, everyone. Are you ready to go?" Ànifa asked as she approached the group.

"Yeah, I'm raring for a fight. This is the strongest I've ever felt," Cecil exclaimed.

"Yttendaus certainly can have that effect," Nayeli said. "She has amazing healing spells."

"Indeed. I was feeling depleted during the fight at Bugenaluf. Now I am quite energetic," Theodore replied.

"We still have one last stop before we head into the forest," Ànifa said. "My sisters suggested we get a guide through the Ytten Forest."

"It is very easy for the Ytten Forest to take advantage of weary or lost souls. The forest may not be big, but once you're in it, it may never let you out," Pearla said.

"That's fuckin' terrifying," Vesten said. "So, where do we find this guide?"

"We don't need to go far," Nayeli replied. "I'll lead the way. But first we need to make a quick stop at my shop."

They followed Nayeli through the town of Ytten to the herbal store she managed—Royal Remedies—where she and Pearla gave them each a simple necklace held together with a brown string. On the string was an assortment of flowers, herbs, mushrooms, and leaves. They were quite pungent—they smelled of dirt and mold. Nayeli explained that the necklace and its assortment of scents would help to ward away the monstrous beasts that prowled the forest.

Pearla stayed at the shop while Nayeli led the group out of town to a nearby field. In the center of the field was a small, shrunken tree. Nayeli knocked twice on the tree and said, "Quaant, are you home?"

"Wait a blubbering minute, won't ya! I'm in the middle of my weekly bath!" came a small, loud voice.

"Who exactly are we meeting up with?" Dasch asked.

"Zir name is Quaant. Zie is a faerie—one of the guardian faeries. The three of us used to spend time out here, talking with zir until late at night," said Princess Nayeli.

"Quaant is quite the character," Ànifa said.

"And what exactly is that supposed to mean?" said an annoying voice. A small nude faerie with dark-brown skin emerged from a crack in the tree.

"Quaant, please clothe yourself. You forget your place," Joan commanded as she crossed her arms and looked away.

"Joan! It's wonderful to see you again!" Quaant exclaimed.

"Put some clothes on, please," Joan said again, shielding her eyes.

"What? I'm not showing anything right now. I'm in my genderless state. Besides, it is you all who interrupted me during my bath time."

The faerie had four small, greenish translucent butterfly-like wings. Quaant was totally smooth where zir privates should have been. As Ànifa studied zir, she remembered little details about zir. Quaant may be a guardian of the Ytten Forest, but faeries were not always fully accepted by the elvish society. Faeries were seen as a devolved form of elf and thus were treated as an obscene injustice. Ànifa had always found them to be knowledgeable and friendly creatures. Besides Quaant, there were other guardian fae, but Quaant was the one she had talked to the most.

"Ah... Ànifa! It's been quite some time. Like what you see?" Quaant asked her.

"Quaant!" Nayeli commanded. "Put on some clothes, now!"

"Fine! Geezy kabeezy, calm your tits!" Quaant exclaimed as zie retreated back into the tree.

"That was... odd," Theodore said slowly, stroking his beard.

"To say the fuckin' least," Vesten added.

"Faeries are quite unique among the elvish varieties," Princess

Nayeli explained. "Since they have the special ability to change genders and body sizes, they can be quite flamboyant."

"Yeah, and much more fun than any crusty old elf," Quaant replied, once again emerging from the tree. This time Quaant was wearing a simple green dress with a brown sash tied around zir waist. "Ah, now Ànifa, where were we?"

"*I* was going to ask you if you could accompany *Princess* Ànifa. She requires a guide to lead her through the Ytten Forest safely," Nayeli said.

"The Ytten Forest is it? A dangerous place, it is. Very dangerous... full of wild fae. Nasty critters they can be."

"You speak ill of your own kind?" Cecil asked.

"Indeed I do, human. Do you only speak praise about your kind?" Quaant asked, studying Cecil closely.

"I suppose not," Cecil replied with a shrug.

"Exactly. Now, what do we have here?" Quaant asked, noticing Druder for the first time. "Why does a vile creature such as this accompany you, Princesses? Humans are one thing... but this—"

"Quiet, you disgusting ingrate," Druder snarled. "I am here by the Queen's command."

"It's true, Quaant," Ànifa said. "He's here to help us."

"So, what's your story, then? Why does the queen command one such as you, dark elf?"

"I do not appreciate that term," Druder shot back. "I am simply an elf."

"An elf, but not an elf. Shit, I'm more elf than you!" Quaant exclaimed as zie suddenly grew to be the full size of a typical elf. Vesten and Cecil gasped. "Like this, I could be mistaken as an elf," Quaant continued.

"Which is why it is against the Code of Ytten for any fae to impersonate an elf," Nayeli said.

"Right, a rule I wholeheartedly agree with. As I said earlier, fae can be quite ferocious," Quaant added as zie shrunk down to the size of a crow. "And yet I thought the dark elves were forbidden from being on the surface of Yttendaus. What happened to that law?"

"My queen mother overturned that law after my father passed," Nayeli explained. "She claimed we needed all the strength we could get, so she sent an invitation to the leader of the dark elves. They met and came to an agreement that allowed Druder and a contingent of others to help protect Yttendaus if necessary."

"I hope she knows what she's doing," Quaant said softly.

"She's our queen, fae," Joan retorted. "We must respect her decisions."

"Right, but even so, I do not take this lightly."

"To the point, then, Quaant," Nayeli said. "Can you lead Princess Ànifa and her companions safely through the Ytten Forest?"

Quaant sighed. "Fine, whatever. I expect just compensation, of course, for my efforts."

"You will get your reward. Oh, and you'll need to wear this," Nayeli added, holding out another of the pungent necklaces.

"Bah!" Quaant said, recoiling from her. "Get that crap away from me! I don't need that. I am part of the forest."

"And yet you do not smell like the forest," Nayeli replied. "Your odor will attract cusith or katsith. You must wear this. I command it."

"I suppose if it's your command, then I must. Why does it need to be so big, though?" Quaant complained.

"Oh, hush now. I know you can easily shrink it," Nayeli said.

"Meh meh meh," Quaant mocked as zie shrunk the necklace down and draped it over zir neck, eliciting a fierce eye roll from Nayeli.

"Well, now that that's all settled, can we be off?" Theodore asked.

"Yes, let's go," Ànifa said. Then she turned to her sister. "Nayeli, take care while we're gone. Keep an eye on mother."

"What's going on with the queen?" Quaant asked, zir interest piquing.

"She's... taking our father's death really hard." Ànifa looked around at her companions.

It's been quite the journey, hasn't it? she thought. *Theodore and Cecil... you've both been with me from the beginning. You too, Dasch and Vesten... it was just the five of us when we set out from Schelff Island. And we're all still together. Of course, we're missing Tyrona, and we have some colorful new additions to our team.*

Druder... I can't read you well. I do not yet know what your intentions are. Why my mother decided to side with you I do not know, although, at the same time, seeing you now... it doesn't make sense why we treated you with such hostility in the first place. We are all elves—we are all the same. Druder, perhaps your presence here is needed more than any of us may know.

And Quaant, you were a good friend to me. I welcome your assistance again. I'm sure that with your help, we will pass through the Ytten Forest with ease.

I still can't comprehend the fact that I'm home again. It feels like this is what I've been fighting for this entire time. Sure, I've been fighting for Eklatros, but in the back of my mind, my goal was always to return home. And now that I am home, it doesn't feel like home anymore. The West Wind is home. This place, while familiar, feels somehow foreign and cold. It's not the home I remember... at least, I don't think it's the home I remember, since I can't really trust my memories. But the feeling of this place... something isn't right. It may have to do with you, Mother.

All I know is that I intend to figure all of this out after we complete our mission. Once Yttendaus is awakened, I should have time to investigate what's going on here.

My sweet sister Nayeli, you were always the strongest. I will need your help the most after all of this is over. Stay strong, sweet sister, and stay safe.

39

BATTLE FOR COMPLETION

Ànifa gave Nayeli one final hug, then set off with the strange faerie Quaant in the lead. She knew she was going to see Nayeli and Pearla again, but she feared that what she was about to do would change everything forever. There would be no going back after this, no matter if she was the victor or if Gnusaramnii was. For better or for worse, Eklatros was changing permanently.

They were eight in total, with the newcomers Druder and Quaant rounding out the team. Quaant continued to lead the way, with Ànifa and Joan following zir. Behind them, Theodore, Vesten, and Cecil followed, with Druder and Dasch taking up the rear.

Quaant bobbed through the air on zir small wings as zie led the team to the Ytten Forest. The floating island of Yttendaus was quite large—slightly larger than the Nibelkaith Volcano. To reach the Ytten Forest, they had to cross through a field of wildflowers of every color of the rainbow in a varied assortment of combinations. There were purple and teal flowers, yellow and blue, green and orange, gold and violet; the flowers stretched on and on. Some flowers were small and low to the ground while others were nearly as tall as herself.

"Wow, these are really pretty," Ànifa commented as she knelt to examine a deep magenta flower.

"These flowers are used in many ways by the elves," Joan explained. "From inks and dyes to powders and medicinal uses; each colored flower is used in a different way. They also produce edible seeds, and those seeds play a large part in the daily diets of the elves."

"Yes. The pink and green ones I like to use as an aphrodisiac," Quaant added. "I think those oneses smell the best."

"Ah, well, that's great," Ànifa said, blushing.

They were quickly approaching the edge of the Ytten Forest. The closer they got to the forest, the denser the flowers became.

"Yttendaus supports all life, and all life supports Yttendaus," Druder said. "I was taught that when I was a child. Only now do I fully understand its meaning."

"What is it you know about Yttendaus?" Ànifa asked, curiously. "You lived within it, which must give you a different perspective."

"Indeed. We who are closest to the core of Yttendaus are taught much about its mystical ways," Druder explained.

"Let's put the plug on any unnecessary speech. We approach the Ytten Forest. We must proceed with respect," Quaant said. "Once we reach the edge proper, I will begin the ritual that will grant us safe passage through the forest."

"Ritual?" Theodore asked. "What kind of ritual?"

"You will see, old one," Quaant replied, garnering a sharp look from Theodore.

When they reached the edge of the forest, Quaant turned to them and instructed the group to remain silent until zie was finished. Without waiting for a response, Quaant spun around in the air while speaking an unknown language. Throughout zir speech, Quaant continually made bodily gestures to emphasize zir message, spinning in the air and even performing somersaults.

When the ritual was over, Quaant turned to them and softly said, "We may proceed. We go in silence."

Ànifa nodded and followed the small faerie into the Ytten Forest. It was as if she stepped into another plane of existence. She immediately felt lighter and everything sounded tinny and distant. There was also a slight pulse, like the beating of a heart.

"*You can feel it, can't you?*" Quaant's voice permeated her mind.

"*Yes, I feel it. I feel the pulse of Eklatros... the rhythmic beating, the essence and flow of life,*" she responded in kind.

"*Good,*" Quaant replied. "*Now call out to your party. We cannot speak out loud—we must communicate only through our spiritual connection with each other.*"

"*Joan, Theodore, Dasch, Cecil, Vesten, Druder... can you hear me?*"

Vesten cursed out loud in surprise, then quickly shut his mouth after seeing the glares from his companions. Yet Cecil, who had never experienced this form of communication before either, knew enough to keep quiet.

"*Fuck!*" Vesten continued silently. "*This is fucking weird.*"

"*Please refrain from such foul language, human,*" Druder replied. "*We are in a holy realm.*"

"*Holy realm or not, that man will speak how he will speak,*" Joan replied, defending Vesten. "*I will tolerate it for the sake of Eklatros, for the sake of our divine mission.*"

"*Say what you will, angel,*" Quaant shot back. "*Yttendaus is not pleased by our intrusion. Our dark elf companion was simply emphasizing this fact. We have been granted passage, yes, but we are not welcome. We do not linger, and we must not stray from our path. Please, everyone, follow me. Only I know the way through this maze... only I can lead you through safely.*"

"*We trust you,*" Ànifa replied, speaking for her party. "*Please, lead the way.*"

Quaant nodded, then set off. Zie led them in a zigzag pattern, turning suddenly around certain trees and even completely doubling back at one point.

"*Ytten Forest is dense on this day,*" Quaant explained. "*It is quite active, and so we must avoid all potential encounters. As a child of the Ytten Forest, I can sense what's around us, and so I know when we get close to a threat.*"

"*Why do you fear your own kind so?*" Ànifa asked.

"*I'm sure you must have many questions about me. You may see for yourself soon enough,*" Quaant answered cryptically.

Ànifa shrugged and continued on silently. As always, if she wanted answers, she would need to have patience.

As they journeyed deeper into the Ytten Forest, Ànifa could feel the pulsing grow stronger. They were nearing Yttendaus' trunk, the source of the rhythmic beat.

Although she hadn't yet seen any of their adversaries, Ànifa could feel them nearby. She was becoming more in tune with the forest with each passing moment. She knew where Quaant would lead them before zie even did so. The necklaces they wore were helping, yet they could not truly protect them now. The forest was too dense—they were running into a creature with nearly every other turn. It took effort for them to avoid being seen, yet it soon became almost second nature to her.

And so, she was just as surprised as Quaant when they nearly ran straight into two powerful gods. They were camouflaged well, both visually and spiritually. Standing before them were Anuwan'sidtsi, the cusith god, and Farreeve'sidtsi, the katsith god. Before they could turn away, they were surrounded by both cusith and katsith.

The cusith were akin to canines and had greenish-brown pelts. Many of the cusith looked more like green, mossy mounds of turf than beast. Their god, Anuwan'sidtsi, looked almost as if it was wearing a suit of armor. Covering its green hide were patches of hardened brown fur. The patches looked like tree bark, making it appear more as a bestial tree rather than canine.

The katsith were akin to felines. They had a varying range of colorations, including purples, blues, and shades of teal. Farreeve'sidtsi, the katsith god, was patterned with a spiral tie-dye. The deep purple spiral began in the middle of its back and spiraled outward, containing greens, blues, and dark-brown and black streaks.

"Welcome, Princess Ànifa Tataluynnia Ekataramnii." The two divine voices communicated mentally as one. *"We mean no harm."*

"You can speak!" Ànifa said.

"We are not speaking, though we are communicating. And yes, here, in this place, we can communicate with you, sister."

"How may we serve thee?" Quaant asked.

"*We come to you now with a warning. There are those in the forest that oppose your presence. As for ourselves, we tolerate you because the forest tolerates you. We see you now as a necessary evil—a foreign presence that serves a higher purpose. Yet not all would agree,*" Anuwan'sidtsi and Farreeve'sidtsi continued as one.

"*Let me guess... the fae,*" Quaant replied.

"*Indeed. The fae vehemently defend this forest. Their blind devotion has made them lose their way. They no longer care about Eklatros herself. They see you only as an intrusion that must be dealt with.*"

"*Sounds about right, honestly. That's why I lickety-split when I was a youngling,*" Quaant added.

"*They lie in wait for you now, in a ring around the trunk of Yttendaus,*" the gods warned.

"*Sounds like they're taking a page out of Gnusaramnii's book,*" Theodore added.

"*In a sense, the fae and the Gnusar are similar. Both act in unison—for a single sole purpose. The fae may not operate under a single mind like the Gnusar, but they work together as a single unit. We come to you now to offer our aid in this fight.*"

"*You fight for us. Does that mean you believe in our cause?*" Ànifa asked.

"*As previously stated, we tolerate you because Yttendaus tolerates you. Yttendaus acknowledges your importance, as do we. Your mission is important for the sake of Eklatros.*"

"*What of the other creatures in the forest?*" Joan asked. "*The griffins or the cockatrices?*"

"*They will stay out of your way. We are all in agreement—you must complete your mission. For the sake of Eklatros.*"

"*For the sake of Eklatros,*" she repeated.

"*Then let us move on together,*" the gods suggested. "*We travel together, as one.*"

"*As one.*"

She smiled as she walked alongside the majestic creatures. They were stunningly beautiful and contained a powerful strength within.

She could sense that their magical abilities could far exceed her and Theodore combined.

They traveled as a pack, with Anuwan'sidtsi and Farreeve'sidtsi leading the way.

Druder felt strange in this foreign land. He was still in disbelief that he was actually on the surface of Yttendaus. When he had emerged from underground it had been late at night, but the bright moon and stars had been more light than he had ever encountered. He'd needed to wear protective eyewear until this morning. The sunlight still bothered him, but he did his best not to let it show. He had to be strong to be accepted amongst these strange individuals.

He had come above ground with six others, all friends and acquaintances. They had been the only brave souls to venture out and to heed the summons from their supposed queen. At first, they had laughed off the message. They already had a ruler—the Supreme Leader Eridame III, who had been in power for close to two centuries. Never before had they had any communication with the land-walkers, so they had been more than ready to simply ignore the summons.

The village elder said differently. While the village elder was not their Supreme Leader, everyone looked up to her. Her words carried the same weight as a direct command from the Supreme Leader. She was the wisest among them and knew everything there was to know about both Eklatros and the Ekataramn.

She told them that they had to answer the call. Eklatros needed them to rise up once again. And so, a flash election was held, and seven candidates were chosen. Druder hadn't been surprised that he'd been chosen, although he had been hoping to remain behind. He was well known in the community as a strong worker and for his sharp mind. The others chosen were priests, educators, and community leaders.

They had selected Cardinal Abbey to speak on their group's

behalf. When it came time for them to meet the queen, the cardinal had been nervous. He kept stumbling over his words, so Druder had interjected and took control. He wasn't the best at explaining things, but he was the only one among them standing straight and tall. Druder was the only one who engaged in full eye contact. He might as well be the representative if he was already the strongest and most capable.

After meeting Queen Stella, Cardinal Abbey had returned to their village, leaving Druder and the others behind as Queen Stella's newest personal guards and counsel. Cardinal Abbey was to report back on everything they had learned about their new foes and the imminent destruction of Eklatros.

Druder had known for a while that things were getting bad. Being so close to the core of Yttendaus had made his kin more attuned to its subtle voice. And lately Yttendaus had been in distress and pain. Druder never would have imagined the situation would be so dire.

During his short time on the surface of Yttendaus, Druder learned much about his newfound allies. Most of the surface-dwelling elves carried a strong animosity toward them. He heard whispered insults and name calling—among those names were *shadow* and *dark elf*. Among his clan, they were simply elves.

He had also come to realize that the surface-dwelling elves believed he and his kind to be evil and untrustworthy. The only ones that were kind to them were Queen Stella, Princess Nayeli, and Princess Pearla.

And now Druder was in the presence of yet another princess, Ànifa. She was much different from her siblings, but he couldn't pinpoint how just yet. All he knew was that her aura was stronger, as if she held an innate power that other elves did not have.

Whatever the case, Druder found his new companions quite peculiar and foreign to him. He had only ever heard stories about humans and angels, and now he had met both species in a single day. One of the humans, the elderly man in the blue robes, seemed to be a magic user. He had been taught that magic was no longer accessible to humanity. Of course, he had also been taught that everything lived in harmony with each other, which he quickly learned was not the case. At least he seemed to be tolerated by his newfound peers. The half-elf Dasch especially intrigued him, although all of his companions were fascinating in their own way.

When they had run into the cusith and katsith gods, he had been ready to defend himself. Yet his companions had reacted much differently. Sure, they had all been surprised, but never at any point did any of them stop to think that they were being tricked.

While he wasn't familiar with cusith or katsith, he was familiar with the ursith. The ursith were magical beasts, like the katsith or cusith, yet these were ursidae—large, bear-like creatures with dark gray fur. The ursith were well known for their treachery and deceit. He would never have trusted an ursith if one had spoken to him.

His companions had been ready to trust these two beasts, so he went along with it. He gripped his spear tightly in case the beasts turned on them.

***

Ànifa followed the gods Anuwan'sidtsi and Farreeve'sidtsi as they led them deep into the Ytten Forest. This time, they simply plunged into the forest—no more zigzagging to avoid running into anything. Now it was the other way around—the other creatures of the forest were actively avoiding them. All except for the fae. She could tell that they were being tracked from a distance. There were many watchful eyes on them. It was almost as if they were being herded forward into the awaiting ambush.

"*We near the protective ring of fae,*" Anuwan'sidtsi and Farreeve'sidtsi said as one. "*Our packs converge. All you need to do is break through. We will hold them off for you.*"

"*Sounds easier thought than done,*" Cecil thought. "*Or at least, that's typically the case.*"

"*The fae are not to be taken lightly, that's for sure,*" Quaant replied.

"*Indeed. They have amassed in strong numbers,*" Anuwan'sidtsi and Farreeve'sidtsi thought together. "*We will do all we can to help.*"

"*Thank you. I really appreciate it. I know you don't think—*" Ànifa thought.

"*How we feel about the matter is of no importance now. Now, we fight. The fae come. Prepare yourselves,*" Anuwan'sidtsi and Farreeve'sidtsi warned.

She barely had time to ready her bow before the first fae charged her, screaming wildly while sporting a set of sharp teeth and claws. She evaded the first attack by stabbing it in the face with an arrow.

"For Eklatros!" Ànifa shouted aloud, prompting screams and replies from her party.

The fae exploded out of the forest in front of them, wailing a high-pitched screech. Then, from nearly all sides, cusith and katsith roared out from the depths of the forest. The cacophony was nearly deafening and slightly disorienting. Ànifa couldn't focus enough to alight her inner flame, so she had to resort to hand-to-hand combat. She held two arrows in each hand, each pointing in a different direction as she slashed and stabbed with them. They were nearly impossible to track—she had to watch for the movement and strike when the moment was right.

Beside her, Cecil resorted to a similar tactic—a small hand-axe in each hand. His large battle-axe was too slow and cumbersome in a fight against such swiftly moving creatures.

"Die you freaks!" Quaant roared in laughter as zie slashed at zir fellow fae with large cat-like claws.

Dasch and Vesten were both using daggers, while Theodore slung lightning and fire spells. Druder was managing himself well, using his spear like a bo staff, jabbing with each end, then periodically slashing it downward or upward to push away the stream of fae.

It didn't take long for the assault to thin out. Ànifa looked around and saw the cusith and katsith were actively keeping fae away from them.

"We must go, now! Come on!" Ànifa cried, urging them to take the window of opportunity granted to them.

They all charged off into the forest together. The fae continued to charge at them, but before they could hit, a cusith or katsith intercepted the attack.

"How far until the trunk?" Vesten asked, a little out of breath.

"We're near!" Ànifa replied. "I can feel it!"

It was as if she was running into the warm embrace of an old friend.

Yttendaus... it is you. I return to you now, she thought. *Forgive me that I could not be here sooner. I am here now. Let us end this war together.*

40

INTERLUDE: IVY HEDERA

Declassification Disclaimer: the following document has been declassified for this usage only and has been sanitized. It has been translated accordingly for your understanding. To access the complete records, please contact Councilmember Ducutyk. His contact information can be found at the end of this document. Sanitized copy approved for release 82017/13/34.

From the desk of Professor Maximilianus Peal. Eklakiln, Caranar 17, 82002 08:00:38:72.

Today is the day. We are starting on a new test subject. It's been a month and a little over a week since we worked on our last subject, Newtus. Since then, we have been monitoring and observing our successes. The results have surprised and pleased us all. Everything is advancing well. All but the Zubba, Blood Bat. He can still only speak in garbled phrases, yet he can speak all the same.

A few days ago, my entire team and I witnessed Professor Clums conclude his work on the Eusphyrchiian named West Kilinder. I am told that this Eusphyrchiian was once an IBHA agent and that he will be added to our ranks as a security guard. It's all quite exciting, really. Professor Navacus Clums and his entire team have been doing really fascinating work with biomechanics. Seeing them work up close was truly inspiring.

However, our Eusphyrchiian test subject is much different from Professor Clums'. For starters, this subject has no name, no background—no identifying traits at all. This body should not be alive. It has no head, no legs, no hands—it is just a husk of a former Eusphyrchiian. And yet, it has a heartbeat, brain waves, and all major organs are functioning adequately. What's missing is a consciousness. I hope that once we finish our experiments, the body will regain awareness.

Supposedly, this body was found on a riverbank within the Ijurvollian capital city of Warae. It had no identification and no identifying marks. Additionally, there were no missing person cases in Warae or any of its surrounding suburbs that matched this body.

We received the body about a week ago. We finally have put together a solid plan of action, which I will outline now.

To start, we will incorporate the strange ivy we harvested during our trip to Acampachetli. We have paid little attention to it since then, as we have been putting our efforts toward monitoring our fauna subjects.

Only Elizabeth Surridge, our resident flora expert, has been keeping tabs on this strange plant. In her latest observations, the ivy plant mimicked her movements, and even responded to her vocal commands. We believe we can use this ivy to reconstruct the Eusphyrchiian's legs. By attaching the ivy to its hip joints, in theory, we believe the ivy will respond to the subject's movements and mental commands.

Due to this ivy playing a large part in our test subject's operation, we have decided to name the subject Ivy Hedera. I know this is premature, but we have a lot of hope for this subject. It won't truly be Ivy Hedera until after we complete it.

The ivy is not the only piece we'll use in this experiment. We are also going to incorporate the two Dark Therid spiders that ultimately survived our tests, Ados and Adok. Both are speaking well, and their variety of silk strands seem to be multiplying by the day. In terms of their speech, they have begun doing something quite peculiar. Interestingly, the two Dark Therid spiders do not move their chelicerae to speak—they simply speak. Somehow, they can vocalize without actually physically speaking. We are unable to find out how, but this adaption will work to our advantage.

So, since our newly named test subject, Ivy Hedera, has no hands, we are planning on using Ados and Adok as its hands. The spiders are large, and each of their eight legs are strong. They will serve as Ivy's new fingers. Ados and Adok will cling onto Ivy's wrists using their fangs, pedipalps, and chelicerae. As I previously mentioned, they don't need to use the latter to speak.

We are going to use an experimental procedure to link their consciousnesses together, so that Ados, Adok, and the Eusphyrchiian will all share the same mind. Ivy Hedera will then, ultimately, be able to see, hear, and speak freely through the Dark Therid spiders. In the best-case scenario, the ivy that we are using as Ivy Hedera's legs will also link its consciousness to the Eusphyrchiian, so all four different components will be a single functioning unit.

This is why I was hired—this is my specialty. I have only done this once before, and the test subjects—an Ancilsan and two underdeveloped Harmertians—did not survive for long after the experiments; however, this body is different. It clings to life already when it should not. It is a special specimen and one that we should take care of and treat with respect.

Work will begin at the top of the hour. We will need all hands on deck here—even Mahlvern and Walverm. I do not have the time to outline the details of what each of us will be doing, but it will test the strength of our teamwork like never before. All in all, today will be exciting.

From the desk of Professor Maximilianus
Peal. Eklakiln, Caranar 17, 82002
23:52:11:60.

It's been a long day. I would honestly have preferred to work through the night, but Kalosse called it. And, I suppose, it was a good call. We were all physically and mentally exhausted.

For starters, the ivy took almost three hours to get under control. Three full hours. That was most likely one of the roughest three hours of my career. And that includes the three trips to Acampachetli.

We couldn't sedate the ivy like we had when we harvested it. If we had, it would have torn the subject to pieces. That was one of the first things Surridge learned about the ivy—when it is in duress, it flails violently and uncontrollably. And when it wakes up after being sedated, it can remain in duress for well over six hours. The subject would not have survived.

Instead, we had to calm it down—much easier said than done. First, we tried to recreate the small terrarium where we keep it. Surridge and Mahlvern discovered how to keep it calm by recreating its natural habitat, including sounds, smells, temperature, humidity, and light.

So, we prepared the room, doing everything we could to create its natural habitat before we even brought in the ivy. That took about a half hour. Once the ivy was brought into the room, it became uncontrollably violent, so we attempted to strap it down, but it broke through three different restraints. At that point, we left it alone for a little while. After it settled down, we slowly and calmly reentered the lab. While it reacted to our entrance, it didn't start flailing. It stayed calm for the first twenty minutes or so. After that, it began attacking us intelligently, striking to kill. At the high point, it strangled me for a good thirty seconds. Since we couldn't hack away at it, Kalosse, Mahlvern, and Walverm had to pry it off my neck. I hope to never experience that again.

Strangely, shortly after that violent outburst, it calmed down and cooperated. We could finally run some final tests to ensure that our plan would actually work. The tests took the rest of the day and were quite successful. In the end, we made the ivy stand straight for a full minute and take on many different shapes. The full report is in the database.

After that, we could finally introduce the Eusphyrchiian specimen into the fold. Luckily, the ivy didn't overreact and try to kill the body. Instead, it reacted in a nurturing manner. At this point, the ivy was very responsive, and we were able to make it attach to the specimen's hip joints and twist to form two legs, just around the Eusphyrchiian's natural leg length by our estimations.

And that's where we left it. We are going to leave the ivy and the specimen together overnight. We hope the two will bond together naturally. Then we will do what we can tomorrow to connect electrical signals to spark in response to the specimen's nerves and mental commands, so it can use the ivy as if it were its own, natural legs.

Only after the ivy is in place will we introduce the Dark Therids, and that won't happen for a couple of days.

From the desk of Professor Maximilianus Peal. Dunakiln, Caranar 20, 82002 19:75:31:20.

Today was a successful day. We managed to get the ivy and the specimen's body linked together.

We used a series of electrical pulses and signals to activate the nerves in the specimen's hips, and when we did so, the ivy responded appropriately. It was able to bend and twist like a typical Eusphyrchiian leg. After a long day of tests, we believe the ivy has completely adhered to the specimen's body. All the details can be found in the database.

Tomorrow we will work on integrating the Dark Therids. Until then, we will work on maintaining the unique environment we cultivated for the room.

From the desk of Professor Maximilianus Peal. Melrikiln, Pjorkiln, Caranar 21, 82002 19:42:09:62.

Once again, it's been another successful day. I have to admit, I'm thrilled things are going according to plan. What we are accomplishing is absolutely groundbreaking.

First thing this morning, we introduced the two Dark Therid spiders into the lab. We let them loose before any of us were in the room, allowing them to adjust to their new surroundings. Keep in mind that while Ados and Adok can speak, they are still exceedingly dangerous. We had Kamarial enter the room first, since she is most familiar with them. For the most part, they simply ignored her, which was our best scenario.

After that, Kalosse and I entered. The three of us were able to coax the spiders onto the table with the specimen. We had to incentivize them using the special flowers that the spiders are oddly attracted to. We asked Ados and Adok about the flowers previously, and they have yet to give us a solid answer on why they are attracted to them. All we know is that they like to rub against them. I collected some of these flowers on my second trip to Acampachetli.

The flowers worked well—the two spiders finally got onto the table. Once they were on the table, we quickly removed the flowers, then lowered a special contraption I designed, encasing all four components together. We then allowed the rest of the team into the room and began working in earnest.

Using a computer module, we targeted the spiders, the ivy, and the Eusphyrchiian and individually sent them targeted sound waves and shockwaves. This step allows for the consciousnesses to be susceptible to melding. Then, using a special frequency, we were able to successfully meld their consciousnesses together, even the consciousness of the ivy. We confirmed our results by running dozens of successful tests.

At this point, we want to allow some time to ensure the connection remains stable. We don't want to put too much stress on all the parties involved in this experimental procedure.

From the desk of Professor Maximilianus
Peal. Rikiln, Caranar 22, 82002 21:07:11:33.

Nothing is communicating correctly anymore. No part of the specimen's body is reacting to any of our prompts. Our theory is that its missing consciousness is the issue. I plan on speaking with Professor Bodeelch and Head Professor Yilvin about this tomorrow. Hopefully, they will have a solution for the issue because this is far beyond my area of expertise.

From the desk of Professor Maximilianus
Peal. Ramnkiln, Caranar 24, 82002
14:02:41:39.

We are moving our operations to another space within the compound. Where we are going is still a mystery. Professor Bodeelch just told us to start packing. A very strange request, but he is my superior. I just hope the move does not jeopardize our subject.

. . .

For all inquiries, please use the contact information below:
Ducutyk@icos.gov
FBI@icos.gov
Please keep your messages under 500 characters. Attachments not allowed.

41

BATTLE FOR EKATARAMN

Ànifa pushed through the last of the trees and brush of the Ytten Forest and emerged in a small clearing. Before her stood the colossal trunk of Yttendaus. From her point of view, the trunk could have stretched on for nearly a kilometer. In comparison, it seemed to be only about a hundred meters tall, with a canopy nearly as massive as Roheefy's. It was strange to her how something so massive could be so hidden.

While she stood there admiring it, her companions formed a defensive perimeter around her.

"Come on, we have a mission to complete," Joan said, urging her forward.

"Right. Can we all go?" she asked.

"That's your call," Joan replied.

"Then let's all do this together. I wouldn't have made it here without you all. So, we should complete this together," she said with a nod.

"After you, then," Theodore replied softly. "We will follow."

"Right, let's go," Ànifa said as she took a step forward.

As she approached, a vine descending from the canopy above

caught her eye. She glanced at it and saw a small, green, human-like head dangling from the end of the vine.

She nearly stopped, but a slight sensation in her lower back kicked her forward a few more steps. She tripped on something and stumbled.

When she looked up, she stood face to face with a beautiful divine being. She looked around and found that everyone had disappeared—it was just them, alone. They were standing on top of a white cloud with the open blue sky spread out before them. She couldn't see the ground, and she wasn't entirely sure if this was real.

"Welcome, Ànifa Tataluynnia Ekataramnii," the feminine entity said to her. The being was made of pure light, yet it stood in human form. "I have been waiting a long time for this meeting."

"So you're... you are Yttendaus?" she asked.

"Yes, I am Yttendaus de Ekataramn. I welcome you here—to the realm within my mind. We stand now above Schelff Island, above the Mason residence."

"So, is this real? Or are we in your mind?"

"Can both not be real? We are in my mind, and we are standing on a cloud above Eklatros. We are here, now. Not physically, but spiritually."

"Yes, I suppose both can be real," Ànifa replied. "Where are my friends?"

"They are near to us and safe."

"Can they hear us?"

"Do you want them to hear us?"

"Yes, I do. I would never have made it to you without their aid."

"I understand. They can hear us now. They will hear and see everything that will transpire between us."

"Alright, that's good," Ànifa replied. "Are we safe from the battle?"

"Do not concern yourself with the ongoings of the mortal realm. What transpires here will be mere seconds of your time. I can assure you none of you will be attacked or assaulted during this conversation."

"Good... that's good."

"Why are you stalling?" Yttendaus asked. "Ask your questions."

"I have many," she replied.

"And we have much time. Ask."

"Where to start? I suppose I want to know what Gnusaramnii actually is. Where does it come from? And why is it so intent on destroying our planet?"

"The entity known as Gnusaramnii originates from a faraway planet known as Melridion. While life still thrives on Melridion, it has changed much since Gnusaramnii's self-imposed exile, which is to be expected—planets never stop changing. And while its home world is not the same as it was, it is still highly important. Those that have appeared in your dreams—Navacus Clums and Maximilianus Peal—reside on Melridion. Also, your friend and ally Tyrona is waiting for you there."

"Tyrona! Wait, how is she there? How do you know where she is? And how do you know about my dreams?"

"Please be calm, my child, and listen well. There is much I must tell you, much you must know before you can truly begin to understand the reason behind Gnusaramnii's attack on Eklatros and your importance in the matter."

"I understand. My apologies."

"There is no need to apologize, my child. Now, listen well. I will start at the beginning. Before I start, you must understand where my knowledge derives from. Understand that I am Yttendaus—one of the Ekataramn. The Ekataramn *are* Eklatros. Eklatros, in and of itself, is one with the Universal Consciousness—the conscious single entity that surrounds us and connects us all together. More simply—all is one, and one is all. I am but a thread in the fabric that makes up the Universal Consciousness. My knowledge derives from the Universal Consciousness, since I am one with it. Do you understand?"

"I... yes. At least, I can understand the concepts behind what you're talking about."

"That'll do," Yttendaus replied. "Let's move on. A long time ago, soon after the creation of this universe, a solar system was born. This solar system was and still is located at the center of the universe—the point at which the big bang originated. Surrounding this solar system was a ring of wormholes, leading to every corner of the rapidly expanding universe.

"In time, intelligent life would evolve on five of the planets in the system. The first of these—the first biological intelligent species to grace the young expanding universe—were the predecessors of Gnusaramnii, a species known as the Lakinceitians. In fact, Gnusaramnii itself *was* one of the original Lakinceitians. Another of these original Lakinceitians is known as Mau, who resides within me.

"The Lakinceitians have a complicated history. Some minds that mingle among the Universal Consciousness, and myself among them, believe the Lakinceitian species was inherently flawed from the initial creation of the species. Before the Lakinceitians were fully evolved, they were molded and crafted together by powerful entities simply known as Light Beings. I have taken the appearance of one of these beings now, in the hope that you may better understand what I tell you now."

Ànifa studied the being she faced. The figure took the form of a human and was encased in a bright light. The light was not blinding —in fact, she realized the light was akin to her own blue flames, Joan's white flames, and Dasch's golden flames. What she was seeing was the pure spiritual energy of the being—a soul in its raw form.

"And so, it was these Light Beings that created the first intelligent biological life, purely by accident," Yttendaus continued. "The Light Beings had found this strange, multicellular living substance. And they used it to play and craft other life forms. They found that by using this strange matter, they could easily create all forms of different life.

"During their play, this shapeless, formless matter discovered its consciousness and retaliated. The Lakinceitians were born from this single mind, this single living mass.

"After the Light Beings had seen what their tampering had done, they retreated and let nature take its course, which, as I stated, I believe they should have done in the first place. My apologies. It's a subject I am passionate about. Being connected with the Universal

Consciousness has its benefits, and all the conflicting thoughts and minds can really harden your own beliefs.

"The Lakinceitians grew naturally for a few hundred years on Melridion. They were intelligent, peaceful, and completely independent. Sure, they were ruled under the guidance of their high matron, Mau, but all Lakinceitians had their own lives, paths, and dreams.

"Yet there was one Lakinceitian that believed this way of life was wrong. This one believed the Lakinceitians, who were born from a single consciousness, should remain as a collective, singular mind. This Lakinceitian—Gnusar, as he was known then—started his own sect. He quickly grew a small following of devoted members, and it was soon clear to him that the Lakinceitian species as a whole would not completely convert to his way of thinking. So, he determined he needed more power. If he was more powerful, he could forcefully make his entire species submit to him, so he, the all-powerful Gnusaramnii, would be the sole consciousness of all Lakinceitians."

"That's... that's horrific," she replied.

"Horrific, but a correct approach to his problem. He did simply need more power. And so, Gnusar and his followers left Melridion, commandeering a modified spaceship left behind from the Ancilsan migration—which is a whole story in itself. All you need to know is that Gnusar left his solar system through the ring of wormholes surrounding it.

"Now, that ring has dried up. The wormholes have since degraded into black holes. Nothing can travel to and from the Vortex Solar System easily anymore, including Gnusaramnii. While Gnusaramnii is currently powerful enough to complete its initial goal of possessing the minds of its kind, it is completely barred from returning home. And so, Gnusaramnii has attempted to gain even more power by consuming full worlds and subjecting all kinds of species to its collective mind. You've seen this happen here, in the form of the Gnurargurts and Gnureavers that have attacked you throughout your journey.

"Throughout this aggressive consumption of life, Gnusaramnii learned about this world and the unique power of us Ekataramn. And so, Gnusaramnii attacked. As you know, it was repelled once. Now Gnusaramnii has returned and the tides have turned. Gnusaramnii is much stronger than it was before and Eklatros is much weaker.

"Which is why we needed you, my child, to awaken us. We have known of Gnusaramnii's return for a long time, and we have been preparing for this day... preparing for you to awaken us all."

"But why me?" she asked.

***

Theodore could barely believe what he was hearing. They were finally learning the truth behind their enemy. And yet, Yttendaus had mentioned Tyrona. How was she connected to all of this? How was she on a distant planet?

He wished he could call out to this being and ask his own questions, but he was trapped, imprisoned in this strange limbo. He floated in an ethereal realm. Beside him were his friends and companions. They were all here, even Quaant and Druder.

Tyrona! Where are you, Tyrona?

Wait, Yttendaus... is it true? Did you hear me?

***

"I will get to that in a moment, child. There is still something I must explain to you first. And it is about your friend, Tyrona Knorse," Yttendaus said.

"That's right, Tyrona! What does she have to do with all of this?"

"In a way, everything. As a payment, to fully awaken Panabeeta and Alakana while dropping the magical barrier around Bugenaluf, Tyrona was needed. To generate so much power, there had to be another source of power. So, we teleported Tyrona to Melridion, with aid from Mau, causing a massive outburst of power that we used to our own benefit. I can assure you Tyrona made it to Melridion safely.

In time, you will all be able to reunite with her. You simply need to speak to Mau, and Mau can take you there."

"That's all a bit confusing, but you're saying that we can see her again?"

"Yes. After the battle is over here, you may all go and see her. That much is important to understand. Also understand that I have, in my past, teleported other individuals to other places across Eklatros, by borrowing Kalahsem's power. I helped return Charlotte. That is why you had to physically touch Kalahsem. Only through direct contact could your consciousness access the Ekataramn's consciousness, thereby granting you access to my consciousness. In that moment, I helped Kalahsem return Charlotte to you."

"I see. Why do I have the feeling that all of this has a deeper purpose?"

"You are quite perceptive. Now we reach the heart of the matter. Ànifa, your whole life, you have wondered who you are and what your purpose is. Those yearnings did not stem from your memory loss; you've always felt like you were meant for more. And you were— you are. Ànifa, do you understand?"

"No... I mean, kind of yes, but no. I know I've always felt that way. What does that have anything to do with who I am?"

"Because, Ànifa, you are not the daughter of Stella and Vyereth. You are my child. A child of Yttendaus—a child of Eklatros."

"What? What are you saying? What does that mean?"

She looked around her, at the white fluffy cloud beneath her feet and the blue sky that stretched toward the horizon.

This can't be real, she thought. *None of this can be real. Even this, right now... everything must be a dream. That's the only thing that makes sense, right? That this is a dream? Or I'm dead. Yeah, maybe that's right. Maybe I'm dead. Because... because how? How can I be a child of a planet?*

42

BATTLE FOR UNDERSTANDING

"Ànifa, you are not dreaming, nor are you dead. You are my daughter. You are my seed, my child," Yttendaus said in the form of a shimmering Light Being.

Ànifa stood on a large white fluffy cloud with endless blue sky surrounding them. "I am your daughter?" she repeated slowly.

In a flash, memories flooded into her mind. Memories that were not hers, but Yttendaus'. Yttendaus was showing her the truth about her past.

She was seeing things she shouldn't have been able to see. She saw her embryo growing in the womb of a young human woman. The woman had chestnut skin and dark-brown hair. She was smiling warmly—she was happy.

Another flash, and the scene changed. Suddenly, she was outside in pouring rain. The woman was clutching her stomach. She was bleeding heavily and crying. Understanding dawned on Ànifa as she watched her almost-mother sob into the rain as a man held the woman tightly.

Another flash, and the scene changed. She saw the embryo once again, only this time it was encased within an acorn that hung from

Yttendaus' branches. The embryo matured within that acorn and the acorn grew in size accordingly.

Another flash, and the scene changed. Ànifa watched her own birth, but it was more like watching a chick hatch from an egg. She watched as a small child ripped out of the acorn, the shell of the acorn having become soft and papery. Soon after, a young griffin picked up the child and set it outside of the Ytten Forest. The child lay on its back in the dirt and cried under a tree.

She was not alone for long. Soon after her nativity, she watched as a young elvish couple came to her aid. Then they brought the child to the palace.

"So that's how it all happened," she said stiffly. "My birth... you took me out of the womb, my true mother's womb, when I was... when I didn't even have a form yet. And I grew out of an acorn... so, I truly am the daughter of an Ekataramn."

"Ànifa, I really am so sorry. I am sorry for stealing you away from the life you were meant to have. I'm sorry for your chosen destiny—" Yttendaus replied.

"Who was she? Who was my mother, my human mother?"

"Yes, your mother was human. She was chosen randomly out of all the pregnant women at that point in time. I let the choice be made by chance. I could not choose myself. Know that this woman has been deceased for hundreds of years; there is no way for you to find her.

"Ànifa, please understand. I did not make this decision lightly. Only one blessed with the power of Eklatros herself can complete this task. You are that one. Your power... I have watched as you have honed your abilities. You still have much to learn, but you are progressing well. In time, you will learn to wield the full power of Eklatros, and, in turn, the full power of the Ekataramn."

"Yes. I understand. I understand the logic and the reasoning," she replied. "And I'm not mad. Not really. I'm just tired. I'm tired of running toward a goal and not fully knowing why I'm even running toward it in the first place. Help me understand. Help me, Mother."

"Your memories. Let's start with your memories. Everything will be properly restored, perhaps more than you could have remembered on your own."

A lifetime of memories flooded back to her. Her lifetime and her memories.

She had lived a good life. It had been peaceful and sheltered. She learned only what her elders taught her, and she had always been educated alone. Her sisters had participated in Yttendaus' school and had grown up alongside the other young elves. Not her. Ànifa had always been told she was different, that she was special. She had always been told that it was because she was being groomed to become the next queen of Yttendaus, and even at a young age, all young potential queens had to be educated separately.

She knew the truth now. She was indeed different. She was not an elf, nor a human, nor an Ekataramn. She was the only of her kind, so she was treated as such, as the alien she was.

"Did they ever fully trust me?"

"I do not know," Yttendaus replied. "I cannot see the inner workings of anyone's mind but your own. But, I can tell you they loved you. Especially your father."

"Yes, my adoptive father, officially," she said. "King Vyereth Ekataramnii... I remember him well now. He was kind and gentle, helping everyone in need, no matter how small or large the task. He was a loyal servant of the people, and a wonderful father and king."

"And Queen Stella Ekataramnii. What can you tell me about her?" Yttendaus prompted.

"She was... she was always more distant, more aloof. But even so, I have some happy memories with her. My fiftieth birthday. The opening day of my sisters' medicine shop. The day I was selected as the official heir to the throne."

"Yes, in all of those memories and more your mother was there, smiling and laughing along with everyone else. She was always happy to be with you."

"Yes, yes she was. She always had a smile on her face when I saw her. She loved me. I know she did. And yet..." Ànifa trailed off.

"Now you are truly beginning to understand."

"The only thing I still don't fully understand is why I had to physically be there to awaken the Ekataramn."

"My child, that should be the most obvious answer of all. Only by coming into direct physical contact with an Ekataramn can your inherent and natural powers awaken the sleeping behemoths."

"Then what about Bugenaluf?"

"Bugenaluf was awoken by Alakana. Upon rooting into the ground, Alakana sent out signals to the rest of the Ekataramn. Since the Great Barrier around Bugenaluf dissipated, he could hear Alakana and slowly awaken from its call. Only when you neared Bugenaluf, aflame in your blue energy, did Bugenaluf fully awaken from its dormancy."

"I see."

"Indeed. Now, you understand everything."

"I... I do. I understand what I must do next. It's so obvious to me now."

"Then you do understand."

"Yes. My adoptive mother, Stella. She is the one I must face. She is consumed by Gnusaramnii. And under the power of Gnusaramnii, she killed my father. Say what you will about how my mother felt about me, but I know how much she loved the king, my royal father. They were made for each other. She would never harm him, and yet she killed him. Gnusaramnii killed King Vyereth. She must be in turmoil."

"Indeed. Stella is fighting a great conflict within herself. She has put up a good fight, but she's not strong enough on her own. Even though Gnusaramnii isn't yet physically on Eklatros, it will be soon. It has used your mother's body as its main conduit, and soon it will completely take her over. I don't know exactly where Gnusaramnii is —it has learned to mask its presence from the Universal Consciousness—but it is near.

"You and your friends are our only hope. Only by ridding Stella of Gnusaramnii's presence can Eklatros truly be free from its grasp. Without a presence here on Eklatros, its minions will no longer be a threat."

"Then we will do what we can," Ànifa said with pride. "All of us, together. I know you can hear me, everyone. Listen well. We will cast Gnusaramnii out of Stella's body. We will save her, and we will save Eklatros in the process. And we can only do it together."

"Right, only together can you succeed. It will not be easy—do not take this task lightly."

"I understand. Thank you truly, Yttendaus—Mother. You have returned my memories to me—my knowledge. I now know who I am and my purpose in all this. And afterward, I will return here and hash it out with you. I don't forgive you for what you did to me."

"I never expected your forgiveness. Now that you understand, I will bear whatever punishment you deem fit."

"I... well, I don't want to punish you. I guess I don't know what I want."

"You will know when you return. You will."

"Yes, when I return—"

A blinding flash of white assaulted her senses.

Joan wasn't sure how much her companions could take, but she was strong. She was an angel of Eklatros.

When Yttendaus said they would witness everything, she wasn't lying. Joan saw everything—from Ànifa's odd birth to the flood of memories that came roaring back to her.

Joan absorbed everything. All of the knowledge, all of Ànifa's memories.

Upon gaining this knowledge, Joan grew angry. She was angry at Queen Stella, who had deceived her, who had deceived everyone. But even more than that, she was angry at herself. How had she not seen the deceit, the evil festering within her queen?

Joan could only give Ànifa her deepest condolences. She understood Ànifa's grief and distress upon learning of her true nativity, and yet, everything now made perfect sense. Ànifa had always been different, but now she knew just how unique she was.

Ànifa—if Ànifa was queen, then Yttendaus could truly prosper.

Ànifa was back inside her body, her hand still on Yttendaus' trunk. She looked around and saw that the rest of her team were all reorientating themselves.

Around them, the battle between the residents of the Ytten Forest raged on. Cusith and katsith were fighting with the wild fae, the cacophony ringing in their ears once more.

"Are you all okay?" she asked everyone.

"I am physically unharmed," Dasch replied.

"I feel mentally scarred," Quaant said, as zie trembled and clutched zir head. "What was that?"

"That was Ànifa's birth," Joan replied. "Ànifa, our true leader and savior."

"So, you saw everything, then?" Ànifa asked. "What about... what about my memories?"

"Yes, all your memories are now floating around in my skull, uninvited, of course," Druder said.

"I'm sorry. I suppose I did ask Yttendaus to let you all see everything. I guess that meant literally everything."

"What memories? Some of it got a little hazy for me," Cecil asked.

"Yeah, same here," Vesten said. "Although, it sounds like we were better off for it."

"It's a lot to process," Theodore said slowly. "But now, many things make more sense."

"I agree," Dasch replied.

"You mean like fuckin' fighting against your possessed mom? Or, shit, I mean your adoptive mom," Vesten said.

"Yes. Like that," Ànifa replied. "We must face her. We must face Queen Stella."

"And how do you suppose we go about doing that?" Druder asked. Everyone looked at him. "What? I know I'm new here, but I'm involved now, for better or for worse. If I don't see this through, these memories that are not mine will haunt me until the end of my days."

"I can't say I agree with that," Quaant said, still trembling. "I... I can't frickin' handle this!"

Quaant flew into the air and screamed.

"Hey, the forest. It's quieted down," Dasch said quietly into the growing silence.

"Yeah, it sounds like the fighting has stopped," Cecil replied.

"Is Quaant gonna be alright?" Vesten asked.

"No!" Quaant screamed in reply. "I am not going to be alright! How is it that you are alright? What we witnessed was not natural! *She* is not natural!" Quaant yelled, pointing at Ànifa.

"You saw the truth, the same as us," Joan said calmly. "She is the true daughter of Eklatros. She is more natural than any of us."

"Lies. It's all lies! Find your own way back. I'm out!" Quaant exclaimed, flying off into the forest.

"Um, yeah... so, is Quaant gonna be alright?" Vesten asked. "Should we go after zir? Zie helped us get this far."

"I don't think that would be wise," Druder replied. "I know the fae. Some dwell underground with us. And what I've gathered is that these fae are just like the fae underground. They are stubborn creatures through and through. If Quaant wants to, zie will know how to find us."

"I agree," Ànifa replied. "I feel awful, though. I never meant any harm."

"None of this is your fault, Princess," Joan said softly. "It was a lot of information to absorb in such a short period of time. Not everyone's minds can handle such an information overload."

"What about the rest of you, then? Are you really okay?" Ànifa asked.

"I don't know how I feel about this situation," Druder said harshly, "but I'm seeing this through, like I said earlier."

"Yeah. I'm with you until the end. Besides, if I stick with you, then I'm sure to see Tyrona again," Theodore said.

"I'm fine. I've navigated through muddier situations than this," Dasch said with a nod.

"All fuckin' good here," Vesten said with a thumbs-up.

"Yeah, I'm all good, milady," Cecil said. "For Eklatros, am I right?"

"We're all okay, Princess," Joan said. "What about you? How are you handling it all?"

"Well, I feel like myself again. For the first time since I can remember, I actually feel whole. And yet, I feel like everything I ever knew was a fantasy, constructed to make me be who they wanted me to be."

"In a way, you're right," Joan said softly. "And I had a large role to play, so for that, I do humbly apologize."

"There's no need for apologies. You didn't know, just as I didn't know. We were both doing what we thought was right, I suppose."

"Yes, I suppose we were," Joan replied.

"Does anyone else find it fuckin' creepy how silent it is now?" Vesten asked.

Ànifa looked around and saw no other souls. It felt as if they were the only ones in the entire forest.

"Let's leave this place," Dasch said, breaking the silence. "We are not welcome any longer."

"How are we going to make it back? Quaant led us here," Cecil asked.

"I know the way out. Yttendaus will show us the way," Ànifa said, her hair the color of the shimmering sea.

They followed Ànifa out of the clearing and back into the Ytten Forest proper. Eerily, there were no signs of living cusith, katsith, or fae, only the scores of bodies that littered the ground.

"How horrible," she said softly. "I wish that none of you had to die at our expense."

"It's the way of the forest," Dasch replied. "Nature is cruel."

"It is, and that will be us if we don't leave this forest soon," Theodore said.

"Exactly, we mustn't linger here," Druder said.

"Princess, we must go," Joan urged.

"Right. I'm sorry, please rest in peace," she said to the cusith, katsith, and fae alike.

She felt Joan's hand slip into her own, and she allowed her guardian angel to lead her away from the carnage.

They left the forest without coming across any wildlife. No cusith or katsith, no fae or cockatrices. Even the gods Anuwan'sidtsi and Farreeve'sidtsi had disappeared. It was eerie and unsettling, especially after such an intense conversation with an all-powerful entity. It was as if Yttendaus herself was quieting the forest and allowing them through. If that was the case, she was glad for it. But something felt off. They had only been gone for mere seconds, but, for some reason, it felt like years.

She shook her head and kept moving forward. She'd go crazy if she kept analyzing the situation. She realized she was still holding Joan's hand and gripped it tightly. Joan returned her grip.

"Joan, you can hear me, right?" she thought.

"Yes, Princess. I can hear you," Joan replied.

"Is this Yttendaus' doing? Or something else?"

"I cannot say. I cannot get any response from Eklatros. Let's just focus on leaving," Joan said.

"Yeah, this place is quite eerie," Theodore chimed in.

"Theodore…" Joan began, then trailed off.

"Yes? What is it?" Theodore asked.

"I'm glad that Tyrona is safe. From what it sounds like, at least."

"Thank you. I am as well. I only hope that she is safe."

"I'm sure she is," Ànifa replied. *"And we'll see her again, soon."*

"Oh shit!" Vesten exclaimed, interrupting their silent conversation. "We're here. We've found the fuckin' exit."

"Hush, human!" Druder exclaimed. "You forget yourself."

"No, not really. But noted. I'll restrain myself," Vesten replied.

Ànifa giggled softly, then burst out in laughter. She couldn't help it. Suddenly, the whole situation seemed comical to her. Vesten stared at her a moment and then he, too, began laughing. The others simply stared at them.

"What? I'm sorry. It's just—this is so messed up, isn't it? It's so ridiculously messed up. Like, I grew out of a freaking acorn. I honestly don't know how I feel about that yet. And now, I have to essentially rid my queen mother of an evil entity that possesses her. And on top of all that, everything that we did to get here. It's just—"

"It's what needed to happen," Joan said bluntly. "I understand your hysteria, Princess. But this is not funny. We must be cautious. We don't know if Stella has any allies."

"Right... right. You are right, like you usually are, Joan," she replied. "It's just, I love you Vesten. I'm so happy you're with us."

"Thanks!" Vesten replied with a wide grin.

"Are you done? Can we focus?" Dasch asked harshly.

"Yes. We can do this. We should do this," Ànifa said, trying to reassure herself. She was completely terrified. Now that she had gotten the laughter out of her system, she was struck with fear.

Joan put a hand on her shoulder. "It'll be okay, Princess. We're all here with you, by your side."

"Yes, you're right. Thank you, all of you. Let's go face our final battle."

Thank you, Yttendaus, she thought. *Thank you for showing me the truth about myself. I'm glad I know everything about myself now. I'm glad that I'm finally me again, at the very least.*

What happens if we fail? This is our last chance, isn't it?

Yttendaus, Kalahsem, Roheefy, Bugenaluf, Panabeeta, and Alakana... all of you I have awoken, and I have not done so in vain. You will remain pure and uncorrupted. I will save Eklatros. We will save Eklatros. And together, we will save our universe.

Together... Tyrona, you are alive. Yttendaus said you are on a planet called Melridion, the same planet where Professor Navacus Clums is. Navacus—I know he is important. He must be, otherwise, why would I have dreamt of him so often? He has to be connected to all of this in some way. Him, and the human professor, Professor Peal... what is their purpose in all this? Tyrona, once we reunite with you, I'm sure you can tell us everything you know.

43

BATTLE FOR REVIVAL

With her memories fully restored, Ànifa continued to lead her party as they exited the Ytten Forest. It seemed so strange to her that she had forgotten Yttendaus, her home. *West Wind* still felt like home to her, but this was her true home. And she was happy to have it back in her life.

And since this was her home, she was going to do everything she could to protect it. If her adoptive mother, Queen Stella, was truly possessed by Gnusaramnii, she would save her, even if it meant sacrificing her own life. She was ready for anything, as long as it meant her family and friends were safe.

She led her party through the field of wildflowers that lined the outer rim of the Ytten Forest. As they neared the fork in the path that would take them into town, they saw a small faerie hovering over the path, zir small wings beating furiously. Quaant looked nervous as zie darted back and forth, contemplating whether or not to fly back to zir small withered tree.

"Ànifa!" Quaant exclaimed once zie saw them. "Ànifa, there you are. Come quick, you must hurry!"

"Quaant, I thought you left," Joan said.

"Yeah, I did, I totally did. And don't you forget it! But now is not the time for silly little feuds. There is something very wrong with the town!"

"What's going on?" Ànifa asked. "Can you explain on the way?"

"Yeah, sure. Let's go," Quaant said, zooming away from them quickly, then darting back, urging them on.

"We're right behind you," Ànifa said as she followed Quaant.

Quaant nodded in satisfaction, then continued. "You see, after I left you all, I was confused and distraught. I thought I would go speak to the Queen about the matter, but everyone is acting strangely. It's as if they've all lost their marbles!"

"Everyone in town? Are my sisters okay?" Ànifa asked, looking up at Quaant as she quickened her pace.

"I do not know. I did not see them," Quaant replied. "But I saw Queen Stella. She was standing in the center of town, beckoning everyone to her. It was all rather creepy."

"Right, Gnusaramnii must be making its move," she said.

"Princess, we must be careful. Anything could happen," Joan warned.

"I'll be ready to cast a protective barrier if needed," Theodore said as he jogged along with them.

"Great, we may just need it," Ànifa replied.

As they rounded the bend that took them alongside the outskirts of town, Ànifa felt a strange feeling wash over her. It was as if darkness was trying to take control of her as it gripped at her mind and her heart.

She stopped in the road and staggered to her knees. "Does anyone else feel this? Like there's an evil hand grasping at my essence?"

"I feel like killing something. I have a powerful urge to kill right now," Cecil replied with no hint of malice in his voice. He gripped the hilt of his battle-axe firmly.

"Aye, me too," Vesten replied. "I feel as if everything must fucking die."

"It's Gnusaramnii. I can feel its vile tendrils creeping into my mind as well," Joan said. "Hold on everyone, I'll resolve this."

Joan took out Halahkahna, the Divine Shield of Protection. She held it out in front of her, the face of the shield facing toward her. Joan closed her eyes and muttered in an ancient language. A bright light washed over her. She opened her eyes, then spun the shield so it was now facing the group. The pattern on the shield was waving and dancing.

"Now, Ànifa, place your hand in the center of the shield," Joan prompted as the imprint of a hand appeared in the center of the shield.

Ànifa looked up from the ground, still on her knees. It took almost all of her effort to lift her hand from her side. Her hand floated in the air, shaking and trembling.

"I... I can..." she said, her voice trembling.

Quaant sighed and rolled zir eyes. "We don't have time for this!" Zie darted over to Ànifa and pushed her hand forward onto the face of the shield.

Upon touching it, a sharp pain tore through her body, and Ànifa cried out. Once the pain receded, a feeling of euphoria washed over her. She felt fantastic. Her body felt strong and capable, and her mind was sharp and calculating.

"So that's what's going on," Ànifa murmured. "Joan, Quaant! We must help the others!"

"Who the fuck are you looking at?" Vesten threatened as Ànifa looked at him.

"Hurry, before it's too late," Joan urged. "The spell only works with direct contact."

Ànifa took Vesten by the arm and shoved his hand onto Halahkahna. Vesten cried out for a moment, then looked at Joan in fear.

"What in the living fuck just happened?" Vesten asked.

"I'll explain later. Quick, help me with the others!" Joan cried.

They were in terrible shape. Cecil was gripping his battle-axe, his eyes growing wild. Theodore was on his knees, his arms in the air as he cried out to the skies. Dasch and Druder were facing each other, glaring intensely into each other's eyes as they prepared to fight.

"It was similar to when I first fell off Yttendaus and into the ocean below. It felt like I was drowning then, since I suppose I was, but the sensation this time was similar. Gnusaramnii is using its powers to corrupt the mind of any person who comes near it. By now, I'm sure everyone in Ytten is a slave to Gnusaramnii," Ànifa explained after everyone was back to normal.

"Somehow, Joan and Quaant were immune. We are grateful for that," Dasch said softly. "I was nearly lost with madness."

"But you never truly lost yourself," Ànifa said. "You clung on, even through it all. I'm proud of you."

"I wasn't really immune," Joan added. "The initial spell I cast was for myself."

"I guess I'm the lucky one, then," Quaant replied, beaming as zie pointed a thumb at zir chest. "I didn't feel anything at all. Still don't."

"Let's hope it stays that way," Theodore said. "Thank you for helping us."

"It really wasn't a problem or anything like that," Quaant replied, zir cheeks growing red.

"We'll need your help again, Quaant, if you'll lend us a hand?" Ànifa asked.

"Of course I'll help. Why else would I have decided to align myself with you again?"

"Great," Ànifa nodded. They continued to stand in the path, just outside the outskirts of town. It was eerily quiet, with only the sound of the wind as it howled through the grassy fields. "We'll split into two teams," she continued. "Since there's eight of us, we'll divide into two teams of four. Joan, I want you, Druder, Quaant, and Vesten to help revive the town. Use Halahkahna to purify everyone. And if you can, please find and save my sisters."

"Of course, Princess. We will find Princess Nayeli and Princess Pearla and save the citizens of Ytten," Joan replied.

"Thank you," Ànifa replied. "And please, be careful. Look after each other. We don't know what it will be like around bigger crowds.

Theodore, Cecil, Dasch, and I will go after Queen Stella. We need to end this *now*."

"Shouldn't Joan help you with the Queen? If her shield can help us, can't it help her too?" Druder asked.

"She's too far gone. I doubt it would be effective," Joan replied.

"Exactly, which is why I need her helping the townsfolk. Does anyone else have anything to add? I'm welcome to any suggestions."

"It sounds like a solid plan to me," Cecil said. "Let's go save the queen. For Eklatros!"

"For Eklatros!" they cried out as one.

"For Eklatros," Ànifa said again softly, after the chant. "*Joan, stay in contact.*"

"*I will, Princess. Please take care, and stay safe.*"

Joan looked back reflexively to check on the others. Vesten followed close behind her while Druder and Quaant stayed a few paces behind him. They were in the midst of sneaking behind the shops that lined the town center. The promenade was densely packed with corrupted elves. They were gathered together in a large circular formation. Joan knew they were all recently turned Gnureavers. But they did not look like the human Gnureavers she had fought before—these still retained their original bodies. Yttendaus was stronger than the other Ekataramn, allowing them to be turned, but they were not close enough to become twisted and deformed.

There was no weak spot for them to start with—they would have to pick their poison and choose whatever spot she deemed would be best.

Joan spotted an area in the crowd in which some younger elves, each less than fifty years old, lined the outer rim. She would start there. She passed through a small alleyway, inching toward the crowd.

"Alright, is everyone ready?" Joan whispered to her companions.

"Ready as I'll ever be for something I really don't want to be doing," Quaant said quietly. "So, yes."

"For Ànifa. Let's do this shit!" Vesten whispered loudly.

"They seem to have their guard down," Druder added. "We should be able to sneak up on them."

"Yes, let us do this quietly," Joan said. "Purification commence!"

Joan rushed out from the alley as quietly as she could, Halahkahna in hand, with Vesten, Quaant, and Druder following her. The crowd had their backs to them, allowing them to sneak in unseen.

Once she was standing right behind the crowd, she murmured silently to herself. Halahkahna activated a moment later. Joan burst into soft white flames, temporarily increasing her strength and power. It was time.

"Now!" she whispered loudly to her team.

Vesten, Quaant, and Druder each grabbed the hand of a different elf and brought it into contact with the face of Halahkahna.

Each of the three elves regained their composure and looked utterly bewildered. A moment later, Vesten, Druder, and Quaant had another elf in hand, beginning the long and arduous purification process.

It didn't take long for the crowd to notice. The elvish Gnureavers swarmed around them. Quaant screamed and grew nearly three meters tall. "I'll protect you all! Continue the purification!"

"Thank you, Quaant," Joan called out.

Among the fray, Joan spotted not just elves, but angels and dark elves as well. It was as if Gnusaramnii had gathered all the residents of Yttendaus together for its ultimate attack. She was saddened to see that her fellow angels had been possessed but knew that without Halahkahna, she would have been as lost as them.

Notably absent from the crowd were other fae, which must have been why Quaant had been overlooked by the initial wave that had struck them all. Gnusaramnii had made a terrible oversight, for Quaant was ravaging the possessed elves that swarmed zir as zie continued to grow—zie was just over five meters tall now. Joan had never seen a faerie grow so big. She didn't even know that they could grow that large.

Meanwhile, Vesten and Druder continued to shove the hands of corrupted elves onto the face of Halahkahna. Each elf they purified, while confused and disorientated at first, joined in to help them once they realized what was going on.

The purified elves helped to create and maintain a bottleneck so the flow of the Gnureavers could be better managed, but it wasn't a simple job—they had to fend off their friends and acquaintances. Those that were too emotional were gently pushed into focus by their fellow elves around them. They were all going through this terrible experience together, and it was only together that they would succeed.

Quaant continued to be a distraction, luring others to zir so that they wouldn't be so overwhelmed.

Joan held her shield firm and continued to give it all she had. This effort may just kill her, but it would be worth it.

"Ànifa, our job is going as well as we could have hoped for," she thought. *"I have yet to see your sisters, but I am keeping a watchful eye out for them. I hope you fare well, and that our efforts are helping you reach your goal."*

"Don't worry about my sisters, Joan. I have found them," Ànifa replied telepathically.

Ànifa stood alongside Theodore, Cecil, and Dasch as they watched the crowd swarm toward Joan and the others, allowing them to glimpse the center of the fray. She spotted her queen mother, her arms raised in the air. Stella seemed to be chanting something. Her sisters and Raveen surrounded the Queen. They were all possessed— they were all one with Gnusaramnii.

"Right. Remember, she may look like my mother—the queen— but she is fully Gnusaramnii reincarnate."

"We understand, Princess. We'll help you save your mom!" Cecil said as he gripped his battle-axe. After a few moments, it burst into golden flames. "Ha, I knew I could do it! All that practice paid off!"

"Very nice, just don't get cocky now," Dasch said with a smirk.

"You know, this is my fight. I'd be okay with it if—" Ànifa began before Dasch cut her off.

"Don't even finish that thought. We're here. We're with you until the end."

"This is just as much my fight as it is yours, Ànifa," Theodore retorted. "We're all in this together."

"Right... right. Thank you. I love you all. Now, I'll stop delaying the inevitable. Let's do this. For Eklatros!"

"For Eklatros!" Cecil, Dasch, and Theodore shouted in unison.

Ànifa readied her bow and notched an arrow while the others readied their weapons—Dasch with his golden flaming sword, Cecil with his magnificent golden flaming battle-axe, and Theodore with his scarlet staff. They were ready for the fight of their lives.

She sprinted into battle. Gnureavers lunged at her but she was faster, evading them just in time. It was Joan's job to deal with the civilians. Ànifa's focus was on Queen Stella.

"Mother!" she cried out.

Stella locked eyes with her. Emanating from her mouth was Gnusaramnii's foul laugh.

"Ha ha ha ha ha... Ànifa!"

"Gnusaramnii!" she yelled, firing an arrow as she ran.

Stella leaped high into the air, dodging the arrow and kicking it into the chest of a high elf.

As she and her loyal companions rushed forward, possessed elves surrounded them. They did not attack—they were merely creating a perimeter, making sure they could not escape.

Stella stepped forward, Gnusaramnii's vile laugh continuing to fall from her mother's lips. Behind the queen stood eight other elves —among them Nayeli, Pearla, and Raveen. The remaining five were dark elves.

"I welcome you, Ànifa, to your imminent death!" Gnusaramnii said through Stella. "But first, I must thank you for awakening the

Ekataramn! My power has grown exponentially since you awoke the first one. Now, I grow stronger by the second as I slowly drain the life force out of every remaining elf and angel! Thank you for serving as a worthy pawn in my plans. Now, embrace your ultimate defeat!"

"You really have never understood me, have you? You've been in my head for a long time now, but you still underestimate me. I will be the one to defeat you, here and now."

"Ha ha ha... yes, let this ultimate battle decide the fate of your sorry little planet!"

She notched an arrow and fired, striking Stella in her left thigh but bouncing off as if it had struck stone, not flesh. Beside her, Dasch lunged forward, prompting Cecil to begin his charge. As Dasch attacked, Stella looked at him and grinned menacingly, causing Dasch to stop in his tracks. Theodore hurled fireballs and lightning bolts at Stella, but she simply batted them away like flies as she shoved Cecil aside.

"Dasch, come now. Are you going to be a good boy?" Stella asked.

"Dasch, focus!" Ànifa urged.

She drew two arrows, holding each one in each hand. She focused within herself, making each one burn brightly in blue flames. She willed those flames into the arrows themselves, hardening each arrow into a blue crystal. Finally, she burst into blue flames herself.

"For the royal Queen Stella of Yttendaus!" she cried, then lunged forward, pushing past Dasch, who was still frozen in place.

Stella's speed was nearly incomprehensible. She dodged Ànifa's attacks with a liquid dexterity, calculating each movement perfectly.

Yet, she was Ànifa, child of Eklatros. She was the only one capable of matching Gnusaramnii's speed. Much like her arrows, she hardened her flames, creating a blue shell around her body. Encased within this shell, her speed tripled.

She swung and slapped Stella across the face with a crystal arrow. Stella snarled, then struck back, but Ànifa dodged the attack and landed a punch to Stella's stomach.

Stella became berserk with rage as she lashed out. All she could do was defend herself from each blow.

"Ànifa!" Dasch cried as he snapped out of his daze.

"Come on, man. We've got to help her!" Cecil yelled. He had laid his golden flaming battle-axe on Dasch's back, returning him to normal.

"Together then," Dasch said, nodding.

Ànifa watched as Dasch and Cecil sneaked up from behind, then attacked Stella's exposed back. As their blows landed, Theodore threw out a combined elemental attack of lighting, fire, ground, and wind, striking Stella in the back of the head. She turned, her eyes wild.

"Go away, you pests!" she snarled.

The five dark elves that had been watching them closely threw themselves into the battle, fighting off Dasch, Cecil, and Theodore.

"Ànifa!" Theodore called.

"It's okay! I can handle her alone," she cried back.

"How confident. It's a shame you're wrong. I'm stronger than you, and I am wiser than you. There is no possible way you can defeat me," Gnusaramnii proclaimed.

"I am the *only* one able to defeat you. You said so yourself," Ànifa replied as she attacked with each arrow.

"Ha ha ha! You can never defeat one such as I!" Gnusaramnii shouted back while parrying her attacks.

"We'll see about that!" she cried. She exchanged a few more blows with her possessed adoptive queen mother, predicting her moves. She was preparing for the right moment to strike. Now!

She parried, then faked her next attack, placing her foot down instead, causing Stella to trip over it. She stabbed her mother in the stomach with one of her crystal arrows. Once lodged in her stomach, her crystallized powers were injected out of the arrow and into Gnusaramnii.

"You fool! You use your life force?"

"It is not my life force, but that of Eklatros. For I am the child of Eklatros!"

"Indeed, you may be, Ànifa," Stella—Gnusaramnii—said as she staggered to her feet. "But children can sometimes be weaker than their parents!"

Two long, dark purple tentacle-like appendages grew out of Stella's back and lashed out at her. Ànifa cried out and created a protective barrier above her, causing the shell that surrounded her to dissipate. Stella screamed at her in return. The two tentacles morphed into wings and she flew high into the air.

"I am all-powerful! This planet is mine!" Gnusaramnii shouted at her in its vile voice.

Time seemed to slow. Ànifa looked over and saw her friends fighting fiercely against the five possessed dark elves. As she watched, they moved in slow motion. Simultaneously, she could also see their future movements. She read the entire battle before it played out in full. If she didn't do something soon, Theodore would be killed from a knife to the back of his neck. Cecil would go down two moves later. The time was now.

She turned and looked at the terrible monster that was swooping down upon her. More appendages were sprouting from Stella as she flew toward her, each one sharpening into a fine point.

"*Joan, protect the others,*" she thought.

"Ànifa!" Theodore cried.

"It's okay! I can handle her alone," Ànifa yelled back.

Beside him, Dasch grunted in satisfaction, then swung his sword, matching the blow from an attacking Gnureaver. He slid his sword down, knocking the weapon out of his opponent's hand. He screamed, then sliced off his opponent's head, his golden flaming sword slicing through like butter.

"Dasch! We should attempt to refrain from killing them," Theodore shouted.

"You want to die? They are not hesitating to kill us!" Dasch replied as another possessed dark elf bore down upon him.

Beside him, Cecil fought valiantly, still awash in golden flames as he parried and attacked with the same movement. Theodore was throwing his usual lighting and fire elemental attacks. He was holding back his power.

"Theodore," Dasch argued. "Do not hold back. Use your full strength."

"You must, my dear friend!" Cecil added as he neatly sliced off his opponent's left arm.

Theodore cried out, casting his most powerful spell—the combination elemental attack made of lighting, fire, ground, and wind. It hit the attacking dark elf square in its chest, punching a hole clean through.

"*Ànifa... I'm sorry! It's the only way!*" he thought.

"*It's okay, Theodore. For Eklatros,*" she replied.

The monstrosity possessing her queen mother's body was nearly upon her.

She closed her eyes and steeled herself for the attack. With perfect timing, she stepped away, then shoved her final crystal arrow into her mother's heart, burying it deep. Once again, the powers drained out of the arrow and into her mother's body.

Stella cried out in pain. It was her own voice this time, not Gnusaramnii's.

"Mother!" Ànifa cried, lunging forward to catch her mother's grotesque body as it fell to the ground. She cradled her mother's head in her hand as tears welled in her eyes. Now that she had heard her mother's voice, all of her pent-up emotions came flooding to the surface.

"Ànifa... it is you. Thank you."

"Mother! I'm so sorry. I did what I had to. You were possessed."

"I know this. I caused a lot of pain."

"It's okay, you can rest now," she said with a shake of her head.

"Ànifa!" Dasch cried as he rushed over to her. "Watch out! She's still—"

Gnusaramnii burst into a fit of maniacal laughter as Stella sprouted wings. She grabbed Ànifa and flew into the air.

"Ànifa!" her friends shouted after her.

"*I'll be fine. Take care, Theodore,*" she thought, as the monstrosity carried her away.

"*Ànifa!*" Theodore replied.

She felt the link between them sever.

"*Your friends cannot help you now,*" Gnusaramnii said inside her head.

"You're right. They can't. It's time for me to do this on my own," she said aloud.

Gnusaramnii laughed as it dropped her into an open field.

She landed hard in the grass. The fall knocked the wind out of her and it took a few moments for her to catch her breath and reorient herself. They were still on Yttendaus, far from Ytten. "You are weak. You will never defeat me! Now, witness my true power. Witness the most powerful being in this universe, Gnusaramnii!" her enemy shouted at her.

This is it, she thought. *This is the moment I've been waiting for. We're finally alone, just the two of us. I will not hold back any longer. This ends now!*

44

BATTLE FOR FREEDOM

Ànifa was on the ground, propped up on her elbows, looking into the sky above her. Dark clouds had gathered overhead while thunder boomed and rolled around them.

The monstrous Gnusaramnii hovered in the air above her, still using her queen mother's body as its vessel. Sprouting from her mother's body were wings and grotesque limbs that writhed and slithered in the air. One of the tentacle-like limbs took hold of the crystalized arrow buried in its stomach and tore it out in one quick movement. After that, it removed the arrow lodged in its chest and Gnusaramnii's vile laughter could be heard over the thunderous sky.

"Ha ha ha ha! I really have to thank you, Ànifa. Without you, none of this would be feasible!"

"I suppose I have to thank you too, then."

Gnusaramnii laughed. "What did I do to deserve your thanks? Using this vessel, I slew your royal father and corrupted everyone in Ytten."

"Thank you for taking us away from town," she said as she stood and brushed the loose grass off of her trenchdress. "I won't need to hold back now."

Gnusaramnii laughed. "Yes, come at me, you pesky flea!"

She smiled and burst into blue flames.

"Your vile reign ends now!" she shouted. Ànifa leaped into the air and flew toward Gnusaramnii, using her flames to propel her through the air.

"So reckless. You waste your life force with every effort," Gnusaramnii laughed as it easily dodged her attack. "You'll surely be dead by the end of this day!"

"I know. I've made my peace with my death. I think I've known for a while now that this is the only way I can defeat you. I am prepared to pay the price," she said softly as she floated above the ground.

"Ha ha ha... very good!" Gnusaramnii said as it swooped on her. She dodged, having anticipated the attack, and counterattacked with another crystallized arrow she'd prepared during their conversation.

She swung the arrow and hit true, piercing her mother's back, right where she guessed the spine might be. Gnusaramnii screamed in pain.

"You witch! I'll show you!"

Gnusaramnii plunged to the ground. From above, Ànifa threw another arrow, this time a normal arrow just for the sake of it.

She had nearly won. The moment of her victory was near.

Now that it was on the ground, her mother's body twitched violently as more limbs and appendages burst out of her body. Gnusaramnii was finally revealing its true self. Until now, Gnusaramnii had been controlling her mother from afar. Now it was coming, transitioning from one body to the next. And during this transition, Gnusaramnii was vulnerable.

She had to time her attack perfectly. She hovered in the air, still in the spot where she'd thrown her last arrow, and began to slowly descend as she prepared for the right moment.

Her mother's body became lost within the mass of wriggling, grotesque flesh. Gnusaramnii expanded in size, growing much larger than Stella. It was expanding still, growing to be three to four times the size of a Gnusar.

It looked much like a typical Gnusar, with only a few differences.

Its scales were thinner and seemed to be covered in a fine sheen of slime. As it grew and expanded, it rumbled with a deep laugh.

I'll shut that vile laugh up for good. For Eklatros!

A few moments before the last fragment of her mother's body became lost to the grotesque mass, she dove toward the ground. She energized her life force until her body turned into pure energy and flew into Gnusaramnii.

Rather than colliding with it, she passed into it and found herself in a dreamlike state.

This was the ethereal plane. She knew it well. She had been using it to communicate with Theodore and Joan telepathically, as well as the Ekataramn and Gnusaramnii. Now, she stood within its dark slushy mist facing Queen Stella.

"Mother!"

"Ànifa! What's going on? Where are we? I'm scared," Stella whispered.

"There's no need to be scared anymore. I'm here for you."

"That vile creature... it slipped into my mind... into my soul."

"You are not free of it yet. Come, take my hand."

Her mother grabbed her hand. It was cold and firm. In this place, her mother once again was in her own, true skin.

It was time.

She turned within herself and gathered the well of life force that remained within her. She took a deep breath—her last and final breath, and pushed her life force out of her body and sent it into her mother. Stella screamed in agony and bliss as she took her daughter's life force, absorbing it like a sponge. Upon injecting her life force into Queen Stella, Ànifa forced out Gnusaramnii completely, banishing it from her mother and from Eklatros.

Suddenly, there was nothing—just darkness. Cold, freezing darkness.

This is it... goodbye.

Quaant hovered in the air above the open field that had become the scene for the final battle. After Ànifa had been taken, Joan had commanded zir to follow her. Zie cared little for Ànifa, having recently absorbed all of her memories, but zie still cared about her well-being, so zie followed, discreetly. Zie had shrunk zirself to the size of a butterfly and remained far behind.

All Quaant could do was watch as Ànifa turned herself into a flaming javelin and pierced Gnusaramnii, who had morphed out of Stella's body. Zie held zir breath for a harrowing few seconds, waiting for something to happen.

Gnusaramnii glowed a bright blue. Its skin boiled as its hideous laugh turned into a twisted scream. Suddenly, Gnusaramnii exploded.

Quaant shielded zir eyes as a blob of steaming flesh smacked into zir chest. Zie expanded zirself to normal size, then brushed the slime off zir body. Zie looked at the ground and gasped in surprise.

For every elf Joan, Vesten, and Druder purified, it felt as if ten more corrupted appeared. There was no end in sight, and even with help from the purified elves, they were still at risk of being completely bowled over. The corrupted elves seemed to be getting stronger by the second. It was no longer a simple task to grab the hand of an elf to place it on the shield—every new gain was a battle in its own right.

Joan was exhausted, but there was no stopping now.

"Vesten!" she shouted as he fought against a particularly strong Gnureaver, his scimitar in his right hand and a dagger in his left. Vesten looked over at her, then took a hit directly in the face that sent him crumbling to the ground.

"*Vesten!*" She watched in horror as the Gnureaver balled its fists together and raised them high, preparing to land another heavy blow.

Suddenly, the Gnureaver froze. Joan looked around in bewilderment—all the corrupted elves had stopped fighting.

"What's going on?" a middle-aged male elf asked.

"Hold steady!" Druder shouted, his hand raised in the air. "Be prepared for anything!"

The corrupted elves stood in place for another few seconds, their eyes glazing over. Then they all dropped to the ground.

Joan looked around wildly, then spied Theodore, Dasch, and Cecil making their way over to them through the throng of bodies.

"It's Ànifa!" Theodore shouted. "She won! She defeated Gnusaramnii!"

"I knew she could do it!" Joan replied. She rushed to Vesten's side.

"Vesten! Are you okay? Vesten!" She shook him where he lay, her voice full of concern.

Vesten sputtered, then coughed as he opened his eyes.

"Oh shit, Joan? What happened?"

"I think you fainted. Can you stand?"

"Umm, fuck... aye, I think so. Just a little sore," Vesten said as he propped himself up with his elbows.

"Come on," Joan said, extending her hand to help him. Vesten took it and got to his feet.

"Hey!" Cecil exclaimed as he approached them. "I'm glad you're all okay!"

"Yes, same to you," Joan replied. "I'm going to go check on Ànifa."

"Do you know where she went?" Theodore asked.

"I had Quaant follow her after she was taken, and I have a general idea where they went," she replied.

"Great, which direction?" Cecil asked.

"About northwest. I'll report back if you're still here," Joan said, leaping into the air.

"Wait! Fuckin' take me with you!" Vesten shouted.

She spun around and scooped up Vesten.

"Let's fly!"

"Ah, well, they're gone," Theodore said.

"What was all that about?" a female elf asked Theodore as she sat up, clutching her head. "What's going on?"

All the recently possessed elves were starting to wake up, adding to the overall confusion.

"Right, we have some explaining to do. Well, now what's the best way to go about doing this?" Theodore muttered to himself. "Dasch?"

"I'm leaving this to you," Dasch replied.

"Oh, such help you are," he said sarcastically. "What about you then, Cecil?"

"Don't look at me," Cecil said. "I'm not the best at explaining things."

"Hey, Ànifa's friends!" came a familiar voice. Princess Nayeli, Princess Pearla, and a male elf he didn't recognize approached them.

"Princesses! How are you?" Theodore replied.

The crowd parted silently to clear a path as Princess Nayeli and Princess Pearla approached.

"We're a bit frazzled, but well," Princess Nayeli replied. "I think we'll all be okay. Now, we beg of you, please check on our sister."

"I'm glad to hear you're well," Theodore said. "But we don't really know where they went."

"Come with us, then. We'll enlist some aid for you," Princess Pearla said, grabbing him by the hand.

"Ah yes. But as to this woman's question, they deserve an explanation," he argued as he wormed out of Pearla's grasp and motioned to the elvish woman who had spoken to him earlier.

"Yes, I agree. And they will," Princess Nayeli said, then turned and faced the crowd. "Everyone, if I could spare a moment of your time. I will personally explain everything that has transpired soon. For now, please return to your homes. You need rest. We've all been through a great ordeal. We'll ring the summoning bells when we are ready to provide you with a thorough explanation."

"Thank you, Princess. We will await your call," an elderly male elf said, then turned to Theodore. "Thank you... thank you all."

"We're just doing our job to protect Eklatros," Cecil replied.

"Thank you, saviors of Eklatros!" a woman shouted.

"Hail, Saviors of Eklatros!" came a shout.

"Hail! Saviors of Eklatros!"

Within moments, the entire crowd was chanting their praises.

"Ah, well, this is unexpected," Cecil murmured to Theodore.

"Agreed. I don't really know what to do with myself now," Theodore replied.

"Yeah, this is awkward," Cecil said.

"Thank you! All of you!" Princess Nayeli said loudly, raising her voice to be heard above the clamor of the crowd. At this, this crowd quieted. "Now, our Saviors of Eklatros need your help! I call upon the aid of the angels. Those of you that are near, please, come hither!"

"Keep an eye out for Quaant," Joan said to Vesten, holding onto him as she flew over the outskirts of the floating island. "I'll scan the ground for Ànifa."

"Right. Sounds good... babe," Vesten replied.

"Don't... don't call me that. I think I'm going to have to teach you a lesson before all this is over."

"Oh yeah? What kind of lesson? A kinky lesson?"

"Just keep an eye out for Quaant," Joan replied with a smirk.

"I am! I can multitask. Now—oh shit, wait! It's Quaant! Over there!" Vesten said, pointing to the faerie as zie darted back and forth nervously in the air. When zie spotted them, zie hurried their way.

"Joan, vulgar human! Come now, with haste!"

"What the fuck did you just call me?" Vesten said under his breath, prompting Joan to chuckle softly to herself.

"Quaant, where is she? Where's Ànifa?" she asked.

"Just down here, come on!" Quaant said, urging them to follow. "I'm glad you're here. I had no idea what to do."

As Joan followed the babbling faerie to the ground, she saw what zie meant.

Joan landed on the ground and let Vesten go, squeezing his hand before letting him step away. They stood next to a weeping Queen Stella as she clutched Ànifa's body.

"My Queen, what happened?" Joan asked.

"My—my dear Ànifa!" Queen Stella wailed. "She's gone!"

"What? She's dead?" Vesten exclaimed. "Fuck no. She can't be. I don't believe it."

"Who are you now?" Queen Stella asked Vesten harshly through her tears.

"My Queen, this is Vesten, a companion of Ànifa's. He helped us on our journey across Eklatros. But the Princess... is she really..." Joan trailed off, unable to finish her sentence.

"Yes... she's gone," Queen Stella sobbed.

"What the—" Vesten said as he approached Ànifa.

"Vesten," Joan said, placing a hand on his right shoulder. "I'll check on her myself."

She knelt and placed her hand on Ànifa's forehead. It was cold and lifeless. Her essence had left her—her once vibrant hair was now pure white.

"My Queen, how did this happen?" she asked.

"Ànifa, my gracious daughter... she saved me. I was... I had been consumed by that evil monster, and just when I thought my end had come, there was Ànifa. And she... she gave me her life's essence. It is only because of her sacrifice that I still live."

"Gnusaramnii... did she defeat it?" Joan asked.

"I believe she did. I feel no lingering trace of Gnusaramnii."

"I saw the whole thing," Quaant said. "Ànifa... she became a flying torch and flew into Gnusaramnii just as it was coming into its true form. Then Gnusaramnii started glowing blue, and then it exploded. It was really gross. But after that... where Gnusaramnii had been, were Queen Stella and Princess Ànifa."

"So, she won, then. She won, sacrificing herself in the process," Joan said slowly, piecing it all together.

"But she's Ànifa! I don't... I fucking don't believe it!"

"Vesten, it's true. She's gone," Joan said, embracing Vesten in a hug. He cursed softy to himself as he held her tightly.

A few moments later, four angels arrived, each holding on to someone. They landed in the grass next to them. Joan's sisters had arrived—Beatrice, Isabel, Priscilla, and Regina—carrying her new family. Theodore, Cecil, Dasch, and Druder each broke free of their respective angel's grasp.

"Ànifa!" Theodore shouted as he rushed toward them.

Joan released Vesten and turned to face Theodore.

"I'm sorry," was all Joan could say to the wizard. She turned to her angelic sisters. Each wore armor similar to her own.

"All of you... thank you for bringing them here."

"It wasn't a problem, really," Isabel replied, shaking her head.

"Speak for yourself," Priscilla said harshly. "I'm going to stink—"

"Shush, sister, you forget yourself," Isabel interrupted as she brushed a lock of brown hair out of her face.

"We should return to Ytten. There's nothing more we can do here," Beatrice commanded.

"My Queen, do you wish to return with us?" Regina asked.

"No, I wish to stay here with my daughter."

"I understand, Your Grace. We'll be waiting for your return," Beatrice said.

The four angels flew off together, leaving the group with Queen Stella.

"Ànifa..." Dasch said softly. "I had been hoping to talk with her, after all this was over."

"As did we all, my friend," Cecil said. "She brought us all together... united us so we could all aid in this victory."

"Yes, that's right," Joan said. "This victory—it belongs to all of us. Ànifa... she didn't want us to grieve. She wanted us to live and to be happy. To see this new world forward, together as one."

"Together as one..." Queen Stella repeated. "Oh, Joan, I've been such a fool. It's all my fault."

"My Queen, nothing is your fault. Of that much I can assure you. Ànifa acted on her own accord. She saved you. Be thankful for that," Joan said.

"I did not deserve to be saved," Queen Stella moaned.

"Of course you did. Everyone deserves a second chance," Joan said softly.

"Everyone here... did you all help Ànifa?"

"Yes. I've been with her since the beginning," Theodore said.

"And I'm only here on your orders," Druder said.

"I'm sorry, who are you?" Queen Stella asked. "I apologize, I remember little from before."

"Don't worry about that now," Joan said. "We should get back to the palace. Everyone's waiting for us."

"Yes... I suppose we should. I don't think I can face everyone just yet, though."

"It's okay. I understand. Besides, you have the walk over there to decide," Joan said.

"Right, yes. That's true," Queen Stella said.

"Before we go, I just ask one thing from everyone," Dasch said.

"What is it?" Cecil said.

"In my time, when a close friend perished in battle, we had a tradition. Without disturbing where they lay, we would recite a prayer to help ease their passage onto the next plane of existence."

"That sounds nice," Joan replied. "Could you start us off, Dasch?"

Dasch cleared his throat and began. "Repeat after me. Mother Eklatros, who binds us all, blesséd be thy name..."

Joan smiled to herself. She knew the prayer well. Though her version differed slightly from Dasch's, she repeated it in full.

"Mother Eklatros, who binds us all, blesséd be thy name. When our time has passed, to your abode do we return. Forgive us in our misdeeds and praise us in our successes. Judge us fairly, oh holy Eklatros. Only you see us for who we truly are. Our loved one returns to you on this day. May you help grant their soul passage so they can achieve glory in their death, now and forever."

When the prayer ended, no one spoke. They wept together, and then gathered themselves. Joan gently picked up Ànifa, taking her out of her mother's arms. She began leading the way back to Ytten.

Ànifa... my dearest friend, she thought. *Fare you well into your next existence. I pray we meet again someday... perhaps in another life.*

45

BATTLE FOR LIFE

Joan solemnly carried Ànifa's body back to Ytten. There was little conversation to be had on the way back. No one was in the mood to talk. Once they returned to the palace, Joan led the party to the spiritual attendant. She gave Ànifa's hand one last squeeze before she laid her body on a table. Theodore, Cecil, and the rest of the group gave Ànifa their final goodbyes. A prompt from the spiritual attendant reminded her to empty Ànifa's pockets. Joan handed Theodore the miniaturized backpack while she took Ànifa's bow and quiver. When she found the letter she had sent with the bow, she held it close and breathed in its scent. No one was ready to say goodbye, but the spiritual attendant quickly ushered them out of his space. Not even Queen Stella could convince the spiritual attendant to give them more time with Ànifa.

Upon leaving, Queen Stella led them all to her private chambers. Before they could settle down, Queen Stella ordered them to change out of their soiled clothing and into fresh, temporary clothing so their regular outfits could be washed.

With that taken care of, they gathered together in Queen Stella's private quarters with Princess Nayeli and Princess Pearla. Queen Stella thanked each of them personally by handing out unique rewards. She gave Theodore a holy relic of the great war—King Waesjeon's golden arrow—to thank him for being the first official member of Ànifa's team. For Sir Cecil Kloud, she decreed that all residents of Yttendaus were now members of the Guild for Eklatros and gave him the entrance fees for each and every new member. The koda was stored in a magical coin purse. She gave Dasch the crown jewel, the only surviving piece of King Waesjeon's crown, in thanks for his service, both in the past and the present. For Vesten, she promised that her best architects and engineers would construct him a new ship. In response, Vesten argued he didn't want to part from *West Wind*, to which it was then decided that they would simply enhance and fortify *West Wind*. Vesten agreed on the condition that he would supervise. As for Quaant and Druder, Queen Stella promoted them to each be the official ambassadors of their clans.

Finally, Joan was officially given her own living quarters in the palace, along with a new wardrobe and personal attendants. Before, Joan had lived in Ànifa's quarters; the rest of the angels lived outside of the palace. While Joan wasn't sure what her future held, she graciously accepted the invitation.

Theodore carefully placed King Waesjeon's golden arrow and crown jewel into the backpack. Once the gifts had been handed out, Queen Stella sent everyone away except for Joan and the princesses. When only the four remained, Stella officially handed the queenship over to Nayeli. While she wanted respite from her responsibilities, she also knew that she was no longer fit to be queen. Plus, Eklatros was beginning a new era, and it made sense to usher in this new era with a new queen.

Nayeli humbly accepted, then turned to Joan. As a new queen, she would need all the help she could get, so she wanted to make Joan her chancellor. Joan smiled and accepted the offer.

Queen Nayeli stood in the Grand Hall and awkwardly adjusted the silver-blue tiara atop her head and brushed her dark green hair out of her face. Now that she was Queen, Nayeli was able to wear her hair however she wished, so she decided to wear it down. It nearly reached her waist. She took a moment to scan the crowd and saw many familiar faces. She took a deep breath and smiled.

"Citizens of Yttendaus—my friends. I have known many of you for as long as I can remember. And none of us have ever had to face anything of that magnitude before. As your new queen, I can assure you all that the threat has passed."

Upon revealing her queenship, gasps of surprise and murmurs erupted from the crowd. Queen Nayeli raised her palm into the air and the crowd quieted.

"I know you all have many questions for me, and I will do my best to address each in time. Understand that while I am your new queen, my royal mother is still alive and well.

"It is only thanks to my dear sister's valiant sacrifice that my mother still lives. You see, some time ago, Stella fell under the influence of an evil entity known as Gnusaramnii. This is the same vile creature that attacked Eklatros all those years ago during the Dark War. Under its command, Stella committed unspeakable acts— including murdering my father, King Vyereth."

The crowd erupted in shouts and cries of pain. She raised her palm into the air again.

"Please understand Stella had no control over her actions. She passed the queenship to me to atone for her actions.

"My sister, Ànifa—Princess Ànifa Tataluynnia Ekataramnii—gave up her life to defeat the vile Gnusaramnii and banish it from Eklatros. All of us owe her our lives, for without her, we all would have perished.

"While Gnusaramnii may be gone from our world, we fear it will be back, and soon. We must remain resilient and vigilant.

"And it will be I, Queen Nayeli Autumnia Ekataramnii, who will lead us forward together in this new age. The Ekataramn are awakened. Eklatros is reborn. Our world will never be the same again."

Joan stood behind Queen Nayeli as she made her inaugural

speech from the throne. To her left stood Theodore, his robes washed and pressed, and to her right was Sir Cecil Kloud, his armor spotless and shimmering. Dasch, looking immaculate in fresh green elvish robes, stood on the other side of Theodore, while Vesten stood on the other side of Cecil. Vesten's green dragon vest was now spotless and accented his full red beard. Druder and Quaant stood nearby. The entire population of Ytten stood in the Great Hall of Yttendaus before them.

As Queen Nayeli finished her speech, the crowd erupted in cheers and applause. Joan curtsied along with Queen Nayeli and the rest of her party. Even without Ànifa, they were still bound together.

"Before we move on, please understand that while today's ceremony is in honor of Ànifa, we will hold a proper ceremony for King Vyereth in due time. Now, everyone, bow your heads for a moment of silence. I have spoken for long enough. It is time that we pay our respects to my dear sister, Ànifa, and all of those who gave their lives yesterday for Eklatros' prosperity."

After a minute of silence, Queen Nayeli silently made her way forward, down the steps of the throne and through the crowd. Joan followed, and the party fell in behind her. As they walked through the crowd, those they passed fell in behind them.

It was tradition to hold funerals outdoors to ensure the soul of the deceased could find its way back to Eklatros. As Queen Nayeli led the crowd outside, a string quartet played the traditional royal send-off song, a harrowing and solemn tune. They entered the town square— the same place where the corrupted elves had gathered. The string quartet was set up beside Ànifa's casket. On the other side of the casket was a podium, where former Queen Stella stood, ready to oversee the next phase of the ceremony.

Queen Nayeli led them to Ànifa's open casket. It was time for every citizen to pass by the casket and pay their respects. While they honored Ànifa, Joan and the rest of the group gathered alongside Stella on the stage. Even Quaant and Druder, who both initially refused, were coaxed onto the stage with them, for they were now official members of Ànifa's team.

Joan stood between Vesten and Theodore. She was discreetly holding Vesten's hand as they watched the elves pass by the open casket. Privately, he had told her that he was going home after the ceremony, because his home was where his cousin, Patsy, was. Joan couldn't deny him this, of course. She had only just met Vesten and had heard of his search for his lost cousin. Besides, she shouldn't have feelings for a human, especially not one as crude and vulgar as Vesten. But he was sweet and caring, and she couldn't help the fact that she enjoyed carrying him as she flew. And yet she was happy for him; happy he had found his family.

She subconsciously squeezed his hand, and he gave her a squeeze back. She smiled softly to herself.

From the podium, Stella cleared her throat and addressed the crowd. The music faded, and then stopped altogether once she began speaking.

"Everyone... thank you all for being here today to pay your respects to Princess Ànifa. Now, I know I don't deserve to be speaking to you all like this. I don't deserve to face any of you. I wronged you all. I tarnished my rule by even allowing Gnusaramnii into my mind. I want to tell you all that it happened unconsciously. And yet a part of me wanted its power. I regret that now, with all I have left to give.

"Your new Queen Nayeli urged me onto this stage. And since I stand here, I will share with you these words:

"Ànifa was not my true daughter. She was brought to me as an infant by Thedro and Heira, your local bakers. They found the child alone under a tree and brought her to Vyereth and me. Our own children were infants at the time, and so we raised Ànifa as if she were our own child.

"Yes, it is true that we gave her a different upbringing than our other daughters. We didn't know where she came from, and so we were cautious. But I loved her, deeply and dearly. She often surprised and delighted me in a myriad of unexpected ways. She was kind and generous and was quick to make good friends, as you all can see from everyone that shares this stage with me.

"Ànifa saved my life. I deserved to die, and yet she saved me by sacrificing herself. I vow here and now to you all that I will spend the rest of my days honoring Ànifa's sacrifice by atoning for my misdeeds. That is why I had to step down from being your queen. This is a personal journey I must take, alone.

"I now pass the podium over to the first of our special speakers, Sorcerer Caldwell of Ajenti."

Stella moved aside and allowed Theodore to step forward.

Theodore cleared his throat, then began speaking. "First of all, I want to thank you for even allowing me on stage. As I understand it, we are the first humans to step foot on Yttendaus, so I thank you for allowing us to stay.

"One of your own was a dear friend of mine. Ànifa truly meant a lot to me. Not only was she bright and kind, but she had a way about her that made you want to follow her. When I first met her, she only knew her name. She knew nothing of who she was or where she came from. But she certainly wasn't lost. In fact, I would say that upon finding me hiding in that mound of snow, she found herself. It was as if she knew that we'd become friends. She was my twin wand.

"Anyway, while she didn't know much about herself, she was a quick learner, and soon discovered her true powers after her friend Charlotte was abducted by a Gnusar.

"Traveling with her, learning from her, and growing with her was a blessing and a gift. She changed my life for the better.

"I love you, Ànifa. I'll never forget you," he said, choking on his last words as he stepped away from the podium.

Cecil awkwardly made his way to the podium. "Uh, yeah, hello. I'm Cecil Kloud, knight and guildmaster of The Guild for Eklatros... of which you are all now a part of. Officially. I'm sorry I'm not very good at this," he mumbled, looking down. After a moment, he looked at the crowd. "Ànifa made me into a different person—a better person. Back when I was in exile with Theodore, I drank far too much. But once I met Ànifa, all of that changed. I mean, the last heavy night of drinking I had was the night I met Ànifa. That night... I'll never forget that night. That was when I was invited into her fold. It felt good to be needed and to have a bigger purpose. I mean, Theo and I had been gallivanting off looking for the Great Barriers, getting nowhere, mind you, until Ànifa showed up. And shortly after that, we got a map that led us to each of them.

"Without her, we never would have won. We relied heavily on her powers and skills throughout our battles. I call myself a knight, and yes, I am a strong fighter. But I'm nothing compared to Ànifa. She was a wonderful leader and an even better friend. Thank you, Ànifa, for without you, our world would be lost.

"Henceforth, the Guild for Eklatros will be dedicated to Ànifa's memory!" Cecil said, raising his fist into the air. "Ànifa, you return home now."

Cecil stepped away from the podium, allowing Dasch to step forward.

"If not for Ànifa, I would still be held in repose in my underground prison. Her presence awakened me and allowed me to atone for my sins in my previous life. I will miss her dearly," Dasch finished, then stepped away.

It was Vesten's turn. Joan squeezed his hand one last time before she let go. Vesten wrung his wrists together as he stepped forward.

"I guess I don't really know where to... where to begin. I'm Vesten. I'm sorry if... if my speech seems broken and disjointed as I restrain myself.

"Sorry... I'm just nervous is all. You see, I had resigned myself to a life of solitude before all of this. I was searching for a lost family member, but I think I had more or less given up on that. I was just coasting through life... but then I saw Ànifa. At the time, Theodore was injured and was being carried by Dasch, my companion who spoke before me. Cecil was there too, and there was just... just something different about them. It wasn't like me, but I had an urge to help them. One of their own was hurt, and they didn't have anywhere to go. So, I took them in. And they've been my newfound fuckin' family ever since. Sorry... I let one slip. But it's... it's true. Ànifa is my family, and I will miss her as such. If not for her... I don't think I ever would have been reunited with my cousin. Ànifa made everything better. Especially when it came to riding on the back of a giant spider. Or a wyvern. Or any of the gods and creatures we were forced to partner with.

"It was certainly a journey. I am so thankful to have been a part of her party, and I am grateful for your attention as us strange humans tell you about someone you must have freakin' revered. I wish I could have seen her as a princess, as she was before all of this. She was special. That's for... that's for sure."

Vesten stepped off stage. It was Joan's turn, and she brushed Vesten's arm as she passed by.

"As you all may know, I am Joan de Ligtheramnii, and I was Ànifa's guardian angel. I was by her side day after day since she was young. Remember how scornful you all were of me back then? No elf had ever received a guardian angel before. Angels were supposed to keep to themselves, only checking in on important holidays and events.

"And yet, Queen Stella and King Vyereth had come to me with their newfound child, asking me for my assistance. Well, they didn't come to me directly, but to the angels. I was the only one willing to help back then. The first time I laid eyes on Ànifa, I knew she was special. So, I agreed to be her guardian protector.

"The day Ànifa fell from Yttendaus was one of my darkest days up to that point. I was completely lost. I wanted to help, but I was instructed to let her be. She had to find her own way, the King and Queen told me. I was only to intervene if she was in any real danger. And that's what I did. I saved her and her companions from certain death.

"I saved her then, although I could not protect her. In the end, Ànifa made her own journey. She set her own path and did what she believed was the right thing to do. We must all respect that decision and honor her for her ultimate sacrifice.

"Ànifa, I love you, and I will carry your memory forward into the future," Joan said and stepped off the podium.

Vesten's hand slipped into hers the moment she returned. She smiled and squeezed his hand in response. She could feel how quickly his heart was beating—he was still anxious from speaking earlier. She sent him her soothing, healing energy so his nerves could calm.

Taking her place at the podium was Druder.

She only half listened to his brief speech. Quaant finished the round of eulogies and then they all said their final goodbyes before Stella closed the casket.

The spiritual attendant made his way through the crowd, slowly wheeling Ànifa's casket toward the palace. Stella, Joan and the others followed. Unlike before, the crowd wouldn't follow them back to the palace. Now it was time to lay Ànifa's body to rest in the palace crypts, alongside the former kings and queens of Yttendaus. In a few days, King Vyereth would join her.

Only the spiritual attendant and members of the royal family were allowed in the crypts. Joan could accompany Ànifa no further.

Goodbye, my dear friend.

The party gathered together for the final time in the palace atrium, surrounded by the statues of former kings and queens. For the first time, Joan felt like an outsider looking in at the majesty of an unknown culture. Nothing would ever be the same after today.

"That was a beautiful ceremony," Theodore was saying to the group. "I felt like I rambled on for a bit, though."

"You all pretty much did," Dasch retorted.

"I'm sorry that all of our speeches couldn't be less than fifty words like yours was," Cecil joked. "But what are we doing now?"

"Tomorrow, I will lead a party to see Mau, the ancient one. She's the one you need to talk to in order to be able to see Tyrona again," Joan explained.

"Tyrona!" Theodore exclaimed. "Finally I'll be able to see her again."

"Theoretically, of course," Dasch said.

"No matter what the chances are, I'll take them," Theodore said. "I'll search across the universe for her if I have to."

Cecil placed his hand on Theodore's right shoulder. "I'm with you, my friend. Until the end, I'll travel with you."

"What about your fuckin' guild?" Vesten asked.

"The guild can take care of itself, I'm sure. What about you, Vesten? What are your plans?" Cecil asked.

"I'm fuckin' going back to Sathon tonight. I've already arranged it with that angel Isabel. She'll be taking me down there in a few hours. I have plans to meet up with Patsy at the Sathon Inn."

"I understand. You will be missed, my foul-mouthed friend," Cecil said as he walked over and embraced him in a hug. Vesten awkwardly hugged the full-armored knight back.

"That's it. You, Vesten. I'll leave the Guild for Eklatros in your hands," Cecil said as he broke away from Vesten.

"I don't know the first fuckin' thing about running a damn guild," Vesten replied as he scratched at his beard.

"I don't either."

"Also, I'm not a knight. Are you sure it's okay?"

"Of course it is. I'm the guildmaster. I get to appoint anyone I want to in my stead. And there's no other person I'd rather pass this title off to. Of course, when I return, I'll be the guildmaster once again."

"Oh, fuck yeah, it's yours. I'll just be filling in," Vesten said.

"So, you agree, then?" Cecil asked as he searched his trousers for the coin purse.

"Fuck yeah, I agree. I suppose I can always ask Patsy to help me out too."

"That's the spirit," Cecil said with a big smile. He handed Vesten the coin purse. "Thank you, Vesten. Take the koda Queen Stella gave me. I'm not going to need it where I'm going. Now, what about the rest of you? Who else is coming with us? Dasch?"

Dasch coughed, then cleared his throat. "Yes. I will accompany you all. With our task now complete, I am simply a man out of time. I do not belong here."

"Right, I get that," Cecil said. "Great, that's three of us so far. Joan?"

"My job is to lead you to Mau. I cannot go any further than that. It is now my duty to support Queen Nayeli."

"I understand," Theodore said. "I'll tell Tyrona you said 'hullo.' Same with you, Vesten."

"Fuckin' A. Thanks," Vesten replied.

"So then, that leaves the two of you," Cecil said, turning to Quaant and Druder, who had both been silent.

Quaant shrugged as zie flapped around in the air. "Yeah, I appreciate you all including me in on this, but I was never part of your crew. Besides, I'm fae. I may not be like the rest of my kind, but I'm still fae. Yttendaus is my home. I will never leave this place."

Druder nodded. "I feel similarly. I don't belong in your group. And yet, if you'll have me, I would be honored to join you."

"Of course we'll have you," Cecil replied. "And you are one of us. Same with you, Quaant. We would never have completed our mission if not for both of you."

"Right. You both never met Tyrona—she was only with us for a short time. Even though she's not with us now, she's still a member of our party. You both are as much a part of our group as she is," Theodore said.

"What happened to her?" Druder asked.

As Theodore began to tell Druder and Quaant about Tyrona, Joan pulled Vesten aside and hugged him.

"Are you sure you don't want me to take you to Sathon?" she asked. "I'm sure the Queen would allow it."

"She might, yeah. But, shit, if you took me... it would be too much of a temptation to stay with you. I don't want to leave you, Joan. But..."

"I understand. Your family is important to you. You're a good man."

"I'm sorry, Joan. I'll miss you the most," Vesten said, squeezing her tighter.

"You'll be in my thoughts," she said, holding back her tears. There really was no reason for it, but she loved this man. "Besides, we'll see each other again one day. Of that, I can be sure. I'm sure Queen Nayeli will allow me to visit."

"I fuckin' hope so," Vesten replied softly in her embrace. "I really do."

She pulled away from Vesten and looked at the others who were engrossed in Theodore's story. She let him finish, then said, "So, it'll be the four of you, then—Cecil, Theodore, Dasch, and Druder. Meet me here tomorrow morning at sunrise, and I'll lead you to Mau."

"Sounds good to me. Tyrona, here I come!" Theodore pumped his fist into the air in excitement.

She smiled. A handmaiden came to fetch Joan. Queen Nayeli needed her. She apologized to everyone and said her final goodbye to Vesten.

And so, just like that, our party splits up, she thought. *We were all bound to go our separate ways eventually. Best of luck to you all—Cecil, Theodore, Dasch, and Druder. You're continuing the mission we started, and for that, I truly commend you all.*

46

BATTLE FOR EKLATROS

Vesten held on tightly as Isabel carried him off of Yttendaus. Now that Yttendaus was awake, the Great Barrier surrounding the floating island had weakened considerably. It hadn't gone away completely like the other Ekataramn—there was still a thin barrier of fast-moving air that generated its own electric current. Isabel had no problem flying through the barrier, but Vesten nearly got thrown out of the angel's arms. Luckily, Isabel had caught him in time before he was thrown to his death.

Being carried by Isabel didn't feel the same as when Joan had carried him. Joan had been much gentler, but firm at the same time. When Joan had been holding him, it was as if they had been embraced in a long hug. Isabel held him more like a sack of potatoes —he was just cargo to her—but Isabel had been the only angel willing to take him to see Patsy. She was even the one that arranged their reunion.

Once they neared Sathon, his ride became calmer, and he could speak to Isabel.

"Hey, thanks again for taking me. I really fuckin' appreciate it."

"For me, it is no problem. I find your kind fascinating, whereas our leader, Juliana, doesn't want anything to do with your kind."

"I also got that vibe from your pal Beatrice," Vesten replied. He used his free hand to wipe a bug off of his goggles.

"Yes, Beatrice and Juliana share much of the same beliefs. Both of them have essentially cast Joan from our clan, simply because she is independent from the rest of us."

"So other angels really aren't guardians or protectors then?"

"It's... complicated. Our role is to be the protectors of all life on Eklatros, but it is angelic law to not interfere with the daily goings on of its citizens. Joan has broken that law many times over."

"You must be breaking that law too, then," Vesten said, as they approached the ground. They were just outside Sathon. It had been years since Vesten had been to Sathon. He had only visited the small town a handful of times after he had been separated from Patsy.

Now, as they approached, Vesten could see Sathon was still in shambles after the battle that Dale, Briggs, and the others had told them about. Some houses were completely leveled to the ground, while other structures only had minor damage. Amazingly, the only building that looked relatively unscathed was the largest in the village—the Sathon Inn and Pub.

"Yes, in a way I am," Isabel answered as she landed in an open grassy field. "We're here."

"Thank you, Isabel," Vesten said as he stepped out of her arms and took off his goggles. "Oh, right, Queen Stella... well, the former queen before she stepped down... she fuckin' promised modifications for *West Wind*. Will someone be in touch with me about that, or how is that all going to work?"

"If that is the case, it's likely the crew will be waiting for you upon your return to your ship."

"Aye, thank you, Isabel. I... take care. Give Joan my best."

"I will," Isabel said as she turned and looked at the sky. She opened her wings, preparing to take off, then looked at him. "You know, I can tell why she loves you. You're a kind soul, Vesten, and a true man to be able to steal the heart of an angel."

Before he could reply, Isabel leaped into the air and flew away.

"She... she fuckin' loves me, does she?" he said to himself. "Joan, I love you too. I hope that you're right. I hope we'll see each other again."

"... and then Money and Annalyse just swooped in from behind, catching the... what the fuck are they called again? Gnusar? They caught it off guard, with Money burying the handle of his ice pick into its back, and tore it clean open. Hey, world to Vesten, are you listening?"

Vesten glanced from the table and looked at Patsy. They sat together, alone in a calm corner of the Sathon Pub. According to Patsy, the entire village of Sathon had been engrossed in a celebration that had gone on for days. The bar was quite rowdy at the moment as a pair of intoxicated men sang horribly at the top of their lungs while spilling beer all over themselves. Surrounding the pair were other men, whooping and hollering along in a broken, off-beat tune. A few tables away from them sat Dale, Tushar, and the rest of Patsy's crew.

He looked at Patsy apologetically. It was true that he'd been barely listening to her. There was a lot going on in his head.

"Yeah, fuck. I'm sorry Patsy. I'm happy to be with you again, I really am. This is what I've been wanting for so fuckin' long now—to be reunited with you. And yet, I left my companions behind, to be here with you."

"What do you mean? I'm sorry, I've been commanding the conversation this whole fuckin' time about stories from the battle. What's going on with Ànifa and everybody else?"

"Ànifa... she's fucking gone. She sacrificed herself to kill that Gnusaramnii monster and save her mother."

"What? Are you shitting me? She's dead?" Patsy was aghast.

"Yeah, Patsy. She's gone, and some of the others are continuing on to the next fuckin' part of the journey. But I chose to stay behind so I could be with you."

"That's... that's sweet, Vesten. I'm happy we can be together again too. I mean, fuck, I was looking for you too. Everywhere we went, I would keep an eye out for you. I've wanted you back in my life, but I never meant for you to abandon your friends."

"No, it's okay. I mean, fuck, they're on their way to a different world. I don't want to leave Eklatros. Besides, I fought long and hard to protect our planet. I'm not about to leave it."

"Yeah, I don't know what the fuck you mean by that—going to a different world and leaving Eklatros and all—so I guess I don't blame you. I didn't realize that anyone could even leave Eklatros."

"I've learned a lot about Eklatros on my journey—a lot of knowledge I never would have known. I mean, in a way, Eklatros is a living creature—we're just all living on it. Sorry, I don't mean to be getting too fuckin' deep into this shit right now. I just want to forget about it all right now and be with you. I'm sorry about not really listening to you earlier."

"Vesten, it's okay. You've been through a lot. You can rant to me all you want," Patsy said.

"I know. But right now, I think I need your help with something else. So, Cecil kinda made me the guildmaster of his guild. And I don't know how to be a fuckin' guildmaster."

Patsy laughed, annoying him to the core. "What is so fucking funny?" he asked.

"It's just... you, a guildmaster? That's fucking rich. Everything you've done lately has been insane, so hey, why not be a guildmaster while you're at it."

"Yeah, fuckin' right? It's been crazy, that's for sure. But, Patsy, how 'bout it? Let's travel across Eklatros and preach the guild's philosophy. With your crew and my ship, *West Wind*, we can continue to make this planet better. Our fight for Eklatros is over. Now it's time for this world to be enlightened."

"You're serious, aren't you? I mean, hey, why the fuck not? It'll give us something to do. Which actually reminds me—I meant to tell you about the World Summit."

"Oh, that fuckin' thing? Dale and Tushar filled us in when we met them in Pikkul Harbor. Sounds like all they did was talk about us."

"Right, and I was on that fuckin' stage telling the entire room about you. It was pretty fuckin' weird. But that's all beside the point. That guy—Rear Admiral Briggs—he was there with us, partaking in the revelries. I was with him this morning. He was saying goodbye, ready to return to Port Columbo, when a message arrived for him. Apparently, the summit was a fuckin' disaster. It highlighted just how unprepared we are for something like this and how broken our world has become. And so, after it was discovered that Sathon was under attack, those that remained behind continued talking. They decided they are going to take drastic steps to create a centralized government. The letter didn't say much more than that, and they were calling back those of great influence to help create this new world government. The message was supposed to be confidential, but Briggs wanted you and—you to know."

"Fuck, really? A world government? Shit, six months ago I would have argued against such a thing. But now it makes sense. Perhaps things would have been different..." Vesten said, trailing off.

"Right, that's the whole fuckin' thing. Three entire towns have been wiped off the face of the planet, and Sathon was almost the fourth. Hundreds of people have died at the hands of those disgusting monsters and thousands more have been displaced. If there had been a centralized government in place, able to launch a quick militarized response, then maybe Kalah, Seaside, and Runti would still be thriving today."

"Who knows? But hey, that only makes me more fuckin' enthusiastic about our new mission. Maybe the Guild for Eklatros can be that response team. If we can set up an outpost in each town, then every town would have, at the very least, some sort of defense system in place."

"Alright, that sounds good to me. Let's fuckin' do it then, cousin!" Patsy exclaimed.

"Great! First stop, Fort Turner, to let them in on our plan. If we're to do this, they need to know."

"I agree. Let's finish our drinks and get the fuck out of here," Patsy said, clinking her mug against Vesten's as she took a deep drink.

"Hey, let's get your crew over here. This is a celebration, isn't it? I say one more round with everyone, and then we get the fuck out of here."

"Fine by me!" Patsy said, raising her empty mug in the air.

Vesten took a deep drink. The cold ale was delicious and refreshing.

Thank you, Ànifa, he thought. *Thank you for showing me the way, for making me a better person. I owe all that I am now to you. Cheers to you.*

Cecil followed Joan through the thick forest. They once again had to pass through the Ytten Forest, but this time they were in a completely different area than before. Here, there were no signs of animal life. The five of them were the only souls around.

"This place... it feels strange to me," Cecil muttered.

"Yes, this area is protected by a powerful spell, similar to that of the Great Barriers. And yet, what we approach is not an Ekataramn," Joan replied.

"Where are we going?" Theodore asked.

"Remember when Ànifa was speaking with Yttendaus and we were listening from the ethereal plane? Yttendaus explained to Ànifa about the origins of Gnusaramnii, and how it once belonged to a species called the Lakinceitians," Joan said.

"Yeah, I remember all of that," Theodore replied.

"Me too," Cecil added. "I was able to listen to that part, at least, before it got all fuzzy."

"The entity known as Mau, as Yttendaus explained, is also an ancient Lakinceitian," Joan said. "And she guards an important relic that only few know about."

"What relic? And how is Mau here, on Eklatros?" Theodore asked.

"She'll explain all that you need to know once you arrive," Joan answered.

"Hmm, I do not like this. I sense danger approaching," Druder said.

"I feel it as well," Dasch replied, placing his hand on the hilt of his sword. He was back to wearing his dark green robe that he had obtained in Ajenti.

"Please refrain from drawing your weapons," Joan said, turning back to them. "What you sense is simply the barrier that we pass through. It seeks to deceive you and ward you away. Ignore it. Just follow me and everything will soon make sense."

Cecil followed Joan silently, fighting the urge to run. Sure, he felt imminent danger, but it was more than that. Voices whispered to him from the fringes of his mind. It didn't matter that they weren't saying anything intelligible; it was simply the presence of these voices that haunted him. He kept his mouth shut and trudged on.

It didn't take long for them to reach their destination—a small, shrunken tree.

"This is it. This is where I must leave you all," Joan told them.

"This tree? Do we... do we speak to it?" Theodore asked.

"Have patience. Mau knows of our presence. She'll reveal herself when the time is right."

"Understood," Dasch grumbled.

"Everyone... it's been an honor, truly," Joan said to her friends. "Traveling with you all has been one of the highlights of my long life. I'll never forget any of you."

"We'll see each other again, though, right?" Cecil asked.

"That is not certain," Joan said, shaking her head. "There are no promises, fair knight. Your future is highly dependent on many factors."

"Right, and anything could happen at any point in time. I understand that, my angelic friend." Theodore walked over to Joan and held out his hand. "It's been a pleasure. Thank you for everything and I'll see you when I see you."

Joan clasped Theodore's hand within both of her own. "Thank you, Theodore, for being there for Ànifa at the very beginning."

Cecil approached Joan and said, "I'll miss you, Joan. Take care."

"You as well, Sir Cecil. Lead the party well in Ànifa's stead."

"Me? You want me to lead?" he asked as he pointed at his chest and took a step back. "I'm no leader."

"Sir Cecil, you are and always have been a leader. You are the guildmaster of the Guild for Eklatros. You need more confidence in yourself," Joan told him.

"Yeah, you're right. I'll do my best," Cecil replied with a firm nod. "Thanks, Joan. Thanks for saving our lives back then, and thanks for continuing to support us. We never would have made it without you."

Cecil watched as Joan walked away, her wings bouncing ever so slightly with each step. She soon disappeared from sight.

Without warning, the atmosphere changed. Cecil turned around, back toward the shrunken tree, and gasped. He watched in grotesque fascination as the small shrunken tree morphed into a small elvish woman. Covering her body was a thin layer of moss made to look like a pale green dress.

"Greetings. I have been expecting you," the strange woman said to them. "I am Mau, the one you seek."

"Mau, it is a pleasure," Cecil said, stepping forward and extending his hand. "I am—"

"I know you all well, Sir Cecil Kloud. I have been observing you for some time now. I am sure you must have many questions for me, but please, allow me to explain who I am first.

"I am Mau, one of the original Lakinceitians. I am this world's gatekeeper. For thousands of your years, the gate has been dormant, much like this planet's true power.

"Throughout your journey, you have wondered as to the true purpose of awakening the Ekataramn. True, with the majority of the Ekataramn awake, Eklatros is stronger and more able to defend itself against any external attacks, such as Gnusaramnii. Yet, the main reason for awakening the Ekataramn was to bring this gate out of its dormancy. Remember, Eklatros is linked to the cosmos."

"So that's how we'll travel to where Tyrona is?" Theodore asked. "By going through this gate that you speak of?"

"Yes. Soon now, I will show you the gate you will use to travel to my home world, Melridion. That is where your friend Tyrona Knorse is now. You will need to hurry if you are to save her."

"What? She's in danger?" Theodore exclaimed. "There's no time to waste then. We must go now!"

"The time is not yet right," Mau said. "First, you must understand the reason behind your otherworldly expedition. As Joan explained to you earlier, I am akin to Gnusaramnii. We are both Lakinceitians, yet, we differ greatly. As you witnessed, I am a shape-shifter. Gnusaramnii once had this ability as well, but he has since diverged into something else completely. Once he discovered how he could clone himself by shape-shifting a piece of his own body, his will became corrupted. Now all he can do is make copies of himself—the subspecies known as Gnuelry and Gnusar. And they, in turn, create Gnureavers and Gnurargurts. Gnusaramnii has become an unstoppable force. It was only through your combined efforts and ultimate sacrifices that you prevailed.

"Gnusaramnii may be gone, but it will be back. Now that the gate is open once again, Gnusaramnii can return to Melridion. Understand that the gate you will pass through has a source, and Gnusaramnii will turn its attention to finding that gate once it regains its strength.

"The four of you must warn everyone you can of Gnusaramnii's coming. It is not an *if*, but a *when*. Gnusaramnii will return to Melridion, and in doing so will ravage the entire Vortex Solar System. The only way this can be stopped is by uniting a fractured system."

"Quite the daunting task. Can the four of us really do this?" Druder asked.

"You must. If the Vortex Solar System falls, then the entire universe will be next," Mau replied.

"It's not just us. Tyrona is there too," Theodore said. "And if she really is in danger, we must hurry."

"Hang on, what about Eklatros? You said Gnusaramnii will be back. How can we be sure that once we leave..." Cecil trailed off.

"Sir Cecil, thanks to you, pieces are in motion that will build up Eklatros' defenses. Eklatros will be ready for Gnusaramnii's return."

"Thanks to me? Wait, do you mean Vesten and the guild?" he asked.

"Precisely. Now, one last thing to keep in mind. The modern-day Lakinceitians differ greatly from Gnusaramnii and myself. They have grown weak and foolish, but do not underestimate them. They are cunning creatures.

"Now, come. The time is ripe. The gate awaits you," Mau said. She turned into the same twisted tree as before.

"Wait!" Theodore called.

"Quiet," Cecil commanded. "The way will be clear to us. Have patience, my friend."

"R-right," Theodore said, then whispered, "Tyrona."

A moment later, a strange feeling washed over them. It was as if the air had suddenly been charged with a dense cloud of static electricity. Cecil looked around him, and then a sharp sensation made him turn and look at Mau. The twisted tree was changing its shape once again, this time morphing into a golden archway. Once the archway was complete, a powerful surge of energy pulsed out of the gate. Forming in the center of the archway was a spiral of air. It grew in intensity until it became a spinning wheel of wind and energy.

"*The time is now*," Mau's voice said in their minds. "*Go forth and deliver my warning.*"

Cecil looked back at the others. Theodore, his eyes wide with awe, was smiling. Dasch looked at the gate, his hairless brow furrowed as he mumbled softly to himself. Druder wore a determined look on his dark face as he stared into the whirlwind.

Sir Cecil Kloud nodded and took a step toward the energetic gate.

This is it then, he thought. *Time to be a leader.*

EPILOGUE
INTO THE VORTEX

"Alright, what about this one? A Human woman, a Nioavellian woman, and a Kolythoanthaean woman walk into a bar—"

"Heard it," came the fierce, grunt reply. "Don't care much for it."

"Comedy is truly lost on your species, isn't it?" West replied sadly. "I was hoping I could educate you."

"We know humor. I just do not appreciate vulgar jokes," Bsarg said curtly.

"Why not? You're as vulgar and hideous as they get!"

"Hey, shut it! Professor Durrist is due by any moment now with Carl, so please shut your mouth."

"I don't actually have a mouth, you know," West replied, knowing his response would only annoy his bulbous friend even more.

If he could smile, he would have. West Kilinder enjoyed messing with Bsarg, especially since he was so easy to mess with. Being in the Intergalactic Bounty Hunter Association had hardened him and shaped him into the intelligent and capable person he was today. But it was also where he had gained his sense of humor. Bounty Hunter humor was something else entirely. The jokes he tried to entertain his new partner with were tame in comparison. His plan was to ease

Bsarg into this humor, but it was not going well. Bsarg simply didn't seem to understand humor, even if he said he did.

The large stone gate they were guarding suddenly began making noises, which wasn't supposed to happen. They were only guarding the gate for appearance's sake since Carl Feng was still there. As Bsarg had explained it, they were supposed to guard the gate at all times, but they were so understaffed it simply never happened. Now that Carl was there, and since West was the newbie, he was assigned the task of gate duty. And since Bsarg was still training him, they were stuck together, for the next few days at least.

"Um, Bsarg, what's going on?"

The deep, royal-blue Lakinceitian looked at him, his black eyes wide. "It's activating. The gate is activating."

"What should we do?" he asked.

"Be prepared for anything," Bsarg replied. "The safety and security of this facility are paramount. Whatever happens, it is our job to protect it."

"Right," he said. West began charging the weaponry on his Life Support System. The LSS was a truly amazing system. It was how he was able to see, hear, and speak. It regulated his breathing, his heartbeat, his brain waves, his blood flow, and a myriad of other internal systems. And on top of all that, it could be used to fire short, powerful bursts of energy that could stun and incapacitate any target. Or so Professor Clums and his team had promised.

"And call Svetlana," Bsarg continued. "Tell her to find Professor Durrist. They need to get here as soon as they can."

"Right, sure thing."

Currently, Svetlana Slesarenko was in charge of security for the entire underground facility. She may have started her training around the same time he did, but even with no experience whatsoever, she was already in command.

West activated the call center on LSS and was patched through to Svetlana.

"Hey boss lady, something is going on with the gate."

"West, is that you?" her soft voice crackled through.

"Yeah. Find Professor Durrist. You both need to get here quickly."

"We'll be there momentarily," she replied, then cut off her signal.

While he had been speaking to Svetlana, the gate had grown more active and violent. He took a few steps back while double-checking that his LSS was charged. A strange feeling washed over him. Something was coming.

***

"Isn't this all so exciting? Just remember that everything is top secret. You cannot tell anyone else, not even Professor Qymberkon. But of course, that's partially what makes this all so exciting!" Professor Randall, a tall, wiry Human said enthusiastically. His brown hair was cropped short, and he wore a pair of black-rimmed spectacles along with the standard white lab coat.

Professor Randall and his partner, Professor Durrist, were the two head professors who ran the secret underground laboratory. From what Navacus had gathered, Professor Randall was a step below Professor Durrist, much like how Professor Qymberkon ranked slightly below him. And yet, Professor Randall had done most of the talking so far. Professor Durrist—a large, dark green Lakinceitian— simply led the tour. There were five of them total—himself, Professor Durrist, Professor Peal, Professor Randall, and Carl Feng.

It was Navacus' first time in the underground facility. He had only learned of its existence the day prior. Although, it appeared as if Professor Peal had been working down here for some time already. So far, it was all quite overwhelming—and utterly massive. He estimated that the facility was at least three times larger than the entire main compound. During the tour he had been shown numerous test subjects, such as an Ancilsan with the ability to shape-shift and a Eusphyrchii with spiders for hands and ivy for legs, which had been one of Professor Peal's subjects before being transferred underground.

Currently, they were on their way to see a mysterious woman who had appeared out of thin air just over a week ago. Professor Randall was explaining that this woman possessed peculiar abilities. She had created an energy barrier and generated a high-pitched frequency that disabled everyone except for Svetlana, who promptly knocked her out cold. They were planning to see if they could take her powers and implant them in a less violent test subject.

"If you're lucky, maybe I'll even show you the security footage one day. It's absolutely classic!" Professor Randall whispered loudly to him.

"Speaking of which, here comes Svetlana now," Professor Durrist cut in.

The tall, blond-haired cyborg approached them, eyeing Navacus curiously.

"Professor Navacus, it's good to see you again," Svetlana said.

"Yes, likewise. I wasn't aware you were down here. Or that down here even existed," he said.

She waited for him to finish, a courtesy she may not have extended to anyone else judging by her stare. Then she turned to Professor Durrist and Professor Randall. "Bsarg has reported activity at the gate."

"I knew it. Just as I had predicted. Come, we must hurry," Professor Durrist said.

"R-right! The tour shall be put on hold," Professor Randall said.

"Randall, I need you and Peal to hurry on over to the Titans. Make sure they don't get too excited," Professor Durrist commanded.

"Ah, yes. Good point. We'll catch up with you later," Professor Randall said, then hurried off with Professor Peal.

"Should we be concerned?" Carl asked.

"Let's see what we're dealing with first," Professor Durrist said. "Come, Professor Clums, we need to hurry."

Navacus shrugged. He wasn't sure what was going on, but everything was brand new to him. He hurried after Svetlana, Professor Durrist, and Carl, going back the way they had come. Or so he thought. This laboratory was like a labyrinth.

It felt as if his mind was being ripped into a million pieces, then stitched back together in a completely different order.

The golden whirlwind-gate Mau had morphed into had sucked Cecil in, and now everything was in shambles. And yet, as soon as it began, the agonizing nightmarish journey ended.

Cecil found himself in a large open room with stark white walls. Two alien beings stood in front of him. Both seemed to be in shock, yet it was the Gnusar—no, not a Gnusar, a Lakinceitian, they were on the Lakinceitian home world now—that recovered the quickest upon eying his battle-axe.

"Drop It! Drop the weapon now!" the blue slug-like Lakinceitian screamed at him.

Cecil froze and looked around him. He watched in strange fascination as Theodore appeared next to him. A moment later, Dasch and Druder appeared. Cecil had to step forward a bit to give them room.

Cecil looked around—there was so much going on it was almost too much to take in. He decided to take it one step at a time. First, the deep-blue Lakinceitian, whom he could somehow understand. Second, the strange alien that was by its side. It was strangely human-like, only with a hard white shell instead of skin. It wore a large white hat that hid its face, and attached to its chest was a strange mechanism he had never seen before. The device was black with multiple blinking lights and gauges—and it was speaking. Last, he was in a large room filled with strange devices he had never seen before. The devices seemed to be connected to the gate they had emerged from.

"All of you, drop your weapons now! Please, we do not want to treat you as a threat!" a strange inhuman voice said, emanating from the device on the alien's chest.

Cecil looked at the battle-axe in his hand. He turned it around, feeling its weight.

"Can they understand us?" the Lakinceitian asked its partner. "Maybe they speak a different dialect? Or maybe our universal translators aren't working?"

"We can understand you," Cecil said, looking at them. "I'm sorry. It's been a lot to take in. My name is Sir Cecil Kloud and these are my companions, Sorcerer Theodore Caldwell, Dasch the Destroyer, and Druder the Decimator," he said, making up the titles on the fly.

I might as well mix things up a bit, he thought.

"Please drop your weapons this instant!" the inhuman voice asked once again.

"Yes, of course. I'm sorry. We come in peace," Cecil said.

He dropped his battle-axe to the ground with a loud clang, then nodded to the others. They all put their weapons on the floor.

"I don't like this," Dasch whispered behind him.

"I'm sure a destroyer like you can handle it," Theodore whispered back, mockingly.

"Shush it!" he commanded, harsher than he had meant to. "I'm sorry. You see, we're here on a mission, to warn you of an impending attack to your system."

"What kind of attack?" the Lakinceitian asked. Cecil mentally noted that, while he had shared their names with them, they had failed to return the courtesy.

"It's known as Gnusaramnii and it comes with an army of dangerous monsters. This threat is unlike any we've ever faced before. We—"

"You fought Gnusaramnii?" the Lakinceitian asked excitedly.

"No, not directly. Our leader did, though, and she gave her life to defeat it," he said harshly, his eyes narrowing on the Lakinceitian. His question had been rather specific.

"The threat may be gone from our world," Theodore added, "but it is not defeated. As soon as it regains its strength, it will once again turn its focus toward your system."

While Theodore spoke, four more people entered the room. One was another Lakinceitian, another was a strange bird-like creature, and the remaining two seemed to be human. The bird creature may have been the same one Ànifa had dreamt about. The black-haired man with small thin spectacles was definitely human, but the blond-haired woman, while she looked human, was composed of strange mechanical parts along with her human flesh.

Before Cecil could do or say anything else, the black-haired man pointed an odd weapon at Theodore and fired. The dart hit Theodore in the neck and he hit the ground face first.

Cecil bent down and grabbed his battle-axe. Before he could make it back to his feet, Dasch and Druder were on the ground.

"Wait!" Cecil cried. "We bring a warning!"

"I'll see about that," the black-haired man said, then fired his weapon again. Cecil attempted to cut the dart out of the air, exposing an open joint in his armor. The dart struck true and he fell to the ground, joining the rest of his party.

"Crap, why'd you do that?" Professor Durrist roared. "He was about to tell us something useful!"

"You don't know that," Carl replied harshly. "Besides, he was armed. He was a threat."

"He only picked his weapon back up to defend himself. And I wasn't threatened by him," Professor Durrist replied. "Bsarg, West, did he talk to either of you?"

"Yes, he spoke to us," Bsarg replied.

"I can replay the entire conversation. As you know, LSS records everything," he added.

"Yes, please play back the conversation. I am curious as to what he told you," Professor Durrist commanded.

He looked at Professor Clums, who nodded to him as he spun through his eternal datalogs.

"Alright, here you go," West said.

After he finished playing the recording, he shut it off, then walked over to Professor Clums.

"You came at a crazy time," he said to his favorite professor in the compound.

"Certainly seems like it," Professor Clums replied. "Hey, what's going on with Svetlana? She doesn't seem like herself."

"Now's really not the time," West said.

"Gnusaramnii... Carl, did you hear that? They mentioned Gnusaramnii by name!" Professor Durrist said excitedly.

"They certainly did. The prophesied time is soon upon us," Bsarg replied.

"What is it?" West asked. "I've never heard it before."

"Carl, contact Lord Foxaire right away," Professor Durrist commanded.

"I believe he's indisposed at the moment, but I'll contact Sid," Carl said as he walked off to make the call.

"Right, so who are they?" West asked, pointing to the strangely dressed Humans that lay on the ground. "Who's the Gnusaramnii thing—"

"Quiet, Bounty Hunter," Professor Durrist said, cutting him off. "I do not have the time to educate you right now. We have work to do."

<hr>

As she floated into the upper atmosphere, she looked around at the world below her. Everything was distant and familiar. She had been part of the world once. Now she was moving on to another world, another life.

Space was cold, dark, and lonely. As she drifted through the cosmos, a soul called out to her. It was close. It needed her.

No longer aimless, she spurred on through the stars toward this soul. She didn't know who it was, but it needed her, and so she would be there for it. That was now her purpose.

<hr>

He awoke with a splitting headache. His mouth was dry and he was groggy. He had no idea where he was or what had happened.

Theodore was lying on a hard metallic surface. He sat up and looked around. He was alone in a small room. The walls, floor, and ceiling were all metal, and there were no doors or windows in sight. There was no furniture—only him.

He realized he wasn't wearing his clothes. They had taken everything from him, including his staff and the miniaturized backpack. All he was wearing was a thin white robe that fell to his knees. Not only that, but his beard was gone and his hair was cropped short. The cool air felt foreign on his exposed face.

"What is this? What's happening?" he screamed, his words echoing around the small metal box. "This isn't right. We didn't leave Eklatros just to be thrown into some alien dungeon! Ànifa! Joan! What's going on here? Why were we sent here? And Tyrona... where are you, Tyrona? Where are you...

"Cecil! Dasch! Druder! Where is everyone? I'm sure... I'm sure they find themselves in a similar state. Tyrona, did they put you in a box like this one? Tyrona... I wonder..."

The hours passed by slowly. As time drew on, he felt himself losing his sanity.

When he came to, he realized he was screaming Tyrona's name. He shut his mouth and looked around the room. He didn't know what had roused him out of his stupor. Then he felt it—a presence.

"Tyrona?" he whispered, his voice hoarse. No, it wasn't Tyrona.

"Ànifa?" he said aloud.

A loud bang against one of the walls made him nearly jump out of his skin. A moment later, a grumbling voice announced that his meal was ready.

A hole opened in the wall, revealing a tray of unknown food and a tall cup of water. He ignored the food and gulped down the water, soothing his dry throat.

"Hullo? Who's there?"

Whoever had delivered his meal was gone, and the hole in the wall had closed as soon as he had removed his tray. He was once again alone, with only mysterious gruel to sustain him.

The gruel and a spoon. A spoon!

Since he no longer had his staff, he had no conduit through

which to conjure a spell. A small metal spoon certainly didn't compare to his staff, but it would have to do.

Theodore stood and held the spoon in front of him. He would try to create a small energy barrier in his fist. He held out his left hand, cupping it open, facing upward. Closing his eyes, he focused on the energy in his hand. Nothing. He couldn't feel anything. Normally, he could always feel the energy flowing around him, but he couldn't feel anything in this metal box.

He tried again, and again, and again. Then he tried some more. Then he screamed in anguish. He slumped to the ground and threw his spoon at the wall across from him.

What's going on? he thought. *I can't feel the energies as I could before. It's like this metal box is cutting me off from everything, stopping me from using my innate magical abilities.*

Tyrona, was it like this for you too? Where are you?

Ànifa, was that you earlier? I felt your presence with me in this room a moment ago, but now, as fleetingly as it came, it has disappeared. Or was that just now? I don't know how long I've been here. Time seems to move differently on this planet—that or it's this metal box.

I really hate this place. I want to go home.

GLOSSARY

Time Period: Ektember 5th to Ektember 28th, 8880

<u>Dramatis Personae - Eklatros</u>

<u>Ànifa's Party</u>
Princess Ànifa Tataluynnia Ekataramnii
Theodore Henry Caldwell
Sir Cecil Johnathan Kloud
Dasch Valentine
Vesten James Teixeira
Tyrona Claire Knorse
Joan de Ligtheramnii
Druder Nanasazii
Quaant Yttenramnii [Pronouns: zie, zir]

<u>Patsy's Crew</u>
Patricia Judith Matros (Patsy)
Dale Lovett
Trevonn 'Money' Hillside
Annalyse Skye
Tushar Kothari
Anqi Gan
Martin Greene

<u>Residents of Port Columbo</u>
Sarah Kloud Mont Simmons
Rear Admiral Brigsby Mont Simmons (Briggs)
Wedge Jess
Captain Ledger
Lieutenant Leonhart
Officer Hood
Officer Berry
Officer Gillian
Alexia Barro
Roxanne Shuck

Givers of Advice and Counsel

Sage Christian Barthandaedlus Mason

Dante Suebsanguan

Charlotte Evelyn Tuesti

Tanaq Jayne Farag (The Bishop)

Afyna Lucarieo

World Leaders

Baron Von Skyock [Port Gall]

Residents of Ajenti

Headmaster Giovanna Kalherd Glauss Barrow

Grand Master Kyle Chinn

Speech Master Elbert Fritta

Spell Master Jamm Prander

Scout Master Murdock Everhart

Medicine Master Kaila Gomez

Eric Franklin Mason

Kelso Mackenzie Spinner

Selma Wingert

Cedric Caldwell

Residents of Yttendaus

Queen Stella Tshaila Ekataramnii

King Vyereth Ekataramnii

Princess Nayeli Ekataramnii

Princess Pearla Ekataramnii

Raveen Narfidaus

Supreme Leader Eridame III

Cardinal Abbey

Juliana de Ligtheramnii

Beatrice de Ligtheramnii

Isabel de Ligtheramnii

Priscilla de Ligtheramnii

Regina de Ligtheramnii

Donatella de Ligtheramnii

Lucretia de Ligtheramnii

Human Foes
Danai Simasathien
Bartholomew Hobbs
Beck Welsch

Historical Figures
Kieth Mason (Kieth Angelcross)
Lindserick the Lancer
King Waesjeon Ekataramnii
Eliziana Lockhart

Ancient Lakinceitians
Gnusaramnii
Mau

Ànifa's Dire Wolf Spider
Chitter

World Terms - Eklatros

Ekataramn
Kalahsem – spirit
Roheefy – rhythm
Panabeeta – mind
Alakana – space
Bugenaluf – reality
Yttendaus – life

Variations of the Gnusar
Gnusar: aka Scaly Monsters. These creatures are covered in hard green scales. They have the power of speech and are immune to fire. They have two small feet that hide beneath their bulk.

Gnuelry: aka Jelly Monsters. These creatures come in many variations and colors depending on their viscousness.

Gnurargurts: These creatures are animals and gods that have been killed and reanimated as minions for the Gnusar.

Gnureavers: These creatures are mostly humans and elves that have been possessed and corrupted to become fiercely intelligent warriors. Can appear to be grotesque creatures or can look like a normal human or elf, depending on the circumstances in which the individual was possessed.

Gods

Abbitarasquos: Toad (Suriaddon) God
Aerigasus: Winged Ram God
Alicinustros: Kangaroo God
Amphoaries: Sheep (Lafhreep) God
Anuwan'sidtsi: Cusith God
Carchaselachii: Shark God
Carnivexion: Thylacoleo God
Chactochactas: Scorpion God
Colvadersk: God of the Land; Jackhorn God
Drakorillasaurus: Dragolum God
Farreeve'sidtsi: Katsith God
Ganhandramii: Elephant God
Glyptotros: Armadillo God
Hartipavoh: God of the Skies; Peafowl God
Kaalhcalodju: Wolverine God
Kadopodzi: Woolly Rhinoceros God
Karcincerii: Crab God
Krakuluthosii: Squid God
Lykotahogna: Spider God
Maqinjinarii: Sloth God
Mawsonii: God of the Seas; Fish (Coelacanth) God
Mochelioidae: Sea Turtle God
Morokomii: Wolf God
Mystiterachii: Whale (Blue Whale) God
Notremoglossii: Echidna God
Nuralagusamii: Rabbit God
Ornithor: Platypus God
Pulmoniserum: Snail God
Qirinocorn: Unideer God
Quohuatzin: Quetzalrong God
Sparassotereon: Lion (Sabertoothed Lion) God
Strigiformii: Owl God
Tesuindae: Tortoise God
Tododaru: Diprotodon God
Urodianusii: Salamander God
Ursiownii: Bear God
Uswassisbaena: Wyvern God

Weapons

Ekatalal: the divine hammer of justice
Halahkahna: the divine shield of protection
Skimither: Vesten's Scimitar
Ytteniron: the material from which Joan's armor is made

Geographic Locations

Landmasses
Schelff Island
Gallheim [made up of three pieces—Heiaam, Khall, and Alabatik]
Roffen
Panna Isle
Sortuga
Yttendaus [Floating Island]

Schelff Island
Sathon
Pikkul Harbor
Charlotte's Tent
Sage Mason's Tent
Schelff Gulf
Samial Mountain Range
Watthana Mountain Range
Bugenaluf

Gallheim
Grethossii [Ancient city—now in ruins]
Fort Turner
Rampa Bay
Port Gall
Galstrom
Dante's Cabin
Kalah
Grethos Mountain Range
Heiaam Woods
Shippo River
Shippo Bridge
Eladali Forest
Kohaku Bridge
Kohaku River
Gatelceous Jungle
Chrevans Grasslands
Lafhreep Mountain Range
Morai Mountain Range
Alabatik Desert
Kalsri Forest
Kalahsem

Roffen
Port Columbo
Ajenti [Formerly known as Cascagrada]
Tora
Haymath [Destroyed]
Hay's Revival
Seaside
Nora's Docks
Noroff Glacier
Poyfenn Bog
Rosemenov Desert
Turquold Mountain Range
Compass Crossroads
Great Roffen Plains
Haymath Orchard
Heefae Forest
Oterrock Canyon
Nicolah Mountain Range
Lopan Sea
Roheefy

Panna Isle
Runti
Heerenditheer
Beetaramn
Nibelkaith Volcano
Panna Peaks
Panabeeta

Sortuga
Sortuga Bay

Yttendaus
Ytten
Ytten Forest

<u>**Ajentian Guilds**</u>
Guild of Seafaring Knights – purple plumes
Guild of Exemplary Knights – light green plumes
Guild of Chivalrous Knights – dark red plumes
Guild of Ajentian Knights – orange plumes
Guild of Policing Knights – light blue plumes
Guild For Eklatros – rainbow plumes

<u>Past Conflicts</u>
War for Equality
The Dark War

<u>Ships</u>
West Wind
The Sundering

<u>Other</u>
A Collective History: The Magical World of Eklatros – A collection of fictionalized historical stories that tells Kieth Angelcross' story. Is also used as scripture for the The Holy Church of Eklatros.
Blue Dream – A species of special herb that Sage Mason grows.
Forest Diesel – A species of special herb that Sage Mason grows.
Koda – The currency used on Eklatros.
Shuyukuii Mushrooms – Mushrooms that, when eaten, induce dreamless sleep.
Tarnight – A foul-tasting medicine that can induce dreamless sleep.

<u>Dramatis Personae - Vortex Solar System</u>

<u>Professor Navacus Clums' Staff</u>
Navacus Clums [Yggdrazim]
Fumalli Qymberkon [Nioavellian]
Sylcertiverner [Kolythoanthaean]
Grasberg [Nioavellian]
Kurjon [Kolythoanthaean]
Mac [Harmertian]
Poi [Harmertian]
Lyd [Harmertian]

<u>Professor Maximilianus Peal's Staff</u>
Professor Maximilianus Peal [Human]
Kalosse [Nioavellian]
Kamarial [Eusphyrchiian]
Elizabeth Surridge [Human]
Mahlvern [Kolythoanthaean]
Walverm [Kolythoanthaean]

<u>Compound's Management</u>
Head Professor Yilvin [Kolythoanthaean]
Professor Bodeelch [Kolythoanthaean]
Professor Dea [Eridavlos]

Underground Staff
Professor Durrist [Lakinceitian]
Professor Randall [Human]

Security Guards
Bsarg [Lakinceitian]
Nijork [Lakinceitian]
Jakog [Lakinceitian]
Sharg [Lakinceitian]

Foxaire Biotech Industries' Leadership
Lord Foxaire [Lakinceitian]
Carl Feng [Human]
Sid Heigel [Human]

Senators
Senator Ducutyk [Kolythoanthaean]

Others
Kate Thomas [Human]
Doctor Sareyse [Nioavelli]
Doctor Poulson [Human]

Compound's Test Subjects
Svetlana Slesarenko [Human]
West Kilinder [Eusphyrchiian]
Norman Harrison [Human]
Ivy Hedera [Eusphyrchiian]

Named Acampachetlian Test Subjects
Salty Susan [Curik Subject #7]
Stick-Brain [Phasmatodaedalus Subject #4]
Denoptace [Phasmatodaedalus Subject #5]
Ados [Dark Therid Subject #1]
Adok [Dark Therid Subject #4]
Penny [Dark Therid Subject #6]
Blood Bat [Zubba Subject #7]
Sassafrass [Loxocemae Subject #3]
Newtus [Neutortous Subject #1]

World Terms - Vortex Solar System

Intelligent Species

Ancilsan (*An-sill-san*): Refugee Species, hailing from the planet Strutheine. Humanoid species, covered in light- to dark-brown fur with short, squat bodies and strong limbs and jaws. They are more comfortable in trees than on land.

Eridavlos (*Eri-daav-lowse*): Refugee Species, hailing from the planet Strutheine. Humanoid species with no limbs. They use a mysterious organ to levitate above the ground.

Eusphyrchii (*Yous-fur-chee*): Native Species, hailing from the planet Ijurvoll. Humanoid species with hard white or gray exoskeletons. They have the ability to regrow lost limbs.

Humans: Native Species, hailing from the planet Carange. Regular humans.

Harmertians (*Har-mur-shun*): Refugee Species, hailing from the planet Strutheine/Mishunaed. Humanoid species. They are short, growing only about fifty to seventy centimeters tall. They have light- to dark-gray skin.

Kolythoanthaean (*Koly-tho-anth-ee-ā-an*): Native Species, hailing from the planet Mishunaed. Humanoid species standing on average around 180 centimeters with light- to dark-gray skin and have six digits on each of their hands and feet.

Lakinceitian (*Lake-in-set-ee-an*): Native Species, hailing from the planet Melridion. Gastropod species with two small arms and two legs that are essentially useless as they are hidden beneath their bulk. They also have small, short tails.

Nioavelli (*Nigh-oh-ah-vell-ee*): Native Species, hailing from the planet Clendenic. Humanoid species with blue to light purple skin tones and egg-shaped heads. They have two arms and three legs.

Yggdrazim (*Yigg-draaz-em*): Refugee Species, hailing from the planet Strutheine. Avian based species, with large flat beaks and white to light gray plumage.

Acampachetlian Species

Curik (*Curr-ick*): Beetle-like insects that are unable to fly.

Dark Therid (*Dark There-id*): Specialized spiders that have about thirty spinnerets and four extra silk glands. A single bite from a Dark Therid can kill a fully grown Ancilsan.

Grumantrus (*Grum-an-trus*): Praying-mantis-like insects.

Loxocemae (*Locks-oh-sem-eh*): Snakes with blood-red scales. They are independent from birth and their fellow hatchlings are their first meal.

Neutortous (*New-tur-toos*): Giant lizards. They are deep purple to dark blue in color. They prey on Loxocemae.

Phasmatodaedalus (*Fas-mat-oh-day-dal-us*): Stick-bug-like insects that do not stop growing. While mostly independent, they live in social groups with a queen.

Zubba (*Zoo-bah*): Zubba have the body of a bat, with the bat's wings and furry head. The bat half is fused onto the back of a large scorpion. The scorpion part does not have a head. The scorpion's and the bat's coloring are always different, and each one seems to have their own personality.

<u>Zubula</u> (*Zoo-boo-luh*): Zubula are very similar to Zubba. The main difference is the scorpion part has a head, and they command the Zubba.

<u>**Planets of the Vortex Solar System**</u>
<u>Acampachetli</u> (*A-comp-ah-chet-lee*): Jungle world where Dark Therids, Zubba, Loxocemae, etc. reside
<u>Mishunaed</u> (*Me-shoo-naid*): Kolythoanthaean home world
<u>Carange</u> (*Cuh-raange*): Human home world
<u>Melridion</u> (*Mel-rid-ee-on*): Lakinceitian home world
<u>Clendenic</u> (*Clen-den-ick*): Nioavellian home world
<u>Strutheine</u> (*Struth-eyen*): Home world for refugee species, such as Yggdrazim, Harmertian, Ancilsan, and Eridavlos
<u>Ijurvoll</u> (*Idge-or-vull*): Eusphyrchiian home world
<u>Dunartera</u> (*Do-nar-terra*): Gas giant

<u>**Cities and Regions**</u>

Melridion
Nalpetalis
Volgash Desert
The Compound

Carange
Delgrious
Starofsky
Bahutenrut

Strutheine
Yolavien
Ligthuria

Ijurvoll
Warae

Clendenic
Kelhorr
Kelhorr University

<u>**Businesses and Organizations**</u>
Foxaire Biotech Industries
Intergalactic Bounty Hunter Association

Melridion Time

Days - Each day is 25 hours long with 80-minute hours:

1. Eklakiln
2. Sarkiln
3. Melrikiln
4. Dunakiln
5. Pjorkiln
6. Rikiln
7. Gnuakiln
8. Ramnkiln

Months - Each month is 40 days long:

1. Vuhardeena
2. Heinineara
3. Lakinar
4. Teinianar
5. Kampanar
6. Julinar
7. Caranar
8. Ohocinar
9. Tsenar
10. Drazineara
11. Zaltrineara
12. Kiliranar
13. Gardevinar

ACKNOWLEDGMENTS

Life is a journey. This story has been with me since I was a young child and has grown and evolved as I have grown and evolved.

First and foremost, I want to thank my family, friends, and everyone I have known and befriended throughout my life. All of you have influenced my life in one way or another, and in turn, many of you have influenced this book in more ways than one. Even if we haven't spoken in years, know that I still cherish the time we had together.

I want to thank my wonderful editor, Erika M. Weinert, dba The Werd Nerd, for all of her helpful edits, guidance, support, and advice. Thank you for believing in me and in Eklatros. You have made me into a better writer, and I could not have done this without you.

Thank you, Derek Van Skyock, for the amazing book cover, for wonderful Dungeons & Dragons sessions, and for your friendship. Navigating your unique, custom-built world through the eyes of Thedro Silkweaver helped me create and build Eklatros. While I'm at it, I want to thank my second Dungeons & Dragons campaign crew as well (Shout-out to Bart, Brownie, Veronica, Kali, and of course, Uisce!)

A huge shout-out to Polly Letofsky with My Word Publishing, who is stunningly beautiful and smart, and to the entire My Word Publishing community for their advice and guidance as I navigated my way into the self-publishing world. And, even though I only got the one opportunity, being able to read aloud a few pages of my book at the Open Mic Night was an unforgettable experience.

I want to thank the two artists who illustrated my characters for me. While the illustrations did not make it into this book (and ultimately were never meant to be part of the book), they helped me all the same. Having those illustrations inspired me to visualize my characters as they traveled across Eklatros. So, thank you, Austin Weeks, and the second artist who wishes to remain anonymous.

Thank you, BMR Williams, for creating the map of Eklatros. Out of all the illustrators on Fiverr, I'm glad I picked you. To find BMR Williams on Fiverr, search for mitsumightous.

I want to give my deepest gratitude to LEGO. A number of characters exist only because of LEGO—Navacus Clums, Professor Dea, Ivy, West, Norman, Mac, Poi, Lyd, Sassafrass, Blood Bat, Councilmember Ducutyk, Theodore, Cecil, and Tyrona. In addition, there are a number of characters yet to be introduced who were originally LEGO characters. In a very real sense, this story would not exist if not for the freedom of expression and play that LEGO inherently provides, brick by brick.

Last, and absolutely not least, from the bottom of my heart, thank *you*. This book is for you. Thanks for following the adventures of Ànifa and her party, and I hope you look forward to the second book in the series, *Escape from Melridion*.

ACKNOWLEDGMENTS

Life is a journey. This story has been with me since I was a young child and has grown and evolved as I have grown and evolved.

First and foremost, I want to thank my family, friends, and everyone I have known and befriended throughout my life. All of you have influenced my life in one way or another, and in turn, many of you have influenced this book in more ways than one. Even if we haven't spoken in years, know that I still cherish the time we had together.

I want to thank my wonderful editor, Erika M. Weinert, dba The Werd Nerd, for all of her helpful edits, guidance, support, and advice. Thank you for believing in me and in Eklatros. You have made me into a better writer, and I could not have done this without you.

Thank you, Derek Van Skyock, for the amazing book cover, for wonderful Dungeons & Dragons sessions, and for your friendship. Navigating your unique, custom-built world through the eyes of Thedro Silkweaver helped me create and build Eklatros. While I'm at it, I want to thank my second Dungeons & Dragons campaign crew as well (Shout-out to Bart, Brownie, Veronica, Kali, and of course, Uisce!)

A huge shout-out to Polly Letofsky with My Word Publishing, who is stunningly beautiful and smart, and to the entire My Word Publishing community for their advice and guidance as I navigated my way into the self-publishing world. And, even though I only got the one opportunity, being able to read aloud a few pages of my book at the Open Mic Night was an unforgettable experience.

I want to thank the two artists who illustrated my characters for me. While the illustrations did not make it into this book (and ultimately were never meant to be part of the book), they helped me all the same. Having those illustrations inspired me to visualize my characters as they traveled across Eklatros. So, thank you, Austin Weeks, and the second artist who wishes to remain anonymous.

Thank you, BMR Williams, for creating the map of Eklatros. Out of all the illustrators on Fiverr, I'm glad I picked you. To find BMR Williams on Fiverr, search for mitsumightous.

I want to give my deepest gratitude to LEGO. A number of characters exist only because of LEGO—Navacus Clums, Professor Dea, Ivy, West, Norman, Mac, Poi, Lyd, Sassafrass, Blood Bat, Councilmember Ducutyk, Theodore, Cecil, and Tyrona. In addition, there are a number of characters yet to be introduced who were originally LEGO characters. In a very real sense, this story would not exist if not for the freedom of expression and play that LEGO inherently provides, brick by brick.

Last, and absolutely not least, from the bottom of my heart, thank *you*. This book is for you. Thanks for following the adventures of Ànifa and her party, and I hope you look forward to the second book in the series, *Escape from Melridion*.

ABOUT THE AUTHOR

Alex Galassi was born in Littleton, Colorado in the early 1990s and has lived in Colorado his entire life. He received his Bachelor's Degree at the University of Colorado in Boulder in the School of Journalism and Mass Communication. Currently, he works as the Lead Developer at Blue Zenith Design + Strategy, a small business started by his mother that creates websites and helps small businesses with their digital branding and marketing. When he is not at work making websites or writing fiction, he enjoys hiking and camping in Colorado's beautiful mountains.